P9-ECO-016

Once in every person's life,
comes a shining year that casts its glow
over all the long years after...

"FIRST-RATE...LIVES, BREATHES, ENGAGES US."
—*The New York Times*

"A SUPERB NOVEL THAT TELLS THE STORY OF THE JOHN KENNEDY GENERATION WHO, FOR A BRIEF MOMENT, KNEW THERE WAS A CAMELOT...A BIG BOOK!"
—*The San Diego Union*

"MAGICAL...AN ELOQUENT, MARVELOUSLY WARM AND COMPASSIONATE STORY!" —*The Denver Post*

"THE STORY OF OUR YESTERDAYS!"
—*John Barkham Reviews*

"EXHILARATING, SEDUCTIVE...EMINENTLY APPEALING TO WOMEN!" —*Cosmopolitan*

"A DAMN FINE STORY, RICH IN MOOD AND DETAIL."
—*The Philadelphia Inquirer*

"A FASCINATING NOVEL...IF YOU ARE A ROMANTIC, AND MAYBE IF YOU ARE A REALIST, IF YOU REMEMBER THE 40'S AND THE GLAMOROUS CONVERTIBLE WITH ITS TOP DOWN AND DANCING TO THE BIG BANDS..."
—*Detroit Free Press*

"NOSTALGIA, LOVE, DRAMA, HIGH HOPES ...MYRER HAS THE GOLDEN TOUCH ALL THE WAY!"
—*Publishers Weekly*

"WARM, NOSTALGIC IN THE BEST SENSE OF THE WORD...AND VERY MUCH WORTH READING!"
—*Miami Herald*

"BEAUTIFULLY WRITTEN, HEARTBREAKING, SOARING...ONE CAN ONLY WISH THAT THERE HAD BEEN ANOTHER 500 PAGES TO READ. IT IS THAT KIND OF, AND THAT GREAT, A BOOK." —*Mobile Press Register*

"A SEDUCTIVE AND ROMANTIC NOVEL OF LOVE, FRIENDSHIP, YOUTHFUL PLEASURES, WRONG TURNS AND THEIR AFTERMATH ...MYER IS ABLE TO SWEEP YOU UP INTO THE LIVES OF HIS CHARACTERS..." —*Kansas City Star*

"AS FITZGERALD BECAME THE VOICE FOR THE FABULOUS TWENTIES, MYER MAY STEP FORWARD AS SPOKESMAN FOR THOSE OF US WHO CAME OF AGE IN THE BIG BAND ERA ...A RICH, ENTERTAINING AND PERCEPTIVE NOVEL." —*Palo Alto Times*

"READ IT. TURN THE PAGES SLOWLY. YOU WILL RECOGNIZE YOURSELF AND ALL YOUR FRIENDS." —*Sacramento Union*

Berkley Books by Anton Myrer

THE LAST CONVERTIBLE
ONCE AN EAGLE

THE LAST CONVERTIBLE

ANTON MYRER

A BERKLEY BOOK
PUBLISHED BY G.P. PUTNAM'S SONS
DISTRIBUTED BY BERKLEY PUBLISHING CORPORATION

for
PAT

Copyright © 1978, by Anton Myrer

All rights reserved

Published by arrangement with G. P. Putnam's Sons

All rights reserved which includes the right
to reproduce this book or portions thereof in
any form whatsoever. For information address

G. P. Putnam's Sons
200 Madison Avenue
New York, New York 10016

SBN 425-04034-8

*BERKLEY MEDALLION BOOKS are published by
Berkley Publishing Corporation
200 Madison Avenue
New York, N.Y. 10016*

BERKLEY MEDALLION BOOK ® TM 757,375

Printed in the United States of America

Berkley Edition, FEBRUARY/MARCH, 1979

The author wishes to express appreciation for permission to quote from
the following songs:

"I CAN'T GET STARTED"
Ira Gershwin-Vernon Duke
Copyright © 1935 by Chappell & Co.,
Inc.
Copyright Renewed. International
Copyright Secured. All Rights Reserved.
Used by permission.

"RACING WITH THE MOON"
Words, Vaughn Monroe, Pauline Pope
Music, Johnny Watson
Copyright 1941, renewed 1969,
ROBBINS MUSIC CORPORATION,
New York, N.Y.
Used by permission.

"INDIAN SUMMER"
(Al Dubin, Victor Herbert)
©1919, 1939 WARNER BROS. INC.
Copyright Renewed
All Rights Reserved
Used by permission.

"GOIN' TO CHICAGO BLUES"
By: James Rushing-Count Basie
© 1941 by Bregman, Vocco & Conn, Inc.
© Renewed 1968
All rights reserved. Used by permission.

"NO LOVE, NO NOTHIN'"
By: Leo Robin-Harry Warren
© 1943 by Triangle Music Corporation
© Renewed 1970 by Bregman, Vocco &
Conn, Inc.
All Rights Reserved. Used by permission.

"CARELESS"
(Lew Quadling, Eddy Howard, Dick
Jurgens)
Copyright © 1939 by Bourne Co.
Copyright Renewed. Used by permission.

"SENTIMENTAL JOURNEY"
by Bud Green, Les Brown and Ben
Homer
Copyright © 1944 Morley Music Co.
Copyright Renewed.
Used by permission.

"BLUE CHAMPAGNE"
By: Grady Watts, Frank Ryerson,
Jimmy Eaton
Copyright © 1941, Renewed and As-
signed to Dorsey Brothers Music, a
division of Music Sales Corporation,
New York.
Reprinted by permission of Music Sales
Corporation.

"SENT FOR YOU YESTERDAY AND
HERE YOU COME TODAY"
By: James Rushing-Count Basie-Ed
Durham
© 1938 & 1939 by Bregman, Vocco &
Conn, Inc.
© Renewed 1965 & 1966
All Rights Reserved. Used by permis-
sion.

"MORE THAN YOU KNOW"
Words, William Rose and Edward Elis-
cu
Music, Vincent Youmans
Copyright 1929, renewed 1957, MIL-
LER MUSIC CORPORATION,
New York, N.Y.
Used by permission.

"THESE FOOLISH THINGS"
(Holt Marvell, Jack Strachey, Harry
Link)
Copyright © 1935 by Boosey & Co., Ltd.
Copyright Renewed. Rights for United
States and Canada assigned to Bourne
Co.
Used by permission.

"SKYLARK"
Johnny Mercer-Hoagy Carmichael
© 1942, George Simon, Inc.
© Renewed 1960 by John H. Mercer
U.S. rights controlled by Mercer Music
and Carmichael Publications. Used by
permission.

"ALL OF ME"
(Seymour Simons, Gerald Marks)
Copyright © 1931 by Bourne Co.
Copyright Renewed. Used by permis-
sion.

"WHERE OR WHEN"
Rodgers and Hart
Copyright © 1937 by Chappell & Co.,
Inc.
Copyright Renewed.
International Copyright Secured. All
Rights Reserved. Used by permission.

"I CRIED FOR YOU"
By: Arthur Freed, Gus Arnheim and Abe
Lyman
Copyright 1923, Renewed 1951, MIL-
LER MUSIC CORPORATION,
New York, N.Y.
Used by permission.

"THERE, I'VE SAID IT AGAIN"
By Redd Evans and Dave Mann
Copyright 1941 and renewed 1948 by
REDD EVANS MUSIC CO., INC.
New York, N.Y.
International Copyright Secured. Made
in U.S.A. All Rights Reserved. Used
by permission.

"DON'T GET AROUND MUCH ANY-MORE"
Lyric, Bob Russell
Music, Duke Ellington
Copyright 1942, Renewed 1969, ROB-BINS MUSIC CORPORATION,
New York, N.Y.
Used by permission.

"BLUES IN THE NIGHT"
(Johnny Mercer, Harold Arlen)
© 1941 WARNER BROS. INC.
Copyright Renewed
All Rights Reserved
Used by permission.

"I'LL BE SEEING YOU"
Irving Kahal-Sammy Fain
Copyright © 1938 by Williamson Music,
Inc.
Copyright Renewed. International
Copyright Secured. All Rights Re-served
Used by permission.

"BODY AND SOUL"
(Edward Heyman, Robert Sour, Frank
Eyton, John Green)
© 1933 WARNER BROS. INC.
Copyright Renewed
All Rights Reserved
Used by permission.

"CALDONIA (WHAT MAKES YOUR BIG
HEAD SO HARD)"
(Fleecie Moore)
Copyright © 1945 by Cherio Corp.
Copyright Renewed
Used by permission.

I am indebted to Richard R. Lingeman's *Don't You Know There's a War On?* for several anecdotes of the Hollywood home front during World War II.

Golden lads and girls all must,
As chimney-sweepers, come to dust.

Cymbeline.

I

Racing with the Moon

1

"ALL RIGHT," Nancy said. "What's everyone going to do today? First you, young lady."

"Yes *ma'am!*" Amanda shot me that quick, mischievous glance and raised her fork like a baton. "You see, George Segal's zipping by in his Learjet and we're going to buzz over to the Cannes Film Festival."

"George Segal!" Peg said. "I'd think you'd want Robert Redford."

Amanda stuck out her lower lip and eyed her older sister and then Ron Dalrymple, who was ladling into his scrambled eggs. Amanda takes after me; her face is homely in a way, bones too prominent—my genes—but unlike me she's never let it bother her. The kids are so much more assured these days, I can never get over it. Then she blinked and gave a shivery little giggle. "Well see, that's because my tastes are kind of kinky."

"Don't use that word, Amanda!" Nancy said in her Regimental Adjutant voice.

"Why? What's wrong with kinky? Kinky's just—"

"We've been over this before. It's offensive."

"Your mother feels it has lascivious connotations," I said, remembering a moment long ago.

"No, but suppose George Segal *did* swing by in his Learjet. How would you play it?"

Her mother watched her a moment. "You're barely sixteen. That's an academic question."

"But pretty soon it won't be. You know?" And she gave me that merry, defiant look again—the one that enchanted and scared me at the same time.

"Amanda, please." Nancy shifted to her Circuit Court voice. "I've things to do, and I need to know."

Amanda stuck out her lip again—then gave it up. "I'm going over to Ginny's and mess around. Play records . . . *I* don't know. Okay?" She picked up the paper and started reading.

"George, how about you?"

I looked at Nancy over the coffee cup's rim. That rounded, well-bred face, still smooth (though some of that was moisturizing cream, of course, applied each night and morning with the precision of a chemist); her hair graying now, a rather pleasing silvered blond, perfectly in place—she was the only one of us dressed and ready to go this raw February morning; she was always the only one—her brows raised in that curious expression of expectancy. First college date, wife of my bosom, mother of my children. Ordering, organizing, planning. For what? Still, she'd asked Amanda first, me second. That meant she had plans for Peg; maybe even for Ron. There was always a pattern behind her order of interrogation.

"Oh, Dad's going out to the old workshop," Amanda said, turning the pages of the *Globe*. "As usual."

"Yes, as a matter of fact I believe I will." Actually, I hadn't planned anything at all. It was that time of year free of pressures around the place—no wood to cut or leaves to rake. There wasn't even any snow to shovel. A Saturday hanging between seasons, a dead-center time.

Nancy nodded. "Well. I'm going in to town. There's a sale on at Stewart's." She clasped her hands under her chin and I knew what was coming. "How about you, Peg. Want to come along?"

"I don't know, Ma. Maybe." She gazed across the table at Ron, who was mopping up a second helping of eggs. That boy must be hollow right down to the heels. He raised his eyes to Peg and smiled with that special intimacy of theirs, but gave no other sign I could detect, though I'm not entirely up on today's nuances. I did know they'd talked till after two, down in the living room.

"Ron: how about you?" Nancy was smiling pleasantly enough, but her voice had that faint, firm edge to it. Nancy had just about given up on Peg and Ron. She insisted on maintaining the fiction of separate bedrooms although they'd clearly been sleeping together for some time now. We'd had an argument about it two nights before—her voice, hissing in my ear, had snapped me awake.

"George. George. He's gone in."

"Gone in what?"

"Into her bedroom. I heard him."

"So what?" I murmured. "They're old enough to know their own minds."

"You may be that emancipated, but I'm not."

"You're trying to tell me you don't know how things are between them? Come on, Nan."

"It's wrong, all wrong. Peg's so damned *willing*..." She jerked herself up on one elbow, and I knew we wouldn't be getting back to sleep for a while. "Either he intends to marry her or he doesn't."

"They don't think that way, the kids nowadays."

"Ron's no kid."

"He had a little thing like Vietnam."

"Yes, and you had a little thing like World War II. You didn't let it paralyze *you* for ten years..." I chose not to reply to that one. "He's never going to do anything," she said implacably. "He's—he's unsound..."

"Chandler likes his work. He told me so."

"Do you expect Chandler to tell you he's incompetent?— What if she gets pregnant. Have you thought of that?"

"No," I said. "No, I haven't."

"Well, you'd better. You're the one who'll have to deal with the consequences."

"Maybe she's taking the pill," I said irritably. "Aren't they all?"

"I don't know, she won't confide in me—you know Peg. She never has. Not in that way."

"It's a good way," I said.

"What?"

"Nothing." That wasn't a subject I wanted to pursue either. "Why don't you just leave them alone, Nan?"

"Just let events take their well-known course."

"Look," I said, wide awake now, and edgy, "are you going to tell them they can't see each other, they can't be in love with each other? That it?"

"Keep your voice down, George. Please. If he were in love with her, *really* in love with her, he'd have asked her to marry him years ago. You know that perfectly well."

"He was trying to get his feet under him..."

"No," she said. "It's not that. It's something else. He's not—serious."

It was her most damning accusation, the Supreme Court one, the one that allowed for no appeal. It always made me angry.

"God damn it, he *is* serious!" I hissed back.

"George, hush... Why do you indulge him so? Aren't you angry simply because you know I'm right?"

In a deliberately level voice I said: "I just happen to believe they love each other."

"Love," she snorted, "—what a multitude of sins *that* word covers! He's taking advantage of her. A snug harbor, with no responsibilities."

I wrenched around in the bed. "Have you forgotten? Us? That time down by the lake? In the Empress?"

Silence then, while the alarm clock ticked away ominously and the radiator pipes tapped in uneven rhythms, and my daughter and my best friend's son made love—were they?—in a room down the hall.

"No," Nancy said in a low, hurt tone. "I haven't forgotten... That was different."

"Sure," I muttered. "It's always different." And always the same, too, I thought. That afternoon by the lake was not one I particularly wanted to remember—it brought up half a hundred charges, extenuations. But there are just so many things you can say. Aren't there?

"Just—leave them alone, Nan. Let them work out their own lives. Like the rest of us. Why condemn them out of hand?"

"I'm not condemning them."

"Yes, you are. You're judging them without right of appeal. You always *judge* people so."

"Yes," she said, and now her voice was bitter with finality, "yes, and *you* never judge them at all..."

Now however, this drizzly morning, Ron surprised us. He said, "No thank you, Mrs. Virdon. I think I'd like to hang around the house for the day. That is, if Mr. Virdon's going to be here." And he looked at me with those dark, intense eyes.

Nancy got that all right, she can pick up that sort of thing with no effort at all—the Cosmic Scanner, Amanda calls her. She nodded pleasantly and said: "Fine. Fine." She threw me one of her most significant glances. "Peg," she coaxed, "come shopping with your old Mom, give me some advice. Won't you?"

Peg turned that steady gaze from Ron to her mother. "All right. If you want, Ma."

"Good, then. We're all decided. More toast, Ron?"

"Well, what do you know," Amanda said, reading from the *Globe*. "There aren't going to be any more ragtops."

"What's a ragtop?" I asked.

"Oh Daddy, honestly. It's a *convertible*—like the Empress. Cadillac's turning out the last one this year."

"Let me see that." I said.

"In a minute. I want to read *Peanuts*."

"And good riddance," Nancy said.

"Why good riddance?" Amanda asked. "What's wrong with convertibles?"

"They're a silly affectation, for one thing. Always were. Look at your father." Nancy gave what I like to think of as her heedless laugh. "Would anybody in his right mind pamper an outworn relic for thirty-five years?"

"I don't know," Ron said, and smiled that sudden, charming smile. "The Empress is an antique—she's real class... We had some good times in that old boat, didn't we, Peg?"

"Absolutely."

"So did your mother," I told them. "She's just choosing not to remember, this morning."

"I remember freezing half to death going back to college, I'll tell you that," she said, getting up to clear away breakfast. "Convertibles are foolish and they're dangerous. It's a wonder we didn't all get killed, the way some of you drove."

"We were careful enough, as kids go," I answered.

"Uh-huh. Especially the romantic Mr. Currier."

"We all could have died a thousand times," I said lightly. "In a thousand ways. And we're all going to die some day."

"Daddy, you're such a spiritual comfort," Amanda said.

"Let me see the paper. If you've sufficiently memorized *Peanuts*, that is."

Yes. There it was. Cadillac was ending production in two months. There were to be 14,000 Eldorados, and that would be it. "There's a lot of nostalgia attached to the convertible," Edward C. Kennard, General Manager of Cadillac, was quoted as saying. "They're the last of a magnificent breed." Amen to that, E.C. The identity of the last car was to be deliberately obscured, however. There would be a final run of 200, painted white and decorated with red-and-blue stripes—a Bicentennial touch. Each car would bear a plaque proclaiming it the last of the convertibles.

"You'll have a whattamacall, Daddy," Amanda said. "A—you know, an heirloom or something. The old Empress. It'll be, you know—"

"—*Unique*," I said. "That's the word you want."

Everyone had left the table. This seemed to he happening more and more—I'd find myself sitting alone at the table mornings, sipping my coffee; it's the most piercing sign of getting older. Nancy was charging around marshaling the troops. Peg had gone upstairs to get dressed. Amanda and Ron were rinsing the dishes with a ferocious clatter.

I pulled on a jacket and went outside. A still, overcast day, vaguely threatful, the old snow sunk in grayed scarves and windrows in the sheltered places. The kind of weather we used to have back home in Skamondaga, where the clouds made up over Lake Ontario and shouldered their way in across the drumlins day after steely day; only there was always more snow there than here, just outside Boston. The east wind took care of that, the sea wind. A car passed down on the road, and beyond the cedars the Varnums' setter whined and fretted, trying to dig his way into an abandoned chuck hole.

The workshop—I'd built it myself from the timbers of the old barn—was in its customary late winter chaos: skis, worn tires, wheelbarrows, snowblower. Peg's '62 MG was on the near side, with its guts all over the bench; she'd got herself a Honda but I couldn't bear to give that little MG away. It was a Mark II, last of that lovely A series; I was going to fix it up for Amanda to take to college, next fall.

I picked my way gingerly through a jackstraw tangle of rakes and shovels till I reached the Empress, and flipped back the poly cover. There she was—the long, angular hood with its louvered radiator grille, the beautifully flaring fenders, the long, low, rakish chassis: all the proud elegance of the classic Packard design. The paint job wasn't quite right—I'd never been able to get the exact, shimmering iridescence of that deep original green. But she still looked glorious to me. I'd put her up on blocks and taken out the battery, but I knew if I hooked her up she'd turn over on the second try. She always did. If you looked hard enough, there was the shadow of the crease Jean-Jean had put in the trunk, and the new right front fender from that fear-laden rainy night in Mattapan, and the faint wavy place where they'd hammered out the ridge Russ made when he nicked the guard rail on Pearl Harbor evening, he and Kay fighting like cats and dogs, and the snow swirling around us in a dreamy white tide. The top was down now, folded neatly under its boot, but I knew where the mend was, where thieves had slashed the canvas and stolen Russ's manuscript the night Jack Kennedy won his senate seat. All those fond and foolish times... Were they?

I heard voices outside, near the garage—Nancy calling, and then Amanda. The door banged and the Pontiac wagon started up. Nancy raced the engine—one, two, three fierce bursts, the way she always did, no matter how often I told her one steady, even acceleration was better for the car—and then they roared off down the driveway, and it was quiet again.

I opened the door of the Empress and got in behind the wheel. The door closed with a fine, solid *ta-tchnk* sound. No car door has closed with that sound in 30 years. The dark green leather was faded now, and a bit cracked in places, but there was still that wonderful, dense, smoky leather smell. The gearshift knob was an old brass lion's head Russ had found in a San Francisco antique shop. The five indicators on the dash panel were large and round, supremely functional, the way a decent car's ought to look. There was the cigarette burn Kay Madden had made on the front seat at the Yale Game in '41, and the darker oval on the edge of the back seat where Dal's hand always rested on the runs out to Wellesley; the portable bar with its little silver ice bucket and red-and-gold glasses was set in the back of the front seat. And folded over the leather robe rail hung the frayed steamer rug the girls had huddled under on New Year's Eve of '41, and which Terry had sat on during the first triumphal parade for JFK ten years later . . . the faded plaid made me think of beach picnics, and spring dances, and late-night necking parties under the maples. So evanescent, all of it—and so innocent, for all our play at sophistication. Yes. Innocent. And the vividness of those days! The ineffaceable joy we'd felt driving to the stadium, or rolling head over heels down the high dunes, or dancing to the big bands; the astonishing intensity of our fervor . . .

"No," I heard myself say, aloud, my hands on the wheel. "No, Mr. Edward C. Kennard. No, you all-knowing automotive hot-shots. You're wrong. All of you are wrong. *This* is the last convertible. And there will never be another one like her."

"You bet."

I looked back, startled. Ron was standing just inside the shop door, watching me.

"Caught me that time." I grinned, but his face was solemn. "Slobbing down memory lane, as Mandy says. I guess the family's right: I'm turning sentimental in my declining years." He made no reply and it irritated me. I got out of the car and shut the door with a bang. "I guess you think I'm one, too."

"No, I don't. What's wrong with memories? Long as they're good ones." He leaned against a fender, looking around aimlessly, his fingers drumming on the metal. It was clear be was nervous; he'd set up the day and come out here, the two of us alone, and now he didn't know how to bring it up. Which was curious—there was so little his generation had found difficult to broach.

"I think I'll build us a fire," I said. "Only take a minute."

He watched me while I fed the stove some paper and scraps of kindling until it was roaring softly and the old iron began to snap and creak; then I shoved in a piece of oak.

"Mr. Virdon, I have a problem."

"Join the club," I said, and eased onto the high stool near the workbench. "What's on your mind?"

But he just looked at me—that deep, intense gaze again, eyes very dark, mouth working at the corners. A strange, unsettling glance. I'd have liked to help him out, but talking to your future father-in-law about marrying his daughter is one of the few things in this world you have to do absolutely alone.

"You've been awfully good to me," he murmured in a speculative tone, as if examining the relationship. "Like a second family, in a way. I don't mean secondary," he amended, with his mother's smile. "Giving me the run of the house the way you have, ever since I came east to school. Letting me use the old Empress before I went to Nam. Couple of times I was scared I'd bash up a fender and you'd write me off, you know?"

I laughed. "She's got her scars. I'm not that obsessed about her."

"You've gone out of your way to make me feel—you know, completely at ease, and everything..." He kept looking awkwardly around; I waited in silence. "I mean, you didn't have to do it. Even with the Fusiliers, and Mother, and all that. Did you?"

"Why no," I answered, "of course not. We're fond of *you*, Ron. We're all fond of you—you must know that."

"You know I'm grateful. Particularly that heavy time. That summer before I went into the Army."

I shifted my feet. He was watching me with a curiously wary expression now; his dark eyes quick and alive again. I said softly: "You don't hold it against me, do you? what I said that night?"

He shook his head vehemently. "No, no. Why should I? You were wrong—Nam wasn't like your war. Not remotely like it. But what the hell, you couldn't know that. And it probably turned out for the best. Maybe. I guess. I don't know."

"I felt the way you did about it, Ron—you know that. Stupid, vicious business...At least you didn't have to rot away half your life up in Saskatchewan somewhere—"

"Sure, I know." He waved a hand slowly in the air as if to wipe something away. "All's well that ends well." He turned abruptly and began to inspect the Empress, passing his fingers over the silver swan mounted on the radiator cap, the gleaming vertical blades of the grille. "No, you've been straight with me. Looked out for me. Almost as if I were part of the family. And I could always count on you for an honest answer, no matter what. No matter what," he repeated.

Jesus, kid, I almost said aloud, *come to the point, will you?* Only of course he wasn't a kid any more, I only thought of him that way. He seemed—I don't know—permanently arrested in my mind at the age of nineteen. It was as if the intervening years had sneaked past me somehow. Well, they had, truth to tell.

"You see," he said in the terse, flat tone, "I have this problem. I have this thing with Peg... The fact is I'm in love with her. For a while I thought it was—you know, feeling affection for all of you, my other family. Good vibes. But it isn't that. It isn't that at all. I'm really and truly and totally in love with her."

"Is that a problem?" I inquired.

He turned then, quickly, straightening, almost as though he were afraid of being hit—there was that sudden tensed setting of his body. "That's just what I don't know, Mr. Virdon," he said. "Do you?"

"Look, son, if you're asking me what you ought to do about Peg, you're way off base. This is something you've got to—"

"Mr. Virdon," he said slowly and quietly, "who is my father? My real father?"

I stared at him, looked away.

"I thought so," he muttered.

"What are you asking me?" But I was too late. "Your father's your father. Why are you asking me—"

"Because I want to know," he almost shouted. "I've got a right to know. Now."

"What gave you this idea?"

"Look"—he was shaking his head back and forth with fierce weariness—"I know, that's all. Let's just accept the fact that I know."

"Did you ask your father?"

"No," he answered, and his eyes narrowed. "I didn't have to ask him."

"What about your mother, then?"

"That's just it. She told me to ask you."

"Me?"

"Yes—come to you and ask you."

"That's all she said?"

He nodded rapidly. "That's it."

I looked down at my shoes. Let George do it. I could see Chris sitting somewhere, bent forward, long hands clasping her knee, her eyes shining—that animate, utterly compelling glance that could make your heart leap. Even if you thought it might never leap again. So she'd put it up to me. As though I were some kind of celestial arbiter. Goddamnit. God damn you, Christabel. After all this time—after all these light-years of silence...

The boy was still watching me—and now the corners of his mouth had drawn down, his eyes had turned flat with disappointment. No, it was worse than that. It was contempt, a mounting contempt.

"I'm sorry, Mr. Virdon," he said coldly. "I hoped you'd be straight. Really straight."

"No more and no less than the next man, I guess."

"I wanted to think that." Then he struck his thigh and cried: "Jesus Christ! I'm in love with Peg—your *daughter*... Have you got the balls to face up to it or don't you? You *are* her father, aren't you?"

I found myself gaping at him: a looming consternation—flooded all at once with light. "You—you think I..." I stammered. "You think *I'm*—"

"I want it now, chapter and verse. If you've got the guts."

I couldn't laugh. I couldn't even laugh. I drew in my breath. Then anger rose in me too, like a foul gas. "—Do you mean to stand there and tell me you actually think I'd have let you fall in love with Peg if *I* were your father?"

"... I don't know. I really don't know. I've tried not to believe it."

"Well, then you're a fool! And sick in the head. If you—"

"Listen." He was on his feet again, but the hand he thrust in my face was open. His voice was low and savage. "You listen. I watched a sergeant arrange the death of our own company commander while he was eating out of his mess kit. Another man, a man who saved my life, rented out three Vietnamese girls by the night. A friend, a good friend, swore to me by all he held sacred he'd never fragged a hooch full of civilians, but he had—I saw him! Men do what they want in this world—for their own private reasons. Lie and cheat and kill. Why not you?"

"—Because I am not like that," I said, and my voice was shaking with old emotion. I could not control it. "There are—well, standards. You don't—"

"Oh, sure. I've seen the games people play! In war, in business. Don't talk to me about standards..."

I ran my hand slowly along the cool chrome of the Empress' grille. In the corner the stove soughed and crackled; it was burning itself out. The world had changed, the world was burning itself out... Perhaps if I'd been more ruthless, everything might have been different; I might have solved it all. The trouble was we hadn't been taught how to cope with reality—the reality under the reality, the one that mattered...

But for this boy actually to believe that I—

Ron had walked to the far end of the Empress. When he turned, his face was impassive, almost expressionless. "I think it's time to knock off the Victorian crap, Mr. Virdon. All the window dressing. Let's have the truth."

She'd put it up to me. Ah Christabel. After all these years. Why not herself, for God's sake? or Dal? And this boy half out of his head with thoughts that might have sickened Caligula... But I knew why. I was only stalling. "Funny you should ask me that out here," I said. "Right here, I mean. Because she caused it all—or might have." I slapped the headlight, the one that got smashed that heart-sick, rainy night in '42.

"The *car*—!" he exclaimed.

"Yes. Funny isn't it?"

"Mr. Virdon, I don't know whether it's funny or not."

"I'm sorry," I said, and caught myself up. "I'm sorry, Ron. I'm not playing with you. I'm not the type, whatever you think. I just needed to get my breath a minute." I went over, built up the fire with chips. "All right. I'll tell you," I said. "On one condition."

That disdainful half smile crept back on his face. "And that is?"

"That you let me tell it my own way. And that you don't leap to any conclusions until I'm finished. It's more complicated than you think, Ron. Most secrets usually are, you'll find."

"I'm waiting," he said.

2

THE FOUR OF US were trying, not too successfully, to move a couch through the narrow outer door of the entry. That's the way it began. The couch was Terry Gilligan's; it was blue—a rather shrill royal blue—and it was enormous. Two men from Terry's father's construction firm had unloaded it half an hour earlier on the black-top outside the entry with contemptuous haste, and driven off again. Terry had asked us to give him a hand.

"What a monster," Ron Dalrymple said. His face was broad, with curiously high cheekbones; he wore glasses and had the habit of squinting when faced with a problem, which made him look vaguely Asiatic. He hefted one corner and grunted. "What—a—monster. Custom?"

"What?"

"Is it custom built?"

Terry shrugged. "I don't know. I guess so. Mother wanted to get rid of it."

"I can't imagine why."

"You know, it looks like those big sofas out at Norumbega," Russ Currier said. He was good-looking, with a long, straight nose, and his eyes, deep-set and dark, came alive the way they did whenever he was excited about something. "Totem Pole. Ever been there, Virdon?" I shook my head. "What a ball park! Dance your fool head off. All the big bands..." His voice had that tart, faintly formal edge of old Boston, but it was only a trace—the quick enthusiasm had a broader origin. Bending over he flicked the blue fabric with his fingers. "Yale's colors, I see. Treason, Gilligan, treason..."

"I'll dye it crimson for you," Terry answered. "With my fine Irish blood."

We laughed awkwardly; we still barely knew each other. We'd arrived in the Yard the day before from our various compass points, registered and tried to seem casual during two disorganized meals at the Union, and that had been about it. The sense of newness, of sudden, boundless adventure lay over us like the golden autumn sunlight; those first days at Harvard were like that, like moving through an immensely golden dream. At least they were for me. After all, it was what had lain there glowing at the base of my heart for half a dozen years, this moment...

"Well, let's get the show on the road," Dalrymple said. "Up on end. That's the way it's got to go."

"I don't think so," Russ answered.

"Sure it is. Trust me, Currier. Trust me." Dal organized us: Russ and I took the front end, he and Terry the rear. We got our end lifted, panting and straining, and started through the doorway. All at once it stopped, wedged tight, and Russ gave a quick gasp and muttered:

"Jesus!"

Dal said: "What's up?"

"My hand—it got jammed in the casing." Russ was holding the back of one hand, which was skinned and bleeding.

"What's the matter—you disaster-prone, Currier?"

"Yeah." Russ scowled at Dal's square, grinning face. "If you hadn't been in such a God damned hurry—"

We stood there sweating in the warm September air. Across the Yard in Thayer someone uttered a high-pitched rebel yell, incongruous under the feathery canopy of the elms, and in the next entry Jimmy Dorsey's band was playing *Frenesi*.

"—It isn't going to go, anyway," Russ said suddenly, in a different tone.

"Why in hell not?"

"Why? Because this little old sofa is smarter than you are, Dalrymple." Russ was smiling now, his eyes wide; he was absently wrapping a handkerchief around the injured hand. "Because this sofa isn't going to let any big-deal clown from Chicago tell it where to go or how to get there. That's why."

"Now listen, Currier—"

"Who appointed you straw boss of this caper? It's Gilligan's sofa."

"All right, you handle it." Dal's eyes were squinted, the cleft in his square chin looked deeper. "But you can lay off Chicago..."

"Look, why don't we try crabbing it?" I said in the silence. "At an angle, like this? Why don't we try—"

But nobody was listening. Dal had straightened just then, he was saying in an awe-struck whisper: "Jesus, will you get a load of *that!*" We all turned and looked.

The car was gliding gently toward us along the walk. It was a convertible, a '38 Packard Super Eight, and it was the most beautiful car I'd ever seen. It was green—but a deep, shimmering green that made you think of antique armor, or the carriages of European royalty. Its hood was long, outrageously long, its gleaming, angular, utterly distinctive radiator grille was like a ship's prow, an image heightened by the slender vertical louvers and the rakish tilt of the two-panel windshield, which flashed and flashed in the sun. The fenders swept down and away magnificently, the twin side-mounted spares rode in their front-fender wheel wells like Viking shields; the tires were six-inch whitewalls around hubcaps stamped with the scarlet hexagon of Packard. The canvas top was down, the fold-down luggage rack held a trunk splashed with the labels of a dozen foreign hotels, the back seat was a gorgeous jumble of matching Louis Vuitton luggage, tennis rackets in presses, a fencing mask and foils. It was a royal dream of all convertibles ever made, and it had stopped at our entry.

The driver got out. A slender figure, lithe, graceful, wearing a rainbow-striped shirt with a very broad collar open at the neck, covert-cloth slacks, black loafers.

"F Entry?" he inquired. His voice was low and even, with a French accent.

"You've got it," Dal said.

He walked up to us, his hand extended formally. "Jean Roche Gilbert Rigord des Barres." He was a handsome devil, to go with everything else—he had that drawn, hollow beauty of the French aristocrat. Yet it was a strong face, almost stern. We introduced ourselves with varying degrees of assurance, shifting uneasily on the worn ballast brick.

"You drove up alone?" Russ asked him. The rest of us had been settled in by our parents, with the attendant embarrassments and confusions of entering freshmen. There was something almost heroic about driving off to college on your own; and in *this* car.

Jean threw open his hands. "As you see."

"You mean that's *yours*?" I said, pointing at the convertible. For a kid who'd resurrected two jalopies out of wrecks and nursed them through a season or so, it lay on the edge of fantasy that someone my age could actually own this prince of cars.

He nodded—then his face broke into a smile that would have melted the heart of a master sergeant. "You like it?"

"Like it!" Russ cried. "For Christ sake—I'll get down on my knees and pray to it, every morning at sunrise..."

We all laughed. Jean offered us cigarettes—Benson & Hedges cigarettes, out of a cardboard box—and lighted them for us with a slender gold lighter. He said to Russ: "Take it for a run tomorrow if you want."

"You mean it?"

"Why not? That's what it's for."

Russ raised his right hand and chanted: "I solemnly swear to hold my running speed below five miles an hour and under no condition to turn a corner!" and we all laughed again.

"You're kind of late, aren't you, chum?" Dal said in that flat, measuring tone I'd already noticed. "Registration was yesterday."

"Yes I know."

"I hope they don't burn you." Dal had a little Ford runabout. Up till then he'd been the only man in the entry with a car of his own at college, and he was squinting a bit, caught between admiration and resentment. "I'd hate to see that dreamboat go bye-bye..."

Jean watched Dal a moment, his lips curled in a faintly deprecatory smile. "Perhaps they will forgive me—if I forgive them."

We were silent—we didn't know how to take that. Jean des Barres was a student, a first-termer like us—and yet he wasn't; and the difference was vast. His eyes, smoke-blue and very steady, roved from one of us to another. "Fair Harvard. I am happy to be here, a student here. But you understand, if there *were* no Harvard..."

"—it would be necessary to invent one, yes!" Russ broke in, laughing boisterously.

Jean beamed in delighted surprise. "You are a true Frenchman."

"Well, not exactly—"

"Yes. *Courier*. They've forgotten how to pronounce it. You have French blood. I am never wrong." Abruptly he reached into a teakwood compartment set in the back of the front seat and came up with a silver flask engraved with an elaborate coat of arms. The cap was an eagle's head. It looked as if it had been wrought by Cellini at least. He produced half a dozen little silver cups nested in a velvet sack with a drawstring and said formally: "Will you join me?"

"Right here?" Terry demanded incredulously. "In the *Yard?*"

"What better place?"

"For pete's sake, Gilligan, don't be a peasant," Russ said; but he was impressed, too.

Jean filled the little cups and murmured: "Santé." We touched them lightly around, murmuring, and drank. It was Scotch—a very dry, smooth Scotch. I had never tasted Scotch like that. It made a slow, fine cone of heat deep in my belly. I was conscious of other new arrivals watching us, and a trio from Holworthy—attracted by the car, perhaps—started toward us, and then stopped. Standing in the warm, dappled light beneath the great elms, watching the clouds drift lazily above the slate roofs I was filled with a sudden fierce emotion—affection, pride, defiance, I didn't really know; or care. But it was real. That I knew.

"What a chariot," Dal was saying, shaking his head at the convertible, which was standing there sparkling and pristine, the epitome of all automotive elegance. Maybe it was the Scotch, but his resentment was gone; he was all wonder now.

"That's no chariot," Russ retorted, "—that's the Empress of all the French."

"Vive l'Impératrice!" Terry said, and raised his cup.

"Vive l'Impératrice!"

We all had another drink on that; and then for a warm, happy moment we looked at each other.

"You know what I think?" Russ demanded. His head was back, his eyes held that wide, magical gleam—it was the first time I ever saw it—his free hand extended as though to fashion something out of the very air. "*I* think we're the brightest, handsomest, most sophisticated crew to come down the avenue in a long, long while. I think we're going to make history..."

There are only moments. They like to tell us that time runs along in even, ticking measures, minute to day to month to decade, but that isn't true. It's like a groping journey in the fog, hiking up Bootspur Trail on Mount Washington in bad weather, nothing around you but the rock of the trail and the ghostly shadows of the firs—and all at once you reach the summit and it's blown clear and the sun is blazing down out of a vibrant, rain-washed sky and everything is new and full of clarity; and time does have a stop, just as the great man said. Moments like that, few and far between, clearings in the fog, on the high ground. Even now, whenever anyone speaks of some kid going off to college I see this moment, seized out of time, the five of us standing there outside Fox Entry, glancing at one another in happy, budding congeniality. One minute we were a group of awkward, ill-at-ease strangers thrown together by chance, on the point of getting into a row; the next we were a *force*—comrades, partners, band of brothers, call us what you will.

It sounds silly putting it this way now—a thousand years later—but it was there. All of us were touched by it, even though Russ was, typically, the one who put it into words. As for me, I couldn't have said anything. I was not that bright, I wasn't handsome at all (I was homely, in fact), and the last thing you could have called me was sophisticated. I was on full scholarship; I owned exactly one sports jacket and two suits; my spending money would be what I could earn over and above board and tuition. I was all too conscious of the gulf that separated me from the others in a thousand and one ways... but

in that one lightning moment I'd been included in this particular
fraternity: I'd touched cups with the others and put my hand on
the convertible's gleaming green hood; and that was more than
enough for me.

3

THAT WAS HOW it started: the best, freest, happiest year of my life, with everything rich and strange and wonderful. The fact that I was the only one on scholarship (I was also the only one of the five who'd gone to a public high school except Dal, and he'd had a year at Choate) only made it all the more entrancing. Harvard is a unique place—at least it was in those days. It was so secure, so pre-eminent and venerable it could sit back, like some fabulously rich-and-powerful indulgent old uncle, pat you on the shoulder and say: "Why now, be anything you like, my boy—a grind or a jock, a social fop or a politician, an esthete or a dilettante, or any combination of these; you may even turn into a boozer or a bore, though I fervently hope you won't... But one thing you *must* do: you must grow up enough to choose what you will be..."

Some men found the sudden boundless freedom oppressive and drank too much, or got involved catastrophically with waitresses or strippers, or simply wandered aimlessly around for weeks and flunked out at midyears. But for me it was college life as I'd dreamed it might be, through a decade of evenings in the cramped bedroom back home . . . During the war I found myself in an allée somewhere in southern France, a moonlit mall that ran between two rows of plane trees, where nightingales poured their liquid song, and at whose far end stood a classic temple, pure as ivory against the night sky. This year was like that—I actually saw it as an enchanted stroll towards truth and beauty, the promise of all good and radiant things. I did.

At the center of the wonder was Jean-Jean des Barres. I have to call him Jean-Jean from here on—Russ had given him the nickname in protest at one of the Frenchman's formal introductions ("Too many, entirely too many names! We'll have to call you Jean-Jean, that'll do it"). Jean-Jean was not only impossibly handsome and awesomely wealthy but, most important of all in those distracted, quicksilver days before Pearl Harbor, he was already invested with a romantic past; he'd been a flying cadet during the phony war. He'd got out of Paris just ahead of the Germans, like Bogey in *Casablanca*, had made it to Lisbon and then to the States, where an aunt had opened one of her homes to him. And here he was among us, a Harvard freshman of all things (his gentle, deprecatory smile could convey just that shade of astonished amusement), enrolled improbably in some philosophy and government courses (which he rarely attended), scanning an out-of-date copy of *Figaro* over interminable cups of black coffee. Most often we would find him sitting on a couch with some girl, his head engagingly close to hers, murmuring in low, seductive, crooning tones. Such nonstop eloquence mystified us.

"What do you *say* to her?" Dal once asked him in exasperation. "All that time—!"

"What one always tells a young woman." Jean-Jean regarded Dal with gentle tolerance, as though indulging a backward pupil. "How attractive she is, how intelligent and graceful, how eminently seducible—"

"The hell you say."

"You are so naive, Dal. So unformed. You will never melt hearts."

There were any number of girls: there were sultry French emigrées with marvelous legs, there were publishers' secretaries and designers' assistants up from New York; there were dark little Cliffies with diamond-drill minds and harsh voices, and the earnest, well-bred products of Wellesley or Smith—and they were all wild about him. He found time for them all too, somehow. Trained as we had been to involve ourselves with one girl at a time, we were bowled over by such versatility. When we learned Jean-Jean had casually rented an apartment across the river in Back Bay, we were stunned—so *that* was why he hadn't been in his room for three nights running. A private apartment—! Jesus H. Christ...

"But what if they find out about each other?" Terry Gilligan demanded. It was not the sex but the promiscuity that outraged him. "What then?"

"It's a matter of discretion, Terry."

"But—you're not being fair! Each girl thinks she's *your* girl. Doesn't she?"

"I have no idea. Each girl is happy when she is with me—at least I'm reasonably sure of that." Jean-Jean smiled his charming smile. "Isn't that what life is all about? You're the sociology major."

"That isn't sociology, that's—that's sexual bingo!"

It was fascinating. We would shake our heads and grin at each other. He was shocking—deliciously shocking. Virgins ourselves, most of us (though not for long, not for much longer), we envied and indulged his bland indifference to classes and books, his mysterious departures and reappearances, the giddy parade of feverish, captivated girls who were continually phoning or dropping by the entry on the flimsiest of pretexts.

"What Jean-Jean's got is *style*," Russ said during one of our interminable nocturnal bull sessions, when Jean-Jean was clearly in his apartment over in the Fensgate, fleshing out our cartwheeling fantasies. "Boy, has he ever got style!..."

Which did indeed seem to sum it all up. We were enchanted by the way he would talk with a cigarette in his mouth, flipping it disdainfully against his lower lip or holding it centered between his teeth; or the way he turned up his jacket collar in sunny weather. He wore paisley cravats, and suede shoes, and sweaters with raglan sleeves. He slurred certain consonants, he had the habit of prefacing his wittiest observations with a short, abrupt "Mnnnh—"; he never seemed unduly surprised by anything that came up. We couldn't be like him, of course—too many centuries of civilized power precluded that—but it was something to aspire to . . . especially if you came from Skamon-daga, New York.

And there was something else, too. There would come a moment when, listening to Edward R. Murrow's sonorous warning tones or looking up from the savage blare of headlines to see the first leaves fluttering down on the still, pewter surface of the river, we would think of Jean-Jean's family seat (a lordly pile near Moreuil replete with towers and a reflecting pond, he'd shown us snapshots), a Wehrmacht officers' billet now, his uncle a prisoner of war—and the thought would nudge us: Maybe he's only a few months ahead of you, maybe he's only the first to be touched by the fire; maybe you're drifting toward the cataract, too—only you just don't know it yet . . .

Meanwhile there were the football games. Clear, hard autumn mornings—there wasn't one rainy Saturday that fall of '40—or if there was, I don't remember it.

"Come on, you guys," Dal would call, "time's a-wasting. If we're going, let's *go* . . ." We would come thundering down the entry stairs and there was the Empress (everyone called her that now, Russ's nickname had stuck), standing there with her top neatly folded under the boot, the sunlight dancing on her mirrors, her chrome, her arrogant silver prow. We would pile in, the five of us, and Jean-Jean would drive her smoothly across the river and over to Brookline, everyone talking a blue streak. Everyone but me, that is.

"What's the matter, George? Cat got your tongue?"

"Virdon hasn't waked up yet. He can't get used to this decadent way of life."

Which wasn't true—I'd been up since seven. I ran the newsstand concession at the Union, they knew it. No, I wanted to hold it in: it was like the kids' game of holding your breath until spots swam before your eyes and you turned slightly dizzy—I had the absurd and happy conviction that if I didn't do or say anything this moment would last forever; the freeze-frame in a movie, as Russ would say. I wanted it to last forever, with all the high, vibrant promise of the day, its surprises and excitements, hanging in the wings. The Worcester Turnpike rose and fell like a sedate roller coaster, the gold and scarlet foliage slipped by, the wind tugged at our foreheads, the radio was playing and Bunny Berigan was singing huskily:

I've flown around the world in a plane;
I've settled revolutions in Spain;
The North Pole I have charted—
But I can't get started
With you . . .

And that was just what we wanted to hear—all the heroic and sophisticated things we'd done, but for all that we hadn't (except of course for Jean-Jean) brought our girls to sweet surrender. But we would, perhaps this very evening; all things were possible on such a day . . .

We swung off the Pike, and the Empress glided through the village, a resplendent gondola; Russ called, "Welle*sley*—first stop *Well*esley . . ." in rising and falling inflection, like a train conductor; Jean-Jean spun the wheel and we moved along the gently meandering paths past the lake, past gaunt stone buildings whose sheer gloominess only a New England Seven Sisters' college can achieve.

The girls weren't ready. They were never ready, they weren't expected to be—that, too, was part of the ritual. We stood around in various poses of restlessness and boredom in the crisp, achingly clear October light; and the girls who weren't going to the game came flocking around us.

"Love—that—convertible!"

"Oh-my-God, it's *smooth* . . ." The word drawn out sensuously, in slow rapture. Their hands caressed the side-mounted wheel covers, the walnut window moldings as though they were a kind of talisman. There were other cars, other convertibles and we nodded or waved to them in carefree magnanimity: *we* had the Empress, we were with Jean-Jean; most of the girls were crowded around *us*. We talked of dances and courses and bands and nothing at all—it was a kind of preening-and-display dance, like those gyrations the Pacific gony birds indulge in. Madge Henderson wasn't going, the dramatic club was putting on *The Seagull* and she had the lead; Beth Nowden had a crucial paper she had to finish, Babs Darcey was going to the BU game.

"BU—!" Russ exclaimed. "Not *B U!* . . ."

"Don't be patronizing, lover."

"I'm not, I'm really not, I was *going* to BU as a matter of fact, I almost did—"

"Come off it."

"—gleaming gospel, ask my flint-eyed father, I was going to confound them all—only then of course I wouldn't be standing here beside the old Empress consorting with a sterling, peerless, transcendent bunch of bums like these..."

That's the way it went. No one really believed anyone—which is to say that everybody believed everybody: for we were the most naive, the most credulous of all the unready American generations.

Liz came out then, followed by Nancy, to a pleasantly derisive chorus.

"I'm sorry," Liz said. "It's impossible to get up Saturday mornings."

"Perfectly fine," Dal said, "perfectly okay—it's only the most crucial game of the season, that's all."

"There's plenty of time. You want me to look glamorous, don't you? You don't want me to shame you, do you?"

"The hell with me, baby—think of the Empress."

"I have been. Every night I crouch at the edge of my bed—don't I, Nancy?—and mumble: 'Don't let anything happen to the Empress, don't let anything bad happen to the Empress,' twenty times."

Liz Payne and Nancy Van Breymer were roommates. I'd met Nancy as a blind date through Liz, who was Dal's girl—and they were as unlike as two girls could be. Liz was tall and angular, with good, faintly hawklike features. Even her clothes seemed chosen for line, simple and somehow elegant. When she moved she made you think of a greyhound—she would have made a fine athlete, but her interests lay elsewhere. She was an art history major, and wanted to be a museum curator.

Nancy was short, with a heart-shaped face and deep blue eyes that drooped ever so slightly at the corners.

"Hi," I said. "You look terrific."

She smiled—a slow, almost secret smile that intrigued me. "Thank-you-kind-sir-she-said."

"I mean it. You look—as if you just waltzed out of a Peck and Peck ad in the *New Yorker*." It was true, in a way. Her blond hair was a perfect page boy, straight and silky, curling in prettily at her throat; her lipstick was perfect, not too much, not too little; her fingernails—her hands were small, I could never get over how small they were—were a soft rose, with perfect moons. I listened to her, smiling, and thought how lucky I was, how fantastically lucky. Anyone who looks the way I do—bony-faced, chin too hard, mouth too wide, ears too big—and poor as a church mouse into the bargain—for someone like me to be dating Nancy was riotous good fortune. She came from Lancaster, Pennsylvania, where her father owned a department store, and she was a superb dancer—much better than I was. Who could ask for anything more?

We were on the way to Chestnut Hill, to pick up what Russ called Jean-Jean's Girl of the Week (Jean-Jean almost never took out the same girl on successive dates). Denise Brasseur went to Smith, but was staying with friends; like Jean-Jean, she had left France, though earlier, during the phony war—her father had been with the French embassy in Washington, before Vichy. She greeted us in a torrent of French and English and kissed Jean-Jean with a quick, sure passion that startled us. She had a sultry little street-urchin's face, wore much more make-up than the girls we knew, and had terrific legs.

"Who will explain football to me?" she called above the music and chatter.

"I will!" three of us said at once.

"It's really very simple," Russ added. "Just think of it as sexual: the ball is thrown through the air and embraced by another player, who is thrown prostrate on the ground by—"

"No, it's not—it's sociological," Terry broke in. "The linemen are the proletariat, groveling in the mud. The backfield are the aristocracy. They're the only ones who can handle the ball, which of course stands for wealth and position—"

"You're both wrong," Dal laughed, "it's financial—the quarterback is chairman, the backfield are his board of directors, the object is to impose your will on the competition..."

"Isn't it wonderful?" Liz queried wryly. "I mean the fantastic advantages of a Harvard education?"

We were back in Boston now, had turned off Brookline Avenue and were speeding down Commonwealth, past indomitable Lief Ericson, to Garland School. Terry ran in, came out with Ann Rowen. He never went with anyone else. She was a good-looking, quiet girl who loved to ice skate; the most amazing thing about her was her ambition—she wanted to be a great chef.

By now the Empress was very crowded. The girls were sitting on our laps in the deep back seat, and this too was part of the ritual: the unwritten law here was that sardine togetherness in so fabulous a vehicle as the Empress was infinitely preferable to spacious comfort in any other mode of conveyance. The sole exception lay in the case of a blind date, where another unwritten law held that lap familiarity wasn't quite cricket, first time out. Ah, so long ago.

"And we're off," Russ chanted. "To the Cliffe, the Cliffe!"

This was one of the matchless advantages to matriculating in and around the Athens of America. As Dal would say when he assumed his phony-locker-room manner: "It's a buyer's market, fleshwise." There were so many women's colleges, and so many girls at each one of them. Nights we would theorize interminably, categorizing and classifying: Smith girls were good-looking but arrogant and unapproachable; Wellesley girls were only fair on looks but good dancers and good sports ("good on a date," was the way we put it); Mount Holyoke girls were dumpy and arty; Bennington girls had "a good line" and were wild (good) and unpredictable (bad); Radcliffe girls were brainy and belligerent but were not all crows as generally supposed; Vassar girls were brainy, belligerent *and* crows; Sarah Lawrence girls were cold and affected; Simmons girls had no line and were (unpardonable sin) terrible dancers... We loved to generalize, pronounce irrefutable judgments—and then blithely scrap them all as soon as one of us encountered some gorgeous, lively exception.

We were on our way back to Cambridge now, the sun in our faces, following Memorial Drive, with the sailboats rocking and dipping in the Basin like cubist cutouts; over the Cottage Farm Bridge, the Empress' tires moaning on the steel web, and now the Harvard towers slid into place like fanciful marble and jade and garnet jewels against the blue sky. It's the loveliest urban vista I've ever known. Along Mount Auburn, past the final club mansions whose interiors we were never to see, through the crash and clatter of the Square, on up Garden Street to the Radcliffe dormitories.

Russ reached over and honked twice—the Empress' horn had a fine, deep resonance, like hunting horns far-off—the door flew open and Christabel Farris came toward us quickly, hands behind her back, her face stern as a jailer's—all at once raised in both hands a placard painted with the legend: *Dartmouth men use woad.*

"Tell 'em, lover!"

"Wullaga-wullaga—"

"Hey now, clamber on board this heavenly express!"

"*Now* we're ready..."

Laughing, she climbed in on Russ's lap, blowing kisses to all of us; and it was true, what Dal had just said: *Now* we were all together, now the show could go on. A game, a dance, an outing of any kind without Chris was unthinkable. She was beautiful—anyone would have called her beautiful—but you didn't think of her that way: it was too unconventional a beauty. Her hair was a deep brown shot through with rich reddish lights, and unlike the other girls she wore it brushed back from her forehead in a loose and pleasurable disarray. Her clear brown eyes had tiny green flecks in them, and sparkled and flashed with exuberant high-spirits; her skin had a fine, warm apricot glow, as if the sun had warmed it; seeing her you thought of sunlight dancing on water, catching the undersides of leaves. She meant—well, *life;* what it offered, what it promised. It was in the way she moved—that swaying suspension that originates in the small of the back; she moved with an abiding awareness of her body, very erect, floating like a ballerina, which was one reason she was such a superb dancer. Her voice was low, like dark music, her laugh deep and ringing—a fine, committed laughter that made you realize at the moment you heard it that you had never heard anyone laugh before, and wonder how anyone on this earth could be sad or sullen. She was laughing now, at something Jean-Jean had said, including us all in the moment of merriment, inviting us to share in it. There was such promise in her eyes! She made us complete, somehow; I think we all sensed it in a funny, inarticulate way; even Jean-Jean, even Nancy.

And yet it was so natural, this exuberant gaiety of Chris's—as though there were no other way to be; now and then, watching her, laughing with her, you could almost touch the nakedness of it, the raw vulnerability, and you felt obscurely afraid. At least I did. But maybe it was only me—I'd had a grimmer childhood than the others. Depression's Baby, Russ had called me once, but with a certain tender edge in his voice—for all his wealthy Brahmin background Russ could fool you. And it was true, I'd had to grow up in a matter of days, I'd already had to grapple with consequences...

"Come on, J-J," Russ was saying, "speed is of the essence. We'll miss the bleeding kick-off..."

"Now Courier, why the haste? Harvard will defeat Dartmouth, Dartmouth will defeat Harvard. Mnnh—will you be a better lover after it is over?"

"I will," Russ declared in the laughter. "I definitely will. After all, if a redskin killed an enemy, he assumed the victim's virility. Or take cannibals. The underlying gestalt was: each part strengthened a part. Consequently, after you'd bashed the poor sod's head in, you munched on his reproductive organs, if you catch my drift."

"Russ," Nancy protested, "that's revolting..."

"Just passing on some of the hard truths."

"Did it work intellectually, too?" This from Terry.

"*Intellectually!* Don't shy away from the subject. We're talking about sex. All life is a series of sex duels, didn't you know?"

"And where do we come in?" Liz demanded.

"You're the objects, the booty..." And Russ gave Chris a powerful squeeze.

"Try not to be too impossible," she chided him. "This is your day to be magnanimous, remember?"

"Why? Why should I be magnanimous?"

"Because you're such a sensitive soul and everybody loves you." And her brow touched his, her lips brushed against his cheek. She was simply, unalterably Russ's girl, had been ever since they were kids together, summers on the Cape. Her father was Chandler Farris, the distinguished oceanographer at Woods Hole; her mother had died when she was three, and she'd been raised mainly in the company of men, which may have accounted for that warm candor of hers, her utter lack of artifice. Girls like Nancy didn't know quite how to take her, at times.

"Actually I'm unique," Russ was saying. He raised his arms like a conquering hero. "We're all of us unique."

"The five conquering musketeers," Liz said drily.

"Alliteration, alliteration! We're the—we're the Five Fabulous Fusiliers of Fox Entry, with our F—"

"Watch it..."

"—with our Fantastic, Furry Females."

"Russ, that's disgusting!" Nancy cried.

"Ha-*ha!* Trapped you. What's wrong with being furry? Furry, like a little bunny. It's all in your leering imagination..."

It was too late for lunch by this time, but nobody cared; we'd pick something up at the game. We were deep in the easy processional headed for the Stadium. The old grads called it by its proper name, Soldiers' Field, but we refused to. Other convertibles swayed past, their occupants waving enemy banners; smothered under our women, the crease vanishing from our trousers, our cheeks delightfully chafed by angora, we shook our fists happily and chanted along with Johnny Mercer:

Sent for you yesterday, heah you come today—
If you can't do bettah, might as well just stay away...

while pedestrians smiled indulgently along the route. A kinder age than this one, grownups forgave us our absurdities. Or perhaps they sensed something, too. For there was an intimation, even then, that something was about to happen— and to all of us, drifting toward the Stadium...

The game *was* important, though—Jean-Jean's amused detachment notwithstanding. Bred to the ephemeral we cared passionately about sports, even the nonathletic among us: we loved the fugitive achievement, the lost gesture. Sitting in a tight little phalanx we roared, "Our team is re-e-e-ed *hot!*(Clap-clap-clap-clap.) Our team is re-e-e-ed *hot!*"—agonized over fumbles and dropped passes, hugged our girls ecstatically and passed our flasks around at every score. This was not for warmth (that would come later, with the chill November twilight of the Yale game); flasks conferred status, defined style. Russ's flask was his grandfather's, antique glass covered in alligator with a pewter top, Dal's was slender and curved and chrome, with shot-cups fitted cleverly in the cap; but Jean-Jean's was of course the pièce de résistance, with its coat of arms—a stag's head with a coronet hovering between the antlers. Tilting it skyward, your eyes stinging, you felt like d'Artagnan...

And finally the game was over—we didn't win, but we hadn't expected to—and we straggled back across Larz Anderson Bridge to the round of house parties, the girl's voices ringing brightly in the cool dusk. There was a bash in Holworthy, there

were others in Thayer and Wig; Rhino Tanahill and Mel
Strasser were throwing one downstairs in our own entry. We
would descend on one in a babble of overanimated greetings and
the staccato wail of some big-band riff tune, perch there a while
and then fly off down the stairwells like a flock of crazed
swallows—only to alight in some other room exactly like the one
we'd left. The pathways through the Yard were filled with small
groups crossing and recrossing—a festive migration to nowhere
at all. We were seized in restlessness. Every campus in America
was, that sweet, fugitive autumn... Only after some hours did it
wear off, and we found ourselves sprawled in Rhino's room,
drinking planter's punches, bound in a momentary discontent,
trying not to listen to the evening news. An unexploded bomb
had been found in the rubble behind the ambulatory of St.
Paul's; the draft lottery would be held the following Tuesday;
John L. Lewis was urging all members of the CIO to vote for
Wendell Willkie; Hitler and Marshal Pétain had met in the
Fuhrer's private train somewhere in France—Pétain said they
had agreed on full and amicable Franco-German cooperation to
reconstruct peace in Europe.

"Cooperation." Jean-Jean uttered his explosive, mirthless
laugh. "Cooperation—with the Boches! Filthy swine..."

"But the Germans will listen to him, won't they?" Chris
asked. "They respect him, don't they?"

"They respect nothing," Denise said sullenly.

"But—he's a great national hero..."

Jean-Jean's lips curled. "Hero to my *father*. Not to me.
Doddering old fool—they put him there to sugar the pill, that is
all."

"Yes," I said, "but if it could mean peace for—"

"There *is* no peace, there will *be* no peace until that odious
little maquereau is wiped out! For the love of God, Georges,
don't be so naive..."

"What what what?" Russ called, turning from the phonograph. "Harsh words among the Fabulous Fusiliers? Nonsense,
nonsense. Jean-Jean is *morne*," he proclaimed, accenting the
word hugely. He became even more loquacious when he was
high. "And can you blame him? Jean-Jean is sick and tired of
playing nursemaid, Dutch uncle, cicerone to a clutch of callow,
sallow, fallow—"

"Don't be superior, darling," Chris said.

"Superior! Ha—it is to snigger. If I were *Jean-Jean* I'd feel superior though, you mark my tintype. If I were Jean-Jean I'd tell off the lot of you. I'd sink to my knees in a pile of black panther skins, run my fingers through a trayful of emeralds the size of grapefruit, and then fling myself in silken dalliance beside the most beautiful, the most versatile, the most lusty of all Persian princesses—"

"I'm hungry," Liz broke in, with a yawn.

"So am I," Dal said. "Come on, you guys, if we're going to get over to town let's get organized . . ."

And Chris coaxed and cajoled Jean-Jean out of his morne, and Terry talked Russ out of another drink, and I got the girls' coats, and Dal made a reservation at the Fox and Hounds— which would put me in hock for a solid month, but I didn't care—and we were off in the Empress again. We were an oddly disparate group, when you thought about it—maybe that was why we got on so well together: we balanced one another's backgrounds, we complemented one another's moods. Russ certainly could have forsaken us for the Brahmin-final club crowd if he'd wanted; but he had nothing but scorn for them, and on this point openly defied his father, a reserved, punctilious State Street banker, who was clearly disappointed in what he saw as his only son's destructively unconventional ways. Russ was his mother's son. She was Italian, from a proud Florentine family, a celebrated pianist, and had been a great beauty—there was a portrait of her in the house on Mt. Vernon Street done not long after her marriage; twenty years later you could see that the painter had had no need to flatter his subject. From her Russ got his flamboyant imagination, and his defiant recklessness. "Frattee-babies," he called the final club men—they *were* the nearest thing Harvard had to fraternities—and once got into a fist fight with a member of Porcellian named Lawring. "I believe they're under the impression their urine is perfumed." He wanted to be the world's greatest novelist and playwright, nothing less—he was certain he was going to be. He would stay up half the night reading *The Red and the Black* or working on a short story—and then sleep through a crucial history lecture, and then work up a towering rage because none of us had waked him for it. Ten minutes later he would have us all roaring with a hilarious imitation of his tutor.

Russ's headlong romanticism was balanced neatly by Terry's

dry, sardonic wit. Terry was a native son, too—but intensely Irish, as the Boston Irish always are. His father had made a lot of money in the building trades, and Terry had even gone to Andover, but he was amused by the social pretensions of other Irishmen. *"Lace curtain,"* I heard him say once of a boy across the Yard named Callahan. "Just what the devil is that supposed to mean? We're all immigrants, courtesy of the potato famines or British savagery. We all came ashore without a dime to our names..." And then the lean, wry smile. "Jesus, the human animal's capacity for self-deception is unfailing, isn't it?" Cool and detached, he was often silent until a discussion was under way. Then his pale, rather sallow face would tighten, his deep blue eyes would darken, and he would bring that cold sociological analysis to bear on the subject with surprising fervor. It was quite a long while before I saw it was a mask for something very different, and more disturbing.

Dal stood somewhere between them—he took issue with both Russ's violent romantic attitudes and Terry's gentle skepticism. He was a sturdy pragmatist; careers were forged by planning, the realization of concrete goals, not mercurial bursts of energy. Dal was one of the few men I've ever met who knew exactly where he was going. His heroes were not Tolstoy or Pasteur or Freud but the Rockefellers, Carnegies, Mellons—the captains and the kings of industry: he had their biographies down pat. He was going to make a lot of money, a great lot: then he would do big things with it. "It's the only way, George. All these dreams of glory, immortality—it's a fool's paradise." The full, square jaw would jut out a touch more, he would nod slowly. "You need leverage to accomplish things; and money is the best and biggest lever of them all."

I understood him all too well, I knew exactly what he meant. His family weren't poor, as mine was, but for all his life Dal had been surrounded by the wealthy—which develops its own peculiar sense of lack. He envied the final club men, the sons of the merchants and brokers of the Northeast, the fearful head start they had on him—once in a while it would surface in a thinly veiled resentment of Russ; and I understood that, too. Harvard in those days left you startlingly free—but it left you just as free to *observe,* to become conscious of every nuance of social distinction, financial gulf, the hierarchies of privilege. Maybe it's all for the best. The world is rife with such distinctions, it runs on them for better or worse, and perhaps it's just as well to come to terms with them in your teens.

But it was such a dramatically illustrated lecture! At the top (if that is the word) were what we called "the St. Grotlesex crowd," a portmanteau embracing the four haughtiest preparatory schools, whose products by and large kept to themselves, dined and hung out at their exclusive final clubs, took a very casual attitude toward classes and grades, and very nearly constituted a college within the college. A Groton man sat next to me in a course on the Hapsburg Empire and never said a single word to me. Not one. It wasn't that he cut me, exactly—I don't think he ever even saw me. Some, like me, can accept it with equanimity, and go their way. For others—and Dal was one of these—it eats away at the vitals like acid: they may suppress it, but they never get over it.

Next there were the larger, prestigious prep schools of the Northeast, such as Choate or Milton or Andover. Their graduates were better mixers, but their attitudes still carried a slight, indefinable sense of difference: generally they roomed together, dated in groups, chose one another's company even on athletic teams or in classes. After them came the lesser provincial prep schools, then the big suburban high schools across the nation; at the bottom of the ladder were the boys from the local Boston public schools, without money or family, who commuted to college from home.

Putting it this way I can see I've overdone it. There were continual overlappings and blurrings; sports, the *Crimson* and other extracurricular affairs broke it down some, and there were those unconfined spirits who refused to be bound by any barriers—our own group was a glorious example. But the hierarchies were always there, the slights and misunderstandings cut deep. Many an undergraduate turned recluse, rebel or cynic who might never have done so at, say, Syracuse or Chapel Hill. But then they had their own fraternities of another sort altogether; all America was a fraternity then—part fraudulent, part real . . .

And I—where did I fit in with all this? Holding down two jobs, racing late to classes, all too often scanning books I wanted to read with care, having to slight things that drew me, clawing incessantly for time; struggling to maintain the dean's list grades on which my scholarship depended, neither athlete nor artist nor intellectual, I brought nothing to the group that I could see. Except loyalty: I had that all right, and to spare. I was, simply, so overjoyed at being accepted, one of the Fabulous Fusiliers, sitting there in the Empress laughing at some outrageous remark of Russ's, exchanging a slow wink with Dal. It was such a magical, utterly unhoped-for investiture I never once questioned it—not then; I only wanted it to go on forever. It sounds mawkish and juvenile, I know; but there it is.

And so my role became defined almost without my knowing it. Now and then I would find myself mollifying Jean-Jean's sudden, unfocused rages over the progress of the war, tempering Terry's acid observations about the rich and privileged, playing buffer in the moments of tension between Russ and Dal. A Horatio (Kay Madden called me that, one turbulent and drunken night), an attendant lord to princes—it's true, I fitted the description. There's always been that tendency to defer judgment, to suspend action, hear out still another side of the story. It's not a very heroic quality—once I was even accused of harboring ulterior motives. But that's wrong, it was never a case of seeking favor. It was something else . . . I had so much to *learn*. They all seemed so sure of themselves, in their wildly divergent ways—and I was sure of almost nothing at all. Except that things were never what they seemed to be . . .

"The contacts you make at college will stay with you for the rest of your life," my father had told me. "They'll be the cornerstone of your future." But his voice lacked conviction even as he spoke the words; they were as gray as his face. I didn't really believe him. I'd stopped believing him since the afternoon nine years before when I'd come running in from school to find him sitting in the old captain's chair beside the kitchen stove with his head in his hands. He was a superintendent—he was management!—and he had been fired, nearly everyone at the plant had been fired. There was no work to be had. He was shaking his head slowly back and forth in his hands as if he would hold it together, and weeping. I had never seen my father weep; it was inconceivable to me that he *could* weep. I stood there in the kitchen, watching him, watching my mother, listening to the beating of dark and terrible wings. Life was not a pleasurable, carefree path toward adulthood, but a patrol through an immeasurable minefield in the dead of night, where one sidelong glance, one misstep would spell disaster.

My father got work, here and there, fitfully, but he was never again gainfully employed, as we say. He was really still sitting in that chair by the stove, unable to believe that this thing had happened to him. He didn't give way to rage, or flight, or drink; he was simply broken. We could never rely on him again. It was up to me, now. My mother quickly made that clear. Up to me, and to her. She had been a pretty woman when I was small, with soft, glowing eyes and a pear-shaped face and the most beautiful hands—I can remember the rings she wore and how her hands adorned them, made them look even more beautiful. She was from Rochester, and she'd married beneath her, I overheard Aunt Edna once say of her; but before long all that was meaningless, anyway. She got a job in Mr. Gratiot's real estate office, typing up forms till all hours and answering the phone in that new, deferential voice that always made me sad. I mowed lawns and shoveled snow, worked first in old Mr. Rossini's grocery store and later in Tolland's Paper Mill, shoveling steaming hot stock into the beaters until the sweat poured down my backbone in a greasy river. The years went by, all too fast; there was never time to keep up with them. I watched my mother's hands grow thin and veined and the beautiful rings disappear from them, one by one (I knew where they'd gone) until only the wide, dull wedding band was left. I made the minutes count, as Mr. Gratiot had warned me to do; but there was more to it than that. Under everything else, like a bed of banked coals, was that hot, hungry need to discover what it was that led people to do the crazy things they did—which is only a kid's way of describing history.

"You're a born scholar, George." Mr Lamprey, our high school principal, his bony fingers in a laced dome in front of his chin. "You have that disinterested pursuit of truth for its own sake. It's a rare gift, George. Very rare indeed." I didn't know anything about that, but I did know that was what I felt, all right. His washed blue eyes rested on mine with affection, and a kind of regret. "Why don't you apply to Harvard?"

"Harvard!" That haven of the rich, the favored, the secure; the idea had never once occurred to me.

"Why not? They take a fair number of scholarship students. And they have what they call a Highest Seventh Plan, tailored for boys from small regional high schools."

Harvard University. Its faculty held the giants—Merriman,

Brinton, Fay, Langer—I knew them, their names were on the title pages of the history texts I grappled with nights after work; it had the mightiest library in the western world. The truth I hungered for was there. Veritas, veritas!

"Well—if you think I've got a chance, sir..."

"I'm sure you do, George. A good chance."

That was incentive enough. I stood at the top of my class, and when I graduated I applied for Harvard—and wonder of wonders, was accepted. My mother smiled her worn smile, her mouth working at the corners.

"I'm so pleased, George. So terribly pleased."

"I know." This was the single, solitary chance of my young life, there wouldn't be another. She didn't have to tell me: I knew. And I was going to be equal to it. I was going to Cambridge, to become a student—and then a master—of history, I was going to do it because my desire and my discipline ran deeper than it did in most other kids my age, and I knew that, too. It was my crossroads. Life was never what it seemed to be—but life was nonetheless what you made of it, what you gave to it; what you salvaged from its shocks and offerings... Junctions, time. Junction. *Tuxedo Junction*—

"What are you thinking?"

Nancy's voice, against the backdrop of music and laughter. We were in the Empress, we'd been dancing to Glen Miller at the Fensgate, we were in the Empress driving back to Wellesley. Her head was near mine, her breath warm against my forehead. I couldn't see her eyes in the dark.

"Oh, one thing and another," I answered.

"No, I mean really... You're so quiet sometimes," she added. "If you don't say what you're thinking, how can anybody know?"

Dearest smooth immaculate Nancy, I'm in love. I'm hopelessly, irretrievably in love with this moment—with the Fusiliers, and the Empress, and Harvard, and Glenn Miller's *Tuxedo Junction,* and you, and I wish I were caught in a time bubble or I could sink into suspended animation or some glorious, goofy Buck Rogers trance so this night would never stop... How could you say that, or anything remotely like it, without proclaiming yourself certifiable? Kidding, yes, horsing around the way Russ did—but not dead serious. And I was dead serious. Your holiest secret dreams are always ludicrous. I'd said something to that effect one night to Terry and he'd replied: "Precisely— why do you think we've been given the ability to conceal our thoughts?"

"Jean-Jean," Chris called; her hair was whipping around her eyes in the night wind, her head was back, her eyes sparkling in the lights of oncoming cars. "Jean-Jean, will you will me the Empress? If I'm good?"

"*Good!*" Russ shouted. "Think you'll get it for being good, do you? That's not the way the game is played, Miss LaRue."

"Jean-Jean will, *because* I'm good . . . Oh, look!" she cried, "—the moon, the moon . . ."

And there it was, a slender silvery sickle gliding along with us behind the trees. It looked as though it had just been stroked into being.

"One new moon, to order," Terry observed. "We spare no expense."

"Oh, you're all so crass," Chris said, and tossed her head gaily. "It's beautiful!"

"*Ra-cing with the moon,*" Dal sang in a dreadful sonorous Vaughn Monroe imitation, off-key. "*Far-above-the-midnight bluuuuue . . .*" and we all joined in, the girls' voices high and clear and fragile on the night air. I gave Nancy a squeeze, singing along with the others, though my voice is almost as bad as Dal's, and watched the stars hanging close above us. That was the real joy of the convertible we knew: it was a car and yet it wasn't—it was a space ship, a phaeton, a prairie wagon, a sloop running before the wind; it was everything we were and wanted to be. The openness, the proximity to rushing earth and sky was unique, unmatchable. The very songs we sang seemed to have been written for it: we had the wind and the rain in our hair, we were high on a windy hill, we built a lovely stairway to the stars, we were racing with the moon, we could hear the angels sing . . . Someone would think of another, and still another, and we sang them all, swooping and swaying through the October night. The convertible was freedom, it was youth, too—all our youth, all the youth we were ever to have, though we didn't know that then . . . When we pulled up before Tower and the girls dismounted, calling softly to one another: "See you . . . see you," it was as if we'd just returned from a voyage to the most enviable isles.

"It was wonderful," I murmured to Nancy at the doorway.

"It was. Lovely." She looked just as band-box fresh as she had that morning. How could she look that way—so untouched, immaculate? It was entrancing. We kissed once, her hands flat against my chest; then she drew away. It was our pattern. "Phone me."

"I will."

Then we were gliding back to Cambridge, Chris singing a blues song in her lovely vibrant contralto, with the stands of the Longwood Cricket Club looming hollow and withdrawn in the fine, cool dark.

4

"I LOVE THIS CAR," Russ was saying. "I mean *real* love. None of this passing-infatuation jazz."

"We'd never have suspected it," Chris said.

"I want to make her my mechanical mistress. In fact, I hope none of you will be unduly shocked if I tell you I'm hot for her transmission."

Chris sighed. "Sometimes I'm not sure you've got all your marbles."

"That's because I'm a *curriolator,* actually."

"A what?" I demanded.

"Jesus, you're ignorant, Virdon. For a straight-A history brain. That's chariot-worshipper in Latin." Russ thumped the wheel's silvered spokes with the heel of his hand. "Yessir, when I'm tooling along in the old Empress I feel irresistible as Cary Grant. In fact I *am* Cary Grant."

Turning, Chris said to Nancy and me: "I knew Harvard would spoil him rotten."

"But you *do* find me irresistible, don't you, mmmh?"

"Of course I do, lover. Now watch the road some of the time, won't you."

We had just left Seiler's Ten Acres, where we'd been dancing to Gene Krupa, and were now wandering around somewhere south of Framingham. I had no idea where we were, and I wasn't sure Russ did, either. Jean-Jean had loaned Russ the Empress for the evening. Midyears were just over; we'd done pretty well, all things considered, and we wanted to celebrate. Earlier that day we'd taken the girls to see Cary Grant and Joan Fontaine in *Suspicion,* which was exactly the kind of sophisticated, was-he-or-wasn't-he thriller we loved, and after that to a North End restaurant Russ knew called Monte's, whose proprietor looked like a Mexican general and who personally served magnificent spaghetti vesuvio in great blue bowls.

All this, however, was to be mere prelude.

"George," Russ had said the night before, "I've had my eye on you for some time now. And I think you're ready."

"Great," I said. I was making out orders for the newsstand supplies. "Ready for what?"

"Sex, you fool, sex! You're not concentrating. Tell me honestly now—no evasions, no extenuations: don't you want to get laid?"

"What? Sure, I do. Of course I do. Only—"

"Okay, then. Let's make a pact. Like suicide, only with a future." He ran a hand through his dark, silky hair; that infectious excitement was working in him like yeast. "Let's go all the way. Tomorrow night. What do you say? I know a place on Lake Cochituate, it's a drive off the road with a view, very secluded."

I stared at him. "You mean, in the *car?*"

"Why not?" He laughed boisterously. "What do you suggest—a suite at the Ritz? a roadhouse on the Pike? I don't think they'd go for that..."

I laughed now. "Come off it. That's ridiculous."

"All right, *stay* a freaking celibate the rest of your life, see if I care. See if Veronica Lake cares." He pounded on my desk with his fist. "Courage, mon vieux! Faint heart ne'er crossed home plate."

"But the four of us in a car—"

"Just tell me you'll try. Really press for the extra base. We'll set the stage—Hollywood and jungle tom-toms and dancing and lots of booze. Are you with me or against me?"

"Okay." I shook my head, grinning at him. "I'll give it a try."

He slapped me on the back, cigarette clenched between his teeth. "That's all we're asking: the will—to—*win*..."

But the weather had refused to cooperate. We came out of the movie into raw, blustery night. It was sleeting fitfully—"a typical lovely New England February evening," was how Nancy put it; and it got worse hour by hour. The roads were treacherous and dark; cones of wet air swept back and forth under the Empress' canvas top, the heater was woefully inadequate. The radio was playing Artie Shaw's *Nightmare*. Everyone's spirits began to flag.

"Russ, where *are* you going?" Chris said irritably.

"It's a promontory, a lakeside vista." He might have been selling resort acreage. "It's quite imposing, actually."

"Oh, well. As long as it's imposing..."

"How you doing?" I murmured to Nancy.

"Frankly, I'm freezing to death."

"That's just what I wanted to hear, sweetheart. We'll have to do something about it." This sounded just right to me, both suave and masterful: Cary Grant and Bogey combined. I eased my arm around her and drew her to me in a completely suave and masterful way. Her lips were cool and firm, faintly caked with lipstick. Her beaver coat tickled my throat. After a certain amount of fumbling I managed to ease my hand inside her coat and hold one of her small, very round breasts. She seemed to be plucking at my arm and I started to withdraw, but apparently she was only trying to draw her coat around the opening I'd made. Was she kissing me more ardently now, opening that small, symmetrical mouth a trifle? I couldn't be sure. Her breathing was still perfectly even.

What to do next? After some confused thought I abandoned that approach, withdrew my hand from her breast, being careful to draw her coat snug about her throat again, and put my hand on her knee. I would have liked to keep one hand on her breast and put the *other* on her knee but my left arm was pinned behind her; in fact it was going to sleep—there was that dry, pins-and-needles tingling just above the elbow. No, it had to be one place or the other. I crept through the layers of clothing—fur of coat, wool of skirt, lace of slip, silk of stocking: textures, each more exciting than the last—and slowly inched my way along her thigh. She definitely stiffened this time, there was no mistake about that, shifting her legs slightly as though to move away from my hand. Advance or retreat? Her thigh was firm, much firmer than I'd thought it would be, and longer; a great distance really.

All my previous experience of sex had been confined to two inconclusive sessions with a girl back in Skamondaga named Josephine Holtz, who giggled uncontrollably whenever I put a hand on her breast. It sounds ridiculous, but the fact was I'd simply never had time for much sexual adventure—which is of course to say I'd never had the opportunity. Advance or retreat? Faint heart ne'er crossed—

I was flung against her; our heads bumped, we bounced against the corner of the seat.

"—What the hell, Russ," I said. I'd lost my tenuous beachhead in the commotion.

"Sorry. It's rustic, a rustic path..."

We were rocking and bumping down a narrow, rutted lane, the headlights dancing on the slick black poles of tree trunks. It was sleeting harder now, driving spikes of light at the windshield, spattering on the Empress' hood like flung sand. We dropped into a hole, bounced up out of it crazily.

"Damn it, Russ!" Chris exclaimed. "Is this trip necessary?"

"Almost there. It'll be worth it when we arrive, you'll see. It's only to be compared with the Hanging Gardens of Babylon."

"Hanging, all right..."

Finally we stopped, and Russ killed the engine. Irritably I looked up. There was nothing. Absolutely nothing. Some bulging masses darker than others, and that was all. No lake, no moon, no vista whatever.

"It *is* imposing," Chris said in her low, musical voice. "Especially if you're claustrophobic. I like particularly the way the moonlight weaves a pattern of gossamer below the chateau..."

"*Looming mass* of the chateau. I knew your heart would dance!" Russ uttered his short, boisterous laugh; sobered again under the pounding sleet. "It's a night for clandestine assignations, outrageous deeds. Women flung in riotous abandon on tiger skins, bodies throbbing with desire. You get the picture."

"If you ask me it's a perfect night for catching bronchial pneumonia."

"Nonsense! Behold the Eskimos, the orgies they contrive in

the steamy heat of the igloo during the long—"

"Turn it off, Russ, will you?" I broke in.

"You wish me to cease and desist?"

"That's the general idea."

"Then why didn't you say so, old Grog?"

Russ had given us nicknames—all the Fusiliers, nicknames that rhymed; he'd worked them up one evening. Jean-Jean was Frog, for obvious reasons; Dal was Wog, because he "looks like a Chink or an Arab or something"; Terry was Trog because he was so cerebral; I was Grog because of my first name and because I was always drinking coffee or cokes to keep awake. We pretended to disparage our sobriquets, but secretly we liked them hugely.

The music ended, the late news came on. British troops had captured Benghazi, the House had passed the Lend-Lease Bill, 260—165, FDR had named Winant to succeed Joseph Kennedy as Ambassador to Great Britain. Wendell Willkie on leaving London declared that all German-Americans hated tyranny and the Nazis.

"*All* German-Americans," Russ scoffed. "Und how does der Schmalzkopf know das, eh? I, Obergeneral Bruno von Kurtschticker, *love* tyranny."

"They all want war," Chris muttered against the gravel patter of sleet. "They can't wait to get you all into it . . . " She switched stations again, a band came on playing a tune I didn't recognize, and she said: "Oh good. TD."

"No, it isn't."

"Yes, it is. I know it is."

And sure enough, a few minutes later a soapy, urbane voice cut in: "—emanating from the Astor Roof, high above Manhattan, the music of that Sentimental Gentleman of Swing, Tommy Dorsey and his orchestra!"—and then that trombone— a fuller, dreamier tone than all the others—and Russ said:

"The winner and still champion. Come right over here and collect your door prize."

The conversation stopped for a while. Laboriously I began all over again. After twenty minutes or so I'd managed to maneuver Nancy into a semi-recumbent slump on the broad green leather seat. My left arm had gone completely to sleep by now, but I couldn't remove it without giving up precious ground. My hand had again cleared away the layers of fabric

and reached that point on the inside of the thigh where it swells
enticingly. Nancy pushed my hand away slowly. I moved it back
and she murmured, "No, George," but this time she let it remain
there. And we writhed and groped like some drugged undersea
creatures, bundled up in polo coat and beaver, sniffling a little in
the thick, dense air from the heater.

"...I love you," I whispered, my lips moving over her neat
little ear.

"You're sweet."

"I want you so."

She said nothing to this, stirred beneath me again; whether it
was resistance or acquiescence I couldn't for the life of me tell.
The code we honored in those dear, dead days prescribed that
the boy went as far as he could until the girl stopped him; then he
dutifully stayed within those bounds. If he was a "nice" boy, that
is, and she was a "nice" girl. But there was the pact I'd made with
Russ. And there were the couples who went "all the way," who
even enjoyed a kind of undefined distinction among us. And of
course there was Jean-Jean—worldly, all-victorious Jean-
Jean...

"*Of course* she will protest, Georges." His smoke-gray eyes
sparkling in quiet amusement. "Society demands it. It is the
nature of woman to resist, and of man to overcome that
resistance. It is a convention, don't you see? Like certain dances.
Underneath the—the ritual, she *wants* you to make love to her,
she desires it as much as you do. Even more, perhaps..."

Was that true? Possibly. Maybe. I could hear sounds coming
from the front seat now—the rustle and creak of rhythmic
movement, heightened breathing, the very softest of moans. Hot
and heavy, I thought, distracted; hot and heavy. Chris wasn't
like the other girls—cool and measured and careful; I thought I
could tell. There was that boundless openness to life, the lifting
groundswell of passion deep in her swaying walk, the dance of
her green-gold eyes, the fullness of her lower lip. And she loved
Russ, without reserve or calculation—she wanted him. Was that
true? What was going on there, then? Were they actually—

For some reason this threw me into a transport of passion. I
covered Nancy's smooth, invisible face with a storm of kisses,
stroked her thigh in a silent frenzy. I had reached the stocking
top, the garter fastening—then a hard, elasticized ridge. Girdle?
Panty-girdle. Of course. Only how the hell did you cope with

that? After more effort I'd succeeded in partly unfastening the stocking and rolling back the light girdle, had reached inside it. I was there, my hand cupped awkwardly in the small, curving hollow, though there seemed still another—oh my God, still another—barrier: some lacy, gauzelike fabric. Nancy was breathing quickly now, her body pressed hard against my hand. I was there! Panting and half dizzy, my loins throbbing with pain, I began to think that it might, incredibly, all take place. There was a condom in the side pocket of my jacket, bought expressly for the great occasion, and I thought of it now with mounting dismay. How the devil did you ever deploy it so the girl didn't see you? How could Houdini himself ever bring that off? My mind began to wander, I forgot I was supposed to be kissing and caressing passionately. I thought of Dal, who was always going out and buying fresh packages of condoms and throwing away the old ones.

"For Christ sake," I'd once exploded, "you haven't even used the ones you've *got* . . ."

"It's like an army, George." He'd given me his genial, coony look, his eyes slitted. Dal had had sex with several women—two girls back in high school, a waitress, the wife of a shoe salesman; unlike Jean-Jean he'd told us about them in some detail. "You may not need to use it for a long while . . . But when you do you've got to be ready. Know what I mean?"

Nancy was hugging me tightly now, nonetheless. She loved to kiss. We kissed each other so long and ardently we ran right out of breath and the low canvas roof of the Empress whirled close around us like a Bedouin tent. It was possible, it was going to happen. Why not? We were adults (well, nearly), we were in love, we wanted each other, and time was sifting through our fingers like diamond dust. It was the moment now, the moment to invade the awesome mystery. Bud Logan, who'd worked beside me in the beater room of the mill, had told me it was so wonderful you couldn't even describe it, you couldn't half imagine—

The sudden uproarious laughter, so wild, so near, made me jump. Russ, peering over the front seat, all eyes and pointed nose: a comic-strip drawing in the near blackness.

"Grog, you old contortionist!"

"For pete's sake, Russ," I complained hotly. Nancy had wrenched away, muttering something. Chris was saying:

"Russ, *stop* it now..."

"No, but have you ever thought how ridiculous we are?" He was still gasping with laughter. "I mean the four of us, bundled to the ears, groping around—"

"God damn it, Currier," I said. "Now shut up, will you?"

But there was no stopping him. That fanciful, headlong extravagance of his could always spill over into something outrageous, without warning, and then he was gone.

"—the high, cosmic grapple for the grail—"

"Russ," Chris said sharply, "that's enough!"

"—and yet at the same time we're terrified, yeah!—of that holy-of holies, the cavern measureless to man, the ethereal, sanctified female va—"

There was the sound of a slap then, sharp and flat—and a short silence, graced by far-away music; and then Russ's voice, now utterly subdued:

"—Wow. Chrissie..."

"All right. I said enough!... What's the matter with you?" she cried softly. "What makes you do loony things like this?"

"It just—I don't know, suddenly struck me as so funny, the way we—"

"You find the damnedest things funny, Russ. Just because your father puts you down now and then, that's no reason to humiliate the rest of us."

"Chris, it was just a momentary—"

"You *hurt* people when you do things like this, can't you see that? Hurt your friends. Hurt me, hurt—well, a moment like this. My God, you'd think you were one of those sherry-sipping phonies like Fletcher..."

"I don't know," Russ said softly after a moment. "I don't know why I do the things I do, sometimes."

"I don't either."

"...I'm sorry."

"You might apologize to George and Nancy."

"It's all right," Nancy interrupted tensely; she'd pulled her coat close around her again with a kind of relief and was dabbing at her nose and cheeks with a Kleenex. "Let's forget it."

"No, I'm sorry, Nancy," Russ said. "I am. I just got carried away somehow, and—"

"It's all right." Her voice was flat and hostile. "Now, if it's all the same to everybody I'd like to get back to school."

"Right.—Grog? Forgive your old Fusilier pal?"

"Sure," I said wearily, "sure, I guess so. Let's go before we get snowed in for the winter."

Back at Wellesley I walked Nancy up to the great oak door. She gave me a quick, perfunctory kiss.

"Hey, I'm awfully sorry about tonight," I murmured.

"It's all right." She was sniffling repeatedly.

"I hope you didn't catch cold. The Empress is a bit drafty this time of year."

"That's the least of it."

"No, I really feel bad about everything . . . I wouldn't have had it happen for the world."

"It's all right."

I should have shut up then; kissed her once more, chastely, and left. But the old need to patch up, to reconcile everybody to everything, was on me. Cursed are the peacemakers. I said: "Don't let it bother you, Nan. He didn't mean it, really. It's his way—he doesn't see the con—"

"He's an insufferable jerk," she burst out in a hard, threatful undertone I'd never heard her use before.

"What? No—"

"If he thinks just because he's from an old Boston family he can act like that, he's got another thought coming. You can tell him for me he's an arrogant, dirty-minded jerk! And you're another for going around with him. Good night, now."

"No wait, Nan—I'll call you tomorrow—"

She had swung away, shaking her lovely blond hair back from her face, her eyes wide with indignation. The great oak door banged shut. I took hold of the knob, which was slick with ice; took my hand away.

On the drive back to Cambridge it started to snow in earnest. We sat three abreast; Chris and I were silent. Russ drove with exaggerated care, entertaining us with a nonstop farrago of jokes, anecdotes, snatches of song. At Radcliffe he saw Chris to the door. It was considered bad form to look in the direction of your friends and their dates at that moment, but I was angry enough to watch them anyway. He started to take her in his arms but she held him off, not in a petty way but directly, earnestly; she was speaking to him, her face upturned to his, white against the hooded portico. Then she too had turned and vanished, leaving Russ standing there, hands hanging at his sides.

Back in the car he slapped the wheel, gunned the engine with a sudden thrust of his body. "Got told off again. Fire and brimstone." He seemed oddly purged by the incident, both soothed and exhilarated, and that angered me more than anything else. "Cheer up, Grog-o. She'll get over it. They both will. As a tangible matter of fact—"

"As a tangible matter of fact, why don't you dry up! If she does get over it, it'll be no God damn fault of yours. Not that it would make any difference to you."

He looked at me in astonishment. "What the hell, you stuck on the dame or what?"

"Maybe I am," I answered hotly, "if that's any of your business, which it bricking well isn't. Just who do you think you are anyway, Currier? What gives you the right to talk like that, with the girls there?"

"Oh hell, they've heard all the words, they've got their own hen—"

"That's not the point! The *point* is you upset people, hurt them for no reason at all..."

"Okay, okay."

"No, it's *not* okay!" I've always been like this: I'll swallow my feelings for a thousand years—good, steady, reliable old George, the loyal subaltern—and then finally something somewhere vital lets go and I've had it. I couldn't stop myself if I tried. "If you think something like that's funny you've got a really diseased world outlook, friend, believe me. What's eating at you under all that fancy horseshit? A night of romance and high adventure, a pact, for Christ sake—and then you pull off this kind of crap! I'll tell you what's wrong with *you*, chum—you've had everything handed you on a big, silver platter so long you take it all for granted. You're not serious when it matters. You don't even know how bull lucky you are."

He put out a propitiatory hand. "Look, I'm sorry as hell, George. Really I am. I'll call Nancy if you want, I'll—"

"The bloody hell you will, you're not calling anybody! You'll only invent a goofy way to turn *that* into some kind of vaudeville gag... An absolutely wonderful girl like Chris—a guy could consider himself lucky just to go out with her once in a lifetime!—and you come up with a stupid, insulting kid stunt like that. I hope to hell she won't even *look* at you for a solid year of Sundays! Jesus, you're a trial, sometimes..."

I ran down after a while. Russ sat hunched over the wheel, the Empress creeping along Garden Street with the snowflakes whirling up eerily against the windshield, showering crystals under the street lamps.

"You're right," he muttered. "I just didn't think. It was pure impulse."

"You *never* think. Why don't you try it some time? Take off those lavender Beacon Hill glasses of yours and see how the rest of the world lives? There's a whole lot of us out here, you know?"

"You're right. I acted like a bastard. A real bastard." He was as contrite now as he'd been reckless an hour before. "I didn't realize it would hurt anybody, I swear I didn't. I'll make it up to you, all of you; that's a promise . . ." Then the sudden droll twist to the mouth, the hilarious sally I knew was coming, that I could never withstand. "Don't write me off, young master—you can have my copious notes on Tudor England. Or the toilet chain which Claus of Innsbruck cast in bronze for me . . ."

Then he gave that up, too, and tossed his slim, handsome head. "What the hell, let's drop in at the Bick. I'll buy you a Maltese Danish. Never had a Maltese Danish, have you? An acquired taste. But hell, aren't they all?"

5

IN JUNE, AFTER FINALS, Russ invited us all down for a week at his parents' summer place in Brewster. He'd managed to patch things up with Chris, even with Nancy, months before, and the line-up was the same as the one at the Freshman Jubilee Dance, except that Jean-Jean brought Gwen Carrington, a pretty girl with bright green eyes, who worked as a fashion photographer in New York City. Russ's parents had gone to Mexico, which gave us the opportunity to roam through the fine old Cape Codder's beam-studded rooms, lounge around on the trellised verandahs and croquet lawns, and dream over the magnificent view of the Bay. We dug clams, or hunted down horseshoe crabs and raced them, or sailed out to wild, lost Billingsgate Island and watched the herring darting over the sunken lighthouse, its foundations wreathed in seaweed, and thought of Jules Verne and *Undine*; but mostly we let the air out of the Empress' tires, and swooped and swayed over the ocean beach at Nauset, where we found a secluded stretch of sand. The water was cold, even for mid-June, and we thrashed and roared and raced out again, while the girls taunted us, bobbing serenely up and down in the swells.

"What softies! No fortitude!"

"Don't hand us that—women have more fat!" Russ shied a hand at them. "Five extra layers of *fat!*"

"Softies, softies! If it weren't for women the human race would have folded long ago."

"Oh, you think so, do you?"

"We know so!"

Dal then and there suggested a softball game, boys against girls. Liz demanded that the boys bat lefthanded, and that the girls be allowed to pitch overhand, points Dal magnanimously granted. That was where he made his mistake, because Liz revealed herself as a holy terror on the mound.

"Hey," Dal called, after missing a pitch by half a foot, "you're really serious about this."

"You bet." Liz wound up like Dazzy Vance and let fly. With a grunt Dal popped it up; it hung in the off-shore breeze and Chris caught it easily.

"I instinctively distrust a girl who can throw like that." Dal peered at her under his hand. "You *are* a girl, aren't you?"

She stuck out her tongue at him. "That's for me to know and you to find out, buster."

"Those babes in the Berlin Olympics, they found some of them weren't females at all, you know..."

"Listen to that," Chris hooted. "If we're any good at sports we've got to be men! Mow 'em down, Liz."

She did. She fanned Terry on three pitches, and got Russ on a topped ground ball that skittered right back to her.

"What do you know," Russ muttered. "Looks as if we've got ourselves into a sit-u-ation."

Things went from bad to worse. Gwen turned out to be even better with a bat than with a camera. Chris couldn't throw as well as Liz but she was a hitting fool, and Nancy had gone to summer camp in Maine since she was seven. To add to our troubles, Jean-Jean had never played ball and threw wildly on every occasion—even into the water once; and Terry dropped a wicked line drive from Liz's bat that really opened the gates. After two innings the girls were leading 6-0 and chattering like monkeys.

When Dal came up again Liz took one look at him and said: "Oh no, you don't. I wasn't born yesterday. Bat lefty."

"And now *cheating!*" they screamed.

"Didn't they ever teach you how to lose?" Dal demanded.

Liz grinned at him, rubbing up the ball between her hands. "They tried."

"I know what you mean. Jesus, what a bunch of vindictive Amazons."

"Fight fiercely, Hah-vahd!" Chris needled. "What a lot of rotten sports. What the hell, fellas. It's only a game."

"Only a game, hell!" By now we were furious and sweating.

"Let 'em hit a few, Liz," Nancy said. "They'll be in a lousy mood all weekend if you don't."

Liz turned and glared at her shortstop, hands on her hips: Whit Wyatt at the Polo Grounds. "Forget it. I've waited seventeen years for a chance like this."

Trailing 14-3 after five ragged innings we conceded, and Dal and I were ordered to build the fire and cook the hamburgers as forfeit. We weren't doing too well until Chris knelt beside me and handed me a beer and said: "Oh, all right—come home, all is forgiven." She was wearing blue denim shorts and a bright yellow halter and she had a slender, sun-bleached fishbone stuck barbarically through her copper hair, which kept whipping around her face in the wind. Her skin had that high apricot glow, but deeper now; her lovely long legs were smooth and brown. She was the only girl I'd ever known who literally didn't care what she looked like—and who looked perfectly stunning anyway.

"Start the buns, George," she said. "I'll turn the hamburgers. What've you done with the spatula?"

Behind her shoulder, far up, beyond the rolling ridge of dunes the great diamond kite still hung, rocking gently, bluer than the sky's blue. She and Russ had built it together, years before. The two of them had got it out yesterday and brought it here to Nauset, running hard through the witch grass, shouting, their voices blown away by the wind, while the big kite plunged and reared, waggling its head like a hooked fish—finally leaped upward rocking, higher and higher, while we all clapped and cheered. Standing in the shallow water I'd watched them still running along the crest of dunes, silhouetted darkly: the first man, the first woman. They stopped, became one, they were holding each other hard, they were kissing—

"All right, that's enough of that!" Dal called, but they couldn't hear him, went on embracing while the big blue kite lifted toward the sun and the gulls wheeled and fell away downwind, screaming defiance. Then Chris broke away, her arms wide, and Russ chased and caught her; it was like a dream, a shadow play, their two figures joining and parting and joining again, until they both fell rolling and rolling down the tawny sweep of sand and lay there together at the bottom... and all at once I felt myself trembling a little, more stirred than I had ever been. I looked away as though I'd intruded on something I shouldn't have; near me Liz, scowling and shading her eyes, was saying in a funny, wistful voice:

"It's—as though they were meant for each other, somehow. Isn't it?"

"Yes," I said.

She looked at me. "Do you believe that? The destiny thing?"

"I don't know," I answered. When I looked back again they were running toward us, their arms locked around each other; Chris's face was turned toward him, her throat long and pure in the sunlight, and she was laughing that happy, heedless laugh, like angel scales...

"What are you staring at me for?" she was saying now, her eyes holding mine with that steady, guileless gaze.

"Nothing," I said.

"Now George, you know it's not polite to stare at the beach."

"You're so at home on the beach," I said.

"I ought to be. I've been on one all my life. I was sailing my own little catboat when I was seven. We used to build rafts—Russ and I—we built a houseboat once, but it sank. Remember the houseboat, Russ? Sometimes I think if I had to be away from the sea I'd die."

"You'd adapt," Terry told her.

"I'm not so sure of that."

"Everyone adapts. Sooner or later."

"Not me, pal." Russ was standing in front of us, beer bottle in hand. "I'm not going to adapt to anything I don't want to, and neither are you. Why should we?" He threw open his hands. He looked romantic and handsome in a scarlet sports shirt, his black hair tousled from swimming. "There's nothing we can't do if we put our minds to it. The horizons are unlimited..."

Terry smiled his secret smile. "Not true."

"What do you mean—*not true?* You sound like a bearded soothsayer or something."

"All right, graph it. Take your social and economic roots. Add the pressures of society, schools, friends. You'll find your choices are very circumscribed, buddy—in fact your whole life is perfectly predictable."

"Nobody's life is predictable," Dal broke in.

"No, look at you," Terry went on, still staring at Russ. "Beacon Hill, St. Marks and Harvard. Your father and grandfather, too. Summer home on the Cape, going with a Radcliffe girl from the Cape—"

"Ha! That's her problem."

"—the patterns are already set. As a reasonably competent sociologist I can project your entire life quite accurately."

"Okay, go ahead. Roll out the crystal ball."

"Oh good!" Gwen cried; she'd got out her camera and was moving around, snapping pictures of us. "I love fortune-telling."

"I don't think you ought," Ann said suddenly. "Really, Terry."

"Why not?"

"Well, it's—" she glanced at us nervously. "It's tempting fate, that's why. Playing God."

"Oh come off it, Annie. You know I don't buy that hocus-pocus any more."

"No, let him go," Russ declared. "I want to hear this. Come on, Gilligan. Lay it out."

"All right." Terry pushed his thin white legs back and forth in the sand. "You will graduate from Harvard cum laude—"

"That's a prediction?"

"—and get a job teaching literature at your old prep school."

"Never!"

"You'll marry Chris—"

"How do you know she'll have me?"

"You'll have three children, buy an old colonial house in Lincoln, do some of the restoration yourself..."

"I hate carpentry. *And* kids."

"Return to Harvard in the comp lit department, work your way up through the ranks thanks largely to Chris's tact-and-charm, until you're head."

"A maverick like me?"

"You'll buy a summer place in Wellfleet and sail a modest sloop in the Sunday regattas. You'll be a stern father to your son, overly lenient to your daughters. You'll drive a fashionably shabby station wagon—"

"Ridiculous!"

"Ultimately you'll join the Union Club, and the Somerset. You'll even be a vestryman at the Mt. Vernon Church."

"Oh, come on..."

"You'll publish one novel and three historical works—the second of these will get you a nomination for the Pulitzer, though it will go instead to an ambitious scholar at NYU. You'll become a faculty eccentric, given to battered felt hats and unbuckled overshoes, famous for the irreverence of your lectures. You'll drink a good deal, but not too much, and die a Brahmin patriarch, surrounded by adoring grandchildren, recipient of a few honors and full of days."

"Provided this doesn't interfere," Jean-Jean said flatly.

We all looked at him. He was holding out the Sunday paper. The headline blared: HITLER INVADES RUSSIA. *Thousand mile front aflame.* For a moment no one said anything. It had just happened that morning. An argument had started at breakfast, and Russ had decreed a moratorium; but its shadow still hovered over the lazy, sunlit day.

"Gloom-and-doom time at old Nauset," Russ complained. "Come on J-J. Not today."

"If you say so."

"We don't have to get into it," Chris broke in. "Miserable, rotten European wars. They never learn..." Her hazel eyes flashed passionately at us. "Why should we get drawn into it?"

"Because it's in the cards," Terry answered with his pale, cool smile. "Don't be naive, Christabel. That's the way things are being arranged. It's another of John Bull's wars, and John Bull *wants* us in there, to bail him out again."

"You're unhinged on the subject of England, do you know that, chum?" Dal said. "Unhinged."

"What do you call Lend-Lease, then? Or the extension of the convoy zones? It's all the thin edge of the wedge, anybody can see that."

"No," Jean-Jean said in a dry harsh voice. "It has nothing whatever to do with John Bull. That swine Hitler wants it. He *wants* everyone and everything to be destroyed." He shifted sand through his slender fingers, watching it intently. "It is his consuming, twilight dream..."

"Oh, come on, Frog-o," Dal said. "You're just sour-ball about everything because you got yourself on pro, that's all."

"Pro-*bay*-tion." Jean-Jean's beautifully chiseled lower lip went slack with derision. "Do they expect me to stand barefoot in the snow, in sackcloth and ashes?"

Jean-Jean had changed during the spring. He would fall into long, morose spells and then burst out in uncontrollable flashes of rage. He quarreled with Denise, he quarreled with Dal and me and even with Russ, whom he liked most of all of us; he got into a shouting match with his tutor and narrowly escaped expulsion; he'd backed the Empress into a stone post and dented the trunk. After each of these explosions he'd be gone for days at a time and then reappear just as suddenly, looking gaunt and contrite, and with gifts for everyone—a pigskin wallet for Dal, a leatherbound volume of Maupassant for Russ, a silver belt buckle for me. His grades were terrible; he'd been instructed to stay on at summer school to make up two courses, and the dean's office had informed him crisply that in any event he would be on probation for the fall term.

"Don't be blue, J-J," Russ coaxed him. "Have another hamburger. Have another beer. Have another willing dame."

"*Russ,*" Nancy warned him.

"Shakespeare, Shakespeare! Macbeth, Act Four: *Your wives, your daughters, your matrons, and your maids, could not fill up the cistern of my lust; and my desire—*"

"Russell, we've *read* the play..."

"But did you take it to heart? Did you realize that at any moment I, or Jean-Jean, or Prince Dal, here, might exercise the droit de seigneur, mmmh?"

"One of the unforeseen advantages of democracy," Liz said dryly.

"In fact, right now I *feel* a droit coming on." Shuffling along on hands and knees he came up behind Chris and gave her a hug, beaming at us all. "Hey, babe: how'd you like to be a consenting adult?"

"Simmer down, darling," Chris said, though she was smiling. Those green points in her eyes seemed to deepen whenever he touched her. "You're sex-starved, do you know that?"

"Then un-starve me. Let's indulge in some farouche fornication."

"Russ feels if he uses a three-syllable Latin derivative he's beating the system," Terry remarked.

"It's the truth!" Russ laughed, delighted, and helped himself to another bottle of beer. "I'm incorrigible, actually. Especially in June. Now what *is* so rare as a day in June?"

"I hate June," Jean-Jean muttered, sifting sand.

"Oh, no!" Chris protested. "Jean-Jean, *nobody* hates June..."

"Nevertheless. I do."

"All right," Russ proclaimed. "If Frog wants to hate June, that's it. June is hereby declared hateful."

"You guys certainly stick together," Gwen said.

"You bet. We're the Five Fustian Fusiliers of Fox Entry."

"Why do you call it *Fox* Entry? It's just F Entry, isn't it?"

"F for Fox," Dal said. "International call letters. Able-Baker-Charlie-Dog," he chanted. "Get it? For calling in coordinates."

"Coordinates?"

"Artillery. For plotting targets. On maps."

"Goodness!" Nancy said. "Where'd you learn all that?"

"ROTC."

"You're in ROTC?"

"Sure he is," Russ answered. "Trust the Wog. It's part of his Grand Design. Don't you know about Dal's Grand Design?"

"No. What's that?"

"He's got it all mapped out. Do you know who his personal culture hero is? You'll never guess. Andrew Carnegie."

"*Andrew Carnegie*—!"

"Dal, is that true?"

He grinned, biting on a cigarette. "Matter of fact, it is."

"You mean he's your *ideal?*" Liz demanded. "A money-bags capitalist?"

Dal stuck out his lower lip and squinted, the way he did when he was aroused. "He was no pirate, you know—like Morgan. Or a simple exploiter like Frick or Harriman."

"No, he was a *complicated* one," Terry rejoined.

"He was the first American millionaire to decide that the rich were responsible for their money—they ought to use it for the public good."

"After he'd smashed the unions and sucked all the blood out of the miners and steelworkers, that is."

"That's business."

"I'll say."

"Dal's got it all diagrammed, on the wall of his room," Russ went on. "You know, like Monopoly: Take a walk on the Boardwalk, elect yourself chairman of the board, collect five million dollars. Do not go to jail."

"You mean it's all on a *chart?*" Chris asked incredulously.

"Smoking gospel. Busy School degree by age 22. $30,000 a year by age 30. His own firm by 35. Corporation head by 40. Millionaire by 45."

"44," Dal said, and we all laughed.

"I'm sorry. 44. Timetable on a graph. Just like the German General Staff."

"Have your fun," Dal retorted; he grinned at Russ, though his eyes glinted behind the glasses. "You'll see. I'm going to be cruising the Caribbean in my own private yacht when you're starving in a garret, drinking dago red."

"Forget it. I bet I have a play on Broadway before you're dragging down thirty grand a year."

"You're on. Case of choice."

"Case of choice."

"I didn't know you were in ROTC," Chris said in a quiet, musing tone.

"Complete ROTC," Russ dictated. "Pass Go. Collect AB degree. Assume officer club status."

"All right, what's wrong with that?" Dal answered in the taunting laughter. ROTC had taken some abuse recently—not a few undergraduates considered them élitist as well as opportunistic, a hedging of one's military bets in case we did get into it—and Dal was touchy on the issue. "At least I'm facing up to it, pal. At least I'm going to be ready for the old clambake when it comes."

"It *isn't* coming!" Chris said frantically. "It can't, it doesn't have to—we're three thousand miles away..."

"You will not be any more ready for it than anyone else," Jean-Jean said flatly to Dal. "War. You think you are learning what war is, do you?"

"Sure I am, of course I am."

"Gold epaulets and jackboots, and the ladies in moiré. Your arm in a sling, maybe, the dear old oriflamme waving prettily, there."

"Look, I didn't say—"

"You know nothing about it at all. You are learning nothing."

"All right, how come you know so much about it?"

"Dal," I said in warning, but he was sore now; it was always his way to hit back when attacked.

"No, how about it, des Barres. Why aren't you over there right now, doing battle? Especially if you know so much about it."

There was a little pause, while the two men stared at each other. A piece of leftover hamburger turned black on the grill, hissing, and the newspaper flopped idly to-and-fro in the fitful gusts of wind.

"Let's drop this," Chris said. "Who wants to go swimming?"

"No, it's a good question. A perfectly good question." Jean-Jean was watching Dal with that faintly derisive grin. "Do you want to know what I was doing last year? today last year? when the Germans took Rouen? I was sitting in a café terrasse, drinking pernod. Seven of us. That was because there were no planes to fly. We were pilots without planes. Isn't that amusing? And the Boches were in Rouen. Birthplace of Gustave Flaubert," he said to Russ. "A cultural note in passing."

Then his lips pressed together again, his face became stern and suddenly much older. "And so we decided we would fight anyway. Why not? Your homeland is invaded, you go out and fight. We would fight and die like good Frenchmen. Like Russ's Fusiliers. We swore on it. We went to the armory and broke in, there was no one there anyway, and took rifles out of the racks. But we couldn't find any ammunition. You see? It was already starting comically. But we would get ammunition when we got to the front. We left anyhow for Rouen. I had an open touring car, a Delage D-8 120, a beautiful thing, and the seven of us got in. Like the football games, Dal. Allons, enfants! Off to the front.

"But the roads were full of people. We hadn't foreseen that. The whole world was running south. Camions, bicycles, wagons, wheelbarrows—anything on wheels. It took us four hours to reach Louviers, where we heard the guns. At a carrefour there an officer stopped us. A fine, tall, handsome major. Like Errol Flynn, Russ. 'Where are you going?' 'What do you think, commandant? To fight the Germans.' He laughed pleasantly. The officers with him laughed, too. 'Kindly tell me what is so comical, commandant,' I said. Then he stopped laughing. 'I am requisitioning this vehicle,' he said, 'get out.' 'The devil you are,' I said. 'On whose orders?' He put an automatic pistol in my face. 'On these orders. Get out.' Then to the others: 'Take their rifles.' 'You will hear about this,' I said. 'Perhaps,' he said. 'Meanwhile you are under arrest, all of you.' Then they got in my lovely Delage and drove away, honking the horn fiercely. Drove south. To Bordeaux, to Algiers, to Timbuktu . . ."

Everyone was quiet now. Russ cleared his throat as though starting to speak, said nothing.

"You see? I told you. It is not what you thought. Is it? The glories of war. We cursed them and cursed them. And then we started walking north, toward Rouen. But it was hopeless, the roads were jammed with people, we were walking in the ditches and we got separated from each other trying to fight our way through.

"And then the planes came. Out of nowhere. Right down the road and gone again. Another and another. And the screams began. Near me in the ditch there was this little girl in a Paris blue dress but it wasn't blue any more, it was soaked red and she was screaming and screaming. And finally I got her hands away and her insides were all out over her dress and legs, and I didn't know what to do, she was screaming so, and no one would stop to help. And the planes came over again, and now there were heaps—piles—of people crawling and groaning under the carts and wheelbarrows. And it grew dark, it began to rain, and I had no coat and no rifle, and my country was beaten, and the little girl was still screaming and I didn't know what to do, I couldn't think what to do, there was nothing at all to do!"

He broke off, his eyes flashing wildly in the hot light. Then he looked down, and tears began to run evenly down his cheeks.

We sat there motionless, transfixed, watching Jean-Jean while he wept in perfect silence and the surf seethed and pounded hollowly and a herring gull beyond the breakers kept making its reedy cat's cry. No one knew what to say.

Then Chris got up and went over and knelt and kissed him on the cheek. "It's all right," she said softly. "You did what you could, all you could, it wasn't your fault. You're right, Jean-Jean. We don't know, we don't know anything about it at all." She put her arm around him. "We love you, Jean-Jean, and we always will. Don't blame yourself, Jean-Jean. You mustn't blame yourself any more."

And sitting there gripping my knees, still rigid with pity, and a curious oncoming dread; watching her holding Jean-Jean, the tears hanging in her fine hazel eyes, her lips curved in troubled affection, the wild copper hair blown back from her brows, it hit me like a blow over the heart: I knew I loved her; I knew I wouldn't ever love anyone else again. I felt scared, and delighted, and deeply ashamed. I glanced at Russ but he was looking out to sea, his hands helplessly rubbing his thighs. My best friend's girl, and I was in love with her. Impossible. I raised my eyes again, and Nancy was staring at me: a slow, curious look. I couldn't even smile.

"Let's go back to the house," Chris said abruptly. "We've all had enough beach for the day. Let's go back and shower and get dressed and run over to the Whaling Museum in New Bedford. I've always wanted to see the Whaling Museum in New Bedford. Haven't you, George?"

"Yes," I said. "Yes, I have."

"Liz? Come on, let's go."

"New Bedford," Russ said. "New Bedford, that's seventy-five—"

"Well, that's where we're going. Right? Right. Come on. Stir your stumps."

We collected the food and beer bottles and blankets and trooped back through the soft sand, complaining of sunburn and cuts on our feet, watching the terns diving for tommycod, calling each other by Russ's goofy nicknames a bit too boisterously; there was a relief, a sense of companionship even in good-natured griping at that moment. I think we felt more together than we ever had before. Something—we couldn't have pictured or described it remotely, but we knew—had moved a pace or two nearer over the slowly sparkling, sliding sea. There was a compelling temptation to look over your shoulder as we shuffled up the last dune toward the Empress' proud silhouette. Directly above her the great blue kite weaved restlessly back and forth in the rising wind.

6

THE MOMENT I saw the postcard on the hall table I knew who it was from, and why. It had only one line, made up of letters of different type faces cut out of magazines and pasted together, like a ransom demand. It said: BG—TP—8/9—SB: DOBYS-FFF. It had a Brewster, Mass. postmark.

"It's addressed to you," my mother said doubtfully. "I couldn't help looking at it. I must say it doesn't seem to make a great deal of sense."

"That's okay." I could feel myself grinning. "It's a kind of code."

The following evening of course there was another postcard, typed on a German typewriter. This one read: *Oberhauptkommando Fuchs: Benny Goodman at Totem Pole on August 9th. You are hereby ordered to Stand By, preparatory to Dance Off Both Your Shoes. Und remember: zee importantistisches ding ist zu BE THERE, ja? Herr Unterfeldmarschall Bruno von Langendobber.*

I pulled off my work clothes and went into the shower, already trying to figure things out, already on my way there.

Half the fun was planning it. I think we got as much pleasure out of putting together an evening like this as we did from the evening itself. We worked up incredibly complex schedules, shot back and forth letters, cards, cryptic wires—we all hated the phone. And we weren't so scattered, really, that summer, the last summer we were all together, the last summer America was all together, that summer of '41. I was working in the beater room at the paper mill again; Russ was down at Brewster writing a mountainous historical novel about Voltaire and Frederick the Great; Dal had a job as barboy at the Annisquam Yacht Club. Jean-Jean was at summer school in Cambridge, making up those courses he'd flunked. Only Terry was loafing ("and proud of it") at his family's summer place in Scituate.

The girls were harder to round up. Chris was on the Cape, of course, and Ann was working as a receptionist in Boston; but Nancy was a counsellor at a girl's camp in Pennsylvania and couldn't get away; and Liz, out in Michigan, sent Dal a terse one-liner, straight wire: ARE YOU SANE NO QUESTION MARK CAN HEAR BG ANY NIGHT FROM FRONT PORCH. But after more frantic correspondence Ann got me a blind date with a girl she said was "barrels of fun and a really groovy dancer," and Dal was bringing a suave number he'd met at the yacht club. No one knew who Jean-Jean had decided to favor.

We were to rendezvous at Russ's home in Boston at noon. Wally Hannon said he'd take my tour at the mill on Saturday in exchange for a day later in the month. I'd picked up a '32 Dodge sports coupe that had been in a wreck, and had been working on it in my free time. One of the springs was badly cracked, she had a tendency to overheat, and two of the tires were doubtful, but I figured she'd make the trip. Jean-Jean and Dal weren't the only ones: I was going to drive up in style with my own convertible.

I was on 3-11 shift that week, and got away just after midnight Friday, running east along the canal, past those thunderous Revolutionary names—Oriskany, Herkimer, Fort Plain—in the clear, cool night. I had coffee at an all-night diner in Scotia and crossed the Hudson just as first light was breaking over the Berkshires, singing to the radio.

It was just east of Pittsfield that things began to go wrong. The fan belt broke in Cummington, but I'd anticipated that, I had a spare and changed it myself. Then just outside of Leicester the spring let go; after a lot of fussing and fuming I jacked her up, stuck a 4 x 4 block between the axle and chassis and wired it snug and she held, though every time I went over a bump it was like jumping on an anvil. A thunderstorm caught me in Marlboro and I got drowned before I could get the top up; it was three in the afternoon before I pulled into Boston, dangerously close to boiling out.

The Curriers' house was on Beacon Hill. Bulfinch had designed it himself. The front portal was flanked by two graceful Ionic columns, the panes of glass in the bow windows were purple with age. I shut off the engine and wiped my face against a shirtsleeve, feeling wildly out of place.

"Grog boy! What took you so long?" Russ was standing on the front steps. He looked tanned and fit, his hair loose over his forehead. The silver plaque centered in the great front door said *Currier* in fine Spencerian script. "Come by sea?"

"Ran into a little shower," I said.

"Ah, the open road . . . Did you drive it or did you push it?" He came down to the car and peered at the steaming radiator. "What's its name?"

"I was waiting for you to give it one."

"Words fail me." He yanked my father's old Gladstone out of the seat. "I haven't got *that* much imagination."

Inside it was cool. We climbed the curving stairs with their fine emerald-green carpet, and now, sliding my hand on the rosewood banister I could hear the rattle and thump of talk and music, and above it, around it, the voice I wanted to hear most of all. As I came in Chris leaped to her feet and came up and kissed me once lightly, on the cheek.

"George! Did you have an accident?"

"The whole trip was an accident," I answered, and everybody laughed.

"You look beat," Ann said. "Here, I want you to—"

"No intros," Russ broke in. "Let him go upstairs, dry out and loosen up. Or do you need a complete overhaul?"

Half an hour later, shaved and showered and dressed in my one good cord jacket and slacks, I came downstairs and met my date.

"I'm Bunny Delahoyde," she said. She was a short, chunky girl with a funny button nose and a wide mouth; her eyes crinkled up into slits when she laughed. "I'm going to BU in the fall. Ann says you drove all night. Aren't you tired?"

"Never felt better in my life," I answered, which was true. "I wouldn't have missed this for all the oil in China."

"Loyalty, thy name is George," Terry murmured, but he smiled at me.

It was lovely sitting in the great double living room. The ceilings were high, incredibly high, there were black marble fireplaces, the doors were of mahogany and had silver hinges, the bow windows ran from floor to ceiling. Curriers in frock coats, in wigs, in judicial robes stared testily down from the dove gray walls. There aren't homes like that any more, anywhere, even on Beacon Hill; they've all been broken up into apartments or gussied up with circular iron staircases and kitchenettes; but whenever anybody speaks of a house being elegant or distinguished it's the Curriers' I see, like some old Flemish interior you remember, cool and quiet forever in the mind. It was all I would ever have wanted for a home, and it was in the heart of the city I loved more than any other in the world.

The couches and chairs were covered with muslin for the summer, which gave the rooms a curious atmosphere: stately and festive at the same time. We sat around and sipped Tom Collinses or rum-and-cokes and played records, and everyone talked at once. We'd been separated for a thousand years, we'd hardly been apart at all. Dal came in with his yacht club date, a voluble, leggy girl named Sue Hazlett, who went to Bryn Mawr and had her own 31-foot sloop. Jean-Jean finally arrived, looking pale and drawn, bringing Gwen. The late afternoon light glowed on the portraits, the breeze sighed in the elms on Mt. Vernon Street. We talked about next year at college, danced fitfully and carelessly, and laughed at one another's jokes, no matter how stale; and the girls' faces flushed with sheer pleasurable anticipation.

"Where'll we eat?" Dal demanded. "I'm hungry."

"You're always hungry," Terry said.

"Well, we ought to get the show on the road, hadn't we?"

"Don't rush it, Wog baby," Russ said. "Let's not rush off. Let's let it build a little."

"Let what build?"

"Oh—the evening, life in general. Let's let it *intensify* a bit."

"You and your crazy romantic notions," Dal retorted; but he

subsided. He'd felt it too. Together again, encased in these sedate, gracious rooms where no harm could ever befall us, with the big-band revel still ahead, we wanted to hold the impending moments, sustain the fond, fatuous illusion that we could slow down time itself, fix it in amber.

"You look terrific," Dal was saying to Chris. "Really and truly sensational, do you know that?"

She did. Her face was tanned, not too heavily; the whites of her eyes were achingly clear, her lovely mouth soft as velvet. Her long legs and high-arched, slender feet were smooth and brown in white sling pumps; sitting there so erect and proud in her white sharkskin dress she looked—oh grace, thy name is Christabel...

"Am I?" she said happily. "You know, it's funny. I went into Jordan Marsh yesterday and everyone kept saying, 'You look wonderful! You look wonderful!' and I took one look at *them* and decided I did, after all."

"Christabel should have a statue of her own around the fountain there, in the Jardin de Lux," Jean-Jean murmured. "Among the great ladies of France."

"For God's sake, don't spoil her any more than she is already," Russ complained. "Chief Atwood stopped me speeding outside Falmouth and she talked him out of it. 'Any boy going around with you would be the right sort, Miss Farris.'"

"I always speak French at such moments," Jean-Jean observed. "No matter how distraught the gendarmes get I continue to speak French. Very rapidly. It baffles them."

And finally the sun dropped behind the stately narrow façades across the street, and we got ourselves together and milled around outside; there were devastating comments on my battered old Dodge, and I pretended to be deeply hurt. Russ had his father's Buick, and Bunny and I rode with him. Dal was in his Ford, and Terry and Ann shared the Empress with Jean-Jean. We had dinner at the Old Oyster House, where the air was full of the odor of fish and brine, and the fans blew densely over our heads, and sawdust lay on the floor in soft, ocher trails. Then we took off for Norumbega Park.

The amusement section came first—"to get us in the proper frolicsome mood," as Russ said. We sauntered along the concessions alley, choosing various challenges at random. Chris won an enormous panda in the ring toss game, Dal cleverly manipulated a remote-control grapnel and brought up a Mickey Mouse wrist watch and a yellow comb and a Brownie camera. In the shooting gallery Terry amazed us all: the Messerschmitts and Focke-Wulfs dived and zoomed crazily across the blue screen, faster and faster, and he shot them all down until the machine glowed red, white and blue and registered three free games and we all cheered. Then we climbed into cramped little beetle-boats and raced around a rink, shrieking and howling. It was revealing, the way we drove: Terry avoided all collisions, Jean-Jean rammed everyone in sight, Russ raced against the tide, Chris kept trying to slip between vehicles, Dal picked one target and pursued it relentlessly; I seemed to get hit incessantly from all directions.

After that we squeezed into bomblike gondolas suspended on steel cranes of arms that whizzed round and round till Norumbega was one long blur of crazy-quilt bands of colored light; and finally Russ said:

"All right, children, that's enough fun and fury, what do you say? Let's go over and catch The King."

Of all the dance pavilions we loved the Totem Pole best: a vast, softly lit amphitheater with couches flanking small tables that descended gradually to a dance floor smooth as old horn. It was exactly what we required: a wide floor, crowded but not packed; good dancers, we rarely bumped into one another. And above the floor, seated behind their gold music shields was the reason we'd put it all together. Our wrists stamped with the invisible ultraviolet colophon that allowed us to come and go, we entered the hall. The rhythm reached out to us like a dense, quickened, cosmic heartbeat, and Chris cried:

"Oh, Jackson! Listen to that heavenly sound . . ."

"What's your favorite band?" I asked Bunny.

"Artie Shaw," she answered without a second's hesitation. "Do you know *Octoroon?* Do you know *Non-stop Flight?*" Then she ducked her head and grinned. "But—well, when you've said everything there's only one BG."

The bands—we were forever arguing about them. We all had our individual preferences and put-downs. Artie Shaw had a terrific sound; yes, and sexy as hell, but at times he was obvious, even crude. Tommy Dorsey was smoother, but sometimes he was *too* sentimental. Well, if it was a question of musicianship, Ellington had the great sidemen—and besides, he'd invented a new kind of music. No, the Duke was too effete, too sophisticated—dancing to Ellington all evening was like trying to drink a gallon of elegant syrup. Count Basie was the best; no, he wasn't—Basie was great all right, he had the solidest rhythm section in the big time, terrific drive, but he lacked—well, something. Glenn Miller was unbeatable in certain numbers, but there was that tendency toward the cute; he put too much emphasis on vocals, and so did Jimmy Dorsey. Well, so would anyone who had Bob Eberly *and* Helen O'Connell. Harry James was exciting, so were Woody Herman and Gene Krupa. They had their great soloists, their own indelible styles; but when you added it all up, somewhere along the line they lacked—well, something.

But the band we could all agree on, for a long evening of dancing in all moods and tempos—jump and shag and glide—was Benny Goodman's. Year in, year out, it remained for most of us *the* band—full of invention and vitality and sheer overpowering musicianship; the sound that most vividly recalled an evening, a moment in time. The very ease with which the band could give up its great stars—Krupa, James, Rollini, Elman, Stacey, Wilson—and replace them with exciting new talents had something grand about it, like an indulgent emperor scattering handfuls of gems over a multitude. And the replacements were so good we forgot our dismay, even the purists among us, and listened for fresh nuances, different styles of shading old tunes. No music could envelop you more securely, more compellingly: the urge to dance was almost irresistible. In a galaxy of jazz nobility, of Dukes and Counts and Earls, the proudest title was Goodman's. He was The King, and there was no more to be said.

Now we moved out onto the great smooth floor like children in a trance, while Peggy Lee sang to us in that faintly mesmeric, subtly forlorn tone of hers of betrayal and desire, and Cootie Williams' lean gold whip of a horn slipped here and there in rippling, muted obbligato, and young Mel Powell dropped piano chords like tolling bells, fathoms down...

> Oh, how I'd cry, oh how I'd cry
> If you got tired and said goodbye;
> More than I'd show—
> More than you'd ever know...

Then the mood changed, the saxophones burst out in cool, pulsing melody and the brass team rose above it, martial trumpets challenging some barbaric citadel, blowing down its walls; and we spun our girls out and back, stamping out our shifting, weaving patterns, and shouted our delight at the end of the solo rides. *King Porter.* Bunny was a good dancer—Ann had done all right by me, I signaled her as much over a forest of heads—we caught on to each other's styles quickly enough, and the music took us. We only went back to the table when the band made its breaks. Nobody wanted to drink really, not even Russ; we talked about Lou McGarity's driving trombone, and this brilliant new kid Powell—where had he come from?—argued happily about bands and tunes and other evenings, and waited for the music we loved more than anything else to start again, welding us together, beating around us like golden rain...

When the dance contest was announced we were surprised, suddenly audacious, on our mettle. Art Draper, the pavilion's major domo, blew into the mike—everyone always blew into a mike before he used it, those days—smiled his genial, boyish smile and laid down the ground rules.

"Now, there've been a lot of complaints that some recent contests have been tilted in favor of the professional jitterbugs and the Latin lovers (faint applause and whistles), so we've decided we're going to find out who the *real* all-around, gold-plated dancers are among you out there (laughter). The band will play eight different dance styles—fox trot, rhumba, waltz, shag, tango, Lindy, conga and Charleston, not necessarily in that order. Now some of you may not know every single style, and it's perfectly okay if you want to try to fake it (more laughter and catcalls). Our floor umpires are very sharp and will probably spot it, but good luck anyway.

"Then, after we've eliminated the clodhoppers and hand-pumpers and walkarounds (laughter and moans), we'll get down to business. The band will play the same styles again, for the survivors, and the winners will be selected from the five or six finalists left on the floor. Remember, you will be judged not only on how well and inventively you dance each style, but on how smoothly you make the transitions (more groans and applause). All right: the contest will begin in five minutes: good luck to all of you!"

The ten of us held a rapid huddle. I said to Dal: "You going to try?"

"Try, hell! I'm going to win it."

"*I'm* going to win," Russ announced. "With a little help from old tanglefoot, here."

"You!" Chris laughed, shaking back her hair. "You never saw the day you could keep up with me."

"How about the conga contest at Belden's Blue Rajah, how about that, who swept them off their feet that evening, mmmh?"

"You and your sensual Latin blood."

"You said it, I didn't."

"Can you tango?" Terry asked me.

"Hell, I thought it went out with Valentino."

"I am the only one of you barbarians who can tango," Jean-Jean said.

"How do you do it?"

"You go into a kind of a slinky crouch," Dal said. "Like this."

"Buddy, you look like a de-eyebrowed Groucho Marx!"

All around the floor couples were trying out steps and laughing.

"That's Dick Fallon over there," Bunny told me. "I don't know the girl." She pointed out a stocky, good-looking guy in a ducktail haircut who was talking to a girl in a swing skirt with brilliant red hair. "He goes to BC. They're fantastic. They won last month at the Riverside."

"Charleston," I said suddenly. "Did he say Charleston? I can't Charleston."

"Just knock your knees and kick up your heels," Chris teased me, her eyes dancing. "Don't be so serious!"

It was a nice moment: like a carefree athletic contest without losers. Only Jean-Jean and Gwen had decided to sit it out. Chris caught my eye again and winked; that lively, devilish, impulsive mood was on her. "Are you ready, Georgie? *really* ready?"

"Wait'll you see my double entrechat."

Goodman started us off with a fox trot, which was merciful, then switched to a waltz, and couples began to drop out. I caught glimpses of Russ and Chris moving with light grace, and Terry looking very courtly and solemn. Then came the rhumba. The uniformed umpires were moving quickly among us now, tapping shoulders. Dal and Sue went out here, Dal could never rhumba decently. Then came the shag—oh God, the shag was fun, if only you kids *knew*—and after that the tango, and Bunny and I were quickly tagged.

"Sorry," I said. "My dance education is incomplete."

She shrugged and grinned her little helpless grin. "We did all right."

"Conga!" Art Draper called, and slender, haunted-looking Davey Tough started rapping out that rolling, insistent rhythm. The floor was less than half full now, with contestants steadily dropping out. Terry and Ann were still there, though, so were Russ and Chris. The revolving lights were flicking sharply over the couples, splashing them in golden spangles. Then, "Lindy Hop! Lindy!" and the band went into *Undecided,* the reed row driving the rhythm and the whole floor obedient to the spin-step-spin. There was Fallon with the red-haired girl, dancing superbly, and a thin man in a powder-blue jacket doing short aerial stuff with a girl in a matching dress, and a tall black couple dancing in straight-up, Chicago style, and maybe a dozen others. Chris and Russ swept by, her gored white skirt swirling like a matador's cape, and we shouted encouragement.

"They can do it!" Dal said. "Look at that! Look at that..."

"One—more—time!" Art Draper's voice boomed, and the band started running through the medley again. Terry and Ann had been cut in the Lindy, and came over to us. We stood there at the edge of the floor as couples kept dropping away, watching Russ and Chris spinning, then double-spinning in the conga to scattered clapping, then shagging to *Stompin' At The Savoy* in perfect easy bouncing unison.

"Where'd he learn to do that?" Dal shouted. "I never saw him do that before."

"They're good," Bunny was saying, "they're really good! Have they been—you know, going around together a while?"

"Yes," I said, "since they were kids. They've always—"

"That's it, then."

"Yeah, but it's more than that," Ann said. "Chris is—oh, look at that!—she's got that thing..."

Only eight couples now, then six, then five. The band lifting into *Roll 'Em,* Tough driving them, picking up fiercely, and Draper calling "All *right!* Let's see your variations...Stomp! Suzy-Q! Boogie! Shorty George!" Now there were only three couples left: Fallon and his redhaired girl, the black couple, and Russ and Chris. Draper conferring with the other two judges on the stand, pointing, nodding, shaking his head. Lou McGarity slamming into a wild, raucous ride, great gold trombone all aglitter. Russ, slim and hipless, dipping almost to his knees in a series of semi-splits and bouncing perfectly erect again, Chris's

face glowing with that high excitement, her lips parted—
smiling! she was smiling, on the edge of laughter—spinning and
swirling so fast her lovely thighs gleamed like bronze under
gauze.

"Our team is re-e-e-ed *hot!*"

"Pour it on!"

We were all shouting now, clapping to the beat. The brass
team was on its feet, all five of them, horns swinging in unison.
We were swallowed up in rhythm; it washed over us like frantic
surf. There was one final, thunderous chorus, the drums
rumbling and crashing in climactic avalanche, and the number
was over.

The roar was deafening. Art Draper was pointing down to
Russ and Chris, calling to them; then they were on the
bandstand, with the other two couples, Art was handing Chris
the gaily-colored little totem pole and calling over the mike:
"—and first prize to Chris Farris and Russ Currier, of Falmouth
and Boston!" The other prizes were bestowed; they were shaking
hands with the other couples, Chris had embraced the little
redhead, the tall black girl, then they were shaking hands again
with Art Draper; then the moment was over, the band went off,
and Russ and Chris came up to us in an uproar of
congratulations and hilarity.

"He did it!" Terry cried. "The old son-of-a-gun—he said he'd
do it and he did!"

"I like that," Chris said, and Dal retorted:

"The hell you say—Chris carried the club." He gave her a
bear hug and a kiss. "You were great, babe. Nothing less than
legendary."

Russ was mopping at his face with a handkerchief. "Actually,
she was just a touch ragged in the tango..."

"—and what about the Charleston?" she cried, her hands on
her hips, her face flushed, eyes sparkling in the gold light from
over the bandstand. She had never looked so beautiful; not even
at the Yale Game; not even on the beach at Nauset.

"It's a question of poise," Russ declared. "Poise under
pressure. All it is." He picked up the gaily painted little totem
and studied it, bear over owl over lynx over eagle. "This means
more to me—this little trinket means more to me even than my
Ralston six-shooter. Than my Special Agent's G-man badge.
Curiously phallic, isn't it?"

"Russ!"

"Idle surmise, purely." He downed what was left of his drink and ordered another round. "We're just too fast. Too fast for the old track, podnuh."

"Looks like it." And she smiled at him—the kind of smile between a girl and a man that means only one thing; for all the world to see.

"Of course I'm keenly disappointed in you all—I was hoping for a Fox Entry sweep. But some got it, some ain't, as Bismarck once said to George Sand."

"Don't gloat, darling. Modesty in triumph."

"Who will sing my praises if I do not, mmmh? Well," he ran his hand through his hair and his eyes took on that mischievous stare, "now we've established the old pecking order beyond the shadow of a doubt, let's get down to a little *serious* rug-cutting..."

The band came back and we went on dancing, nodding now and then to other contestants on the floor. It made for a loose, easy feeling, a kind of unforeseen camaraderie. The band ran through a flawless *Changes*, and then Peggy Lee sang a moody, moving *It's Been So Long*, and then Goodman stepped out front, in earnest, and showed us all why he was master of the blackstick, holding in a precarious balance between exuberant abandon and a crisp, disciplined elegance the music we loved at times more than anything else in our strained and slipping world.

The winds of March that made my heart a dancer—
A telephone that rings, but who's to answer?
Oh, how the ghost of you clings—!
These foolish things
Remind me of you...

The evening lifted away. We changed partners, and finally I found myself dancing with Chris to *Moonglow,* Goodman weaving the simple little melody into something almost painfully poignant against Tough's feathery brushwork and Powell's somber blues chording, the wide hall moving in dreamy acquiescence under the golden spangles. Dancing with Chris was literally like walking on clouds—you had no sensation of stepping or turning, moving your body. To this day I can never hear *Moonglow* without seeing her face that night.

"You looked wonderful out there," I murmured. "Really and truly marvelous."

"It was fun."

"You were smiling. As though you—" I stopped.

"As though what?" She leaned back and looked up at me. Her eyes were filled with those tiny green lights.

"As though you knew you were going to win all along." It wasn't what I'd been going to say. I couldn't say what I'd been going to say.

"Maybe I did." She laughed, that low, even laugh that had all kinds of hidden deeps in it. "We were just—you know, stepping it out, concentrating on switching styles, loving the music—and then I noticed the floor was getting awfully empty. And then all of a sudden I felt we could win: I could feel it in Russ's hand—right there, in the small of my back. You know? We were going to win, there wasn't any doubt about it. Silly, isn't it?"

"No. It isn't silly at all." *Nothing you could ever say or do could ever sound silly to me.* But of course I didn't say it. She was my best friend's girl and she was in love with him fiercely, unalterably, irretrievably; I knew that because it's even more true what they say about lovers than it is about thieves; and that was all there was to it. I shut my eyes and drifted in a kind of foolish, holy agony while Benny Goodman's clarinet told its tale of lost love, the melody piercing and exultant and wistful by turns, and the revolving lights stung my eyelids.

And finally the band played *Stardust,* that rapturous, bitter-sweet valediction for all dances of my generation, and after that their going-off number, *Goodbye,* the saddest tune ever written, and we stood and applauded softly now, almost regretfully, and watched the musicians packing up, and then strolled back to our table. Jean-Jean was sitting there and saying tersely to Terry:

"Well, if they've reached the Black Sea, if they've actually cut the Kiev-Odessa railway—"

"No war talk," Russ protested. "Hey, not tonight, okay? We agreed. I know, I know, Germany's swallowing up the whole bloody world and we're all going to be drafted and have our hair cut off. But not tonight, okay?"

And Jean-Jean smiled up at him, that charming, indulgent smile, and said: "Yours to command, oh king of the jitterbugs. What is your pleasure?"

Russ shrugged and grinned. "Well, we can't quit now. Where'll we go?"

We stood around in the warm night air, being intolerably witty and profound, and laughing at everything and nothing. We drove to an all-night place Dal knew where they served eggs benedict; and then Jean-Jean wanted to see what Massassoit really looked like, so we drove over to Plymouth to look at his statue, and as long as we were there we ran down to the shore to show Jean-Jean Plymouth Rock; but it was too dark to see it. Finally we wound up at a small, deserted beach near Scituate where we went swimming, and huddled in towels and blankets sat on a low rocky cliff while the stars fell away one by one and the sky lightened to slate, to dove, to salmon, and in the ragosa and bayberry thickets the birds began sleepily to stir.

"That's Minot's Light," Ann said, pointing. "I love you."

"You do," Terry answered. "This is so sudden."

"No, see? One, four, three—the flashes. *I—love—you ...*"

"That's the kind of lighthouse I can identify with," Russ said. "By God, I think I've finally achieved it."

"What's that?"

"What's the Aristotelian definition of happiness, Gilligan?"

"Complete and habitual exercise of one's functions."

"Oh well, if *that's* all it is, we've all made it, we've arrived."

"Speak for yourself, buddy," Dal said. "Happiness for me is fifty thousand a year and a seat on the stock exchange."

"Don't be crass, Dal," Chris pleaded. "Not tonight."

"That's telling him, babe." Russ took a histrionic stance, arm upraised. "A hundred years from now, when the big ledgers on these times are tallied, let no one forget the stand made by this fine young American girl, and how it aroused the con—"

Without warning the sun broke up out of the sea like a huge topaz medallion, pouring gold toward us in a shimmering, quaking river.

"Make a wish!" Chris cried.

"You don't wish on the sunrise, silly," Ann said. "It's the first *star* you see, not the sun ..."

"Not me. I wish on the first sun of the day."

"There'll never be another night like this one," Russ said; his eyes searched out each one of us. "This is the peak. Do you realize that? From now on it's all downhill."

"The original Nostalgia Kid," Terry remarked lazily.

"Today's vicissitudes are tomorrow's good old days."

"Let's make a pact," Russ went on. "We'll meet here—ten years from today. Right here. What do you say? Let's swear on it."

"Ten years," Jean-Jean began, and shook his head. "In ten years, mon vieux..."

"We can do it. All it takes is—is firmness of purpose and great desire."

"And a little luck," I said.

"All right, and a little luck." He waved the brightly painted wooden cylinder above his head. "Come on, now: swear, by the sacred Totem Pole of Norumbega!"

We all swore.

We straggled back to the cars then and got dressed and said our goodbyes; and still we hung around, leaning against the fenders, smoking, chatting, caught in a light-headed elation that wouldn't leave us. Finally the others all rolled away. And in the fresh, clear morning Russ and Chris and I looked at each other.

"What fun," Chris murmured; she slipped her arm around Russ's waist and glanced up at him happily. "What wonderful fun we all had."

Yes, that was the line. It summed it all up.

I put a towel over my head, rubbing my hair with it. The sun was already hot on my shoulders; I knew it was going to be a scorcher. I thought, all at once and for the first time in hours, of Nancy. I hadn't missed her at all. I felt guilty for not feeling guilty.

"I didn't get my wish," Russ said in a lugubrious tone.

"You took all the marbles," I said, turning. "What in hell *was* your wish on the sun?"

"That it would go on forever."

He laughed and climbed into his father's Buick.

II

I Don't Want to Walk Without You

1

"COME *on*, GEORGE," Russ hissed at me. "Crawl out from under that damp rock and greet the bright new day." He'd just come up from running cross-country; tanned and lean, his hair plastered close to his head from the showers, he looked like an Indian—a very handsome Ivy League Indian. He peered around the house library, squinting in the gloom. "Hell, there's nobody in here, anyway," he remarked in a normal voice. "Who with any good sense would be? Come on, let's eat. It's after five."

"Right with you," I said. I put away the marking inks, clipped the out slips together and locked up, and we walked across the grass where the first fall leaves lay like buff and ocher flakes, stirring in the light breeze off the river.

"Summer, you old Indian Summer," Russ sang, arms over his head. "Just *breathe* that lovely fetid paludal air."

"Paludal," I said.

"Swampy to you, pal."

"Then why don't you *say* swampy?"

He shook his head at me wearily. "You just don't understand. Never use a simple word when an esoteric one will score. Howja expeck ta git a gent's grayde?"

We passed through the high wrought-iron gates. We were upperclassmen now, pleasantly settled in one of President Lowell's ivy-bound answers to the clubmen and their rathouses, those sumptuous dormitories known as "the houses" that sprawled along the banks of the Charles: Russ and Dal and I rooming in one suite, Rhino and Mel next door, Terry and Jean-Jean on the floor below. The entry was lettered K but we blithely, stubbornly persisted in referring to it as Fox.

"Let's look in on Jean-Jean and Trog," Russ was saying. "Give them a royal hard time. Have you seen the new chick J-J's surrounded? Ava something. Tits like pack howitzers." His eyes rolled, he went into a little shuffling dance. "My God, wouldn't you give your bicuspids to climb in with that, wallow in the celestial syrups? Ya-hoooo!"

"Well," I said. "I thought you've been running your heart out, all over Melrose."

"I have, I have. What's that got to do with the price of fish? An inexhaustible fund of misplaced sexual energy. That's what Mel Strasser says I've got, and he ought to know, he's the medical genius."

"Where I come from we called it just plain horny," I said.

"Yes, well, you're not where you come from, ace. Here there's a term for everything and everything in its term. Conversely."

We climbed the entry stairs to a medley of music, shouts, curses, radio voices pounding out the evening news. Russ flung open the door—nobody ever locked his door in those days—and cried:

"Froggy-bo! What's the hue and cry? What mesial groove are we tracing this evening?" Then he dropped his hands. Clothes were all over the place, draped on the furniture, spilling out of that gorgeous Vuitton luggage. There was a liquor carton on the floor half filled with books. The radio was playing *Cherokee*. "Hey, what the hell's going on?"

Jean-Jean leaned out from the bedroom. *"Joie,"* he said. "The password is *joie*." He came up to us in his quick, darting run and hugged Russ, then me. "Deliverance, renaissance, whatever you wish."

"What goes on?"

"I am leaving, mon vieux."

"Leaving! But you just moved in, we've just got rolling—"

"True. True."

"Jesus, J-J, have you got yourself canned?—*already?*"

"No-no-no." He laughed, wagged a forefinger at us, back and forth. "Nothing so sordid. No, it is voluntary. Purely voluntary."

"But why?"

"Because that is how I am." He laughed again, his eyes shining. The transformation was unbelievable; he looked like a younger, happier, more resolute brother of Jean des Barres. "You wouldn't want me to get stodgy, would you? set in my ways?" Then, very quietly: "No, I am going to Brazzaville."

"Where?"

"To join de Gaulle."

"For—Christ—sake..." Russ was gazing at the luggage, at the fencing mask lolling in a corner of the room. There was a look of boundless consternation on his face—I'd never seen it before; he was chewing at his lower lip. "But—you *can't*..."

"Nevertheless. I am going." And all at once he snatched a pillow from Terry's great blue couch and flung it at the ceiling. It caromed off the mantel; a bottle fell to the hearth and smashed. "Over!" he cried. "The minuet is over."

"Oh, come off it, J-J," Russ said. "Stick around. At least till midyears. At least till the Yale Game. Don't you want to find out how we do against Yale?"

"You can write me, mon vieux. With all the ivy-covered news." He put a cigarette between his teeth, groped in his pockets for his lighter. "No, I have sulked in my tent long enough. Mnnh—a classical allusion, Russell. You see?—my Harvard education has not been entirely wasted."

His eye caught mine, he winked; a droll, solemn Frenchman's wink. I went up to him and grabbed his hand. "All the luck," I said. "All the luck in the world."

"Thank you, Georges. It is possible I may need some of it."

"But look, you can't just go like this," Russ broke in; he'd recovered himself, but his eyes still darted hotly. "I mean, not without a—Christ, not without some kind of a farewell gathering, the clan all gathered round—"

"A ceremony," Jean-Jean said, and winked at me again. "Of course. Who am I to deprive you of ceremony?"

Two nights later—a Friday, fortunately—we began to assemble at Jean-Jean's apartment in the Fens. The preparations had been frantic: Russ gave out orders like the commander of a battalion about to be overrun. "Now it can't be a surprise bash, that's out. But I want it to be something Jean-Jean will remember the rest of his life. It's got to be the load of all loads, absolutely. Nothing left to chance. Right?" He personally bought an awesome three cases of the best liquor Scotland and Kentucky could produce. Terry was ordered to spare no expense with food, Dal was to make certain there was plenty—and he meant *plenty*—of ice, I was charged with rounding up phonograph records from everyone, with duplicates of Jean-Jean's favorites in case of incidental breakage. The girls were told in no uncertain terms to make themselves available or forget about the rest of the year—or the rest of the decade for that matter. It was Russ at his wound-up, extravagant, romantic best: we dropped everything else.

That afternoon I got a kid named Schilz to take over the house library for me; and proud as a margrave and nervous as a cat I drove the Empress out to Wellesley and got Nancy. It seemed odd not to be picking up Liz, too; she and Dal had parted company after June, Dal said he'd lost interest in her.

"She's a strange one," he'd offered late one night. "I don't know—I'm not sure she's all there. As a broad, you know what I mean?"

"You're just pissed because she showed you up in the softball game," Russ had taunted him.

"No," he'd answered, without heat, speculatively. "No, she's cold . . . No, it's not that, she's not frigid, actually—it's as though she's got her mind on something else. It's unnerving . . ." Then he'd grinned his Oriental cat's grin. "What the hell, maybe it's just chemical. Anyway, it's time for a change."

But when I came into the lounge Liz was there, talking with Nancy. Nancy gave me a quick, perfunctory kiss. I could see she was irritated; that thin, perfectly straight line had appeared between her brows. Liz shook hands straightaway, her full arm extended, like a boy's.

"Hi, George."

"Hello, Liz."

"Tell Jean-Jean good luck from me, will you? And the crowd."

"Absolutely." I didn't know what to say. At first I'd thought she'd decided to show up out of defiance, but now it didn't seem like that at all. I felt off-balance, a bit contrite. "Hey, we'll miss you, Liz."

"Sure you will."

"No, I mean it."

She smiled easily. "The world isn't going to crash, George. Give Dal my best." She laughed naturally, watching me. "Let me know how he makes out with that little old Monopoly game of his sometime, will you?"

Driving through Wellesley Hills Nancy said: "Who *is* Dal bringing, by the way?"

"Girl named Kay Madden. Bennington. I haven't met her."

She was silent. I felt vaguely distressed: the old need to soften, propitiate, bring it all around again. "Sorry it turned out this way, Nan."

"No problem. That's how it goes." But she was staring straight ahead at the traffic, her hair lifting gently in the wind.

"Is she—taking it hard?" I asked.

"What a silly question! Honestly!" Her blue eyes flashed up at me, away again. "She's been seeing someone else for quite a while now. Boy from Amherst she met last spring. Whatever made you think Dal's such a prize, anyway?"

I started to flare up at this. Where did my loyalty lie?—to Nancy, or the Fusiliers?

"Liz is a *very* appealing girl," she said, and gave me her most significant glance. "She's also very self-possessed—"

"Of course, Nan. I didn't mean to imply—"

"She knows what she wants to do with her life, and she's going to realize it. All of it. You'll see. If someone doesn't have the brains to appreciate her, that's their hard luck. There are plenty of others who will."

"Sure, of course," I repeated with a touch of irritation. "I think Liz is terrific, I always have—you know that."

"Well, you don't sound like it, George."

"All I meant was I wish things could be—you know, the way they were."

"Well, they can't. Don't worry about it, George." She ran a thumb over the perfectly manicured nails of her other hand. "Tell me about Jean-Jean. How's he going to get to Africa? He'll be an officer, won't he?"

I dropped the subject after that and we talked about de

Gaulle, and Africa, and what we'd done and hadn't done all summer. I'd written her about the Totem Pole evening, playing it down a good deal—it had seemed somehow obscurely disloyal to make too much of it—and her reply had been rather noncommittal. Now however she wanted to hear more about it, especially the dance contest.

"Chris and Russ were fabulous," I told her. "Really beyond the fab. They got better with each number—you should have seen them in the final set. They were like one person, like dreaming your way through a dance."

"I didn't think they were that good, actually."

"They were, though—especially Chris. We all were. It was alchemical, as Russ says. Even Terry and Ann lasted till the last 12-15 couples. We'd have finished in the top three if you'd been there, I know we would."

"Don't be silly."

"No, it's true. You'd have carried me on the tango and conga, and we'd have made it. They watch the girls mostly, you know."

"Silly," she repeated, but she was pleased, and her mood lifted a little on the way in to town.

Jean-Jean's apartment—his pied-à-terror, Russ called it—was in a remodeled old mansion; it had high ceilings with roman arches—there were no doors except for the bathroom—and it looked northeast over the feathery green sweep of the Fens toward the golden dome of the State House and the accusatory finger of the Custom House tower. God knows what it cost. It had rattan deck chairs from some old Dutch cruise ship, and a sectional couch done in Madras stripes, and a gigantic record player where, encased in glass, chrome arms and levers could change or invert twelve records at a time, with the softest click and hum of its hidden machinery. It was playing now—*Avalon*, a particular favorite of Jean-Jean's—and things were already in a high state of exuberance.

"Hail, Grog!"

"Always room for two more..."

Terry and Ann were dancing, Chris was doing a lively imitation for Jean-Jean; Mel Strasser, looking solemn and medical, had brought Marge Feldman, a warm, steady girl from Radcliffe; Rhino Tanahill was there—a mighty tribute, because he was playing against Cornell next day—with Prill Harms from Vassar; Fletcher and Bierce were there, so was a diffident

French boy named André Mortier, also a refugee from the Wehrmacht, whom Jean-Jean occasionally went around with. And people were still coming in, to a chorus of hooted greetings and the tinkle of glass and the shivery laughter of the girls.

I went over to Jean-Jean and handed him the car key and said: "Thanks, J-J. I felt like Blériot."

He nodded. He was wearing one of his beautiful French shirts with the long cuffs turned back now on his forearms. The wide collar was open at the throat.

"Georges is a traditionalist," he murmured to Denise. Out of all his frieze of ladies he had invited her, possibly because of his return to Free France. "Georges remains faithful to the old standards of decorum. He will make a wonderful archivist."

"I like tradition," Denise said; yet her smile seemed forced. One foot rapidly tapped the parqueted floor.

"So do I, so do I," Jean-Jean nodded somberly. He was already a little drunk, but the only way you could tell was his eyes: they darkened to a deep, moist slate. "Without tradition there can be no—no—I don't know *what* there can be."

"There can be no salvage," Chris finished for him.

"Salvage?"

"Yes—nothing would be held to, carried forward."

"Merde!" Russ broke in loudly, waving his glass. "Tradition is the swamp we're all drowning in."

Jean-Jean smiled. "You will learn, mon vieux."

"If I *was* a French nobleman like Jean-Jean," Chris cried. "I'd never want to change anything!"

"Were, *were*," Russ corrected. "Condition contrary to fact."

"You!" She laughed, gazing up at him happily. "*You're* a condition contrary to fact."

"I am. It's true."

"But I love you anyway. Isn't that ridiculous?"

And then—right then, right at that instant, eerie as it sounds—I felt a sudden little flurry of excitement behind us, a heightening of voices punctuated by bursts of greeting; and I turned and caught my first glimpse of Kay Madden.

She was very thin, with fine slender legs, and she was handsome all right—the faultless confectionary symmetry of the professional model: aquamarine eyes with high arching brows, a full, sensuous lower lip held in a gently provocative pout; her blond hair was swirled low over one eye and curled in prettily at her throat. Only two small crescents at the corners of her mouth marred the conventional beauty of her face. But it was her manner that seized and held you: that faintly imperious, faintly bemused look that leaps out at you from the fashion pages of the big magazines. Yet there was more, too—an audacity beyond challenge, a defiant self-assurance that proclaimed she held the world solidly in her hand. For two strokes of a metronome she measured us—celebrants, well-wishers, satellites and stars—and found us just a touch wanting.

Then she shrugged out of her coat and passed it back to Dal in one easy, careless gesture and moved straight on into the room. She was wearing an electric blue shirt of raw silk and a swing skirt and spike heels.

"Hello, J-J," she said; her voice was high and clear, with a metallic edge. "Hail and farewell, is it?"

"Hello, Katherine." He made his quick, courtly little bow, though she pressed inside it and kissed him. "Are you amusing yourself, chérie?"

"You know I am, lover. That's my mission in life." Abruptly she turned to me. "And you're George."

"Right," I said. "How'd you know?"

"Simple. You're the—well, the *serious* one."

The quick, presumptuous glance, the bullying beauty; then she turned away, took someone's hand provisionally even while she spoke to someone else, and watching Dal following her, off-balance, his Chinese face frozen in a prideful, nervous grin I thought, Christ, he can't handle her; and then I looked at the rest of us and thought, Christ, *nobody* can handle her. Nobody around here, anyway...

"And this is Chris Farris," Dal was saying, a little too loudly. "And this is Russ Currier, the dancing fool."

"Oh—" her aqua eyes brightened, the lip pouted a shade more. "You're the one that had that short story in the *Advocate*."

"I'm the pigeon." Russ's lips closed over his cigarette. "How'd you happen to see that?"

"Oh, I always get seated before the main titles."

"Bennington, isn't it?"

"That's it. Bennington."

Russ still hadn't taken his eyes off her. "What'd you think of it? the story?"

"I liked it. I liked it a lot." She brought her chin down, studied him from under her brows. "Fooled you that time, didn't I?"

He laughed and nodded. "Matter of fact, you did."

"Actually, I think your power is visual, not linear. Films, not prose."

"That right."

"Yep. I do a little writing myself, a little reading."

"Up in Bennington."

"Up in Bennington. And elsewhere. Ever thought of doing a screen-play?"

"Oh, sure." That madcap, maniacal glare had flowed into his eyes. "Yeah, as a matter of fact me and Doré Schary and Preston Sturges are putting together a swifty about this Russian lady who falls in love with a guards officer and throws herself under a train. We're calling it—"

"Choo-Choo, Anna Baby," Kay broke in flatly, and everyone laughed.

"Kay knows what's she's talking about, Russell," Jean-Jean said. "Her uncle is Lorenzo Flagler."

Russ started. "The producer—the Hollywood producer?"

"There wouldn't be two of them," Kay answered. "Not this karma. No, seriously, that scene at the end of the wharf: it's a two-shot, close-up and reaction. It's pure moom pitchers."

"I don't think so," Chris said suddenly; she was smiling but her eyes were grave, unsure. I'd never seen that look in her eyes before. "There's a lot of interior thought, whatever you call it—people thinking, feeling. You couldn't do that on film."

Kay looked at her a moment—the measuring glance, supremely confident. "Maybe you're right, sweetie. It was just a thought." Abruptly she turned and said: "Dal, be a local hero and bring me a Gibson, will you?" And to Jean-Jean: "I ran into Alexis two weeks ago. In the city. He's doing guess what? Drinking carrot juice. Yes!" She laughed, a high, hard metallic laugh. "Gallons and gallons. He's obsessed with joining the RCAF. They've got him staring at wheels that sparkle and flash, he says they make him seasick. He's even wearing a patch—he looks like a parfit gentil pirate. How are you going to get over there, sweetie? Dakar?"

That's how it went, the rest of the evening. Later on I saw Russ making a Gibson, and later still I caught a glimpse of him talking with her on the balcony, his hand near his forehead gesturing, the way he did when he was excited about something. Wherever she was, people clustered, gestured, argued. What was astonishing was the way she could convey the sense that there was this really important world out there beyond where you were, and that she personified it. One word, she could say one word—and you felt you had to prove yourself somehow, like those men who actually leapt to their deaths in the sea at ancient Cnidos when they first saw the statue of the incomparable Aphrodite...She was so certain of herself! I got Jean-Jean talking about her—I knew better than to try to engage her in conversation. She came from Santa Barbara, her father owned one of the big aircraft plants out there; she loathed Bennington, and flew down to New York City whenever she could. She knew Joan Crawford and Cary Grant and David Niven and Alan Ladd, she'd been to Antibes and Klosters and Taormina, she had been places even Jean-Jean hadn't been, and knew people he didn't know.

What with the music and liquor and Jean-Jean's departure it was all too much; everything seemed crazily off-balance. We were too wound-up, too on edge for real hilarity. Our world wasn't our world any longer—there was this other mightier, glittering world of Kay Madden's and it was all there was. It made for an aura of dissatisfaction, a testy, combative atmosphere in which for the first time we forced our gaiety, blundered into misunderstandings, sulks, apologies. The lights came on over Boston, sparkling blue in the fall air, the big band riff tunes we loved bathed us in their pulsing thunder, people came and left and came back again bringing friends, but we found no comfort in any of it. Jean-Jean was going to the war. The war was out there roaring away, a cosmic forest fire raging utterly out of control now, sweeping across continents and seas, and he was going—and *he was the first*. The first of us. The thought dogged us as we drank, danced listlessly, laughed too loudly at the wrong things, quarreled too quickly over the right ones...Later, much later I seemed to be sitting on a leather hassock in the connecting bedroom watching Denise holding Jean-Jean by the arms and saying frantically:

"Crazy, it is crazy. What can you do? in Brazzaville?"

"Probably nothing," he answered stolidly; he was very drunk, but his enunciation was perfect. "Nonetheless."

"You hate hot weather anyway, jungles. *Why* must you go?"

"Because—I like to do things on impulse. Like all good Frenchmen."

"Don't joke with me, Jean. Not with me. Not now."

"It is difficult..." He passed his fingers along her cheek and neck with a practiced grace I found enviable. "It would be patriotic, it would be soul-stirring to say it is because of the formation of the National Council for Free France." Then his smile vanished, he dropped his hand. "But to be truthful, to be absolutely truthful with you, chérie, it is because one hundred and fifty citizens—and I assume that includes women and small children—were rounded up on the streets of Saumur three days ago and machine-gunned to death. For being on the streets of Saumur."

"Ce n'est que folie, que sottise romantique..." She had reverted to French now, speaking rapidly, a torrent of entreaty, but my French was pretty good, I got most of it. "It is not your war, you have risked enough, suffered enough, you have lost enough—you know that."

"If it is not mine, whose then is it?"

"It is not yours, that's all I know. Let the Americans do it, the Americans who have everything, who are so sure of everything—yes, and who know nothing..."

"Enough," he said sharply; he could tell from the look on my face that I understood. "Their turn will come. That has nothing to do with me. Be quiet now, dearest."

Denise looked at me with sudden, intense hatred—it was as though she had just become aware of me—then her sultry little gamine's mouth drew down and she burst into tears. "I'm sorry," she said thickly. "George, I am sorry. For what I said. I didn't mean what I said."

"It's all right."

"Tell him, tell him..." But she was gazing past me, to where Russ now stood in the doorway, a drink in each hand.

"Tell him what, baby?" Russ said.

"He listens to you, he likes you, you're the one he cares about most, I know." She put her arm on his now and I saw what I'd always felt—she was deeply attracted to Russ.

"I tried, Denise, I *tried* to tell him—"

"Tell him he must stay, it is hopeless, they are only a handful, a handful! In the jungles, there... Tell him it is—"

"Enough," Jean-Jean said again in a different tone. "There,

now. That's it." He looked at Russ, at me, and smiled—but his face was altered, everything was altered. I'd had too much to drink, but it was still true, I wasn't imagining it. He was no longer roommate, classmate, brother Fusilier. We were nothing to him now, somehow, and there was nothing to be done about it.

"I'd give everything I own," Russ muttered after a pause, nodding at Denise, who was sitting on the bed now, wiping her eyes with a handkerchief. "Everything I own to keep Jean-Jean here. I mean it. I'd even—"

There was a crash of glass, concussive, glass thrown not dropped, then Kay's high metallic laugh; and over it, over all the voices now subdued, Dal's voice, shocking and harsh:

"—now you can take that back, you lousy yellow son of a bitch!"

I swung through the arch, and it was like a tableau—a badly rehearsed scene: Dal, his face slick with sweat, drunker than I'd ever seen him, pointing threateningly at a silent, recoiling Terry; the others grouped loosely, stopped in a dozen attitudes. I saw Nancy scowling in disgust, Mel blinking with solemn alarm, Kay Madden's eyes dilated in sudden high excitement; but no one moved. Only the silver levers of the record changer swung and dipped behind their glass like the arms of a somnambulist robot.

"I'm sick and tired of your God damn cute sentiments, Gilligan, I'm sick of your cheap shots at England, what a bunch of suckers and slobs we are, ROTC, the rest of it . . ." Two white spots had appeared at the corners of his nostrils, a bad sign with Dal. He was swaying on his feet, his pale eyes slitted behind his glasses. "All right, come on, you got the guts to put 'em up, step outside a minute? or you want me to call you a chicken-livered, loud-mouth in front of all these wonderful people. Ah?"

The phonograph started to play another number, *I'll Never Smile Again;* perfectly logical. Terry was staring at Dal, all the blood leeched out of his face. His lips worked but no words came.

"Well, come on," Dal taunted thickly. "Coming or aren't you?"

I walked up to him and said: "Take it easy."

"You go to hell," he muttered, but without conviction.

"Look, let it go now. He didn't mean anything, it was only—" I glanced back at Terry. He threw us all one wild, wordless glance—then whirled around and ran out of the apartment.

"Terry!" Ann called.

"Let him go," Dal shouted. "Good fucking riddance..."

"Relax, will you?" I said.

"Come *on,* Wog." Russ was there now, everyone was talking at once. "Have a drink and sober up. You're wrecking the party."

"And you?" He squinted cunningly at Russ. "How about you, hot shot?"

"Having a good time," I said. "A good time will be had by all. Now calm down, will you?"

It went on and on, all out of balance, maudlin and affectionate and irascible by turns. A serious young man in steel rimless glasses from the floor below came up to complain about the noise—I don't know why everybody in Greater Boston didn't—and was persuaded to stay on and join the festivities. And Russ thought of somebody who ought to be here, a good man, to celebrate, to do Jean-Jean honor, and called him up, to find curiously that he was in bed and sound asleep. And the uproar climbed and climbed, the jostling and embraces and pointless stories and spiraling laughter...

And suddenly, very suddenly it seemed, there were only half a dozen of us, and in a mountainous disarray of glasses and spilled liquor and dirty plates Russ was standing on the leather ottoman with a glass held high above his head and shouting over the music:

"And here's to the man, a final toast, to the best, the finest of us all, the man who made it all possible! I give you—the Frabjous Frog! Mitt the crowd, Jean-Jean."

We murmured something; we were too tired to cheer.

"A few words, a few words, Jean-Jean baby."

"What a great one you are for ceremony, Russell. You would have made such a good *Frenchman.*" Jean-Jean looked at us fondly, but that distant, alien look was in his eyes. "Once when I was eight years old I went to stay with my grandfather at his home near Cognac. There was this park filled with beautiful exotic birds that were so tame you could go up and touch them, if you were careful; and not far away at Ile d'Oléron was the sea; I had never seen the sea, and I petted the peacocks and pheasants and played in the sand and found sea shells, and I always thought of it as the best time I'd known... But this year has had a quality all its own. You've made it bearable for me, all of you."

"Dear Jean-Jean," Chris said. "You always know what to say."

"No. I mean it. But even good things must end."

Russ cried. "No, no!"

"Yes, yes. And so, Russell—because you love ceremony so dearly." With one deft, careless motion he lifted something out of his pocket and tossed it high in the air. It hung there, arching, glinting—I recognized it at once: it was the key to the Empress on its gold chain. Russ snatched at it, dropped it, picked it up, looking at Jean-Jean with a puzzled expression.

"Yes. For you."

Russ stared at him now, almost sobered. "The car? You mean you—you're—"

"Why not?"

"But you can't—just give away the Empress..."

"Why not? Who will love it as much as you? I very much doubt they will let me take it to Brazzaville."

Someone gave a short, wordless exclamation, and Kay Madden said: "J-J, you've had seven too many."

"No. I was afraid someone might think that, and so I took the liberty of doing this." He went over to his jacket and lifted out a paper and handed it to Russ. I saw a red notarized seal in one corner.

"Crazy," Nancy murmured to me, "that's crazy... Isn't it?"

Russ was hefting the key, the notarized deed, shaking his handsome head in disbelief. "I'm... I'm..." He stopped. "I haven't anything to say."

"Famous first," Chris said, and we laughed.

"Beau geste!" Kay said. "Now I know how the phrase originated. Only why not me? I'd appreciate it more than anyone, lover."

"Oh, but Katherine. You already *have* everything God and the devil can grant. You don't need anything. Do you?"

"Dear Jean Roche Gilbert Rigord." Those two small crescents tightened around the corners of her mouth, and I realized he knew how to handle her—or at least fight her to a stand-off. "You're beautiful and titled and decadent but you haven't the palest idea about what I have—or need, either. Russ does, though. Russ understands because he's essentially creative."

"What do you need?" I asked her. Sober I wouldn't have said it. Sober I wouldn't have said anything.

She gazed me out of existence. "You're a dear boy, and you mean well. Make me another Gibson and maybe I'll tell you. Where in hell has Dal wandered off to?"

"In the bedroom," Russ said. "Among the fallen."

"Well, someone better resurrect him, because I've got to roll in before three."

We got Dal on his feet more or less, and got the girls back wherever they had to be, and made it back to Cambridge without getting pinched or wrecking the Empress, a minor miracle in itself. I made a bicarbonate of soda, set the alarm clock for quarter to seven, and fell into bed still wearing my shorts and socks. The bed kept upending itself, whirling slowly back and back on some mythical central axis, a highly unpleasant sensation for which I'd never found any remedy. But finally I got off.

And then I came awake with a start. There was a slow, persistent tapping at my bedroom door.

"George," a voice whispered. "George..."

I got up and staggered against the desk, found my study lamp after some more fumbling and snapped it on. It was almost four-thirty. I opened the door. Terry was standing there fully dressed, with his jacket collar turned up. He was shivering and I knew he'd been walking around outside.

"George, I've got to talk to you. I've got to." He gave a cough that turned into a sob, and tears started running down his face. "What am I going to do? What can I do, George?"

"It's all right," I said. "Sit down." I shut the door again and handed him the bicarb. "Here, drink this."

He emptied the glass obediently, and peered at it. "I just—couldn't move. Couldn't act. With everybody there watching."

"Forget it. Everybody was squashed."

"No. They'll all remember. Everyone. Something like that." He was shivering all over, rubbing his face with his sleeve. "I should have hit him, tried to, anyway... Now I'm finished."

"Don't be silly."

"No, I am. I know I am." He gave a long, shuddering sigh. "The fact is—I'm afraid of fighting. Always have been. My father used to put on the gloves with me but it never did any good. I was always scared. When I was nine a bunch of kids picked a fight with me in Dorchester, knocked me down. Ever since then I—well, just freeze up, all over...That doesn't condone it, of course."

"Nobody's drawing any dark conclusions."

"No. I'm a fucking coward, George. Yellow. Just the way he said."

"Look, Terry, you're still half-shot and you've got everything all out of whack. Nobody's going to remember half of what went on tonight."

"They'll remember this." Doggedly he shook his head, his voice hoarse. "I might as well wear a sandwich board all over Harvard Square: *My name is Terence Gilligan and I've got a yellow streak a mile wide right down my back.* In our society only prowess in—"

"Will you turn off the sociology crap and *listen* to me?" I demanded. "Everybody's afraid of something. Dal's scared witless of water—you saw that yourself. Out at Billingsgate. *I* can't stand heights—if I'm on a fifteen-foot ladder I start to shake like a leaf. You can't take—"

"It doesn't matter. In our society—"

"Fuck our society. Everybody's got his weakness—that just happens to be yours. Besides, Dal passed out in the bedroom ten minutes later. Christ, we practically had to treat him for the bends."

I rattled on for an hour or more, and finally got him calmed down. I resolved to have a talk with Dal and make him apologize to Terry if I had to beat him over the head with a shovel. Still talking, I walked him back to his room and put him to bed.

"You're a good guy, George. You're as good a friend as a guy could want." His eyes searched mine, unhappy and pleading. "I won't forget this. Ever."

"Don't worry about it," I said. "Sleep well."

I guess I'm as callous as anyone else underneath all the layers of loyalty. Going back to my room I wasn't thinking about Terry at all; what my mind kept stopping on, running and stopping like a broken filmstrip, was Russ bent over Kay in quick, voluble excitement, and that look of growing dismay on Chris's lovely face.

2

"NEXT REHEARSAL HE came on like Dracula," Noel Baxter said. "Shoulders hunched, eyes rolling, hands pawing at the air. I said: 'Al, you're a telephone *repairman*—it's just another phone, you've repaired millions of them.' 'That's not the way I read this character,' he says."

"Oh, that's gorgeous!" Kay Madden cried, laughing.

"And off he went into a long harangue about how *this* telephone repairman has always wanted to be a research chemist, and how one of his hands has been crippled on a previous job and he's just discovered his wife's been doing tricks all over town. I said, 'Al, it's *two lines,* he's just there to fix the *phone...*' 'Just a simple repair job,' he says. 'That's the trouble with you intellectuals, that's all you ever see.'"

Baxter paused, watching our reactions, sipping his drink, a stinger, foamy amber in an outsize old-fashioned glass. We were all drinking stingers because he'd simply gone ahead and made them. It was a drink I'd never had before, but I could taste the brandy and I decided to take it very slow and easy.

"Bix, honey," Natalie Baxter said, "these kids don't want to hear about the weirds of Al Dempler."

"Oh, we do, we do!" Kay exclaimed. "I remember I met Al when he had that bit in *Now Voyager*. Please don't stop him, Tal, it's hilarious. Go on, Bix."

"No, I'm boring you," Baxter said. He was a tall, emaciated man with deep-set onyx eyes and a drooping black mustache. He looked a little like Eugene O'Neill—but only at first glance. He was wearing a lemon-yellow cravat and a blue blazer with a coat of arms over the breast pocket I couldn't quite make out.

"You're *not* boring us," Kay protested. "Is he, Carole?"

"Not me," Carole Rivers said; she glanced nervously around. "I'm loving it."

"We never get to hear anything zazzy any more. Stodgy, stupid old New England. Are you bored, Russ?"

"No, it's fascinating," Russ answered; and he meant it, I knew. He was sitting hunched forward, hands clasped in front of him, the way he always did when his interest was aroused.

"You see?" Baxter murmured, pleased. "These young people don't seem unduly depressed. Maybe it's diagnostic of you, darling." He smiled blandly at his wife, who made a face at him and finished her stinger. She was short and stocky with blunt, rather attractive features; Kay had told us she'd danced in the front line in Busby Berkeley musicals in the early Thirties.

Noel Baxter told another story and I pretended to listen, studied the house instead. It was the kind of aggressively modern structure that somehow manages to look barren even when it's crammed with furniture. The ceiling soared off into complicated open-beam vaulting and clerestories; vast panes of glass and brushed aluminum sliding doors gave on a redwood deck, a flag terrace complete with outdoor barbecue, covered now for winter, and an almost intimidating view of Pleasant Bay—now a still, steel plate under low-shouldering clouds; a lobster boat hung in its gray expanse, bound to neither sky nor sea.

Across from me Carole Rivers, my date, shivered once and pressed her arms against her sides. It was drafty in the great barn of a room in spite of the open fire burning fitfully under its massive triangular bronze hood. Malibu on Cape Cod. Every now and then a downdraft would send smoke out into the room in rolling gray clouds. This would be a cold house in winter—it was already chilly and it was only early December. The Baxters didn't know it yet because they'd bought the place on a balmy August afternoon with the sundeck filled with tanned, half-naked bodies, and there had been something pleasingly incongruous about this California beach house thrusting its batwing roof and plexiglass bubbles above the pines and scrub oak of Chatham—a home away from home. Baxter was working on a play with a New England setting, and he'd wanted to be "near the city" (by which of course he meant New York City) and it had all seemed providential.

"Russ wants to be a writer," Kay was saying in her bright, conversational tone, "in fact he's already on his way. He's had several stories published in the *Advocate,* and he's going to win the Houghton Prize for fiction."

"Oh, come on, now," Russ demurred; he gave me an embarrassed glance, and shrugged. It was odd to see him so ill at ease.

"Of course, you are, darling. It's fated. I'll send you a story he wrote, Bix, it's awfully good."

"Fine—I'd like to see it." But a certain edge had crept into Baxter's voice now; I had a sense of the interminable avalanche of material that must be foisted on a playwright and director of his notoriety.

"No, look, it's kid stuff," Russ protested. He'd caught that note of forced interest, too. "I'm just getting started, really—just feeling my way."

"Nonsense," Kay interrupted him. "Tell Bix what Professor Purcell said to you."

"Old Blinkers Purcell," Baxter murmured, and shook his head mournfully. "Still padding the ivy halls, sucking hind tit to Doering. Kind of makes you choke up, now, don't it?"

"Eh, what's Meyer doing now?" Kay inquired in a surprisingly good Brooklyn accent, and she and the Baxters laughed. Kay was always saying things like that—the tag lines of jokes, perhaps, or Hollywood anecdotes. Russ was watching her unsurely, raking his hair with his fingers. I felt angry with him—I wanted to haul him out of this cockeyed architectural transplant, drag him out on the flagstone terrace and shake him back to his senses. But he didn't see me, he didn't see anybody, he hadn't for weeks. His eyes were on Kay—they were always on Kay now, in a kind of fevered, apprehensive absorption. Since the farewell party for Jean-Jean they'd been seeing each other incessantly—in Boston, down in New York City. He'd gone to bed with her, he'd told me one night late, in confidence. I'd tried to stop him, I hadn't wanted to hear about it but he'd insisted, naming times and places, as if that might make it more tangible to him somehow.

"She's—it's just overwhelming, Grog. I—I simply can't describe it. The things she does—! It's like riding a golden boxkite over the Grand Canyon, diving and diving... What's the matter, you don't believe me?"

"Yeah. I guess so." Watching the restless glitter in his eyes I knew suddenly that he'd never made love to Chris, not fully—and this made me angrier at him than anything else. Then before I could speak he tried to swear me to secrecy: Yale Game weekend was coming up, and Dal mustn't know about Kay—nor Chris, nor Terry.

"Why all the subterfuge?" I demanded. There was an air of exultant mystery about the whole affair that irked me. "Why all the cloak-and-dagger?"

"Well—" he looked troubled, his eyes shifting "—it could break up the group, the Fusiliers..."

"The Fusiliers."

"Dal's already asked her. His feelings will be hurt."

"Dal!" I said hotly. "Fuck Dal! How about *Chris's* feelings—you spent any time on that?"

"Oh well, Chris, of course..."

"What do you mean, *of course!* What the hell's the matter with you? Jesus, how can you even look at Kay when *she's* there, right there?" I pointed aimlessly in the direction of Radcliffe. "When she's anywhere at all?"

"I know..." He shook his head, almost as though to clear it. "I know."

"You ask one hell of a lot of your friends, Currier."

He glanced at me in surprise—I almost never called him by his last name—and then that burning, desperate look crept into his face again. "I can't help it," he whispered. "I can't help myself—that's all there is to it. I'm sorry. Now will you back me up or won't you?"

And so Yale Game weekend had been ruined; at least for me. A solid, surprise victory over the Eli, our own Rhino Tanahill one of its heroes, a merry round of house parties culminating in

Gene Krupa's band at the Copley, the Oval Room . . . and yet for me it was all strained. artificial, unsure. An unsuspecting Dal had brought Kay, Russ was with Chris, but it was all façade; and Chris knew better, too—I was sure of it. There was a moment, during the roaring victory party in Mel and Rhino's room across the hall when I'd caught her eyes resting on Russ with a still, grave expression, and my heart turned on itself. Where did loyalty bend, at what point would it break? At what point *should* it break?

"How about you, George?" Natalie Baxter was saying now; I saw she'd been watching me. There was something in her bold gaze I didn't like, I didn't know what it was. "What do you plan to do with yourself?"

"I'm not sure, Mrs. Baxter. Teach history maybe, or foreign service."

"For heaven's sake, George, *loosen up,*" Kay demanded. "Call her Tal. George is a demon for formality." Kay loved to explain you to other people as though you were dead or far away. "He's not a proper Bostonian like Russ, he's from some Indian village near Canada actually, but he *wants* to be one terribly. So he overcompensates."

"I'm sorry," I said to Mrs Baxter. "It's just how I was brought up."

"George is terribly strait-laced," Kay went on. "He thinks a sexdigitist is someone who can do it six different ways in one night."

I laughed along with the others, but I felt mulish and resentful. I had not been at my best all that weekend. I was angry at Kay for her random assaults and her incessant manipulating, and at Russ for his infatuation or consuming passion or whatever the hell it was, and I was most furious of all at myself for letting him talk me into this whole idiotic weekend down at the family house in Brewster, when I ought to be back in Cambridge studying.

Kay had engineered it all, of course. Wouldn't it be fun, just the four of us, down there in the winter and wild weather, Cape Cod battered by an angry sea? I could imagine her working on Russ. And George, why didn't she bring a girl for George, one of her best friends at school was an awfully smooth dancer—just the four of us together in the wilderness. I'd wondered why she, the glamorous city girl, certainly no nature lover, had pushed so for the trip; now, watching her flirting with Baxter, drawing him out, laughing at his stories, I knew why. And Chatham only a stone's throw from Brewster.

"George is really a boy at heart," Kay was telling them all. "Isn't he, Carole? A play-time, sleigh-time kid. But loyal. Loyal to the end." Eyeing me she laughed her quick, metallic laugh, and I knew, too, why she'd wanted me along on this junket. As I've said, I'm not terribly quick; but I get there, in time.

The return to fundamentals had not gone well. The house was cold and damp, Kay was an indifferent cook—her idea of a meal was a western sandwich and a plate of potato chips. She and Russ were continually disappearing in one of the bedrooms upstairs, or huddling around the fireplace discussing movies or plays. The afternoon before, sick of Kay's nonstop performance, I'd gone for a walk over the dunes with Carole. Like Kay she wore more make-up than the girls we usually dated, and her clothes were expensive. But something about her—the occasional flicker of an unmotivated smile—disturbed me. Like Kay, she was always using snips and scraps from some private code, or leaping off into an analysis of someone present; but unlike Kay, you had the sense that those assaults were turned inward.

The beach was empty of life; the wind was light but the very air seemed to sink into your vitals and hold there. I took her hand and we ran along the firmer sand at the sea's edge; when we stopped I hugged her, almost automatically. She kissed me then, with a frank, fierce passion, her tongue licking under mine. Astonished, I straightened.

"What's the matter?" she said in a faltering voice.

"Nothing."

"Don't you like me?"

"Sure I do. Of course I do."

"No, you don't, I can tell you don't, a woman's never fooled about things like that—I can see it in your eyes." Her own had filled, suddenly. "You find me repulsive."

"No, Carole—"

"You do, you do!" And now, incredibly, the tears were streaming down her cheeks. "Then why did you lead me on like this, let me think you were attracted to me, that's a perfectly rotten thing to do!"

"Look, Carole, it's nothing like that at all." I was getting alarmed; the loops and shifts in her mind were disconcerting. Was she going to turn violent?

Then I had an inspiration. Well, it wasn't even that really, it was as natural as breathing. I thought of Chris—always when I was at the beach I thought of Chris, running with the great, blue kite, or kneeling at the fire, or wading in the shallows, bent over, her face so serious and intent—it made her look even more lovely when she was absorbed in something—hunting for some shell for her collection...

"It's nothing I can help," I heard myself saying with a strange, deep pleasure. "There's this girl and I'm in love with her, totally in love with her, and it's hopeless, I can't even tell her I am—she doesn't know I exist. I'm sorry."

Her attitude changed instantly: her gaze softened, she sank her teeth on her lower lip. "You, too," she murmured. "You know, then, you've been there. Don't you get sick of the whole stupid game?"

I shook my head. "Never. Just being around, near her, makes it all right."

"But if you can't tell her—"

"It doesn't matter. Every now and then I see her, I'm in the same room with her. And then it's all worth it."

She gave her bitter little smile. "You've got it bad. You're worse off than I am. But—how can you go on like that?"

Now I grinned. "I haven't any choice."

We sat then, in the lee of a dune, and talked. For hours. At a dance last summer she'd fallen in love with this boy and they'd been pinned—and then he'd broken it off with no explanation, nothing; and on and on. I listened with a kind of weary fascination, a little ashamed.

It grew late, the sea turned mauve, then black as tar; half frozen, we ran back to the house. No lights were on. Carole slipped into the bathroom. All my thoughts centered on getting warm, I went quickly down the hall into the living room—and there they were, Kay and Russ, locked and swaying on the rug, the firelight flaring on their naked flesh like stripes from a lash. For the merest part of a second, to my stunned senses, they looked as if they were actually on fire, and I drew in my breath. But they were oblivious of me, their slender bodies rocking in quickened rhythms, beautiful and savage and numbing; I was conscious of an utterly childlike guilt—looking on what I shouldn't, punishment would follow—and then I had swung away, but not before Kay's eye had caught mine in one swift, triumphant, mocking glance...

"Tommy Buckler flew up last week," Baxter was saying now to Kay.

"Really?" Her head whipped around.

"He was asking about you."

"What's he doing in the east?"

"Odets wants him for the lead in the new play—or somebody told him he did. He wanted my indispensable advice."

"What did you tell him?"

"To forget it. He's a film actor, always will be. He'll make a fool of himself on Broadway."

"And not much of a film actor, either," Russ said suddenly.

"Don't be jealous, lover," Kay retorted. "Russ is feeling churlish because Tommy's an old admirer. Tommy is one gorgeous hunk, I mean."

"*Ni*agara Falls!" Carole chanted, and everyone laughed.

"God, how I miss the Coast," Tal was saying. "All that glorious sun, taking a dip in the pool year round." She turned up the thermostat in a little spasm of vexation. "This is all very picturesque, very cultural, etcetera. But after September you can have it."

"Darling, it's only for a year," Baxter said irritably.

She sighed, her lips pinched in dissatisfaction. "Well, I want some excitement, anything..."

She turned on the radio, a lavish Stromberg-Carlson, switched from the symphony to Helen Forrest who was just winding up *I Don't Want to Walk Without You.* Harry James's trumpet started its solo, a little too sentimental—broke off all at once in the middle of one hard, piercing note, and as if on Tal's cue the voice broke in, the tension bleeding through the carefully controlled professional phrasing: the words that changed all our lives.

—*Sunday,* I seemed to be thinking; *on a Sunday*...I was the center of an empty panic that swung round and round the thought: I'm not ready. Not ready for anything like this. I had set down my glass and locked my fingers together. I thought: you silly son of a bitch, get hold of yourself! You knew it was coming, any five-year-old kid knew it was coming, what's the *matter* with you? And yet the eerie, engulfing sense of panic swelled and swelled—

Then it passed. There was a moment of release, giddy and equally empty, like a leap high through space; and after that a cold, sharp certitude, overlaid with boundless regret. No more wait-and-wonder, then. It had come, it was here. As we knew it would. I looked at Russ. Watching me silently he nodded several times; his eyes were flat and hard.

The voice stopped then, the music returned; but to this day I've never been able to recall the new tune or what band played it. All I remember is the six of us caught in that moment, looking at one another as though expecting some irrefutable, divine answer, that swiftly congealing sensation of angry certainty, and outside the clouds beating inland, looking grimmer now, a dirty, leaden apron; the lobster boat, still suspended between earth and sky, seemed not to have moved at all. Staring hard at it I thought—I know it sounds utterly crazy at a time like that, but it's the God's honest truth—I thought, What is she doing, right now? Chris? Where is she, what is she thinking, hearing this?

"What fabulous timing, Tal," Kay said with a forced laugh. "Will any of us ever listen to Harry James the same way again?"

"... A gag?" Baxter murmured, his head cocked. I stared at him. "Like that Mars invasion thing Orson did—"

"No. It's no gag." Russ was on his feet, twisting the signet ring with his family seal round and round on his finger; that hard, tensed expression on his face. "Let's go," he said.

"Right." I got up. I understood him perfectly. This was no time to be with strangers; it was a time to be with your own kind, people you knew and trusted, whose fate was going to be yours. I felt exactly the same way.

"Go? Go where?" Kay demanded.

"We've got to get back."

"But what's the sense in running off? Okay, so the Japanese have bombed Pearl Harbor, what's so—"

"That's right."

"—why all the hysteria? It's as if you—"

"I'm not hysterical."

"Yes, you are, you certainly are. Sit *down,* Russ! Jesus squeeze-us, you'd think it was the end of the world."

He turned and looked at her then, and I could see the hot resentment in his eyes—and more: the defiance, even hatred. "It *is,* baby. Oh, it is. Ours, anyway. Just wait and see." He swung away from her. "I'm sure the Baxters will forgive us if we rush off."

There were a few more exchanges, but it was over. Russ was adamant, the weather was turning bad, the Baxters themselves were shaken, arguing over what to do, when to return to the Coast.

We packed in a hurry and closed up the old house. As we drove through the withdrawn little Cape towns in the Empress the traffic thickened suddenly; everyone was hurrying now, hurrying north. Storm clouds kept shouldering in out of the Atlantic; Manomet Headland loomed up across the Bay like a hostile shore. The end of things, the thought kept beating in my head, a senseless refrain: the end of things. There were a thousand words Russ and I needed to say to each other just then, yet I couldn't think of one of them.

But Kay wouldn't let it alone: Kay wasn't through, not by a long shot.

"I can't say I was thrilled with the way you acted at Bix and Tal's. I wonder if you realize how rude you can be. I suppose it's another of the Boston Yankee graces." Russ said nothing, watching the road. "Russell's a purist," she went on, turning to Carole and me. "Russell feels if he takes a *really* dramatic stance, never mind over what, everybody will fall on their knees and cry: 'There stands a man of action!'"

"It's all right, Kay," Carole said pleadingly.

"What's all right, darling? Jumping to our feet and running out of the Baxters' like a bunch of scared kids?"

"Well, I think they wanted us to go. They—"

"—I've never been so humiliated in my life." She bent that imperious, measuring ice-blue gaze on Russ again. "You still sulking away in your baby carriage, there?"

"How about dropping it, Kay," I said.

"Enter sweet Horatio, attendant lord."

At the Sagamore Bridge we were stopped in a crush of cars. An army truck had just pulled off on to the shoulder. Soldiers were flipping back the canvas and jumping down from the tailgate; they were wearing helmets and carrying rifles.

"They shutting it off?" I said. "Closing the bridges?"

"I don't think so," Russ answered. "Putting a guard on the Canal, more likely."

We were moving again. An MP strode toward us, his head up, motioned us through with harsh, peremptory gestures. One of the guard detail whistled as we passed, and several others grinned, their eyes glinting under their helmet rims.

"Soldier-boys," Kay observed, "already playing at their little war games. Heroes every one, as I live and breathe."

Russ's hand shot in front of Kay so fast I thought for a moment he'd hit her. "You know something?" he said in a low, furious tone. "There could be German subs *right—out—there.*" His finger jabbed at the Canal entrance. "Right now. Has that thought occurred to you?"

"Don't be ridiculous. We aren't at war with Germany. We aren't at war with anybody at all."

"Yes, well, we will be."

"Jesus lord, what a pessimist. —Hey now, wait," she protested, as Russ swung the Empress around the bridge circle and started down Route 6 toward Buzzards Bay. "Where are we going?"

He looked at her. "Back to Bennington."

"But we're going to Hugo's, we talked about Hugo's, we decided, don't you remember? I'm in the mood for lobster."

"I can't see it, Kay."

"What do you mean, you can't see it? *Can't—see it,*" she hissed, and picked a piece of tobacco off her lower lip. "Look: I want to eat lobster at Hugo's. Would you mind giving me six reasons why we can't?"

"Well, for one thing I don't think any of us feel like it."

"We'll take a little vote on that."

"And for another it's expensive."

"All right, so it's expensive. So what."

"I'm broke, Kay."

"I see. You might have thought about that on Friday, mmmh?—How about you, George?" Her fingers tapped the back of the seat, her cold blue eyes appraised me, found me wanting.

"I agree with Russ," I said.

"Now *that's* a fresh approach. Really bracing. I suppose if Russell started sucking on an ostrich egg you would, too."

"And I'm broke, too. Incidentally." Words have such different meanings for different people. Russ could say *I'm broke* and mean it—but it wouldn't mean remotely what it did to me. Even so, I knew he'd been running through his generous allowance at an alarming clip since he'd started going with Kay—he'd been borrowing from both Rhino and Terry. "It's out of the question for me."

"Please, Kay, it doesn't matter," Carole said nervously, "it's getting late anyway."

"Look," Kay raised her voice, "I'll *pay* for the God damned meal, if that's what's worrying you."

"No, you won't," Russ retorted. He was barely hanging on to himself. "There isn't time."

"Charming. A date with the gracious Ivy League."

That's the way it went, mile after somber mile. Taunton was in a convulsion of movement. Everyone seemed to be going somewhere, doing something in frantic haste. Patrol cars swooped here and there, sirens wailed, a fire chief's wagon almost ran us down near Foxboro. Official America was out in the streets, gesticulating, burning up gas, ringing bells, setting off alarms. Crouched in the drafty back seat, tense and depressed, I knew how they felt: there was a certain blessed release in any activity, however aimless. The radio kept repeating the first bulletin and adding others. Wake Island was under attack—precisely where *was* Wake Island?—and so was Guam, and Clark Field in the Philippines. The panic was gone now; what remained was a cold, hollow dread. What was going to happen? What was going to happen to us all? Abruptly—like that—it was dark; the countryside looked bleak and cheerless, as if disaster had already struck; the lights in the farmhouses seemed meager.

Near Shrewsbury Russ stopped at a diner. It was an unhappy choice. The air was heavy with steam and fried grease, the tables were dirty, the juke box kept playing *The Hut-Sut Song* over and over. Everyone was talking about the Japanese attack. The waitress came up and Russ said: "How about hamburgers all around?"

"I don't like hamburger," Kay said. "Do you have veal?"

"Nope."

"Well, do you have roast beef?"

"Nope."

"Well then, just what *do* you have?"

The waitress, a big woman with a mouth like George

Washington's, pointed to the placards above the counter. "It's all up there, miss."

Kay picked up her fork, waggling it between two fingers. "Sometimes it's nice to wash the silver after someone's used it. Didn't anyone tell you?"

The waitress' head came up. "Now listen, Suzy, if you don't like it—"

"No, I don't like it."

"You snotty college kids, you can—"

"It's all right," Russ broke in tensely, "we'll take four hamburgers, four coff—"

"Oh, no, you won't—you can take your fancy butts some place else!"

"My sentiments exactly," Kay said.

"My God—and at a time like this, too."

We went out to the car in silence. Just outside Athol it began to snow—light, tentative flakes, probing. A few miles farther on it thickened suddenly, lying on the road in long, snaky trails. Russ was driving too fast for this—the Empress was without snow tires. I started to say something, said instead: "Think they'll make landings on the west coast?"

"I don't know. They could. All that ocean out there..."

"Invade—you're talking about invasion?" Kay demanded.

"You feel we're privileged. Off limits."

"Oh, turn it off! I'm sick of all this talk, talk, talk of war. Can't you think of anything else?"

"Not tonight, Josephine."

"Tell me, Mr. C., is it your bean-and-codfish ancestry that makes you so engaging? or is it that hot Italian strain?"

He glanced toward her, the muscle in his cheek flexed tight, and I knew it was a final appeal. "Let it go, can't you, Kay?"

"Let what go, exactly? Your war obsession? I suppose you realize you just blew the biggest *chance* of your life."

"Is that right."

"You don't just walk out on Noel Baxter, you know."

"Look, we've been all over this."

"Just what do you feel gave you—"

"—Because *we're* the ones that are going to get our asses blown off, that's why!" Russ shouted. It was the first time he'd raised his voice. "Baxter won't, that's for sure." He was driving still faster; I felt the rear end of the Empress lift and sway subtly on a curve.

"Russ," I said, "hold her down."

"It seems I was wrong about you," Kay went on in that bright, assertive tone. "Really wrong, buster. Not the common, chuckle-headed Harvard jock but different—a little ambition, a sense of how things work. A little drive. But no, you're just like all the others. Aren't you. Well, aren't you?" Russ said nothing, his shoulders hunched, glaring into the whirling curtain of snow, and his silence seemed to sting Kay physically.

"Russ!" I shouted, "Now *slow down!*"

Kay was laughing, a low, indulgent laugh, her head back against the seat. "Well, let me cue you in, sweetie, a short communiqué: next time you get involved, I mean emotionally in—"

We skidded then. I felt her go, wrapped my arms around Carole and pulled her in behind me. There was that light-sick gliding surge with no sensation of movement, only a buoyant whirling—and then the slam and recoil, and a series of grinding shocks; and silence. We were stopped. Russ was shouting something and Kay was shouting back, Carole was screaming and clutching at my arms and neck; around us the snow drifted dreamily down in the headlights' glare, oblivious.

"Let go, Carole," I muttered. "Let me go, now." She was sobbing, gasping for breath. I pried her hands away and pressed on the door handle; it wouldn't work. I stepped across her and got out on the driver's side. Russ was standing by the fender looking straight up into the falling snow. Kay was bracing herself between seat and dashboard and staring at us; her face looked white and wild under the canvas.

"You all right, Russ?" I said.

"I've had it," he breathed. "Had all I can take. *All* of it!" He struck the fender with his fist.

The Empress was resting with her trunk against the guard rail, facing upward across the highway. The rider's side was scraped across both doors and the rear fender. There was no other damage I could see.

"We're lucky," I said. "She's all right. Come on," I told him. "Let's go—someone comes around that curve now they'll pile into us. Russ!"

He seemed to be pushing against the fender. Then I saw he

was hanging on to it; he was shaking like an aspen leaf.

"You want me to take her?" I asked.

He nodded dumbly, gripped his hands together. "Should—have put snows on."

"Yeah." We got in, Russ in back with Carole; I took the wheel. Carole was sobbing, "Oh, I can't stand this, I can't *stand* it!"

"Well, you'd better," Kay answered in a voice like flint. "That son of a bitch nearly killed me." Her fingers lightly traced the side of her face—a soft, affectionate gesture that set my teeth on edge. "Let's see if these heroes can get us home in one piece."

We took off again. Heavy and beautifully balanced as she was, the Empress felt mushy; anything over 20-25 and her rear end started to throw. I held her down, taking the curves as full as possible, shifting on the downgrades, fighting off the dreamy, mesmeric upsurge of snowflakes against the glass. I'd turned off the radio and for a time there was silence; even Kay had subsided. The maples gave way to birch, to firs, the grades got steeper. There seemed to be just the four of us, creeping through a universe of gently falling snow.

At Williamstown Kay said: "Can't you go any faster than this?"

"Not without piling into a tree."

"Then we're going to be good and late for signing in."

This produced a new rush of lamentation from Carole. "Oh my God, we'll be expelled," she moaned.

"So what?" Kay retorted. "There are other institutions of higher foolishness."

But we *were* late, very late. Coming into Bennington there was a feverish council of war.

"We can sneak in through Clark and McKee's window," Kay was saying. "Once we're inside we can bluff it out." I was to park behind a clump of bushes she knew, Russ was to reconnoiter the ground first. They went on conspiratorially until I said:

"Forget it."

"What?"

"Forget it."

"Then just what do you suggest, Horatio?"

"We're going to see the Dean," I said. "Where's the Dean's house?"

"You're out of your mind!"

"We're going right to the Dean and explain the whole thing. We got caught in heavy traffic because of the Pearl Harbor attack, and the snow slowed us down. And that's it."

"Well, I can tell you right now *I'm* not going over there—insufferable creep, he's just *waiting* for a chance like this to burn me."

"All right," I said, and now for the first time I was good and angry, "then you can get out here and walk the rest of the way. In the snow. Which way do you want it?"

At the Dean's house I pulled up to the front door, swinging the Empress around so the dented side was away from the entrance.

"See, the lights are out!" Kay hissed at me. "Of all the stupid hair-brained—"

"Of course they're out. They're upstairs, going to bed. It's late." I got out of the car and faced them. "Well, are you coming or aren't you? I'm damned if I'm going to do this all by myself." We trooped up to the front door and I rang the bell. There was a substantial wait, then the porch light came on, and then the hall light inside, and a slight figure in a paisley dressing gown opened the front door and said irritably:

"Yes, what is it?"

"Dean Cairns?"

"None other."

"I'm sorry to disturb you, sir. At this hour." I introduced Russ and myself. "We were delayed—the traffic is fierce—because of the attack, I guess, and the snow storm. We're late getting the girls back."

"I see."

"I hope you won't campus them or anything. It's no one's fault."

The Dean peered hard at me for a moment, then smiled. Two tufts of hair stood up on both sides of his head like gray horns. "I'm happy to see you're in good hands this time, Miss Madden." His eyes rested on Kay with a cold glint; I realized he thought I was Kay's date—I wanted to laugh out loud. "Even Bennington hasn't been permissive enough for you. But I'm glad my suspicions were misplaced. For once." He sighed. "Well. It's been a terrible day, a terrible day."

We thanked him and drove the girls back to their dorm. Carole shook hands with me awkwardly, Kay and Russ parted with a few words and nothing more. Watching his stiff, stricken face I didn't know whether to feel happy or sad.

Anyhow I took the Empress on in, slapping my face briskly every now and then and singing along with the radio at the top of my lungs, with Russ curled up in the back seat, sound asleep. I hit Mt. Auburn Street at exactly 7:30, pulled up in front of Porcellian or Sphinx or Onyx or whatever one of the hotsy-totsy final clubs it was, and went straight to work, my jaws sore from yawning. If they wanted to impound the Empress for being illegally parked and toss Russ in the can for good measure it was perfectly all right with me.

3

RUSS HAD THE crease in the Empress' side hammered out and refilled and repainted; he ran hard over in the cage afternoons and spent his evenings down in the house library; he began going up to Radcliffe again to see Chris. He never once alluded to the weekend: it was as though it had never happened. Not only had he turned taciturn but he showed an uncharacteristic self-discipline—which was weird, because everyone else had been thrown wildly off-balance by the war. Even I—steady, staid, sober old George—had to wrench my mind away from the parade of calamity in those weeks following Pearl Harbor, when Guam and then Wake fell and Singapore and Malaya tottered, and the battered, exhausted lines on Luzon shrank, and buckled, and shrank again.

"What are *you* going to do?" That was the query you heard all around you—there was little talk of anything else. A few were all for enlisting right away; others claimed that was a sucker's game: the services weren't equipped to absorb us anyway, they'd call us up when they needed us, it'd be a year or more before the country was adequately mobilized, if at all. But most of us—like the rest of the country—drifted into a middle course: we'd complete the fall term, midyears were only a few weeks away; and then we'd see...

And we were beginning to have a pretty good idea about what we'd see: it was going to be a long war, a very long war, with fronts on half a dozen continents, 10,000-mile supply lines, forgotten garrisons in Kirghizstan and Bora Bora...and somewhere at the end of the road (if there *was* an end of the road) lay the inevitable assault on a Europe already held by the professionals, the masters of modern war, and then that necklace of islands slung from the great belly of Asia, and its flat-faced, unflinching people who would never, never give in. A far-away, interminable war. They were going to get around to us all, sooner or later; any number could play. And so we waited, and argued, and for the first time in our heedless young lives read the morning papers more carefully than our history and economics texts.

What was most curious of all was that everyone underwent a monstrous sea-change. Stolid Rhino Tanahill got up out of bed on the Wednesday morning after Pearl Harbor and, unshaven and without jacket or tie, took the subway over to North Station and enlisted in the Marines. Dal, the fire-eating Anglophile, became one of the loudest proponents of watchful waiting. Terry turned tight-lipped and angry whenever the subject of Japan came up, talked of joining the submarine service and bit Russ's head off when Russ showed amusement at the idea. Everyone went out of character.

For instance, it was Dal—of all of us the one who cared least about the group, who now and then had even ridiculed "this asinine Fusilier crap"—it was Dal who became positively obsessed with the idea of a formal New Year's Eve party. Count Basie was going to be at the Cocoanut Grove. What could be more fitting than for the group to toast in 1942 with the swingingest, guttiest band of them all? It was a natural.

Russ and I exchanged a glance, and Dal caught it. "What's the matter with you guys?"

"I'm not all that sure everybody can make it," I said. "It'll be the holidays. The girls—"

"Of course they can. What've they got better to do? Look,

you've been roaring away about taking off for China and Africa, for pete's sake, and you're worried about a little thing like a run back to Beantown after Christmas?"

Russ had picked up a magazine and was pretending to read it. I said carefully: "I'm not sure it's such a hot idea, Dal."

"Why in hell not?"

"Everybody's all torn up."

His slanted eyes shot back and forth from me to Russ. "Torn up? Over what?"

"Well, the war and everything."

"All the more reason! Christ knows where we'll be a year from today. Rhino's going in on the 15th, Bierce and Blazer are gone already. Time's a-wasting. One last big bash—let's pull out all the stops. Go formal. What do you say?"

"I'm stony broke," I said. "For one thing."

"Oh, Jesus." He pursed his lips in disgust. "You going to put it on *money*, a thing like this? I'll carry you, then."

"Out of the question," I answered sharply. "We've been over that before."

"Okay, then make it a loan—you can pay me back when, as and if. Hell, pretty soon you'll be making fifty a month, clear. For years and years." He stopped grinning, glared at me and then at Russ, who was gazing out of the window. "What's got into you jokers? You're always yowling and howling about the Frazzle-ass Fusiliers, one for all and all for one, and then you get a chance like this and you sit there like a couple of cigar-store Indians. Currier, you listening to me?"

"I'm listening."

"Well, you don't look like it. I thought you'd rather dance than screw. Maybe our last big get-together, and you act like a couple of numb assholes. I just don't get it."

Watching his square, exasperated face, edged now with suspicion, I thought of Chris spinning and swirling under the golden spangles at Norumbega, her lovely face rapt in sheer, open delight. *I could feel it in Russ's hand—right there, in the small of my back.* Was that what she'd said? Would it make her happy? It could—it should. What the hell: if it would start those tiny green points of light dancing in her eyes again...

"Okay," I said. "Count me in."

"That's more like it. Rusty?"

Russ had glanced at me again—a look filled with alarm, and

something else I couldn't read, something wistful, pleading. "I don't know," he muttered, "I'll have to see. The old gentleman's giving a party—"

"Bugger the older generation. It's our turn now."

"Chris'll be down the Cape."

"You ever know her to pass up a big-time dance? And with *Basie?* She'll make it if she has to walk it on her hands and knees. Come on, Currier, don't be a pooper. Join the parade."

"I'll try—see what she says."

Then to our amazement Terry embraced the plan with a vengeance. It was terrific, a five-alarmer; we'd gather for dinner at his parents' home, the whole crowd, and go in to town from there. He wouldn't hear of it any other way. Dal had apologized to him months before for the shouting match at Jean-Jean's— I'd seen to that—but even so Terry's enthusiasm floored me.

Of course he knew nothing about Russ and Kay. And neither did Dal, who was almost certainly going to invite her. Twice out of sheer apprehension I started to ask him, and stopped—it sounded too artful. Also, I didn't want to know: it was better simply to hope that she'd be caught up in some theater party down in New York. Russ said nothing, only that Chris was coming, with bells on. Rather diffidently I invited Nancy, and got still another surprise when she told me she wouldn't miss the evening for worlds, she'd buy a new dress for it, she'd come back from home in plenty of time. Everyone seemed bewitched, compelled to do the reverse of what you expected.

The afternoon of the 31st came on cold; very cold. A steel-gray sky without a trace of wind, the thermometer at 6° above zero, the kind of day people back home used to say it was too cold to snow—and knew better. For the first time the Empress refused to start. Bundled to the ears Russ and I fussed over her, finally removed the air filter and held open the air intake valve until she caught. Russ was preoccupied, almost surly.

"Who's Dal bringing, you know?" he said in an elaborately casual voice.

"No, I don't. I didn't feel like asking him."

"I suppose he'll bring her."

"Maybe not—she may not be available." I paused. "That actor's in New York."

"Tommy Buckler?"

"There was a picture of him in the papers, Tuesday."

He nodded grimly, staring at the road. "Well, let's pray."

"Yes, let's."

Nancy was wearing a pale blue gown, and a thin chain with a sapphire pendant glittered on her throat; she looked supremely immaculate and pretty, and I hugged her in a little spasm of affection and chilled bones. And Chris was—well, Chris, glowing away in a simple white strapless gown that set off the high apricot luster of her cheeks and throat, her hazel eyes. Her hair brushed in a Lauren Bacall way just to her shoulders. Crimson satin sandals made even her lovely feet festive. I gave a low, deeply appreciative whistle and she grinned back at me and cried: "Say it again! Why don't Harvard boys wolf-whistle more?"

"They're too high-born," I told her, "they haven't put in enough time around corner drugstores."

"Well, they should. How else is a girl going to know?"

The Gilligans' house was a big, new structure in West Newton, huddled behind a forest of foundation shrubs. Inside a fire was roaring and the looping chains of light in the Christmas tree threw a rainbow glow over the girls' flushed faces. A nervous black maid served us eggnog in small silver cups, a sprig of mistletoe hung invitingly from the overlarge center chandelier. Dal and his date hadn't arrived. I stood, near the tree, feeling a bit awkward in my father's tuxedo—among us only Russ could wear one with perfect ease—listening to Mr. Gilligan, and waiting for the other shoe to drop. Would she come—would she actually have the poor taste, the brass to show up after that weekend? Carole had written me two weeks before, a brief, disjointed note saying that Kay had gone down to the city that weekend to see Buckler.

"Ah, they can't hold out," Mr. Gilligan was saying, clenching his great red hands. "Once we start pouring out those tanks and planes and the air raids begin in earnest, their production'll start falling off. They'll have to call it quits."

"Have the Russians?" Terry asked him brightly.

"Have the Russians what?"

"Called it quits? They haven't got any production at all, half their country's overrun. I don't see them caving in. Why should the Germans or the Japanese?"

His father stared at him for a moment, his rough, pocked face sober. "For the simple reason, Terry, that we will give them no choice. They can't match our industrial potential. Why, in France the last war we had stuff stacked up to the skies, miles and miles of it. Wait till we get rolling. They'll see the folly—"

"You mean they'll send emissaries. A negotiated peace, Pop. A nice, 19th-century settlement. That what you see?"

His father laughed then and shook his head, but his eyes glinted. "Ah, you double-domed intellectuals! I mean they'll quit because it'll be their only way out."

"Their only way out from what, Pop?" I'd never seen Terry like this: defiantly at ease, rocking on the balls of his feet. I stared at him. "You're wrong," he pursued. "You know that?"

"You think so, do you?"

"Yep. Dead wrong. This is the new stone age. Total war, total destruction. No survivors. New rules."

"Please, Tom," Mrs. Gilligan protested, "these young people don't want to talk about war—they're going to a dance!" She was a small, birdlike woman with fine brown eyes and beautiful fair skin. She was wearing an amethyst brooch that made me think of a ring my mother had once owned. "What a pity it's so cold out tonight," she said to Chris.

"Oh, it'll just make us dance faster than ever," Chris answered. Her eye caught mine, she winked merrily and held her eggnog very near her ear. "Do you think they'll play a tango tonight, George?"

The bell rang, the maid moved toward the front door. I forced myself not to turn my head. There were voices, a short pause, and Dal came into the living room, preceded by Kay Madden.

In the brief silence the only sound was the dense rustle of the girls' gowns. Everyone's eyes were on her—everyone's eyes were always on her, she had that unerring faculty for drawing attention, maybe certain people *are* invested with some mysterious magnetic force—and she paused for just the slightest of moments, measuring us all in that imperious, supremely confident way she had. Her eyes were like a northern sea. She was wearing a perfectly molded black strapless gown with some kind of deep gold thread running through it, she had her pale hair up, and she looked stunning. As usual. I stole a glance at Russ, and caught the flicker of something anguished and despairing—instantly supplanted by a perfectly impassive expression, almost stern. Watching him, the wary, uneasy faces of the girls, I thought, This is going to go badly, very badly; there must be a way, some way to avert it—

But Kay fooled me, she fooled all of us: it was her forte. She went straight to Mrs. Gilligan and greeted her warmly, then Terry's father; only after that did she turn to the rest of us.

"Why, George—you look so debonair. You *do*." Her eyes went over me like a beacon flashing, moved on to Russ. "The impeccable Mr. Currier."

"Hello, Kay."

"Going to win the dance contest tonight?"

"I guess not." His lips barely moved. "No contests tonight."

"What a shame. Dal thinks he and I could give you a good run for your money." Abruptly she swung around to Terry and smiled. "And *you've* got a secret."

His face broke open in delighted astonishment. "Hey, what makes you say that?"

"Just a shot in the dark."

"Terry's always got a secret," his father rumbled. "Always did."

"Oh, but that's good!" Chris cried. "What's that saying about secrets? Keep one, you're its master; reveal it, you're its prisoner. Who wants to go around with everything on a sandwich board, for all the world to see?"

Remembering that gray dawn after the Fens party I glanced sharply at Terry, but he was nodding and grinning away like the proverbial cat.

"A man can hide all things but two," Kay recited. "That he is drunk and that he is in love."

"But wine and anger betray all secrets," I added.

"No, no, no," Chris broke in, "it's time and chance, somebody said."

"Wonderful," Mr. Gilligan said, shaking his big craggy head. "What a bevy of beautiful girls—and witty, too. What have you boys done to deserve them?"

"Clean living and a fast outfield," Dal said; and relaxing now, everybody laughed and sipped at the eggnog.

For dinner there was a huge rib roast and baked potatoes like bursting bombs, and deep red wine in long-stemmed glasses; we beamed at each other through the candles, above the holly-and-ivy centerpiece. I found myself seated between Ann and Terry's sister Sheilah, a gawky kid of 14 with her teeth in braces who went to Concord.

"But I'm going to New England Conservatory soon."

"You're interested in music?"

She nodded rapidly. "I'm going to be a great pianist."

"You tell 'em, honey," Russ said from across the table, smiling. "And don't you let anybody stop you."

"Oh, I *won't!*" Gazing at him she flushed a bright crimson from her forehead right down to her slender little throat, and dropped her eyes to her plate in confusion. I recognized the symptoms. Another girl in love with Currier, still another: it amused and irritated me.

"God, how I envy you boys," Tom Gilligan was saying. "I'd give anything to be your age again."

"So would I," Terry said.

"No, I mean it. It was the biggest thing that ever happened to me: Paris, and the Argonne. You'll see, when this thing's over the old USA is going to come out the single big power in the world. It's going to be the new American century, a real one, with full control of world markets—a man will be able to make a fortune in ten years' time."

"You think so, sir?" Dal asked.

"I know so."

"And just think," Terry broke in, "us chickens will have made it all possible—simply by going out there and getting ourselves blown neatly into bits!"

"Terence," his mother said.

Mr. Gilligan watched Terry with raised eyebrows, and I thought of the boxing sessions, the wild exchanges, the naked fear. "You're in fine fettle tonight, lad. Very fine fettle."

"It's his secret," Kay said. "It's given him a strange power, as Chris said." Smiling she raised her glass. "Here's to the new American Century!"

"That's my kind of girl," Mr. Gilligan said.

Dutifully, a little self-consciously we drank, and looked at each other around the table. It seemed strange, in this long, still room with its imitation Sheraton sideboards and French doors and flickering tapers, that there should be a war anywhere at all, that there were other houses, other streets where people were dying grotesquely, horribly in a thousand ways. God rest you, merry gentlemen, let nothing you dismay—

"By golly, that's what we need more of," Dal was saying. I could tell he was well on the way to getting plastered. "Solid, honest-to-God optimism like Mr. Gilligan's here. You know, it occurs to me that's the best definition of happiness: optimism in the face of adversity."

"And thank—you—Ralph Waldo Platitude," Terry said.

"You'd do well to take hold of a few of those sentiments, mister," Tom Gilligan retorted. "I like this boy, Alice," he went on, indicating Dal. "He's got a head on his shoulders, he hasn't swallowed all that rose-tinted, ivory-tower baloney they're peddling over there across the river. Dalrymple—that's an Irish name, isn't it?"

"Well, partly, sir," Dal answered, and Terry guffawed:

"Irish!—he's a coony Scotchman."

"The Irish and the Germans made this country," his father said doggedly, "do you realize that? The two most despised races in the world, and they made America. Their blood, their sweat." His blue eyes rolled round to Russ, he caught himself up. "No disrespect meant, you understand. That's simply how it's been. That's why we've had to prove ourselves, over and over again, in the face of you Puritans."

"Tom," Mrs Gilligan murmured.

"You speak my language," her husband said to Dal. "When this thing's over you come around and I'll give you a job. A good one."

"Oh, Wog'll never be content with something like that, Pop," Terry broke in. "He plans to be head of General Motors."

"I'd be honored to have the chance to break in with your firm, sir," Dal said. "But I'm afraid that's a long way off right now."

"Well spoken, son." Mr Gilligan regarded his own offspring with a puzzled air. "How did I father such a cynic, I wonder?"

"Oh, he's no cynic, Mr. Gilligan," Kay said. "Actually he's the biggest optimist of us all. That's why he acts so cynical—it's to cover up all that potential disappointment."

"Hey, that's one on you, Terry," his father said, and laughed his booming deep laugh. "You've got a wonderful girl there, Dal. Looks and brains and a fine wit. I'll bet *you're* part Irish."

Kay smiled at him prettily. "Yes, I am, Mr. Gilligan."

"I knew it! Tongues of angels. She's my kind of girl."

It went on like that—Terry ebullient, Russ constrained, Dal deferential, Kay congenial and warm: everybody completely out of character. Was it catching? After dinner we wrapped ourselves up in coats and scarves—no one wore a hat in those days, we'd have cheerfully frozen to death rather than wear a hat—piled into the Empress and less impressive cars and drove through the icy dark to Boston's South End, tawdry and tough, with the old newspapers stirring in the gutters. The hat-check girl said, "Hi ya, boys," the maître said, "Yeah, we got it, right this way," and led us to a large, dim table near the wall. New Year's Eve, and the Grove was roaring. There were only a few uniforms—a major, three navy ratings, two armored forces men—yet they seemed to dominate the lush, hot room. At the next table a man with a purple complexion and two great gold teeth poked his companion in the ribs with his knuckles and said: "When you going to get rid of that alderman, Grace?"

"Who *are* these people?" Kay demanded. "This looks like an abandoned set for Edward G. Robinson."

"Takes all kinds, baby," Dal said.

"Here's your new American Century," Terry rejoined slyly. "The Arsenal of Democracy, cranking up."

"No, but it's the band!" Chris said. "The band is everything."

And the Basie orchestra came on right then, as if on cue, and slammed into *Roseland Shuffle*. Chris's eyes started dancing, she cried: "That *beat!* Come on—everybody up for the kick-off..." We took to the floor and after a while, swinging and stomping, shouting our approval at the solo rides, we got it all together again. Nancy, her little round face flushed with pleasure, surpassed herself—she made me sorry she hadn't been with us at Norumbega after all. Between numbers we simply stood and clapped, waiting for that formidable, fantastic rhythm section—the best rhythm section there ever was or ever will be—to catch us up and send us spinning and rocking all over again. The Count was the past-master of contrasts, and to hear him was always more exciting than you'd remembered. To say they were arrogant was putting it too strongly: they didn't need to be. It was the sublime self-confidence of the team that knows it's going to win. After all, they'd defeated the legendary Chick Webb in a battle of bands, on his own home ground at the Savoy—something even the best of the great Goodman bands had failed to do.

Between sets we drank and switched partners. Kay moved with an electric, sinuous force on the floor—she could make a good dancer even out of Dal. She was cool with me but pleasant enough: we talked about *Citizen Kane*, and the army; they were the safest topics.

"Why didn't you enroll in ROTC, George? the way Dal did?"

"I don't know. It's not my way, I guess."

Her even white teeth pressed down on her lower lip. "You feel being an officer is vaguely sinful. That it?"

I grinned. "Maybe I do, at that."

"George, that's a ridiculous romantic notion."

"You're dancing with a ridiculous romantic character."

"You can say that again."

We were under the bandstand. She glanced up with her quick, dazzling smile and waved, and Jo Jones, proud as an Ashanti warrior, grinned down at her, ripped off a furious drum-fire break and flashed one stick over his head, the other blurring over the sock-cymbal. *Jumpin' at the Woodside*. The rhythm drenched us, pounded up and down inside our veins.

"How about Nancy, George?"

"Okay. How about her?"

"Have you reached for the brass ring together? gone over the falls, as Russ puts it?"

I could feel my face stiffen, I couldn't help it. "That would be telling," I said lamely.

She laughed. "Oh, come on, you can tell *me*—after all we've been through. Pearl Harbor and all that. You know, you could go a long way, Grog-o. If you'd free yourself of certain fixed ideas."

"I guess that's true of everybody."

"Yes, but it's particularly true of you." Her eyes turned utterly flat, depthless. "You could play *first* fiddle. You know?" And laughing she swung out and away from me again, her hips moving like a stripper's.

Dancing with Chris half an hour later was coming home.

"Having a good time, George?"

"Fabuloso. And you?"

"Groove. As always." Her eyes rested on mine steadily; she was smiling, lips parted, but that shadow still lay deep behind her eyes. What was it? Uncertainty, resignation, fear? But Chris would never be afraid, she was all sheer, vibrant heart. Uncommon valor. I spun her out with the heel of my hand, she slipped out under my arm, off to my right and back again with that floating ballerina grace that made me tremble. And the shadow was still there. Nothing would ever be the same for her again. Would it?

"You so mean and evil, you do things you ought not to," fat Jimmy Rushing sang in that wonderful, piercing tenor, his eyes glinting and sad. *"But you got my brand of honey, guess I'll have to string 'long with you..."*

"Well, I'm glad to hear it," I answered, a touch late. "As a matter of fact, nothing I can think of would make me feel better."

"You're a good man, G.V. You don't have to say anything, you know."

"I *want* to say it, I mean it."

"I know you do. You're a good man, George. Good and true. I only hope Russ Currier knows what a friend he's got."

"Of course he does—I tell him every morning while we're shaving."

The number ended in a die-away wail of brass; the crowd clapped and cheered while the band went off. Back at the table Kay was saying:

"I should think you'd *all* want to, it's like turning yourself into a god any time you feel the urge."

"What's like being a god?" Chris asked.

"Flying. The sea all kinds of crazy blue and amber, and the Corniche like a wrinkled old lizard's skin below—God, there's nothing on earth like flying, I can't imagine why you don't all become pilots. If I could fly a plane I'd be the happiest woman in history."

"Who do you think *was* the happiest?" Russ said. He was always asking questions like that. With the dancing and liquor and Kay's astonishing geniality he was more relaxed now.

"Penelope," Nancy said.

"Why?"

"Because all her waiting, her sacrifice was worth it in the end."

"What? With a husband who'd slept all over the Mediterranean? Do you think after he'd wrecked Troy and sacked in with Circe he'd ever be satisfied with *her* again?"

"Sure he would," Nancy retorted, and her blue eyes began to shine. "Of course he would—all he wanted was to get home to her, really."

Russ said: "Now who was the unhappiest?"

"That's easy," Chris said without a second's pause. "Cassandra."

"Cassandra!" Kay exclaimed. "Why on earth that old crow?"

Chris looked at her—a long look, very steady, very brave. "Because that's the most terrible thing of all—to know exactly what's going to happen and not be able to do anything about it."

"I see."

"And on top of that for nobody to believe you when you tried to tell them."

"Nice point," Terry said. "Nevertheless, she asked for it."

"How?"

"You can't take on the gods' attributes without getting burned, *you* know that. What Ann calls playing God. Right, Annie?"

"Something like that," Ann said uneasily.

"Like the way you predicted my life," Russ said to Terry. "That afternoon at Nauset."

"That's right. And nobody believed me, either."

"Least of all Jean-Jean."

"Ah yes—Jean-Jean!" Kay exclaimed; his name seemed to have released a spring deep inside her. "Suave, masterful Jean-Jean. What do you suppose he's doing right this minute? Let's all guess. Dal, what's Jean-Jean doing now?"

Dal laughed uneasily. "Well, he sure as hell isn't playing leapfrog with some luscious Manhattan model, that's for sure."

The band had come on again, the management was setting up for the midnight broadcast, running in microphones. Ten minutes to midnight. Drinking too much of too many kinds of alcohol always made my imagination jump around in outlandish ways, conjure up absurd and dangerous images. I shut out Kay's bright, metallic voice and watched Buck Clayton holding his trumpet, his slender fingers fluttering over the valves.

The edge of something: we were on the razor edge of something. Waiters were setting party hats and noisemakers at our places, Nancy had put hers on her head, a toy soldier's scarlet visored képi; Dal was wearing a green-and-gold derby that made him look surly and tough. Nothing can give you so powerful a sense of division, of rupture and change as New Year's Eve, with its Janus-faced instant that compels you to

glance back with regret, forward with apprehension . . . Why did
I think that? 1942 was coming, on raven wings: what did it have
in store for us, any and all of us? I thought again of Nauset
Beach, but now it was Kay riding the great blue kite, soaring and
rocking like a bird of prey—

I yanked myself back to the table again. Kay was saying:
"You guess, Russ. Tell us what J-J's doing right this minute."

He was holding a golden stovepipe hat in both hands; his eyes
rested on hers with a kind of wary appeal. "I'd rather not."

"Why's that? You're the creative one. Isn't he the creative
one, George?"

"Indeed he is," I said.

"Isn't he the talented one, Dal? the one of you with a future in
lights?"

"Oh, I don't know about *that*."

"You don't?"

"No, we've got a little wager about that." Dal had picked up
one of those curled gadgets that unravels and was blowing it in
and out rhythmically. He winked his coony wink but Russ did
not smile. "About future plans and who's going to set the world
on fire."

"Yes, well, all that's kind of in cold storage now," Terry broke
in. "For the doo-ration. You know?"

I'd had too much to drink: far too much. There was that
unpleasant distance to everything, things were moving along
independent of me. And they were going to keep unreeling and
there was nothing anybody was going to be able to do about it.
Least of all me. Nancy said something to me and I smiled
numbly, understanding nothing, and gazed at the bandstand.
Basie, looking like a genial, beneficent uncle, nodded once and
began striking blues chords softly, over and over. He seemed
very far away.

"Oh, but Dal, how silly of you," Kay was saying in that
terribly bright, terribly clear voice. "Russ's an artist, and you
know you can't beat an artist."

"Sure I can."

"No, you can't.—Been writing, Russ?"

"Not very much." His face looked stiff and drawn.

"I wouldn't imagine so. Not in a world at war. That'll be for
later."

They were broadcasting now. The m.c. was speaking into the

mike, his voice inaudible, and Jo Jones was beating off the seconds on the sock-cymbal: *tssh—tssh—tssh—tssh*. The last seconds of 1941, going, going—

"Or maybe you'll throw it all over, just to prove your independence. You think he will, Dal? There's always that need to prove his independence. From what, I wonder?"

"Getting to midnight," I said suddenly. I had to say something and I couldn't think of anything else. My face felt numb.

"Loyal George," Kay went on; her ice-blue eyes fastened on mine, moved on again. "Our good Horatio. No, there's a certain perversity in Russ. He wants something, wants it terribly—and then he has to throw it all away. Have you ever noticed that, Dal? Now, you take that writing room of his—you know, the one at the end of the Brewster house, over the trellis. That's a sacred grove, no hankus-pankus in *there*, kids. No, that's only for other rooms... but when it comes to the real thing, when *push comes to shove*, no pun intended, when it's a case of really taking a girl over the rainbow—"

"All right, let's drop it, Kay!" I heard myself say, too loudly. The m.c. was audible now, calling out something about 1941, Jo Jones was still back there tapping off the seconds on the high-hat. Dal's face was white, white as old bone, his eyes wide behind his glasses, staring full at Russ. A still, awful moment, everyone frozen staring, and Kay's voice riding over it all, cutting through the saxophones, the quickened cymbal heartbeat:

"—and poor George, blundering in at a time like that, really hilarious, the *look* on his face!"

"*Now shut up,* Kay!" Russ was on his feet, so was Dal. Those pale white blotches had appeared around Dal's nostrils.

"You son of a bitch," he breathed—I could see his lips moving. "You sneaking, no-good son of a—"

The cymbal beat ended in a rippling crash of drums, there was a blare of horns and shouts; people crowded high around us, embracing, waving, the band plunged into a crazy, jazzed-up rendition of *Happy Days Are Here Again*. Balloons floated drunkenly in a haze of smoke, colored lights played over us like fire; a chair fell over beside me. And now the club exploded into full hilarity—roars and catcalls and whistles and tin horns bleating like lost demonic sheep, heaving shoulders and upraised hands:

"*App*eeeee Noooooyeeeeeerrrr!..."

And the eight of us stood or sat or crouched in all this giddy rejoicing like an island of wooden figurines: Russ stricken and angry and shamed, Chris with that sad, acceptant shadow in her eyes, very grave and steady, Kay's eyes glinting like hard gems, her face wreathed in that triumphant smile. No one could ever say her timing wasn't flawless. Dal was still saying something, I could hear his voice but I couldn't make out what he was saying.

Then he moved, around the far side of the table, toward Russ: a sudden, heavy rush, bumping people who turned to him laughing, brandishing glasses, whirligigs and horns. I knew I could never reach him, started out behind Nancy toward Russ—and saw Terry spring to his feet and wrap his arms around Dal, wrestling him backward. There was a great commotion, the man with the wide purple face was shouting at them angrily; a waiter had his hand on Dal's shoulder, pushing. By the time I got past Russ it was over. Dal had reached Kay, had seized her by the arm. She was glaring at him, twisting and glaring.

"Dal, look out, you're hurt—"

"I said we're *leaving!*" he shouted. "That's it!" He pulled her away. They were there, and then they were gone. It was all over.

We looked at each other uncertainly. Russ's face was like a thundercloud. Very gently Chris removed her bright green conical party hat and set it on the table, gazing down at it; then smiled at me—the fondest, saddest smile.

"I don't imagine we've any more use for that, do you think, George?"

"No," I said. "Not right now."

All around us couples were still embracing wildly. One of the armored forces sergeants had lifted his girl to his shoulders and was spinning round and round with her while she laughed hysterically, her head back and her eyes tightly shut. The band was playing *Cherokee*, Harry Edison's horn blasting high and raucous above the reeds.

"Let's get out of here," Terry was saying. "This place has lost its charm. Let's go over to the Statler Bar."

"All right."

Disconsolately we collected our coats and straggled out into the cold—to run right into Kay and Dal. They were arguing violently. She pulled away, he caught at her arm and muttered something, his face close to hers. Then he spotted us and his head came up again.

"There he is!" he shouted at Russ. "Kid Galahad. King of the Ferking·Fusiliers! All for one . . ."

"Oh, shut up, Dal!" Kay cried, but now he ignored her completely, swung away from her.

"You're not worth her big toe," he snarled, his teeth bared. "You know that, chum?—and you never were." I realized with a swift shock he meant Chris, not Kay. "Leave her for this slut . . . You're not fit to be in the same *world* with her! You underhanded son of a bitch—"

They went for each other this time: a silent rushing together, the thud of blows, gasps, a muffled groan from Russ. Then Terry and I were between them; Terry again had hold of Dal and was clutching at him, trying to pin his arms.

"Let me—*go!*" Dal roared. He broke loose and clipped Terry in the face, but to my amazement Terry held on and got hold of him again. I had Russ securely. He was wiry and quick but I was stronger than he was and I held him. There was a bruise on his cheek and his mouth was cut. Beyond him I could see Kay standing a little apart with that superior half-smile, enjoying it. The evening, opening pianissimo, hadn't been a waste after all.

"You crummy Beacon Hill creep . . . Too good for us all, aren't you? You see what he *is*, don't you?" he cried, panting, gazing straight at Chris now. "Don't you?"

"Dal—"

"Oh, the fucking hell with it!" He wrenched out of Terry's grip and took off down the street.

"Dal!" I shouted. I ran after him. The air poured into my lungs like burning, my eyes were streaming water. Jesus God, it was cold. I was almost sober. At the street corner I stopped, peering around. There was no sign of Dal anywhere. You too, I thought, gazing into the bitter dark. You too, old buddy. Join the club.

I walked back to the Grove. The girls were all clustered around Terry. His face was streaming blood, his nose was already swelling. Ann was dabbing at it with a handkerchief and making distressed sounds.

"Terry," I said. "You all right?"

"Yeah!" He laughed wildly, wagging his head "Dizzy bastard... Think it's broken?"

"Broken!" Ann said.

"What a wallop!" He was still laughing, irrepressible; the transformation was astonishing. "Jesus H, what a clout..."

Everyone was talking at once. Kay was saying: "Well, *someone's* got to get me out to Milton, I'm not going to stand *here* for the rest of the night."

"Where's his car?" I asked her.

"How should I know?" She disclaimed any knowledge of it with a gesture. "He's got the keys."

"Take her home, will you?" Russ said; his face had a pleading look. "Just get her back to wherever she's staying. We'll find a cab."

We broke up quickly, then. An eerie drive: Nancy stiff with anger, Kay making terse, flippant observations as though nothing at all had happened. Only Terry, in the back seat with Ann, was bubbling over with high spirits. I kept worrying about Dal, careening drunk around the South End.

At the place Kay was staying I got out and walked her to the door.

"What a pity," she murmured. "What boors you all turned out to be."

"Yes," I said, "we're terribly naive."

She looked at me in surprise, as though seeing me for the first time. "Why, Grog," she said, "I do believe I've misjudged you."

"No," I said. "You'll never do that." I looked at her—the bullying professional beauty, the absolutely depthless aqua eyes. I wanted to hurt her really badly; then it passed. I said: "It won't work, you know."

She smiled her rapt, superior smile. "Want to bet?"

"Sorry," I said. "I never bet against my friends."

"Faithful to the end... You think I can't read you? It's all over your face—every time you look at her."

"Good night, Kay," I said.

It got even colder on the run to Wellesley—it must have been 15° below zero that night. The heater was barely working. What was most surprising was Nancy—after Kay's departure she turned light-hearted and convivial. Huddled together under the car robe with Ann they joked and sang and did imitations of

Kay, and shouted loud and contradictory instructions to me. At the dorm Nancy embraced me—a quick, sure clasp and a passionate kiss that amazed me.

"Hey," I said, "you ought to live in Siberia."

"I know!" She laughed merrily. "The cold—the cold always brings it out in me."

"Brings what out?"

"You know! But tell me."

"Anything."

"How is it you devoted Fusiliers never get together without trying to knock each other's blocks off?"

"Oh, that's to prove our underlying solidarity."

We laughed, and kissed again. Her lips were soft and full, her body curved in and in to mine.

"My God," I murmured, "what's got into *you?*"

"Impulse, I guess."

"A long locomotive for impulse: one—two—"

"Ssh..." She giggled. "I feel crazy."

Another car pulled up to the entrance. We kissed again and she slipped inside. After we'd dropped Ann off at Garland Terry insisted on buying me breakfast at the Hayes-Bickford's in Harvard Square. His nose had swollen hugely, one eye was a mere slit now; blood was spattered all over his dress shirt.

"Jesus, you're a mystery," I said. "You won't battle with Dal when he's falling-down drunk and keep me up half the night worrying about what a gutless wonder you are—and then you hold him down when he's in a murderous rage and laugh like a hyena when he pushes your face in."

"That's how life is. Full of surprises."

"I guess so."

"Don't grieve, Grog." He sipped at his coffee gingerly, as though it might be contaminated. "The evening wasn't a complete bust."

"Is that right."

"This party: it was really for me."

"For you?"

"That's correct." His one good eye shot up to mine, he gave me that sly, triumphant smile. "I've gone in, old pal."

I gaped at him. "In? In where?"

"Army Air Corps. If I'd heard that bitch on flying earlier, I'd have picked another branch."

"What? When did you do that?"

"Two days ago. You're feasting your eyes on Irish Terry Gilligan, Air Cadet."

"*For—Christ—sake.* But you were the one that—" I broke off.

"I know. I know."

Neither of us said anything for a moment.

"But why in hell didn't you tell us?" I demanded crossly, to cover up the silence. "We'd have put together a brawl, the biggest ever, we'd have—"

He waved a hand in my face. "No no, that's just what I didn't want. It was better this way. Don't you see?"

"No. I don't see. What about midyears?" The idea of throwing away a term's board and tuition horrified me.

"Screw midyears." He clasped his hands around the chipped coffee mug. "I wanted this to be private, too: my own celebration. My own private pact with myself."

"That's a lot of mystic crap!" I said loudly. "And coming from you! Hell, you're still a Catholic after all, you're still religious as hell, for all the sociology bullshit." Several breakfasters looked around disapprovingly—I recognized a horse-faced clubman named Conger I disliked intensely; I lowered my voice. "Why didn't you wait until they grabbed you? They'll get around to everybody soon enough."

"It wouldn't be the same." His eye held mine. "I had to do it this way. Don't you see, George? I'll never know about myself—really know—unless I do. Never."

"That's ridiculous. What'll you prove? I told you— *everybody's* afraid of something."

"*It'll prove something to me,*" he said, and now there was a sudden heat in his voice. "And that's the name of the tune." Then he turned irrepressible again. "Besides. Remember the shooting gallery at Norumbega? They need me up there."

"Up where?" I said irritably.

He raised one finger portentously, like a benediction—only it was the middle finger. "The wild blue yonder. That great fly-swatter in the sky. You name it." He winked—or maybe he just blinked, I couldn't be sure. "But that's where I'm heading, daddy."

4

"NOBLE OLD Forester." Dal held his drink up to the stand lamp; the cubes stirred gently, rocking; crystals in amber. "Man's best friend."

"They're going to stop making it soon," Russ murmured.

"The hell you say."

"No, they're not," I said, "it's going to be rationed or confiscated or something."

"What in hell does that mean—just the generals and admirals get to booze?"

It was exam period. We were supposed to be studying hard for midyears—the three of us had one coming up the following day, as a matter of fact—and we were going to take another stab at our notes later on; but right now, after dinner, we were slumped in the living room talking about nothing at all. The panic and rage of Pearl Harbor had turned into a chronic malaise: we would waste hours on crossword puzzles or witless games of dice baseball or hearts, with one ear cocked for the news over the radio.

And now, as a final, irrecoverable distraction, the letters had begun to filter in. Rhino's were filled with comically gruesome tales of boot camp, close-order drill amid clouds of sand fleas, frantic calisthenics at midnight and something called "cat fever." Terry's world seemed to be filled with song—a farrago of marching bands, lusty chanting in cadence along the Miami strand—and study and more study ("Ah, call back halberds and broadswords—do you jokers realize that if this keeps up, war is in danger of becoming a bleeding *anachronism???*"). Jean-Jean's dispatches sparkled with droll observations on the grand parade of foul-ups and absurdities—supplies delivered to the wrong continent, composers commanding assault units, ex-prizefighters who collected butterflies ("Drôle de guerre, mes enfants. Voltaire, I am happy to inform you, was right. But here, alas, the only garden to cultivate is a decaying rubber plantation run by a mad old Belgian who wears a pith helmet and jodhpurs.").

We weren't Harvard undergraduates any more, we were amoebae dividing and subdividing. Each of us was in a dozen places now, here and "out there"—Georgia, Hawaii, Africa, Australia. We talked listlessly about shortages—tires were frozen, as were cars, gas was going to be rationed soon, so were sugar and beef and just about everything else. But we didn't believe in either the commodities or the shortages; all that really mattered this evening was what lay out there ahead of the prow of your ship, the nose of your plane, the sights of your rifle. Everything else was simply irrelevant, and there was nothing to be done about it.

"I'll clue you in, fans." Dal gave us his sly, sleepy grin. "There's one hot commodity that isn't *ever* going to be rationed. You dig?"

"That's right," Russ answered. "And where they'll be shipping you, you won't be getting any of that, either."

"Dry your eyes, ace. I'll be getting that wherever they send me."

They locked eyes for a moment, half-glaring, half-grinning, then looked away. I'd managed to pull things together since New Year's Eve—that is to say they were walking around each other like two strange dogs. But it wasn't really healed over. Once certain things have been said, that's it: there's no going back, however much one might like to think so. Dal felt he'd been royally suckered and bamboozled (he quickly came to the conclusion that I'd been in on it, too, and his attitude toward me cooled perceptibly); and Russ seemed to be torn by guilts and rages with no object. So we'd rocked along through January, and here it was exam time, with everyone even more tense and distraught (if that were possible) than before—and abysmally unprepared.

"Ah, they're all teasers basically," Dal said, and gulped down his drink. "Even when they put out, they're still playing with you."

"Not all," I said.

He glanced at me sideways. "No. Well—almost all of them. That satisfy you?" He yawned and stretched, cracking his knuckles above his head. "We're well rid of her, you ask me. And I know, nobody did. But it's true. Cheap, conniving bitch..."

"Rid of who?" Russ demanded suddenly.

Dal stared at him. "Little Miss Killer from Bennington. Who'd you think?"

"What about her?"

"She married him. Buckler." Still staring, Dal swung an arm toward the heap of papers and periodicals on the table. "It's all over the papers—where you been?"

Russ was on his feet. "Buckler—you're telling me she married Tommy Buckler?"

"That's right. Big deal, at this playwright's house in Connecticut."

"You're crazy, Dalrymple! She *couldn't*..."

"I'd like to know who would stop her, short of artillery. What the hell's the matter with you?" He was watching us both now. "Didn't you see it? It was in this morning's *Herald*, it's right there."

I picked up the paper. Yes, there it was, on page three. A nightclub shot: Tommy Buckler, his square, hard, strangely boyish face staring uncertainly at the camera; and Kay, more stunning than ever, her eyes resting on him adoringly. TOMMY BUCKLER WEDS BENNINGTON CO-ED. A caption she wasn't going to like very much. It had been a small private ceremony at the home of Mr. and Mrs. Noel Baxter, old friends of the bride (Darien was apparently a good deal "nearer the city" than Chatham). After a few days in New York the newlyweds were flying back to Hollywood, where Mr. Buckler had been cast in—

Russ jerked the paper out of my hand. All the color had drained from his face as though he'd been slapped, hard.

"She wouldn't have done that," he muttered.

"She *did* it." Dal scowled at him. "I tell you, you're well out of it. Look, you think she ever gave a green shit about you? You were a fill-in, that's all. A short wait between trains. Just the way I was. She played you like a trout."

"Why don't you shut your ugly face!"

Dal laughed once, but in amazement, not malice. "You're crazy in the head, Currier, you know that? Fletcher ran into her down in New York two weeks ago, he says she's been telling tales all over town about the snot-nosed blue-blood she had so much fun with..."

Russ was still glaring at him, the paper in a crumpled wad between his hands, his eyes wild; and I braced myself for trouble. But all at once he flung away the paper and ran off down the hall; the door pounded shut.

"For Christ sake, Dal!" I said hotly. "What did you have to bring that up for?"

"I thought he'd seen it. Why all the goofy care-and-feeding—isn't he supposed to know about her?"

I ran into my bedroom, threw open the window and looked down. It was snowing again, tentatively—the street was already a broad, straight band of white. While I peered down, blinking, the Empress' lights went on; the engine roared twice, gustily, then it swung out and took off toward the Drive, spinning wheels and slewing on the snow.

"Dizzy bastard." Dal had thrust his bulk into the window beside me. "Where's he bound now? He's got an exam tomorrow."

"We can't let him take off like this," I said. "Christ knows what he'll do, the state of mind he's in. We've got to catch up with him."

"Are you kidding?—I'm not his God damn nurse-maid...Hell, he's probably running over to Boston, to his parents' place."

"No—he wouldn't go there now. Not now." I thought a minute. "No, where he's gone is Woods Hole. Chris is down there, she finished her last exam day before yesterday. Come on, let's roll it."

He grabbed my shoulder, pushed me back. "Are you serious? You want us ·to drive down to Woods Hole on the chance that . . . Virdon, we've got a humping exam tomorrow morning!"

"All right—you'll flunk it anyway. Or you'll pass it. Dal, he's in trouble."

"You trying to tell me he's really and truly *hung up* on that bitch?"

"No, he's taken off for Cape Cod the night before a midyear exam at ninety miles an hour in the snow because of the lure of the open road. Jesus, you're dense!"

"Grog, it's snowing, they say we'll get—"

"I don't care if we get three feet—you owe him this much!"

"*I* owe him—why *me?*"

"Because you brought her to the farewell party for Jean-Jean."

"She was some friend of his—that's how I met her. Jesus-please-us, I didn't know Currier was going to go over the falls about her. I didn't know he was going to get himself involved with a five-alarm barracuda."

"Maybe he couldn't help it!" I shouted at him. "Maybe we can't always *plan* who we're going to get involved about! That ever occur to you?"

He stopped then, shut off whatever it was he'd been about to say. We looked at each other a moment—thinking the same thing, maybe; maybe not. I couldn't tell.

"All right," he muttered, and pushed his glasses up on the bridge of his nose with his thumb, "if you're damn fool enough to try to track him down, I guess I'm double-damn fool enough to drive you there."

Dal's Ford was parked around the corner on Plympton. He'd left one of the windows half open and snow had sifted in thickly over the seat. I brushed out as much of it as I could, while Dal ground away on the starter. She caught twice, and quit, and finally started running, rough as a cob, bucking and coughing her way along.

"She's just cold," he said.

"The hell she is. Don't you take *any* care of this heap at all?"

"She's been running fine."

"I'll bet. Ignition coil is shot. Or the distributor cam. *Something's* wrong with her."

"How was I to know we were going to take off cross country... How do you know he's headed for Woods Hole, anyway?"

"Because I do, that's all."

It was snowing harder now—tiny, obdurate flakes that stung the glass like sand. The radio was spouting its customary fountain of good news: Rommel was 55 miles from Tobruk, the Japanese were 8 miles from downtown Singapore; General Hershey had announced a plan to draft men previously deferred because of dependents or physical defects.

"How do you like that. Now it won't do you any good to rupture an ear drum."

"Or knock up a broad, either."

The radio cut out right after that, and I couldn't get a peep from it. Dorchester looked deserted, blinds drawn against war and night and winter; a ghost city. I thought of Russ without an overcoat, out ahead of us somewhere, pushing those 130 rearing horses, glaring at the dreamy, white-carpeted highway, raging away, accelerator foot pressing down, down...

"Pick it up a little, can't you?" I said.

"Grog, she won't do it, I can hardly hold her now."

In South Quincy he took the wrong turn and was half way to Nantasket before I got us turned around again. Then just below Assinippi the engine quit, dead. We coasted in to a store, which was closed. I got out and flung up the hood.

"Maybe I can fix it. Give me the flashlight."

"I haven't got one."

I started waving my hands. "Jesus Christ, Dalrymple, what good are you! Can't you do anything right, anything at all?"

He grabbed me by the shoulder again. "Take it easy, Grog."

"Why? Why should I? Give me three reasons."

"You're wound up like a top over this."

"Yes—and *you* couldn't care less!"

"No, Grog-o, don't say that."

I pulled away from him angrily and started off down the road.

"Where you going?"

"To get some help," I snarled, "—you want to sit there on

your ass forever?" By now I was frantic—I was convinced something terrible had happened to Russ. I stomped on down the road, the snow driving into my face and neck, cursing Dal, internal combustion engines, newspapers, Kay Madden. Look at her—she could turn us all inside-out, even after she'd swooped away out of our world; maybe she *was* a goddess incarnate, a God damn sorceress—why not? Anything was possible in the winter of 1942...

At the crossroads I found a diner with an open pay phone, and called Woods Hole.

"Yes?" That voice I'd know anywhere, any time, on earth or above it; subdued now, edged with concern. "Who is it?"

"Chris? This is George. Has Russ—have you heard anything from Russ tonight?"

"Yes—he's here."

So much for presentiment. I slumped against the phone box, half-sick with relief. "He's all right, then?"

"He's asleep. He's sick—he sounded half out of his head when he came in. He's running a fever of 102°."

"Do you need help?"

"No. Dad's sent for Doc Snow." There was a voice somewhere on the line, laughing breezily, a mix-up, and she said: "George? Where are you?"

"Assinippi. I think."

"*Assinippi!* What are you doing in Assinippi?"

"We were coming down—Dal and I. The fact is, Russ left in a rather disturbed frame of mind."

"I know." And that shadow was back in her voice. I could see her standing there by the telephone stand in the front hall, her head cocked prettily, holding the receiver against her ear like a shell.

"Chris—"

"Yes?"

"Chris, don't... It's nothing. He'll be all right."

"Will he?"

"Look, I don't know how to put this—"

"You don't have to, George. We read the papers, even down here in the sticks. Aren't we all lucky? Or unlucky, as the case may be..." She broke off, with the strange voice laughing along merrily, and I could see her bent forward now, holding the back of her hand pressed against her mouth.

"Chris—"

"Just kidding," she said a moment later, her voice brave and steady again. "Just whistling my way past the old burial ground, Georgie."

"You and all the rest of us, kid," I said, as though I didn't know perfectly well what she meant.

That's the way it was during midyears. Curiously enough—for everyone seemed compelled to stay out of character, all the dials had gone crazy—that night I borrowed a flashlight from the short-order cook in the diner, found the break in a lead wire to the coil, cut a six-inch piece from the panel wire and spliced it, and got the Ford going again; and we made it back in time to take the exam—in which Dal got a better grade than I did (even though he kept himself awake by sipping bourbon surreptitiously through a straw planted in a coke bottle in the breast pocket of his jacket). Russ was really sick; he came back to Cambridge a week or so later, hollow-eyed and pale, and shut himself up in his room. We left him to his own devices.

March was as mean as February—snow and sleet and more sleet; the dirty ice in the gutters never melted, it wore away like stone. More people were leaving—restlessness was a virus, and we'd all caught it. Ann left Garland and joined the Waves, Rhino was sent up to some gelid swampland in North Carolina, from where he related very unhilarious tales now, involving hand-to-hand combat drills and crawling under live machine-gun fire. Terry was washed out of flying school—something to do with his depth perception, we gathered—and was assigned to gunnery school. Jean-Jean's most recent letter made casual reference to a change in location; the sheets of paper were deeply creased and stained, as though they had been carried for some time in a sweaty shirt pocket; one corner was smeared with mud. What new location? The Free French were fighting in North Africa now—against Rommel: that tough, wily, superbly competent, invincible Rommel. Clearly things were not as drôle as they had been...

No point. There was no point in staying on in college, no point in doing anything that didn't have to do with grenades or rudder bars or landing craft. You could tell yourself that *The*

Scarlet Letter or French foreign policy under Mazarin mattered, but it wasn't true. The war and the winter had taken over everything.

And then one evening I came in from closing up the library to find the room dark. On the phonograph the Quartet was playing *Memories of You*, Benny Goodman's clarinet soaring up out of the piano and vibes, utterly simple, unbearably poignant; Russ's favorite recording. I hung there in the doorway. A cigarette end made a slow, descending arc at the far end of the couch.

"Nobody in here but this chicken." Russ reached up and switched on the lamp. "Just wanted to hear a few. Last time around."

"What do you mean?" I said.

"You know the slogan: *Join the Navy and see the World*. Well, I did and I will." He seemed delighted by the expression on my face. "120 Causeway Street, tomorrow morning at oh-six-hundred hours," he chanted happily. Then he sobered. "Imagine: *six o'-frigging-clock in the morning*. I haven't got up that early in all my life..."

"—Navy," I said.

"It's my sea-faring blood a-calling. The old forebears were big in the China trade, you know: 'round the Horn, opium and silk, beating the little yellow devils on the belly with bamboo rods. Discipline, Virdon!" He clapped both hands on his thighs, and I saw he was smashed.

"But we said we—" I fell silent, conscious of a sharp stab of betrayal. Only two weeks ago we'd decided to sign up for the Enlisted Reserve Corps, which would allow us to complete this term, and go into the Army together.

"I know, I know. But why grope around in the mud when you can have nice, clean decks under your feet, three hot meals a day, everything spick-and-span? That's the way to fight a global war, Grog-o."

"Sure."

"Anyway, I can't wait till June. I'm sick to creeping death of this place—I want to get a million, zillion pinwheeling miles away—and the old Navy's just the ticket. Maybe they'll even ship me to Kolombangara. Ever thought of that?"

"Where's Kolombangara?"

"Beats me, dad. Honorable Nipponese know, though: honorable Nipponese are sitting there, right now."

"Well, hey," I said after a little pause, "let's get up a farewell bash, I'll round up some of the—"

"No. No party. I don't want one. I'll just—fold the old tents and slip away. Far from the customary skies." He nodded toward a half-empty bottle of Cutty Sark on the coffee table. "Join me in a small libation though, will you?"

I poured myself a drink, a big one. BG took the final chorus, wound it up on one plaintive, sustained note.

"Oh, Mr. Goodman," Russ murmured. "You'll never know the pleasure you've given me. Isn't that sad?" He snorted, slapped his thighs again. "Well: here you go, daddy. This hurts me more than it does you." He held up the key of the Empress, watched it swaying on its gold chain. "But all good things must end. In 1942 they must, anyway. She's all yours."

"You mean it?" I said.

"Of course I mean it, why wouldn't I mean it?" He sang off-key: *As a dollar goes from hand to hand, so the Empress goes from Fuse to Fuse* . . . That's short for Fusilier."

"You're tank-o."

"Am I not, daddy."

"Thanks, Russ." I hefted the key gently in my palm. "I'll love her and cherish her till your return."

"Good show. Well, I guess it's time to ring down the curtain. Where's that miserable son of a bitch Dalrymple?"

"Maybe up at the OG. Or McBride's."

"Well, tell him au revoir but not goodbye. That bastard. Cut my mouth, broke Terry's nose. I ought to hate his guts, you know that? But I can't. Hell, he's just as simple-minded as the rest of us, for all his big-deal, financial-wizard bullshit. Just as confused . . . You realize that, don't you?"

"I realize that."

"Old Grog. Not a hell of a lot gets by you, does it? You're slow as molasses in January, but you get there. You get there."

The Quartet was playing *Body and Soul* now, and we drank and listened.

> *My heart is sad and lonely,*
> *For you I sigh, for you, dear, only—*
> *Why haven't you seen it?*
> *I'm all for you, body and soul . . .*

"We had the best of it, Grog. You know that? It'll never be so wonderful again."

"Sure it will."

"No, it won't. You know it won't.—Norumbega. That was the high point: when everything..." He stood up suddenly, swaying a little. "Well. Got to take hold. Got to get over to venerable, insufferable Beacon Hill. The Old Gentleman wants to have a heart-to-heart. Probably about life insurance—new low rates, you understand."

"Where's Chris?" I asked him.

"Beats me. Up at the Cliffe, I guess."

"I'd think you'd be seeing her tonight."

"Can't. Not right now. Can't."

"But—you've *got* to..."

I hadn't meant to put that much heat into it. He looked at me—a glance of sudden sharp surprise, a touch of fear; was it? Then his lips came together again. "Said our goodbyes, Grog. One way and another. There are certain things you can't—

"Kee-rist, I'm loaded. The old boy isn't going to like that. One bit. But he'll forgive me. We're in a period of—of universal forgiveness. You noticed that? Forgive us our sins as we enlist our bodies. Jesus, you should have heard old Smirker Smedley up at the Dean's Office: 'It's gestures such as yours, Mr. Currier, that will keep this country a bastion of liberty.' *Ta-daaaaa!* I told him: 'Smirker baby, you're a bit of a bastion yourself.'"

"The hell you did."

"I did. I most certainly did. I said: 'Smirker baby, you ought to run for Congress. Or start a night-club act. I'm not sure which.'" Abruptly he started off toward the door, whirled around again. "Christ! Almost forgot. I'm drunk as a bastion. Here. I want you to hold this for me." He handed me a fat manila envelope, clasped and sealed.

"You mean send it on to somebody?"

"No no no," he said irritably. "Hang on to it. If I should—what'd they say, last war?—go west. Then open it. Will you?"

"All right. If that's what you want." But I felt suddenly cross with him—the careening melodramatics, the self-concern. I said: "How do you know *I'll* come back, for Christ sake?"

He smiled at me fondly. "You will. It's your destiny."

"Bullshit." I fingered the envelope. "Don't you want your folks to have it?"

"Absolutely not. They wouldn't know what to do with it.—You're my family, Grog."

"You're plastered."

"Check-O. But it's true, just the same. Best friend an impossible, insufferable, arrogant jerk could ever have...No: my father never says anything; my mother always says everything, with full orchestration. The Lost Generation, they called them. Maybe they were. Well, we're the Ruptured Generation. Hung up between a wet dream and a bad dream."

He stood there, one hand on the door jamb, staring at nothing. "I've got a confession to make, Grog. When I went over there this morning I was full of piss and vinegar, I was gong to take out the whole Jap navy in one salvo. Now, I'm—well, I'm just—scared." He tried to smile. "There seems to be no other word for it. Scared as hell...You ever feel that way?"

"Yes. Plenty of times."

"The old five-ply intellectual with all the answers—and I don't know a God damned thing. About myself or anything else. Who the holy hell do I think I'm kidding?" He turned then and looked at me slowly—a look I'd never seen on his face before. After a moment I saw his eyes were glittering. "Why do I do it, George? Why do I spread so much misery around?"

I tried to say something and I couldn't. I wanted to say it wasn't true, he didn't bring misery or if he did it was only because he gave people so much happiness, too; that it was because he was Russ Currier—impulsive, creative, high-strung, because he wanted so *much*, because he was different from all the rest of us and had to be judged by different standards...I wanted to say all that, and I couldn't. It would have cheapened that moment, the anguished torment in his eyes. I know he was disappointed in me, but I couldn't help it.

"I don't know, Russ," I said. "I don't know why."

He stared at me in hurt, surprise, almost fearful recognition—then grabbed me, a sudden harsh embrace; broke away just as violently. "So long, George."

"So long," I said. "Good luck."

5

I ALMOST DIDN'T answer the phone. It was a warm, humming May afternoon, I was deep in the intricacies of Bismarck's scheme (unfortunately, successful) to unify the German people, and on Jean-Jean's gleaming, glorious record player Edythe Wright was singing *Music, Maestro, Please*. But the phone kept ringing and ringing, and finally I went over and picked it up and said: "Cambridge Sand and Gravel!" It was considered very jazzy that year to answer the phone with a different and supposedly hilarious response each time you picked it up.

A girl's voice said: "What? Who *is* this?" A French accent, faint and far-away. Denise.

"Hi," I said. "I'm sorry—I was being funny. How's everything?"

"But who is this?"

"George," I said. "You remember old Tio Jorge, the keeper of the seal. Where are you calling from, Alaska?"

"No, no—Washington, I am in Washington. I must speak to Russ. Is he there?"

"Sorry. He's gone bye-bye."

"What?"

"Gone—the Navy, he's in boot camp. Didn't you know? Hey, this connection is terrible. You don't suppose the Japs have got a tap on it, do you?"

"A trap?"

"Forget it. No, there's only Dal and me holding the fort now. Have you heard from Jean-Jean? Listen, we got a letter last week, week before last I guess, he's in North Africa. He's driving a Bren gun carrier."

"Georges—" She was still rattling along, but I couldn't make it out. "Jean—he—"

"Seems weird, doesn't it? After the Empress, and that Delage. One of the supreme sacrifices in a world at war—Jean-Jean on a Bren."

"No, *no,*" she said, or may have said, "you don't hear, not clear, oh Georges..."

"What?" I shouted, fearful all at once, on the edge of a sudden gaping precipice. "Look, I can't *hear* you, I can't—"

"Killed!" she cried then, and now I heard her clearly enough, "he has been *killed*—at Bir Hacheim, the filthy Boches—oh Georges..." and now she was crying, sobbing and sobbing, her voice hoarse and shrill. "He is dead, Jean is dead! In a battle, there..."

"Jean-Jean?" Not Jean-Jean. It could not be Jean-Jean. "You're sure? *You're sure?"*

"My father learned, through the embassy, oh God, it is terrible, terrible, oh if only I could talk to Russ, I want to talk to Russ..."

I don't know what else I said. I couldn't think of anything to say. Anything. I heard her voice running on, hoarse and despairing, and I didn't hear it at all. There was a tear on the chair arm where the purplish upholstery had burst through, an ash tray swiped from the Savoy, a volume of Dal's rebound in black and titled *Shifting Economic Patterns of the Twentieth Century*... I said something, I know I said something finally, I gave her Russ's address in Bainbridge, Maryland and she sobbed a goodbye and hung up.

I sat then, and smoked a Chesterfield down to the bitter end while a slow, hollow, sick sensation washed up through my guts and belly and chest, and made it curiously hard to breathe. I was sitting here. Here with the sunlight blazing in from the river and the empties on the mantel with their inscription—H-13, Y-O; *Jubilee Bash— Fusiliers Forever!* and the signatures; the gaily painted little totem pole from Norumbega, the poster of Georgia Southern artfully divesting herself of the first of 15 veils, the polished round wooden seat Dal had lifted from beneath the buttocks of a streetcar motorman in Boylston Street station; the framed montage of snapshots Gwen had taken of us grouped in front of the beach fire in Nauset, mugging, sassing the camera—

It couldn't be. It could not be. Jean-Jean was here, right here, the door would swing back and he'd come in with that quick, lithe stride, wearing one of those beautiful striped shirts open at the throat, a cigarette bouncing between his chiseled lips and say, "Bonjour, Georges. And have you been taking to heart my advice about the fair sex, mmmh?"

I got up and ran out of the room, took the entry stairs three at a time. The sun was bright with no breeze, but I was cold, quite cold. The iron gates looked shiny and very tall.

"Hey!" someone yelled, "hey, Virdon! What's the matter, you deaf?" Fletcher, in a fringed straw hat and purple vest, a Scollay Square mummer.

"Fuck you, Fletcher," I muttered. I had no idea whether he heard me or not. The Empress was parked down the street, under a scarred elm. I got in, dropped the key on the mat, picked it up and started her and drove quickly up Plympton, along Quincy, past the Faculty Club, Fogg Art Museum. Floating strangely, somebody else driving, somebody else who was me watching me driving past Mem Hall, looking gloomy and arrogant in the spring light. There would be a plaque in its echoing corridors for this war soon, another plaque with rows and rows of names...

At Cabot I parked illegally and half ran up the walk. The sweat was slick on my forehead now, and my neck but I still felt cold, and faintly dizzy. Marge Feldman was at the desk: broad, Slavic face, warm candid eyes. Mel Strasser's girl.

"Chris? You want to see Chris? She isn't here, George."

"When'll she be back?"

"She's gone home for a few days. Woods Hole."

"Oh."

"What do you hear from Russ?"

"Nothing much. At all."

"Say—" Her eyes very wide and dark and direct. "You, okay, George?"

"Sure, fine..."

"You look as if the law is after you or something."

"No—nothing like that. See you."

Back in the Empress again, off through Brookline and out the Turnpike, the tires shrieking on the curves. His hands were on this wheel, placed like this, his fingers splayed on the silver spokes with the thumb hanging loosely; shifting gears with two slim fingers, an almost disdainful ease, *you have no right to drive this car*... Switching lanes, running the lights, I'd never driven like this before, steady prudent old George, but I didn't give a damn; memories kept brushing close around my head like clouds of deadly gnats, and it seemed to me I could keep ahead of them—barely—by driving fast. I didn't even slow for the speed trap on that long, wooded curve at Chestnut Hill where they'd nailed Russ one night; but no patrol car was there now. Russ was always getting speeding tickets, Dal was too coony to get caught, Jean-Jean had been stopped by the law on Memorial Drive and had said to them rapidly in French, smiling charmingly all the while: "All right, you've snared me, you pimps without mothers, defilers of sisters, you've ambushed me properly, now what do you intend to do about it, mmmh?"

Off the Pike into Wellesley Hills, where the matrons all wore Peck & Peck shirts and heels just the right height, who had not had to pawn their family rings one by one, who laughed in their well-bred Seven Sisters way and gossiped and pointed firmly to the choicest cuts of meat, and then got into their paneled station wagons and drove back to their colonial-style homes and their healthy, overprotected children destined for St. Mark's and Andover and Choate—who would never, never have to work in a gas station or a paper mill...

Welles*ley, Welles*ley. Now the green-arched college walks and ways so neatly meandering. Girls in jeans, in plaid skirts, in cardigans, worn backwards this year with the inevitable single strand of pearls, in loafers and saddle oxfords just properly scuffed, walking in twos and threes; their eyes rolled out at me, covertly envious. I was a pampered aristocrat swooping grandly through their domain, one of the favored, the élite.

You have no right to drive this—

And there she was, walking along by herself, books and

notebooks hugged to her neat small breasts, her skirt swinging nicely, her blond hair lifting prettily at her shoulders. Nancy. Dear Nan. I slowed, a touch too sharply, and she turned—her little round porcelain face broke into surprise and delight.

"George! How funny. I was just thinking of you."

"I'll bet."

"Cross my heart. Even if you *have* caught me looking a perfect wreck."

"You look fine. You always do. Hop in, I'll drive you anywhere you want to go."

"Anywhere?"

"Anywhere."

"That's tempting." She gave me a slow, quizzical look and swung in beside me, running her hand over the sea-green leather. "That's right—now she's yours."

"Not really. On temporary loan, I guess you could say."

"Isn't everything? I mean when you take the long view, as Terry would say."

"I suppose so."

"Whew!" She plunked her books onto the rear seat—a gesture very unlike her—and threw herself back against the leather, her eyes closed. "This is the life. I tried to become a greasy grind, but it just didn't work. This spring weather makes you *unstrung*. I can't keep my mind on *anything*. Maybe I ought to get a job in a defense plant. Liz is going to, in spite of the fact she's a brain. Or maybe I'll join the Waves, like our illustrious prexy. If Liz went into the Waves she'd be planning the invasion of Europe. I don't see why women can't be generals and admirals, we're every bit as competent... What is it, George? What's the matter?"

"Nothing. Nothing."

"No. Tell me."

"Nothing. I—"

"Please tell me."

I did, then, driving I didn't know where, along those beautifully edged paths, looking like a scion of the rich and favored and hating myself for it; trying to beat down fear, and dread, and a mounting burdensome guilt that left my hands clammy on the wheel. Gliding endlessly under the maples and elms all washed and vibrant in the lemon spring light, where nothing terrible could ever happen; where there would never be the shrill moan and crash of high-velocity shells and the animal screams of men in great pain and a Bren gun carrier lying on its side, smashed into junk, with one wheel still foolishly spinning, while its occupants groped in the sand like crushed beetles—

"Oh, I'm sorry, George," Nancy was murmuring. "So deeply sorry. Oh, I know how you must feel."

Did she? Maybe she did, it was possible she did, why couldn't she? *Jean-Jean* . . .

She was talking to me softly, her little round face long with sorrow, her eyes wide with sympathy: the clearest, deepest blue. I wasn't hearing what she said, only the sound of her voice. It was not the voice I wanted, needed above all others—but it was sweet, it was soothing. Her voice, running softly above the Empress' engine. We were on a road that led down to the lake, a rutted, lonely road where trees closed over it arching and the sun filtered through in sliding lacy shawls of light. Nothing stirred. The water was still as still. I shut off the motor and took her perfectly manicured little hands in mine.

"Nan," I said. "Nan, I just don't know. I just don't—"

And I began to tremble. Now, not moving, not racing along the Turnpike, the swarm had caught up with me; I was open to it. I was more afraid than I'd ever been in my life—more afraid than the afternoon my father had been fired, or the night Louis LaBrache had fallen through the ice. All that mattered now was that my friend, the man who had welded us together and made us a happy, prideful band of—yes, brothers—had ceased to exist. He was dead. And if he had been killed . . .

You have no right—

"George. I wish there was something I could say. Or do. I mean it." Her face was close to mine, her eyes filling with tears. "I always thought I was good at times like this. But I can see I'm not . . . There just doesn't seem to be anything anybody can say."

"No," I said. "There doesn't."

"He was such fun. I was afraid of him, a little—he was so, you know, knew his way around so. All those girls. I know he's French, but it kind of took your breath away . . . It just seems *impossible*," she murmured, and tears began to run down her smooth little cheeks and catch in the corners of her mouth. She looked all at once very plain, almost ugly—yet I'd never felt more drawn to her. "He was here, right *here* with us only a few months ago. Only a few months! The way he'd say drôle—that is so drôle. You are so drôle, chérie. Remember?"

"I remember everything," I said.

I don't know how it happened. To this day I don't know, there wasn't any easy sequence of events. You hear some poor son of a bitch convicted of murder say he can't remember how it happened to do what he did and you think, Uh-huh, sure—but it's true, it can be like that: there are times when you simply don't know. One moment I was sitting there, my eyes full of tears, bound in a kind of shame (at being here, alive, in the Empress, in this leafy lush Wellesley springtime) and a kind of gladness (at being those very same things): fear and sorrow and a confusion that knotted my guts, and Nancy was saying, "Oh darling, I'd give anything, just anything on this earth to keep that look out of your eyes—I would . . ."—and the next moment I was kissing her wildly, holding her hard to me, and suddenly it had nothing to do with making out or scoring or any of the other hot-shot sophomoric stratagems we regaled each other with up in the dorm during the late hours but only a need—a fierce, inarticulate need to make love, to consummate, unite, make complete . . . No, it was more than that, I can't explain it really; but it was the most needful thing I'd ever felt.

"George," she gasped. "George . . ." And then: *"Wait—"*

But that was all she said. She swung away from me, not recoiling, drew her sweater over her head, and bent forward and slipped off her bra. We undressed with a swift, silent purpose that was like a dream, afraid to look, afraid not to, and turned toward each other again. Unclothed, her body seemed smaller somehow, more fragile, with its pale blond wedge of fur, the absolutely round, solid little breasts. I felt bold and suppliant all at once. I kissed her firm coral nipples gently and caressed her thighs, I remembered even then to touch the sweet vulnerability of her . . . oh, it was a tender effort, as tender as I knew, but she remained tight—dismayingly tight; I couldn't seem to enter. The constriction became greater and greater, we were caught in an agony of trembling. I thought, What's wrong; what's wrong? She cried out once, a muffled word or phrase I couldn't decipher, was it a warning?—and then she gave a low moan and her body released at last, a tidal channel into open waters, and everything floated in tremulous bands of light and shadow . . .

And then there was no sound at all except our rasped breathing and the gentlest of breezes stirring the leaves overhead. Light and shadow played over our bodies. We lay sweating lightly, transfixed, and gazed at each other in a way we never had before. There was nothing to say. Her skin was so white and firm—like alabaster tinged with rose. Very gently I put my hand on one of her breasts, held it suspended in a strange, fugitive peace. The world had stopped, everything had stopped.

Then there was a clatter in the branches above us and a jay flew up like a toy kite with a hoarse, high scream. The undersides of the leaves tossed in a shower of silver, and out across the lake there was the sharp, rhythmic slap of rudder lines and a girl's voice was chanting shrilly: "—*Eight! Eight! Eight!*"

We moved then, both of us at once.

"George—would you dress outside?" Nancy said. "Outside the car?"

"Sure." I slid out from behind the wheel and dressed quickly and walked off a bit into the woods. The branches swayed under my hands, their leaves limp and finely veined; beyond them the lake glittered like memory. I felt altered, a completely different person. *Jean-Jean is dead, we are alive, in the midst of death we are in life,* the inversion beating in my head like a litany.

When I came back to the Empress, Nancy was fully dressed, combing her hair. As I got in she stopped, uttered that same inexplicable little sound and put her arms around me, but differently.

" . . . I don't know why I did that," she murmured. It was the most honest thing she'd ever said to me. Maybe it was the most honest thing she was ever to say in all our lives.

"I don't either," I answered. But that wasn't true: I knew—or thought I did.

"George . . ." Her eyes moved over mine in a kind of pleading search, a fear, a claim. "I love you, George."

"I love you, Nan."

"Oh, darling." But her body was strangely still. She was afraid now, deeply afraid. I could feel it, a minute trembling. "George, you didn't—wear anything. Did you?"

I shook my head.

"Well." She frowned, counting. "It's near my period. Fairly near. I think."

"It's all right," I told her. I felt oddly confident, flushed with certainties. Of what? "It'll be all right."

"We've got to get back," she said suddenly.

"Sure. If you want to."

"No—stay here. Let's stay here. Just a few minutes longer." And she seized me around the waist—a fevered little clutch that was fiercer than when we'd been making love, far more passionate now. "Oh, I'm so mixed up—I don't know what's happening. It's crazy."

"No, it's not."

"Yes. Crazy." She pushed back her hair, a sharp, distraught gesture.

"It's all right, Nan. Don't worry, now . . ." Holding her I grew hard again, which amazed and pleased me. I wanted her again—a slower, more voluptuous progression this time. But I only stroked her head, trying to reassure her. So quick, I thought inanely; over so quickly.

"I don't know what happened to me," she muttered, staring down at her hands. "I've never done a thing like this. Never."

"I'm glad we did."

"Are you?"

"Yes. Oh, yes."

The jay shrieked at us again, bouncing on a near branch, and I thought of the great blue kite at Nauset, and Russ and Chris tumbling over and over down the open face of the long dune. They had made love together the week he'd been down at Woods Hole, after he'd heard about Kay and Tommy Buckler. I was certain of it. So had Rhino and Prill. Everyone was reaching out, touching, cleaving to one another as the current quickened, the angry roar came on—

"Thank you, Nan. You're wonderful," I murmured, and pressed my lips against her silky golden hair. For all the awkward, strained brevity of the act I nonetheless felt shriven, anointed. We had confirmed the ancient union: man-woman; together; one. Hadn't we? But Nancy troubled me. Surely she must be feeling the same time-old link to all beginnings; yet there was that still, indefinable tremor throughout her body, and a sadness that seemed half-guilt, half-accusation. But I hadn't taken advantage of her—at least I hadn't meant to. It was . . . two people who simply needed each other, that was all it was. Well, wasn't it? And it had made a bond between us, of course it had done that . . .

"I'll never forget this moment, Nan. You're wonderful."

"You'll call me," she said, searching my face again. "Tonight. You'll phone me, won't you?"

"Of course I will."

"Do you love me, George?"

"You know I do."

"I just want to hear you say it. Silly, I know. Everything's so silly, isn't it?"

Watching her solemn blue eyes, feeling the new pressure of her hands on my arms I thought: I've crossed a line. An invisible, immeasurable line, and nothing will ever be the same again. Nothing.

Yet it was Chris I thought about on the drive back to Cambridge that afternoon; and that night I phoned her at Woods Hole to tell her about Jean-Jean. She wept, as I knew she would, and then (as I knew she would) she said the words that comforted me. I no longer remember what they were, but they eased as nothing else could the storm of guilt and sorrow, the climbing dread.

6

THERE WERE SO many things to do, and I didn't seem able to do any of them. Turn over my newsstand concession to an earnest kid named Prentiss, break in Schilz on the library routine, send home the junk I'd accumulated, see Nancy. At times I felt like some 19th-century type making final arrangements before fighting a duel—only it was a duel I'd had no hand in, I certainly hadn't been given the choice of weapons.

All that work, was all I could think, all that work and it's been for nothing. Why had I raced from jobs to classes to other jobs, or sat up till 2 A.M. with a wet washcloth pressed against the base of my neck, struggling with Machiavelli's sardonic advice to budding heads of state? Maybe Socrates had been willing to die, but I sure as hell wasn't. It's all right for them, I'd say to myself hotly, thinking of Russ and Rhino and Terry, the wealthy and favored, it's easy enough for them, they can come back after it's over and pick right up where they left off; but what about me—I've got more to lose... Then the sheer maudlin absurdity of it would hit me and I'd mutter, What makes you think you're so bloody special? what gives you the idea you'll *come* back—that any of you will come back? No, let it go; cut the hawser and put it all behind you. I was eager to leave, I was wild to stay on in the only world where I'd been completely happy; I was in a perfect turmoil. Out there somewhere were shaved skulls and sergeants and icy replacement depots, and beyond them silent, menacing shorelines and the blinding flash of high explosive and the terse, grim commotion of field hospitals—things I could only guess at, late at night, when I would fall prey to moments of boundless dread and my guts would turn moist and hollow, churning on themselves, and my mind would be flooded with the old, unanswerable infant cry: *What is going to happen to me?* Things real and unreal at the same time—I'd passed into Russ's Limbo Zone, floating, impatient and afraid ...

And then the day before I was leaving for home and a week before I was ordered to report at Camp Devens, I heard someone coming down the hall, a lighter, different step, and there was Chris standing in the doorway. She looked thinner, and tired; her eyes seemed overlarge and brilliant against that lovely skin. She hadn't been out in the sun at all.

"Chrissie!" I called. I felt that sudden rush of exuberance, serenity, sheer delight her presence always brought me. Lovely, lovely Chris. That crazy obsessive voice had already begun its refrain: *Nothing can happen to you, friend, nothing—do you realize that?—now she is here.*

"Hello, George." She was the only one of us who never used Russ's nicknames. Then her face went stiff: "You're *leaving* ..."

"Sure am. ERC, baby."

"When?"

"Next week. I'm taking off for home tomorrow."

"But I thought you could stay on longer."

"Only to end of term. Which has just ended. Three A's and a B. How do you like that? As if it mattered at all at all." I popped four more books into a carton. "They can do without me no longer. The war must be brought to a speedy and successful conclusion."

"You don't have to be funny," she said. "*Everybody's* trying to be funny. Why?"

"Beats me. Laughin' to keep from cryin'. Stiff uppuh

lip—and all that. Why aren't *you* lying on the silken sands?" I seemed to be compelled to bat along like this, talking all around the only thing we both were thinking. Were we? "Chasing the golden sandpiper over the—"

"Cut it out." She laughed, but her voice was sharp. There was a funny, feverish look in her eyes that unsettled me. "Look—I came over to see you. Are we alone?"

"Yes. Dal's joined the fitness brigade. Running in place, deep-knee bends, hubba-hubba, he wants to be in tip-top shape for the old confla—"

"George, I've got to talk to you. Sit down. Come over here and sit down. I can't do this number standing up." She took hold of my hand, my wrist really, as if she needed to hang on to it, the way a child does. I felt that fearful, pleasurable surge deep in my belly. But her mind wasn't on me. Or her heart, either. Any plain stupid fool could see that.

"Yours to command, lover," I said.

"George, I'm in trouble. Big trouble. I'm pregnant."

Her mouth closed then, as though that was all there was to say. Which was probably true. I stared at her. Ridiculous, it seemed completely ridiculous, the kind of thing that could happen to other people—not to us, here, in this splendid college room with its view of the Charles... *The son of a bitch!* I thought with automatic savagery. *The lousy, selfish—*

"George, you've got to help me."

"I see." I didn't, though. I couldn't seem to collect my thoughts. I sat there beside her, watching her eyes, thinking of Kay Madden's high, hard laugh, Russ and Dal roaring at each other, trading insults. Everything seemed crazily altered, the way a familiar vista reflected in a mirror becomes alien and menacing. I said: "Is it...uh, are you—"

"*Yes*, I'm sure," she snapped in quick, angry tones, "and *no*, I haven't just skipped, and *no*, I'm not going to tell him about it, not a God damned word. My God—he doesn't even know I'm alive. Or care either. *You* know that."

"No, don't say that. If he knew, if you told him—"

"Oh, don't be so stupid," she nearly shouted. "Don't you think I know how it is? I knew last fall, at Jean-Jean's apartment, I could tell the way he looked at her, the way his head swung around...I may be dumb but I'm not *stupid*, for God's sake. And neither are you."

"But he'd honor—"

"Oh, stop using words like that! Jesus, George!"

"I'm sorry."

"So am I," she answered after a moment. "I'm—just wound up a little, that's all. He isn't going to know about this," she said quietly. "It's my problem and I'm going to solve it my way. But you've got to help me. You've got to find out about somebody."

I felt scared, then—sick-scared. "You mean," I said very slowly, "you want me to get the name of some—some—"

"Abortionist, that's what they call them, George. Yes. You're just terribly perceptive." Her voice was half an octave higher than its customary soft cello tone. There were short deep blue lines under her eyes, her face was gaunt—and she looked more beautiful than I'd ever seen her.

"Look, Chris, this is serious..." She stared at me as though I were some kind of mental defective. "I mean, are you sure you want to do something like that?"

"Yes. I'm sure. I've thought about it fifty nights, fifty times a night, back and forth, pros and cons, and I'm *sick* of thinking about it ... Please, George. There's no one else I can ask. I trust you—more than anyone else. You could find out about someone, couldn't you? Couldn't you?"

"Yes," I said after a time. "I think so. I can try. Only—"

"Only what?"

"Well—it seems wrong. The wrong thing to—"

"Oh now *look*, if you're going to go all moral on me, if we're going to have a bull session about it, you can forget it! This"—she jabbed at her belly in a blunt, hard manner that upset me—"this doesn't mean anything to me. Animal, vegetable, mineral—I don't know what it is and I don't care. Maybe it's already got an identity and an imperishable soul and a social security card and a God damn MA degree in sociology—all *I* know is it's great big trouble for the rest of my unnatural life. Now do you want to argue that?"

Neither of us said anything for a moment. On the floor below a door slammed and someone—it sounded like Walt Fenstermacher—thumped his way down the stairs, braying in Vaughn Monroe's nasal bass: *"Forgive meeee—for wanting you-so—but one thinggggg—I want-you-to-know..."*

"Well," I said. I couldn't keep from glancing idiotically at her belly. "Well—it *is* life..."

"That's easy enough for you to say." And there was hatred in her eyes now, a hatred older than any of us. "There's life in the *zoo*, for God's sake! Governments all over the world are just begging their loyal, patriotic citizens to slaughter as many people as they possibly can. Sure, *you* can talk about it till the cows come home, you're not stuck with the lease...It's an accident," she burst out, "an accident, can't you get that through your lofty male head? Or do you want to theorize a while?

"I knew a girl," she muttered; she was bent forward, her hands wedged against her knees. "Back home. Noble Lochinvar lover went wheeling back into the west again, or Buzzard's Bay or wherever he came from. She couldn't make up her mind about it, she *theorized* all over the place, and then it was too late. Everybody shunning her and just loving it. Well, it's not going to happen to me," she said in the hot, threatening tone, and fixed me with her eyes again. "I'm not throwing away my life because of one stupid, unnecessary—"

She broke off, gave me that morose, wry smile. "I keep forgetting. He's your best friend. Isn't he?"

I nodded. "But that doesn't mean—"

"I suppose you're wondering whether it was my fault or his."

I shook my head. "I figured it was his."

"Well, you're right. I guess...Oh, it's such a mess, a mess!" she cried, and tears stood in her eyes for the first time. "I wasn't trying to trap him, that's the last thing I wanted to do, you must see that. I know he's very passionate, very sexual. Well, so am I, he's not the only one. All those wild, fantastic things he says, it's not just talk—never was. And then she'd dropped him, obviously thrown him over, any idiot could see that. And then when he turned to me again, I thought—with the war and everything falling apart...well, what was the point of holding out when other girls were giving it to him? And I love him. More than anything in the whole silly world. I *wanted* him...

"I'm sorry," she said, and turned away and blew her nose. "True confessions. You don't want to hear all this drivel. The only trouble is, I can't seem to think about anything else. I'm all apart, I've been sitting up there in the God damn Widener reading room until I'm half loony."

"You need a drink," I said. "A stiff one." I went over to Dal's liquor cart and poured some of his precious Old Forester into two glasses.

"You pay for everything." She was holding the glass in her two hands as though to warm them. "Don't you. Payment in full, they never taught us that, and it's the one, black, rock-hard thing you need to learn, under all the technicolor slush. The world, they say. This isn't the world—" she pointed to the record changer, the windows, the river; then pressed her fist against her belly "—*this* is the world. Right here." She took a sip of her drink, another. "Yes, liquor does help, doesn't it. You feel it's going to, so it does. Mind over malady.—You see, it's not just—this business I fear, George. What I fear has already happened. It's—it's loss of love itself. Loss of what I *am* . . .

"You will get hold of somebody," she said, more quietly. "You will, won't you, George. You won't let me down. I trust you. More than anyone."

"All right," I said. Watching her lovely, gaunt face, the hunted look in her eyes I thought, This is how she'll look when she's middle-aged . . . and I'll love her as much then as now. Anyone would. Anyone. I was swept with overpowering sadness. "I'll see what I can do. You go on back to the dorm. I'll give you a ring later on."

Mel Strasser was sitting at his desk, tilted way back in his chair, snapping a large rubber band between his fingers and staring at the wall. There was a black medical tome in front of him but I knew he wasn't studying.

"My God, Virdon—you still here?"

"I keep telling myself if I don't leave Cambridge it'll all go away."

"Maybe you've got something there." Mel and I had a lot in common: like me, he'd gone to public high school and he was on scholarship. He was on the edge of a group too, a loyal spear carrier. There were things we never needed to say to each other.

"Do you know there's no medical answer to dengue fever? No serum, antidote, remedy—nothing whatever. And half a million clean-cut American boys are going to come down with it, sure as fate. Old Rhino's probably got it right now."

"Hell, Rhino's indestructible," I said.

He shot me a glance, pursed his lips. "You realize I'm going to be the only poor sod left in this place? Along with Thornhill and Conger and a couple others. The presto-change-o class of '44. Now you see it, now you don't." He slammed the medical book shut and flung himself forward. "Come on up to McBride's. I'll buy you a beer if you'll buy me one."

I said: "Mel, I need some help. There's this girl and she's pregnant."

He put his hand back on the book softly. His eyes were like ripe olives, dark and depthless.

"Jesus, George. I didn't figure you were the type."

"I'm not," I said. "That's why I'm asking you. I thought you might know of someone who could take care of it."

He snapped the rubber band at the wall. It bounced off the plaster and he caught it deftly, a reflex action. "Yeah, I can give you a name." He puffed out his lips. "You might be well advised to give it some thought, George."

"I have."

"I mean, maybe you—maybe there's—well, some other solution."

He'd first assumed I was the father and the girl was Nancy—then he'd decided it must be some other girl. Hot Jock George, the Big Time Lecher, banging the Seven Sisters silly. To tell him I wasn't direcly involved ("Actually it's another guy, Mel, a good friend, I'm just doing this for a friend") would sound even more fantastic. I thought of Nancy then, with sudden light dread, remembering the afternoon by the lake. Suppose she was pregnant too, right now, only she just didn't know it? Jesus, how many girls were there, all over America, knocked up and desperate, and either hounding the guilty guys or seeking illegal abortions? And why in hell did I use the word *guilty?* Weren't we simply the untutored, the unwary? the most naive of all the unready American generations? I shut it out of my mind and said:

"It's the only way, Mel. That's the way it's got to be."

"I see."

"There's not one hell of a lot of time. I'm going in next Thursday and I've got to get home soon as I can." I could see his expression change. I realized that sounded unpardonably callous. "Well, there's a need for haste on all counts."

"How far along is she?"

"Fifty-nine days."

"She in good health?"

"Sure—I guess so."

"You guess so. I'm talking about heart, blood pressure,

kidneys." His eyes shot at me again. "You've got to think of these things. *They* won't..."

He wrote out a name and a number on a pad, drew a line and wrote another name below it; tore the sheet off. "Here you are. Use this name when you phone. Not mine. This one. I don't have to emphasize the need for discretion."

"Right. Thanks, Mel."

"Don't thank me. Or anyone else. Where do you plan to take her afterward?"

"Afterward?"

"Sure—maybe she can go dancing at the Terrace Room, but I wouldn't count on it. They'll simply want to get rid of her the minute they're through. They'll shove her out that door and it'll be up to you, kid. Better nail down a room somewhere."

"All right. How much will it be?" I said suddenly. "The—the fee?"

"It varies. Two-fifty, maybe three. Can you swing it?"

"I don't know. I'll have to see."

"I can lend you fifty if you can't raise it any other way."

"Okay—thanks."

"There's no guarantee with these bastards, you know. She may still need a D and C."

"D and C. What's that?"

"Oh, Christ." He struck the chair arm. "This lousy frigging medieval puritan country! Look, be sure to have stuff with you. In the car."

"Like what?"

"Like blankets, for Christ sake—she's going to be in shock, mild shock anyway. Think! Ice, and towels. Pads."

"Pads?"

"*Sanitary* pads, Virdon. You've heard of menstruation?"

"For Christ sake, Mel, don't be an asshole." But my voice lacked edge. With his sense of decency, his good clear head and his sober concern he'd made it seem dangerous in a way nothing else had. Treacherous and lonely. I saw he was steadier than I was, and harder—his medical studies had equipped him for the world far better than any puny gov or history courses. It was his world all around us now—the world of pressure points and femoral arteries and scalpels and plasma...I got to my feet, working the slip of paper into smaller and smaller folds, peering down at it. "Okay, I'll see you around."

"George?"

"Yeah?" I turned at the door, angry at my boundless ignorance and fear, a bit resentful of his tough expertise.

"Look . . . call me if anything goes wrong." His eyes were dark and very steady on mine. "If there's prolonged bleeding, or she starts running a fever, things like that. I mean it. Call me and I'll get to you as fast as I can. Promise me."

All the antipathy ebbed out of me—I felt a quick, deep wave of affection. "Sure. I will. Thanks, Mel."

That evening I made a series of phone calls. First the number. It rang five times, seven, eight. At ten I started to hang up and a voice, a hearty, soft, sales executive's voice, answered. I asked for an appointment and gave the name. There was a pause, and then the man said:

"What is the time situation?" I told him. "All right. Give me your number and we'll be in touch."

"But when?" I didn't like the vagueness of that. "It's important to get this settled."

"In an hour or so. What is your number?"

I gave it. "What will the fee be?"

"Three hundred. Cash, of course." The voice was hearty to the point of joviality, as if about to burst into laughter. "We'll be in touch soon."

"But—how about my client? Don't you want a—preliminary interview?"

"That won't be necessary. I'll get back to you in a little while."

Then I called home and listened to my mother's troubled, solicitous voice, feeling more unreal than ever.

"I'd so hoped you could be home tomorrow, dear. Uncle Jim is here, and the girls. I've used all our points for a roast—"

"I'm sorry, Mom. I really am. I'll be home as soon as I can, you know that."

"Is it something bad!" Changes in plans meant trouble: she knew. I saw myself reflected in the window glass, sitting by the phone: the Ivy League sophisticate, in button-down Oxford shirt and seersucker slacks, suave and casual and debonair. Well you see, Mater love, there's this chick who's just a touch *enceinte* and I simply can't leave her swinging on the garden gate. In point of fact I'm arranging for a swifty, you know how it is . . .

"No, it's the Army," I said aloud, lamely, falling back on the military expedient for the first of many times. "They want me to take more tests, there's no way out of it. I'll see you soon. Love to everybody, now."

Then I called Chris. Then the jovial, hearty voice called me back, set a time for the day after next, and gave crisp, precise directions. Then I called a cheap little hotel I knew and reserved a room. Then I called Chris again. Then I picked up my three-gallon ration of gas in a jerrycan and poured it into the Empress' tank, and checked the Greater Boston road map in the glove compartment. Then I went back to the room and fell into bed.

Thursday was a raw, indeterminate day, the kind of day that can fall in March, or November, or even June, which it was. By evening it was raining—a steady, sullen easterly downpour, and cold. I ran by Radcliffe just after eight, and beeped twice quickly, and immediately Chris let herself out and came down the path with that light, springy walk. She was wearing dark glasses and had a kerchief over her head; she was carrying a little bag. Our first date together, I thought bleakly. Of sorts.

"Hi," I said.

"Hello, George."

I went around and opened the door for her and she ducked inside, swinging her legs in neatly, her knees together. I always loved the way she did that. She had the most beautiful knees, I'd told her that once and she'd laughed wildly and said, *"Knees!* What a ridiculous idea, beautiful knees, you're a subterverted *pre*vert, George..."

She tossed the little bag into the back seat and said: "Well—on to Berlin. Or some place." I handed her an envelope. "What's that? Oh, of course—the entrance fee." I'd raised a hundred and fifty, seventy-odd of my own, fifty of Mel's, and the balance from Dal. I'd told him it was a personal loan I had to pay off right away; he hadn't made any comment.

While I drove down Garden Street she rummaged about in her purse—whipped off the dark glasses with a muffled sound of exasperation. "How can they *see* anything with them?"

"What are you wearing them for?"

"I don't know. The better to cloak myself in anonymity. Is that why Hollywood stars wear them? cheaters? so when they retire into Tijuana for their quote emergency appendectomies unquote nobody will recognize them?" Her face looked still more hollow, brushed with deep blued lines. "Ah, it's all so glamorous..."

I was silent, watching the road, the sinking leaden sky. On our left the Harvard towers slipped away, looking toylike and trivial, a confectioner's joke. Last run down Memorial Drive, up and over the Cottage Farm Bridge, the tires moaning, the Empress swaying slightly on the slick iron. Last run. I felt freighted with sadness, anger, a barely contained panic, cold dread.

"Leaking."

"What?"

"It's leaking, somewhere. The top."

"It can't be..."

"Well, it is." I could hear her fussing about like an animal making its nest. "One of the seams, I think. Blessed are the dead the rain falls on..."

"Don't say that!" I snapped.

"Sorry. Slipped out. Things keep slipping out these days. It's a slippery sort of time, wouldn't you say? I would."

We slid through Kenmore Square, swung right on Massachusetts Avenue and ran past the tawdry shops, past Symphony Hall where we'd heard the Duke one night, across Huntington, Columbus, the tavern signs glowing hotly. It was raining harder. Cars streaked by like menacing fish, forty fathoms down.

"Savoy," she murmured; she'd seen the festive red-and-blue marquee. "Remember the night with the Father? *Play it till 1951,*" she sang softly. "Who was that singer with Hines? Sexy girl, sang *I Must Have That Man.* Ginger—Ginger something. Russ said she was better than Lena Horne, better than Billie Holiday even, remember? Russ tried to talk George Frazier into featuring her one night..."

"She's beautiful, isn't she?" she said in another voice, and I knew who she meant.

"No, she's not."

"Yes, she is. She's beautiful."

"The hell she is. She's not in your class, she never will be. *You're* beautiful, she's not. You can take my word for it."

I felt reckless, all my senses inflamed and careening. I'd had a terrifying dream the night before. We were at the beach at Nauset, all of us, climbing these high-tension steel towers, laughing and calling to each other, Russ up ahead, taunting us on. And then Chris had fallen, her naked body was bouncing on the wires, spread-eagled and writhing, blood pouring from a dozen places. In a high, sick horror I scrambled down toward her through the steel, mortally afraid of falling, and above me Dal was screaming, "No, no! *Live!*—they're *live!*" and I hung there, shaking, afraid to descend farther, afraid to withdraw... A real lulu. I hadn't been able to get back to sleep for hours. Now, as if to atone somehow, I felt bound to say what I really felt, whatever the consequences.

"She's got conventional good looks. If that's what you mean. It has nothing to do with beauty."

"No, it's more than that. She takes her risks. Remember that."

"*Risks*—her father's a millionaire!" I said with hot resentment. "Her uncle's a bloody movie tycoon—where's the risk there?"

"That's not what I mean. I mean she has the courage to act out her fantasies. That's something. Most people don't, you know: they lie in a thicket somewhere, waiting to pounce—and then they never even pounce when their chance comes." She fussed with the leaking roof, stroking the canvas with a rag she'd found on the floor of the car. "She's got—psychic influence. That's what I couldn't match."

"She's got *what?*"

"She can get people to do what she wants. That's what the world runs on, that's the two kinds of people the world's divided into—the ones that can bend others to their will, and all the rest of us. Where did Jean-Jean meet her, anyway?"

"I don't know. Some hot-shot New York party, I suppose." I felt more subdued suddenly, thinking of Jean-Jean somewhere deep in the Libyan desert, turning to dust, to sand, to nothing at all. We were moving now past Franklin Park, gloomy and bedraggled in the cold rain, getting nearer.

"Good old New York City. That's what he's always wanted. Russ isn't a rock-ribbed provincial Bostonian at all, that's the shell. I saw that a long time ago—underneath it he's roaming up and down Fifth Avenue, Scribner's Book Store to the Plaza. The center of the diamond... You don't suppose it's like a fever, do you? Burn itself out and he'll be rid of it? or is it more like leukemia, incurable?"

I made no reply, there was no answer to that one that I could see; turned right on Blue Hill Avenue, past rows of dreary frame houses huddled densely. A corner of the city where neighbors suspected and feared each other, where furtive, dangerous things were done. It was raining really hard now, and dark.

"Where are we?" she interrupted herself irritably. "Where is this, anyway?"

"Mattapan."

"Mattapan. I've never even heard of it, and I've lived in Massachusetts all my life. Still, I suppose if there weren't a Mattapan it would have to be invented, you know?" She was talking faster and faster, the rain was washing in greasy, pulsing waves over the windshield. I could hardly see the road. "What's that? That gloomy building there?"

"Boston State Hospital," I answered.

"Well. That's convenient. I mean, just on the off-chance things gang aft a-gley. Sort of a back-up pattern. My Grandpa Gos—that's short for Gosnold, can you imagine being christened *Gosnold?*—my Grandpa Gos used to say, 'The operation was a complete success, but unfortunately the patient—' "

"Chris, for *Christ sake!*"

"Just running on, just rambling, it doesn't mean anything." She could not stop herself now; I could barely say a word. "So many phrases they have for it. Knocked up, duck in the oven, letter in her letterbox, FOB Dee-troit, all so comical, really a riot, anyone with half an ounce of humor can see that. Ironies, the world is crammo-jammo with them, Russ is right about that, bless his stony heart. When you think about all the people dying in London, in Hamburg and Hankow and Leningrad tonight, just tonight, thousands of them, burned and bombed and shot full of holes, children especially. Russ would write an epic about it, wouldn't he, these two homeless urchins in Zagreb, say, eating grass and garbage, fighting just to stay alive, and here in America, in jolly old Mattapan—you can *feel* the irony, can't you, it jumps right out at you, terrific really, a theoretician's *dream*, and what a movie it'll make!—you know, cast of thousands, she'll introduce him to her Uncle Lorry it she hasn't already, and she'll star in it herself, I mean that's part of the plan, isn't it? and their futures will be assured, in glorious technicolor, and in twenty years, when all the—"

The car ran out at us from the right. Peering hard at street signs, struggling to see, I braked—in the flash of a second it struck me that he wasn't going to stop, that I wasn't going to be able to stop either, there wasn't room. Or time. I swerved violently left, the tires squealing, his headlights swept over us like a beacon. A slow-fast dream passage as he glided monstrously, impossibly near, the lights dipped out of sight below the right fender. Then the shock and recoil. Chris cried out sharply, an animal cry—I saw her body slam forward against the windshield. Then we were stopped dead, there was a thin, festive tinkle of glass, and I could see the driver's face like a frightened fish, pop eyes and mouth gaping, a perfect black O.

"Chris!" I shouted. "You all right?"

"Sure—yeah." She was panting as if she'd struggled up a cliff, her hand to her head.

"You sure?"

"Sure. Just a clunk."

I pushed out of the car and ran around to the right side in the rain. The car—a '36 LaSalle—was embedded in the Empress' fender, its radiator hissing and steaming in the dull dark. There was no one anywhere in sight. The driver had opened his door, then stopped. While I watched he eased out one foot, a shiny black shoe, cracked across the instep.

"What the hell were you doing!" I shouted. "Coming out of there like that? Come on, let's go, let's go—you think I *like* standing in the rain?"

He got out of the LaSalle like a sleepwalker. A flat, pasty face, a mouth like badly healed surgery, currant eyes that darted left, right, left again. He pointed vaguely behind him.

"Well now, the right of way—"

"—was mine, it was mine! You were whipping out of a side street, there..." I looked back. Chris was rolling down her window. I saw a shadow on her face, moving, a ribbon. Blood. She was bleeding, her face was bleeding. I leaned in toward her. "Chris! You're hurt. You're—"

"It's nothing. Bumped my head somewhere. I'm *all right* ..."

I whirled around again. The driver hadn't moved. I grabbed him by his coat lapels and shook him, shook him again. "You've hurt her!" I shouted in his face. "Do you realize that? You could have killed her! You God damn, stupid son of a bitch!"

He put his hands on mine, almost gently, swayed back and

forth, his head rocking a little. "Now," he said gravely. "Now. Least we can do is—is be gentlemen."

I saw all at once he was drunk. Stewed to the eyeballs.

"You bastard," I gasped. Rain was beating into my face; my eyes were stinging.

"Now," he said.

"You stupid, *stupid* idiot!" I wanted to hit him, smash his pasty, shifty-eyed face to rotten pulp, I would have killed him if I'd had a weapon in my hand, anything. I know I would. I slammed him back against the car so hard his hat fell off on the hood.

"—George," Chris was pulling at my arm, she'd got out of the car. "George, come on..."

"Get back in the car," I said roughly. And to the driver: "Your license."

"Now, there's no need for a lot of—"

"Give me your fucking license!" I screamed. "And get the hell out of my way..." I crouched down in the water, peering, studying the collision by feel. The cars weren't hung up on each other, which was all I cared about for the moment. The Empress' fender was driven in hard around the wheel; the LaSalle's radiator was shot, spilling water, steaming on the macadam. The driver was fumbling about in his wallet and muttering something. I shoved him aside, started the LaSalle, and backed it off to another shower of falling glass, got the lug wrench and a tire iron out of the Empress' trunk and after a good deal of panting and sweating pried the fender away from the wheel. Lucky enough. She'd drive, she'd still drive.

I ducked inside the Empress and wrote out the man's name and license number on the blue Cape Cod Bay area of the map. He was hovering around me now, thick white hands opening and closing like a spastic's. Even drunk as he was he must have realized he wouldn't get 500 yards with that radiator.

"All right." I handed him back his license. "Now go home and sleep it off."

"But—what am I going to do?" he faltered, pointing.

"Anything you like," I snarled at him. "Push her over a cliff. Jump off it yourself. Have another twenty drinks. Just anything you like—only get out of my way!"

I started the Empress, put her in gear. The steering felt all right, if the alignment had been affected it was minor. That great Derham custom body. We'd lucked it out. Beautiful, glorious, indestructible Packard car—*Ask the Man Who Owns One*...

"It's all right," I said, as evenly as I could. "All right. That son of a bitch." I was seized with a fit of cold trembling; water was streaming through my hair into my collar. "She'll drive. We've got time. I allowed a little extra. We're almost there, don't worry now."

"I'm not. I'm not worrying," she said.

"You sure you're okay?"

"Yes. Fine."

"Is it deep? still bleeding? You must have—"

"No, it's fine.—Turn around," she said.

"What?"

"Turn the car around. I'm not going."

"No, look, there's time, we're practically—"

"Not going to do it, George."

I pulled over under a row of spindly, drooping trees and turned off the motor. All the houses on the block seemed to be watching us.

"But you said. You said your mind was made up, no matter what."

"Well. I've changed it. Woman's prerogative." She laughed once—a single gasp of mirthless laughter. "The *hell* with him."

"Chris—"

"I'm not going through with it. He can go fuck himself!" Then, again more quietly: "I'm going to have this baby."

"Chris, honey, you—"

"No matter what. No matter what." And now she was crying, quietly, her voice roughened. "Even if he never knows. Or cares. Especially if he never... It's part of my love. The realest part. Don't you see, George? Don't you see?"

And all at once we were holding each other, hard, her head pressed against my cheek; holding each other and rocking back and forth a little, she was sobbing her heart out, and the tears were running down my face now, and all I wanted to do on this earth was protect her, comfort her, hold her and shield her from all unhappiness, all harm, all foul betrayal...

Finally she drew away and blew her nose hard. "It's true," she murmured. "That's all that counts."

"No, but your father," I said, "back home—"

"The hell with them. It's my choice. Mine."

"They'll can you at school."

"It doesn't matter. This matters."

We were bent forward, conspirators in some most dangerous game: each speaking for the other now, all the counters reversed. The rain thundered on the roof.

"But what will you do?"

"That's my problem. I'll solve it."

—*I'll marry you.* I nearly said it. I very nearly said it, bent toward her in the cramped dark, my hand on her shoulder: I'll marry you, Chris, I've loved you for months and months, I've always loved you and always will, you don't know it but it's true—I was starting to say it. And then like a stab I thought of Nancy, the lost, blind grappling by the lake, and her silence. I didn't have the right. I'd made another commitment, I must honor it, that was the way the game was played. Wasn't it?

And so I sat there, sat silent. It's as I've said—for me there are only commitments and consequences: that's all I've ever seen. Ever since my father came home that afternoon and sat weeping in the captain's chair by the stove, weeping and weeping. I just can't see anything else. It's bad, of course, it paralyzes you, it silences you those rare-as-emeralds moments when you *should* speak out, when you should take it all in your two hands, take the wild, impossible leap of deliverance, the leap that would transform your life. You hesitate—and you are lost. And yet, without it you become—well, like Russ... Don't you?

But I would have asked her if it hadn't been for that hour by the lake; I know I would.

Then she said: "I'll never love anyone else. Never. Not like that. I know you can't understand that, George, but that's how it is, and there's no changing it. The very idea of—" She broke off. "Life's minor compensations. Or maybe they're major, I don't know. Anyway, that's how it is." Her voice was perfectly steady now. "I'm going to have this baby. Period." She gave my hand a quick, firm squeeze. "You've been a good friend. The best friend anyone could ever have. Putting up with all these hysterics and everything... Now let's go home, okay?"

"And besides," she laughed softly, a shade of her old sweet laugh. "Think of the money we've saved..."

She was quiet most of the way back to Cambridge. She seemed utterly drained of all energy, all emotion; for a while I thought she'd actually fallen asleep. In contrast I was forcing my mind to take its disciplined course, to cope, trying not to touch her as I ached to do . . . I'd take off for Skamondaga tonight, the midnight bus from Park Square. I couldn't get the Empress repaired, there wasn't time, that'd have to be up to Dal. Then in one week it would be Devens, and basic, and the Great Unknown. Chris wouldn't get to graduate. Now she'd be drummed out of Radcliffe, the subject of locker-room asides. Laughing, vibrant Chris, who tied her hair back with beach-grass stems and ran along the shore calling to the herring gulls . . . Chris, oh Chris.

On Memorial Drive I switched on the radio. All the news was bad, worse than it had ever been, almost the worst you could imagine. Rommel's armored units had captured El Gazala and claimed 3,000 prisoners, the Germans had launched a massive new offensive near Kharkov. A huge sea battle was raging at Midway.

"Midway," Chris said. "Midway—that's near Hawaii, isn't it?"

"Yes," I said. "Very near."

"God . . . You don't suppose we could lose this war, do you?"

"I don't know. Tonight I swear I don't know. Come on up to the room," I said. "Let me give you a drink."

"All right. Yes, I could use a drink. I really could. And anyway, now I don't have to worry about the bloody rules. Do I?"

G Entry gate was open; I slipped her quietly through the entry and up the stairs.

"It seems like nothing now," she whispered, giggling. "It used to be so scary. Everything *is* relative, as Terry used to say. Isn't it?"

Dal was slumped on Terry's monster blue couch reading a fat gray book. Jean-Jean's 12-record changer was playing Benny Goodman's *String of Pearls*.

"Well . . ." He swung himself to his feet and his narrow eyes began to gleam. "If we must die tomorrow let's live tonight, eh? What have you two been doing—gigging frogs in the Charles?"

"Had a little accident," I said tersely. "Drunk son of a bitch hit us, over in Mattapan."

"Mattapan! What the hell were you doing in Mattapan?"

"Slumming," Chris said. "Latching on to some local color."

"Chris got hurt," I said.

I watched his expression change. "Hurt? You hurt, Chris?"

"No—he's making a lot out of nothing. I just bumped my head. On the dash."

"No, come on, let's take a look."

We sat her down and Dal examined her. "Say, that's a nasty cut." He looked at me crossly. "What were you doing—burning up the track?"

"I *told* you—this drunk came barreling out of a side street and clobbered us..."

"It wasn't his fault, Dal. George was doing everything he could—" she broke off, ran on without a tremor "—the rain was terrif. You couldn't see a thing."

"I don't like the looks of it. It may need stitches."

"No, it doesn't need *stitches*. Good Lord, you're making a mountain out of a mole hole."

"The hell I am." He said abruptly: "I'm going to get Mel."

"No, wait—" I started, broke off.

He turned and looked at me. "He's right next door, for Christ's sake. What's the matter with you? Suppose it gets infected—don't be so God damn callous..." And he was gone down the hall while I stared after him.

Chris smiled up at me, shrugged. "What's got into him?"

"Well, maybe he's right," I said lamely.

"Nonsense." But she seemed obscurely pleased. Anita O'Day was singing *Skylark* in that fine, husky contralto, and Chris sang along with her, absently:

> —*Have you anything to say to me?*
> *Won't you tell me where my love can be...*

And I thought of the night out at Seiler's Ten Acres dancing to Gene Krupa, and later in the buttoned-down Empress with the sleet drumming on the canvas like a snare, and Russ peering at me over the front seat and laughing. *George, you old contortionist, you!* God damn him, I almost said aloud, God damn him to hell and back...My God, had all that happened a year and a half ago?

There were voices in the hallway: Dal came in, followed by Mel Strasser, who said: "Hello, Chris." Then he saw me—there was a flash of surprise and then his olive eyes turned darker and without depth. He bent over Chris.

"Good and clean," he said. "Got iodine, Dal? Band-Aids, the

wide ones? Won't even leave a scar." I watched his fingers move along her temple: deft, gentle, sure. He would make a good doctor—he would drive himself through the long hours, save lives. All at once I envied him fiercely. "Right where the face-lift incisions are," he was saying. "Here, and here."

"Just what I need—" Chris laughed wildly "—a face lift!"

"You'll never need one, baby," Dal said.

"Won't I?"

"No," I said, "you won't, ever."

"You're both loony," she exclaimed; she was holding her head tilted, the slender throat arched in that way she had—still laughing while Mel penciled the cut with iodine; she never once flinched, though her eyes were blinking rapidly, narrowed. "Sometimes I think you Fox Entry types carry loyalty too far."

"You look run-down, Chris," Mel said in a preoccupied tone, bandaging the wound.

"I *am* run down—so would you be if you'd had four exams in six days."

"You ought to take vitamins: you know, B-complex, minerals..."

She raised her head and looked at him. "Maybe I should at that."

He straightened then, and turned to me. "How about you, George?"

"Me? I'm fine. Nary a scratch."

"You were lucky. Both of you were." His eyes darkened again, shining. "You going down to DC?"

DC. I watched him, thinking rapidly, remembering the other night. "No," I answered, holding his eyes. "There's no need to."

"I see." He nodded. "Good."

"He's reporting at *Devens,*" Dal broke in. "What's all this about?"

"There was talk about some of us being sent down to Washington," I offered casually. "Some classification deal."

"Stick around, Mel, have a cheering cup with us," Dal said.

"No, I've still got a paper to hand in. Thanks just the same." He grabbed my hand in both of his. "All the luck in the world, George."

"Thanks," I said. "For everything."

Dal made us drinks and we sat around listening to records and talking aimlessly.

"What were you reading?" Chris asked Dal.

"How to make a cool million in the stock market."

"Beautiful."

"Yeah, there's really nothing to it."

The rain had let up again and the air blew in cool from the river, stirring the curtains. I felt numb, frozen in this terrible day, like one of those prehistoric mammoths caught forever in the ice. Had I actually held Chris Farris weeping in my arms, urged abortion, turned away from my own deepest, green desire? Around us the house seemed hollow, holed with vacancies. A skeleton garrison now. For most of us the waiting, the dreamy limbo time, was over. I understood how Jean-Jean had felt, and Terry, and Russ. Chris—slipping away from me now, lost to me—and Dal, sitting together on the couch, seemed like another race of anthropoids, locked behind a film of glass.

"The way it works is this," Dal was saying to her. "Your bear sells what he doesn't own in the hope that, before he has to deliver, he'll be able to buy back at a lower price, thus making a profit. You follow me? You're selling in the hope prices will fall."

"Sounds risky."

"Sure, the risks are big, but the profits are bigger. Because stocks tend to decrease in value faster than they rise in value. See, a falling market spreads fear. And hope is less suddenly contagious than fear."

"That's true, isn't it? Then it's all psychological."

"Well yeah, I suppose you could say that. You know the definition of a pessimist: a guy who wears both belt *and* suspenders. Your bull, on the other hand, doesn't wear anything to hold his pants up."

"Why are they called bulls and bears?"

"Function. Your bull tosses his victim in the air—drives prices up; the bear knocks his man down."

"Oh. I thought it meant something else."

Dal laughed, his Chinese eyes narrowed still further. "That's your sensual mind. I know what *you* thought."

I got up and wandered down the hall to my room. Everything was packed and gone: my old cracked Gladstone—my father's, from his palmy days—was lying open on the bed. I sat down at my desk, put my hands on the worn cheap wood. Unreal. The desk, the room, the college, Dal and Chris laughing in the common room, Dick Haymes singing *I'll Get By*.

Well; it was stupid to go on sitting here. Say au revoir but not goodbye. I shut my bag, picked up my soggy trench coat and went back down the hall. Dal was bent forward, his big arm lying along the back of the couch; Chris was facing him, one leg tucked under her, a hand at her chin. She was nodding, a faint smile at the corners of her mouth.

"You off?" Dal said.

"That's it." I handed him the key to the Empress. "She's all yours. By right of accession."

"God damn. Who'll *I* give her to?"

"Beats me. There must be one 4F in the class. Sorry about the fender. I want to pay for it, Dal."

"Forget it."

"No, I mean it. What the hell, I'll be making all of fifty a month, clear."

"This is all wrong," Chris said suddenly. "Your going off like this. No farewell party, no brass band for George..."

"Well, it's sort of lost its distinction," I answered. "There'd have to be a bash almost every evening."

"Even so, it's not fair." But I could see she was relieved. I was a reminder now. Never be a party to someone's sharpest pain: you may not be forgiven for it.

"Hey," Dal said, "can't I run you in to the station?"

"No—I'll take the subway. 'Harvard-Central-Kendall-Park, through the subway in the dark'... Take Chris home. Get her out of here without being compromised—"

I stopped awkwardly: I didn't realize how it would sound.

"Unless she wants to be, of course." Dal grinned his sleepy Chicago grin. Old hot-shot on the prowl. Then he turned solicitous again. "Hey, going to miss you, old buddy." He glanced around the room—I think it had only just occurred to him that he'd be all alone after tonight. "Who the hell am I going to drink with?"

"That's what you get for joining ROTC. Well, see you around."

Chris came up to me then—that lithe, eager way—and put her arms around me and kissed me: she had never kissed me like that—certain, sure, tender. "So long, George. Be good. And thanks for—well, everything."

"My pleasure." Why was it when I most wanted to show how I felt, I always blew it? But I couldn't say anything more—it was as though a crack had opened up, running the length of me, all the way down into my guts, and I couldn't quite hold it together.

"Wait—" She reached into the pocket of her jacket then, drew something out and put it in my hand: a small oval shell, fawn-colored. So tiny and so perfect. It felt made for my palm. I couldn't look up from it.

"Little deer cowrie. They say it has life-giving properties. Lucky." The green points of light in her eyes were moist now. "Dear George. To remember me by."

"Take care of yourself, Grog-o." Dal was pumping my hand up and down; and all at once his eyes were glistening, too. "I mean it. You take care, now."

"Only the brave deserve the wicked," I said. "And conversely."

"And conversely."

They followed me to the door. I was walking out of the only world I'd really loved, heading for Christ knew what. It had been so *short* a time! My throat felt tight, my sinuses stung again. Jolting down the stairwell I looked back. They were standing in the doorway watching me: Dal had his arm around her waist. He murmured something I couldn't hear, she looked up at him—a new, strangely expectant glance. I started to speak, waved my hand instead and moved off down the stairs. Something in the way they were standing there reassured me—and wrung my heart.

III

Don't Get Around Much Anymore

1

"—But she *couldn't* have done that!" Ron cried. "She couldn't! Not Mother..." He was still leaning against the fender of the Empress, one leg crossed over the other, hands sunk deep in his pockets; but his face was wild with outrage, his eyes snapping blackly. "Why, she didn't love him at all! Dad. She just latched on, she just—*used* him. My God!"

"That's enough, Ron," I told him sharply. "You don't know what you're talking about. Anyway, I'm not through yet."

"What could change *that?*—what do you expect me to think?"

"People do things they wouldn't ordinarily do, in times of stress. Isn't that what you were just telling me?—about your friends in Vietnam?"

His head came up again. "That was different—that was life and death."

"So was this," I said softly. "Oh, so was this. And don't you forget it." I shivered once, shook my shoulders inside my jacket. The stove had run down again, I was chilled from sitting and talking. "You going to hear me out, Ron? That was the condition. Remember?"

"Whatever you say." But he'd made up his mind. I could tell. Dear God. Spare us the impatient, cruel verdicts of youth. Our own youth.

"You keep your shirt on," I told him. "Let's go inside—I'm freezing to death." We plodded along the flag path to the back door. It was raining again, a fine cold drizzle locked in spooky swirls of ground fog. A day like Mortellange. Ron was following me in silence, heels sucking in the wet. I felt harassed and vexed. I decided he was going to get the rest of the story whether he wanted it or not. All of it I could tell him, anyway.

In my study I felt better: the scarred old desk awash in manuscripts and galley proofs, the massed bookcases, the prints and photographs. I could always cope with things in here. Well—almost always. Ron was peering at a framed montage of snapshots, the corners of his mouth drawn down again.

"Those taken at that picnic? the one at Nauset Beach?"

"Yes."

"He's one cool dude, that Jean-Jean. Funny... you all look so young."

"We were."

"No, I mean—*young* young. I don't know, I can't explain it."

"You don't have to." I opened the cabinet beside one of the speakers, pulled out an accordion file and handed it to him. "Here you go. Some primary sources. Why take my word for it?" I grinned, although I still felt provoked. "Here it is—World War Two. *Our* World War Two, anyway. Help yourself."

He began to finger the files. "They're in order. Chronological order. Postcards, letters, little phonograph records..."

"V-records," I said. "And V-mail. V for Victory."

He whistled, looked up at me. "Hey, you really *are* the keeper of the seals, aren't you?" he asked, and I couldn't for the life of me tell whether his expression was admiring or derisive. "The way Jean-Jean said..."

"There's not so much there, really. When you think of all that happened.—You do want the truth, don't you?"

He frowned, and lifted out the first letter. I leaned back in my work chair, my hands laced behind my head, and stared at a framed front page of *Paris Soir*, frayed and stained with something, maybe old wine, whose headline said: *PARIS EST LIBRE! Le Traître Laval et sa clique ont suivi les Boches.* I closed my eyes. When I opened them they fell on a piece of ancient marble molding that always rested on the far corner of my desk...

Grog Boy!

I know, I know, you've just been double-timing 30 miles with full pack & running obstacle courses all day & doing KP all night, & you're beat & royally teed off at the whole cruddering US Army & the LAST thing you want to hear is a raft of poop hot from the Home Front.

Well, forget it. Forget those aching doggies, those blood-drinking drill sergeants. Shove all that mud, sweat & tears behind you for a 2-beat & tune in on the BIG NEWS OF 1942:

Flash! CHRIS & I ARE MARRIED. Wedded, espoused, joined in holy (more or less) matrimony, spliced. What do you think of *that????* And you are looking at one deliriously happy character. I still can't believe it—in my plain frazzle-assed good fortune.

It was all so sudden. (To coin a phrase.) We were out at the Totem Pole (yeah!) with Mel & Marge, & Woody Herman & the Herd beating out *Woodchoppers' Ball*. And I felt something between us, I can't explain it. The thing I felt the night you took off for Uncle Sam. One of those magic ripples. I know I sound like a goofy monk or something, but there you have it. And I thought, what the hell, over the falls, in for a dime in for a dollar, a cat can look at a king, right? And I said it: "Marry me, Chris."

Yeah, just like that. She stopped dancing (can you imagine Chris *stopping dancing?*) & said, "You're crazy." I said, "The hell I am." "Dal," she said, "you're just in that mood." I said, "I've been in love with you ever since I met you." She blinked at me then, & her face got that lovely deep color—you know, like ripe peaches or something, that glow, & she said, "You're serious. You're really serious." "Just because I never *said* anything doesn't mean I didn't *feel* anything," I told her. "Everybody thinks I'm only a hot-rock but I'm serious as hell about this. I want to marry you." She just stared at me, shaking her head slowly, & then tears came into her eyes & she said, "You're a good man, Dal. An awfully good person." Which shook me up, because *you* know & *I* know nobody's ever called me *that* before.

Well, we talked till 3 AM, & I really poured it on. Remember I once said you can sell anybody on anything, it's simply a question of empathy & eloquence? Baloney. She said she'd have to think it over. After all that. Which really threw me, dad. I didn't even go to bed at all, just walked all over Cambridge, I was half off my trolley. Next day soon as I got a chance I hot-footed it up there to the Cliffe & finally tracked her down in Widener (Jesus, THE WIDENER READING ROOM) & dragged her out & lured her down on the river & started in all over again. And you know it's funny, right in the middle of it I realized I'd never wanted anything so much in my life, nothing had ever meant this much to me. I got scared, all the way down in my guts. I'd never felt like that before, I thought I was going to blow apart, right there on the sunlit banks of the Charles.

Anyway, to make a long story earth-shattering she finally said YES. And here we are, an old married couple of 16 days.

Now DON'T BE SORE, Grog. I know you've got a right to be, but don't. I *wanted* you to be best man, so did Chris. But we figured: time's a-wasting, Uncle Sam is breathing harder on the back of my neck, rumor is they're shaking up all the reserve programs, you're only young once, & WHY WAIT. And I knew you'd never be able to wangle a leave during basic. And the rest of the gang scattered all over, what the hell.

AND then things REALLY started rolling. The ceremony was going to be down at her Dad's place in Woods Hole. By that deep blue sea she's so hung up on. And no gas for the Empress, all I had was 3 A-coupons. I tried to use Mel's & an officious son of a bitch over in Somerville called me on it. "Coupons can be used only in connection with the vehicle described on the front cover, can't you read?" I said: "Jesus, Mac, have a heart—I'm getting MARRIED." He gave me one of those sourball Somerville looks & said: "Tell it to your draft board." Hah—hah.

So then I did some frantic sleuthing & found out about this guy in Watertown, a shady joker in a derby hat & green suspenders who was selling black market gas at *35¢ a gallon*. But price no object. So I got 10 gallons & started up the Empress & was just about asphyxiated with this weird stink, like cleaning fluid. I said: "What'd you give me?" He said: "Naphtha."

"*Naphtha!*" I screamed. "You crazy bastard, it'll wreck the frigging engine!" "Look," he said, "do you want to get there or not? Just hold your speed down. And put in a quart of # 10 oil." I said: "In the *tank?*" "Sure," he said, "it'll float on top, keep the stuff from evaporating." So we got there, but we both smelled like a dry cleaner's, & it pretty well burned up the muffler & tail pipe.

My folks came on from Chicago. They were kind of surprised by it all, as you might imagine, but they swallowed hard. And they love Chris. Especially Dad, who adopted her on the spot. Oh, I almost forgot. During the ceremony the minister came to the place where he says, "If there is any man who feels this couple should not be lawfully wed, let him step forth now or forever hold his peace." Well, right at that point this little cousin of Chris's was holding his grandfather's cane & he dropped it on the floor. It sounded like a gunshot & everybody jumped & looked toward the door. I half-expected—well, never mind what I expected. You know.

Anyhow, that's my story & I'm stuck with it. And loving it. Hell, I'm walking on air. There was no honeymoon, sorry to say: 3 days in New York City, & 3 more back at Woods Hole, & then it was back for summer session (accelerated schedule to you, son). We're camped in a beat-up flat over behind Dunster with a silver tea service, 2 toasters & 5 Ronson lighters (wedding presents) & a bed & 2 camp chairs (Morgan Memorial). It's hardly a palace over in the Fensgate, but it's home. Chris has quit Radcliffe & is working at the Coop.

Got to run. Chris sends you love & kisses. (After me you come first.) She has written Russ. We thought it was better that she do so, given the circumstances. Hope he doesn't take it too hard, but what the hell, he had his chance & he blew it big. I've no regrets. Not after New Year's Eve. He's still hung up on that Madden bitch, who is *Launching a Career in Films*, according to a squib in the *Globe*. Do you hear anything from Gilligan? That guy is the world's worst correspondent.

Shake it easy, dad. Really wish you could have been here for the ceremony. Wish you could be here right now to hoist a flowing flagon with us. We got sentimental the other night & phoned Nancy in Lancaster. She misses you a ton (as you know), is working hard in a hospital there (as you know, too) and likes it. Liz has gone to work in an aircraft plant. The women of

America are AROUSED, Grog: they are going to *win this war* for us & I for one think it's a great thing. When do you make field marshal?

Dal.

Dear George,

It's a beautiful summer afternoon and I'm sitting on the lawn behind the house writing this. Mother is working in the Victory garden and Duchess is lying here beside me, her nose on her front paws and her eyes rolling up at me every now and then. It's so peaceful. And it's so hard trying to imagine what you're doing right now. I mean of course I *know* what you're doing from the newsreels and LIFE magazine and your letters. But it all seems so far away this afternoon. So unreal.

You're right, I do like working at the hospital. It's hard work, but I like it. And it's great experience. I'm getting awfully good at it if I do say so. Miss Hatcher, the head nurse on our floor, has let me give IVs and help prep for surgery, stuff like that. She says I have the temperament to be a topflight nurse, the dedication and discipline (her words) for surgery and everything. Should I be thrilled? or horrified? Well, I've got to confess I'm thrilled right now. Miss Hatcher wants me to enroll in the RN course, but right now I can't make up my mind.

Isn't that fantastic about Dal and Chris? I didn't believe it at first, I thought it was some kind of practical joke. You know Dal. In fact I still don't understand it. Have they been, you know, attracted to each other for some time? It seems so strange—I thought Chris was really deeply in love with Russ. A woman's never wrong about something like that. And then after that ghastly New Year's Eve it looked as though they were back together again, I mean, weren't they? It kind of takes your breath away, if you know what I mean. And right after Russ had gone into the Navy, too. What do you hear from him?

But it's you I'm thinking about. All the time. You do know that, don't you, darling? You have to. Duchess has just poked my elbow with her nose, as if she's cross with me for writing about everything but the thing I care about most. And that's you. I miss you so, darling. Sometimes at night I just ache for you so I can hardly stand it, I have to get up and read or something. Such a crazy, crazy thing we did that afternoon by the lake. And yet I'm glad we did it. If you are. If we build on it, I mean, if we make it stand for something. Oh, I don't know what I mean, I'm so mixed up about everything. I don't know whether to go back to school in September or not, Miss Hatcher notwithstanding. Liz says she's not going back. She says it's a dishonest dream world crammed with all the wrong values. Is that true? I don't know. Liz is so *sure* of herself, I wish I could be like her. I know what she *means*, I guess, but the fact is I love the place: the hen sessions in the dorm late at night, trading lasts and gossip and even the courses. I don't want to do something rash and then regret it.

But next fall you won't be there.

All this sounds pretty silly to you right now, I know, and I don't blame you. I worry about you—so many GIs seem to get hurt just during training—though I know there's no real need to, George darling. You're so capable and steady. You're more competent than the rest of the Fusiliers. I know you don't think so, but it's true. You know how to hold things together, keep them all rolling along. And I admire that more than anything. But darling, *please, take care.*

All my love,
Nancy

Dear Dogface:

By the time you read this we'll be at sea again. Yep, I put in for sea duty and I GOT sea duty, right off the bat. A can (destroyer-minesweeper to you) on Atlantic submarine patrol. She's old, a 4-stacker retread from World War I (or maybe it's the Mexican War) named the *Tolliver*. She's top-heavy, there seems to be something wrong with the starboard screw (that means a propeller, not what YOU think), her armament is pitiful, she's dissolving in rust; but she's all we've got and we love her and call her the *Tolly*.

Found myself back near our old stomping ground on our last run! "That's Highland Light over there," Chief Lonborg told me, pointing E by N to the blue pin-prick flash. "Right, Chief," I answered. Won't catch *me* saying, "Sure, Swede, revolving lens set in a bed of mercury, shines 42 miles out to sea, second most powerful light on the Atlantic Seaboard, I grew up on that beach below the cliff . . ." None of that. An apprentice seaman is what I am, the lowliest of the low, and nobody is going to label *me* a pop-off college kid too big for his breeches.

And oh God, have I been sea-sick. Yeah, the old sea dog of Cape Cod Bay. Horribly, interminably, gaspingly sick, dry heaves and all (without benefit of a grand and glorious drunk, either). Punishment without crime, you might say. The Chief found me on my hands and knees, hanging onto the weather strip for dear life and retching like a sick cat. "You want these." A bunch of soda crackers in one enormous red hand. They might as well have been scorpions crawling on a pancake of seagull shit. "I don't want anything," I croaked, shuddering to my innermost innards. "I said you want these, Currier. *Get 'em down.*" "Right, Chief." And you KNOW I did. And of course they came up again. But the third batch didn't, and after that I was okay. Just a case of getting my sea legs, heh heh heh.

Well, a lot more has been rough besides the weather. There are sinkings all around us, all the time. The U-boats just sit out there and pick up the tankers and freighters silhouetted against the glow from the coastal cities and knock them off. Just like Terry at Norumbega. It's murder. And we tear away after them at flank speed, and never see them—only where they've been. A deadly spoor of rafts and swollen bobbing bodies and life jackets and mattresses and buckets and bits of planking. Last patrol we picked up a life raft with four men in it: three days in the 2x4 raft, in that sea. Two of them were too weak to climb the ladder, one with a leg smashed all to hell. His face was blue, actually blue. Chief said the Captain took one hell of a chance sitting there dead in the water while we got them on board, but thank God he did, anyway.

Jesus, how you get to hate the subs. Black obscene things, coffins, cigars, pricks, you name it, hitting without warning in the dead of night, and then fading away into nothing. Once in a while—once in a great, great while, after days and weeks of chipping and swabbing and watch standing—the terrible general alarm goes off—nang-nang-NANG-NANG-NANG!—always around 2 AM when you're NOT on watch, and you come out of your sack in a flash of pure burning naked panic and snatch up your jacket and race to battle stations. And the sonar people report a contact and the ship heels over wildly, chasing echoes, zigzagging through the chill dark. And then the attack run and the depth charges—thoom, THOOM—shaking the old *Tolly* like a cosmic fist... and then nothing. No sonar echo, no seething convulsion of air bubbles, no oil slick. Nothing. And finally the word comes over the squawk box to secure, and you stumble below again, your feet and hands numb and your belly griping and growling, and nothing in your heart but a grinding hatred for this enemy who hits so cruelly and slips away; who never, never shows his face. Before I went out on patrol I used to feel a certain grim pity for them—the cramped quarters, the furtive subaqueous rituals, the terrible black strangling conclusion. But no more. No more. At times, glaring out at the heaving black sea with the wind tearing at your eyelids, you could choke every submariner to death with your bare hands...

But the real war is with the weather. Rust and salt. Salt and rust. "Only thing that's holding this old bucket together is rust," Chief says. "Rust and a whore's prayers." Which just about says it all. No wonder everything looks so spick-and-span on a ship—you're forever scrubbing and chipping and painting and holy-stoning all day and half the night. Eternal vigilance is the price of buoyancy. And you chip and you chip until your forearms are one throbbing ache, and the red rust creeps into your ears and nose and under your nails and stays there forever.

But what's hit me most of all these past months is how much I *don't* know: about ships, guns, mines, communications, weather—you name it. I wonder if you've felt the same thing. Christ, Groggy, why didn't we learn Morse, those feckless, wasted evenings? or read up on 40 MMs, or isobaric lines and Polar air streams? What the hell were we DOING??? Heinie Koch, my bunkie, is a scrawny, rat-faced little guy with one year of high school, 50 odd jobs and 2 cases of clap—and he's 10 times the sailor I am. Make that 20. It's mortifying, but there it is.

But I'm learning. Fast. I see why, even back in boot camp, they made us wait-and-then-rush, wait-and-then-rush. Because that is what our war is going to be—interminable periods of boredom lanced with sudden violent action, when we must respond automatically, do the right thing and do it quickly. The fucking Navy is right, after all. Well, some of the time, anyway... And then there are moments, golden moments, some early evening with the sky streaked in gold and vermilion and sienna washes and the marble-and-onyx sea sliding and rolling away easterly, a dream of an impressionist master, and Pinky Kraft comes up and says those magic words, "I relieve you," and you lay below and climb into your sack, swaying with the ponderous heave and sink of the ship, and you're filled with a kind of goofy fierce joy at being a member of the crew, bound together in this rolling world of ⅝" steel, and you think, "I'd die for her, our beat-up old *Tolly*." Would I? Chief says, "I'm living for the day I step off this whore's bucket," but he doesn't mean it; she's his *Tolly*, too. We hate her and we love her; we feed her, she sustains us. It's a perfect marriage.

But Jesus boy, it looks like a long war from here. A grim, dirty, everlastingly long war...

I suppose you got the word about Chris and Dalrymple. It hit me, I don't mind telling you. Really shook me up for a while. I had no idea there was anything there. And *marriage*, for God's sake. At a time like this. We spent half our lives together, Chrissie and I, all those years at the Cape, I can hardly believe it. If old Stockyards thinks he's going to beat the draft with it he's got another thought coming, they'll grab him up right along with everyone else. You'll see. I know Chris and I parted under rather strained circumstances, what the hell, I tried to be straight with her. But *Dalrymple*. Jesus Christ. I just don't get it. After all the brawls and bull sessions and dances, all those times together ... Hell, there is such a thing as loyalty, isn't there?

Well, isn't there?

Well, the hell with all that. I'm a sailor now, and I want to be a good one, and that's all she wrote. Period. Hope you get intelligence school, it sounds like a slot where you could be doing something valuable—which is more than I can say at this point. But you've got to start somewhere.

My Blue Heaven in '47—
Swab-jockey Russ

George—

I never was much of a letter writer, and now I've collapsed completely. Mea culpa. Too much going on. I am, to coin a phrase, Somewhere in England. Wouldn't you know they'd ship me to the one country I've hated with a passion since infancy (perhaps before???).

I'm waist gunner on a Fort. Our pilot is a mammoth feetsballer from Wisconsin about twice Rhino's size named Hacklund who drinks Black Velvets and is *the best*. I mean. The ship is named *Stompin' Sal*, after his sweetheart, a prom queen at U. of W. who addresses letters to him with a lipstick pencil and is said to be a great dancer. Originally Hack christened the plane *Shaggin' Sal*, but some RAF high brass were here on an inspection tour and there was a terrific commotion we couldn't figure out at the time. Seems "to shag" has a wholly different meaning in the UK. While for us it only signifies a dance step, over here it means SEXUAL INTERCOURSE—and raunchy S I at that. Ah, the Old World is so much more sophisticated than us frontier barbarians.

Actually I *may* have to abandon my prejudice against the British (it'll cost me my Boston-Irish citizenship, I know). They're pretty great, on all counts. And the girls are SENSATIONAL. In point of fact I've met one named Rosamond—well, enough of that, I'll go into R another time.

Thanks for relaying all the Scoop on the Group. The Dalrymple nuptials were (are) a bombshell. (I heard from Dal.) I think he's completely off his chump, but if he wants to put it in the old noose it's his red wagon. Yeah, I figured it was all over between Chris and Russ—at least it was when I left. Actually I thought if Chris married anybody, it'd be you. That's right. But you can't always call them.

All for now. Duty calls. What the hell are you doing, DIGGING CULVERTS! Don't you know there's a war on?

Terry

Grog-o:

Have you ever tried to write with 2 hands, & steady the pen with your OTHER 2 hands at the same time? No? I thought not. Well, that's how it looks from here. "From here" being a magic phrase, connoting approximately 5,000,000,000,000 light miles. Well actually they're *heavy* light miles. I'm unable to give you the exact figure because (a) my slide rule is down at the shop having its vertical-horizontal hair calibrated (and YOU KNOW what calibrating hairs can do to you, mmmh?); & (b) my vision is currently a bit clouded.

Please do not wax over-hasty in your conclusions. By clouded I mean (1) there is a great deal, a very great deal of atmosphere in the air, & (2) I am *watching* myself write this from that 5 quadrillion miles away. The precise formula, in case you're interested, is $B^{16} \times 3.1417 \div S 2$. B = Bourbon (or Booze, as the case may be), & S equals less than 2 hours sleep over the past 24.

Or, put in simpler terms, my efficiency ratio is very low. Very low indeed.

BUT all this is preamble to the universe-boggling fact that at

2:11 AM (it is now 4:30 AM) Chris bore down with all her might & main & GAVE BIRTH to a bouncing baby boy. YOWWWWW!!! Weight 7 lbs 12 oz, length 20½″, bald as a billiard ball & screaming like the proverbial banshee. *I am a father before I have graduated!!!* First in the class. (I think.) Sorry I can't send you a cigar, but you were never much of a smoker anyway. Also, please remind me before I finish this letter that I've just promised to send cigars to Brad, Doris & Archie. (Never mind who they are. Who are they?)

And also, Mel is home in Cleveland & I have no steadying influence. Beyond my own right hand. Or left rather.

ANYWAY, it's all fab-u-loso. Chris was wonderful. Lying there all sweaty & dreamy & pleased as punch with herself. You know what the first thing she said was? You're never going to believe this. She said: "I wish George could see him." Yeah. *"George,"* I said, *"George VIRDON?* Grog-o? Why George?" "Because George would love to see him," she said. I understood her perfectly. When you're married you'll be able to follow this kind of logic without skipping a beat. But imagine: her first words! How do you rate that?

But then she did throw me—she absolutely REFUSED to name him after you. I pleaded, threatened, cajoled: no dice. "There's only *one* George," said she. You see? It's perfectly clear... And you wonder at the fact that I've had a drink or two. Or three. "We'll name him Ron," she said. "Well sure, fine," I said. "You sure you want to? It's not the jazziest name in the world." "Yes. But not Dal. *You're* Dal. *He's* Ron." Personally I think the chick was still gassed. But that's the way the dialogue went.

I DID get one bill through committee, though—you're his godfather. This entails absolutely no obligations, aside from his prep school & college tuition, summer camps, grand tour abroad, a few incidentals here & there UNTIL HE'S ON HIS OWN TWO FEET. (And if the war lasts long enough, we won't have to worry about the grand tour abroad.)

Jesus, I wish you were back here on the gelid banks of the Charles. I even wish that crazy asshole Currier were here. No, hell, I'm just shooting my mouth off, I am, I'm all over that hassle, I was months & months ago. YOU talk to him, I've written until I've come down with writer's cramp, first class. If he wants to hole up on his 4-piper quinquireme & sulk away the hours it's his business. Apropos de boxkites, did *Carib Song* hit the Saddy night flicks down there at Tarleton? It did a 2-night stand here at the UT. We almost missed it—I didn't bring it up for obvious reasons, & Chris didn't think *I'd* want to go, ditto. After we got all THAT straightened out, we went. And there she was, little old deadly Kay, in the flesh—& I *do* mean flesh. A blonde Ava Gardner on the prowl, as Chris said; her performance did strike this reviewer as what old MacCausland would call FLAWED. Which is weird when you think about it, because KM is such a consummate actor in *real* life, don'tcha know. Maybe she was just miscast, & next time out they'll give her a more sympathetic role, such as Goneril.

You see?—I've been sitting here scribbling so long I'm actually getting SOBER. The Entry is a tomb—I looked in on it the other day. Everybody's gone now except us fascist-officer types & a few haunted souls (4F deferments). Great to hear you're in special weapons. I always knew you were special, Grog-o, & how in hell are we going to win the war without weapons??? Joke. Bad. Chris sends lotions of love, my son & heir an enormous howl & a wet diaper. *I AM A FATHER.* I keep sitting here, waiting for the shock waves to catch up with me. Now I've GOTTA achieve 5-star rank, & fast. You see how it is.

                                                                                Dal Baby.

_____Everywhere around us was the interminable sighing of the blowers, and the cat's-eye bulbs that bathed the troop hold in a weird orange glow, and the almost solid stink of damp clothing and cosmoline and stale cigarette smoke and vomit and sweat... and something else, too—an odor you couldn't place, couldn't for the life of you identify, that had been getting stronger day by day, and was strongest of all this evening, this final evening drawing near the coast of Italy.

"Now hear this," the PA system hissed and thundered. *"Now hear this. Darken ship. Darken ship. The smoking lamp is out."*

"Smoking lamp," Arnie Oppenheim echoed with gleeful scorn. "*What* lamp?" He gave that nasal, whinnying laugh of his; the bunk above mine creaked and his head leaned out, foreshortened, hanging down toward me. "Jesus, aren't they quaint, Vird? Don't they just tickle the old gonads?"

"Such language, for our brother service," Sabotnak, one of

the veterans, muttered from a bunk across the narrow aisle.

"No brothers of mine. Rope-yarn Sunday," Oppenheim chortled with exasperated hilarity, and slapped the steel frame. "Scuttlebutt, Rocks and Shoals—*listen* to the donkeys! Every God damn one of them thinks he's Horatio Nelson. Shot in the ass with Those Glorious Days of Sail."

"Show some respect," I said. "My best friend is in the Navy."

"Well then he's another fuck-up. Just like you." And he grinned down at me, his head crooked like a hanged man's. To Opp the Navy was a playground for a club of wound-up automatons who reveled in wasted motion and eerie passwords. In addition to which he got seasick. He'd been sick as a dog through most of the Atlantic crossing six weeks before, and he'd been sick off and on ever since we'd left Oran. "I suppose we ought to get some sleep, Vird. You know?"

"Yes," I said.

"Can you sleep?"

"No."

"Me neither."

His head was still hanging over the edge of his bunk and for a long moment we stared at each other; but in the morbid yellow light I couldn't see his eyes. Opp and I had been together ever since basic. He'd put in for motor transport at the same time I'd requested intelligence; we'd both been made casuals for our pains, and then sent to special weapons school, and then unceremoniously yanked out of that and shipped out to North Africa as infantry replacements. No one knew why. The Division had swallowed several hundred of us in one fierce gulp; and here we were. The stanchions creaked, the blowers moaned without ceasing, shadows loomed over us blackly and swept on, as men went to the latrine or simply roamed through the five-tiered gallery of the troop hold in a nameless, interminable quest for nothing at all; the ship heaved and sank like some immense animal, gripping us in its iron belly.

"Rolling," Opp said irritably. "Why does the fucker have to *roll* all the time? Boat this size . . ." His head popped back out of sight, his buttocks pressed a tight ball of canvas close above my chest. I put my arm over my eyes, but my eyelids were still laced with crazy slashes and splotches of light.

. . . It had all come to pass, with the arching, inexorable symmetry of a Russian novel. The enemy coast was out there, right out there somewhere, full of menace and things unimaginable, just as my mind's eye had conjured it back at my desk in Fox Entry, evenings; in a few hours we were going to land there and try to take it by force of arms.

It was no good telling myself I just wasn't sleepy, that the lights and the continual roaming and talk were disturbing me. I was afraid, as I had known I would be. Not panicky, or hollowed out with dread. Just scared of what was out there—how it would come at me, how I would meet it. Would I measure up to it? Would I? I was a replacement, around me in the foul, saffron gloom were veterans of El Djerdou and Kefala Pass, and a thousand-mile-wide gulf separated me from them; their smiles, their glances, the movement of their hands had made that clear enough.

I pulled the fawn-colored shell—Chris's shell—out of my pocket. Its smooth, hard surface was cool at first, but it warmed in my hand, like the sand at Nauset . . . I found myself holding it tightly, repeating with a blind, incantatory fervor: Let me do this beachhead right, God. Please. No matter what happens to me, let me measure up, don't let me let the others down, the platoon; that's all I ask, I mean it—

Yet there were things, too, I hadn't foreseen. Back at Benning, at Tarleton all the excited talk had been of divisions activating, crack combat outfits, the gleaming spearhead of the war against fascist aggression, and the shoulder flashes its members arrogantly wore—wild cats and lightning bolts and timber wolves and flaming swords—caught at our hearts; most of us tried to join them. But at the specialist schools—I'd attended one long enough to hear it—the baleful admonition had run: *Foul up here and you ship out.* Ship out where? Why, to one of these crack combat divisions that had been formed so proudly. It was a punishment then, to be in combat, a combat infantryman. And the tech sergeant at the repple-depple in Oran had passed his eyes over us with amused contempt. "Now, you want to get a few things through your stupid heads. You've been reading *Time* and crowing your rocks off like that frigging rooster on Pathé News and you think you're going to be lapping up vin rouge and pronging Hedy Lamarr in between accepting the surrender of thousands of dumb, yellow Krauts, and you think that's the way it's going to be all the way to Berlin. Well, I'm here to tell you the Krauts are *not* dumb, they're *not* yellow, they're one hell of a lot better soldiers than you poor sad bastards will ever be. Also, there are very, very few Hedy Lamarrs hanging around waiting to get pronged, and *they're* going to be shacking up with some bird colonel in Supply. Not you. The fact is, you're replacements, and there's nothing lower than a replacement except a hound bitch with the mange. You're fuck-ups, you're the slobs nobody wanted for something better, and that's why you're standing here listening to me rather than splicing field telephone wire or overhauling the carburetor on some six-by. Some of you have got plans for sliding out of here and looking up a little of that red-hot Casbah loving, and some of you think if you fuck up and dump your rifle or your gear you'll get sent somewhere else, somewhere a little bit safer. Well, I'm also here to tell you there's no place lower than this—this is the end of the line, from here you're going into the first wave on Rome or Genoa or Marseilles or wherever they've got planned for your sorry little asses. So you will—repeat, *will*—take care of your rifle and your gear, and you will go where we send you. And that-a is that-a."

This was more than the old *"You'll be sor-reee!"* that greeted all recruits at basic; this went deeper. It was great to be in a red-hot combat outfit at Benning; it was punishment to be sent to join one in North Africa. The same outfit. Was that because Benning had been deep in the heart of *Life* and *Time* and the newsreels, 5,000 miles from the war? Maybe. Or was it—

"Now hear this," the squawk-box rumbled now. *"We have just received a flash from General Eisenhower's headquarters. The Italian Government has surrendered. Italy has surrendered unconditionally."*

A moment of silence—then a bedlam of shouts, roars, rebel yells.

"That's *it*, that's *it!*" Locatelli cried. He was dancing up and down in the pinched alley between the stacked bunks. "It's all over!"

"What's all over, kid?" Platoon Sergeant Duchemin said from the bottom bunk.

"The war, Sarge, the frazzle-ass war!" Oppenheim vaulted out of his sack and grabbed Locatelli around the waist. "They're cracking, and it ain't from shacking, baby..."

"Hold your water," Duchemin said.

"Ah, come on, Dutch! It's over—they've thrown in. We'll be

packing away the lasagne verde and boffing some delectable quail by tomorrow night. Bet, Sarge. Want to bet?"

Duchemin grinned up at him—that slow, half-mournful, half-sardonic grin that usually gave us pause. "That appeals to you, Oppenheim?"

"Hell, yes, I'm nobody's frigging hero. And anyway, I want to find out if it's true what they say about Italian broads."

"Tail," Ensor muttered sourly from below me. "That's all you ever think about, Opp—tail and more tail. Jesus, what a one-track mind."

"Find me a better track, I'll run on it." Hands on his hips, Opp grinned down at Ensor; all he was wearing were his underdrawers and socks and he had his inflatable lifebelt cinched around his waist; his hair, curly and a brilliant red, was standing out from his head like a Zulu's. "Can I help it if they all go wild about me?"

It was true; it had been the same in Trenton, in Columbus, in Fayetteville. He loved women, women loved him; he walked up to a girl, gave her that crazy Bronx spiel and she melted; he was always the first to get a dance, a date, a shack-up. It drove us frantic.

"He will," Locatelli was saying, picking at his nose and laughing. "He'll be groping a fucking contessa before they've got the joint secured."

"How do you rate it?" I taunted him, pointing. "Look at you—skin and bones, ears like a pregnant elephant. Now if you were like my old roommate at college, handsome, charming, I could see it. But what in holy hell do they see in *you*?"

Opp threw back his head. "If you got to ask, Vird, I'll never be able to tell you. Hell, it's got nothing to do with looks and build—you know that. Those hairy Hollywood types—Victor Mature, Jon Hall—they couldn't get it up if they had to. I could beat any one of them out any day in the week. And so could you if you weren't such a morbid bastard."

"You must have a king-size drive shaft, all I can say."

"Crude, Virdon, pretty crude. Especially for a Hah-vahhd man." He threw out his arms. "Hello out there, you luscious, full-assed, balloon-breasted cheesecake—I'm on my way!"

"You can't even speak the language, like Locatelli, here,"

Opp narrowed his eyes shrewdly, a speculative merchant. "I'll cut you in on something, Vird. The Jews and the Italians have always been sympatico. It goes back to the Ark—Mount Ararat was really Vesuvius. Actually, the Neapolitans are descended from one of the Twelve Tribes."

"Jesus, what a crock," Ensor said.

"You could look it up, Frank."

"Now hear this, now hear this: all staff NCO's will report to their company commanders, on the double."

Sergeant Duchemin slid his massive body out of the bottom sack and clapped his helmet liner on his cropped head. "The word," he declared.

"At this hour, Sarge?" I asked him.

"Not all that late, kid." He winked at me slowly. "Don't go away now, will you, Harvard."

"Jesus, what a card old Dutch is," Opp said. "Real hoe-down, corn-pone humor, you know?" He stood there above me, his slender, bony body swaying with the ship's roll, watching the quiet, purposeful movement of men toward the companion-ways. The moment of jubilation had died away completely. Opp ran his hand through his kinky red hair. "You think it's true, Vird?" he said. "You think it could be over? or what?"

"Deeper," Platoon Sergeant Duchemin said.

We stared up at him, panting. Ensor's face was powdered white and streaked with sweat; a sad mime's with the make-up running.

"Jesus, Sarge," I said, "it's all rock, nothing but rock and—"

"*I* don't care if it's poured slab," Duchemin said. "You go down another two feet, hear? Jesus, you kids." He moved off along the line of foxholes in a shambling crouch while we glared after him. Off to the right, toward Battipaglia, the sound of firing flared up again like grease popping in a pan, and now another sound, a curious subterranean rumbling, untraceable and oddly disquieting, bowled on beneath it. Dust sifted over us in the hot puffs of wind.

"Lousy fucking dictator," Ensor muttered, and banged his shovel against the side of the hole. Behind us stood a crumbled section of ancient wall built of the same white, flintlike stone we'd been digging, and near it an olive tree, stunted and contorted on itself like some old German engraving, its leaves crisp and shiny in the sunlight; far off in the grayed haze we could make out a gaunt rim of mountains.

"Hey, Vird!" I turned. Above the next foxhole Opp's great beak of a nose, shiny and red under the helmet rim. "You know you always wanted to see sunny Italy."

"Fungoo," I said.

"That's *Italian?*"

I shied a hand at him and went on digging, listlessly. It had been a day of surprises. The Italian Government had surrendered all right, but the Germans had not; and the Germans were running things here, the way they were just about everywhere else. The operation was still on as scheduled. We'd gone over the side into the boats, milled around in the chill dark for hours, and finally came in to the sound of artillery fire and a beach awash with overturned landing craft, with crates and blue life jackets and shattered planking. And two bodies rocking in the shallows, over which the gentle undertow ebbed and surged. Helmets, leggings like ours. GIs, like us. Dead.

"What are you waiting for?" Duchemin had roared at us. "Now move your asses, hear?"

We moved on. There were trees that looked like poplars, only with curiously scaled and mottled trunks, there was an orchard of olive trees, there was an old farmhouse, spilling its guts of stone and mortar, there was plowed ground, hard ground. Nobody seemed to know what was going on, or where anybody else was. We were halted at the edge of the olive grove and told to dig in, and ten minutes later ordered out to this slope above the broken wall and told to dig in all over again. And all the while there was the uneasy sense of a forest fire somewhere out there ahead of us, crackling and hissing away, bearing down. Lieutenant Dodds left us and returned, left again. We watched the old men out of the corners of our eyes, envying and disliking them, and tried to find out from their reactions how things were going. When did it start—when was something going to happen?

We ate a K-ration tin of ham and egg yolk, cold, swapped entrenching tool for shovel and went on digging, deeper now, prying out the lumps and slivers of white stone. Earth broken and tamped for thousands of years. Etruscans, Romans, Carthaginians, Goths and Visigoths and Huns and Vandals, Greeks and Vikings and Christ knew who else. They'd come and gone, and what had it proved? That men lusted for more, always more, extended their control, tyrannized over their—

A squarish chunk of stone hit the forward lip of the hole,

dropped to my feet; I ducked instinctively, looked up. Opp, grinning at me again.

"Piece of the Coliseum, Vird. Souvenir."

I picked it up. A section of molding, V-and S-scroll. From the entablature of a temple. Was it? A temple to Neptune, or Apollo, where robed figures once made obeisance and guarded the mysteries. There was an indisputable thrill, holding this fragment of carved stone, its dusty, grayed surface, thinking of Carthage, and Troy, and Atlantis; the lost lovely cities—

There was a whistling, a high dread inhalation, hovering. We raised our heads, listening. Someone shouted: *"Take—cover!"* a tone of angry concern, threatful. There was a terrific detonation that seemed to come from behind my right shoulder, and the earth leaped up and then fell away so fast my head slammed against the leading edge of the hole. Jesus! I was down in the hole, knees against chest, one arm clamped against my neck, with no idea at all of how I'd got there. Another explosion, harsh and tearing, another, another—the world was full of crashing things. The earth jarred and wobbled foolishly, the air melted into vivid blue and yellow bands, laced with darting red flares. A wall of grinding, terrible pressure had fallen on me. Things whizzed and moaned with incalculable menace. What were *they?* What—

Something struck my helmet with a clank that terrified me utterly, drove my face into the dirt. Blood. My nose was bleeding. Slowly I felt the helmet. A faint dent. My head here, inside it. Jesus. Nothing could stand this, nothing anywhere ever. Someone was yelling at the top of his lungs, *"Stop it, stop this crazy shit!"* My voice. I was the one yelling. Both my hands were clamped around my helmet rim. An avalanche of railroad cars, boilers, tractor bodies flung down a mountainside of old iron by a race of giants. My God, *nobody—*!

Now get hold of yourself. My voice again, a stammering over-rapid exhortation. All right. Shelling. You're being shelled, that's it, you see, 88s, they told you, Sergeant Duchemin said shelling was to be expected and this is it you see that don't you pure and simply a case of artillery fire no problem just hang in there and Jesus *God—*

A blast drove me down like a monster fist, earth showered over my neck and hands, cordite fumes swam into my throat and lungs. I was strangling, I was going to choke to death here. My body was hurling out of itself somehow, expanding, gas-laden, my ribs were going to burst like a grenade. But I couldn't unclench my jaws, couldn't free them, they were locked in some impossible way. My teeth hurt, and my neck. That was because my hands were locked there, gripping it. Of course. Steel and stone whined and hummed, and then the whipcrack and concussion waves like titan hands. They can't ask this of anybody, anybody at all, I don't care who they are, they can't...

The din increased, but higher now, arching, a *choo-choo-choo* sound of great wings beating, of phantom sky-borne trains; the grinding, crashing pressure lifted, swung away. I looked up, dazed, panting as if I'd raced up a mountain of loose rock. My head was aching so I couldn't see or hear: sounds came and faded, bands of light and dark raced across my eyes and fluttered slowly, clearing. I was all right. Perfectly all right. No problem.

"Ensor?" I said, or thought I said.

"Look!" Someone—it seemed like Locatelli but I couldn't be sure—was pointing, waving his arms. "Dizzy swabby bastards—look at 'em *go!*"

I glanced toward the sea without thinking. A rolling edge of cloud, a cloudlike fog, and a prow sheared through it thin as a knifeblade, vanished again and reappeared, and bright orange flames burst from the turrets. Destroyer. Ours. Another one, following fast through the smoke screen, heeled over wildly, careening, all its guns blazing in wild festivity; and the pulsing freight-train *whoosh* of shells passed overhead. A high, pure-white plume of water rose beside the lead ship, another still higher; there was a flash like an acetylene torch just below the bridge and the knifelike prow shuddered and dipped; but still its guns flamed in quick, eerie rhythms, and the smoke tore away from its funnels, black and savage.

"Give it to them! Good old fucking Navy—"

"Bet your ass!"

"Pour it on..."

We were all shouting now, waving our arms. Up on the gaunt blue rim of the mountains now we could see the pin-prick flashes come and go.

"Russ!" I yelled to Opp. "He's out there! My best friend..." I was certain, pointing, that Russ was out there, manning one of those guns; I never doubted it for an instant. Ensor was still crouched in his corner of the hole, his feet doubled up under him.

"Frank!" I yelled. "Get up—they're giving it to them. Yeah! Come on, we're out of it. Jesus, that last one was close, wasn't it? Close as a—"

Too still. He was too silent, crouched there. Something was wrong; terribly wrong. I reached out and took hold of his belt, his shoulder, pulled him over gently. A great curved tear in his chest and throat, white wires and bits of gristle soaked in blood. Blood was pumping thickly from his throat, over his jacket, seeping through his trousers, his shelterhalf, soaking into everything, too much of it, far too much, oh Jesus Jesus. His eyes rolled up at me once, white and staring, fluttered closed, rolled open again.

I jerked back, my hand at my mouth. Somebody was calling something but I didn't hear what it was. So much blood. What could you do against all that thick scarlet rush. I don't know how long I stared at it, watching it sliding around his knees, the soles of his boots, sliding and filling the pits in the grayed stone one by one.

"All right, sound off! Let's hear it, now!" Sergeant Duchemin's voice, monitory and terse, and then the responding chorus:

"Ramsey!"

"Oppenheim!"

"Locatelli!"

"Connors..."

My voice came back, then. "Medic!" I screamed. "For Christ sake, medic—!"

Duchemin was glaring at me, his eyes slitted. "Ensor?" he called. "Ensor?"

I nodded, turned away, swallowing. Beyond the shattered wall the mountains looked like armor plate in the September haze.

We were shelled again late that afternoon. Westphal, in the same foxhole with Oppenheim, was hit in the neck and hand, Connors in the back. I moved in with Opp, I couldn't stay in the hole Ensor and I had dug, it was out of the question. We ate another tin of K-ration, pork and egg this time, and at dusk we got the word to be alert, elements of C Company were going to be passing back through our line. They did, moving down through the olive grove with the uneven, crablike gait of people who don't want to seem to be in a hurry but who are in a great hurry all the same. Behind them the desultory chatter of gunfire had swelled to a deep, rolling roar that blotted out nearly everything else. Two men passed between our foxhole and Ramsey's, lugging a bazooka and shells, then another man without a helmet, holding his arm hard against his body, gasping, followed by another burdened with a sack of grenades, who sank to one knee beside us, panting dryly.

"How's it going up there?" I heard myself say.

"It ain't." He cleared his throat harshly and spat, panting. "Tell you, Mac, it's one hell of a shit-storm up there." He hitched the swollen sack on to his other shoulder and moved off again.

I looked at Oppenheim, who was staring at me strangely—an expression that it suddenly struck me must be on my own face.

"What do you think?" I muttered.

"Think? You're not getting paid to *think*, boy—you're here to spread democracy among the peasantry ... How in hell should I know?"

Ten minutes later a .30-caliber machine-gun squad came hurrying down and began to set up in my old foxhole with a lot of cursing and banging around. The uproar of gunfire was worse now; tracers began soaring overhead like some terrible new race of supersonic insects. This was bad, this wasn't going at all the way it should be. How could you tell if—

"Here you go." Sergeant Duchemin, looking enormous in the deep dusk, handing down two cloth bandoleers of clips. "Hang these over your shoulder. And keep your eyes peeled, now."

"Sarge, what the hell's going on?" I said.

"World War Two. Land of vino rosso and big-assed broads, remember? Open the flaps on the right side of your belt."

"Sure. Why?"

"So when you stand on your head the clips will fall out on the ground and you can play fifty-two pick-up. Jesus, you kids."

"But what's the scoop, Dutch?" Opp asked him. "Where's the front line?"

Duchemin grunted. "We are, kid. We're the front line. Now work it out between yourselves which one's going to stay awake and when. Point is, I want *one* of you awake all night, hear?"

"Right, Sarge," we said together.

He turned away, then swung back again and clapped me on the shoulder. "Take it easy, Harvard," he said. "You'll do all right."

He moved away down the line like a shaggy old bear. The firing was intense now, a furious crackling punctuated with heavy bomblike explosions. I watched the machine gunners setting up, the assistant stamping the trail shoe into the hard ground, the others throwing up earth, feeding in a belt; the desperate haste of thieves certain of capture. This wasn't the way I'd foreseen it at all; not remotely. What the hell was really going on? A tremor slid through me, a faint light shuddering. *The front line* . . .

"You nervous in the service, Vird?" Opp's face, pale and unreadable in the almost-dark. "Better you should enjoy a big bowl of my Ma's gorgeous chicken soup with matzoh balls. You sleepy?"

"Sleepy!"

"Yeah—shut-eye, sack-time. Well, I am. I'll take it in two hours." He nestled deep into his poncho, rifle between his legs, the barrel pointing absurdly out behind his ear. "Wake me at 155th Street, conductor—it's been a long day."

"Vird! *Vird—!*"

I came awake in a flash of naked terror. A cold blued light swaying, streetlamp flickering, everything swaying underwater, upside down, all of it swallowed in one continuous coughing roar, and here and there high-pitched shouts and cries. Opp's hand was still jabbing at me.

"—What's the matter?" I gasped. At the same instant I heard Sergeant Duchemin call:

"—Line! Now up on the *line!* . . ."

Another flare burst high overhead then, and began its dreamy descent, and tracers burned their red and orange wires, at-me-and-away, at-me-and-away, curving upward at the last second. I gazed at them in a trance. Opp yelled then, and pulled me down. There came a series of smashing shocks at the edge of the hole, and dirt sprayed on my neck and hands. Then it was gone. I raised my head again. Opp had pushed his rifle up in front of him on the tamped earth; his hand looked white as paper against the stock.

"Come *on*, Vird!"

I was quivering, my whole body: a shaking I could not stop. Silly. All perfectly silly. I clamped my arms together but my head was waggling uncontrollably now, a palsied chilled wobbling that would not go. I gripped the rifle with all my might but my hands went on shaking. What did you—

There was a figure. Dancing at the edge of the woods. No, running. A man. Another. Then a cluster of figures tossing and jouncing, flat wide helmets and tight tunics black in the crazy blued light of the flares. *Germans*, a voice somewhere said very seriously. But that was all. Nothing followed. I could only stare at them, shaking, thinking: Jesus. Germans. Running. Right there. There was no need to be here, no sense in staying here, right here, while Germans—

"Fire, now!" Duchemin was roaring. "Fire, fire, *fire—!*"

The blast of the M1 shocked me. Opp, firing, his whole body lifting and dropping with the recoil. An ejected shell struck me on the cheek, a sting I never felt. In a trance, bound in Duchemin's harsh command I raised the rifle, aimed it wobbling and dipping at the swelling, jostling cluster of figures, squeezed the trigger. Nothing happened. I was flooded instantly with panic—all at once remembered the safety, pushed it off with my knuckle and squeezed off again. Too high. I'd fired too high. But with the gun's kick I was all right. The panicky trembling was gone. I was calm as calm now. I emptied the clip, inserted another swiftly, aimed at a tall figure rushing near, dangerously near, his mouth gaped wide, distended. I fired, the man leaped upward twisting, his back arched fantastically, and fell away out of sight. Only a few now, dancing, bobbing: three, then one. Then none at all. Over on the left they were running back toward the woods and I tracked them, glad of the jarring, comforting kick of the rifle, seeking it. Now there was nothing but shadows that swayed and slid under the slipping, dying flare.

"Knock off!" Duchemin bellowed. "Now, *cease firing...*"

I leaned back from the rifle. I felt tired, elated, vaguely sick; my hands were numb.

Dutch's voice again, flat and peremptory: "Sound off, sound off!"

"Sabotnak!"

"Ramsey!"

"Locatelli..."

I called my name without thought, as he'd taught us, and

turned. Opp was staring at the long slope through the olive trees; his lip was slack, saliva was running in a thin shiny stream from the corner of his mouth.

"Opp," I said. "Opp!"

He swung his head, and threw me one long wild agonized despairing glance. I had never seen a look remotely like that on anyone's face before.

"Hit?" I almost whispered. "You hit?"

He shook his head once, his jaw still hanging, his face caught in that white mask of anguish and supplication.

"Sound off, you people!" Duchemin thundered.

"Oppenheim!" I called, and looked down. My hands were perfectly steady now. I ran a new clip into my rifle and closed the flaps on the right side of my cartridge belt _____

2

Dear George—

Christ knows when I wrote you last, if at all or ever. I might as well begin with a confession. (You can take the Irish Catholic boy out of the Church, but you can't, etc., etc.) Anyway I've prevailed on a friend who's going stateside to take this epistle back with him and mail it to you on his own—I don't want anybody else to read this but you. I, Terence Xavier Gilligan, am in love. Yes. And with an *English girl*. Can you see Pop's face on learning this? If he knew, that is—which he doesn't and won't. Her name is Rosamond and she works at the base here, a plotter. She's short and plump and wears her hair parted neatly in the middle and has these great soft clear brown eyes. She's quiet and sweet and gentle, and she has this slow smile that turns everything, absolutely everything in the world warm and fresh and enchanting, just like that. It's true: nothing, no, nothing fazes her, not all the savagery and misery rained down from high heaven for a million million years.

There's something almost frightening about this—this quiet English fortitude in the face of catastrophe. You find yourself thinking: My God, what right have they got to react this way? who in holy hell do they think they are? Which of course misses the point, because it's nothing idly or arrogantly assumed, they've earned the right to it. My God, what they've gone through! Her mother killed in an air raid in '40, father on a minesweep somewhere, uncle blown to atoms trying to defuse a bomb down in the City (probably seeking to save the fucking Bank of England with his last heartbeat). Her husband is in Italy, where you are (roughly); he hasn't written her in over two years, she says they married too early, didn't know what they were doing.

Do I feel guilty? Not one iota. And neither does she. And you know what's really crazy? I haven't gone to bed with her. (I told you this was going to be one hell of a confession.) It's curious—I just want to be with her. Just sitting there in that shabby little room with the cracked walls and taped window panes and this weird philadendron plant groping its way to the ceiling, and the tea kettle whistling its heart out like a brave little tugboat—one of those battered old buckets that bucked and rolled their way across the Channel and picked up the army at Dunkirk, say. I sit there for hours while her aunt prattles away pleasantly and Rosamond knits and now and then answers. And I set down my teacup and look up and there she is, her hair parted so neatly above that high, ivory brow of hers, and those tremendously wide, clear eyes. So clear! Watching her I can feel all fear and rage slough away like some foul fungus. Well, I can't describe it really. And I can't tell anybody else but you—somehow I have the feeling you'll understand this. In fact I know you will.

For the rest...well, for the rest, the same wretched litany. I'm tail gunner now. Morris was hit, and Hacklund said he wanted somebody out there he could count on to protect his ass. Which suits me fine. I can curl up out there in my plexiglass penthouse with all the privacy in the world. The farther away from the whole wild-blue-yonder, mom's-apple-pie, our-team-is-red-hot shit the better. Out at the end of the line...

Remember that conversation we had, the last one we had alone, that New Year's Eve? about proving something? You were right. It hasn't proved anything—only that you can be as miserable and terrified as anyone else. (Except for the ones that love it, revel in it all—I imagine you've run across a few of those jokers yourself by now. For them I feel only something halfway between contempt and pity—they're dead already, dead to everything good in life and they don't even know it... Well, and a sizeable chunk of fear, because they're the *real* enemy: they want everyone else dead too, along with them.)

No, it's luck mainly. Luck, good or bad. Whether you're hit or not, whether the 109s are out in force that day or not, whether an engine winds up or not and you abort over the Channel and run back to base, feeling guilty and savage with yourself for feeling guilty. I was heartbroken when they washed me out of pre-flight, I felt ashamed, I couldn't even write any of you back there, I got a room in a fleabag in Orlando and stayed stupid sodden drunk for three days... But not any more. Now I just want to last it out. Just last it out as best I can.

Until it's over. Yeah. But it's not getting over (as you bloody well know yourself), it's light-years from ever being over, the 2nd front has been postponed again we heard—still again, Jesus—and nothing's even remotely near to *beginning* to be over. What a dreary, deadly treadmill, and no way off it either. We crawl out in the raw damp dark and sit there in the briefing room sipping foul, watery coffee and trying to look halfway conscious while a character playing Robert Taylor, pencil mustache and all, tappy-taps a pointer against the map and outlines the mission (obliterating the iron works at Essen or pulverizing the aircraft engine plants at Dusseldorf, something modest like that, don't you know). And then we stand around the ship like the snow removal gang at Kerry Corner, talking about nothing in particular, while the sky turns a sickly gray-green. And finally we take off and form up and head out over the North Sea (the coldest, deadest ocean in all the world, don't let anybody tell you different) and the clouds come bowling their way toward us out of Norway; and then the sun, below us, far below us, shoots its yellow rays straight up, bathing the Forts' undersides with cold fire. An upside-down world, everything upside-down.

But all the early elation is gone, the breath-caught majesty I used to feel, the sense of floating in the heavens' glory, washed in it, rocking near the highest throne... now it's all tightness, hollow dread, jittering bands of fear like oncoming surf, no end to it. And the cold. If only you weren't so frigging *cold*. And then the fighter escort falls away astern, your heart sinking away with them, and high up now the fat dots like bee clusters that swell with monstrous speed to Jerry fighters arching, twisting, skidding down—here-and-gone, like that, here-and-gone, the gun bucking like a cold, hellish animal and the shells spattering against the blister in an amber brass rain; and then the run on target, with flak in dirty gray bursts skidding and drifting by too, the interminable run with everything in the hot, hellish world focused on *you*, a single spot at the base of *your* legs, your crotch, your very roots; and finally, finally the ship's lurch and heave on release, and the agonizingly terrifying slow turn and the run through the gauntlet again...and after a thousand thousand years that cold dead empty sea slides up under the starboard wing, and you realize you're soaked in sweat, and chilled to the bone through the sweat, and your eyes burn and your head aches rackingly, and you're wallowing in a goofy welter of relief and gratitude and nausea and despair and everything else a poor, fouled-up human being can feel without actually shooting right out of your quivering skin...and that night, say around 2 AM, unable to sleep, sitting in the latrine (for want of anything better to do) all the losses crash in on you, all the guys you've known and lived with, gone now, vanished, plucked away into that vast, gray-green obscurity as though they'd never lived, never been at all—and you find yourself gripping your bare knees in an agony of fear and trembling rage and thinking, It must be for something, it's got to be, all this misery, this terror; some fairer world has got to come out of those ruins we've made down there below us, or it would be better, really better, to be out of it all...

Enough of that crap. Got carried away. Shit, I can't write this to anyone else but you, George, only because I know you're feeling it, too. Anyway, forgive the blather. Consider it all part of the confession. You'd have made a good priest, George, you know that? Yes really, no sarcasm intended. You know how to forgive—trespasses and derelictions and everything else. It's why we all sought you out. But who in Christ's name ever listened to *you?* We never thought of it, did we, any of us? What was eating *your* vitals? What selfish bastards we were (are). Will we ever be all together again in one room? Tonight, here, now, it seems impossible, the most absurd fantasy, like a kid's dream of heaven...

But we will. We've got to. For love of God, take care now.
Hope you've managed to liberate some Soave Bolla, if not (dare
I say it?) a few of those lush Italian broads. (Or so they say.)
                              The Fensgate in '48 (not 'arf likely)—
                                                      Terry

Dear George,
   It's one of those glorious days you only get on Cape Cod in
mid-autumn, everything white and old-gold and a blue so deep
it's actually painful, the whitecaps galloping in across the
Sound, white steeds of Mananaan, as dear old Yeats would say.
Remember him? Not that I'd blame you if you didn't,
considering where you are right now. But he is a comfort—I find
myself reading *The Green Helmet* and the other ones, the civil
war ones, at 2 and 3 in the morning, when Ronny's waked me up
and I can't get back to sleep. He felt things so deeply, agonized
over them—and yet he was so wise, too. Oh I know, he was
probably hot-tempered and selfish, the God damn biographers
are always dying to tell you what a sonofabitch anybody you
love *really* was... yet you know you could talk to him, he
wouldn't laugh at anything you might say. And sometimes late
at night I find myself talking to him, telling him my
troubles... See what a muffin-head you're liable to become even
back here on the old Home Front, with everybody gone, in
England and Italy and Africa and Oceania...
   Well. First of all: A report on The Beloved Empress, who is
now comfortably hors de combat for the duration. I have to tell
you, though—first I did a goofy thing. The top was still down
from Dal's last trip here in June before he took off for OCS; and
I just got in and started driving on down the Cape. And oh God
it was good, just feeling the sun beating on your face again and
the wind whipping your hair around your head, the lovely
rushing *freedom* of it. The radio was playing *Stairway to the
Stars* and I kept singing along with it at the top of my lungs, the
way we used to do, a crazy wonderful half-hour... and of course
I paid for it, too—when I looked at the tank it said empty and I
ran out of gas in Waquoit; and I'd be there yet if a nice chief
warrant officer from Camp Edwards hadn't come by in a jeep
and pushed me all the way in to Woods Hole...
   ANYWAY. I did everything you said to do in your letter
(*when* did you find time to write it?), in fact I handed your list to

Clarence Horton who came over from Crowell's Garage. He said: "Thorough one, aint he? (He pronounced it *thuh*-ruh, the way we do down here.) You'd think she was the lahst cahhh in cree-yay-shun." "She is, Clarence," I said, "she is—the last and the loveliest. Now help me fix her up, just the way George says." And he did, even if he is browned off at everybody these days because he's 4F.

God, if this war will only end. If it ever will. Everybody *is* bewitched, as you said once. The dials have all been turned up past tolerance. You know. The thrifty have turned so grasping and miserly they'd terrify old Scrooge, saving ration stamps and hoarding; the timid are in a perpetual panic of foreboding, racing down cellar every time there's gunnery practice or depth-bombing out in the Bay, or peeping out behind their black-out curtains; the church elders have all become air raid wardens now, stumbling over garbage cans and threatening everyone with jail; the carefree have gone crazy wanton wild—lonely women perched on bar stools or hanging around the USO looking for a pick-up, a dance, even a cigarette together, their eyes sad and frightened and bold...

Well, I'm no one to talk. Am I?

Anyway, back to the dear old Empress. We jacked her up and put her on blocks, disconnected the battery and drained the radiator and engine. Clarence removed the spark plugs, put oil in the cylinders, and turned the motor over so it would force oil into the valve stems (whatever they are). He also put oil in the intake manifold (ditto). Oh George, darling. You *are* funny. And I depressed the clutch and wedged it down with a stick of wood. Clarence was very taken with this last touch. "I see. Keeps the clutch plate from rusting to the fly-wheel. Got a head on his shoulders, ain't he?" "You bet," I said. "Everything would go to hell in a bucket if it weren't for George." I vaselined the chrome, especially the radiator vents. And then we put the top up and covered the floor with mothballs, and put an old bedspread over the seats. And there she sits, looking sleek and proud and very, very hurt. "Don't you worry, honey," I told her, "this God damned war will be over some day and you'll be out on the road again, making all the rest of 'em look sick." And Clarence looked at me as if I'd lost my mind (which maybe I have), and then he burst out laughing and said: "Maybe she will, at that, Chrissie. That's some cahh..." And then after he left I sat there alone, remembering Jean-Jean. God, it was only yesterday.

I'm working at the oceanography lab with Dad afternoons. Just sort of a lab assistant while he runs tests, but I love it. I love sea life more than I ever did—the glorious unquenchable variety of it, its inexhaustible *life*. Rhino sent me some shells from Vella Lavella (sp?) for my collection, fantastic murexes and cowries, incredibly beautiful. I'm afraid he's on Bougainville now. He says he saw a tridacna shell 2 feet across, but he couldn't figure out a way to ship it back. He says the King of Ulithi actually bathes in one!!! I'm spending a lot of time reading seriously about shells these days—maybe I'll even harden my own. (Shell, that is.) Anyhow I'm actually cataloguing my old collection.

But Ronny is what really matters. How I wish you could see him! He's a joy and a delight, even when he's wicked, which is quite often. (Alas.) He's actually trying to talk already, can you imagine that? And he's full of the devil. His eyes—well, you'll see when you get home. I wonder what you think of me, George. I mean really, not just the all-for-one Fusiliers junk. I hope it isn't all bad. You know, I've worked up a theory—it goes something like this: The stupidest things we do can turn out to be the best and wisest, and the cleverest actions can have the most disastrous results... so it doesn't matter *why* we do something initially, it only matters what we make of it later. Does that make any sense? Probably not. Well, I wasn't ever profound. I suppose I ought to feel guilty about everything, but you know, I don't at all. Oh, regrets of one kind and another, sure. But not guilt. I'm not falling for the life sentences—at least not the self-imposed ones. There are enough of the others to go around. I'm going to try with all my might to be a good wife and mother, a good friend. What can you do that's better than that?

Dal's still at Camp McMeachern, he seems to be doing (a) guard duty (b) KP (c) washing his clothes. He's furious because he hasn't been sent to Fort Sill. I reminded him of how you did KP and dug ditches for months, and he wrote back: "Sure, but George has the *temperament* for it." (!!!) Personally I think it's good for him—I told him he was lucky as sin to be an officer—when he gets to be. Ann says Terry's flown 32 missions, and he's been awarded the air medal. I think of him a lot—so cool and cynical—but that wasn't Terry at all, was it? it was only what he *wanted* to be. And I think of you even more, dear George—I see by the envelope you've made corporal: why didn't you *tell* anybody you were promoted? I have the feeling you're holding your squad all together just the way you did the

Fusiliers—bucking up Terry, slapping down Dal, soothing Russ. Picking up the pieces... I know.

Thanks for the word about Russ—we've heard nothing. He still hasn't forgiven me, I guess. Isn't that a laugh really? Well, maybe he will some day. It works both ways, doesn't it, chum?

Oh George, all this must sound so silly to you where you are now, what you're going through, it must sound completely nuts. But it's all there is to write about. What we had—the picnics, the dances, the runs in the old Empress, the closeness among us, *that* was real for all its foolish happiness (even the hurts were real enough, weren't they); and what we hope for later—gorgeous kids and high-powered jobs, holidays in the sun—that's real too, even if we can't really see it. But *now* is only a kind of numb floating, purposeful sleep-walking through the days and nights... Or is that me? Liz is full of purpose, Nancy's full of plans—and yet only half of us is here. You're the other half, the healing, fulfilling half that we need to make us sane and whole and alive again...

Crazy. Don't pay attention to any of this loony drivel, it's just your old ex-Cliffie blowing off steam. Actually we've got everything perfectly under control. Perfectly. You'll be devastated to hear that Alice Faye has been stripped of all servants except her nurse, and has offered to combine households with Mrs. Tyrone Power, who still retains a gardener, and Mrs. Henry Fonda, who still has her cook. Something called "Imitation Whisky" has been found to be ½ whisky, ¼ orange juice, and ¼ anti-freeze. (At least you won't freeze to death if you pass out from it on the way home.) The OWI says 1 lb of fat contains enough glycerin for six 75-millimeter shells. Is that true? Elvira Tayloe is the queen of all the Allotment Annies—she managed to marry six sailors, and was nailing down the seventh when *two* of her husbands met in an English pub (yes!) and began exchanging snapshots of their devoted wives. Surprise. And Harry James is marrying Betty Grable (*Metronome* headline: LEGS WILL WED HORN.)

All of which will give you a picture of the raddled old Home Front.

Love, and be careful,
Chris

Dear GI Joe—

Home the sailor, home from the sea. Well, not exactly, but I'm walking around on dry land for a while. (Curious sensation—you keep waiting for the deck to start that slow, ponderous heaving...)

And I'm back at school. Yep, communications. I put in for it a good thousand years ago—I decided that for better or worse communications is the heart and soul of naval warfare: if all signals are swiftly and correctly sent (and received) and everybody does what he's supposed to—when to fire and when to turn and when to run away (to fight again another day)—we'll win the war. (He says.) And then I thought no more about it, went on standing my watches and chipping paint and bitching like a good jack tar. But as Chief Lonborg says, "Long as you're in the Navy they're always planning to send you to one God damn school or another." And all of a sudden, out of the blue Atlantic, I got orders to stow my gear, don dress blues, and stand by for transportation to San Francisco! "And for Christ sake, Currier, try to *look* like a sailor for once in your life." "Right, Chief." And by Neptune, I did. I shook hands all around, saluted the OD and the flag with monumental precision, and climbed down the ladder into the boat, while the guys lined the rail—Heinie Koch and Wildruss and Pinky Kraft and the others—calling down all kinds of obscene suggestions.

And then (you won't believe this) gazing up at them all, grinning, I found myself on the edge of bawling like a baby. Yes, real tears, I couldn't stop them. Crazy, I know, but there it is; make of it what you will. All those months with them, the stinging gales and bleak watches, the lousy chow and endless working parties, and now I'll never run across any of them again except by wildest accident... And if I *were* to run into them we wouldn't have a thing in common except those aching cold hours, the crud details, the pinched, frantic liberties ...Friendship: what is it? can you analyze it? What I felt that morning for them is nothing like what I felt for Jean-Jean or what I feel for you, and Terry, and even that hot-shot bastard Dalrymple—yet it's more, too: poorer but sharper. You know what I mean.

And so I'm in regress—a student again (of sorts), up to my ass in procedure (the Navy is *big* on procedure), semaphore,

flaghoist and blinker. Flaghoist is a breeze, thanks to some
practice I got on the *Tolly*; and I love semaphore, the sheer
flamboyant archaic drama of it. The instructor flipflaps his flags
at one end of the field and we answer as smartly as we can, and
then he chews us out fortissimo. Blinker, however, is a terror.
You crouch in a big darkened barn of a barracks and glare at the
shuttered flashes until your eyes feel as though they're going to
pop out of your head like hard-boiled eggs. Curiously, I find I'm
much better at sending than receiving. Why? I know, I *know*
what you're saying. And fluck you, mate.

But San Francisco! What a dream of a town. It's all golden,
not just the Gate, white and festive with its white cubist houses
and its hills and thousands of green parks. Glorious and raffish
and exotic—Chinatown savory with delectable restaurants and
shops, North Beach like your private idea of Napoli. (Well, not
your idea of Napoli, I know—I meant the Shelley-Byron
version.) And the music! You'd go crazy, Grog. You're rolling
along in the late night fog, and all of a sudden you hear it—a
blasting chorus of *I've Found a New Baby*—and we turn like one
man and barge into the gin mill, and there they are—trumpet,
trombone and clarinet flanked by piano, drums and guitar: the
classic sextet, stripped to essentials. I'm becoming addicted to
New Orleans jazz—its marvelous improvisation, its simple
force. Or maybe it's because its roots run deeper than big band
swing, it's more private and primordial, the heart-and-start of it
all.

Speaking of which, I *have*. (Found a New Baby.) Met her at
the De Young Museum, which only goes to show you that
culture has its rewards. She's Austrian, her family got out of
Vienna in '38. Voluptuosity—thy name is Leni. And man, is she
built! Fab-u-loso. Added to which she has a terrific head on her
shoulders, and she's completely and unaffectedly frank—a
change from that glittery gemstone I've been er, ah, exposed to
in the not-so-distant past. Speaking of whom (which I don't very
often): scuttlebutt has it that her second movie is as bad as the
first—I haven't caught it. She's singing now—a long engagement at the Persian Room last fall—and is making records. She
and Buckler are living in Ramon Navarro's old palace. I drove
by it one day—I got down there to LA on a 72-hour pass. But I
just drove on by the place. Then I got bombed at the Hollywood
Canteen.

But back to Leni. She lives across the Bay in Berkeley. Her father once ran Kempner Verlag, the distinguished publishing firm. People are continually dropping by their apartment—and the talk! It's dazzling. "Then you would hold an entire people guilty, Franz?" "Of course, of course—I am speaking of free will, of the need—" "Ah, but how do you know this 'free will' of yours is not simply determinism on a higher level? What did you do when the last war broke out but murmur, 'Nichts zu machen,' and climb into your uniforms...?" Spengler and Hesse and Koestler and Bergson—the names and ideas flare up like Roman candles. I go staggering back to barracks higher than I could ever be on mere booze.

Well, it's been good for me. Fact is, Grog, I'd just about given up thinking about the war since I've been in the Navy—I mean in anything more than a technical sense. And being with Leni has reminded me that there *are* still principles involved. For her this war's been going on for years, and it's no struggle of abstract ideologies; it has brought immediate and concrete terrors. It's very humbling. You can't separate theory and practice, kid. It grieves me to say it, but old Immanual Kant was as full of shit as a Christmas goose.

And on that morsel of profundity, I'll crap out. Besides, I have to bone up on British semaphore (as though our own weren't confused enough). Thanks for the roundup on the crowd. It *is* gratifying to learn Dalrymple has finally entered the grand conflict—obviously the Second Front Can Now Be Opened. I know this is a shittily wicked letter, spouting off about Frisco and jazz and SEX SEX SEX while you're wriggling around in the muck, but what the hell, you've got to take your kicks while you can. That certainly is some soft underbelly you're poking at over there. It looks as though it would be easier to come down through Norway from the North Pole, or maybe up the Danube. Take it easy now, and join us in our rousing new cheer: *3 dits, 4 dits, 2 dits, dah—Navy, Navy, blah blah blah!*—

Russ on the Beach

————The fountain had been smashed to pieces. Smooth fragments of marble, bits of arms and torsos of nymphs and dolphins lay in the shallow, dirty water, pitted now with rain drops. Now only a lion's head spat a sullen trickle into a broad fluted shell, cracked and chipped, leaking greenish-black stains. It must once have been a pretty little fountain, in a pleasant little piazza. You could see that, even now.

We walked down the street in the cold rain, our boots clacking on the worn stone, till we got to the great oak door we knew, the door that had a brass ram's head for a knocker. Oppenheim raised his free hand and tapped it once, then three times smartly. From deep inside there came a muffled cry.

"It isn't everything, but it's home." Opp winked at me solemnly. Helmeted, in the stained, frayed combat jacket, with the BAR slung barrel-down over one shoulder and a filthy barracks bag draped over the other, he looked like a freebooter, a brigand out of the Middle Ages.

"What makes you think she'll even let you in?" I said. "The way you look."

"Because I'm so irresistible, Vird. I *told* you."

There was a clash and clang of bolts withdrawn, portcullis-and-drawbridge sounds, and the great door swung open. A wizened, leathery face with sweeping pure-white mustachios. Federico, the porter.

"Buona sera," Opp said.

"Vossignori." Federico bowed, his faded gray eyes bored into ours: the bow, the elaborate salutation, the glance a little masterpiece of derision. Federico hated all Americans with magnificent impartiality. Then he stepped back, and we climbed the worn marble steps. At the landing the inner door flew open and a small boy flung himself against Opp's legs and shouted: "Uppeee! Hey, wan' caramella!"

"Hey, there." Opp picked the boy up in his arms. "How's Guido?"

"Wriglee-gum! Caramella, eh?"

"Yeah, later. Where's your mamma?"

There was a bright torrent of Italian—prayers, oaths, rejoicing, something—and Teresina ran toward him then, her arms open.

"Uppy!" she cried. "Uppy, Uppy, ah, grazie a Dio!" She caught him to her and they embraced, all three of them, man woman and child, on the dim, chilled landing. Behind them, in the doorway, I could see Giulia with her arms crossed under her breasts, watching us.

"Ciao, Giulia," I said.

"Ciao, Giorgio."

"Ah, Uppy," Teresina murmured. "I—pray—you be—safe . . . vero!"

He released her then, grinned his quick, lopsided grin. "They can't catch me, I'm the gingerbread man. Don't you know that?"

She shook her head, not understanding, but pleased all the same; her eyes roamed over his face. She was about thirty, with gaunt, bold features—under her jet black hair her eyes flashed like dark mirrors tilted in sunlight; a striking, harsh beauty that made you think of ancient days, men in doublets and hosen competing with quarterstaffs at country fairs.

"Ecco—vieni, vieni," she said, and we trooped into that room that always made me sad, with its cracked, water-stained walls, the ruined makeshift bits of furniture: the room was so beautiful, so grandly and perfectly proportioned, the furnishings so wretched.

"Caramella, carmella!" Guido shouted; he was pulling at Opp's trouserleg. "Ho ancora fame, sai . . ."

"Zitto!" his mother said, and cuffed him affectionately.

"What's that?" Opp said to Guido. He took off his helmet, stood the BAR carefully in a corner, crouched down facing the boy. "Ayyy?" Putting his hand to his ear, squinting, an old upstate wiseacre. "Ay? What's that ye sayyy?"

"Ersee!" Guido shouted, laughing, plucking at Opp's jacket pockets.

"Ohhhhh . . . A piece of genu-ine American chocolate, is it? Well, I just don't know." And he started through his pockets, combat jacket, wool shirt, pants, feeling about with exaggerated care, twisting, while Guido capered about him in a little agony of delight, plucking too at the harsh cloth, his eyes shining. It was the ritual.

"Ecco!" Opp all at once produced a half-bar of chocolate. "Hey! No—what do you say? Guido."

"Grazie mille, signore. Mille grazie!"

"Prego-prego-prego . . ." Opp stood up, swung the battered barracks bag from his shoulder and pulled out two boxes of ten-in-one rations, cans of grapefruit-and-pineapple juice and a tin of British bully beef, and laid them on the battered table. "Reuben's it isn't—but what the hell, it's chow."

"Holy Christ," I muttered. "Where'd you get the fruit juice?"

"Midnight requisition, dad. Targets of opportunity."

"You dizzy bastard."

Teresina was examining the food, her hands fluttering over the tins and cartons as if they were rare porcelain. Marveling, laughing she looked up at Opp. "Ah, Uppy-you-so good, so—" But she had no English word for it, or at least not the word she sought, and she wanted to speak English as a kind of thanks perhaps, I could see that; so she merely threw open her hands, a swift confession of failure—and then she embraced him again, and now she was weeping.

"No," he murmured, comforting her; his eyes rolled around to mine, dismayed. "No, no, Teresina, don't cry, now . . . Doesn't it make you happy, the chow?"

She shook her head, laughing now, still weeping, her voice running liquid, a rushing river of Italian. She always spoke in floods and storms, or at least it seemed that way—derision and hilarity pursuing one another in a torrent. She had such zest, such appetite for life; nothing fazed her for very long. Her husband had been some kind of minor functionary in the town, and had run away north when the Germans pulled out. Teresina loved to utter imprecations as to what she would do to him if he ever had the gall to come back. Her gypsy eyes would flash, the wicked-looking bread knife would flash once, twice above the table. Paf! Paf! Oh, yes! You'll see, you'll see. Prince of cowards, worthless toad!

"And now—" Opp had broken away, his hands raised high above his head, a maestro about to launch the overture, a midway barker—"and now, courtesy of those well-heeled, lovable folks, the Services of Supply: this latest model from Paris." He whistled the old eleven-note trumpet fanfare between his teeth, drew out of the barracks bag a GI sweater, winter issue, went up to Guido and began to wrestle it down over the boy's head. The sleeves hung down over his white hands, the waist came to his knees. "Well, he'll grow into it."

"In 1955," I said. "How'd you come by that?"

He shrugged. "Hickey. Gave him that Kraut dagger for it." He stood up again. "And that ain't all, folks. Who said Santa Claus is dead?" Bending over he plucked out three cans of evaporated milk, a new GI blanket and a can of coffee, to a bedlam of rejoicing, tears and laughter.

"Opp," I said. "For Christ's sake. Opp."

He turned, his hands at his chest, appeasing. "Please. No

lectures, okay? The kid needs his vitamins, doesn't he? What's the matter—afraid you'll lose your corporal stripes, there? Afraid they'll ask you to resign your noncommission?" Then his face flushed all at once. "Look, they're *selling* the stuff in Napoli right now. Making a profit on people who haven't got a pot to piss in—yes! Is it their fucking fault they're hungry, frozen half to death? It could be Nashville, Denver, Buffalo, there, just as easy. Turn it *around!*"

"I know."

"Well, then..." He ducked his head in that funny, birdlike way he had, and gave a shrill exasperated laugh. "Think because I'm a Yid I can't give something away? Go on," he said a moment later, his arm around Teresina, "go comfort Giulia, for pete's sake. Give her a big tumble."

"Ah, mind your own business."

"Don't you like her?"

"Of course I like her—that's got nothing to do with it."

"What makes you so morbidly faithful, Vird?"

"What makes you such a five-alarm tail hound?"

"Crude, Vird. Crude and rude. You know what they say: if I'm not with the girl I love, I love the girl I'm with. All the fun you're missing!"

"Sure."

"Why is it, Teresina?" he asked her in a hoarse stage whisper. "*Why* does Giorgio so stubbornly turn his aching GI back on the very thing that makes the world go round?"

"Ehhh..." She smiled up at him, sensing the meaning of his words. "Giorgio has—fidanzata?"

"No—worse! He just *thinks* he does."

I laughed with the others. It was impossible to get angry at Opp. Besides, there was something I liked about being discussed in this free and open way. I liked being called *Giorgio*: it sounded so much richer, more romantic. Better than just *George*, solid citizen, faithful retainer. Here I was the hero of an opera—a minor hero of course, but still...

Later we ate supper—pasta and the bully beef, and vino rosso—and Opp and Teresina talked a blue streak at each other, while Giulia and I listened. Giulia was around twenty-five and as unlike her sister as she could be. She was short and the soft flesh—the flesh I tried not to look at—was plump and smooth. She had a long, perfectly straight nose, but it was that full Italian chin that moved me. Her voice was low, and she spoke rarely. She had married just before her husband had been shipped out to Africa, where he'd been captured at Mersa Matruh; and that was about all I knew about her. I figured Opp only brought me along because Giulia was there.

After the meal Opp took Guido on his lap and showed him how to do the vibratory trick with the fork and the table edge, and I read my mail. A letter from Nancy about a weekend in Michigan with Liz, the routine at the hospital. And a long letter from Dal, from Fort Sill, which first infuriated me, and finally had me laughing out loud.

"What's tickling your gonads, Vird?"

"It's my roommate," I said.

"The swabby?"

"No, the other one, the ROTC one. He's at OCS now. Learning all about artillery. He says—hey, you'll go for this—he says time fire is 500% more effective with a burst 15 yards off the ground than percussion bursts."

"Jesus, I'm delighted to hear that."

"He says when a shell bursts, its effect is mostly from side-spray, so when it bursts at percussion most of the spray either goes into the ground or up in the air. But when it bursts in the air, the spray flies down from an angle, has time to spread out, and really covers an area efficiently."

"Oh, not really. Not really, now. I can't go on."

We were both laughing now.

"Let me quote: *As a matter of fact, time fire and ricochet bursts are the only satisfactory way of getting at troops who are well dug in, except of course by the very expensive and uncertain means of a direct hit.*"

"Yeah, there's always that. Isn't there?" Opp was bent over the table now, beating his hands on the wood. "Oh, Jesus," he gasped. "Oh, my sagging GI balls."

Teresina popped into the doorway, her head cocked in that attitude of eager expectancy, participation. "What—has happened?"

Wagging his head, Opp shied a hand at her. "Can't explain—too complicated. Can't do it. Give us a hug and a kiss, you gorgeous passionate female."

Of course when things don't, uh, work out as planned, & a few judicious advances to the rear are in order, the surprise isn't

*possible. And that's when your forward observers are
all-important. They stick with the front lines of retreating
infantry (that's you, son) & adjust fire 100 yards in front of them.
And brother, from that distance you can really adjust, I mean.
'There's an enemy truck column passing that road junction.
Knock it out, Mr. Dalrymple.' And if you're not flat on your
belly barking out commands to your radio operator with a
volley on the way in 2 minutes from the guns some 3—4000
yards behind you, you don't get to finish the problem.*

There was a certain grisly gratification, crouching here in this
battered, ancient building in a dirty, ragged uniform, boots
caked thick with mud, after six days on the line and four more
hauling ammunition, picturing Dal in pressed khaki, sitting in
class boning up on the principles of massed fire. It was
outrageous. It was hilarious. The throw of the dice, as Russ
would say—

*What I do miss is Chris. Jesus H. God, how I miss her. You
want to thank your lucky stars you're not married, you've got no
idea what it's like to be married and then get pulled apart like
this. It eats at your guts like battery acid.*

*Speaking of which; thanks for the letter of instruction to
Chris re immobilizing the Empress. For the doo-ray-shun.*

*Well, I hate to have to be the one to write this. But I can't put
it off any longer, & I won't feel anymore like it tomorrow, or a
year from tomorrow. So I better spit it out now. Terry was shot
down. The big raid over Schweinfurt. Wing was on fire, plane all
shot up. Somebody thought they saw two chutes, but then
someone else said no, none. Terry's kid sister Sheilah phoned
Chris, his folks got a letter from Terry's squadron leader. 43
missions, they said he was credited with 4 planes.*

*Jesus, I'm sorry to have to write this, with all you've got on
your mind right now. But I figured you'd want to know anyway.
What a marvelous guy he was. Surprising in a way—he seemed
so, you know, sour-ball & ineffectual, & look what he did. Jesus,
George, I feel lousy over that row I had with him, roaring drunk
and shooting my big mouth off—I'm going to have to straighten
up & fly right. Anyway, take care, & let me—*

"Vird! Hey, read some more, I want to hear more about time
fire..." Then his face changed. "What's the matter?"

"A friend," I said. "Old friend. Shot down over Germany."

The girls were back in the room; they were watching me, their faces somber, drawn, inquiring.

"Un amico," Opp said. "Caduto." His hands made a swift, eloquent pantomime—a plane spiraling down and down and down.

"Ah, poveretto..." They broke into a soft torrent of commiseration. I was amazed to discover my eyes had filled with tears and I ducked my head. If I hadn't been so tired, if the girls weren't looking at me like that, with such sympathy and affection—with such sad wisdom—I'd have been all right. Now I felt shaky and defeated. The wine churned sourly in my belly.

I put my head back against the smooth, damp wall and closed my eyes. Teresina's voice ran on, deep and soothing, and beneath it, behind it, there was the incessant bump-ump-ump-ump of artillery, like sacks of sand dropped from a tremendous height. Six months. Six months since the Salerno landing, and we hadn't got anywhere at all; inching through the dust and then the mud along the narrow valleys, waiting for the inexorable shellfire to come crashing down from the ridge beyond us, and then the next one, and the next.

All wrong. I'd thought war was—I don't know, something *defined.* It had always seemed defined in the textbooks back at Cambridge; violence and killing, moments of stress and fear, yes—but bound in a neat round sum of endeavor: something attempted, accomplished, ended. But that wasn't true. It was never over. Day succeeded bitter day—a roofless farmhouse, a headless Madonna and Child under a little stone hutch, a piece of a sign that read VITA PIU SANA (but *what* made for a more wholesome life?) creaking in a cold wind, concertina wire that tore through gloves, through rags, through everything, and slashed your hands; men were killed or wounded or fell sick, vanished forever and new faces came—frightened, unsure faces, and we hated them, fearing their fear, their dangerous inexperience, and sullenly tried to teach them the little we'd learned.

And what we'd learned, finally, painfully, ragingly was that it would never be over; that the stupid, grinding process would go on until everyone was dead or down, you as well, and no one was left, all were replacements, and only the rear-area commandos in PBS down in Naples selling gas and cigarettes and rations on the black market were happy. On those rare leaves in Naples we vented our hatred on the rear echelon, hating them as we'd never hated the Germans, muscled them off the sidewalks, elbowed them away at the bars, picked fights with them whenever opportunity arose. And that was as stupid and vicious and purposeless as everything else.

The hell with it. The filthy shitting hell with it. I pulled my lucky shell out of a cargo pocket and held it deep in my hand. Chris somewhere, so far away. I hoped the sun was on her hair...Terry. Bouncing up and down at the Yale Game Dance, waving to Anita O'Day swaying tightly up there in front of the band shields, that funny defiant grin on her gamine's face, singing *Let Me Off Uptown*, and smiling back at him. All bony knees and elbows, pushing at the sand, squinting up at Russ, murmuring, "In fact, your whole life is perfectly predictable." Leaning toward me over the table at the Bick, grinning around his broken nose, middle finger upraised, saying, "They need me up there!"

I squeezed the cowrie tight in my hand, and thought again of Chris—of Chris coming into the room after one of the games, her skin aglow, like the heart of one of her golden conches, her eyes full of that high expectancy, her laugh open and free—the way the very air in the room seemed to alter its composition, now she was here...

I awoke with a convulsive twitch that made me grunt. Fading, falling light; I was stiff with cold. The room was empty except for Giulia, who was crouched near the stove, her arms clamped against her sides. Where had someone sat like that, in a gray chill dusk?

"Ciao," I murmured.

"Ciao, Giorgio." And she smiled her sweet, timorous smile.

What was I doing here, dozing and starting, neither drunk nor sober, in the company of this plump, plain girl I barely knew, while my friend was in another room making indefatigable (and apparently matchless) love to Teresina?

"—What do you think of me, Giulia?" I heard myself say in a dreamlike tone; I felt detached, disembodied, as if all moorings had been slipped. "What is your opinion of me, your *real* opinion?—this dirty foreigner sleeping in your home? Do you hate me?—conqueror, still another invader? Do you see me as a magician who can pluck food out of the emptiness around you?

Do you ever think about what your life will be in 1950—or 1970? Assuming of course that you survive. Assuming any of us survives..."

I paused. Her cheeks flushed faintly; her eyes dropped, rose again. I had the distinct impression that she understood me perfectly, though I knew she couldn't have. She answered in Italian, in the same haunted singsong I'd used. She might have been saying: *"I would like to hate you, I was prepared to hate you—but I cannot. All systems are barbaric by definition, my friend. We were once the mightiest power on earth, with absolute dominion over a thousand races from Scotland to the Tigris. And now for centuries we have been divided and despoiled. Only life matters, Giorgio. Each single life."*

Had she said that? any of that? I answered anyhow: "Yes, but systems determine our lives as individuals—you can't escape that."

Her eyes said: *"Yes, but there are always choices. A man can turn his back on any authority. You could desert from your army this very moment if you wanted."*

"I would be caught and punished, maybe put to death."

"Possibly. Very possibly. But you could do it. You have that choice. You are disgusted with the greed of your own army and the stupidity of your officers—I have heard you. Yet you will not desert. The thought has probably never entered your mind."

"No, it hasn't. But I believe in what we're fighting for, more or less."

"Everyone believes—more or less."

"No, our cause is right—more than the Nazis', anyway, God knows. More just than most. So if we commit crimes too, it's wrong, it's very wrong, sure—yet it's for the greater good, don't you see?"

"But what is the greater good? If every system sacrifices its own people to its own ends, and if every system falls, as it certainly will, how can there be any greater good than a man and woman's honest joy together, private pride in work and dreams...?"

Now she was silent, we both were. The twilight deepened, her grave round face was barely visible; softened by dusk it looked pale as marble, pure as a Renaissance figurine; almost beautiful. She was woman, all women, femininity in its terrible vulnerability, its magnificent strength. Was I awake or dreaming? I had never felt like this, not quite like this—unnaturally alert, unbearably alone...

There came a muttering, a low subterranean rumbling that swelled to a pulsing, quaking drone. Planes—not ours. Raid. I was on my feet with no sense of getting there. Giulia too had risen. She was looking up, as though she could see them through the stained ceiling. The thunder was quite near now, burgeoning. I had just time to think, We can't make it to a shelter, a wall, against a wall is best—then the first explosion came, two more; the room shook, and Giulia came running against me. I pulled her down under the massive oak table and we cowered there while the great hellish feet stamped over us in three mountainous, skull-splitting crepitations, and swept on.

I was holding her. Her head was in the hollow of my neck. Her hair smelled of soap, of sweat, of woman, her breath was hot and quick against my throat.

"Giulia," I murmured. "Ah, Giulia. I want you. Now."

She made a sudden low incoherent sound and drew away from me. Dismayed I released her; but then her hand closed on mine.

"Vieni," she whispered. "Presto, presto..."

She led me into her room. I unhooked my cartridge belt and pulled off jacket, shirt, boots, my gear thumping and clanking on the cold stone floor. Then I turned. She was sitting naked on the edge of the bed, watching me, her hands at her full round belly. Her eyes were huge. All at once I felt loutish, confused, angry with myself, and paused. She reached out then and drew me to her again.

"Abbracciami, Giorgio," she whispered, trembling, "*abbracciami, amore...*"

I lay down with her then in an agony of cold and desire. Her breasts were fuller than I'd thought they would be, her legs shorter. I could not control my trembling now. I touched her, caressed her as best I knew how. But when I started to enter her she stopped me.

"No," she said softly, "lente, lente, Giorgio. Aspetta un po'..." Gently, surely she pushed me on to my side, my back, her hands stroking my chest, bent her head then to my belly, my genitals, her lips and tongue moving with light, sweet deference. Her soft insistence held me. She made love to me, and then murmured endearments I didn't understand, and made love to me again . . . I slid into a vale, a haven of perfect ease, of peaceful felicity. All the tensed trembling had vanished. I knelt above her and took her lovely breasts in my mouth and drank at her womanness; I covered her smooth belly with kisses, raised her small furry mount beneath my hands and caressed it, hearing in a rush of pride her soft moans of joy. When I entered her at last it was like a Roman triumph, all purple and crimson banners flowing. She cried out, her thighs flaring in rapture; I made love again, and still again, I was the emperor of all passion bestowed and taken. I had been granted goodness. In the midst of death we are in life. Yes. Oh Terry—grace *can* descend in the midst of hell . . .

She was right, this plain, silent girl with earthbrown hair. The war was there, right up there on the rocky slopes beyond the curve in the road above Minturno, the mud and icy wind and the stramma thorns that tore at your hands and face, and I was going back up there the day after tomorrow—but she was right, all the same: at bottom there were only the moments, the islands of personal truth—those private triumphs of body and body, heart and heart . . .

Outside a heavy vehicle—a six-by-six, a weapons carrier, some kind of convertible anyway, all our vehicles were convertible now—groaned up the street through the piazza; beyond the high narrow window the rain was still falling _____

3

Dear Footslogger:

There's absolutely no sense in trying to tell you where I am because they'd censor it anyway. So let's just say Somewhere in the Blue Pacific, and let it go at that. I know I've been a complete and total bastard about writing. (Christ, I can hardly summon up the pezzazz to get off a communiqué to the Old Gentleman these days.) I'm at sea again, have been for the past 100-odd years or so. Another DD, another old rust bucket, named the *Jennison* this time, fondly (?) called the *Jenny*. I've made signalman 3rd, which has meant more pay (which I cannot spend anyhow) *and* longer watches, increased responsibility (and concomitant ass-chewings), more paperwork and less sleep. Less and less sleep. The burdens of command. A little excitement a good while back, and ever since then we've been escorting tankers, towing targets, or ferrying high-octane gas (a real joy). Not exactly what I had in mind when I joined the Navy; but then, how much of it has been?

One bright spot in a gray season: we put in at Samoa on our erratic travels and I actually got ashore. Passed up the native attractions (Kipling may have found a neater, sweeter maiden in a cleaner, greener land, etc., but it sure as hell wasn't here), found Sadie Thompson's house, and talked 2 shipmates into hiking up Mt. Vaea with me to Robert Louis Stevenson's grave. Nice moment, standing there with the gaunt purple peaks soaring up all around, and the sea, all shimmering turquoise and amber and cobalt bands, stretching off to the world's end (Murph and Westlund cursing me out all the while, complaining of charley horses and blisters)... Old Tusitala, the tale-spinner. RLS was in California, too. Is my life destined to parallel his in some eerie, capricious way? At least I haven't got TB (though if I *did* have I'd be 4F and hence not stuck forever on this sweltering tin can). I can however boast of a rash on my ass and under one arm—jungle crud—which Hendrich the chief pharmacist's mate loves to paint incessantly with salicylic (?) acid, which burns like the fires of Dis for some minutes but otherwise does no good at all that I can see.

Aside from Samoa, not one hell of a lot to regale you with—though there may be soon, if you know what I mean. One funny moment: at an anchorage which had better be nameless there was a terrifying amount of signal traffic, EVERY God damned signalman in the God damn US Navy seems to be faster at this blinker business than I am, I had just got reamed out by some snotty SOB on a light cruiser for lamentable slowness in response... and then suddenly, from a jeep carrier: "STOP... DOPING ... OFF ... YOU ... BLUEBLOOD ... HARVARD ...SON...OF...A...BITCH..." I almost fell off the bridge. It was Richards, from Communications School, who had somehow miraculously kept track of me (which is more than I did of him). Two days later I wangled a quick visit. That's the *real* Navy, pal: ratings and morale and Jap flags stenciled all over the bridge—they're really fighting the war, those guys.

Oh well. They also serve who only shit and sweat.

But as for the easy life—let me clue you in, dad. The fresh water's been strictly rationed. Our sacks are filthy, and sodden with sweat; it's an oven—a dense, reeking oven—below decks and so we all crap out on the decks, around the gun turrets, life jackets jammed under our heads. And then it rains—savagely, without any warning whatever—and you lie there in a trembling chill, drinking in water through every parched and gaping pore... I'm damned if *I* know where the steaks and butter and sugar are going—they sure as hell aren't going out to this asshole end of the world.

But worst of all (while I'm disabusing you about This Pampered Navy Life) is the lack of sleep. You just can't ever get enough of it to function decently. You come off the 12-to-4 and you've just flopped like a Bowery rummy beside a 40 mm gun tub—and it's reveille; or you've just ended a frantic three-hour all-hands-evolution loading ammunition, and the twitching in your back and arms has eased enough to let you drop off—and a hand is shaking you again and again and again, and you finally snarl, *"All right—!"* and stagger to your feet to go on watch. Or that terrible General Quarters klaxon goes off, a hiccuping rattlesnake turned up to 300 decibels, and you can't find your life jacket or your shirt (which you WILL wear because of the danger of flash burns, or go on report) and you grope around in a white-hot panic, with unpleasant images of Jap heavy cruisers or torpedoes or bombers curving in at the hull beside you like Buck Rogers missiles... and at last, after GQ is secured, and you're off watch, and they aren't hounding you for some special shit detail—why then, there's a lovely avalanche of paper work to be tidied up.

And finally you go groping around in a thick pink haze of exhaustion, surly, snapping, committing foul-ups you'd never be guilty of if you could just GET ENOUGH SLEEP. Just 4 hours, uninterrupted. Just 2. In spite of yourself you find yourself nodding off, and then coming to with a flash of pure unalloyed dread. *Asleep on watch.* The cardinal, eternal, unforgivable sin of all shipboard sins. (I remember a guy named Kendall fell asleep on watch on the *Tolliver*, on sub patrol, and how Chief asked Mr. Stramm, the Gunnery Officer, to let him handle it—and how he did handle it.) But it's hopeless: you rub your eyes, chew the insides of your cheeks, do deep-knee bends, pinch your ear and your armpit and your ass, and still you find yourself going under—and nearly an hour to go.

You won't believe this, but we'd been at battle stations almost incessantly, nobody had had any sleep for two days and nights running, and Tico Garcia was taking a station-keeping message from SOPA, and Mr. Carnwright, the OD, snapped: "All right, all right, what's the poop?" and I looked up and there was Tico standing there with the pad in his hand, moving perfectly to the roll of the ship, his eyes glazed and staring at nothing at all. Out on his feet. Absolutely out. "Garcia!" the OD roared, and Tico blinked and came to with a little lurch, and said: "Aye, sir." And of course the OD chewed us both out savagely and put him on report. Which isn't fair, because Tico is the best signalman on board. He was just done in, nothing more, nothing less.

And the worst parts, the most degrading, infuriating parts of it I can't write about. Can't put in a letter, I mean. And I know you know why. Those parts will have to wait for some impossible-to-imagine golden afternoon back at Cambridge, with a cool breeze pouring in from the riverside windows and the record player pounding out BG's *String of Pearls*, and each of us with a tall glass of (forgive me for even mentioning it) Cutty Sark and soda; when we are, fantastically, our own men again...

The doldrums: we're drifting through the doldrums (whatever the hell *they* are), bound in a universe of sliding, oily water and foul, clinging heat. One of Dante's Inferno rings—by no means one of the lowest ones: a subdivison of Ring #2, say. Christ, I've forgotten *everything* I've ever read or learned. I brought *Nostromo* and *The Possessed* on board with me at San Diego and I haven't even cracked them; I find myself flipping listlessly through some idiotic comic book or listening devoutly to *Pistol Packin' Mama* over the bullhorn as if there were some arcane truth to be deciphered there... Have you felt this? this all-engulfing miasma of futility and dejection? as though it didn't matter what you ever did again?... Asiatic. We're all going slowly, inexorably Asiatic—you can feel it happening to you: stealthy, absurd obsessions with things like New Zealand coins or snap hooks or the illustration of a girl you've torn out of a disintegrating copy of *Esquire* or even the *Saturday Evening Post*; sudden terrible rages over trifles, forgotten in minutes; and worst of all, the sense—watching some sunrise of unearthly beauty or a school of flying fish skittering ahead of the ship like handfuls of dazzling silver coins, or some thunderous landfall with tortured magenta peaks and rain clouds boiling up behind them like angry gods—the sense that you are not seeing those things at all, that you are *somewhere else*...

Thanks (yet again) for the word on the old crowd. *Wonderful, wonderful news about Terry*. Thank God he is alive. Thank God. To think he should turn out to be the bloody bleedin' 'ero of us all. I hate to think of him a POW there, deep in Germany. (Oh, for the civilized days when wars were fought by parfit gentil knights and periodic exchanges of prisoners were held, with full military courtesies.) Anyway, the Ferking Fusiliers are still intact.

Except of course for Jean-Jean, God rest his soul.

Got a rather raddled V-mail from Dal, full of apology and solicitude—a tone no doubt influenced by the fact that he's at port of embarkation (ever a sobering moment, as you know) and on his way to the Great Adventure. I ought to answer him, and maybe I will if I can get up the enthusiasm for it. (The idea of his being a husband AND a father AND a bleedin' orficer, all in a year and a half, is almost more than I can stomach.)

Saw Kay M. in a newsreel last month, or some month or other; riding a fucking Sherman tank, legs crossed alluringly, blowing a kiss to some lucky doggies off-camera. Traveling USO show, I think, Somewhere in England. I hear her latest recordings have made her Queen of the Jukeboxes. Christ, if Kay thought Hitler was going to win the war she'd parachute into Berchtesgaden in black bra and lace panties. (Maybe he still will, and she still will.)

Also see by the papers you 'eroes have busted out of the Anzio beachhead and are pounding toward Rome. Delighted to see you made corporal, which gives you something in common with Napoleon; and even more delighted to hear you're still in one piece . . . Jesus, I envy you, George—no, I mean it. I know, I know, the cold and mud and patrols and shelling and all the rest of it. But you're doing something concrete to get it over with (even if it is on that stupid Italian peninsula, where any poor dumb son of a bitch over the age of eight could see—fucking-A *should* have seen—that 20 guys with slingshots could hold up a division); and you're over there where it's all going on—Rome and Paris and London, the Old World, our roots, the fountainhead of everything we are (or aren't). Well: ours not to reason why, ours but to groan and fry.

—And yet, for all the incessant battle stations and watch standing, the ridiculous, rare hours ashore in some sweltering pocket of jungle with a spam sandwich and a single can of beer—for all the boredom and empty futility, I keep being nudged by the thought that (unlike you) I have yet to pay my dues in this biggest and most exacting of all fraternities. I don't know how or where or when, but some time. Soon, I think.

Flowing stein in '49,
Jean Val-Jean Russ

FLASH—FLASH—FLASH—

All right, you coon-assed goldbrickers & yardbirds, you can stack your stacking-swivels & butt your butt-plates: Dalrymple is About to Open the Second Front!!!

Yessir, shipping out as of Thursday. All howitzers processed, equipment crated & stamped, POM requirements met—& we've been sitting around POE for 10 days drinking ourselves into a state of grand physical collapse because some of those royally paid longshoremen dropped one of the howitzers 30 feet into one of the cargo holds & we've been waiting for a replacement. And now we're READY TO ROLL. Yep, the Old Man finally succeeded in convincing one of the boys that shakes the big dice that they had a battery of the most deadly artillery in history at their fingertips, & they'd better use it.

The Old Man is great—I've never met anyone like him. No crap, no flap, it's right on the money every time. Like the first day I reported in. Curious moment, isn't it? It's not like your first drunk because the world doesn't start changing, and it's not like your first day at college because there's no crowd to commiserate & guff around with. Anyway, the scene ran like this:

D (looking sharp as hell, front & center & highball): "Lieutenant Dalrymple reporting for duty, sir."

OM (one glance): "Get rid of that garrison cap, Dalrymple. This is a line outfit. You're not a God damn airplane driver."

D: "Yes, *sir!*" Never let it be said that old Wog is slow to take a hint, especially when delivered with a blow torch.

2nd episode. D, chilled to the bone, half cockeyed from lack of sleep, totally covered with mud from trying to extricate a 13-ton howitzer from a bottomless bog with 4 (yes, 4) 18-ton tractors: "Lt. Dalrymple, reporting as ordered, sir."

OM: "When did you last have leave, Dalrymple?"

D (after the briefest of pauses): "None, sir—since graduation from OCS." (All of 5 months ago.)

OM (one significant glance): "I suggest you apply for one."

D: "Yes, *SIR!*"

This time I took the hint even faster, & was pulling into

Woods Hole 48 hours later. And there was Chris & the kid. Now don't blow your stack, Grog. I know you've been overseas for 101 years & a day, is it my fucking fault you signed up for that stupid ERC instead of ROTC, like the rest of us gentlemen? Anyway, I can't help being a bit of a shit & raving about it. 5 glorious days & I'll never forget a minute of them: we hit the old Capstan Bar in Hyannis (remember?) & we hiked the beach at Nauset, & then went to the Ritz Roof to hear Helen O'Connell singing *Green Eyes*. But without the old crowd it wasn't the same—we looked at each other, & nodded, & left early.

But Ronny. What a wonderful kid. It's all that matters, REALLY matters, Grog, no matter what they say. They can take government policy & the Army & high finance & shove it. Doesn't sound like old Dal, does it? That's how I feel, though. He sits there in my lap & waggles his little round head & yawns & drops off to sleep in your arms & I swear, you feel like the first & last father in world history. He didn't recognize me until I took off my cap & uniform blouse. Personally I think the kid's a secret pacifist. (And after 3 months of wallowing in the mud of Georgia I wish *I* was.)

Well, now it's the outfit, & overseas. And the Old Man has really moved me around. Either he's priming me for something, or I'm no frigging good for *anything*. We'll see. Pretty soon I'll be brushing up on my German first-hand, I think I hope. Hell, I worked for myself all last year, so I guess it's time I started working for someone else, and Ike is as good a man as any. The artillery is the biggest damn holding company in the Army, & the anti-trust law is defunct for the duration. Lot of big deals to be swung, right?

Listen, you selfish bastard, come back because I've got a number of things to thrash out with you over a long Scotch or 2.

See you in Berlin—
Dal

No love, no nothin',
And it's a promise we'll keep—
No fun, with no one . . .
We're getting plenty of sleep!
Our hearts're on strike, and though they're like an empty
    honeycomb—
No love, no sir, no nothin' till our babies come home!
Ra-daaaaa . . .

(Laughter, giggles, background noises.)

Hello, you Fiendish, Fractious, Ferocious Fusiliers out there, wherever you are! This is Chris—

—and Nancy—

—and Liz, pinch-hitting for Ann, who's far away in Seattle—

—and we're serenading you from a *very* cramped booth in G. Schirmer's Music emporium in the heart of downtown Boston. The Andrews Sisters we're not—but what do you expect from a hausfrau, a riveter and a bedpan artist? Anyway, we decided that since you guys are all scattered to the four winds we'd get together and yack about old times. And it took planning worthy of Yale Game Weekend. Can you imagine what getting a hotel room in *Boston* is like? But we did it, and here we are. There's no Scotch in Boston either, so we've been drinking cuba libres, as there is plenty of rum. Plenty of rum. It does very nicely. In fact, too nicely maybe. (More giggling.) Say something, Nancy, I've run down.

Hello, kids—and especially George: hello, darling. We just got this idea of cutting a V-record to you all only a few minutes ago, and we don't know how it's going to come out. Or even if it *is* going to come out. Anyway, long as this is a broadcast, here are a few choice news items from the home front. (Background noises, rustling.)

What's that?

Read it, *read* it . . .

Oh. Okay. "The sweater girl controversy continues to heat up across the nation. It all started when the Vought-Sikorsky Aircraft Corporation sent 53 girls home from its Stratford, Connecticut plant explaining that the wearing of sweaters on the job was strictly forbidden on moral grounds"—did they really *do* that?

For God's sake, read the clip!

"—and that the girls should wear only slack suits or coveralls. The United Auto Workers took exception to this, pointing out that secretaries in the office wore sweaters. 'I fail to see,' Charles G. Manion, a union official, was quoted as saying, 'why sweaters are perfectly moral in the plant's offices and immoral in the plant.'"

I don't believe *any* of this.

That's what it says. "A spokesman for Vought-Sikorsky, who did not wish to be identified, said the firm has been misquoted.

'The action was taken purely as a safety measure, not on moral grounds.' He cited a National Safety Council ruling that sweaters, when caught in machinery, did not tear like cloth and therefore were much more likely to cause injury to the wearer. Asked for comment as a preeminent authority, actress Ann Sheridan declared at a press conference yesterday that the whole dispute should be kept in proper proportion: 'It's quite simple—a little girl in a big sweater might be a safety hazard. On the other hand, a big girl in a small sweater might be a moral hazard. If you see what I mean.'" Oh, that's priceless! (Laughter, rustling of paper.)

Item two. "Actress Dorothy Lamour received a severe shock at a war bond rally in Cincinnati, Ohio, where she was dispensing kisses to all buyers of $25,000 bonds. Herbert M. Riesner made his purchase, stepped forward to claim his reward—and fainted dead away before he could collect. 'I feel quite badly about it,' Miss Lamour said after Mr. Riesner had been revived and led away. 'I do want to be patriotic. I had no idea Ohioans had such vivid imaginations.'" (More laughter.)

Well, that'll give you guys a perfect idea of what you're fighting for. And *now* it's time for the prizes and awards. Liz, will you handle this end of it.

Love to. There's nothing like a prize when you—

Wait—it's the end!—the end of the side! We ought to—

Well, and here we are again. The flip side. Let's see: For Dal, a six weeks' subscription to Madame Lazonga's dance studio. For George, four Tibetan monks specially trained in cataloguing Great Moments in the Himalayan Crevasses...Is this funny?

No—it was all I could think of! (Surreptitious giggling.)

For Russ, a leatherbound copy of Taliaferro Quondam's *Carefree Nights under the Pacific Stars.* For Terry, a catcher's mask, to be worn at all future dances.

Oh hell, forget it. It was just an idea. Hey, we're not terribly funny. We've been sitting around feeling mopey as hell, and drinking cuba libres, and all we want to say is, be careful, all you wonderful idiots, we love you and miss you and want you all home again, and that's all we want—

I love you, George, *please* be careful now. And write me—

And Terry, we're all thinking of you more than anyone else, just waiting and praying for it all to be over, and the day you'll be free and we'll be all together again...

Okay. Ready? One, two, three:
Missed the Saturday dance...
Might have gone, but what for?
Awf'lly diff'rent without you—
Don't get around much anymore...
Goodbye, George, all of you—
Bye, Bye, Fusiliers...
Goodbye...

Ron lifted the V-record from the turntable and peered at it. "Three little chicks on a toot during World War Deuce." He shook his head. "What a flaky performance."

"Flaky time," I answered, "all things considered."

"It's as though you're high all the time," he mused. "High on the Brave New World. America the Bootiful. Yankee Doodle Dong."

"Does it seem that way? We weren't. You take Terry—"

But he didn't want to listen, he was all full of his Research and Analysis. "There's something missing here," he declared.

"Of course there is."

He picked up a sheaf of what he'd already read, and then his eyes fell on me as though he'd never seen me before. "Where are *your* letters?"

"Mine?"

"Yeah—yours. Is that so silly? Where's Uncle George?"

"Well," I muttered, "nothing very special happened to me."

"I'll bet," he said, and the corner of his mouth drew down, his dark eyes began to snap again. "I know the kind of nothing-very-special you're talking about. Sure: you kept everybody else's, but nobody kept yours." He threw back his head and laughed without mirth. "Perfect, perfect!"

"Hold on," I said. "Russ lost his ship, Terry was a POW for years. The others have probably got some—"

"Don't kid a kidder. Dad never kept a letter in his life—not unless it had stock tips or real estate appraisals in it. Hell, he's never even kept any of Mother's... No, it's the same old jazz," he repeated stubbornly. "You kept the archives and *they* all couldn't be bothered. Right?"

"Well," I gave what Amanda calls my wintry smile, "I have my memories."

"Very funny," he said, and picked up the folder again.

Darling—

Mother's got the Stromberg-Carlson in the living room turned up to 500 decibels to catch the war news, but I've got the little white Philco out here tuned to Make Believe Ballroom, and Bob Eberly's singing *Blue Champagne*. Remember?

They just interrupted again with another bulletin. General Patton's 3rd Army is racing across France, entire German divisions are trapped somewhere. We're really winning, aren't we? Oh George, it does begin to look as if it'll be over soon. In the newsreels Saturday night there were shots of GIs riding on the tanks and waving, and one of them looked a lot like you, but I couldn't be sure because of the helmets and all the dust... I always like to imagine you're up there on the screen waving at me anyhow, it makes you seem closer. See how loony your Nan is getting, without you around? I'm certifiable at times, I swear.

Darling, *WHAT* WERE YOU DOING IN THE *HOSPITAL*??? Were you wounded? or sick? or what? I've been frantic worrying. You're so hopelessly laconic or stoic or something. Only Sweet, you've got to let a gal know a thing or two, once in a while; *please*. How I wish I could have been there to take care of you.

Commencement was strange: strange and sad all at the same time. Sad because Liz wasn't there sitting beside me; because you weren't there. Hardly any boys were. Marcia Bryson's date Eustace Conger, you knew him, didn't you? he's an ensign in the Navy, V-12 I think. And two other boys posted nearby who got leave. A lot of fathers were away, too. It seemed so *mistaken,* as though everyone had forgotten to come at the last minute, a grand mixup—it wasn't what I'd imagined it would be like at all. Still, I'm glad I went back to finish.

Dean Marsh was wonderful. "All of you have heard endless talk about the GI Bill of Rights. Well, I want to talk to you about the Wellesley Woman's Bill of Rights. What is *your* Bill of Rights? *Your* post-war planning? The post-war world will be a chaotic one, with all the tensions of reconversion, the hardship of runaway inflation. The boy you dated in '40 and '41 will be coming home a man now—but with a difference. He will be confused at the new world he'll see, resentful at the years he's lost; he will have hardened in ways you won't immediately discover or understand. In great measure it will be up to you to lead, to shape the course of that new world—for him, for you both..." And so forth and so forth.

My God, am *I* supposed to be able to do all that? any of it? My mind kept wandering all through the ceremony, I kept imagining the faces I wanted to see there, Liz and you and Ann and Terry and Chris and Dal, and even crazy impossible old Russ—and when it was over I found myself up in the room bawling.

And here I am, lying on the glider in the sun porch. I've just been stroking suntan pancake on my legs. Like Lucky Strike Green, silk stockings have gone to war, you know. But the effect *is* kind of sexy—wish you were here to help put it on! It's so lonely around here with no place to go and the parade of dreary movies down at the Orpheum. A bunch of us did go to see *Laura*, though. Remember when we went to see *Suspicion* in the Empress that night it snowed, and Russ was so impossible? It only seems funny now, somehow.

Anyway, I'm back at the hospital again, working in ICU, under a wonderful gal named Marge Carruthers. I like the pressure of it, the need for vigilance, I like feeling needed and valuable. At times I feel absolutely heroic—all right, go ahead and laugh, you rat—like the time last week I spotted septicemic symptoms in this boy's leg and notified Dr. Kramer, and we got it before it turned gangrenous. For a couple of days I felt just like Madame Curie. And then at other times I find myself wondering if it's just an escape, so I won't have to think about what I ought to be doing. Only what is *that???*

I'm thinking of going to New York in the fall. Liz is planning to go—she says I can room with her in her aunt's old apartment in Greenwich Village. Wouldn't that be wonderful!!! The defense plants are already beginning to lay off people, there's talk of reconversion. Liz is going to enroll at Pratt, she's decided to become a clothes designer—she's really serious about it, she always did such terrific sketches, you know. She wants to become another Mainbocher, and she'll do it, too—you wait. I'd like to get into magazine work, it's always appealed to me. The essential thing, Liz says, is to get the show on the road. "Sure, the war's still on and everybody's floating around in a state of suspended animation—but what are you going to do with yourself when it's over, and your whole *life* is lying out there ahead of you? Don't duck the issue!" God, she's great.

Another bulletin. We've just invaded SOUTHERN FRANCE!!! Between Cannes and Toulon, it says. Everything seems to be breaking at once. Oh darling, is that you? It is, isn't it? And now it says advance elements of 3rd Army have reached Orléans. I can hear you saying, If only Jean-Jean—

Oh Darling, it *is* going to be over soon, I can just feel it! For God's sake, take care of yourself, let the new men do the hard things now. And don't sit under the apple tree, with anyone else but

Your Nan

_____I watched them climb down out of the six-by-six, one by one, sweaty and dirty, new faces and old; the new ones looked troubled, a bit resentful, absurdly vulnerable and young. When they were all down, watching me, the warm wind plucking at their collars, I called: "Erwin, Koonz, Jason! You're pulling guard duty. Go eat early chow. Now, there will be a weapons inspection at 0730 tomorrow."

"ODs, Vird?" Opp said.

"No. Lieutenant Harding doesn't care what *you* look like, but your weapons had better be clean. Damn clean."

"What we got tomorrow?" DiLeo said.

"Working party again. Rations and water."

"Jeeze, Sarge, when do we ever get to sleep?" Breithoff, the newest of the replacements, asked peevishly.

"You don't," I told him. "Maybe next war."

I'd just let them go when the caravan came tearing up the road—a Packard clipper with its stars covered, two olive-drab sedans, half a dozen recon cars and jeeps—and swept past us. We scattered, cursing; the dust boiled around us in clouds.

"For Christ's sake!" Ramsey roared. "Who's that? Goering?"

"USO show," DiLeo answered. "Rice told me they were coming through."

We all watched them. The flag car stopped at the supply tent, then the rest of the procession, and the occupants began piling out. I saw two forest-green uniforms, a lot of brass and braid, and then a flash of gold hair that gleamed like a helmet in the sunlight. One of the officers called something, and the woman answered, her voice very clear and imperious. A voice that expected to be obeyed. Captain Lawson, the supply officer, hurried out of the tent and saluted smartly.

"It's Danny Morgan's group," Dee said. "See him? Wearing the baseball cap. That's Kay Madden."

"Kay Madden?" Breithoff said in a thin, awe-struck voice. "Hey, is it really *Kay Madden?*"

"No, it's Theda Bara," Ramsey told him, and spat. "So she's gash. She's just expensive gash, that's all."

"No—she's a wonderful person. I read about her—she gives away all her money to an orphanage in Santa Monica."

"Oh, my broken GI balls. They pump out that crap and you swallow it. You silly yo-yo—she puts out every night for the flag rank, like all the rest of them."

"I don't believe it," Breithoff said resentfully.

"You silly yo-yo."

At the same moment she laughed—that high, metallic laugh that ran tantalizingly down the scale. It was Kay Madden all right. They were moving toward us slowly; a tall man with a hawklike face was making introductions. Kay's head was back, her hair flashed and flashed in the September air. Her eyes were masked by a flier's tinted eyeshades, but I'd have recognized her anywhere, any time. She was wearing a smartly tailored suit of pale blue gabardine and walking oxfords, and her legs still looked every bit as terrific as they always had. Then she turned and said something to Danny Morgan and I saw the First Division flash sewn on her shoulder.

"Well, well," I said. "The Big Red One."

"Yeah," Ramsey muttered, "they probably made her an honorary frigging brigadier."

"No—*she* picked it," I said. "She wanted it. Number One. You know?"

They were near us now. Captain Lawson was explaining something to them, or trying to, and Danny Morgan was muttering glumly about something else, or perhaps it was one of his sourball imitations; then one of the two men wearing a green foreign correspondent's uniform murmured in reply, and Kay laughed again and cried: "Oh, if it's against regulations, lead me to it!"

"What gorgeous pussy," Opp murmured, shaking his head. "What a gorgeous, five-alarm, fluid-drive, gilt-edge piece of ass."

"Go on, Opp," DiLeo said. "Snow the broad."

"Yeah, come on, Opp!" Ramsey urged, "pour it on—you're the boy. Take her down to one of the supply tents and boff her till she squeals for mercy."

"Who, me? You kidding?" Opp laughed faintly, ran his hand along the edge of his jaw. All the brash assurance had vanished; he looked just like Breithoff. "That's out of my class."

"No, come on," Ramsey pressed him, "I got fifty says you can't prong her inside of two hours."

"—She's not so special," I heard myself say suddenly. "I've been out with her."

"*What?*" They were all staring at me now, blank with incredulity. "Ah, come *on*, Sarge..."

"I have," I said stubbornly, feeling cross with myself, watching that almost indolent imperiousness of hers, the way she shook back her hair or reached for a cigarette from that thin gold case; thinking all at once of New Year's Eve, the shouting match and the fight in the bitter dark, and her arch, derisive smile. I told myself it was the First Division patch, but I knew it wasn't; it was that flicker of pale diffidence in Opp's eyes. No, I thought, no, by Jesus. We don't back off from *anybody*—

"I *have*," I repeated. "I was dancing with her New Year's Eve of '41."

DiLeo snorted, and Ramsey said: "*You*, Vird? Forget it."

"Want to bet?" I said.

"Hell yes, I'll bet. I've got a hundred says you're full of bull."

"You're on."

They were passing by us now, still walking toward the dispatcher's tent. Danny Morgan looked red-faced and worried, not at all the way he did in his Orphan of Broadway series. I nodded to him, stepped into the group and said: "Hello, Kay."

She turned with that quick, alert snap of her head, frowned, thrust the flier's glasses up on top of her head. She had a light tan, the faintest eye shadow. "Yes?" she said. "What is it?"

She didn't recognize me. It was clear. She wasn't cutting me—she really didn't remember me. Someone behind me—it was Ramsey—laughed once. The major with the handsome, hawklike features said with a trace of impatience: "What's on your mind, Sergeant?"

"George Virdon," I said to Kay. "From Fox Entry days. Cambridge."

Her eyes dilated then, flattened, she laughed and extended her hand. "George—of course! I didn't recognize you, sorry to say. Trop de places, trop de faces..." Then the bemused, supercilious smile, but harder than I remembered it. She was thinking of New Year's Eve, too. Was she? Those two crescents at the corners of her mouth were sharper. "What have you been doing with yourself?"

"Oh, just wandering around. Hoofing it, you might say. Italy, and then southern France. And now Champagne—I guess this is Champagne."

Behind me I could hear DiLeo hiss: "He knows her—he *does!* He wasn't bird-turding..."

"You look primeval, George." Kay always recovered quickly; you had to give her that.

"Yes, well—" I gestured. "The world's work, Kay."

"We were at General Patton's headquarters last week— everyone there looks so smart and confident."

"I can imagine."

Her eyes were cold now, cold as aquamarines. "You're in supply, then."

"Oh no, we're a line outfit. This is just—a sort of vacation, you might call it..." It was odd: I was standing right there in front of her, so close I could smell her perfume; that heady, expensive scent made you think of flowers on some barbaric tropic island—and yet there was this curious sense of *distance*, as through I were peering at her though field glasses from a far-off ridge. "Here," I swung back quickly, gesturing, before she could speak, "I want you to meet some of my boys. They're devoted admirers of yours, to a man...This is Corporal Arnie Oppenheim," I proclaimed, yanking him forward by the sleeve, "my best friend, we've been together ever since Tarleton—"

She smiled her dazzling model's smile. "Hello, Arnie."

"Ma'am." Opp looked at his feet like a yokel, blinking. I could have kicked him in the ass.

"And this is Walt Ramsey, and Dee DiLeo..." I thrust them forward now in a kind of vengeful jocularity, and she greeted them all with that bright, professional eagerness, and something more, too—a touch of demure reticence: American Woman-hood in the War Zones. Only Dee showed any of his casual poise.

"Hey, don't any of you guys want to talk to *me?*" Danny

Morgan barked in his gravelly Ned Sparks voice, and Dee answered:

"Not today, Danny—maybe after we get home, okay?" and everyone laughed.

"Miss Madden, are you going to sing for us tonight?" Breithoff asked her. His glasses made his watery blue eyes look even bigger.

"I sure am, soldier."

"Will you please sing *Don't Get Around Much Anymore?* for me?"

"Why, of course I will. Tell me your name again, and your home town."

"Clarence Breithoff, Zenda, Kansas. That's near Wichita."

"All right, Clarence. That's a promise." Her eyes came to rest on me again—the old measuring, bemused glance I remembered. "You're a sergeant, I see, George."

"Lean and mean."

"How about Russ Currier—what do you hear from him?"

"He's on a destroyer, out in the Pacific somewhere. Signalman."

"Poor, dear Russ. Playing Lord Jim. Of course. Or is it Jack London. And the Irish boy—what was his name?"

"Terry Gilligan." I spelled his last name for her, very slowly. "He's a POW. He was tail gunner on a Fort, he was shot down over Germany."

"Oh, I'm sorry... You Fusiliers—how is it you're all so low in rank? for Harvard men, I mean?"

"Talent," I said, staring at her. "And dedication. Except for Dal, of course—you remember Dal. Dal's made first lieutenant already, he's a general's aide or some God damn thing."

"Well, Dal," she said, and those little crescents at the corners of her mouth sharpened. "He was going to set the world on fire, wasn't he? Does he still want to be chairman of the board of General Electric?"

"Hell, he'll be running Krupp *and* I. G. Farben in a year or so. You watch. He and Chris got married. You remember Chris Farris."

Her eyes widened in their first surprise. "Chris? But she was always tagging after Russ."

I hesitated ever so slightly. "Well. It didn't work out. They have a baby—Chris and Dal. Little boy named Ronny."

"But what about you? If he dropped her, why didn't *you* move in?—you're the one that was hopelessly in love with her." Watching my face she burst out in that hard, bemused laughter. "Oh, you're too fantastic, all of you! Incorrigible romantics..."

"Yeah," I answered flatly, "we're all terribly naive. I told you that once. Remember?"

The hawkfaced major leaned forward then and said, "Kay, I think we ought to be moving along."

"Of course, Adrian." She touched his arm in that possessive way of hers. "George, this is Adrian Hughes, he keeps everything running smoothly for us."

"Major." I saluted powerfully.

"Sergeant." His eyes passed over me, vaguely disapproving, slid away.

"Adrian's positively fabulous—we were the first group into Paris, the day it was liberated. Were you in Paris, George?"

"No," I said. "No Paris."

"What a shame. You should have been there—it was fantastic! Girls throwing flowers all over the tanks and jeeps, climbing up and kissing the GIs, handing around bottles of wine... and then a one-armed man in a beret began to sing the *Marseillaise*, using a wine bottle for a baton, and we all joined in, everybody in the whole Place de L'Opéra, and people laughing and kissing each other—a whole new beautiful world being born, right before your eyes! Wasn't it wonderful, Adrian?"

"A bang-up saturnalia, Sergeant."

"I can imagine, Major."

"I hope somebody got it on film, George, I really do. What a crowd scene it'd make!"

There she stood, her faultless face animated, the bullying, presumptuous beauty, in the tailored powder-blue suit with the First Division shoulder flash; as fresh and bold and alluring as ever—as though there'd never been a Salerno or Anzio or Castelfontana or Fréjus or Montélimar; as though Locatelli hadn't rolled back and forth in the mud, shrieking and moaning, or Tyne hadn't sat weeping, and weeping, and holding his head, or Dutch hadn't lain at the base of the plane tree near St. Durance holding his groin in both hands—Dutch, who'd held us all together, taught us everything, babied and bullied us, and who was indestructible, who couldn't be hit, who *couldn't* be...! At that moment, watching those gem-hard eyes of hers I could have smashed her face in, gutted her with a bayonet, without one single twinge of remorse.

"I can imagine," I repeated instead. "I'm so glad we were able to arrange it all for you. In our humble way, of course."

Her eyes narrowed, the crescents deepened; then the hard, triumphant smile. "Well, that's your job. Isn't it?"

"That's it. To kill Krauts, any way possible. So the high brass can waltz in and liberate the booze and the quiff."

"How vulgar of you, George."

"It's a vulgar war. You know?"

She pursed those sculptured lips. "Come now, George, you really don't need to play the rough, tough sergeant-with-a-heart-of-gold—not with me. This is Kay Madden, who knew you when you were a poor, frightened, small-town boy, in over your depth. Remember?"

"No act, Kay." I smiled now, for the first time. "No role. I'm the real thing. Still pure Skamondaga, New York."

"Kay," the major was saying, "we've really got to be moving."

"Of course, Adrian." Still she hung fire a moment, studying me. "Well, nice seeing you, George. Take care of yourself."

"I certainly will, Kay."

She swung away then, moved off toward the tents surrounded by her retinue: still the center, the object of all eyes—avidity, lust, and just plain sentimental longing; emissary of that gleaming, blatant power that had captivated a continent, dwarfed all its other deeds and dreams. Our Silver Screen. Our Golden Record. Watching her waving, blowing kisses to the GIs calling to her, waving back, I felt more despondent than I'd felt in all the sad and weary way since that last night in Cambridge _____

4

Hubba-hubba, Grog-o!

Somewhere in France is all I'm allowed to say, & at the rate we're moving that's about as accurate an address as I can swing anyway. Just when it looked as if we were going to re-enact Life in the Trenches, World War One style, somebody pulled the Big Plug & since then we've been ON THE LOOSE. What I mean. I haven't slept 2 nights in the same bed. & I *mean* bed. The accommodations 2 nights ago were in some French millionaire's summer spread, complete with canopied 4-posters, parqueted floors, some satirical (& deliciously pornographic) etchings—& a hidden (but not THAT well hidden) stock of flawless cognac. The night before that was a chateau on a river with a God damn DRAWBRIDGE (no shit) right out of *Ivanhoe* & coats of arms chiseled in the stone. Hot diggety Jesus. This may not be the safest way to tour Europe, but it sure as hell is the liveliest.

I do believe I've cornered the cushiest, plushiest job in the Div. The Old Man's been made Asst. Div. Cmdr., which means general trouble shooter and cook-&-bottle-washer extraordinaire, and I'm his aide. Captain R.G. Dalrymple, at your service. Yeah! It's hectic (I'm averaging about 4 hours sleep per night) but it's rewarding. The Old Man is TERRIFIC, I mean: he's everywhere at once, kicking asses, slapping backs, oiling the wheels, anticipating absolutely every problem & solving it. "The Army's like a business, Dal," he told me the other day, "a hell of a lot more than most people care to admit. Inventory, personnel, production, forecasts, distribution—you've got to keep on top of it all, one jump ahead of the other fellow or you'll lose your shirt. Only in this case it could be your ass." And he laughed that explosive laugh of his & we were off again. What a five-alarm ball of fire.

All right, I'm bragging again: but somebody's got to cure you of that overweening pessimism—that last letter was a crepe-hanger. I'm telling you, Groggy, it's going to be over before you know it. Jesus, the stuff we're throwing at them! Fuel dumps three stories high, ammo & supplies stacked in city blocks, tanks & 6x6s racked up hub-to-hub like the parking lot at Midway . . .

And then yesterday at 0600 we were practically blown out of our sacks by the roar of all the artillery in the western world. The Old Man wanted a look at the big picture & we took off in the plane & were treated to the most spectacular demonstration of raw power I could ever have conceived of in my most fantastic dreams. As far as you could see were tanks & smoking towns, & infantry moving on foot between the tanks. The armor would knife around the towns, the GIs would move in & mop up, & then push on again. On the horizon fighters & mediums were pounding away, & in the near background our artillery was sweeping woods, crossroads, anything that looked as if it might hold up the advance. The vast, impersonal power of infinite mass, channeled & deployed. It actually made you catch your breath—in a way it was beautiful.

Yeah, yeah, I know what you're thinking (Currier isn't the only son of a bitch who knows what somebody else is thinking). I've seen the other side of it too, pal. We've driven past the smoking, blasted houses, & the engineers working waist-deep in water trying to hold the only bridge against a flooded river, & the dead Joes still lying where the medics had tagged them & moved on. I've seen the sights. & I know if it weren't for you guys out there on the line we wouldn't be anywhere. I hate the whole business—I mean when I stop long enough to think about it (which I don't, very often); but at times I can't help but be overwhelmed by it. It's big & it's important; as Currier would say, it's history, & we're part of it.

Does any of this make sense? Probably not. Blame it on the cognac I've been nipping since 2300. Anyway, when the Big Hammer fell, & we HAD to change our college routines so radically, HOW we faced the changes is the name of the game. Sometimes I think the war may have been the saving of us—it's taken all the old empty rituals & given them a direction, a force... or it can.

It's funny, the goofy things you find yourself doing sometimes. Example: couple weeks ago we'd just come in from 12 straight hours checking battery dispositions in a driving rain. We were set up on the 2nd floor of an old mansion that had been worked over a bit: leaks in the roof, walls buckling in. Poor tactics, I know, but we'd been out in the rain for three days off & on, & the Old Man said, "Screw tactics, we're going to be comfortable," & I said, "My idea exactly, General," & we moved in. Ed Blake, who's almost as good a scrounger as your old roomy, had come up with a steak & was broiling it in the fireplace, & I'd uncovered some cognac and champagne & was dealing out French 75s, & Ruekuyser, the Old Man's batman, got the generator set up just in time to catch Big Band Serenade on the Armed Forces Network out of Paris. & it was a groove, as Chris says. & 1 thing led to another, & before long we were offering a few toasts here & there, to Ike, FDR, Dorothy Lamour, Chris, Bob Hope, Lena Horne, Chris, Ann Sheridan... at which point some Luftwaffe characters began to circle & drop flares right over town. There was a slight pause, but right then Peggy Lee started to sing *Why Don't You Do Right?* and the Old Man said, "The hell with it. I'm staying right here." "Absolutely," I said. So I got up to propose a toast to the Fusiliers & a bomb hit fifty yards down the road and half the windows blew in, plaster raining down & dust boiling up everywhere, & the Old Man was on his feet like a cat with his hand rotating around his head, roaring "Follow me!" & we all rushed the stairs en masse. No more toasts. Not that night.

Hey, but I've GOT to tell you about the Dreamboat. She's a converted weapons carrier, & she's our pride & joy. She idles at about 65 & features 3 mirrors, a siren, an extra tire rack & fender flaps; & tomorrow we're going to look up this contact I've got over in ordnance & get a .30 cal. mg mounted on her. She's no Empress, but she's a honey in her own right. I'll send you a snapshot of her when I get one.

Wasn't that V-record from the girls a gasser? Personally I think they were slozzled to the eyeballs. Mel's still grinding away at premed, Terry seems to be as well as can be expected in that fucking Stalag. & I got a *letter from Currier,* who's apparently rotting away on a tin can west of Pago Pago. Funny, isn't it?—the only one of us obsessed with dreams of High Adventure winds up in a backwater of the Pacific.

Ronny is WALKING. Yeah! Chris says he is left-footed, ambidextrous, & a great big tease. So you can see he's a real slice off the old ham.

Anyway, we're rolling. Won't be long now, Grog. Hang in there. Be good: & if you can't be good, be careful: & if you can't be careful—well, shit, name it after me anyway...

Jumpin' Jive in '45,
Dal

Dear Sarge—
There is this bed I'm holding down, my right leg derricked high in the air with block and tackle like a great white club, and right above my head a monkey bar I zealously pull myself up on 50 times a day. Another bed on my left holding a guy named Hannon, who has very bad burns, and another on my right with a guy named Klein, who can't use either of his hands. Beyond him a window, and outside it a kind of tree I've never seen before with the most beguilingly beautiful, feathery drooping green foliage that sways in the warm wind, in which two little blue-and-orange birds bob around, chirping happily to each other. And that is all I know about.

Remember what I said a couple of letters and 3,000 years back? about dues being rendered and payable? Well, they were rendered, and I've paid up. Not in full—plenty of other guys have done that. Plenty.

But enough to last me quite a while.

It seems we got caught with our pants down. Or somebody did. They say... well, they say a lot of things. Some day I'll tell you about it. (Not tho' the sailor knew, etc.) There we were, screening the jeep carriers off Samar, in support of the Leyte amphib force. Routine stuff—minesweeping, sub reports, interminable battle stations, no sleep. The usual. And then it came in from SOPA. I was on watch at the time, I took the message:

ENEMY SURFACE FORCE... 4 BBS, 7 CAS, 11 DDS... SIGHTED 20 MILES NORTH... AND CLOSING AT 30 KNOTS.

Yes. Old Giggles Carnwright, the OD, looked at me as if I'd just tweaked his nose for him. *"Battleships!*—You sure of this, Currier?" "Yes, sir. It just—" "Confirm. Confirm!" and in three hops and a skip he was in the Old Man's emergency cabin calling, "Captain! Captain, you'd better hear this..." Outside the blinker came back at me. CONFIRMED... SHIPS HAVE PAGODA MASTS. The Captain came in, rubbing his face with a towel, his hair all sticking up on one side of his head, and glared at the chart table. "Kurita. Came on through San Bernadino after all... But where the hell *is* everybody? Where's the heavies? Aren't they out there?" I'd never seen this expression on his face before, not even the time we got hit by a shore battery off Wokai Point. No one said anything. A long, long moment, with the *Jenny* rolling gently in the swells, and the morning sun glittering on the sea like scattered diamonds, and the water-color smudge of a rainsquall rolling toward us from the southeast... and then without warning the blasting, sonorous nasal of the TBS, and we all jumped:

"Leopard to all kittens, Leopard to all kittens: Small boys make smoke. Prepare for torpedo attack. Big Tom to lead. Get the big ones. It's all yours. Good luck."

"So that's how it is," the Captain said. Then his expression changed again. His eye caught mine, he said, "So you've been bitching for a surface action, have you, Currier? Well, here it is. With bells on."

Out of nowhere. The whole Japanese fleet, and nobody to stop them. But us chickens. The jeep carriers off our port quarter sending up planes any which way, ass-over-teakettle, making smoke, racing away south... and now overhead that pulsing freight-train rumble (you will be familiar: only you've never heard 14- and 16-inch salvos, dad: it's like celestial wings swooping down)—

Well. We went in. Four destroyers and six destroyer escorts, against the giants—zigzagging, flank speed, sneaking in and out of the rain squalls. We closed to 4,200 yards and fired one spread, closed to 3,600 (!) yards and fired another; put fish into two heavy cruisers, our 5-inchers got hits on a Kongo-class wagon, and they couldn't touch us, couldn't depress fast enough. The Captain called: "Full right rudder. Come 2-2-5. All engines full," and stepped over to the TBS and said, as if he were in a barbershop discussing the Red Sox: "Alleycat to Leopard. Exercise completed."

And then we began to take it.

It's funny now, lying here and thinking back: of that whole terrible morning I can only remember bits and pieces, tableau-flashes like camera stills. No sequence, no causality. Which is funny for a joker who's always prided himself on his fabulous memory... a towering plume of boiling water five stories high, so close you could reach out and touch it, and the *Jenny* heeling over crazily, I thought for a second she was going, the whole bridge and forward stack streaming bright yellow from the dye in the burst shell... Lt. Smolka, the gunnery officer, the glasses jammed against his eyes, calling: "Jackpot, jackpot, baby—beautiful! Now *hold* it in there!"... a shattering explosion aft, and the #4 gun, turret and all, tumbling upward and upward like a shattered gray box, the whole fantail, ash-can racks and all, a mass of smoking, twisted wreckage... the blinker on the *Piersall* starting to flicker at me erratically: RUDDER JAMMED HARD LEFT... STAY CL—and then a blinding white flash dead amidships and the blinker went out, and slowly flags began to climb the truck through the fire and smoke. LOST POWER... MY SPEED ZERO... WOUNDED REQUIRING MEDICAL ASSISTANCE... Big Westlund scowling at the wheel, his face rigid with perplexity, saying, "She won't answer, Captain—I've *got* her as hard over as she'll go!"... Strickland, the talker, his voice shrill and very earnest, as though answering a very difficult oral exam question: "After engine room reporting, sir. Bad fire, steamlines burst, badly buckled plates, engine-room flooding rapidly. Three dead, five wounded—"... The Captain saying with just a trace of irritation, "All right then, jettison it! Disarm all tubes," and then turning away, peering through his glasses and singing lustily, *"You took the part that once was my heart, so why not, why not take all—of—me?"*

And then the world blew all apart. It's the only way to describe it. It was like being at the very heart of an erupting volcano—no, it was more like sitting inside a prodigiously big boiler—a boiler the size of Harvard Stadium, say—that has just burst. I was lying jammed tightly against the edge of the pilot house, holding a fire extinguisher, my knees drawn up to my chin. I couldn't see anything, hear anything; then I could. Everything was shattered, battered, flung apart. There was no port bridge wing. None. One moment Lt. Walsh and Dorker were standing there; then they were gone, and so was everything else. Strickland was on his face on the deck, shivering, his whole body shivering, and an absolutely impossible amount of blood was streaming away under him down the slanted deck, mixing with that crazy lemon yellow dye and the water from the near miss earlier. The Captain was hanging to the binnacle, his cap gone, ribbons of blood streaking his face and neck. He was looking at me angrily—it was the first time I'd seen him looking really good and pissed off since that sub surfaced and almost rammed us coming out of Moapora Inlet. And I simply stared back at him. I couldn't seem to do anything else, I couldn't seem to take it in, somehow; what had happened.

Then the Captain said: "Currier. You're talker." I said, "But Strickland—he needs help, he—" and he shook his head at me as if I were some kind of wilfully disobedient pupil and said: "The ship. You're talker now. *Currier.*" And I said, "Aye, Captain," and got up in a kind of loony trance and took the headphones from Strickland, getting the blood and dye all over my hands and face. And there was another explosion somewhere amidships, and a near miss right off the port bow that almost took her over, and for a while—thirty minutes, five minutes, sixty hours—I was talker, receiving the mounting torrent of disasters, fires and explosions and ruptured lines and flooding, flooding, flooding, and relaying the Captain's orders. I have no distinct recollection of anything I heard or said. Fantastic. And all this while the Captain and Westlund wrestling with the wheel, on manual now, and Lt. Smolka propped against the flagbag fumbling with his belt, trying to tie off a leg at the thigh only he couldn't do it because one arm looked as though it was nearly severed, too, and only the Number Two 5-inch was still firing in a slow, faltering rhythm, like a funeral gun...

And then, some time along then, there was a terrific detonation below the well deck and a pillar of pure-white flame and the ship gave an awful, shuddering leap that sent us all sprawling and then fell back again, and the deck began to slant impossibly, the sea rising toward us like a bubbling, heaving black wall. And the Captain said, "Magazine. I was afraid of that," as though someone had just pinched his wallet, and wiped his face on his sleeve. "Well. I guess that's it." Still he stood there a moment, passing his eyes over the whole smoking, crashing, boiling junkyard that had been the stacks and superstructure, and then gazing, his lip slack with contempt, at the smoke-smeared silhouette of a Jap cruiser, her guns still sparkling in continuous fire. "Thought we'd be easy, did you, Mr. K? Well..." Then he said crisply: "Currier. Pass the word. Abandon ship. Abandon ship, all hands." I said, "No power, Captain," and at the same moment Westlund dropped his hands from the wheel.

"All right, then," the Captain said. "We'll just have to—" The #2 gun was still firing, and he said crossly, "Currier, go forward and tell those people to knock off. We're going to be swimming in minutes." I said, "Aye, sir." The ladder was slanting forward through a forest of tangled steel and fires and broken bodies. It was awful. Awful. I'll spare you the details—you've been there and back again. I know. But talk of Dante—this was no Second Ring. This was Ring Seven, complete with sound and color. Oh, yes. Something came down right behind me like an elevated subway platform, and from the hatchway came a terrible hissing, gurgling sound. All I could think was, Our *Jenny*, our swift, slim, beautiful *Jenny* we've worked on so many months, they've wrecked her, they've smashed her all to hell, the filthy murdering bastards. I've never felt exactly the way I did at that moment in all my life.

The steel door to the gun mount was hanging loosely, swinging and banging with the roll of the ship. Inside, in a smoke-blackened mass of shell casings and rags, figures were moving like drunks, like sleepwalkers. Giannelli, the whole side of his body black with burns, Murph with a towel wound around his head, someone I didn't recognize on his knees under the breech. "Murph!" I said, "abandon ship! She's *going...*" He turned and stared at me; his left arm was streaming blood which kept splashing on the brass shells. "Fuck you," he said tonelessly, and turned back to the gun. I remember thinking, *Why not?* just as clear as that, and I went in and helped him lift the shell and shove it into the breech, and slam it shut. I understood them, it seemed perfectly fitting, the most natural thing in the world. We got off one round and then there was a thunderous crash that seemed to come from right behind my left ear, and I was on the forecastle deck somehow, piled into the lifeline chains, and I started to get up and I couldn't make it, and I looked at my leg and I'd had it, I knew I'd had it then. And Christ, how it hurt! And big Gee got me over the side, I don't remember it, only the shock of the water, and trying to get away from the ship, trying to push the oil away, gagging and puking from the oil, there was so much *oil*...

Well. That's my story and I'm stuck with it. As Murph used to say. A hundred thousand light years later the *Jenny* went down stern first, boiling and booming and hissing, holding her chin up till the last, like the proud old girl she was, and taking with her among countless other objects precious and trivial a couple hundred pages of an absolutely illicit, court-martial-offense journal of imperishable prose. Which just goes to show crime does not pay.

And so we lost—but we won, too. Because old fox Kurita turned back right after that, high-tailed it back through San Bernadino Strait. Right then—when there was nothing, absolutely *nothing* between him and the transports and amphibious stuff at Leyte Gulf. *Why???* They say he never knew Ozawa had sucked the BBs away north, that he thought the Leyte airstrips were operational when they weren't—they say we did our job so well he even thought we were light cruisers (!), part of mighty 3rd Fleet and not the lowly little escort we were... And so we stopped them. A faint echo of Thermopylae, and Shiloh. Was it? A part of history—a fragment of a footnote. But it isn't what I thought it would be, any of it. Not remotely, dad.

It's such a bitter thing, to lose your ship. Like part of your body cut away. You feel useless, superfluous, only half a man. I see it now—the ship *was* us, all of us, in some mystical, all-embracing way no one who hasn't been in a ship's crew could ever hope to understand...

Yeah, I got the V-record, but I never had the chance to play it—and now it's moldering away, down in the deep six. Funny, where everything winds up: plans, dreams, memories...you get morbid, lying in sick bay—you feel so frail and fragile, at the mercy of things.

Well: nothing to do now but lie around waiting to mend, and get another ship. It *is* going to go on forever, isn't it? Your friends fall all around you, the flies bite, the wheat is full of weevils, your armor rusts, and Troy never falls. For God's sake, take care, Groggy. Maybe the glorious Tausendjahre Reich *will* collapse by Xmas—in which case you can come on out here and help us wear down pleasing honorable Nippy-Nips. Suiting you?

Sun & fun in '51,
Horatio Nelson Currier

————Jeep engines; you couldn't be wrong about that, even now; drawing nearer swiftly, snorting their way along the rutted, frozen surface of the road. They sounded strangely hollow in the fog.

"Jeeps," I muttered to Opp. We were lying in the light snow at the base of a thicket. Just below us the road forked left and right—to where? to Bodeaux? to Werbomont?—and less than fifty yards away, at the base of a hill, stood the stone farmhouse I'd been watching through the glasses for the past five minutes.

"Jeeps," I repeated. Opp nodded once, mutely; but when I got to one knee he clamped a hand on my shoulder and said: "Wait."

"What the hell for? We'll get the word—we'll hitch a ride, for Christ sake."

And then the jeeps burst into view around the curve in the road, out of the shoulder of the pines, and I saw the helmets; and my guts gave a lurch of sick fear. Opp pulled me flat with one violent jerk of his arm. The jeeps swung in near the farmhouse. There was a command, and two men jumped out and ran forward briskly with two others covering: an automatic deployment, no waste motion, superbly professional. Nine of them. A big man had a Spandau and belts draped all over him, and there was a field sergeant with a Schmeisser in the second jeep. The two lead men had reached the doorway now, one on each side. The first man ducked in and back, then went in, followed by the other. The only sound came from the jeeps' engines, idling. I could see the Division's markings on their hoods. In a moment the two men were out again, their weapons hanging loose in their hands.

"Rein garnichts," one of them called, his voice thick in the cold, sullen air. "Ausgebaggart."

They trotted back to the lead jeep and climbed in, and there was a brief argument, with much pointing. So they're lost too, I thought, hating them; my heart was pounding so it blurred my sight. The desire to shout curses, weep, open fire, throw down weapons and helmet and walk out into the road, get it over with, any way at all, was overpowering.

There were two more exchanges which the Feldwebel ended abruptly. "Na mach!" He pointed to the left fork, southwest, a blunt peremptory finger. "Los, los damit!"

The gears clashed savagely, the lead jeep bucked and coughed, one of the riders laughed. Then they moved off down the road, rocking and slewing on the slick.

I got up then, pounding my hands against my thighs. "Let's get out of here. I still say we take the right hand one."

Opp rose without a word and we went on, toward the northwest, in the direction we hoped and prayed was Ferrières, keeping at the edge of the woods now, well off the road. It started to snow again, fitful swirling bursts that stung our faces. My shoulder was hurting me. Somewhere back there this way there must be Regimental Headquarters, or Division or Corps or somebody; *some* part of the God damned American Army in Europe. Opp's trench foot was worse; he was hobbling frankly now, his whole body heaving and sinking every time he came down on it. The fog kept lifting and settling and lifting again, like a Grade B horror movie, the pines themselves seemed to move, dancing toward us and back, forward and back, a madman's minuet.

A while later—ten minutes, an hour—deep in the woods across a ravine we heard a voice calling: "Harry! Hey, wait up, will you? *Harreeeee!...*" and then the blurred, shuttling yammer of a Spandau and the voice stopped calling. We hurried on faster now, slipping and skidding on the hard, slick ground, glancing back over our shoulders every few steps, while the road curved away northward, between steep little hills, heavily wooded. Cruel country, all rocks and ridges, impenetrable. The cold was worse: it seeped into your vitals and clung there, sluicing along the marrow of your bones until your teeth chattered uncontrollably and your head shook like a palsied old man's. I'd pulled a pair of gloves from a dead T5 near Aunais; they were worn through at the fingers but they were better than nothing. Even walking fast, slamming your boots on the winter earth, your feet stayed numb. If only we had something to eat! Anything...

On a little ridge we sat down behind a fir tree, out of the wind, and Opp checked the compass again.

"What do you make it?"

He shrugged. "Beats me... we've got to hit the river sooner or later, we keep going this way."

"Where the hell *is* everybody? Have they all been overrun?... We've bought it," I said a moment later. "We're not going anywhere."

He studied me a moment, askance. He looked wolfish and gaunt, with the cut over his eye and the dirty red stubble of beard. "You better watch yourself," he said tightly.

"What do you mean by that?"

"I saw you, back there. You took your own sweet time taking cover—I had to *pull* you down..."

"You're full of shit," I muttered. "Let's go."

No warning, I thought fretfully, desperately, tramping on under the massed pines. Out of nothing. Nothing! Only the day before we'd been back in reserve, lined up in the gray fog in front of the battalion field kitchens, the replacements grabassing around, talking about Christmas, talking about Liège... and there had been that mutter of engines from over on the Baugnez road, a deep, premonitory rumble that swelled to the barking clatter of tanks moving fast; several of us had set down our messkits, listening.

"Bolling's TDs," Opp said. "Hitting the road. The glory-humping cavalry."

I said: "I thought they moved out yesterday."

"Well: you ever know anything to get done on the same day, Vird?"

The jeep came by then, tearing along the road at the end of the long field; a staff jeep, its fishpole antenna whipping crazily; it was full and three more were clinging to the frame. Two of them had no helmets, one man was wearing a skivvy shirt only.

"Ya-hooo!" Ramsey yelled at them. "Save me a snort of that, will you?"

But they raced on down the road, heading west toward Stavelot, all of them staring rigidly ahead; not one of them turned and looked at us.

"For Christ sake..." DiLeo's mouth was full of food. "What's the matter with those guys?"

And then all at once there they were, on the road near the woods' edge, rocking and rumbling, their flanks shiny and black against the snow, their guns swinging toward us casually—tanks such as we had never seen before, and DiLeo was screaming: "Kraut!—they're *Kraut!*" and then everything splintered into tumbling kaleidoscopic pieces without plan or purpose. Somewhere a squad cooker soared into the air, turning lazily end over end; a tent went up like a writhing green torch, and figures inside it, all on flame too, capered and danced; Ramsey was standing on a weapons carrier firing a mounted 30-caliber, crying to us, "Take off! Take off, now!" and a second later there was a mountainous sunburst flash and the weapons carrier bounced like a blackened toy and there was no 30-caliber, no Ramsey anywhere at all; something flung me into a stack of pallets so hard I thought my shoulder must be broken; and later there was a ditch into which I threw myself, where Lieutenant Burroughs, looking scholarly and intense, was methodically firing his carbine and telling me to pull everyone back, we couldn't begin to hold them, pull everyone back—and an instant after that his right eye was a dirty, blackened hole streaming blood, welling up and streaming, and the fingers of one hand clawed at the chill mud, clawed and released in furious, quivering little rhythms; we made the woods, then, where the roots of trees twisted over the hard ground like broken arms and legs, and Breithoff was holding his legs and shrieking, and behind me Jilkota and Phillips were out in the clearing hurrying back toward them with their hands clasped behind their heads, and I yelled at them but they kept walking, jerkily, toward the tanks until the machine guns caught them and they both went down together, out of sight.

I emptied the last magazine I had, threw away my Tommy gun and somewhere picked up a BAR from a PFC I'd never seen before. I tried to do the best I could but it wasn't enough. I couldn't seem to pull myself together. I was all right when I knew I was going up on the line, when I could get set for it, even when the planes and 88s worked us over at night... but this!—no warning, no chance to set yourself—it pulled me all apart. I just couldn't cut it, and that was all there was to it. DiLeo was hit in the gut and we tried to carry him and he began to scream with the pain, and we didn't have anything to give him, and we couldn't carry him anyway, we had to leave him there in the snow; and there were the tanks again, still coming on, crushing thickets and snapping trees; Walt Dillon hit one with a bazooka, a perfect shot right at the base of the turret, and there was nothing, a black smudge on the gleaming iron, and the tanks kept coming on, and I shouted at Walt to get out of there, but he stayed, firing and firing at the lead tank until it moved right over him, shuddering; and I ran and fired and ran again until red streaks raced across my eyes and my mouth was full of rotten brass; across a road with telephone poles canted like the masts of foundering ships, along a hillside of scrub oak that tore our faces, through firs massed dark as death...and here it was a day later, and there were just the two of us, Opp and I, cringing and creeping through a wilderness of drifting fog and slick, snow-masked rock, and I hadn't kept them together, I hadn't pulled anyone back at all. And always, behind us, beside us there was the sharp, barking clamor of tanks like tractors working some nearby ghostly field...

Behind me now Opp stumbled, fell to his knees. I hauled him up with my good arm, and he stood there a moment, blinking, leaning against a tree, one knee bent, balancing the bad foot on the toe of his boot.

I said: "Can you make it? with that foot?"

"Never mind my foot!" His eyes flashed at me savagely, flickered away again. "I don't know what *your* plans are—" he began, and stopped.

"I haven't *got* any plans," I said sullenly.

"I'll tell you this, they're not going to round *me* up, Virdon. You can do anything you want to—"

"What the hell are you talking about?"

"—they're not going to shove *me* behind the wire, get their rocks off working me over..."

"All right, *all right*," I nearly shouted.

We checked the compass again, mutely, and plodded on; a furtive, blundering, hopeless business. Past another fork in the road—which way now? west or north?—past a turned field like frozen white waves, through more woods. The trunk of every tree seemed to shift subtly; bits of light kept flashing away from the corners of my eyes. What I absolutely could not rid myself of was the sense that someone was right there behind me, taking slow, deliberate aim at a spot at the base of my skull; just under the rim of my helmet. My shoulder was a cold bar of pain so solid I could hardly think of anything else. Twice more we heard tank engines, on our right now, and veered away. There was no sense checking them out, we knew whose they were.

"To come to this," I said, or thought I said. I realized I was perilously close to weeping. After all this deadly, weary way. Salerno, and the first sick shocking awareness of our own pathetic mortality; and then the long, wet agony of Anzio, and the pitiless indifference of the gods of artillery and chance, the uncaring, capricious swoop of death. Some lived, some died, and all the valor or craft in the universe didn't matter. And after that the Dragoon landing and the headlong rush up the Rhone Valley, the crazy, haphazard clashes with overrun Wehrmacht units, and then the link-up with the Normandy armies and the drive to the frontier in the clear, winelike autumn days, when it did seem as if the war might—impossibly, miraculously—be over by Christmas...

And now, out of nothing, this.

What was the sense of it? in hanging on? We'd paid our dues. We'd given it everything we had, taken our patrols, wire parties and assaults—done every filthy thing they'd asked of us and more besides. Arduously, grimly, we'd learned the lessons they'd never taught us at Bragg or Tarleton: we'd cut our overcoats to hip length for greater mobility, got rid of our gas masks, taped our dogtags so they wouldn't clink together and reveal us, filed a razor edge on our entrenching shovels to make digging faster, put cotton in our ears to deaden the roar of assault bombardments, tied condoms over the muzzles of our weapons in heavy rain; we'd found that leaving dirt on you kept you warmer and less visible, that two light wool shirts were warmer than one heavy one, that burlap is the best of insulators; we'd learned where food—even cognac—was hidden in abandoned farmhouses. We'd taught ourselves how to check for booby traps, to master one another's different weapons, to cover one another, to trust one another utterly—and never, never to volunteer for anything. We had finally, painfully, agonizingly become professionals—as good, we felt, as the formidable professionals we faced. And now it was all undone. In a few, hideous hours we'd been smashed and scattered, we were running and hiding like petty thieves, quarreling, suspecting each other's motives...

What the hell, I thought, tearful and raging, I hung in there on the beachline at Salerno, I saved Locatelli's ass at Caserta, I took over the platoon when Dutch was hit at Montélimar; I did all right... But it wasn't any good, it didn't salvage anything. They'd broken through anyway, they were hunting us, cutting us down; they were still beating us.

Numb with cold, half-starved, I tried to think of Fox Entry days, of Russ in the hospital ward at Pearl, of Nancy, of Giulia, and most of all of Chris... but the trick wouldn't work. All I could think of now was Jean-Jean in the ditch near Louviers; now, now I understood. My God, why hadn't he struck us all dead that afternoon on the beach at Nauset? How could he have endured us?

Loyalties. I'd transferred my loyalties from Harvard and the Fusiliers to the squad, the platoon, the Division, without question or reservation. And now there *was* no platoon—and for all I knew no Division, either. Nothing was left but this deadly, swirling fog and fitful bursts of snow that stung like salt, and the numbing, aching cold that rooted itself in my very guts and made me still more desolate and afraid... Why hadn't they alerted us? An offensive of this size—Jesus God, hadn't they spotted *any* of it? or were they all too comfy in their hilltop chateaux with their titled cunt and their champagne to give a good God damn...?

The dense, massed barrier of the firs thinned and lightened then, began to break up. I slowed instinctively, eased up to the lip of the hill, raised the glasses—saw a little cluster of houses, the river like a dull silver band, a bridge with men moving on it. Men with our helmets. Ours.

"GIs," I said. "We've made it back. We've made it!"

We hurried down the slope and followed the road, the snow squeaking under our boots. I could see two men working under the bridge now, tying charges to the steel. One of the soldiers in the center of the bridge span called something, and a man broke off what he was doing and moved toward us and then waited, a Tommy gun in one hand.

I came up to him and said: "Jesus, am I glad to see you." My knees were weak with relief. "What's the scoop?"

He looked at me, then at Opp. He was a short, stocky man with a single silver bar painted on his helmet, and a growth of stubble. He had a short black empty cigar holder between his teeth. "What outfit are you?"

I told him. "They hit us at Reinanche—near Reinanche. We were in reserve, we didn't even know they were there until they opened up on us. You got orders to blow this? We heard tanks over there, somewhere." I pointed vaguely northeast. "About an hour ago. We've been walking all day and all night." It was absolutely impossible to stop talking. "We'll give you a hand, if you need it."

"You wouldn't have a couple Ks to spare, would you?" Opp asked him. "We haven't had anything to eat since yesterday—day before."

"You want to help us blow it," the Lieutenant said.

"Yes—sure. If you need a hand."

"I see." He looked down, rasping the edge of his boot against the planking—all at once brought the submachine gun up and pointed it at me. "What are you doing with those glasses, soldier?"

I stared at him. "Why—they're Kraut," I said.

"I know that."

"I took them from Burroughs. Our platoon leader. He got killed back there, at—"

"That a fact."

"Hey, what's the matter with you?" Opp demanded suddenly.

"Shut up." The Tommy gun hadn't moved. It was still pointed at my belly. I saw that two other men were holding rifles on us. "All right. Who plays third base for the St. Louis Cards?"

His voice was low, perfectly flat. I was gaping at him now. "The *Cards?*"

"That's right. Come on, answer it! And *don't move your hands.*"

Opp laughed once, harshly. "Spies—you think we're a couple of fucking spies, that it?"

"You see those three over there?" He gestured with his free hand. I saw three bodies on top of each other in the shallow trench by the side of the abutment, where they'd obviously been dragged and dumped. Snow and dirt had caked on the blood, the green-gray hands and faces. "They wanted to help us, too. Only they didn't have any of the answers. Not the ones I wanted. You better have them, boy. The right ones."

"Look, Jack," Opp cried, "—you some frigging kind of nut or something?"

"Give me the answer."

This was bad. I couldn't remember. Third base. I *knew*, and I couldn't remember. All I could see were the Lieutenant's eyes, the web of fine red lines around them and the little white glint at their centers, and the barrel of that gun, big and round as a howitzer, the ugly snout with its flaring sights pointed straight at my belly. The three of them motionless, watching us, the others working in frantic silence below. This was crazy, we'd made it *back*, our own people—

"Look," Opp was saying in a wild, raging voice, "I'm a Yid, for love of God, a *Jew*, check my fucking dogtags—you think a Kraut spy is going to pretend he's a *Jew*—?"

"I couldn't say, fella. I couldn't tell you what a Kraut would do. All right. Now I'll—"

"—*Kurowski!*" I shouted, "Whitey Kurowski, for Christ sake! Marion at shortstop, Cooper behind the plate, Walker Cooper—Musial and Slaughter and Moore in the outfield—that satisfy you?"

"Okay." The Lieutenant lowered the weapon, looked away. "Okay. That's good enough." He waved once. "All right, Walsh. Give 'em a couple D-bars."

"—Oh no," I said, and now I had seized him by the collar before any of them could move, "oh no—two can play at this game! Who led the league in hitting?"

"Jesus, Vird," Opp muttered.

"No, come on!"

The Lieutenant grinned at me around the black cigar holder. "That's easy. Dixie Walker. And Boudreau in the American. Give 'em some chow, Walsh. They look like they can use it. All right, Sergeant," he said to me now, all business, impersonal, as if the last few minutes hadn't ever existed, "take that BAR and set up over there on the other side. Back of that break in the wall, see it? We may need cover."

"All right," I said. My legs were trembling badly, sweat was streaking my neck and sides. Opp handed me a piece of D-bar and I bit into it, the hard, sour chocolate, and swallowed. My teeth ached so I grunted.

We'd just started across the bridge when we heard them: the terrible flatulent barking clamor. For an instant we all stared at each other, our mouths open.

"Drabic!" the Lieutenant called. "How much more time you need?"

"Half an hour, maybe," a voice beneath us answered.

"Well, you haven't got it. Come on! You'll have to shoot what you've wired."

"You're the doctor."

"Come on *out* of there, now..."

Drabic came up from under the bridge, his pants soaked. The tractor clatter was louder now, higher in pitch, as though the tanks had somehow sensed the bridge, their threatening nearness to it. We ran across the worn planking and up the road past the burned shell of a building, and threw ourselves down behind the break in the wall. I snapped down the legs of the gun and set up quickly. It was a good field of fire. I could see the road curving away to the south under the plane trees, the row of houses, barred and shuttered, the wooded hill we'd come down earlier. Opp handed me another piece of chocolate and I ate it slowly, turning it over in my mouth several times before swallowing. It had stopped snowing and the fog had lifted, though it still lay in milky patches over the river. The water swirled blackly around the stone piering of the bridge.

And then there they were again, pushing out from the curve in the road below the hill, looking brighter against the backdrop of the pines; immaculate and gleaming, unassailable, led by an armored half-track. And the disconsolate fear rushed back into my chest and guts again, redoubled. Down below us the Lieutenant threw up his arm, then pumped his clenched fist up and down, up and down, and they came scuttling back toward us while Drabic crouched behind an overturned cart, feverishly cranking the handle on the exploder. If she didn't go, if she didn't go right away, ah God, let her blow now, *now*...I was praying now, almost audibly, watching the oncoming armor, counting them: five, six, seven—

There was a deafening, reverberant roar, black smoke boiled up from a violent orange geyser, and we cringed as bits of stone and steel rained down around us. I raised my head. The dust was clearing, the smoke drifted lazily away northward; the bridge was down in the river except for a single girder which was sagging between the piers, swaying delicately back and forth. I could have wept for sheer gratefulness. The Lieutenant cursed, cursed again.

"No problem," one of the engineers said. "You couldn't get across that with a bicycle."

The tanks came on swiftly, their hatches open, their guns swinging here and there like great rigid snouts. The command half-track was flying a bright little orange pennant at the end of its antenna.

"Christ, what *are* they?" I muttered. "What *are* they?"

"King Tigers," the Lieutenant said. "With those good old 88s. Something old, something new. Give me the glasses."

"No," I said. "They're mine." For some silly reason I'd have fought him for them. I added: "I'll be your spotter."

He gave me a funny look, then nodded.

"Hey, let's get out of here," one of the engineers said.

"Stay where you are," the Lieutenant ordered. "And no firing unless I say so. Pass it."

I raised the glasses. The commander of the half-track was clearly visible now. He was wearing headphones over a visored cap, his gloved hands gripping the iron; a white, narrow face. Smoke and dust were still rising from the explosion, mingling with the drifting skeins of fog. The command car stopped about fifty feet from the wrecked bridge. The commander glared at the stream, then raised his eyes until he seemed to be looking directly at me—all at once struck his fist once against the hatch coaming.

"Missed the bus, did you, Kraut-face," the Lieutenant said. "Beat your fucking meat..."

The commander turned then, making hand signals to the armor behind him, and I saw the black uniform, the twinned lightning-flashes on his collar.

"SS," I murmured. "Waffen SS unit."

"That a fact. How many you make it?"

"Eight—no, nine."

The tanks had fanned out, flanking the half-track, making a kind of screen before the bridge. The commander jumped down from the car and shouted orders, and infantry riding behind the turrets began dismounting from some of the other vehicles.

"What's up?" Opp said.

"Don't know."

More men were in the road now, moving behind the tank screen. They were beating on the doors of the houses. We could hear thumping, a few scattered shots. In a moment I caught glimpses of people coming out into the street: several women and children, an old man in an overlong black coat and beret.

"What are they doing?"

"I can't tell, can't make it out—"

Then I could. Framed by the gleaming iron the commander

was shouting at them. He moved out of sight, reappeared again in front of a young woman with a blue kerchief over her head. He was still shouting, leaning forward from the hips; his arm swept back toward where we were lying on the slope across the river, pointed to two men carrying machine pistols. I could read the pantomime easily enough. How many of them are there? five? ten? Why didn't you stop them? It's your bridge they have destroyed, and you let them do it! A handful of frightened Yanks, running from us, still running like rabbits, we are winning this war now and you did not help! I should have you shot, I could, do you realize that? I could see his mouth gaped wide with rage, his head pump as he made his points.

The woman spat in his face.

He struck her, again, again; short hard blows. She fell to her knees, then hands and knees and he kicked her where she knelt and she fell to the snow, and then tried to drag herself on all fours again.

"—going to kill her," I heard myself say loudly, "he's kicking her, he's going to—"

The commander had whirled around, was gesticulating to the two guards. He stepped back out of sight, and now the Schmeissers began their rippling, shuttling rhythm, brittle as glass shattered, and the little clump of people shook like a bush trampled, buckled and sprawled scattering and rolling away out of sight. And still the machine pistols went on firing, and now screams drifted back to us like children far away playing, like the yelping of pound dogs.

Someone next to me was cursing. I looked away wildly—saw Opp running his left arm through the sling of his M1 and the Lieutenant wrestling with him, shouting, "No! I said no!"

"Let me go!" Opp cried. "I'll kill the bastard, I'll *kill* him—"

"They'll blow the bunch of us to hell and back with one round—you crazy? Now, knock that off!"

Opp stopped struggling then, let go the rifle and looked at me; a look I remembered from Salerno. I gripped one hand inside the other and shut my eyes. The firing had died away now, into echoes and stray shots, like firecrackers, thin and harmless in the cold air. And the fog shut down like a filthy gray curtain.

All day we kept moving north by west. Two men from a disabled tank destroyer joined up with us, half a dozen jittery replacements from the 627th, and a tough little character wearing a Navy watch cap who was carrying a bazooka and five shells. And late that afternoon we found ourselves straggling up a narrow cut between high harsh rock walls. The fog was still heavier, walling out all sight and sense.

"This road ain't leading nowhere," one of the tank destroyer men said; he turned, spraddle-legged, and faced the Lieutenant. "Now don't shit me: you got any idea at all where you're going?"

"*Yes*, I know where I'm going," the Lieutenant snapped. "Up ahead is Mortellange."

"Big deal."

"And after that it joins up with the road to Sprimont."

"Double big deal."

"And after that, if you walk far enough, is Liège." The Lieutenant played the empty onyx cigar holder back and forth across his mouth. "That's what the Krauts want—Liège. Fuel and supply dumps there."

"How the hell do you know all this?"

"Because I know, that's why."

And right then, as if his words had conjured them up, relentless and omniscient, terrifying in the opaque white stillness, the pulsing tractor clatter came again. Behind me Opp made a sharp, incoherent sound. I glanced at him; his eyes flashed at me once, wildly, swung away. He hadn't said a solitary word to anyone since the bridge.

"That sounds like tanks," one of the replacements said in a shrill, hurried voice, "a lot of tanks."

"You noticed," the Lieutenant said.

"They got across," Drabic said tonelessly, looking at the road.

"Sure—somewhere else. You think that was the only bridge over the Amblève?"

"They're on this road," the same replacement said shakily. "Coming up this road," and another one of them cried, "Let's get out of here..."

The Lieutenant said: "Now you stand fast, you hear?"

"Screw that noise," the first replacement said, "we better break up and—"

"*No!*"

I turned. Opp was standing in the middle of the road, his rifle at his hip.

The exodus stopped all at once. The kid with the high, shrill voice said: "What the hell—?"

"I said no! Enough, by Jesus. Enough!" Opp looked gaunt, half-mad, his eyes like bits of cut metal under his brows. His lower lip was cracked and bleeding. "No more running."

"Opp," I said dully. "Opp—"

"Look, Mac," the Lieutenant said to him, "put it away, now. Let's get—"

"No—you look, big shot! Look at this place." Opp waved one hand along the steep black walls of rock. "All we've got to do is get the lead car, that armored half-track. And it'll stop them."

"Look, Mac," the Lieutenant said, "they told me to go up and blow that bridge and I blew it. Now all I want to do is—"

"Stop calling me Mac!" Opp said to him savagely. "My name's Oppenheim... I'm sick of it! Sick of running. Filthy SS bastards... No! We take out that command car and they're fucked—they can't get around it, they can't push it out of the way."

"But *tanks*—" one of the kids breathed. Far down the road the jittering clatter faded and swelled again, like a badly tuned radio.

"What's the matter—you think it's never been done before?"

The Lieutenant walked deliberately up to Opp; his Tommy gun was still slung on his shoulder, the cigar holder was sticking straight out between his front teeth. When he got right in front of Opp he stopped, his hands on his hips.

"Okay, Mac," he said, "let's drop the comedy. I'm giving the—"

"You're giving *nothing*—!" With one quick movement Opp jammed the muzzle of the M1 against the Lieutenant's belly. "*I* say it! I'm sick of this shit. This is the place to get them and you know it and I know it, and *this is the way it's going to be!*"

I could only blink stupidly, watching this exchange. I hoped the Lieutenant would take Opp's rifle away from him, I hoped Opp would shoot the Lieutenant, I hoped the whole fog-laden ravine would vanish, all of us included, into thin air. I didn't know what I hoped. Why the rest of us were all still standing there I couldn't imagine. I'd dropped out of any conscious response; I felt hate for the SS, fear of the tanks, guilt that I was still alive, shame that I hadn't done better back at Reinanche, loyalty to Opp—yet all this wash of emotions lay outside myself, as though some other chilled, famished, exhausted fugitive were feeling these things. What did it matter? The whole German

Army had fallen on us and G-2 hadn't even doped it out, or if they had they hadn't given a damn. We'd had it, we were all through...

"You want to run all the way to Paris?" Opp was saying between his teeth. "To Normandy? start swimming? You want to turn yourselves in, nice comfy POW camp in Breslau—you think they'll read you the Geneva Convention?—you *saw* what they did at the bridge! To civilians... No! We stop the scrimey bastards *right here*, and if you don't like it you can go shove it, you no-good gutless son of a bitch!"

The Lieutenant hadn't moved a muscle. He still had his gut jammed against the rifle muzzle; he was grinning a tight little grin. "Full of piss, ain't you?" he said.

There was the briefest of pauses. The tanks were definitely nearer now, coughing and barking.

"He's right, Wally, " Drabic said in a low voice. "It could work."

The Lieutenant stepped back then. "All right. You for it?"

"It's worth a try."

The Lieutenant nodded to himself. "All right. Suits me. What you got left?"

"Three satchels. But the problem is—"

"I know what the problem is. All right: we'll put everything on the armored car." He turned to the kid with the bazooka. "Can you use that thing?"

"You bet your ass."

"Okay. You take that side." He looked at me. "You set up on the other side, over there." Now for the first time since the quarrel he looked at Opp. "You want to come with me and Drabic?" Opp nodded. "All right. You people take cover up there, on both sides, and pour it on when the BAR opens up."

"You mean you're going to *stay* here?" the first replacement said. "You're crazy—you guys are *crazy*..." He had eased around where Opp had been standing, and now he was back-pedaling up the road, one hand out in front of him. "I'm getting out of here, I'm telling you!"

"Get your ass back here!" Opp shouted, but the boy had swung around, running, and vanished into the fog.

"Stay where you are!" The Lieutenant had the Tommy gun laid over on its side, cradled on his forearm, pointing at the others. "The rest of you stand fast, you hear? Or you take one in the ass!" They watched him a moment, fearfully; one of them started to say something, checked himself. "All right," the Lieutenant went on. "Let's get going." His eyes fell on me, then; snapping a thumb at me he said to Opp: "You trying to tell me *he'll* be any good?"

I put my hands in my pockets quickly.

"He'll be all right," Opp answered. "As soon as it starts." He threw me a look of exasperation, threat, appeal—I don't know what. "He's like that."

"Suit yourself."

The kid in the watch cap took the two TD men for help on the bazooka. I picked what looked like the quietest of the replacements and we all scrambled up both sides of the ravine, clawing at the gnarled clusters of scrub oak, sliding and stumbling on the loose rock. The roar of the armor was very loud now; I could hear the thin, craking squeal of the treads. I found a little natural V between a rock outcropping and some loose stone, ran down the bipod legs and got set up quickly. I decided to switch to a full magazine, but when I pressed the release the magazine didn't drop out and I had to yank it loose, which frightened me still more. Suppose I got a stoppage? It was so God damned *cold*. If there was condensation in the gas port—

"What's the matter?" the kid asked.

"Nothing. Nothing." I was shaking so badly now I dropped the fresh magazine in the snow, pulled out my handkerchief and frantically wiped it as dry as I could, as well as the receiver and guides. I ought to check out the ejector, I knew, but there wasn't time, there wasn't any time at all. I ran the operating handle back and forth several times and inserted the new magazine, praying the poor bastard had loaded it properly, whoever he'd been: and flipped the change lever up to full automatic.

"What do I do?" the replacement asked.

"Here." I handed him two magazines. "Slap these into my right hand when I tell you. And if I get hit she's all yours."

"Mine? The gun?"

"What the fuck do you think?" My head was trembling too, now; I knew I was making him even more scared than he was but I couldn't do anything about it.

"But I've never *fired*..."

"Well. It's like the M1."

"I never fired the M1. Not since Kilmer." I looked at him.

"I'm in cooks and bakers. They just came and got us and gave us rifles and put us in these trucks..."

"Well—" God help you, you poor son of a bitch, I thought; God help us all. Right now. "Just watch me. If she jams, pull the operating handle back and then forward. What you saw me do. Tap up your magazine, like this, and fire again—that'll probably clear it. But she won't jam. She won't jam."

He nodded rapidly, his mouth open. I looked away. Opp and Drabic and the Lieutenant were crouched behind a boulder 20-odd feet ahead of me, their helmets bunched together, and beyond them a kid was lying on his side, not using cover at all; I had the crazy idea he'd just been hit, his position was so strange; and then I saw that he'd frozen that way, his hands clamped across his chest, gripping his shoulders.

The engine roar was huge now, deepened by the fog, accented by the slithering, pulsing squeak of the bogies, as the tanks strained on the upgrade. Coming. They were coming now. Ahead of me the Lieutenant raised his palm toward me, his arm stiff, and I answered in kind, my hand wavering in the air.

"Sarge," the kid was saying in a thin, shrill voice, "you think we can stop them?"

"Of course, *of course* we'll stop them! Shut up!" Oh Jesus God, help me, I began to pray over and over, helplessly, oh help me now. But it was not for safety, I'd given up on myself utterly, I only wanted to get that half-track first. The sweat was running down into my eyebrows now, down the sides of my throat. I tried to swallow, could not. I thought of the scene at the bridge, the Belgian civilians wilting under the Schmeissers, and Dee lying in the snow looking up at me—oh God the look!—and Breithoff and Koonz and all the others I couldn't save, couldn't hold together after all this time and I said with scornful, raging despair, All right, now as good a time as any, good as any, fuck it, *fuck it all to hell*—yet even then I was swept with the feeling that someone else was doing all this, feeling all this, some perfect stranger lying here sweating and shaking on the cold rock, bound in measureless, leaping fear and sheer uncaring hate—

And then there it was. All at once, spawned out of the fog, its smoothly sloped hull and turret slick with rain, the terrible 88 with its bulbous muzzle-brake probing the mist. Tank. *A tank.* Not the armored car. Tiger leading. Oh no. Oh no Jesus no. The little orange pennant was flying at the end of its antenna now. It came on, shuddering and rocking; impossibly big, impenetrable, filling up the ravine. No Jesus. I wrenched my eyes away. The Lieutenant was glaring at me, swinging his hand, palm-down, back and forth, back and forth. I clamped my left hand over the small of the stock, pressed my cheek against the knuckles, lined up the narrow rectangular driver's port and opened up. She fired. I watched the quick, firefly dance of sparks on the slope plate just below the port and pulled down with my left hand, still firing, conscious of the turrent turning, the 88 swinging lazily toward me like some very clever, all-powerful being. The machine gun too in its snug little ball-turret was firing. But I was all right now. I ducked, reloaded—saw a bright yellow flash on the front slope plate and the tank rocked gently and came on again. Bazooka shell. A waste—it would never penetrate, he'd have to go for the treads. "Lower!" I screamed, knowing he couldn't hear me, nobody could ever hear me. The earth under my belly was vibrating from the armor. The 88 was swinging back now, toward the bazooka. I put ten rounds right into the driver's port; the tank stopped momentarily, started again. There was another flash on the skirt just above the righthand tread. The 88 fired then—an all-engulfing *whipcrack!*—then there was an onrushing dance of little geysers in the rock and snow in front of us and I pulled the kid down with me, cringing and gasping—raised my head again to see the tank still coming steadily up the draw, followed by the others.

All wrong. We were too high. The bazooka man couldn't get low enough. We needed to be underneath it, not above. Too late. They'd never be able to get the satchel charges down there. I saw Drabic poised in front of the boulder, reaching out awkwardly—then he swung back and down, clutching air, rolled out of sight. The tank came on again, flaming and grinding. I could see the massive towing bolts welded on the front plate, a series of Roman numerals stenciled over the driver's port, several cases of our 10-in-1 rations lashed to the side pannier. It was no good, no good, we couldn't stop them, couldn't get—

Someone was moving, sliding and skidding down through the brush. Opp. It was Opp. Down there on the road now, all alone, scuttling in toward the tank—he had thrown a satchel charge right in under the lefthand tread, another. There was a roar, a vaulting black geyser and the monster lifted and settled in a little sea of smoke and dust. Then slowly it thinned, sifted away uphill. The tread was lying in the road like a shattered conveyor belt; the tank kept beetling forward on the good tread until it was nearly at right angles to the road, the great gun muzzle jammed against the rock. In the ditch at the edge of the draw there was something. A shriveled mass of rags and pulp, a mashed scarecrow. Nothing else at all.

Oh you motherfuckers. You filthy no-good bastard bitches. Another bazooka shell hit the bottom of the gun mantle, and the 88 drooped forward drunkenly, then began to rise again, wavering. Hand-traversing now. *All right*. The turret hatch swung back, a figure came up bareheaded, the Schmeisser in his hands winking hotly. I hit him in the chest, the face, the chest, and he poured back down inside the hatch like gelatine. Another one rose up and I shot him too, another; and now men were coming up the road, clinging to the skirts of the following tanks, and I got them all, swept them away like maggots. One of them threw down his weapon and knelt by the treads with his hands in the air and I shot him too, reloaded and went on firing and firing, and a gun was trying for me and I stood up and ran right through another magazine and reloaded and still they wouldn't hit me. And then there was a deep, hollow explosion and white smoke began to seep out of the ports and the open hatch of the lead tank. And now they were backing away, the other tanks, backing off down the ravine, and someone was pulling at me and I was still standing there firing at them, and the magazine ran out, and the Lieutenant was pounding me on the shoulder, the one that hurt so, and shouting: "Hauling ass! We got it, *got* the fucker—! Attaboy, attaboy, all *right*, now!" and I was crying now, I'd grabbed him by the collar and was screaming in his face, "You lousy shit, he's worth ten of you, a thousand . . . !" and he was nodding at me and grinning that tight little grin around the black cigar holder, pounding and pounding me on the shoulder ⸺⸺⸺⸺⸺⸺⸺⸺⸺⸺⸺⸺

5

Dear George—

I've just come in from walking on the beach, and even though it's after 2 I'm still not sleepy. Hence this letter, which may or may not get finished tonight.

It was so beautiful on the beach just now. A full moon (well, almost) and everything silver: silver poured over the dunes and bayberry thickets and beach grass, trailing long quicksilver scarves across the water, sliding and glittering. Everything cold and still with winter. Nothing stirring except the sea itself. All that *life*. I walked and walked, my shoes crackling on the seaweed and bits of shell, watching the moon and the sea, and thinking how it really does unite us, keep us one: there is no barrier from this beach all the way to Cherbourg or Tokyo or Hamburg—only the barriers men have made.

George, dear. Prill Harms was here with me for three days—I told her to come over and stay. Mostly we just walked, or played with Ronny, or sat and watched the sea. She heard from Rhino's father. George—it's bad news, I'm afraid. Very bad. Rhino was killed on Iwo Jima. There must be some more graceful way to say this. But I can't think of any. And even if I did it would only come to the same thing: Rhino has been killed, Rhino is dead. Oh George, I hate to be the one to write this to you, especially where you are now (or where I think—no, I *know*—you are now). But I knew you'd want to know.

So victories everywhere now. So many victories—and all I can think of is Rhino, how big and quiet he was, that soft grunt of laughter when something amused him. How brutal and fearsome he looked in his football uniform, and yet how gentle he was—that special, delicate gentleness big men often have, I remember when I danced with him his hand on my back was less firm than anyone else's.

And after Bougainville, and Guam (he won the Navy Cross on Guam, did you know that?) and now that tiny little island with all its terrible caves . . . It seems so wrong—all a man should have to do is *one* battle, and then someone else should carry it on from there. That's pretty childish and unrealistic, I know, but where has all the maturity and realism got us? What has

[*The following two lines crossed out heavily, indecipherable.*]

Two days later. A mad gale, with tumbling, pounding surf and ragged snatches of cloud tearing by overhead, so low you could reach up and touch them (well, nearly), the gulls screaming at each other like bandits, lurching and flailing through the murk, the sickles of beach grass bent flat under the wind. Angry, warlike day. Ronny loved it, he kept racing up and down in his hooded red jacket like a sea elf, waving his arms and shouting back at the surf. The sea *is* like a child, isn't it?—the way it responds so swiftly and completely to the elements. Yet even in its fury it's so pure; as though it would like to rebuke us for all our calamitous, deadly ways . . .

Speaking of change: I got over to New York for a couple of days last month, and stayed with Nancy and Liz. The apartment's in a lovely old brownstone in the Village: large, airy rooms, the people you pass in the halls very friendly. New York is like a big, noisy family getting ready to move to another town—there's that same atmosphere of bustle and good-natured dissension and expectancy.

And you'll never recognize Liz and Nancy—they're both chic

career girls now! Liz is doing wonderfully at Pratt: I always felt she was the most talented of us, underneath that self-disparagement. Nancy likes her job with *Interiors*—she's started way down on the ladder but you can bet she won't stay there long. I felt like the proverbial country mouse! But we had fun (when we weren't thinking about you and Dal and the rest of the Fusiliers).

It does look as if it must be over soon. It must. Dal wrote me he's in Germany now, so I suppose you are, too. He took off one afternoon in the Dreamboat to look you up, but he couldn't locate you (small wonder); it happened to be just the afternoon the General needed him for something and couldn't find him—and when Dal got back he got a royal chewing-out. But he'd promoted several bottles of Bernkasteler Riesling along the way, so he told the General he was on a scrounging mission for *him*, and talked his way out of it! Dear, irrepressible Dal the Eternal Operator—wouldn't you just know? I miss him.

Oh George. I think of you so often when I'm walking the beach. Sometimes I think I can see you over there, talking to your boys, checking their rifles and packs. No one could be a better platoon sergeant than you are; no one. For God's sake now, be careful. You've done enough, and more than enough. Yes, you have.

And I did hear from Russ, at long last. A very flat, terse letter, not like him at all. Not that I blame him, really. Oh it's terrible, all of it. This *long*, cruel war. Only the Cape helps me get through this time. Looking up, when you see the moonlight washing that silver path across the sea, it's such a comfort to say to yourself, "At least we can't destroy *that*—that's our source, our origin, our true home: it will redeem us, wash us all clean again..."

Love, and be most careful—
Chris

Dear Grog:

Dig this jazzy letterhead, will ya? I tell you, those Nazi bigwigs really knew how to lay it on—eagles & swastikas & crosses, no wonder they began to believe their own press notices.

Well, so it's over, kid. Finally over, & I've got to say I've seen it all. Wehrmacht shuffling along in the dust, thousands & thousands of them, all of a sudden looking like a crowd of broken old Bowery bums. A Russian major at Steyermund with a build like Two-Ton Tony Galento who slapped my back till I thought I had asthma & made me drink half a bottle of vodka chug-a-lug (the old Fox Entry training stood me in good stead). Karl Rudolf Gerd von Rundstedt (who dat?) sipping brandy in a CP at Eschenbach & telling the Old Man & some other high brass precisely why the Great Ardennes Counteroffensive came a cropper. (I'd have given $500 if you could have been there to give old lizard-face the royal word.)

AND I've cruised all over this pretty little province of Hesse-Nassau in the Old Man's Packard Clipper (no Empress, of course, but it has its points) with its castles & farms & picture-postcard vistas, & my majority came through last month (how about THAT), & I've got an office with all kinds of oak paneling & Festung furniture, & I'm billeted in a fucking Schloss run by a gorgeous blond, blue-eyed baroness with a build like Lana Turner's who speaks excellent English (& French & Italian) & who can't, simply can't do enough for you, & the floors echo like gunshots & it has 15-foot mirrors & floor-to-ceiling tapestries of knights in armor & their everloving damsels clinging to them like glue...

AND I'm about as mixed-up & miserable & pissed off as a man can be. Impossible, isn't it? But it's true. I'm Military Government Officer for the area (big deal: nobody else *wanted* the effing job, that's why) & I'm trying to do the best I can, & it's simply not good enough. I'm just not cut out for it.

This problem of guilt, for instance. I know, I know, the Army circulars say they're ALL guilty, across the board: the whole nation backed Adolf, ergo they all ought to be punished. But that's a demonstrable crock & you know it, Grog, & so does anybody who THINKS about it with more than his anus. Is a 3-year-old kid guilty? is a World War I veteran with one leg? Who is guilty? who is NOT guilty? & HOW guilty?

Oh sure, the SS die-hard who's still trying to steal grenades—that's simple enough. Or the party official who left intact all the party records in the Rathaus at Saarbach. When they brought him in & I asked him why he hadn't destroyed the very records he must have known would incriminate him & others he answered: "Ah, but they were so perfect!" It's easy enough to be sure about the SS trooper (Leibstandarte unit) picked up in civilian clothes in Gensdorff who admitted (after questioning—& some rather rough working over—by CIC interrogators) nailing to a barn wall a Polish woman who had been knocked up by a German, & cutting the baby from her belly with a bayonet, & who passionately defended his action: her sin deserved the punishment—she had defiled a man of Aryan blood by sleeping with him.

Yeah. But what are you going to do about the tow-headed kid of 8 who bummed some chocolate from the Divisional G-3, & was caught booby-trapping his jeep the following night? or the farmer who never joined the Nazi party, who was even sentenced to 6 months & stripped of his property rights for speaking out of turn at an SA rally, & who has just been picked up in violation of curfew because he was trying to get help for his sick wife, he says—and maybe he was?

Oh hell, I know you know all this—or worse, for all I know. But you don't have to try to make some sense out of it all day. I don't know what *you've* seen, but I haven't found a single city that isn't the last word in destruction: Aachen, Stuttgart, Mainz, Frankfurt—you name it, we've done it. We took the leading industrial-technological nation & turned it into the World's Biggest Junkyard—& who's going to clean up the mess, get it running again? Answer: we are—unless we want to let the Russians do it by default.

And in the middle of it all, here we sit, in splended isolation. We've pounced on every remaining facility that's still functioning—country houses, resorts, swimming pools; we're doing nothing, absolutely nothing to help them rebuild. We simply sit astride them, in our sheer dead weight of numbers, & snap at them when they do something wrong. And of course no fraternization. Oh, sure. And they *are* fabulous, these Mädchen, I think you'll agree. Jesus H. When some luscious piece of cake trots in & starts pleading with you for a job on the staff, translator, secretary, file clerk, anything, just *anything*, it gets harder & harder to look the other way...

Finally I blew my roof about all this crazy chickenshit—& the Old Man promptly chewed me out. Royally. "You seem to have misunderstood your function, Major. You are not authorized to initiate policy for the Occupying Forces—nor question it either. Have I made myself sufficiently clear?"

What a reaming. But the Old Man's wrong, it isn't that simple . . . It was easy enough during the fighting, operationally I mean—you got the word & you took off, no questions asked, & got on it. You know. But here I am trying to play King Solomon & Oliver Wendell Holmes & St. Francis. It's ridiculous.

So, I'm putting in for redeployment. I can hear you blowing your stack all the way from Bad Hexenkirchen, & I can't defend it, can't even explain it really. I just know it's what I want to do. The Old Man will REALLY ream me out, too—but I'm going to approach him at a propitious moment when he's just come back from the Schloss, full of good will & Kraut wine. I'll work it, you'll see.

Hey, some REALLY good news: *Terry is OKAY!!!* Really, I mean. I twitched a couple of big wires (what's the sense of *having* influence if you don't use it?) & located him. He's in a Stalag in the Russky zone. He's been sick & has lost a lot of weight, but he's all right. I played around with the idea of a fast run to see him, but I'm chained to this fucking administrative crap (Rank Hath Its Burdens). It's a relief to know he's all right.

So it looks as if the four of us made it. So far, at least. Christ knows how long the Jap caper is going to take; personally I think it's nowhere near over—maybe a year, year and a half; & I want to be in on it, when they fold. Unless you want to give me some of your superfluous points, Grog-o. What the hell are you going to DO with all those points? (I know, I know, just what *any* beat-up GI would do, waa-waa.) Even with Ronny (12 HAPPY DIGITS—COUNT 'EM!) I'm still short. You wouldn't want to deal, would you? Tell you what, I'll trade you unrestricted use of a jeep & the address of an absolutely delectable Kraut broad named Hedwig for 20 points. Whaddayasay? Share the wealth...

And remember:　The angle
　　　　　　　　Of the dangle
　　　　　　　　Is in direct proportion to
　　　　　　　　The heat
　　　　　　　　Of the meat

　　　　　　　　　　　　　　　　Dal-Baby

Darling Darling DARLING!!!

It's over. Really and finally and unbelievably *over*, for good and forever. It seems impossible—even after all that's happened today I can hardly believe it. But it's real. Bells are still ringing here and there all over the city, and every once in a while a siren starts wailing for no reason at all, which seems to set off half a dozen more.

New York City went mad: stark, staring, raving, roaring MAD. It came in over the radio at the office, and we ran to the windows and tore up old files and phone books and newspapers and tossed them out of the windows until it looked like a blizzard in August. And Mr. Hines—his sons are both in the Pacific, one of them on a destroyer, like Russ—came out of his office carrying a bottle of very old Scotch he'd been saving for this moment, and made us all have a drink with him, and then he sent Jim Thompson out for some more, and people kept proposing toasts, and the racket got terrific, and finally Mr. Hines laughed and said, "Hell, nobody's going to get any work done today, and why should they? Go on out there, have yourselves some fun, and God bless you—" and suddenly he sat down in Sue's chair and started crying and grinning and shaking his head at us.

Well then Sue and I left the office and started walking over toward Broadway, and the crowds got heavier and heavier and by the time we reached Sixth Avenue it was fantastic. Everybody was kissing and embracing all over the place, total strangers, laughing and crying. A GI was standing under a marquee playing a clarinet, playing *Avalon*—Jean-Jean's tune, remember?—and another soldier and a girl were jitterbugging on the roof of a parked car, and all of a sudden a sailor who looked like Alan Ladd grabbed me by the hand and shouted, "Conga line! Conga line! Let's go, *let's go!*" and we went snaking across streets and around cars and fire hydrants and lampposts, and finally we went right into this hotel lobby and out again, people joining us all the way! And after a while I thought, This is crazy, this can go on all night, and I broke out of it, and took me another hour just to get downtown on the Fifth Avenue bus.

And I'd hardly got into the apartment when the phone rang. Guess who??? *Dal!* He'd put in for reassignment to the Pacific—can you imagine that?—and he'd just got into New York harbor that morning, and they wouldn't give them furloughs yet but they'd all got leave for the night. It was a bit awkward, my rooming with Liz, so I asked her how she felt about it; and she just laughed and said, "Sure, why not? Long as we don't indulge in any pick-up baseball games!" Liz is really terrific, nothing fazes her. She's burning up the track over at Pratt, you should see some of her designs—she's so creative, I wish I had one tenth her imagination and flair. You wait and see, she's going to rocket right to the top once the fabrics and materials start coming in again. She's already had an interview with *Mainbocher!!!*

Anyway, Dal came up for a drink. He's a *Major,* with all kinds of ribbons and decorations—even a French one! He looks different—I don't know, less hotshot, more serious. But he's the same old Dal. Afterward he took us both out to dinner at Keene's, and then to Café Society Downtown, and we heard Josh White and Lux Lewis, and we all got high as kites and phoned Chris at Woods Hole and jabbered at her all at the same time until the operator cut us off. And afterward he hailed a cab and we just drove round and round through Central Park, all the way up to that funny little frog pond at 110th Street and back down to the Plaza, round and round until it started to get light; and people were still out there roaming the streets, snake-dancing, singing...

But all I want to think about is you. Darling, where are you now, and what are you doing, and when are you COMING HOME?!?! Dal says you've got points enough for all the Fusiliers and then some, and I guess that must be true, you've been gone just a hundred zillion years. WHY can't they release you, and right away!!! I know, it's just that I'm half crazy with waiting, and I know you are too. Darling, phone me the minute you get in. I'll throw myself at Mr. Hines's knees, I'll quit my job, I'll hire a fireboat and sail it down the Hudson spraying water in lovely silver fountains in all directions—

Oh Darling, Darling, there's a great day coming, as the song says; and soon. I've just been living for the day you come home...

Love you love you love you,
Your Nan

IV

It's Been a Long, Long Time

1

I DON'T REMEMBER an awful lot about those first months back home. Which was funny—you'd think I would have: I'd dreamed of them often enough. Oh, I went through the rituals, along with everyone else—the elaborate formalities of discharge with the solicitous buck sergeant who wondered if I'd given any thought to post-war planning (as though any of us had thought of anything else), the film shown just before separation (a portrait of the Army so viciously falsified you didn't know whether to roar with laughter or bellow with rage); the brief reunion with Nancy in New York City, a round of absurdly unlikely places such as the Copacabana and the Stork Club, the fevered, incessant talk which raised more questions than it answered—but more of that later; walking up from the Trailways bus stop in Skamondaga that first morning, passing my hand over the feathered hedges and spiked picket fences, with the first ash leaves sailing down through the crisp fall air—amazed to find that my eyes had filled with tears; the loose, bathrobe hang of civilian clothes; the obligatory gatherings with family, everyone disappointed, even a touch resentful, that I'd shed my uniform the second day and wouldn't put it on again. (I never have, to this day, though I've kept it neatly hung up at the back of a closet in a mothproof case.)

Nothing fits, I would catch myself thinking, listening to Uncle Dick holding forth on the boundless possibilities of plastics and television, or helping Wally Hannon grind the valves on a '39 Plymouth down at the shop, or walking along the old tow path by the canal, kicking at cinders; this isn't it, this isn't what I expected at all . . .

It was the Army, the War we had once thought would be strange. And it had been strange enough, all right. Only what we'd come back to was stranger still—stranger because it was precisely what we'd known before. Only now it was fat and rich and brash. A new world on the make, with things to buy and things to take.

Or was it only that we'd been at war so long that, in some terrible way, *it* had come to be true, and everything else fantasy?

The bad time came a week later. I was lying on the hammock in the back yard watching the clouds rolling east over the drumlins, thinking of nothing, drifting on the edge of sleep . . . when I was invaded by a sense of complete and utter emptiness, an immeasurable void stripped of order or purpose or feeling, in which I was somehow the center. Empty. The world—this world, the real world—was perfectly empty, and so was I, bereft of passion and beauty and all value. Everything was futile, a dance of shadows—

I remember leaping to my feet and racing off somewhere—anywhere—then stopping still, panting, sick with a nameless, all-pervasive revulsion. My hands, my feet were infinitely hateful; trees, houses, barking dogs floated by outside me like dream surf. I forced myself to walk, faster and faster, running finally in a distending panic through woods where hawthorn slashed my neck and arms . . . and at last I threw myself down, and muttered names, names, names—all their names—in a terrified invocation to nothing at all . . .

In the Middle Ages I suppose they would have called it a visitation of the Devil; today they'd call it an identity crisis arising from intense alienation and deep psychic trauma. I only know it was a descent into hell. Russ's bottom ring. *Outside,* was all I could think; I was outside everything, body and spirit, love and hatred, good and evil—

. I remember my mother standing in the kitchen and saying, "George? Why are you looking at me like that?" And I remember I shook my head and mumbled something inane, and tried to smile. How in Christ's name could I tell her that I was wondering, quite dispassionately, what she was doing there—alive—this curious biped on our scarred, whirling ball, near the end of the second millennium?

I resented her living, then, when Opp and Dee and Ramsey were dead: was that it? But then, where did you bound that? Millions had died, millions more had lived, myself included—and what did that prove, if anything? Did I actually *want* everybody else dead, too—my own mother, myself?

That frightened me more than anything else; I rushed down to Muldoon's, but Skeets Baumhauer was behind the bar and only wanted to reminisce about Luzon, and I fled back to the house again. "You're home," I kept telling myself savagely, as if I were one of my own replacements just arrived on the line, "it's over, you're back in the real world of jobs and families, you've got to finish your God damned degree, what the fuck is the *matter* with you? Now pull yourself together, Vird, you gutless GFO!" But the harsh command didn't work any better than anything else.

It wore off a little over the next several days while I quite simply faked it, watched myself playing the role of the Moody, Taciturn Veteran; it was the best acting job I ever did—I was disgusted with myself. I read a lot, drank a lot more, and avoided my parents as much as possible. Nancy called twice. I told my father to tell her I'd had to go over to Buffalo. I didn't want to talk to her.

As I said, the homecoming in New York had been a troubled affair. I'd met her after work at the Algonquin—for some reason I'd become obsessed with the idea, meeting her at the Algonquin—and we had dinner at Gallagher's and then went dancing to Stan Kenton at the Hotel Pennsylvania's Café Rouge. Kenton was being hailed as the Band of the Year by the polls, but the music hit me all wrong—it sounded too hopped-up, too frenetic, and then too lead-footed on the ballads; it made me unbearably nervous. I missed the lifting, driving, controlled intensity of Basie and Goodman. We left early, went downtown to Café Society and the Village Vanguard and wound up at Nick's, listening to the brash, honest improvisations of Chicago jazz—and talking, talking, talking all the while.

Nancy was much more articulate and assured than I'd remembered her. She seemed to have everything in hand. She loved her new job on *Interiors*. I gathered she'd got it through Liz's connections. She'd really found what she wanted to do, she said—one day she'd go into design, like Liz; it was really stimulating. Her little, round heart-shaped face was a touch less round and heart-shaped now, her clear blue eyes darker, more determined. She was wearing her hair shorter, in a loose, feathery corona, curiously pleasing; she was every bit as good looking as before, and I told her so, and held her little hand in both of mine across the table.

The apartment she shared with Liz was in the Village—a huge room, obviously a studio in other days, with a bedroom where Liz was now presumably asleep, and a kitchenette where two people could just stand without bumping. We tiptoed around and made coffee, whispering and giggling like kids. When I took her in my arms she kissed me passionately enough; but when I drew her down beside me on the couch and moved my hand over one of her small round breasts she murmured, "Oh darling, we can't."

"What's the matter?" I said.

"Not here. Not now." And with a short, gasping laugh: "She's right in there—!"

"She's asleep. She won't mind."

"Darling, we *can't* . . ."

We wrestled around for a long time, in various strained contortions, a ritual of overture and repulse I found all at once distasteful and silly—we'd *been* through all this a thousand years ago. That afternoon I'd gone up to the Bronx to see Opp's mother—a visit I'd felt obligated to make, that I'd wanted to make, but which had left me in a turmoil of emotions I didn't even want to examine. I finally said, not too gently: "Nan, this is ridiculous, you know that?"

"George—"

"We're not kids any more."

"I know . . . Oh, George," she burst out, "—I wish we'd never made love that afternoon. I mean it!"

"You do?"

"Yes, yes! Or I wish I'd got pregnant. One or the other! Oh, I'm so mixed up, George, I don't know half what I'm doing."

I felt stunned. This was all so different from her last letters I couldn't put any of it together. What had happened? To my complete amazement she began to cry softly, rocking back and forth, her perfectly manicured little hands to her head. "Help me, George. Just hold me and—and help me..."

I took her in my arms again, almost automatically. Well, it couldn't have been any fun for her, either; all that dreary procession of years... I thought suddenly of Giulia in the bare, high-ceilinged room with its stained walls. *Abbracciami, amore.* One tiny island of felicity in a sea of savagery and waste. Where was she now, what was she doing? That girl who had given of herself so freely, so generously, washing me clean of terror and despair... Should I feel guilty about her here, now, holding my first college date, my first love? I didn't. I knew I didn't. Guilt simply didn't apply—it was that simple.

Nonetheless I felt troubled for Nancy, sobbing here in my arms. She resented it, then, what we'd done by the lake: wished it hadn't been. Sex was so *crucial* to us—grail, battlefield, sacrament, trial-by-fire. How had it got that way? Did I owe her something for that bewildered, long-ago grappling? She clearly felt I did. Obligations... to see Opp's mother, to write Dee's wife, to look up Dutch—*those* were obligations; but this—!

Still, she had waited, and written, and said she loved me; it *had* been a long time, and now she was unhappy and confused; like all the rest of us. I stroked her neck lightly, absently, thinking of ten thousand clashing things, and seeing none of them. We dozed, and woke, and dozed again, through that interminable subterranean growling New York makes at all hours of the day and night, like a great metal beast devouring metal, until the long monkscloth curtains turned gray with first light. When I left she embraced me, begged me wanly to forgive her for acting like such a simp, and I made light of it; yet, sitting in the Buffalo train watching the soft, pewter plate of the Hudson, the flint-rock cliffs of the Palisades late that same afternoon I felt deeply resentful, almost hostile. Well: I wasn't the only one who had changed...

Now, tormented by my visitation, I knew Nancy was the last person I wanted to talk to. Lying on my bed, Crane Brinton's *A*

Decade of Revolution discarded, I would look at my hands, the Harvard banner tacked to the wall between the windows and think: Just what the hell do you think you're doing here? With the fervor of an acolyte I told myself I was George Virdon, back home, ready to complete my education, take up my life again...but my very guts knew better; and nothing—for a while, anyway—was going to undo that. When Russ called from Boston and begged me to come over, stay with him a while, I caught the first bus for Albany.

He was waiting for me at Back Bay station. He looked drawn, white, handsomer than ever. He walked with a pronounced limp—he was still in and out of Chelsea Naval for therapy; one arm had that dead, absolutely hairless, waxed puffiness of a bad burn. He laughed too loudly, and was too silent. But I felt more at ease with him than I had with anyone else since coming home. The great house on Mt. Vernon Street was utterly unchanged: still, lordly, imperturbable—the perfect setting for readjustment, you might think; but it didn't work that way. Nothing did.

At meals Russ's parents were quiet, a bit wary. Every topic seemed to have a least five abrasive corners. He and I left right after coffee—to the jazz joints along Columbus Avenue or out in Back Bay, the old familiar places, hunting for the big bands, most of which seemed to have vanished into thin air. What the hell had happened? We talked and drank, drank and talked, and at last we wobbled home and crept up the long curving stairs, shoes in hand, to fall into bed in a near stupor which precluded any thought at all, and few memories.

The explosion came the third evening, at dinner. Mr. Currier was going on about credits—I was only half-listening—something about extension of unrestricted credits to the occupied nations.

"Money?" Russ said suddenly, looking up. "You're going to give them money—the Krauts?"

"It's being explored." Mr. Currier was a trim, bony man with a puglike face and steel-rim glasses; it had always been impossible to think of him as Russ's father. "It will have to be rebuilt some time, you know."

"The Ruhr, you mean? heavy industry?"

"We can't leave an industrial vacuum there. Unless of course you'd rather the Russians filled it instead."

"Well, why not?" His eyes shot over to me, back again. "A

vacuum. Why not? A nice, agrarian vacuum. Where sheep shall safely graze."

"Russell," his father said, "you are talking about one of the most highly developed industrial centers in the world."

"Jesus, I'm sorry—*I* thought I was talking about the most highly developed mass-murder machine in the world. Ask *him*—" he said with a harsh laugh, pointing at me "—he's been bucking it long enough! . . ."

"Russell," Mrs. Currier said, "I don't really think this—"

With a weary patience I found almost as exasperating as Russ had, Lyman Currier said: "It is a question of economic recovery. For all of Europe. If you simply wash your hands and walk away—"

"Oh no, I can see it's infinitely preferable to build it all up, so they can do it all over again."

"Come, now: there will be safeguards." His father smiled. "And how about our own people, who still have pre-war agreements with the German and Japanese firms? Have you thought about them?"

Russ pressed both hands, hard, against the edge of the table. "No, I haven't, you know?" He grinned through his teeth. "I just haven't—thought—about—them—at—all. Isn't that disgustingly irresponsible?"

"Russell," his mother murmured.

"You don't feel, then, that the German people are capable of rehabilitation?" Lyman Currier asked him.

"Capable—how in hell should *I* know? I'm not God . . ."

"That is hardly an intelligent—"

"All I *do* know is, you simply don't give a bunch of loony-farm inmates a lot of guns and tanks to play around with. They just might decide to have themselves a high old time using them again . . . Jesus!" he cried suddenly, "haven't you learned *anything*—?"

"That's perfectly ridiculous," his father said hotly. "You don't know what you're talking about!"

"Lyman—"

"No, hell no, of course not—I've only been busting my hump for the past four years so *you* would be free to make all these fine, mature, sensible decisions for all the rest of us!" Russ flung down his napkin and strode out of the dining room. The tapers fluttered once and straightened again.

There was a short silence, broken only by discreet clinks in the kitchen beyond the butler's pantry. The thick green carpeting had muffled Russ's footsteps on the stairs.

"Times of stress." Francesca Currier gave me a troubled smile. Her lovely Modigliani face glowed in the candlelight like ivory; she was wearing the most delicate emerald necklace high on her slender throat; her hair was raven-dark. Everyone's dream of a mother—beautiful, poised, talented, a favorite of the gods; and yet...I thought again, sharply, of Giulia. Where was she now, what was she doing? The coin silver fork I held in my right hand could keep her alive for weeks—and Guido and Teresina as well.

"So difficult to strike the resolving chord," Mrs. Currier was saying. Her beautiful pianist's fingers played aimlessly with a silver napkin ring. Then suddenly, with a tremor of irritation: "He's always been so sensitive, so high-strung..."

"It's a hard time," I murmured.

"You feel the same way, then? the same way Russell does?" Lyman Currier asked.

About what? I thought, wildly resentful now. About setting the Germans up in heavy industry again? about the gulf between this smug complacency at home and the angry returning veteran? about forking rich food into my mouth when tubercular kids claw deep in filthy GI cans outside the mess halls of Minturno or just about any other God damn place you could name? or do you perhaps refer merely to the timeless, reliable war-to-the-death between father and son?

"He just needs a little time, that's all," I managed to say.

"I thought the Navy would've given him a better sense of the real world."

"Oh it did, Mr. Currier," I said, and this time I couldn't keep a trace of heat out of my voice. "I can assure you, it did."

"We've tried our best, George," Francesca Currier said to me, with that troubled smile, "we really have. I know we seem like ogres to you—just going along living here as we have. But what else could we do? One must talk about something. We haven't asked Russell anything about the war itself, the time he was hurt; and he hasn't volunteered anything. Though I don't know why—*you* talk about it enough among yourselves when you're alone together..."

"—*Because we've earned that right!*" I burst out—looked

down at my plate in a torment of angry confusion.

There was an embarrassed silence.

"He didn't mean to get angry just now," I said lamely. "None of us does. It's just that—there are certain things we can't bear to think about right now. And one of them is the idea that this war will be fought all over again in twenty years or so."

"It can't," Francesca Currier said with an odd catch in her voice, and for the first time I caught a flicker of the anguish of a thousand wakeful nights. "This time they really *must* find a way. Can't they this time, Lyman?"

Her husband looked up at her uncertainly. "I don't know, Cesca. I truly don't know."

"It's as though he's blaming us for something," she went on with that sudden hot urgency she'd given Russ. "As though he's already condemned us. For being alive..." Without warning there were tears in her eyes; she looked old, and rather homely—no longer beautiful at all. "Excuse me, George," she said, wiping her eyes. "Everyone is overwrought these days. One way or another."

I put my hand on hers. "I know you care," I said. "He'll be all right. You'll see. He just needs—time."

"Keep an eye on him, will you, George?" Mr. Currier said. He was staring at me, his mouth slack, his eyes diffident behind the steel frames. "You always were a good influence on him."

And who'll keep an eye on *you?* I thought, leaving the table with its chased silver coffee pot, the Sèvres demi-tasses; climbing the long, green-carpeted stairs, my hand gliding up the rosewood banister. Who'll watch the shakers and the makers, the heavy traders...? Russ was slumped in an easy chair in his bedroom; beside him there was an open bottle of I. W. Harper and a badly chipped wine glass, half-empty. "Have a drink," he muttered. "You look as if you could use one."

"I'm okay."

"Christ knows how you stand them—*I* can't. Bullion for Krupp and Company—Jesus! Why don't they just re-equip the POWs right now—all our surplus gear: what were there, eleven million of us?—ought to be enough to go around. Then they could resurrect the dear, dead Afrika Korps, and the—"

"Knock it off," I said in a tone I hadn't meant to use.

"*You* knock it off," he retorted savagely, "you're not chewing out one of your snot-nosed replacements now." But he fell silent, sipping at the wine glass. "I've got to get out of here. Permanently," he said after a time. "If I had any balls at all I would."

"Let's go get the Empress," I said, right out of the blue, with no idea I was going to say it.

"The Empress?"

"None other. Check her out. See if *she's* alienated and maladjusted. Listen to her troubles, get her out on the road again. Why not?"

"She's down at Woods Hole, isn't she?"

"Check-o. Let's go give Chris a bad time."

He scowled moodily. "I don't know. Dal's got her now..." I shot him a quick glance—did he mean Chris or the Empress? But he was staring moodily into the fire grate.

"Screw Dal. Jean-Jean gave her to you. Dal will only smash her all to hell, the way he did the Ford. Come on. You'll only get into another row if you hang around here and get bombed."

"All right," he said. "Sure, why not."

Which was how we found ourselves in the Currier Buick the following afternoon, running down the narrow road through the fire-red of barberry, the wine-red of sumac, up the little rise and through the bleached-silver split-rail fence sections, and there was the house, squat and ancient, set back from the grand old mulberry; and under it a little figure was playing in a pile of leaves, and another larger figure raking up those leaves— a graceful figure that magically, miraculously became Chris. She stopped, waved, moved toward us with her lithe, springy walk, her face alive with that apricot glow I remembered, her hair in soft, happy disarray—and the old sensation swept over me, the still, utterly trustworthy voice that said: *You're safe now; everything is all right—you're here again; in her presence.* A relief, a sense of vast contentment, and more than that—a rushing joyful *certainty,* like sunlight flooding green fields; everything clear and revealed—the discovery of a simple, pure, incalculable treasure... I felt it all, getting out of the Buick, catching my sleeve on the door handle, watching Chris running to me across the leaf-strewn lawn. I saw it all too, then. I had schooled myself deliberately to deaden all emotion, because to feel was to suffer, to go half-mad with grief and loss, and I'd wanted no more of that. After Mortellange I'd built the wall brick by dusty brick, held myself apart from the kids, even the few old men who were left, I'd shunned all overtures, all confidences—and now in one flaring instant the dam had burst, it had all gone washing away.

"George!" She had kissed me, she was in my arms, we were rocking back and forth, laughing and shouting and saying nothing at all. "Oh, George..." She drew back, looked deep into my face; a glance that saw everything, understood everything, forgave everything on earth; the little green points of light were still there, sparkling. She was so *alive*. And now I wanted there to be life again. "Oh, I'm so glad, George! I'm so *glad* you're home."

She turned to Russ then, embraced him quickly, a bit too quickly, as if she struggled for control. That pained shadow flickered an instant behind her eyes; or did I imagine it? "Well. Long time no see."

"Time staggers on."

She exclaimed, as if she hadn't known about it: "You're limping!"

"Yeah—my horse threw me."

"The cane—the cane is terribly distinguished."

"They want me to use it. Tell you the truth, I feel like some kind of a British staff orficer pukka-pukka type." He struck a pose, legs crossed, hand on hip, cane thrust sidewise, his face screwed up in petulant disdain. "Eh—ruddy piece of cake, wot? Oh-I-say..."

—He doesn't feel anything, I thought, watching him. Not a thing... The whole world had just turned emerald green and gold again, the sun and stars had resumed their whirling, majestic courses—and there he stood, doing imitations, smiling that utterly charming smile. You sad sack, I thought for the first time in my life; you poor, benighted, sad-ass sack.

"Grog, tell Chrissie about the drunk at the Bermuda Terrace who thought I was what's-his-name—"

But I was already moving across the lawn to the little boy who was walking toward us unsteadily.

"Hi, there," I said. He looked up at me, squinting. I picked him up and said: "You're Ronny." Soberly he nodded, watching me. Dark, piercing eyes, unmistakable eyes, not exactly pleased with what they saw. "Don't be so *serious*," I said suddenly, "—I'm your godfather!" and I poked him in the ribs. He laughed, then, his eyes still fastened on mine.

"This is George, lovey," Chris was saying now. "You know about George. And this is Russ. They've been far away. Like Daddy."

Russ said: "What do you say, sport?"

Watching him, Ronny's face clouded over suddenly. He looked bewildered, then affronted; he began to cry. I laughed, glancing at Russ and then Chris. An odd moment—I felt like an intruder; then I didn't.

Chris took him from me, his fat little legs straddling her hip. "All these strange faces out of the blue. All right now, buster . . ."

"Well, well," Russ said, shaking his head. "Chris. Chrissie—my old sailing partner . . . I must confess I find it difficult to see you as a mother."

"You must try, Russell." And her eyes flashed like swords. "Funny, isn't it?" she went on after a moment in her former tone. "You're strangers to him. Perfect strangers. Ridiculous."

"Not me," I said, "we've always been buddies. Haven't we? Come on now, take a look at this." I pulled a package out of my pocket and opened it: a carved wooden gryphon, painted red and black with gold wings. "It's from Bavaria. Land of toys. And other things." I wound it, set it on the brick wall and it shuffled along, whirring, a fierce little mythical engine, beaked head bobbing, wings flapping gently up and down. Ronny clapped his hands in glee, reaching down, and I wound it again. We watched it in silence.

"He's a fine boy, Chris," I said. "A fine, wonderful boy."

"Yes, isn't he?" she answered, and she looked straight at me with the gravest, gentlest smile; and I knew she'd forgiven me for that night in the rain, in Mattapan. The night it should have been I, not Dal, who asked her to come away with me, no matter what. No matter what.

"And last but not least, a little something for the long-suffering mother." Russ had come up from the car, holding a small bundle wrapped in blue-quilted Navy fabric.

"For me?" she said.

"A little token of esteem—straight from the Sultan of Palamangao."

Gently she opened it—excelsior, then absorbent cotton—drew out a conical sea shell adorned with delicate whorls and rows of tiny spikes; it lay there in her palm like a crown jewel, glowing from deep red to the palest rose and orange hues, shimmering and quaking in the fall sunlight. Chris had caught her breath sharply. "Conus gloria-maris," she breathed. "My God. A Glory of the Seas... But there are only—I don't know—25, 30 of them in the *world*—"

"You should have seen the one that got away," Russ said.

"I've never seen one—a real one. Only color plates. My God. Where'd you get it?"

"Philippines."

"No, I mean where—where exactly?"

Russ shrugged. "Quartermaster I served with said he got it from a trader on Mindanao."

"Oh Russ—it's beautiful! Fantastic."

"I couldn't let Rhino be the only one to send on the conchological goodies."

"Dear, dear Rhino," Chris murmured and looked away. The clouds rolled on above her lovely, glowing face, above us all, fleecy and white and utterly innocent; the sea beyond the dunes flowed majestically south to Prospero's isle, and the Land of Fire, and west to Samoa, Tulagi, Iwo Jima...

"Well, I guess you want to see the old Empress," Chris said after a moment. "I haven't dared look at her since Clarence and I put her to bed—"

"There's no hurry," I broke in, "no hurry, Chris." Russ glanced at me sharply and I grinned at him. I could have stayed there forever, winding up that ferocious wooden engine for Ronny, watching Chris, listening to that deep, sweet contralto of hers, the dancing laughter that made you impatient with all anger, all solemnity anywhere on earth. We went inside then, wandered through the old Cape Codder, admired Chris's shell collection mounted on black felt in cases: cowries smooth as satin and conchs with outlandish spikes and tails, murexes like mad undersea dreams; there were shells like scorpions, there were shells like turbans and battle helmets and bishops' mitres and spindles and tops, there were shells ugly as misbegotten toads and ethereal as butterflies, there were shells as fanciful as tulip buds and goddesses' ears and minarets—a flamboyant wealth of shapes and colors and markings that would make Caliban himself believe in a Supreme Creator and all His glory. Chris heated a fish chowder she'd made, and I took Ronny on my lap and fed him with a red-handled spoon; we drank vodka and cranberry juice, and watched the bay glittering in the low autumn sun, and caught up on all the news.

Terry for some strange reason had wound up in a hospital outside of Paris—his sister Sheilah had told Chris he was expected home any week now. Mel Strasser was at Harvard Medical, doing brilliantly—he was going into the Army on graduation. And wonder of wonders, Fluffy Fletcher, the Lowell House sherry-sipping esthete and Scollay Square mummer, had just returned after a distinguished career as a Japanese language expert in the Philippines and China.

"I don't believe it," I protested. "Not the Fluff! What's the story with Dal?"

"He's down at Fort Bragg."

"What's the matter with him?" Russ asked lightly. "Doesn't he know the game's over?"

"He promised his commanding officer he'd complete some report or other. He wasn't very clear about it. But he can't get out of it, apparently. I think it's rotten of them just to hold on to him like that."

Russ laughed. "Don't you want him to pull his oar, Chrissie?"

"You're serious," she said after a moment. "You resent his not being in the war as long as you were. Don't you?"

"I just like to see a fair shake all around." He'd dropped into that extravagant Cockney accent he'd picked up in the Navy. "Share and share aloike, mates, all in this together-o, aw, wouldn't ye say, naow?"

"Come on, Russ," I said, "let it go. We couldn't *all* be wounded heroes."

His head snapped around at me, but he caught himself up, and laughed. We talked about the old days, then; Russ told a couple of very funny stories about sea duty, and after that we went out to the garage and pulled the light tarp from a long low shape—and there she was, alert and proud and gleaming, waiting for us; every inch a queen.

"Hello, sweetheart," Russ called out, and kissed the little silver swan on its beak, "here's your daddy come to take you out into society again. Are you ready?"

"I don't know about the tires," Chris said. "They look awfully bare."

"Yeah, we'll have to get tires. What *are* they?"

"750—16s," I said. "We'll find some, if they're around to be found."

I reseated the plugs and cleaned the manifold, we added oil and gas and water, and hooked up the battery. When she caught on the second try we all cheered and laughed, as if we were the ones who'd been reclaimed. She sneezed and coughed a couple of times, then settled down to that low, pulsing *hwiss-hwiss-hwiss* that brought back the fall of 1940 more sharply than anything else. Anything except Chris. We took her down off the blocks, cleaned out the mothballs and camphor, tightened and reconnected and polished and had a great time generally. For the first time we were at ease. And finally we said goodbye to Chris and Ronny and made some confused and tentative plans for a big reunion evening soon, and went out into the cool, rushing dark.

At the car I said suddenly: "Let me drive her back. Okay?"

He cocked his head. "What's the matter? Afraid I'll pile her up?"

"You'll take it too fast—we're going to have to nurse those tires. This time I'd like to take her. You follow me in the Buick."

He shrugged. "Sure. If you want."

I ran back up Route 3 taking the curves slowly, letting the traffic pile up behind me. I felt happier than I'd ever been. A sense of sheer release, a sun-drenched certainty about life's infinite opulence—I don't know what to call it, it's indescribable really, you can't *give* words to such exuberant felicity of mood. Promise. Suddenly everything had promise again. All right, sure, she was married to Dal, she was the mother of Russ's child—I'd always been grateful for small favors: I'd just been with her, she'd held me in her arms and cried my name . . . The Empress' radio was kaput but all the way back to Cambridge I sang at the top of my lungs, weaving in and out of the South Shore traffic, mugging at Russ scowling at me from the Buick:

> *I'll be seeing you*
> *In ev'ry lovely summer's day,*
> *In ev'rything that's light and gay—*
> *I'll always think of you that way . . .*
> *I'll find you in the morning sun,*
> *And when the night is new . . .*
> *I'll be looking-at-the-moon—*
> *But I'll be seeing you . . .*

We left the Buick at Mt. Vernon Street and drove over to Cambridge and parked outside the Oxford Grille. The jukebox was playing *Careless* and I sang that, too, right along with Dinah Shore, and smiled at the waitress, a hefty blond girl named Bonnie, and told her she was looking delectable.

"Hey, have you been nipping?" Russ demanded.

"I'm a maladjusted vet," I told him. "A war-crazed, manic-depressive type. I'm moving just now into the euphoric syndrome."

"Jesus Christ."

"I've been him, too. I'm barmy outa the Army. *Are you just careless as you seem to be,*" I sang along with dear old velvet-voiced Dinah, "*or do you just care less for me?*" and I chucked Russ under the chin. "Do you, Brahmin-baby?"

"Get out of here."

We had a drink or two—for leaving the road, that was—and then a couple more. That snotty blueblood clubman Conger came in, wearing his Navy uniform, V-12 or X-22 or whatever, and I sang out: "Good evening, *sir!*" and smiling genially at him offered a swift and highly obscene salute. He scowled at me blackly and passed on.

"What the hell has got into you? I'm the unreconstructed asshole in this lash-up, Virdon. You're making me look bad."

"You can do it, too. I'll show you. Repeat after me: I'm just a—"

"You dizzy bastard."

"Bastard, if you will. Dizzy, no. Behold, I stand poised on the threshold of a great career. In fact I seem to see it all before me—the whole vast sweep of world history. In the first scene is Ashurbanipal the Hairy, with his braided beard and his harem of hot-and-cold running Babylonian—"

I broke off. Russ had put his hand on my arm. The juke box was playing *Where or When*. Russ's eyes were locked on mine—that hot quick glance. "Kay. That's Kay, isn't it?"

"Yeah. That's her." It was good; a nice mood of dreamy regret, her voice pitched deliberately low, almost a murmur under the reeds:

> *Some things that happen for the first time*
> *Seem to be happening again;*
> *And so it seems that we've met before—*

And laughed before, and loved before—
But who knows where—or when?

"I only heard it once before," he said. "At Pearl. I knew it was Kay, I didn't have to wait for the announcer. I wonder where she is."

"I ran into her," I said. "In the dear old ETO."

He lowered his glass. "You did? Where? When?"

"Fall of '44. Near Vouziers. She was with Danny Morgan. Songs and skits, stuff like that there. She was pretty good, actually. I toddled up and introduced myself."

"You did? What was she like?"

I looked at him. "What makes you think she'd change any? Well, it wasn't the happiest meeting in history—I wasn't at my best, you could say. It was on a bet, sort of. She put me down. You know: Pallas Athene Greets GI Joe. A little touch of Mata Hari in the night. Or do I mean hari-kari?"

"Hara-kiri. The bitch. What'd she want to do that for?"

"Beats me. That's Kay."

"She wouldn't have done that," he said.

"Im telling you, she *did*. Well, we were never that wild about each other."

"I don't believe it. She may be a bitch—"

"Correction: *is* a bitch."

"All right, *is* a bitch. But she wouldn't have put you down. Not at a time like that."

I looked at him again. "Have it your way, dad. Drink up, and let's get something to eat." I watched him pressing his nails with his thumb. "Am I to understand you're not over that yet? Do I read you?"

"What? Sure I am. Of course I am. Just surprised, that's all." But his eyes as he picked up the menu were dark with memory.

2

"THE WAR HAS changed him"—that's what they said about us. Well, we were, and yet we were not. No, in the end we reverted to type—but with a difference. All our pre-war characteristics seemed to be distended, deepened, like the dyes made from those fantastic murex shells of Chris's. Russ turned more mercurial and romantic than he'd ever been, I more disciplined and loyal, Dal still more practical and ambitious; and Terry—sardonic, vulnerable Terry—was dyed most darkly of us all.

The big homecoming party was for him, as it should have been: a glorious, nonstop, three-day bacchanale—for years it was talked about in Cambridge as the big party of "that winter," the maladjusted winter, the first winter back from the war. Russ organized it, of course, and was its host. His parents were away (his father was down in Washington doing preliminary work for the forthcoming ratification of the Bretton Woods Agreements—"making the world safe for King Midas and his Twelve Croesuses," was the way his son put it), and Russ proclaimed a Perpetual Running Open House for All Fusiliers, Old Guard, Auxiliaries and Staunch Friends. We rounded up what pre-war records we could find, lugged in liquor by the case and ice in blocks, stocked the larder. No mustering-out checks were ever put to better use. The bedrooms were outfitted with extra cots, the girls assigned to some, the boys to others. *"While various forms of fraternization are (unofficially) permitted,"* Russ's circular read, *"any scrounging-in-depth must be carried on at the risk of the participants, and the payment of unusual forfeits."* The great front parlor was stripped for dancing, the rosewood sliding doors were opened and the living room behind it crowded preposterously with couches and love seats *"for petting, spooning, cosseting and other intimacies."* We set up the bar on a mammoth marble-topped table in the rear of the room with easy access to the dumb waiter. Nonessential breakables were removed for safeguarding; those portraits of venerable, disapproving Curriers we covered with gigantic blow-ups of Gwen's snapshots of various Fusilier outings, *Lampoon* covers, a poster of Gypsy Rose Lee at the Old Howard, Bill Mauldin cartoons. Russ raced around tense and choleric as a director with an out-of-town opening at the Colonial.

All Friday afternoon they poured in. Nancy came up from New York City with Liz, who looked very hawklike and high-style in a red bolero jacket and skirt of her own design, and a striking military cape. Mel Strasser, solemn and diffident, brought an ebullient Marge Feldman, whom he'd married that summer; Fluff Fletcher came with a charming little Chinese girl he'd met in Manila. Ann was still away in Seattle with the Waves but Denise came, looking stunning in a Trigère dress and a Canadienne, and bringing her new husband, a slender good-looking Frenchman who had fought with Leclerc. There were old track friends of Russ's, and football teammates of Rhino's come to pay tribute. Even Conger showed up in his V-12 sailor suit with his frozen-pudding final-club air and a girl who looked like a member of a Salem witch tribunal; and I greeted them along with everyone else. Coker Blenham, president of the *Crimson* and all-around class operator, brought his round, genial face and deep, booming, politician's voice.

Old rivals, old allies...Chris and Dal arrived around six—the moment I'd been waiting for, with delight and some apprehension; I worked my way quickly up to the hall entrance.

"Chrissie!" Russ was saying. He embraced her. A celadon-green dress clung softly to her slim, full body, its wide neck revealing the slope of her shoulders; her lovely face was glowing from the fall air outside. She looked festive and eager and full of gaiety, and that old feeling brushed me: *Now* we're all together, now the party can begin.

"Chrissie-girl..." Russ was holding her hands in his. It was the first time he'd seen her in Dal's company. "You look dazzle-o. As always."

She laughed. "The party's already well under way, I see."

"No, I mean it. You *do*—just like my old sailing partner..."

"Not this trip, Russ." She smiled, but her voice was level and very firm; she was in absolute control.

Dal and Russ shook hands then, and everyone crowded around them. Dal was still in uniform, he hadn't been separated yet. He'd put on weight—he looked massive, almost bursting out of his blouse; the major's leaves and three banks of ribbons flashed and gleamed.

"Dalrymple Q. Bonaparte," Russ was saying. "When you going to take off that monkey suit and join the rest of the crowd?"

"Just wanted to give you a swift thrill, dad."

The two men surveyed each other with a wary appraisal: two stray dogs meeting in alien territory. It got a little quiet around us. Chris was looking straight at me now—that shadowed, glance behind the heavy eyelids, brave and steady. I winked at her, said suddenly to the men in my old platoon sergeant's voice: "I thought I told you two to stay in the car!" and everyone roared, even Russ; and from then on it was all right—for a while. I turned up the volume on the phonograph, put on Benny Goodman's *Let's Dance,* and we were off.

I danced with Nancy, then with Liz, tended bar for a time—glanced up at a sudden mild commotion, and there was Terry, thin as a rail, being mobbed by everyone. I pushed through the press and called his name. Someone had cut his hair too short; his eyes looked enormous in his drawn, sallow face.

"Grog! You homely hick son of a bitch—what the hell do you think you're doing here on Beacon fucking Hill?"

"You dizzy Mick," I told him, "who'd they bribe to let *you* in—!"

Then we gave that up and grabbed each other. He was all skin and bones, he actually *felt* brittle. I stepped back, people pushed in around me. I thought for a moment I was going to break down and cry, but a girl in a bright red dress had just embraced me and was kissing me on the mouth. I kissed her back with all my might.

"George!" she cried. Everyone around us was whooping and hollering. "Don't you remember me?"

"—Sheilah!" I exclaimed, blinking, remembering now. "I'm sorry... You crazy kid, you've gone and grown up."

She had. All the birdlike child's shyness was gone, the knees-and-elbows gawkiness. In front of me stood a very pretty Irish girl with large brown eyes and a jet-black pageboy that shivered when she laughed. She was laughing now. She was Terry's Celtic fineness turned impulsive and spendthrift.

"You play piano," I struggled, "you wanted to go to New England Conservatory—"

"Total recall! I'm there now."

"Who's this, who's this?" Russ said, moving in on us. "What dis-*crim*-ination—don't I get a great big soul-kiss welcome home, too?"

"Hey, look at—" I began, but Sheilah put her finger to her lips and said to Russ: "If you guess who I am."

"Gee, I don't..." He frowned, his hair swinging in a long wave low over his forehead; he looked more attractive than he ever had; but he didn't remember, he clearly didn't. "Sober I might..." Then his eyes widened; he'd caught the shadow of resemblance. "You're that fidgety baby sister of Terry's—"

"I like that!" she cried.

"Terry's kid sister," he repeated, and his eyes began to darken. "Well," he said. "Well, well, well... *Now* how about my homecoming kiss?"

"You don't deserve one." But she swung in toward him, her lovely piquant face uptilted. They kissed softly, barely touching; she broke away with a funny little gasping laugh.

"Wow," Russ said, watching her. "Resume flank speed. Where *have* you been hiding?"

"On my balcony at the rear of the palace."

"Solid-old-man." Somebody across the room was calling to him, telling him he was wanted on the phone, and he turned away, then back again. "Hey, don't go away now."

"Oh, I won't!" She grinned at me—a quick, impudent grin,

her shiny black hair shivering about her throat, and I remembered the New Year's Eve dinner at the Gilligans', and that deep flush racing in a crimson wave over her face and throat. She'd said the same words that night, hadn't she? and to Russ? *Oh, I won't!*

It was a glorious, tumultuous, heedless reunion. We played through all our records, and then we played them all over again; we broke several, and felt badly, and then forgot all about them. We danced, cutting in on one another outrageously; we formed conga lines, invented new dances, did imitations, made speeches; impelled by nostalgia some of us drove in a caravan of cars, convertibles of all ages, of all shapes and sizes, but led by the Empress, to the Terrace Room (which was changed), to the Totem Pole and Revere Beach (which were closed), and then on north to Salem to see the House of the Seven Gables because Russ said he needed the inspiration; and finally returned to Mt. Vernon Street—was it evening? or early morning?—to find the party still roaring and rattling along, with a couple I barely remembered dancing near the long bow windows to Woody Herman's *Midnight Echoes,* and Fletcher earnestly explaining the pictorial elements of Japanese calligraphy to several mystified souls, and Dal and Blazer Blassingham lying on the floor, the center of a hotly wagering circle, playing a game called *Are You There, Moriarty?* in which both contestants, blindfolded and prone, gripped left hands and tried to clobber each other over the head with furled newspapers.

Sometime after that we played *Charades,* in which Liz caught Dal (whose team was losing) trying to cheat—everyone laughing and pointing at him, while Dal stood there in T-shirt and stocking feet, red-faced and rueful; we played *Who Am I?* and a game I'd never heard of called *Tamerlane,* and much later found ourselves lying on our backs giggling, playing a game we'd invented as we went along, in which the object was to advance, without moving any part of your body except your left hand, a huge, transparent balloon—a balloon of very scurrilous origins indeed—from one end of the long room to the other. And behind us Chid Bierce was softly playing Chopin on the Curriers' satinwood Chickering, while the phonograph imperturbably hammered along...

But what we did most of course was talk. And drink. And talk. Liz and Chris finally protested the war reminiscences; they set a huge Limoges vase on the bar and pasted a sign on it that read: *Fine of 25¢ for ANY reference whatever to the Late Unmentionable,* and we all owlishly agreed: the girls were right, incontestably right, it *was* boring—hell, we'd *put* all that crap behind us, hadn't we? this was the dawn of a new day, a spanking new era...and five minutes later we were buttonholing one another with tales of torrential rains on Funa Futi and liberties in Melbourne and escapades in borrowed 6x6s in Poggibonsi, and the quarters and dimes and nickels kept plinking into the great vase like silver raindrops.

"—so the dizzy Limey took off crosswind, wide open, and lifted her off the runway like there was no tomorrow, and I was screaming, 'Your pressure, watch your *pressure*—you're drawing 60!' and all he did was whip her into a wingover that left my guts back in London someplace—and then I saw this chimney go right past my ear. Christ, I could have reached out and touched the fucker. I screamed, 'You crazy Limey bastard!—you just missed that *chimney,* there...' and he looked back at me, indignant as all hell, and yelled: 'Yer *suppowsed* to!'"

"...and Forward Lookout is hollering, 'They're there, three of them, I can see them!' and Fire Control says, 'Give us some light, now,' and Bridge says: 'Illuminate!' and we're all set for that long, piercing shaft of blinding light to go rocketing out there, the gunners are braced, everybody's hanging there waiting for all hell to break loose—and all of a sudden there's this goofy, dull orange glow, just as if you're sitting inside a God damn Japanese lantern. Everybody, everything a dull orange. Weird. And the Bridge is screaming: 'Illuminate! *Do* you read me, *illuminate!*' and all we keep getting is this crazy dull glow. Some dizzy son of a bitch had forgotten to take the canvas cover off the humping searchlight."

"It was just a little notice, in the Calcutta paper, just a couple lines. *Information desired as to whereabouts of Darcey Hollis, aged 9, last seen on a raft in Sunda Straits.* I've just never been able to get it out of my mind..."

"—and finally we brought the line up from battalion, two days and nights without a break, I want to tell you we were beat. I crapped out right there in the hallway, and was out like a light in ten seconds flat. And the next thing I knew somebody had stepped on me, right on my arm. I yelled, 'You stupid, *stupid* asshole, can't you see I'm lying here trying to get some sleep—!'

and then, Jesus H. Christ, I saw it was General Bannerman. He stood there glaring down at me for a second, then he burst out in that cackling laugh of his and he said: 'Son, I want to shake your hand—you're the first son of a bitch I've run into all day long who knows what the fuck he's trying to do...'"

The girls were pretty indulgent with us really, now that I think about it. We weren't used to drinking either—not at such a Dionysian clip, at any rate. The Pacific Theater men hadn't had any booze at all, some of them. We cursed the bullshit ineffectuality of the United Nations, we waxed hopeful about Cord Meyer and the American Veterans Committee, we attacked and defended John L. Lewis. Everyone talked at everyone else, and nobody listened. It was compulsive, it was absurd, it was as vital as breathing. Nobody was immune. We were all sinners confessing, lawyers pleading, clowns seeking to amuse; and, for the first time, over and under and through it ran the high, fierce certainty that we were going to take it all, now we were home: head the firm, write the masterpiece, isolate the virus—change the very *shape* of things... Were we the most sentimental of all the American generations? We sounded that way; certainly we were still the most fearfully naive...

"What's the form?"

"You will—repeat, will—hold to the last man. Is that perfectly clear?"

"Perfectly, sir. There is only one thing. Personnel has not been able to *locate* the last man."

"Then get those men out of the hot sun. Can't you see they're dropping like flies?"

"Sir, that formation is for General of the Army Douglas MacArthur, sir."

"Then why didn't you say so? Stand fast and carry on..."

Time turned volatile, distending and compressing at whim, or shattering into a rainbow shower of drops, each one isolate and clear as crystal. At one point I remember Dal rhapsodizing about something called a computer age, a glorious, gleaming era in which everything—meals, bills, travel, all money transactions—would be handled by machines, and food (indeed, all biological functions) would become archaic and people would simply deposit tiny, odorless pellets in plastic receptacles; I remember Denise holding the key to the Empress and bursting into tears while everyone crowded around her, troubled and ineffectual; I remember Nancy deep in an absolutely indecipherable argument with Mel over the most effective way to treat spinal meningitis; at some point I remember Liz sitting, still and intent, sketching a handsome Bakota ceremonial mask perched atop a rosewood secretary; I remember Blazer engaged in what he called the Mongolian Sobriety Test, standing on his head in front of the fireplace, his face a dangerously dark red, while a girl I'd never seen before cautiously tilted a glass filled with Scotch into his inverted mouth; and later—or was it earlier?—I remember Chris's lovely face close to mine—we were dancing, weren't we? yes, a rhumba, *Argentina*—and she was saying: "Oh George—did you ever think we'd ever be all in the same room again, ever?"

There seemed to be too many of one particular word in that sentence but I wasn't quite sure which one it was. "I had my doubts at times myself," I said. "But my lucky shell pulled me through."

"Shell?"

"Your little cowrie."

"Oh," she cried, "did you really keep it? Carry it with you?"

"All the way and back again. I'm never going to let it out of my sight."

"George, you sentimental nut! I didn't know you were superstitious—I thought it was only us mad, seafaring types."

Still dancing I led her out into the hall—it was almost impossible to hear anything she was saying in the living room.

"It wasn't superstition at all," I told her. "It was *you*. Your shell."

"Dear sweet George." Her eyes were always so clear!—the whites were so pure they were almost blue; those little green points were still dancing there. She squeezed my hand, a quick, affectionate squeeze. "That accident we had. In Mattapan. I've never been so glad about an accident in all my life."

"Do you mean that?"

"Oh, yes," she murmured. "Oh my God, yes. Was it planned, George? Do you suppose there's some kind—"

There was a thumping commotion right above us—a figure came tumbling and flailing down the long, curving flight of stairs, to land in a ragdoll heap at our feet.

Chris cried: "Oh—!"

It was Fletcher. He groaned something inaudible; one leg

moved feebly, then the other. I bent over him.

"Fluff," I said in his ear. "Take it easy, now. You all right?"

His eyes fluttered open, rolled around like crazy amber marbles. To my surprise he bounded erect, chin up, arms clamped stiff at his sides.

"Just need—little drinkle," he declared. "Regain my equilibrium."

"No, hold on—"

He collapsed against me, all dishrag, boneless. His eyes closed ponderously, and he sighed.

Chris said, "Is he hurt?"

"No—he's swack-o."

"Are you sure? It's such a long flight..."

"Don't you know God protects fools, drunks and enlisted men? Let's put him to bed," I said. "First to fall." I swung him over my shoulder in a fireman's carry and started up the stairs, Chris following me. *They are fools—who fear to speak—for the fallen—and the weak,"* I declaimed in rhythm to my steps. Fletcher felt perfectly weightless, a curious sensation I decided I must examine later.

On the third floor Chris moved toward the master bedroom assigned to the men.

I said, "No—down there," and pointed toward a little-used guest bedroom down the hall. "Get the door for me, will you?"

It was ajar. Chris swung it back, and then stopped stock-still. I put out my free hand to move her to one side, and stopped myself. Light from the hall threw a yellow band across the bed, where two slender bodies were lying, locked together, arms clutching back and shoulder—a thrusting frieze of love: unmistakably Russ, unmistakably Sheilah. I was conscious of her hair flowing dark over his throat, a long, purplish-red scar on his thigh. They had not heard us, frozen there.

"—as you want me, darling," Sheilah was crying softly, "deep, Russ darling, deep and hold—again, oh yes—*again!*—"

Then I moved quickly. I drew Chris with me out into the hall. "Come on," I muttered.

She almost ran ahead of me back to the master bedroom. I lowered Fletcher on to his cot, and went up to her. She was trembling all over.

"It's impossible!" she breathed; she looked stricken, one hand at her mouth. Her eyes were huge. "I can't—I just *can't*—"

"Chris," I said. I took her by the shoulders firmly; she was quivering so violently I was afraid she was going to fall.

"Why do I feel this way, George? *Why?*"

"Chris—"

"For all I know it's a good thing—after all, she's not like *her*—not like... For all I know maybe they'll be good for each other... I'm jealous, I guess." She laughed shakily, caught her breath. "Am I jealous, George? She's so *young*. Isn't she?"

"Chris, don't—"

"Only a few years—why does it seem like so *many?* so awfully many?" She pressed her forehead against my chin. The racket downstairs seemed immensely far away, an upheaval in a foreign country. "Terry," she said then, in sudden alarm, "where's Terry?"

"We'd better get down there," I said.

We hurried down the stairs together. I was in a wild tumult of sensations. Their bodies were so *white*, was all I could think; so white...

We came into the livingroom, the rattle and crash of the party. Nancy was standing just inside one of the great doors, watching us, her eyes speculative and flat.

"Well—you've been up there a long time, you two," she said in a light, sharp voice.

"Yeah," I laughed, "how about that." I realized I was still holding Chris's hand. "You're looking at the old demon lover himself."

But Nancy didn't smile. "A mighty long time," she repeated.

"Hey, Nan—" I began, but her eyes were fastened on Chris. "I thought you were an old married woman now, Chris."

Chris's face went perfectly blank with amazement, she started to laugh—then her head came down. "That's right, Nancy," she said quietly. "I am. An old married woman." She gave Nancy a very long, very steady look, and moved off into the crowd.

"You know, that wasn't a good idea, George."

I laughed again, I don't know why. There was a twinge of furtive guilt about those two upstairs, but I also felt hilarious, imbued with subtle, mysterious powers. Was I more plastered than I thought? Nancy was still watching me, her face set in anger.

"Come on, Nan," I said, "what's this all about? Are you

putting me on? *Chris!* Why, Chris is—"

"I know."

"You don't think—you don't actually think Chris and I—"

"I saw you come into the room—*I'm* not the one looking guilty!"

"Nan, for pete sake—"

"I've seen the way you look at her . . . dancing with her like that—what's the *matter* with you!"

"Nan, we were *putting Fletcher to bed*—he fell down the stairs."

"Oh, honestly! . . . You know there's only been you, George." Her eyes roved over my face carefully—the old look of fear, entreaty, claim I remembered, but harder now. I'd never seen her like this. "All this time. Only you. While everybody else was fooling around, tearing off somewhere, getting married . . . I thought we meant something to each other. Do we, George?"

"Sure we do, of course we do. Nan, you're simply—"

Blazer came up then and asked Nancy to dance with him. Smiling she accepted but her eyes flashed back at me once more, dark with reproach. Near the piano Terry, surrounded by half a dozen people, was telling some story, waving his skinny arms, and at the bar Dal was still arguing heatedly with Coker Blenham about mutual funds.

And finally it was Sunday afternoon—somebody said it was, anyway, and we decided we might as well believe him—and the ragged, stunned exodus began. I drove Nancy and Liz to South Station, watching the somber stippling of uniforms around us and thinking of wartime departures. The girls were affected by it, too; Liz was preoccupied and quiet; Nancy hugged me impulsively and said: "Oh darling, I'm sorry—I don't know what got into me. Write me now, call me, won't you?" She'd caught cold, she was shivering in the raw east wind; she seemed genuinely unhappy about her accusation the night before.

Back at Mt. Vernon Street the great house seemed cavernous, resonant with loss. Only Russ and Sheilah and Terry and I remained to wash the dishes and a hundred glasses of all shapes, our minds as vacant as the dove-colored, high-ceilinged rooms.

Later that evening Russ and Sheilah took off somewhere. I finished up in the butler's pantry and trudged upstairs to the front livingroom, now more or less restored, to find Terry lying motionless on a couch. I thought he was asleep and started to leave, when his head turned toward me.

"How you making it, Grog?"

"None but the brave," I said. "Great brawl, wasn't it?"

"Fab-u-loso." But the expression in his eyes hadn't changed.

I talked idly of school, courses and credits; his silence made me uneasy. After a while I ran down.

"Funny, isn't it?" he said after a long pause.

"Yes." I knew what he meant.

"One part of your brain is thinking: It's just as though none of it ever happened . . . and the other part knows that was all there was."

Outside a truck groaned its way up Mt. Vernon Street.

"I wasn't in hospital at Neuilly all that time," he said. "I was in London. I looked up Rosamond."

I locked my hands together in my lap.

"I was walking up the street toward her place—the flat I told you about, remember?—and this guy was coming out. I'd never seen him before. I didn't think about it one way or the other—and then I did. All of a sudden I was certain. Dead certain. I went across the street to the pub—the *Two Swans,* it was called: isn't that perfect? Jesus—and I drank a couple of ales, and watched the doorway until she went out shopping. I saw her then."

He sighed—a long, low exhalation, and twisted his head on the cushions. "She'd decided to stay with him. 'He has nowhere to go, Terence,' she said. She always called me Terence, I kind of liked it . . . 'I can't let him down, you see.' 'But—he never even wrote you!' I told her, 'it was years and years—' 'I know. But that's another thing. He is here now, he needs me.' '*I* need you,' I said, 'I love you—Christ knows I need you . . .' 'I know,' she said, 'but I am married to him . . . He has suffered so, Terence.' 'Suffered!' I cried, 'you want to talk about *suffering*—' 'And he is English.' 'And I'm Irish,' I shouted, 'a dirty scrimey Mick, is that it?' She looked at me—oh my God, that look. And I calmed down a little. 'You know better than that,' she said. 'I only meant I can't pretend it isn't there, don't you see?' She paused and then she said: 'It isn't as if we'd lived together, Terence—I mean really *together*, you know.'"

He sighed again, and rubbed his nose. "I told her she was all I thought about in the lousy Stalag, all those years, it was what kept me going, the only thing really, the thought of getting back to her, just being with her. You don't know what that means, George, you've never felt it, but it's that simple, it's as absolute and inarguable as—well, as Communion..."

I didn't say anything. His voice was so low now I could hardly hear it.

"'I'm glad of that, Terence,' she said. 'But it doesn't alter things. You have to live out what you've taken on—I can't explain it actually. But I know it's what I've got to do.' 'You're crazy,' I shouted at her again, 'a nut—if your father's a drunk *you're* supposed to be one, if you break your leg at the age of eleven you're supposed to walk with a limp the rest of your life—is that it?' 'I know, you have all the educated arguments, but—' 'You fool!' I shouted, 'you stupid, masochistic fool!' I called her a slut, a teaser, a rotten no-good cold-blooded Limey bitch, I went sort of crazy there for a while, and she just watched me with those clear lovely eyes, without a word, while I shouted at her and pounded the iron railing beside us until I thought I'd broken my hand. 'You don't want to marry me, Terence,' she murmured after I'd subsided a bit. 'No?— how do you know what I want?' 'You want something utterly different—you do.' 'And that is?' 'I don't know,' she said, 'and neither do you. But you'll know when it happens.'"

He raised his hand, let it fall to the cushions. "So that was that. She wouldn't change her mind. So I came home. Why not? *Sweet Thames! run softly—*" He laughed his soft, mocking laugh, and cleared his throat. There seemed to be absolutely nothing to say.

"I broke out once," he said in the old, sardonic tone. "Yeah! The old Air Corps college try. Civilian clothes, forged papers. Out the tunnel, and away—to freedom..." He laughed again, a laugh that turned my blood thick. "What a farce—they picked me up in two days. Just where the fuck did I think I was going, through that armed camp, with about ten words of German?... *And* then I drew 15 days' Vogelkäfig. Know what that is?"

"No," I said.

"It's a little roost for the chickens that try to fly the coop. Only there are no windows, no sounds. No day, no night. Only black silent time—all the time in the universe, or no time at all.

You can take your pick. Very clever, really. If you're the solid, down-to-earth sort you just curl up and have yourself a good snooze. If on the other hand you're the tense, imaginative type—"

He broke off. We sat there, bound in hangover fatigue, awash in memories and regrets. Sunday night after the war.

"Do you know," Terry said in a low, even voice, "there was a time—there was actually a time when I wished I'd bought it when the old *Sal* got hit. That I'd been killed . . . You ever feel that?"

"Yes," I said.

"You know, then." He nodded. "You know. Even now there are moments—"

"No, not now," I said with a hot sense of urgency, "not *now,* Terry—we've got to shove that away. All of us . . ."

"Speak for yourself, chum."

"You can't think that way! Look, it's over, we're out of it, we can go on with—"

But he only laughed softly, a laugh that made me curiously, deeply afraid; for all of us. "Back to Russ's Good Old Days, eh?"

"Well," I stammered, "they *were* good . . ."

"Who was it said simplicity is the mother of disillusionment? Well, he was full of shit, whoever he was. I'll tell you something: *knowledge* is the mother of disillusionment."

"Don't say that, Terry. Knowledge—"

"You want to know something, pal? In the Stalag there was a bombardier named Callender I got to know real well. He was from my squadron, we got shot down on the same raid. He had all kinds of connections. You know what he told me? It's very, very interesting, Grog. Pay attention, now. Callender told me there was this Jerry agent in Germany who was working for British intelligence, and he got picked up by the SS, he was under suspicion—his credibility was showing, you know? And so, Callender said—now mind you, he *said*—our government let him tip off the Germans to *our* raid, so his cover wouldn't be blown. Seven hundred of our people flamed on that one. To uphold that Kraut agent's credentials, you see. What do you think about that?"

I stared at him. I hadn't felt this boundless, desolate despair since—not since Mortellange. No, this was worse than

Mortellange; this was—

"—They wouldn't," I muttered. "I can't believe they'd do a thing like that..."

"It's possible Callender was misinformed," Terry answered in that cold, dead, musing tone. "He may even have invented it. To pass the lonely hours. But somehow, you know?—I think he was leveling. And of course they *were* all up there in force that day, waiting for us—"

"You can't," I cried in a kind of thin panic, "you can't believe that, Terry, you mustn't believe that!"

"Oh, yes I can," he said in a tone that sank into the very stone bottom of my soul. "I can believe absolutely anything I want to. And nobody on this pitiful, fucked-up globe can stop me."

3

IT TURNED INTO a grim winter—blizzards and biting winds—as if to remind us what it had been like that last winter before we'd left for the war. We all caught colds we couldn't shake for weeks; the Pacific crowd got malaria recurrences, and sweated and shivered and shook while we alternately made fun of them and brought them extra blankets and medication. We drank too much, indulged in pointless quarrels and reconciliations; we were always on the verge of settling down.

Harvard was a troubled place that winter—college campuses were, all the way across America. There was a sudden wide mix of students—veterans who had never expected to see the inside of any college, let alone the Ivy League. There were new courses, and compulsory class attendance—an innovation we old men bitterly resented. And there was the overcrowding. Russ and Terry and I, back in our old room, were joined by a tough, quiet kid named Mike Krupsic, a mortarman with the Tropic Lightning who came from Gary, Indiana and who'd received enough credits from Army courses to give him upperclassman status. Russ was very cool toward him at first—Russ was continually affronted by some of the newcomers.

"Jesus, we're getting multifarious around here. Was this one of the Four effing Freedoms we fought for? Where are some of these people coming from—scme Ozark swamp?"

"Careful—you're beginning to sound like Conger and the clubbies."

"You know perfectly well what I mean."

But eventually he accepted Mike because we liked him and because of his war service. This became an obsession with Russ—he was always erecting his own complicated gradations: those who'd been wounded in combat occupied the highest rank; then those who'd seen combat but hadn't been wounded, then those who'd been sent overseas, and so on, right down to those unspeakables like Conger, who had sailed the high seas of Cambridge for the entire war. This sentimental élitism both amused and irritated me—I gave him a hard time about it.

"What if—I mean, suppose a guy got hit by a stray on the firing range at Bragg? or a tank nicked his ass at Belvoir? He's wounded, see? but he hasn't gone overseas."

"Oh, come on."

"Or suppose a conscientious objector in that stockade in Connecticut went on a hunger strike and the MPs roughed him up, maybe broke his arm. Where does he fit on the ladder? He's been in a kind of combat, but he—"

"Bugger off, Grog. Distinctions ought to be made, all I'm saying."

"Are they going to hand you a B in Chaucer because you got some steel in your knee? Look, how many yoyos had any choice? You went where they shipped you, you did what you were told—you know that."

"Not necessarily—"

"Yes, necessarily. It's a myth, your goofy masonic lodge of warriors—"

"You're no better than that snot-ass Conger—don't hand me that! You don't believe it yourself."

Which did shut me up—I was damned if I was going to stand comparison with Conger in *any* way, shape or manner. One fact was refreshing: the power and influence of the clubmen had been hugely diminished in the tidal wave of vets and new enrollment—in this respect at least, Fair Harvard was never going to be quite the same again; and I for one was not desperately sorry. At a thousand colleges across the Republic other brands of fraternities were eroded, too, as the survivors of Okinawa and Avranches, schooled to harsher rhythms, looked cool-eyed at such childish antics and turned to books, to the business of getting on with it, pressing back into life.

We oscillated through all kinds of moods that winter. It was time itself that had altered, and now tricked us: time had moved so fast in that year before the war—and now it passed with a curious indolence. There was time to do *everything* now, it seemed; the possibilities stretched before us—a lordly view from a mountain top... Yet there was a catch—we were still caught in attitudes fashioned before the war. Like a reformed gambler saddled with old debts we were frozen in the 1941 image of ourselves. Some weeks we'd bury ourselves in books and work through the night; then for no reason at all we'd leap into the Empress, race over to town, get roaring drunk and disorderly, hurling threats and insults at this new civilian order; and hours later find ourselves wobbling and wavering over some back country road. And for several days afterwards we'd be sunk in boundless lassitude, hating Cambridge, America, life itself...

Russ was, typically, the most mercurial of us all. He applied for Spencer's prestigious course in the novel and was accepted—then broke with him violently, he never would say why. But he went on writing like a demon—drifting in and out of sleep I could hear the muffled thump of his typewriter through the wall. Mornings I'd find him sitting white-faced and tense at his desk, surrounded by crumpled wads of paper and cigarette butts and half-empty Coke bottles.

"You dizzy bastard. You'll never make it to class."

"Class? Class? What are those? Hey, I'm rolling, Grog-o. I'm getting it! I'm going to get it—the whole crazy Idiot's Delight..."

Dal had enrolled at the Business School, across the river; he and Chris were billeted—there was, alas, no other word for it—in a dreary village of Quonset huts near the Watertown Bridge, with the rest of the ball-and-chain set, as Russ called the married veterans. It was a cramped, icy place crowded with odd sticks of furniture, a two-burner hot plate and toys littering the chewed-up plywood floor. I dropped by whenever I got the chance—as much to see Ronny as anything else, I told myself. Just sitting there with him on the floor, playing parcheesi or helping him through the makeshift jungle gym outside soothed me. He was impulsive, quick, intensely imaginative—always inventing fanciful tales which he utterly believed. He had a slight stammer, which bothered me.

"Don't worry about it, Georgie!" Chris would chide me; and she would snatch Ronny up high over her head and whirl round and round, while they both laughed at each other like banshees. I never knew a girl who was so easy, so good with kids. "He'll get over it—won't you, honey? It's just enthusiasm, just—his nature."

And her hazel eyes would rest on mine with that sweet, shadowed, compelling gaze. I would grin back and make some foolish crack to blunt the quick, deep dart of affection. How I longed to speak to her that winter—if only to tell her how much it meant to me just to see her now and then, be near her, follow the long curve of her throat when she bent over a saucepan, watch the way she would throw her weight on one long leg, as if poised for flight, the way the back of her hand would brush her cheek—an almost dreamy, child's gesture...She was so beautiful, and so gloriously unaware of her beauty—which made me love her still more. If that were possible; which it wasn't. And I almost did speak that winter, once I actually opened my mouth to say—what? *what,* for God's sake? Anyway, somewhere a line would not let go, a cleat held fast. I plodded back through the slush to the house library and checked out the section of *History, Medieval,* sneezing in the thick, mote-clogged air...

Relations with Nancy were—well, troubled. What very nearly broke us up for good was the telephone. I had the poor boy's instinctive distrust of the gadget: you either talked with someone face to face, or you wrote a decent letter, setting down what needed to be said. Phone calls, like telegrams, were for crises—death and accidents and other Acts of God; I could never free myself of a sense of something bogus and disembodied in a casual call—much less endless casual calls. Nancy on the other hand loved the phone; she was always ringing the dormitory. Our conversations were filled—that is to say, empty—with pauses, silences, nonsequiturs and repetitions that set my teeth on edge; more often than not I broke off abruptly, with some invented excuse.

Then Liz up and got married—a sudden, completely unexpected move—to a museum curator she hadn't known very long named Hugh Moncrief. They'd gone out to his family's home in St. Louis for the ceremony; Nancy had been her only attendant. And now the phone calls doubled and redoubled. The apartment was lonely, the job was silly, everything was stupid; couldn't I get away, come down for a few days? just a few days? No, I couldn't, I protested, not right then anyway, I was studying for my *life,* for God's sake...

She showed up at the room one Saturday afternoon—a surprise: that old immaculate band-box freshness but softer again now, in a close-fitting honey-colored dress with rounded shoulders and full hips; she was wearing high heels with slender ankle straps. Russ was delighted with her.

"Hey, Miss Curvaceous! *Dig* that New York lady..."

"Listen to him." But she was pleased, I could tell.

"You've been letting this gorgeous girl sashay around Manhattan all by herself? Shame on you, Grog."

He phoned Sheilah and got tickets for *Call Me Mister,* and we had a wonderful evening roaring with delight at some extraordinarily funny young men we'd never heard of named Carl Reiner and Buddy Hackett. The musical fitted our mood perfectly that winter, it said what we wanted to hear: love us or not, we were back; there were things in America that needed changing, and we were going to change them, too; come what may. Afterward at the Merry-Go-Round Bar, Nancy was relaxed and warm, she even kidded with Russ in a light, casual way. Sheilah put her up, and on the way over to her studio we sang in dreamy, quavering harmony:

> *Never thought...my heart could be so yearny,*
> *Why did I decide to roam?*
> *Gonna take...a sentimental journey—*
> *Sentimental jour-our-ney home...*

and when I saw her off at South Station the following afternoon it was like old times. There still were uniforms, embracing couples, the burst of fetid steam beneath the cars; it took me back to '42 in one giddy rush.

"Hey," I said, "I want to see you."

"Do you?" She was smiling at me, her pale brows raised. "You just did."

"You know what I mean... Don't despise me, New York lady."

"I'm not entirely sure I shouldn't."

"Nan, you're *fabuloso*." I did feel unsure now, at a disadvantage: she was out there in the world, with her magazine job and her Manhattan high-style clothes; and I was—well, still trying to catch up, stitch up those lost years. "Nan, I'm *pinned* here—I'm like a rat in one of those goofy treadmill cages."

"You're a rat, all right."

"I know."

I kissed her, one with the other couples, the waiting train. Ah, trains and departures! What they *cost* us, what the mere sight of them still conjures up. Did those urgent iron wheels, the rushing steam, work like some mad potion in our blood, did they actually *create* romance? *Time's a-wastin', time's a-wastin', time's a-wastin'*... She swayed in to me, a flooding urgent pressure—broke away trembling. Then with a tense laugh:

"I'll see you, rat! You better graduate good and quick."

She climbed the hollow iron steps; her legs looked terrific in the high-strap suede pumps.

"Nan—"

Steam shot at me in a solid white plume and I jumped back. Laughing, she shied a hand at me and moved on through the car.

"It's here, it's here—the greatest show on earth!" Russ was standing in the doorway with Sheilah; they had their arms around each other like a couple in a musical, ready to break into a routine. "Who's coming with us?"

"Where away?" I said.

"Fair Harvard's hat is in the ring." Russ sailed an imaginary boater—he still never wore a hat, none of us did, only the war had been able to make us cover our skulls—across the room and out the window, south across the river, the Stadium, to New York, to Washington. "Yes, sir! That sterling hero of Kula Gulf, Beverly Hills and Miami Beach, John F. Kennedy, is running for the Congress of the United States."

"The hell he is," Terry said.

"Right on top of world events as ever, I see. Yep, he declared himself a candidate—on WNAC, night before last. He's speaking over at Central Square right about now. Come on, let's catch him."

"The God damned fool," Terry muttered. "The poor, misguided son of a bitch."

"*I* think he's smooth," Sheilah cried, and winked at me. Her black hair was tousled from riding in the Empress, her brown eyes were dancing; she looked wonderful and wild. "And sexy—my God! *I'll* vote for him."

"Well, you can't. Yet."

"I will, anyway. What about that story Daddy used to tell, Terr? About the man that voted sixteen times, using dead people's names? I'll wear a different wig and vote for Jack each time. Come on—I want to see him."

"Hoping lightning will strike, babe?" Terry inquired.

"Well—why not?" She glanced roguishly at Russ, who made a pass at her. "He's got to marry somebody..."

"Now, when yez go to the polls," Terry crowed in an outrageous brogue, "remimber ol' Knocko's iver had yer intrists to hearrrrht..." He laughed silently, shaking his head. He'd been sitting in the same chair ever since breakfast doing a crossword puzzle. He'd re-enrolled with the rest of us, but that was about all he'd done. He drifted in and out of Boston bars, the revival movies down on lower Washington Street, he read a lot—but remote, eerie stuff: Kierkegaard, the Bhagavad-Gita, St. John of the Cross, Simone Weil. He seemed to shun everyone's company, yet he was always around—he could neither cling to us nor let us go.

"Just a son of the ooooold sod," he went on mirthlessly, "with a tidy little private bank account of—what? Two, three million?"

"Stop it, Terr," his sister chided him. "You're so cynical. Honestly, you ought to be an undertaker or something."

"The old man's pressured him into it, lads. Old Joe's unconquerable dream. Lose one son, impound another."

"Cynic!"

"Scheming female!" But he got up and pulled on his jacket.

Spring had come early, as if to atone for the winter's savagery; the day was mild, with that silvery impressionist overcast only Boston skies take on with the first warm days. Russ had unearthed two new tires out in Jamaica Plain—God alone knew what he'd paid for them, I didn't have the nerve to ask; we put the top down, the wind plucking at our hair, and the Empress rolled majestically along Massachusetts Avenue as if the grand old car knew she was moving toward a different destiny.

"You're wrong, Terr," Sheilah was saying from the front seat, "Fran Walsh says he's *terrific*. Really on the side of the ex-GIs and everything. She heard him at a house party in Brighton. They're all crazy about him."

"Sure—a bunch of sweet young things, every mother's daughter hoping to waltz into the Kennedy millions. That isn't *campaigning*. What in hell does he know about politics? And *Boston* politics! Heckling's a tradition here, George—it's all part of the game. You should have heard Jim Curley swapping insults with the crowd at Savin Hill... And Cambridge! He thinks it's all an extension of Harvard. Why, those hoods from Kerry Corner will slaughter him. What's he going to say to them? Mike Neville will eat him on toast."

"Your voices!" Russ declaimed, tapping the silver steering wheel spokes in rhythm. *"For your voices I have fought, bear of wounds two dozen odd; battles thrice six have I seen and heard of—indeed I would be consul..."*

"Lot of good that'll do him," Terry snorted. "Some of these guys living down here were *real* heroes—Guadalcanal, Omaha Beach. That won't cut any ice with them. Here it's where do you come from, are you one of us, what are you going to do for us?"

Sheilah said: "But he *was* a hero, wasn't he?"

"Forget it—his boat got run down out in the channel. From behind. Somebody was asleep at the switch, that's for sure. But old Joe got it hushed up." He winked at me—a crafty, Irish politician's wink, cracking his face. "The Forrestal connection. Get me?"

"Oh Terr, you're impossible!"

"All right, ask your Navy boyfriend. Wasn't that about it?"

Russ shrugged, watching the road. "I don't know. I remember there was some scuttlebutt about a court of inquiry, something like that. And then it was dropped." His eyes met mine in the rear-view mirror, snapped away. "It was probably just a foul-up. You've no idea how bloody dark it can get out there at night, at sea."

"I'll bet," Terry said.

"Hell, he was gutsy enough. That long swim, towing McMahon."

"Don't forget the coconut shell."

Sheilah cried, "You're all just jealous because he's so gorgeous-looking! Fran Walsh says he could be in pictures if he wanted."

"Shafty *Kennedy?*" Russ stared at her. "Hell, I ran into him over at Chelsea Naval all last fall. I'm damned if *I* think he's so much on looks."

"You wouldn't!" Sheilah said. "Conceited Brahmin-Guinea half-breed." Reaching down she pinched him on the inside of his thigh; he yelped and let go the wheel and swatted at her and she laughed wildly, ducking away—then kissed him on the ear, and winked at me again. She and Russ had been traveling together for several months now. Spence Talbott, a music major, had told me Sheilah was a very talented pianist, but how she ever got any practicing done was a mystery; she was always in Cambridge. She was more than attracted to Russ—she was shamelessly, irretrievably in love with him. I knew; I ought to know.

"Why do you call him Shafty?" she asked.

"I don't know—everybody called him that in the Navy. He got shafted out of some cush duty somewhere, I think."

"And that's only the half of it," Terry grunted. "Running for the 11th! Why, it's Jim Curley's old district—why, even Honey Fitz lost in the 11th! It'll take more than the old man's bankroll to bail him out of this one."

The Square was nearly filled; we parked and walked up to the edge of the crowd. A husky young man in shirtsleeves was standing on top of a beat-up black '38 Ford, making introductory remarks, and the crowd was buzzing fitfully.

"Kind of overdoing it, isn't it?" Russ said. "Heap like that?"

"Better than a Rolls, wouldn't you say?" Terry answered.

"Well hell, everybody knows his family's loaded. That old car isn't going to fool anyone."

There was some milling around, and then the guy in shirtsleeves got down and Jack Kennedy climbed laboriously up on the car roof. Watching him I was disappointed. I didn't know him at all—I'd only seen him once, before the war, at one of the Princeton games; he was a couple of years ahead of us. He was wearing a dark gabardine suit that looked two sizes too big for him; he had an atabrine tan, as the Pacific crowd called it—that sallow, jaundiced color the drug produces—he needed a haircut, and he was all skin and bones. He didn't look like any matinee idol to me.

There was some applause, scattered, perfunctory, and I saw a couple of homemade placards pumping up and down, forlorn in the crowd. One said: THE NEW GENERATION OFFERS A LEADER. Kennedy started to speak, coughed, cleared his throat and began again. A girl at the rear of the crowd shouted, "Louder!" and he raised his voice with an effort, frowning. Some leader.

It was a terrible speech. Terrible. He talked about the returning veterans and how they'd learned to rely on one another under the stress of a world at war, and something about new political and economic forces sweeping through the post-war world, and so forth and so on. At one point he told a joke, a poor one, and nobody laughed. It was all vague generalities, fumbling, deadly dull.

"Disaster," I heard Terry mutter under his breath.

It was. Kennedy kept pausing, his lips working, glancing around nervously. His hands made awkward, self-conscious little chopping motions, which gave him a curious mechanical quality. It was all like something he'd tried to commit to memory, and hadn't quite. I could feel the mood of the crowd—flat, dutiful, unmoved, on the rim of disapproval. The faces of his own people around the car were rigid with disappointment... He doesn't want to do this, I thought, he doesn't like these Irish and Italian working stiffs and their women, he feels ill at ease with them, superior to them. Poor little rich boy in over his head. Doesn't he realize how he *sounds?* What ever made him—or anybody—think he could get away with this?

"—*Hey, Kennedy!*"

The cry was high, piercing, at the back of the crowd, perfectly timed on a pause. Heads turned. Jack started, he grimaced once.

"Here it comes," Terry murmured in my ear. "Low bridge."

"Hey, Kennedy! Whyn't you go on back to that fancy hotel room they rented for you over in Boston, there? ["Skip McNally," Terry said. "Neville man."] Call yourself one of us, do you?"

"*Yes,* I call myself one of you." Jack peered forward—his

face was all at once alert, tensed, aggressive; the change was astonishing. There was some derisive laughter, but he nodded into it, pointed south. "I was born right over there across the river on Beals Street. You want to see my birth certificate?"

"If you're one of us, why don't you have a home here now? Why haven't you lived here for twenty years?"

"I didn't have a home out in the Solomons either, Skip. ["Jesus," Terry exclaimed softly, "he knows McNally!"] Neither did most of the men right here in this crowd. That's just it—we haven't *had* a home for the past four years—we need one *now* ..." McNally tried to break in but Jack rode through him, his voice sharp and penetrating now: "What do you want us to do—vote only in the Solomons or Normandy?"

Several people in the crowd laughed at this, and Russ called, "Hey, that's pretty good, Shafty."

"No-no-no, we know, you were over there at *Haaaaa*hv'd"— the word drawn out deliberately, the very distension insulting— "we all know you went there..."

"Yes—I went to Harvard and I'm proud of it, Skip. And I'm even prouder of the fact that *every* vet can go there, too, if he wants to, thanks to the GI Bill. Yes, I'm a Harvard man—and I'm Irish and a Catholic, and I'm proud of that, too—does that disqualify me, Skip?"

The crowd was stirring now, laughing and buzzing. Italians love their theater wherever they find it; and in Boston, politics can be rare good theater.

"Beautiful, beautiful! He's quick," Terry was saying, "my God, he's quick!"

"—The Candidate from Miami Beach!" This came from the other side of the Square; a deeper voice, more authoritative. I caught a glimpse of a blunt face, straight black hair, a soft round chin. "You going to tell us how to clip coupons, how to run a bank, *Mister* Kennedy?"

Jack smiled then, for the first time—that quick, boyish smile, with just a hint of deviltry. And now he did look handsome. "Well—the vested opposition! No, I'm not going to talk about banking, Danny—I'm going to talk about Cambridge. I'm glad you came down here today, Danny. Let's *talk* about Cambridge: let's talk about why the minimum wage is only a pitiful 65¢ for a hard day's work, and why a veteran and his wife and baby are all crowded into one room, living with his family because he can't find a house to live in; and why there's no low-cost housing, and why the three-deckers right over there at Kerry Corner are coming apart because there's no lumber available to fix them up, at prices a man can afford! Let's talk about jobs, and why fair employment in Cambridge is a hopeless dream instead of a working reality! [Look at him," Terry shouted in my ear, "look at him *go!*"] Let's talk about why rents have increased 160%—160!—in the past two years alone, and why the Navy Yard has just laid off 2,400 men since January! And how come Mike Neville hasn't been doing anything about all this? He *claims* he runs Cambridge—doesn't he know what's going on?"

"Nobody's fooled, Kennedy," McNally broke in again loudly, "you're not fooling anybody with all that blarney! Your carpetbagging daddy isn't going to buy *this* seat for you with his Hialeah Racetrack bank-roll..."

"Yes, he's such a carpetbagger he's just invested half a million dollars in industry, right here in Boston."

"Half a million, is it? For the—"

"At least he's put his money where his mouth is. But I don't have to apologize for my father or any of the Kennedys—any of them!" Jack looked angry now, fighting mad; all the mechanical hand-chopping was gone. "I'm running for Congress from the 11th. You want to go after my father, Skip, I'll see you later. I'm here to talk to the people of Cambridge about the issues—the mess Boston is in, and what we're going to do about it!"

"He's taking them," Terry chattered excitedly, "they're scared, they're playing his game—he's got them going!"

It was true. The contrast was perfect—old pols and young reformer, smoke-filled room versus the wide-open spaces, pettifogging civilians against openhanded veteran, a new generation on the march. It was like the climax in a God damn Frank Capra movie—

"Sure," the opposition called scathingly, "you're rich, so you *care* about the poor..."

"Yes, I care, I can figure it out—I can see when the cards are stacked against the working man. You weren't in the Pacific or the ETO, Danny, but even you can imagine how the returning veteran feels, with no roof over his head and three mouths to feed and milk—milk, by God!—at 22¢ a quart, and bread at 11¢ and no end in sight...or can you? Maybe you can't—you certainly haven't *done* anything about it..."

"Kennedy, what about that Negro butler you had at *Haaaa*hvd, there?" Another voice, I couldn't see the speaker.

Jack laughed at that, his eyes snapping. He loves this, I thought, he's enjoying it, he's got them going and he knows it. Poor little rich boy or not, he was rolling over them all. He was Honey Fitz's grandson, all right.

"Yeah," he said, "we spent the better part of a year picking up after him!—I and my brother Joe." A two-beat pause to let this sink in. Then: "Sure, a kid of 17 doesn't have all the sense in the world ... But I do now. I think a whole lot of us do, now. We've come home from the war and we've lost a lot of time we'll never get back again—and that's the least of it, the very least. Now we want a fair shake, a *real* say in this post-war world. It's a new world, Danny, make no mistake about that."

His head came up now, he turned from the Neville clique as though they'd never existed. "There's a new spirit everywhere—I felt it at the opening of the United Nations in San Francisco, I can feel it walking the streets of Cambridge here, and Somerville, Charlestown, the North End. Ringing doorbells, talking to people, listening to them, asking them questions. I want to meet every one of you and talk with you personally before this campaign is over—and I'm going to. It's time for a new generation to take the helm—*our* generation—and we're going to do it, too. After all the heartbreak and sacrifices we're going to move forward, and make this city and nation—and world—a proud place for ourselves and our children. And so I ask you for your support as your candidate for Congress!"

He dropped his hands, and smiled. We were cheering, applauding wildly—it came out of us unbidden. This young man would speak for us. It was what we all felt that spring, the first spring without gunfire since '39; and now, here, one of our number was saying it, he was going to try to do something about it.

He'd got down from the beat-up Ford roof now—a jerky, older man's movements, his face stiff with pain; the back was still bothering him—and the crowd pressed in toward him in a babble of calls, shrieks, laughter, a cane-brake of hands reaching. They were his. There was not the slightest doubt about it.

"You know," Russ was saying, "I think he means it..."

"You're God damned right he means it," Terry answered, so hotly that I glanced at him. His eyes were flashing, he was puffing savagely on a cigarette.

Jack was moving toward us now, shaking hands rapidly and firmly, smiling that dazzling boyish smile, his tousled ruddy hair ruffled in the light breeze from off the river. I could hear his voice in the aspirant's ritual: "Thank you, I'll appreciate your support June 18th, thank you so much, thank you for your support—" A girl embraced him, then another, an older woman with iron-gray hair wrung his hand in both of hers; she was weeping and shaking her head and smiling all at the same time. At the far end of the Square a big limousine pulled away fast, heading for Somerville.

"Holy Christ," I heard someone behind me say heavily, "this kid will walk in."

He was very near us now; he caught sight of Russ, his eyes widened all at once. "Tolstoy!" I remembered what Russ had told me about Jack's fondness for nicknames. "How's the gimpy leg?"

"Sound as your aching back!" They laughed together, the two handsomest men in the post-war world: politician and poet, Mick and Brahmin, worlds apart. "Nice going, Shafty. I mean it."

"You're with me, then? Coming over to the party of the future?"

"You know, I might just do that—against my better judgment." They laughed again, and Russ introduced us. Jack's grip was firm and quick, his eyes held on you with sharp interest; well no, it was more than that—you had the sense, for the single instant, that he was concerned with you and only you, in all this hooting, babbling crowd.

"You took them, Jack," Terry was saying excitedly, "McNally, the whole Neville crew. You beat them at their own game! Terrific, terrific..."

That alert, intense, measuring look slipped back in Kennedy's face. "Gilligan," he said. "B-17 gunner. Prisoner of war. Right?"

Terry started. "Why, yes—that's right..."

"I want to shake your hand—you know what it's all about. Are you with me, then?"

"All the way, Jack!"

Kennedy smiled. "Will you come work for me?"

"Why—well, sure, if you feel I could help—"

"Of course you can. I can't do it alone."

"I'll work—I'll slave for you, Jack!" Sheilah cried. "I never heard such a wonderful speech in all my life."

"My impulsive kid sister Sheilah," Terry said.

Jack Kennedy looked at her. "That's what we need—lots and lots of beautiful slaves. Seriously, will you come work for me too, Sheilah? I'm going to win, you know."

"Oh, I will!" And to my amazement she blushed a fiery red all the way into her blouse.

He moved on, shaking hands, people pressing in upon him from all sides, as if somehow to gain grace from his style, gather strength from his very frailty—swung back to us one last time. "I'm counting on you, Gilligan! Come by tomorrow—the Bellevue, okay?" Then he was swallowed up for good in a happy mob of hard-hats, weeping mothers, shrieking girls.

"Fantastic," I heard myself say, as we walked back to the Empress. We were all talking at once. "He's got—I don't know what you'd call it exactly, it's—"

"Magnetism," Russ said. "Intense personal magnetism, charm, psychic force. Some got it, some ain't."

"Well, he's got it."

"How can he lose?" Russ laughed uproariously. "The girls all want carnal connection with him, and the mothers all enjoy sublimating it."

"The hell with that," Terry said.

"It's true—didn't you see—"

"He's a great man," Terry declared in a tone I'd never heard him use before. "He's going to go all the way—he's going to be President of the United States."

"You're crazy—he's a *Catholic...*"

"So am I. An Irish Catholic. Don't you like it, Currier?" And his head came down, his hands came up.

"Terr, for heaven's sake," his sister cried.

Russ was gaping at him. "Oh, come on, Trog, it's a political operation, a con job."

"The hell it is!"

"You said yourself his old man set this up, that PT-boat caper's a crock of—"

"Never mind what I said—I was wrong! You got that,

Currier? Now, you keep your lousy blue-blood opinions to yourself!"

"Terry," I said, "take it easy."

"You want to go round on this, Currier?" Terry said. "Come on, then—"

Russ fell back against the green side of the Empress and slid down to the running board in a gasping fit of laughter. "I don't—just don't believe this. You're a—what are you, Troggy? You're an agnostic—or something. Aren't you?"

"The hell with that."

"Too much, it's—I can't—don't believe any of this..."

"He's going to do it," Terry said doggedly, glaring down. "He's going to wipe it clean—all the old, dirty deals, the graft, the bullshit—everything! You'll see... I'm going to work for him. I'm going to work my balls off for him. And you can knock off the sarcastic wise-guy crap, Currier. All right?"

I couldn't think of anything to say; not a thing. Russ was still sprawled on the running board, shaking with laughter, beating on the side-mounted wheel cover with the flat of his hand. "Whatever you say, Knocko—anything you say. Don't shoot, Knocko baby! I'll go quietly..."

"I HAD FAITH!" Terry cried happily. "I knew he could do it, and he did."

"Listen to him," Russ said, but he was grinning.

"Bricking-sticking-A! They called us chowderheads and punks, they said we didn't have a chance, they laughed at us at the Faneuil Hall rally—and we won. A libation!" He raised his glass, beaming at us, his face dead-white and sweating in the June heat.

"Gilligan, you still can't drink," Dal told him, and Sheilah said:

"Sit *down*, Terr. You make me dizzy."

"A toast, men of Fox: to the winner and champion of the new generation, *our* generation, by God—John Fitzgerald Kennedy!"

"Yaaay, Kenneny!" Ronny, sitting on my lap, crowed, and threw back his head in that complete little surrender to delight.

"Attaboy," Terry glided up to him, tousled his hair clumsily.

"Going to work for us when Jack shoots for the White House?"

"By God, he'll be old enough by then," Dal mused.

"What? Don't be silly. Fifty-six, sixty—maybe sooner."

"You're crazy."

"Will he, really?" Chris asked from the shallow round washbasin that served as a sink. "Run for President?"

"Of course he will. He'll win, too,"

"If the old man's money holds out," Dal said. "They say old Joe shelled out over half a million on the operation. That true?"

"A grand crock. Ask Dalton. Ask Dave Powers. Nobody bought him anything."

"Boys, boys, it's too hot to argue," Chris protested.

"Half a million and a sunk PT-boat," Dal muttered. "That's not a bad return."

"And a million dollars worth of sex appeal," Russ added. "You want to throw that in."

"All right—so he's personable," Terry retorted hotly, "so he used his war record. What's wrong with that? That's politics." He mopped the side of his face with his sleeve. "You sourball skeptics...The *point* is he's changed the face of American politics forever."

"Yeah—it used to be a nice, clean machine-run power struggle and he's turned it into a cheap, glamor-boy, café-society popularity contest."

Terry watched Dal a moment, then smiled. "I declare, Dalrymple. You're turning into a jealous old man. Know that?"

"I'm *not* jealous. I'm merely trying to inject a little common sense into all the sentimental bullshit and hysterical flag-waving."

There came a low barrel-rumble of thunder, far away to the south. "Maybe it'll rain," Chris said, stirring something on the two-burner hot plate. "Cool things off a bit. Dal, Sheilah's glass is empty."

"I'm okay," Sheilah said, "I've had enough."

"Not me," Terry said.

"Yes, you have, Terr. You're fricasseed."

"Nonsense!" He ignored his sister. "Tonight's my night to howl, and I'm howling. Taking it off them all these weeks. Dan Shaughnessy wanted to bet me a thousand bucks Neville would beat Jack two-to-one in Cambridge, and I didn't have the money to put up. Chance of a lifetime! Which reminds me, Wog-o: You owe me twenty."

"Dal!" Chris cried. "Did you bet? Money?"

He shrugged, glaring at Terry. "Just a gentleman's wager."

"You know we can't afford that kind of foolishness! And to bet against your own friends..." She poured red wine from a gallon jug into the bubbling iron casserole with a quick gesture of distress. Playing a fiendish maze game with Ronny, rolling the little steel ball in and out of the dead-end alleys, I watched Chris slice the garlic bread, her face flushed, lips compressed in annoyance, hair damp against her forehead, and thought, She's worn out, worn out with things in this cramped tin shell, away from the sea—and then: No, she's unhappy, deeply unhappy; it's not going well with Dal, she's trying too hard, something... and the realization gripped my heart like a fist.

We were crowded into the Dalrymples' Quonset for an impromptu celebration. The furniture was almost comically hit-or-miss in those days of overcrowding and shortages. There were a couple of ragged canvas butterfly chairs, an ancient Morris chair with half its guts spilling out and a faded paisley shawl draped mercifully over the wound; there were two stools, and a condemned University library chair I'd brought over and repaired one afternoon. Kitchen, living and dining rooms were all one. Grass-mat rugs covered pieces of the plywood floor. The table, which doubled as a desk, was a door Dal had found on the Watertown dump and varnished. Chris had done her best to brighten the tin walls with colorful Japanese dragon kites, and a white rice-paper lantern softened the harsh center fixture; but the atmosphere of pinched squalor stubbornly remained.

And it was hot. Very hot. Tonight we'd taken the windows right out of their frames but it hadn't made any difference: the summer sun cooked the barrel roof of corrugated tin all day long, and the room was like a furnace. Now and then a tiny puff of breeze would stir against the battered screen door, which only made the air seem heavier, more stifling. The bags of ice cubes we'd brought from the new dispenser on Mt. Auburn Street melted before we could pop them into our drinks.

The fact was, Harvard wasn't an institution of higher learning any more. Not really. Like every other college in the country it had turned into a degree factory, a nonstop treadmill of accelerated programs run by suddenly arrogant and

peremptory deans' offices, whose offical attitude was Move It
Or Lose It. To our dismay we saw it was just like the Army: move
out, get it over with—never mind how; shape up or ship out. In
this repple-depple GI Bill world maybe it was inevitable, but that
didn't mean we had to pretend to like it. Even Dal, for all his
hard, pragmatic ambition, felt harassed and disgusted.

And yet it was impossible not to find yourself swayed, even
swept along at times with this rude, prevailing wind. We *had* lost
all that time, life *was* leaking through our cupped hands like
water; hell, we'd seen armies crushed and crowns abandoned—
and here we were, flung back to raw schoolboys again.

Terry alone was jubilant. He'd gone over to Boston the day
after the Central Square rally, and the day after that he'd
dropped virtually everything to work for Jack Kennedy. The
new curriculum suited him perfectly—he'd done the barest
minimum to maintain passing grades. And his new-found idol
had won, and won big: Jack had pulled almost as many votes as
his three leading opponents combined—a stunning upset that
confounded all the experts. Like everyone else I hadn't thought
he could actually win; I felt he might make it close, emerge as a
contender to be reckoned with in future races. But he'd taken it
all, now—he was a cinch for the congressional seat in
November. In one bold stroke he'd become one of the two or
three brightest stars in the Democratic heavens; and he wanted
Terry to serve on his permanent staff.

"—I want to tell you, I was *scared*," Terry was saying. He was
still standing in the middle of the little room, waving his arms.
"Well, five miles, in all that heat, and he was bone-weary to start
with. But my God, he was *blue!* Shivering and shaking— I didn't
think he was even breathing. We stripped him and sponged him
down, somebody called for a doctor, and after a while he came
around. For a minute he looked as if he didn't recognize any of
us, I thought he was paralyzed, or dying or something, and
Mickey Hanrahan said, 'It's all right, Jack, it's all right, boy,
don't move, don't try to move, now...' and all of a sudden Jack
grinned that wonderful grin of his and said, 'What's the matter,
Mick? Afraid it's going to be all for nothing?' 'Don't try to talk,
Jack, just rest,' I said. 'Ah, we few, we happy few, we band of
brothers,' he said. 'Don't worry fellas—they'll hold their
manhoods cheap whiles *any* speaks that fought with us upon
Saint Crispin's day...' And then he closed his eyes again, and

Mickey turns to me and says: 'Who the hell is Saint Crispin?'"

"Harry Plantagenet at Bunker Hill," Russ said; we were all laughing. "Oh, it's too much..."

"Rhetoric," Dal muttered. He'd put on weight over the winter, he looked tired behind that fierce energy, his lower lip thrust out. "A figurehead—that's all he'll ever be. GM, Big Steel, IT&T—that's where the power lies. They tell the Plantagenets what to do."

Terry laughed and shook his head. "That old bromide! Not this time, pal. He doesn't need their money—hell, he's got more than they have!"

"I'll sign that."

"No, he knows just what he wants to do and how he's going to do it. He's got it all diagrammed."

"Sort of like Dal," Russ said.

"Yeah, as a matter of fact it is—and it's all in his head. He's going after the Legion on the housing thing. Can you imagine—the *Legion!*"

"All right, Terr, subside a bit, will you?" his sister said. "You're not the only one around here with some good news."

Terry stopped and stared at her. There was a sudden expectant pause. "What's up? Let's hear it."

Sheilah glanced at Russ. My first thought was, They've got married—or they're going to; then, watching her eyes I knew it wasn't that, it was something else.

"Don't you know, George?" Sheilah asked me. I shook my head. "Don't any of you know?... For pete's sake, Rusty!" she burst out. "Haven't you told them? any of them?"

Russ ran a hand back through his hair. "It'll keep."

"You're crazy... His book!" she exclaimed, "—they're going to publish it! Aurora House."

We burst into a spontaneous storm of congratulations.

"Why, that's wonderful!" Chris cried. "That's wonderful news!" She moved to him with that buoyant ballet dancer's walk and impulsively kissed him on the cheek. "You mean they've accepted the novel, and you've just been *sitting* there?"

Russ smiled sheepishly. "What the hell—it's no big deal. It's Terry's night, anyway."

"The hell it is," Terry said. "That's fabulous!"

It was a funny moment, because from where I sat in the corner by the screen door holding Ronny, I could see everyone:

Chris with a big iron spoon in one band, her face filled with that high excitement again now, that sea-surge toward life's boundless possibilities—but shadowed still; Terry all careening enthusiasm and plans; Sheilah, eyes warm with that adoring passion (she's not in love with him, I remember thinking even then, she's beyond love, it's some crazy obsession, there's no *anchor*); Dal, his face frozen in a half-squint, half-grin, unreadable.

"Now you sweat out the reviews, right?" he was saying.

"Oh, no—first I've got to finish it." Russ shrugged again in his deprecatory way. "They like some parts, they don't like others."

"But they *are* going to publish it," Dal pursued.

Russ looked at him. "Oh, yes. It's set."

"Well, I'll be damned. Sneaky, pretty sneaky, Currier. Sitting there cozy-dog cool, all evening long. Slipping one over on your old pals." Dal's eyes were narrowed to slits behind his glasses. "What we going to do about it, Grog?"

I shook my head, smiling, watched him empty his glass. I had a pretty good idea of what he was feeling. He'd hung in there, freezing and then roasting to death in this corrugated tin hovel, repairing the leaks, plugging the drafts with old rugs, caring for Ronny when Chris was pinned down with other details, marketing Friday nights in Allston to save money, proctoring, grading freshman papers, studying till all hours, grinding out the grades—and in three days two of his three old pals had broken out, with a vengeance. They'd skipped classes, helled around— and it hadn't mattered, they'd made it anyway. They'd outstripped him in a bound. His resentment was almost a living thing—you could literally see him fighting it. Even filled as I was with all possible good wishes for Terry and Russ, I was brushed with a touch of it myself.

"I knew you'd catch it all," Chris was saying, "—the war and everything. All these years . . . What's the title?"

"Full Fathom Five."

"Alliteration!" Terry shouted. "Just can't get away from it, can you! I can see the headlines: Frenetic Fusilier From Fox Fashions Ferocious Farrago of Far-Flung—"

"Terr, *sit down!*"

"What I want to know is, is it liberally peppered with sex?" Dal demanded.

"Every third page."

Terry said: "It's our year! The Year of the Fox..."

What with all the tumultuous news it was another hour and several drinks before we got around to eating. I put Ronny to bed in his crib, which was wedged in a tiny cubicle between the double bed and the back wall. Terry told more stories about the campaign, everyone talked and sweated in the close, damp heat, the radio played the new music called bop—gliding dissonances that jarred on our nerves; the thunder, nearer now, muttered and bumped like artillery. Dal hardly touched his food, drank steadily through the meal. Chattering in a kind of choleric gaiety he stepped on everyone else's lines; he baited Terry about Jack Kennedy, broke in on Chris to tell a long, pointless story about a Wehrmacht officer who'd been discovered in a Paris brothel making a good living as a male prostitute, and finally stumbled into a confused wrangle with Russ over whether Europe or the Pacific had been the more perilous theater of war, while the rest of us listened in boozy resignation.

"—comes to continuous combat, unrelieved pressure—ask *him*." Dal jabbed a thumb in my direction. "He'll tell you..."

"Don't drag me into this," I answered.

"Dal," Chris said quietly, "let's find another topic, all right?"

"I'm talking about sheer, unmitigated pressure, day in day out."

"Well, talk about something else. Nobody's really terribly interested in this."

"Well they should be. Now you—" he pointed at Russ, a quick accusatory finger "—you had one operation, two weeks, maybe three, and then months and months of R&R, some balmy tropical isle, palm trees and the old lagoon—"

"Maybe so," Russ said uneasily, staring at his plate.

"—but in the ETO, baby, it went on and on. On and *on* and on. Artillery alone. George could tell you. If he wasn't such a clam-mouthed son of a bitch. Hell, I remember one time, on the Siegfried Line assault, there were *26 days* when you couldn't stick your ass out of—"

"Oh—what difference does it make!" It was Chris, her eyes burning, one hand gripping the side of her throat; we stared at her, half-sobered by her outburst. "For God's sake, Dal, stop talking about the war, stop *talking* about it!... Did you really love it as much as all that?"

"What!" He rose to his feet, heavily. "Love it—what the hell do you mean, did I love it? What kind of a—what kind of a stupid-ass thing is that to say?"

"Because you act as though you did, sometimes—that's why..."

Lightning flickered once outside the screen door, a blued twilight glow; the paper lantern lifted and danced above the table in a sudden hot gust of wind.

"That's ridiculous," Dal said. "Why shouldn't I talk about it? Give me three reasons. Give me one. Just pretend it never happened—just up and forget it, ah?"

"There's a difference between—"

"Terry hasn't forgotten it. Oh no! He's used it plenty. Tail Gunner Terry, one of Kennedy's heroic vets. Back home. The old—"

"Dal," I said sharply, "let it go."

There was a sudden, brighter flash; thunder broke in a hard, flat report.

"Old Currier's used it plenty, too—look at his war book, here! The Rover Boys in the South Pacific—*there's* mileage, all right all right..."

"Dal," Chris said, "that's a rotten thing to say!"

"Why—just because it's old ivory-tower Russell, with his imperishable prose?"

Russ got to his feet just as the thunder came again in a thin, high, shattering crash. I could see his lips moving; he was saying something to Sheilah, who also stood up.

"What's the hurry, Currier?" Dal's voice roared in on the thunder's fading. "Don't like the hard truths under all the romantic *Farewell to Arms* bullshit—that the ticket?"

"Dal," Chris said fiercely, *"you behave yourself!* These are your friends..."

"Well, this is my house—so-called—and it just so happens—"

"Dalrymple," I said as harshly as I knew how, "you're loaded and you're acting like a shit. Now, *shut up!*"

He stopped dead, gazing at me, his mouth slack, his tongue shoved against his lower lip, while the rising wind hissed against the screens.

"So that's how it is," he said. "You too, Brutus-baby. If you can't lick 'em, sign up, ah? And you *know* better! Well, then you can shove it—the whole sorry bunch of you."

And with a sudden, violent movement he stepped out of the hut, black under the lightning glare. The screen door crashed against the casing.

"Don't go after him, George." Chris stopped me with her hand. "Let him—walk it out, it'll be better." She was blinking hard, her lip was trembling.

"I'm sorry," Russ said. He swung his jacket over his shoulder. "I wasn't going to say anything—I was afraid of something like this."

"Don't be ridiculous. He's smashed... I'm terribly glad, Russ. I am. Dal's really glad, too—you know he is." She had herself in hand again.

He dipped his head. "Well. It's a start."

"The old dream. Remember? Your book in a five-foot pyramid in Scribner's Book Store window on Fifth."

He nodded, smiling. *"The air-built castle and the golden dream..."*

"The maid's romantic wish, the chemist's flame, the poet's vision of eternal fame," she finished, as though it were something they'd said together, long ago. Long, long ago. "Goodbye, Russ."

He stared at her. "Goodbye—what do you mean, goodbye?"

"Nothing... It's the end of something."

"No, it's not."

"Yes, it is. We'll all go to the far corners, now... I'm glad for you, Russ," she said. "Really and truly glad. Make it a good book—a wonderful, terrible, glorious book that'll change everyone's lives overnight."

He laughed. "Hold on, now—I'm just a scribbler."

"No, you're not—you never were... Well, anyway." She embraced him quickly, almost fearfully, turned and hugged Sheilah and then Terry. "Don't worry about this. He'll snap out of it."

They left, then. I stayed on. I couldn't tell whether she wanted me to stay or not, but I'd made up my mind about something. The storm, curiously, had died away; there was an occasional lightning flare, nothing more. Down the row a woman's voice rose, shrill above a man's baritone, both together climbing angrily; then silence. The heat returned.

"Strains of married life in Quonsetville." Chris's mouth

twisted wryly, she tossed her head in that proud way she had, then looked down at the sink.

"I guess we do talk too much about the war," I said lamely. "It's a stupid habit. Like smoking."

"Oh, but *you* don't," she said in the old, soft, musing tone. "You never talk about it."

"What? Sure, I do."

"No, you don't—you're the only one who doesn't. I've noticed. You listen, you even horse around with those nervous-in-the-service routines—but you never talk about it." She turned then, leaned back against the weird little sink, a dish towel held across her hips. "You really want to put it behind you, don't you?"

"It's over, we've had it, forget it."

"Just like that."

I rubbed the back of my neck. "Let's say it's unprofitable."

"You never wrote after that last December. The Bulge. I noticed that, too." Her voice dropped another note, that lovely, ringing cello tone. "You couldn't hold them together, could you, George? The boys you wrote about before. Opp and Dee and the others—that serious kid from Kansas... Could you?"

I shook my head.

"I knew. I knew that was it... It was really very bad there, wasn't it?"

"You haven't got the faintest idea," I said.

"I know, I know that. I knew it then. Following all of you around on those maps, trying to imagine—unable to do one single God damned thing to help you. Those rotten bloody maps! We're so powerless when we most want to be effective, us women. So powerless..."

It was very quiet now. The air was absolutely still.

"I was thinking yesterday—*this* is my World War Two," she said, and laughed once. "Ridiculous, isn't it? The analogies are inescapable, though. The Quonset-half is my tent, the stews are my rations, Ronny's my squad or platoon or whatever, Dal's courses are the campaigns...

"But to lash out at all of you like that—it's wrong!" she cried softly, and her eyes filled now, for the first time. "It's—it's unworthy, of him, of us all. The things we had, the fun, and loony dreams... To begrudge Russ this—"

"Well, there's always been that thing between them," I

murmured. I was only half listening to her now, I was caught up in something else; I felt like a man on the edge of a desperate act—a rescue or a murder.

"I guess I've made a mistake," she was saying now in that sweet contralto. "I guess I never should have done it. I thought—I don't know, I don't know how but I thought we could make a go of it. I know he loves me—he's good, you know, underneath it all; such a *good* man. I thought I could love him, come to love him, you know, and I did—I do love him. You know that, don't you, George. But it's all gone wrong..."

She broke off. She was weeping now, but not like most women, sobbing and gasping; she was merely shedding tears, her worn, lovely face stern, austere, her voice perfectly even, a bit sing-song.

"I had no right to do what I did. I sentenced him for life—I didn't mean to, I swear I didn't mean to, but that's what I did. And he resents it without even knowing it. This blow-off tonight, don't you see?—it was at me, really, not the others."

"You can't think that way," I said with alarm, "don't you see what you're doing?"

"The cruelest things—the cruelest things are the ones we do for the best of motives. Only of course they're not the best of motives at all. Maybe I ought to apply under the Indiscreet Wives Bill. Have you heard about the Indiscreet Wives Bill?—a woman who has a child not fathered by her husband can put it out for adoption without notifying her—"

"Chris, now cut this out..."

"—and the only truth that I can see is that it's better to do the wrong thing for the right reason than do the right thing for the wrong reason. Isn't that profound? Isn't that really deep and profound?"

"*Chris*—!"

"And nothing can undo it, nothing can change it, nothing."

I moved toward her, then. I could no more have stopped myself than if I'd been caught in the undertow at Nauset Beach. I put my hands on her shoulders.

"Chris," I said. "Chris." She came against me, lightly, her head pressed against my throat; she was still weeping in perfect silence.

I said: "I love you, Chris. I've always loved you—from the first day back in 1940. The first time." I hadn't thought I could ever say it, I'd sworn by everything I held holy I never would...and here I was. Saying it. Once I'd started I couldn't stop if I'd tried; it was so ridiculously easy. "Chris, I love you."

"George, I thought I could count on you—"

"You can—that's just what I'm saying..."

"George, I hoped you'd never say it, don't mess up—everybody messes up, all the time! You mustn't, you mustn't do that."

"It's true. I won't ever love anyone else. Ever. I always knew it." I was calm as calm now, holding her, saying at last what had lain like a white-hot coal in my guts for nearly seven years. "Marry me, Chris," I said. "Say you'll marry me."

It was as if I'd tripped a secret spring. She flung back from me violently, almost fell against that crazy Dutch oven, her hand to her mouth.

"George—no, you mustn't say it!" she burst out. "Easy, you think it's that easy—just walk off into the sunset?"

"Chris, I've always loved you, that night in Mattapan I wanted to say it then, I should have said it then." I held her hard against me, but again she drew back.

"*Now,* I'm talking about now! Don't bring that up. There was a time for it maybe but that's gone now, it's past and done." She struck her thighs with her hands. "George, I have a child, a husband..."

"You said yourself you're—"

"Never mind what I said, I'm telling you what I *am*...Don't be like *them!*" she cried all at once. "You're different, you're better than they are. Don't you see that?"

"What?" I protested. I felt all at sixes and sevens. Why were we talking about me? "No," I said, "that's not true—"

"It is, it is! If only because you hold to things—you don't evade or rationalize all over the place, either. You know how to live with what you've drawn, you've always known that."

I laughed then—once and bitterly. "A lot of good it's done me.—And if it's all wrong," I protested, "if it's all a stupid, hopeless mistake—"

"We don't compound the felony," she said slowly.

"Dal doesn't love you—not the way I do," I heard myself pleading. "Oh Chris—give us a chance, I swear—"

"It's no good, George. And you're wrong about Dal, you know. You are. Anyhow, I told you once I was going to try to be a good wife and mother, no matter what. Well—I am."

"But you need me—"

"*He* needs me—he just doesn't know how to show it, he never has. And he was there when I needed him... You mustn't play might-have-been, George. I know! It causes more grief than anything else. You mustn't bring this up ever again. I ask you not to, George."

"You're crazy," I almost shouted, "—you're condemning yourself—you're condemning us both—for a crime we didn't commit!"

She smiled at me—the saddest, darkest smile I'd ever seen. "I have to be the judge of that," she said, and her voice was perfectly steady now. "Not you... And you've got to help me, George. Because I can count on you."

"Yeah," I said after a moment. "Everybody can always count on me."

There was a cry, then—a soft cry from the bedroom. Ronny, waked by our argument, love scene, whatever the hell; or maybe he was having a nightmare. Why not? Why should the kid be exempted?

"That's Ronny." Chris tossed her head briskly, as though to clear it. "I'm sorry about this, George," she said, "I really am—it was my fault."

"Don't be ridiculous, Chris."

"Let's drop it. For good and forever. We must... Please, George." Her gaze was anguished, pleading, quite resolute. "Help me, now. You have to help me." She whirled and went into the bedroom.

Outside the air was just as heavy and foul: the storm hadn't changed anything. I walked quickly along the river, talking to myself. I felt like a man who has just gambled away his entire fortune, put himself in debt for life, on one roll of the dice—I was dizzy-drunk with the sense of boundless loss. "Count on me!" I shouted hoarsely, "oh Jesus, yes, live with it, sure, don't compound the fucking felony, oh Christ!" A couple on the grass near the water's edge were looking at me strangely, their faces blue in the arclight, and I waved to them, laughing, coughing, wagging my head. The bridge, the Stadium, the oil-shimmer of the water all seemed painfully clear, and close, as though I could touch them with the fingers of one hand—there was the same light-headed, breath-suspended clarity I'd felt that afternoon

Denise had phoned me with the news of Jean-Jean's death in North Africa.

At the Larz Anderson Bridge I turned left, toward the Square: I couldn't face Russ and Terry, not now, not for anything. What I needed to do was go to the Oxford Grille and get good and stoned. At the Square I paused—on impulse went down the stairs to McBride's, a smoky roaring din. Friday night in academia. The juke box was playing Glenn Miller's old recording of *Chattanooga Choo-Choo*, and Mike Krupsic and a bunch of ex-paratroopers were crowded into one booth, singing along at the top of their lungs. The bar was three and four deep, cigarette smoke dipped and rose in long, gassy veils. Blazer and Bierce were on the far side, matching pennies—a grim and silent pantomime. I worked my way into the press, ordered an Old Overholt and water, a double—and there at the far end of the bar, wedged in a wall of sweating backs and waving a glass about was Dal, bent over a thin, redhaired girl, who was giggling at him nervously. I pushed my way toward him.

"Ah, come on," he was saying, "don't knock it till you've tried it."

I eased up beside him and said: "Hello, Dal."

He turned—his expression flowed from elation to surprise to hostility. He was blind drunk; his eyes opened and closed like gadgets worked by a child.

"Well—Grog-o Baby. What brings you here, to this iniquous—iniquirous den?"

"You," I said pleasantly. "I was hoping to catch you at your most debonair. And I can see I have."

"Have what?"

"Caught you."

"Grog, want you to meet Arlene," he said, putting his arm around her ponderously. "Arlene, this is Grog."

"Hello, Arlene," I said.

"Hiya!" she said, and laughed merrily. "Is your name really Grog?"

"Really and truly."

"Arlene works in a napkin factory," Dal offered. "In Allston. All kinds of napkins, it seems: table, paper, sanitary—"

"Oooh," Arlene cried, "that's naughty, Russell!"

"Russell?" I inquired. "Who's Russell?"

"Silly! Your friend here. *He's* Russell. Boy, are *you* ever squashed!"

"Oh," I said. "I see. My friend usually uses his middle name, which is Terence."

"Oooh, that's a beautiful name! It's Irish."

"Well, my friend's part Irish. And part Brahmin."

"Brahmin?"

"That's an old Hindu sect."

Arlene laughed merrily again, blowing smoke into our faces. "Aw, you're a kidder!"

"I know," I said. "So's my friend Russell Terence, here."

Dal was grinning at me—his most coony, forbidding Chinese grin, his glasses glinting like mad coins. "A joke, Grog-o. Just a little joke, to pass the time. What's new?"

"Well, several things. One is, that your wife sends her best regards."

"Who?" Arlene said.

"His wife," I said. "W-I-F-E. Homebody. Helpmate. Didn't he tell you?"

"Oh." Her mouth formed a wordless accusatory hollow. "You didn't tell me you were married!"

"He was saving it for a little surprise," I said.

She glared at him, then at me, thrusting herself back, her elbows pumping, through the crowd. "You men, you're all alike—"

"We're bastards," I said.

"Arlene," Dal called, "hey, Arlene, don't rush off..."

"Bye bye, Arlene," I said. "There," I said, turning to Dal, "don't you feel virtuous?"

"Jesus, you're one pain in the ass, Virdon."

"I hope so. I fervently hope so. I hope you get piles with complications."

"Old Tio Jorge. Santa's little helper. You think I can't read you, Virdon?"

"There's nothing to read."

"Oh, no. Sweet Saint George, pure as Galahad." Then with sudden quick savagery: "Why don't you mind your own fucking business, Virdon. Just for once."

"I am," I said. "And you're it."

"Now listen, hot-shot—"

I grabbed his arm just above the elbow, pressed with all my might. "You're going home right now," I said in a very low, very steady voice, "or I'm going to beat the living shit out of you. Every last ounce."

"Is that right."

"That's right. Let's move it."

"Let go me—"

"Let's go." I shoved him through the crowd at the bar, propelled him up the stairs and out into Boylston Street. I didn't care how much of a fuss he made, or how bombed he was either, and he must have sensed it, because he didn't put up any resistance. Outside, however, he flung me off, and plucked off his glasses with one deft, sweeping motion. It was raining now—great warm drops that splashed on the pavement, on our foreheads and hands.

"I'm warning you, Virdon," he said. "Bugger off."

"If you don't go home right now I'll kill you," I said. "I'll break your face."

He studied me a moment: a bull in a pasture, uncertain. I realized I was hoping he'd swing on me, I was praying he would—I was even hoping it would be a long, bloody, grinding battle: I knew I could beat him, and I wanted to fight him more than anything else in the world.

He stepped back, and spat on the pavement. "What a fun evening. Really a riot all around." The rain came down harder now, suddenly chilling, spattering in our faces. Neither of us moved. "Full fathom five thy father lies," he declaimed, nodding. "Doesn't he wish it, though. Chicken-shit snotty bastard—doesn't he realize without his old man he'd be nothing? Nothing! Full fathom five . . . Fuck him!" he snarled, swaying, banging back against the stone. "Fuck him straight to hell and back again . . . Go on!" he shouted at me, "go on back there, kiss his royal ass, you love him so much! Maybe he'll name one of his creepy characters after you . . ."

And now, suddenly, without warning, his eyes had filled. He struck the wall beside him with all his might, swayed against it limply. It was the first time I'd ever seen Dal weep.

I put my hand on his shoulder—gently this time. The rain was beating on us in sheets, in lashing waves.

"You fool," I whispered, "you fool. You've won—can't you see that? *You've won* . . ."

He raised his head and stared at me slackly; his face was drained of all the hot-shot bravura, all guile. It was a look I couldn't read. For half a minute we gazed at each other in silence. I felt close to tears myself.

"I'll tell you about it, Grog," he said finally. "I'll tell you all about it some fine day."

And he swung around and went swaying off down Boylston Street toward the river. There seemed to be absolutely nothing else to do but go back through the rain to Fox Entry.

Two nights later Nancy called from New York. There was going to be a party for Liz and Hugh; wouldn't I come, pretty-please? In a turmoil of anguish and loneliness I told her, By all means, she could count on me, everyone could always count on old Giorgio; I'd be there.

5

"GEORGE DARLING," Nancy said, "this is just like old times. Isn't it?"

"Mmmh-hmmm," I answered. Taking my hand from the silver spokes I placed it on hers, and smiled at her—a rather labored smile; my face was stiff with smiling. Old times . . . Well, it was and it wasn't. We were rolling along in the Empress through drowsy, late-summer countryside, the radio was blaring Tommy Dorsey's *Opus I*, we were headed for a fancy resort by a lake that Nancy knew about.

We were also married. JUST MARRIED. The Empress had been enlisted in an entirely new service. Bedecked in white-and-blue ribbon she was ferrying the newly wed—and their goods: the elegant fold-down luggage rack held Nancy's camp trunk, the rear seat was jammed with cartons of dishes and crystal, silver flatware and clothes—all our worldly possessions, as the saying goes. Sudden? Well yes, I guess you could say it had been rather sudden . . . and then in another way you could say it hadn't been.

But it was going to take some getting used to...

"And *now* what are you thinking?" she demanded, cocking her head at me; that frowning, faintly quizzical glance.

"Déjà vu," I said. "I'm having a funny case of déjà vu."

"Why, how many times have *you* been married before? Now don't brood, darling, it puts lines in your forehead. Want to call it off?"

"And give back all those presents?"

"That would be a drag, wouldn't it? Well, there *was* one moment there I wasn't so sure about you. I wanted to tell old Foxy Elmendorp to hurry it up—you looked as though you were going to yell, 'There's been a mistake, it's all off, everybody go home, *go home!*' Crazy, the outlandish things that race through your mind at moments like that, isn't it?"

But she didn't laugh, and I made no reply. She settled herself back in the green leather seat in that bustling, almost proprietary way she had, and gazed sturdily down the road. The lemon-yellow linen dress made her look cool, completely self-possessed; she was wearing a silk scarf to keep her hair in place, and harlequin sunglasses. I kept wanting to ask her to take them off—for a few moments it became desperately important to me that she remove them; then that mood passed, and I let the narrow country road unfurl lazily ahead of us, smooth black-top ribbon with its fresh white center-stripe and borders; soporific, vaguely comforting.

... I don't know how it all came about really—not exactly how. I'd gone down to New York, to the party for Liz and Hugh; then at the end we found ourselves alone, dancing to the radio, not dancing really, just hovering, indolent as carp in some oriental pool, and Nancy was saying, in low, dreamy tones, "—miss you, darling, oh God, I've missed you so terribly these past months, you can't ever imagine, I tried to be cool and independent and it was all so silly, I can see now it's you, you've always been there, right there behind me like some kind of wonderful anchor or pillar or something—no, it's *true*, it's that simple, darling, it hasn't anything to do with pride or plans for the future, there are always scads of men around, or all that tommyrot, but just—I *need* you so, darling, just to be with you—oh, we've been such lunatics to let all these months go sliding by, all this *empty* time!"—and then I discovered myself holding her tightly, half-crushing her, saying fiercely, almost tearfully, "Yes, yes, it's true, oh God, yes, Nan, yes—!" and then we just stood there, clinging to each other, while out in the river a tanker signaled twice; long, trailing moans...

The wedding had been a strained, convulsive affair; maybe every wedding is, one way or another. We'd agreed, Nancy and I, on a simple ceremony at her parents' home—at least I'd thought we had. And then I got down there to Lancaster two weeks before the wedding to find it was to be a church ceremony, followed by a reception at the country club.

"How'd all this happen?" I asked Nancy in some annoyance.

"Well, Mother says I'll regret it later if we don't."

"But how do *you* feel about it?"

"Oh, I don't know—how should I know?" she said, and her eyes filled with tears. "I'm so tired, George, I don't know, what difference does it make?"

"Well, if it's what you want."

In the end a rough compromise was adopted: the wedding would not be in the church but in the adjacent chapel, and dress would be more or less informal. Mrs. Van Breymer dealt with the florists and caterers and worked out billeting arrangements that would have taxed a divisional G-4. These were clearly perilous, uncharted seas where women assumed command.

Everything, nonetheless, seemed to keep going wrong. Mrs. Van Breymer's father became ill four days before the service, and she wanted to postpone it—but here Nancy, to my surprise, objected so violently and bitterly that her mother gave in. It turned out there was no reservation for my parents at the country club; that mix-up took several hours to straighten out; I was enraged at my father's air of helpless fatalism and my mother's solicitous self-effacement, and suspected Mrs. Van Breymer—probably unfairly, but the late August heat was savage, and I was on edge. Nancy's mother was opposed to the marriage, I knew: she felt I might "do," being white, gentile, and a Harvard man, with prospects (albeit vague ones) of being a good provider—but that Nancy nevertheless could certainly "do better" if she'd only bestir herself a bit. Something like that—it's odd how clearly we read the unspoken messages of this world.

Walter Van Breymer, on the other hand, liked me a good deal—possibly he saw in me some of his own struggling young manhood, his hard-won position. And maybe he saw more than that, too; I've never been sure... Yet his sentiments were overborne. Clara Van Breymer weighed me with those bold bright-blue eyes and found me wanting; and she was so certain! You felt she'd never been oppressed by a lingering doubt in all her ex-Junior League, committee woman's life.

"But where will you be living in Cambridge? I mean, what *arrangements* have been made?" Her expression was mildly peremptory—the face, I saw with a soft, hollow shock, that Nancy's would become in twenty years or so...

And there were other troubles. The gardenias were not delivered as promised, there was a misunderstanding over the rented Lincolns that were to bear us from the chapel to the club. Even my best white shirt popped a cuff button as I was dressing. Seeking help I went down the hallway, heard terse, angry exchanges—women's voices—coming from Nancy's bedroom, and hurried back to my own room and changed shirts. Outside I could hear the seethe of tires on gravel, the slamming of car doors and the false, overbright soprano cries of estranged family members greeting one another. The heat was excruciating.

In the middle of all this Walter Van Breymer invited me to go into the den with him. We'd already had our private talk several weeks before, when I'd declared my intentions and defended my prospects, so I had a pretty good idea of what was coming. He closed the door with an air of both apprehension and relief, and we sat down. He smiled at me once and looked away, fussing aimlessly with a brass elephant on the table by his chair. His sandy hair was parted just a touch to the left of center.

"I'll be frank with you," he began. "You know we're fond of you, George. Now Clara feels you two've got no business getting married, with you still in college and all." I smiled and nodded. "Well hell, Clara's forgotten how it was when we got married. I was clerking at Werthauer's, I had about $300 saved and that was it. Fact is, if everyone waited till they *did* have any business getting married they'd all be too old to care about it any more." He gave a deep, sudden sigh, more to relax himself than out of impatience or distress. "Nan's been up there in New York City, being the independent young career woman. On her own, making her own decisions—she knows what she wants..." He knocked over the little brass elephant, righted it again. His lips under the neat, sandy mustache gave a wry twist, his eyes blinked at me warmly. He'd be a good man to work for—demanding but straight. "And yet she's still my little girl. Going off to school, her hair in pigtails. And I just wanted to say . . ."

He broke off again, now visibly embarrassed. I was finding it increasingly difficult to maintain a properly deferential attitude.

"Well," he said with a kind of summary regret, "you're a man grown, I know that, you've been away to war—France and Italy and everything. So all I want to say is—" his face took on a naked, pleading look "—be gentle with the little girl. Just—be gentle with her, George."

"I will, sir," I said. "I promise you."

"Well, that's it, then." He got to his feet hurriedly and shook hands with me as though we'd just met. "That's it. We'd better get going—Clara'll have my scalp if we don't get on out there."

The ceremony itself was interminable. Utterly and everlastingly interminable, world without end, amen. Foxy Elmendorp the minister, who did look vulpine with his ruddy triangular face and bushy eyebrows, got thoroughly carried away by the occasion; his thin, husky voice, lisping irritatingly on the sibilants, rose and fell in long, labored waves. Time hung from the pinched gray vault of the ceiling like sleeping bats, dripped like stalactites. My nerves seemed on the point of rocketing out of my body. Why did everything have to take so infernally *long?*

I was consumed by the sense that I'd forgotten something—something irreparable, the discovery of whose loss would bring on utter disaster. Was that what it was? . . . *The rings.* No—Russ, standing right here beside me, looking slender and elegant in a new navy blazer from J. Press, had the rings in his right-hand pocket; I'd seen him check just before we came out of the vestry. What, then? All those rows of eyes behind us were riveted on the back of my skull: old friends, new relations. Jesus, didn't *anyone* else feel this? On my other side Nancy looked perfectly composed, in white organdy with the short veil of lace and her mother's single strand of pearls; every inch the Bachrach bride in the New York *Times*. She was following Elmendorp with an earnest, eager expression, her brow perfectly serene . . . *You two,* I wanted to say aloud—very nearly did say—disengaging myself, stepping back, leaving Russ and Nancy standing there; you two go ahead with this, I'll just—

No, that was wrong, too. No, Dal ought to be in my shoes, marrying Nancy, they'd go well together, they were immensely compatible in many ways: they dealt in tangibles, the art of the possible. Yes, and then Liz and Russ ought to pair off—that hot, unreckoning lust for the invisible no one else sees, crossgrained, vulnerable, self-centered; why not? And then Chris, sitting there in the third row on the left of the aisle, would rise as I came toward her, standing so tall and regal and straight, empress and ballerina and watersprite all in one, who trod so sweetly proud—oh, golden Yeats she loved so . . . and I'd say, "You see, it's better this way, better for us all, don't you see, darling?" And she would nod, holding her head in that funny brave archaic way, a woman Homer sung, her warm skin glowing and her hazel eyes glittering with tears—but tears of joy this time, she'd see it too, who wouldn't? Why in God's name not, change partners, dos-à-dos with your partner, breast to breast; lightly, lovingly change partners in this turbulent, mystifying dance—

Something had happened. Had ended. I swam in sudden white panic. Elmendorp's eyes were fastened on me coldly, dilated with expectancy. What was wanted? Russ's knuckles pressed me just under the ribs.

I said: "I do." Not my own voice at all. Nancy was speaking then in a clear, high voice. Russ produced the rings, easily and unobtrusively, Nancy and I exchanged them—it was over. Suddenly, magically, unfairly: over, and I wasn't ready, somehow. We were moving together up the aisle, all the faces turning like flowers, blank blurs. My face was burning; the light outside hurt my eyes.

The reception was better; a little better. At the club we stood with our backs to the windows overlooking the 18th hole and the courts, and the faces slid toward us along the line, facetious or solemn or weepy. Terry, sardonic and pleased; and Sheilah, who hugged me, crying and laughing, and said weddings always affected her this way; and Mel and Marge Strasser, who were living in Brookline while Mel interned at Peter Bent Brigham, and Hugh and Liz Moncrief, and Gwen Carrington, whom Nancy had seen a lot of in New York, who'd been married and divorced and made big money now as a fashion photographer; and finally Chris, who embraced me—a quick, light clasp, her lips brushing my cheek—and said: "I hope you'll be happy, dearest George—there's no one I'd rather see happy than you," and then she kissed Nancy, who looked at her in a kind of cool triumph, turning her cheek; and then Dal, sweating in a gabardine suit as old as mine, was telling me it was about time, after all the cheap procrastination...

There was, mercifully, good champagne, which I drank too much of; there was a cake, a many-tiered affair Nancy and I cut together, and which was filled with dozens of little silver charms—Russ discovered a top hat in his slice, Chris found a star, I drew an old hightop shoe. A photographer, a nervous young man with bulging eyeballs and wearing a bow tie, kept grouping and regrouping us in different false combinations; there was a little band that opened with *Serenade in Blue,* Nancy's favorite, and I led her out on to the floor, feeling curiously wooden and off-balance.

"There he goes—the champ of Norumbega Park," Dal called, and I grinned, but sadly, thinking of Russ, who would probably never dance any more with that knee, and Chris, whirling and whirling under the golden spangles, and Jean-Jean...

Time passed, in the heat. My mother liked Nancy immensely, as I knew she would, and Russ charmed Mrs. Van Breymer, as I knew *he* would, and Dal and Mr. Van Breymer talked overseas markets and reconversion; people kept congratulating us, and I stood there, sweating and grinning like an orangutang and saying to myself, A new life, a new life—

And finally we ran outside through a blizzard of rice to where the Empress was drawn up, all washed and polished fit to kill, and Russ handed me the key, and everyone was shouting and throwing rice at us, and I started to say, "Thanks, Russ, it's really great of you, I won't ever—" and right there in all the bedlam I saw his face was working, his eyes were filled with tears...

"Russ was sweet," Nancy was saying now, as if she'd read my thoughts. "To lend us the old Empress like this. He's changed, hasn't he?"

"Do you think so?"

"Oh, yes. He's so much more—confident, at ease. With the book coming out next spring. Much more considerate—I've noticed. Success makes people better."

"I don't know—"

"Of course it does. No, it's Chris I feel really sorry for."

"Why's that?"

"Oh honestly, George." She gave me her significant look. It

was something I'd noticed about Nancy ever since the war—her habit of stylizing certain glances. "It's called Making the Best of a Bad Bargain. Don't you think *anyone* could see through it?"

I turned and looked at her. It was the first time I'd seen this side. "Chris likes you," I said quietly.

"I know she does, darling. And I like her. That doesn't mean you can't see another person clearly . . . She's going to leave him soon," she said. "Dal."

"Chris?—never," I said.

She threw me a swift, quizzical glance, looked sturdily away down the road again. "Too fast," she said, after a pause. "She moved too fast. Only long engagements make any sense. Like ours. Love at first sight—that's one of the world's bigger and better myths."

I said nothing. We really hadn't had a long engagement; just a kind of—obligation, was it? a sort of commitment? I sighed. That just made three—no, four—assertions of hers I already disagreed with.

We drove in silence for a time. There was a stretch where they'd been making road repairs. I took it a touch too fast, and dust rose around us in swirling hot clouds. The sense of strangeness, of dislocation persisted. Nothing fits, I kept telling myself, the way I had during those first terrible weeks back home; none of this is real, somehow, not real . . .

"Did you hear what Dal called as we left?" Nancy was saying with irritation. "That old bromide about your going right on up with the window shade? Honestly, sometimes I don't think he's got all his marbles."

"It's just the way he is. He thinks it's being witty."

"Bordello humor, I suppose. You'd think a little Harvard polish would have rubbed off along the way."

"Let's don't talk about them," I said suddenly.

"What? All right—yes!" She squeezed my arm. "Let's just talk about us. Nothing but us."

That seemed to change her mood. She turned light-hearted, lying back against the seat, her hands behind her head.

"Let's trade dreams, Georgie. Childhood dreams. You know, like TLs. Mine is what Nurse Hatchér used to call 'competence made instinct.' You know: the catastrophe, right out of nowhere, the nervous hush in the crowd, a voice calls out: 'Is there anyone here with medical training?' And I step forward, perfectly calm and assured, and say, 'Yes. I have.' And there is a murmur of approval, and the crowd breaks back as I move through them to the prostrate figure . . . Slow dissolve, as Russ would say. What's yours, darling?"

"I don't know," I said. "I'm not much on daydreams."

"Now darling, everybody has *one.* You're going to have to stop that dreary anti-social habit, Georgie. Now we're an old married couple."

"What habit's that?"

"Of never saying what you're thinking. It's in restraint of conjugal togetherness. Come on, confess—tell your blushing bride."

"Well, let's see—it's a more or less vague thing," I said with an effort. "There's this war between Austria and Turkey in 1837, and nobody really knows why—not *really* why—and I unearth some new documents, piece together overlooked correspondence and so forth, and come up with the real reason. Not very exciting, I'm afraid."

"Oh, but it is! Much more important than Russ's novels. What are they, anyway, but fabrications? And Dal's dreams of becoming another bug-eyed J. P. Morgan, gloating over his moneybags. Did you hear Liz kidding him, asking him how the old Monopoly do-not-pass-go schedule was coming along? if he'd picked up that Caribbean yacht yet?"

"He'll do it," I said. "He's been working hard."

"Didn't you think Liz looked wonderful? She's going to Europe in October, she and Hugh—Hugh's going to be putting on a big new exhibition at the Met this winter. Gee, I'm going to miss her."

"New York's not so far away," I said.

"Well, you know what I mean."

We reached Lake House in the early dusk. It was a massive, rambling old structure, abounding in turrets and terraces, part castle, part hacienda—a product of the lost, grand, turn-of-the-century summer resort days. It was humming with activity: people hurrying in from tennis, lounging and drinking under umbrellas, hurrying off somewhere else. Our room was large (we'd reserved it through Nancy's father), with a little iron balcony that overlooked a corner of the lake. We unpacked slowly, showered and changed, and went down to dinner. There was a band here too, a better band than the one at the club.

Surreptitiously I tipped the leader to play *Serenade in Blue* and *Stairway to the Stars* and ordered a bottle of Piper Heidsieck, which pleased Nancy; and we danced some, and talked.

When the floor show began I suggested we leave, but she wanted to stay on and watch it. The comedian wasn't very funny, and the imitations of celebrities a woman did weren't very good either, but Nancy laughed, enjoying it—I'd never seen her so exuberant and carefree—and I began to catch her mood. She looked lovely sitting there in her soft voile off-the-shoulder dress, her hair a feathery gold crown in the blued light. She was so—I don't know, so touching in the way she sipped at her champagne, smiling to herself, her eyes roving over the nearby tables. It's such a vulnerable moment, that first evening together after the wedding, with all your life spread out before you like some grand Renaissance painting, or a voyage to far Cathay: so many things to see, feel, surmount together...

She caught me looking at her, and smiled. "The secret life of George Virdon," she said, but her voice was soft this time, low with affection.

A rush of great warmth for her stole over me; I thrust away the sense of baffled dislocation that had held me since the ceremony, took her hand and said: "No secret. I was just thinking how lovely you look right now. And how happy I want to make you."

"Flattery—flattery will get you anywhere, Mr. V." Her eyes turned moist then; she dropped them.

"It's true," I said. And I meant it, too. I wanted nothing more at that moment than to make her happy—I did. That night at Liz and Hugh's she'd said she needed me, and I realized now I wanted that terrifically, I *wanted* to be the person she needed and trusted more than anyone else; we could have a good life together, a full, wonderful life—all it took were warm and willing hearts...

When we finally went up to our room she was in high spirits, doing a series of little dance steps on the stairs. But when I closed the door behind us and took her in my arms she was trembling.

"What is it, sweet?" I said.

"I'm—nervous, I guess. Nervous-after-the-service." She laughed, and looked at me—a funny little glance, rueful and wry and suppliant. "Wedding fatigue."

"I know. I am a little, myself." I did feel a bit unsteady, but I knew its source clearly enough. Watching her downstairs I had begun to want her more and more—I wanted too, with all my heart, to put everything else aside and share a new felicity with her, lead her gently into that high, deep joy... We hadn't made love since that long-ago afternoon by the lake—which is to say we never had, really. On the few occasions we'd been alone together during the past year she'd made it clear enough she wanted it that way; she was determined that we wait; and burdened with work and caught in my own emotional turmoil all spring, I'd been ready enough to accept it.

I kissed her on the lips, the eyelids, the throat. "There's a cure for that, darling," I murmured. "A lovely cure."

But she was still trembling—her hands moved on my back in tense little plucking patterns. After a moment or two she drew away a step.

"I'm sorry," she breathed. "I need to relax—get relaxed a little, I guess."

"Don't worry about it, Nan."

"I know it must seem silly to you—"

"No, it doesn't. Why should it? Don't worry about it, honey." My arm clasped around her shoulder, holding her, I smiled. All right—she was nervous, unsure of things, maybe even a little frightened; it didn't matter. I had tenderness and ardor enough for two, enough to carry her with me, swinging in that golden net, I was certain of it... Haven't I said we were the most unready of all the unready generations? And we were; God knows, we were.

Nancy went in and ran a hot bath while I sat on the balcony sipping at a drink and listening to the dance music drifting up from the ballroom; thinking of Nancy in that tub in there, and then trying not to think of her, focusing on the future instead. We had a Quonset-half lined up; it would be a bit rough but it was only temporary. I'd graduate in February, I'd have my master's in two years; I knew Langer would accept me for his seminar. What would I tackle in my thesis? Something pivotal—my German was good, my French was better. *Operation Sealion,* maybe. Why hadn't Germany invaded Britain? Really why? Why hadn't Hitler sealed off Gibraltar? Chances missed. Had the Thousand Year Reich lost the war right there, in the fall of 1940, the golden autumn we all piled into the Empress and Russ called out, "Welles*ley, Welles*ley!"

and Jean-Jean pulled up at the dorm entrance with a lazy, disdainful swing of the wheel, and the girls came flocking around us crying, *"Love— that—convertible!"*

A shadow passed over me, across the balcony railing, vanished. I turned my head. Nothing. Grazed by some nameless concern I got up and went back into the room. Nancy was lying in bed, hands behind her head.

"Hey," I said with a grin. "What you doing there?"

That look—of rueful resignation, of undefined appeal—was back on her smooth little heart-shaped face. "Just thinking."

I sat down beside her on the bed. "Why didn't you tell me?"

"Tell you what?"

"That you were through bathing."

"I"—she shrugged—"didn't want to spoil things..."

"Spoil things?"

"I mean I just wanted to lie here for a moment and think about everything." Her body stirred under the sheet, as though she were nestling deeper into some burrow. "All the things we're going to do. How we're going to manage. Everything's going to be so different now."

"I know." She wanted to hold the moment, then, like a snatched breath caught, dizzying? I could understand that—I loved her for it. But not now. Not *this* moment. I ran my fingers along the edge of her neck. "We'll talk about all that. In good time."

"Well, I only meant we ought to—"

"All in good time, darling. Now—is another time."

I kissed her then, very softly. Her lips were full, compact and neat: I'd forgotten how small they were. Her arms moved up behind my head, a tentative cradling motion.

"You're all right?" I whispered.

"Yes—I'm okay now. I don't know what was the matter with me."

I began to undress quickly then, automatically emptying my pockets on the bureau. Wallet, change, penknife, key to the Empress. The little cowrie shell clattered hollowly on the glass cover.

"What's that? What's that?" Nancy called tensely.

"Just a lucky shell Chris gave me. Before the war."

"Oh." Then, very flatly: "Surely you didn't carry that silly thing around with you for four years..."

"Yes, I did," I said.

The lamp beside the bed went out. I turned in surprise. Light—blued, vaguely metallic—poured into the room from the balcony. Naked, I swung in beside her. She was wearing a gown, long and flowing around her, which surprised me again—I'd been so sure she'd be naked.

"No fair," I said lightly, "you're all muffled up."

"Silly, isn't it?" She laughed once. "Wait a minute." She sat up and shrugged out of the gown, her head back. Her round little breasts were pale as milk, smooth as alabaster, faintly dusty under my hand. She was so immaculate! Everything had been soaped, rinsed, powdered away; I missed the fine, beguiling scent of flesh, dense woman smell. I kissed her throat, the line of her collarbone, her breasts, took one tenderly in my mouth, felt the nipple rise from a quiescent bud into a tight, small cone. Her breathing came roughly now, heightening—a faint, muffled protest; she made as if to pull away and then abandoned that, and thrust upward with small, troubled movements.

"You're lovely," I murmured, comforting her. "You have a lovely little body, Nan."

"This is our time—our first real time," she breathed hoarsely, "isn't it? This time now, darling."

"All right."

"No, I mean it—I want that."

"All right, love." If she wanted that, why not? In place of that sad, desperate coupling by the lake... This would be our real lovemaking, then. So be it. Her solid little body swelled against me now, the smoothness of her belly, the cradle frame of her pelvis. All surging warmth, rising, coming to meet me. What a mystery and a delight a woman's body was! I flung back the sheet and knelt above her in the pale blued light, kissed her belly, her thighs, caressed her silky fur, those tender, tender petals, slipped my hands beneath her buttocks and lifted her gently toward me, toward joy, to bring her to this bursting joy where all lovers—

"—No!" she was crying, had been crying, "no, no—what are you doing—!"

She wrenched herself away from me, gasping, one hand clenched tightly, covering herself. "What's the matter with you—!"

Hands on my thighs I gazed at her in consternation, in alarm;

she was afraid—my God, she was still afraid. No, it was more
than that. She—

"Nan—"

"You're not overseas now, with one of your cheap Italian
whores... I'm your wife, your *wife!*—remember?"

I felt fury, fear, remorse—a stormy confusion. She looked
threatening now; her face was closed, set, implacable.

I stammered, "Nan, I love you..."

"Love—! You call this *love?* It's—it's degrading!" she cried,
and she clutched her gown around her now. "It's all dirty, it's
insulting!"

"How can you say—"

Snatching up her negligee she swung out of bed. I reached out
to her.

"Nan, listen a minute—please, Nan—"

"No! Let me alone, leave me alone!"

She ran into the bathroom—the door banged shut, the lock
was thrown; I could hear the toilet flushing, then the shower in a
high, thin roar.

Dirty, degrading. No; no, it was not. But it did not look as if I
was going to be able to convince my wife of that. Her voice had
been so wild, her eyes so frightened, so threatening... I could
try; I *would* try; but somehow I felt even then it was not going
to be enough.

I went to the bathroom door, tapped on it lightly, said:
"Nancy. Nancy, please open up and listen..."

There was no answer. The shower was still seething. I pulled
on my robe and went out on the balcony and sat down. The
orchestra was playing *Starlit Hour,* an old Glenn Miller
arrangement.

You're not overseas now.

They had warned the country about us, of course: us
sex-crazed veterans. They'd done their duty. Silver-haired
orators had actually risen on the Senate floor and urged the
creation of "Demilitarization Centers," where the most
dangerous—er—combat types might be—ah—rehabilitated
prior to release. Years ago Uncle Dick had made a guarded
reference to the Army of Occupation of the Rhine as having
been made up mostly of men who had contracted syphilis—I
could still recall his voice lowering on the word—kept there for
the long, painful mercury treatment of those days. Now, one war

later, we arrant American sons had brought home something far more contagious, far more deadly to our puritan shores—that Mediterranean memory, glory in the many mansions of love.

Abbracciami, amore.

The band had quit. Farewells and laughter swelled up in the parking area behind the terrace, died away again. Lights were going off in the wing downstairs. Above the pines the stars hung like soft round globes in the late summer heat; out beyond them the Milky Way arched its course in dusty incandescence through infinity. Gazing at it, smarting and despondent, I thought of Chris standing by that makeshift sink, hands at her sides, weeping; remembered what she'd said about doing the wrong thing for the right reason . . . But she'd been wrong. I'd gone the other way; and it was every bit as bad.

6

WELL: MARRIED LIFE. Bumps, bruises and adjustments. It is mind, not body, that makes marriage last. Time heals all things... Why are the people who coin adages always such damned absolutists? No: time heals *some* things; enough so that we learn to keep it all turning over, restore the amenities, maintain a kind of interminable patrol.

We made it up, of course. What else was there to do? Nancy was cold and forbidding and outraged. I held her in my arms and told her I was sorry if I'd offended her, truly sorry, I'd only wanted to bring her joy: and after a while she wept and said she was sorry, too; and after that she became mollified, and contrite, and still later timidly ardent; and we made love—of a sort. In time she even seemed to enjoy sex—at least I thought she did. Not a rich, joyous celebration but a sort of diffident desire, anyway. But something had rolled down between us with the crashing finality of those iron shutters on the Italian shopfronts, and nothing was ever going to be quite the same again; I knew.

Keep thine eyes wide open before marriage; and half shut afterward. Another adage. Half of it I'd already found to be true, at any rate.

I got off to a good start that fall, nonetheless. The Maladjusted Veteran Syndrome had run its course; everyone was working now, everyone wanted to finish up and get out, to get on with it. My thesis ran on in leaps and bounds—it was almost as if some wiser, more eloquent colleague were writing it. I was doing what I wanted to do more than anything else in the world: I was delving into *why*—peeling back the leaves of that grand old artichoke, human existence itself. At times the hunger to seize the very heart of it, to *know*, would clutch me so I would sit up till two, till three, reading on and on. It was like penetrating the darkest continent of all; my eyes would burn and there would be a bar of solid pain across my forehead, and still I couldn't stop. Langer liked my work and told me so; everything fell into place. I was hitting my stride.

Even living in a drearier, more decrepit Quonset-half than the Dalrymples' didn't bother me much. I'd been used to making do, dealing with pressures; there were only a few more of them now, that was all. It even made for a nice sense of partnership with Nancy, planning shopping expeditions, hitting the laundromat, budgeting, getting by on less. It was only temporary; we were going to lick the world, we knew we were.

One gusty, booming November evening I came in to find Nancy looking very tense and distrait.

"I've got some bad news," she said, after a few preliminaries. "I guess it is. I think I'm pregnant."

I felt a shock deep in my belly, a gathering swell of dislocation, of concern; then a slow, quiet elation. I put my hand on hers. "Darling Nan," I murmured.

"I thought I was all right. Just a skip or something." She gave a deep sigh, slumped forward again. "It should have been all right." She hated to wear a diaphragm, she'd preferred the rhythm system, which had surprised me; now she was blaming herself. It was curious how sexual responsibility for pregnancy had shifted over the past few years: before the war the burden had fallen, unfairly enough, mainly on the man; now, unfairly enough, it lay with the woman. Was some industrious sociologist buried in a stack up in Widener even now, predicting a new matriarchal culture because of it? Probably.

"It *is* all right," I said. "It's great, Nan."

"I didn't want to say anything until I was sure. Bother you. Especially at a time like this." She shrugged despondently. "Poor timing."

"Don't say that, honey." The deep, humming elation had increased—I felt jubilant, invincible, an illustrious father of the race. "It's wonderful, wonderful news!" I hugged her; she slumped against me, drew back smiling, her eyes full of tears.

"You're a good man, George. You really are."

"Of course I am."

"How'll we manage? With a baby...?"

"We'll make out. Look at Chris and Dal."

"Yes. Look at them."

"They're doing fine! And so will we." I hugged her again; I hadn't felt so happy about anything in years. "Now don't you worry," I told her, "you just relax and take it easy, I'll handle everything—the hospital and everything."

She laughed then, and shook her head at me. "You idiot—that's seven months away. *Seven months.*" She stared at the end wall, where I'd hung a battered Mexican serape in an ill-disguised attempt to liven up the room and stop some of the draft. "My God."

"It'll go by like a flash. You'll see."

Actually it didn't—the time that winter moved slowly. Nancy got a job working in the infirmary, and we put aside some money; not much, but some. I worried about her, doing this for my sake, as she often said—I tried to take on as many of her chores as I could. Dal wound up his stint at the Busy School in a burst of glory, and he and Chris left for Chicago and some serious job-hunting.

"I'm ready, Grog," he said. "I'm ready to roll."

"Become chairman of the board," I chanted, "collect five million dollars. Pass go."

"Have your fun," he grinned. "I'm going to burn up the track."

"He will—I really think he will," Chris said.

She hugged me and said goodbye; I buried my face for an instant in that deep, coppery hair, and said softly, "Hey, good luck, good luck..."

Chris was right—we were all heading for the four corners now. Terry went down to Washington as part of Congressman Kennedy's permanent staff. And in April Russ's novel came out.

New York was gleaming, New York was bracing and lively and full of certainty and power. It's hard, in the tawdry, uncaring, murderous minefield Manhattan has become, to remember what a vivid, intoxicating capital it was in the spring of 1947. The little golden Mercuries atop the lamp posts on Fifth Avenue seemed to symbolize it all—its speed and wealth and air-borne grace. There were places to park in Midtown in 1947; waiters in the East Side bistros were polite, and even attentive, and the food was superb; blacks and whites joked with each other in the bleachers at the Polo Grounds, happily passing beer and hotdogs along the rows, couples strolled through Central Park at midnight without qualms; and if some unfortunate soul suffered a heart attack passersby even escorted him to the nearest hospital, where attendants rushed him to emergency without demanding proof of medical insurance. Ah, call back yesterday...

We left the Merchants Limited and came up the ramp into Grand Central Terminal, with its festive animated ads, and its long vaulted ceiling glinting with zodiacal gods, and Nancy squeezed my arm and said: "Let's have fun!"

"Let's!" I said. We took a cab at the Vanderbilt entrance and rolled briskly uptown to Liz and Hugh Moncrief's apartment, pointing at the shop windows and interrupting each other. New York was an adventure, a challenge, a reward for good behavior; your heart picked up a beat in New York those days. It made you feel glad that you were young and healthy and fairly bright, with 40-50-60 years rolling out ahead of you like the Yellow Brick Road. No one was home, but we let ourselves in as Liz had instructed us to, washed up and changed like kids on holiday.

"How do I look?" Nancy asked me. She was wearing a teal blue dress of light wool—she always looked well in blue, with her eyes and bright blond hair; there was just the beginning of fullness high in her belly.

"Scrumptious," I said.

"No, seriously." She studied the gold-rimmed mirror over Liz's vanity with that straight, hard gaze. "I mean for a pregnant old female."

"You'll be the most expectant person there."

"Very funny." But she laughed. "If only I didn't *feel* so unattractive."

"It's all in in your mind. And your tummy-tum. Come on, let's get down there and meet the élite. Sass the brass."

The occasion was the publication of *Full Fathom Five.* Russ's book was already a success—at least the publishers were reasonably certain it was going to be. The advance reviews that had appeared so far were highly favorable; and they were to get even better. "Captures the terror and high courage behind those great naval victories in the Pacific; Currier's swab-jockeys are depicted with rare humor and compassion"... "More convincing battle scenes have not been realized since Remarque and Barbusse"... "Appalling in its impact and brutal in its truth. In one leap Currier has joined that illustrious company of Conrad and Melville and Stephen Crane"... I still remember the reviews.

To Jean-Jean, first of the Fusiliers—who led us into the valley of the shadow, the dedication said; and that too, seemed fitting and good. Russ had lent me an extra set of galley proofs a month before, and I'd read right through till five AM, risking Nancy's wrath and the morning's demands. A lot of it was autobiographical (I knew that from his letters), but far more was imagined. The war was there, it was all there, whatever you'd seen or felt or done. By the time I reached the final scene I was weeping, weeping for the inconsolable losses, the desperate decisions; the long death of innocence...

The party was being held in the executive offices of Aurora House. These were still the days when the emergence of a significant book was an occasion to be celebrated. Nobody referred to a novel as "the property" then—at least they didn't here in the east. There was still the belief that people liked to read, needed to read; that good books mattered, could change our lives... and there was also that year an intense rivalry among the publishing houses over *the* war novel: the one author of *our* generation who would take his undisputed place in the company of Tolstoy, Crane, Hemingway. Aurora House felt they had him in Russell Currier.

Things were at a rolling boil by the time we got down there; the long rooms were studded with small buzzing clusters from which individuals kept breaking away in sudden bursts of merriment, as if the laughter itself possessed some explosive force, and drifted off—to be instantly absorbed by another buzzing nucleus. Bernard De Voto was there, with his dry, barking laugh, and so was Thomas Heggen. I recognized John Hersey, looking solemn and handsome, talking with Eric Sevareid, who didn't look solemn at all—and who looked a lot handsomer. I saw Irita Van Doren, with that sad, fine head, and Virgilia Peterson, as restive and imperious as an osprey. John Horne Burns, whose war novel had just come out, was talking with—or rather, listening to—an intense, saturnine Gore Vidal, who had dashed off *his* war novel (some said maliciously) even before the war had fairly begun. Cass Canfield, very Groton, was there, chatting with Lewis Gannett of the *Tribune*; and Orville Prescott, clearly not a partying man, stood a bit aloof and austere, looking just the way you hoped the *Times* book critic would look.

There were others I couldn't place, though, and no one around me could identify—quick, nervous men in raw silk jackets and Sulka ties. They smoked slender dun cigars and sported deep tans, though it was barely April, and their women were overthin and overdressed and over madeup; their nervous energy was an almost palpable thing in the warm, light air.

And at the center of it all was Russ, looking like a young conqueror in a tweed jacket and whipcord slacks, greeting people with a subdued warmth. Chris and Dal hadn't been able to come east from Chicago—though Dal sent a festive, congratulatory wire—but Terry had flown up from Washington; Sheilah was there, bubbling with excitement, and later Liz came in without Hugh, who had been held late at a staff meeting, and Fletcher, who on the strength of his prowess in Japanese had promoted himself a job on the Far East desk with *Time*. Norris Lydecker, Russ's editor, came up and Russ introduced us.

"George—George is the only reason we're standing here right now!" Sheilah exclaimed happily. "He kept Russ's nose to the grindstone, all last year."

"Sheilah, come on," I protested.

"It's true!"

"Before the war," I said to Lydecker, "I used to ride herd on him now and then. But he worked like a demon on the novel—you couldn't get him to stop."

"George is the mainspring of the Fusiliers," Sheilah added. "You know about the Fusiliers." Lydecker nodded. "Well, George is sort of—our conscience, I guess you'd call him." She winked at me mischievously. "He keeps us all on track."

"You're the scholar in the group." Lydecker was a tall man with a bony face and heavy salt-and-pepper eyebrows; beneath them his eyes held a sardonic twinkle, like Raymond Massey's. He was smoking an unlighted pipe. "Russ tells me you're better read than he is."

"Oh, no—only in history."

"But you've taken a lot of lit courses."

"Yes. I've always believed in that."

"In what, exactly?"

"Well—that people act the way they do because of what they've read, as much as because of what happens to them."

"Climate of men's minds, eh?"

"Something like that."

"Going into teaching?"

"That's it."

"Ever thought of publishing as a career?"

"No," I said, "I haven't."

"It's a growing field." The dormant pipe shifted to the other corner of his mouth. "When this baby boom starts growing up, textbooks are going to burgeon. Good college textbook editors are hard to come by."

He watched me a moment, drawing noisily on the empty pipe. "It'll be a lot more exciting, Virdon. Do you really want to plod up and down in front of the blackboard, in some musty lecture hall?" A handsome woman in a beautifully tailored beige suit came up just then and embraced him. "Why Marya, how lovely! ... You'll never have moments like this," he said to me, and winked; the woman was still holding his hand. "It's also a lot more rewarding financially. Think about it, Virdon."

"I will, Mr. Lydecker," I said, "—I certainly want as full a life as possible." I turned away, laughing—and looked straight into the eyes of Kay Madden.

"Well, George! Of all people ..." She leaned forward in that deft, assertive way of hers and kissed me high on the cheek. She was wearing a champagne-colored tiesilk dress cut in what they were calling the "New Look" that spring—Liz said it had been created by the rising couturier Dior—narrow waist, sweeping long full skirt, and soft shoulders: a very feminine silhouette, pleasing after the military tailoring of the war years. The famous golden hair was gathered in a gleaming chignon, coiled smoothly at the base of her beautiful neck. She looked, needless to say, as stunning as ever. She was smiling winningly. I knew then that she'd been watching me for some time—and that some of the consternation I had felt on seeing her showed. No one should have an open, revealing face, it should be trained out of us during infancy: it leads to so much trouble later on.

"Bix," she was saying, "this is George Virdon, Russ's roommate at Harvard. You remember Bix Baxter, George."

"Indeed I do," I said with forced heartiness, shaking hands. "Nancy and I saw *Sarabande* during its Boston run."

"A terrible week," Baxter said, though he smiled. He looked bigger, sturdier than I remembered him. The gaunt O'Neill look was gone; only the eyes still flashed their restless gleam now and then. The war years had been good to him. He'd had two smash hits on Broadway, and one of those—a rotten war play—had won a Pulitzer. In between he'd written a documentary on General Bannerman they said was a classic of its kind: I doubted it. But then I'd gone to see it with a chip on my shoulder—like most servicemen I had the spiteful suspicion Noel Baxter wouldn't have got anywhere near the preeminence he enjoyed if he hadn't been scribbling away in 4F safety while America's younger dramatists were gassing bombers or clearing minefields...

"Don't you know you never remind a playwright of an out-of-town opening?" Kay told me, laughing.

"Oh—I'm sorry," I said to Baxter, but someone came up to him just then and he turned away. "Anyway," I told Kay, "everything turned out all right."

"Is that your philosophy, George?—all's well that ends well?"

"Sometimes."

"When did we last see each other? Where was it?—Paris?"

"Vouziers," I said. "A field outside Vouziers. Very dusty."

"Really?"

"Oh, yes. You covered us with it when you came roaring into camp. Your triumphal caravan."

"That amazing memory of yours." She pressed her perfect teeth on her lower lip. "I thought I'd find you here."

I smiled. "I wouldn't have missed it for worlds, Kay. Not for worlds."

I'd turned my back fully to Russ—or where I thought he was—without thinking: an instinctive desire to block her off, interpose my body. I know it sounds foolish—it *was*; but there you have it. Kay caught it, of course; the way she caught everything. I saw the little crescents at the corners of her mouth compress once, and release; her pale eyes glinted. She said:

"Tell me all about yourself."

"Not an awful lot to tell," I answered. "Still a schoolboy—graduate school now. Still taking orders. The limits of my capabilities—as you once said yourself."

"I didn't . . ."

"You did indeed. Your very words." I was beginning to enjoy myself a little. "How about you? Are you making a new picture?"

She shook her head, lifted a drink from a passing tray. "No, I'm working with Lee Strasberg. Actors Studio. I may do some summer stock: the Cape Playhouse."

"Back to fundamentals," I said.

"Something like that."

"How's that irrepressible husband of yours?"

"Dear me, you *are* out of touch. Fusty, musty Bean-Town-on-the-Bay." The tiny crescents bracketed her lips again. "We were divorced last year."

"Oh. I'm sorry to hear that."

"Don't be."

"Whatever you say."

The fact was I knew all about it—the quarrels and estrangements between Tommy Buckler and Kay Madden had been grist for the gossip columnists for some time; Kay said he resented her career, that she'd taken third-rate roles only to please him; Buckler alluded angrily to a string of other men, and excursions to Vegas at odd hours . . . Uncle Dick often said it: Always ask a question to which *you* know the answer—you will learn more about your man that way than any other. Was that true? Perhaps. I was really enjoying myself now. Kay had given me a real jolt, and now I was scoring a little myself.

The reversal of roles pleased me. America is such a crazy see-saw: there's never been anything like it in the history of the world—not even the royal courts in the days of the grand despots. Three years ago Russ was a broken body on a sweat-soaked hospital cot—one of many thousands—and Kay was a flaming comet, serenading a million roaring, drooling GIs from Napoli to Liège. Now Uncle Lorenzo was dead—he'd choked to death on a piece of filet mignon at Chasen's—yes, actually—the two films she'd made had been box office disasters, none of the music companies was asking her to record now; the shooting star had fallen, now it was hanging low on the horizon—and here was Russ, the first and most wildly acclaimed of our serious war writers . . . And then too, there was the memory of that dusty afternoon at Vouziers, and Ramsey's bet; and Opp—the temptation was too much . . . Or was I merely trying to exorcize something?

But it is always a mistake to gloat. Always. Nothing so provokes the vengeful wrath of the gods . . .

"But *you've* gone and done it, haven't you?" she was taunting me lightly.

"Done what?"

"Tied the grand knot."

"How do you know that?" I asked in surprise. She might have spotted my ring, though I doubted it; I have the habit of holding my drink in the palm of my hand—a mannerism of Jean-Jean's.

"Easy." She laughed; she was back on top of things again. "The way Nancy—isn't it Nancy?—was looking at you from across the room. There's only one explanation for *that* glance. Ownership, son. Congratulations," she added, with a malicious lightheartedness. "You fooled me."

"Did I."

"Yes—I was sure you were going to pursue Chris Farris. Are they here, by the way? she and Dalrymple?"

"No, they couldn't get away. They're living outside of Chicago now."

"Too bad—I'd like to see them again. Anyway, when you missed the boat there, I figured you'd settle down a confirmed bachelor."

"Horatios never marry, you mean."

"Of course not—it blunts their loyalty!"

She must have been waiting for an opening. Her timing—I've said it before, I know—was always flawless. And she possessed that special faculty of holding your gaze with her own, yet somehow covering everything else in a very crowded room. She laughed her high, shivery laugh—all at once moved adroitly to one side, just as Baxter was disengaging himself, and moved forward a step, forcing me to give way. I stepped back. Russ was shaking hands with someone—some face I'd seen somewhere, in *Life* or the *Saturday Review*—he swung away, his eyes met Kay's. I saw his face freeze in that hot, dark, Italian way, his lips just parted; for a second his eyes seemed to glaze over, like a man hit by a stray round.

Then that burning, desperate look flooded into them, that look I remembered, and he smiled and said, "Hello, Kay."

"Hello, Russ. What a long time!"

"Yes. Isn't it?"

"But what a glorious occasion!" She had brushed her way past me now. "And here's Bix, come to give you his blessing."

"Hello, Currier," Baxter said. "Congratulations."

"Thank you. I'm—touched that you came by."

"It's a pleasure. Wonderful job, really a spell-binder." Baxter was smiling as I'd never seen him. "Picture deal yet?"

"A few offers—nothing definite." Russ looked suddenly gauche, off-balance. I thought of Pearl Harbor afternoon, the big, drafty house with the California hood smoking, the storm clouds low over the bay.

"Don't hurry it. Let the excitement build, and hold out for all you can get. The war'll be good box office for some years yet, or I'm very much mistaken."

"I suppose so." Russ's eyes flashed at me once, went back to Kay. People kept crowding around him. Charles Jackson, and the woman who wrote *Forever Amber,* and the editor who'd worked on *Memoirs of Hecate County,* and God alone knew who else. It was all heady and exhilarating and exhausting, and we all talked too much and drank even more, and promised vehemently to keep in touch with people we'd never seen before and probably would never see again.

And finally it did break up, and several of us—the group included Kay Madden—walked over to Fifth Avenue through the soft, damp April evening to look at Scribner's window, where *Full Fathom Five* was stacked in three awesome pyramids 20 copies high, backed by a mammoth blow-up of the jacket. It was marvelous—Salter at his best. A sailor stripped to the waist was lunging wildly toward a gun in a milky blued murk of cordite fumes . . . but a second glance belied the image: the atmosphere was denser than that, much heavier—it was water, *under*water, the ship had been sunk and the sailor was trapped there, his eyes staring blankly, his hair floating, his arms flung suspended in the channel tide; his gestures were not the violent contortion of battle, but the abandoned somnolence of death. *Of his bones are coral made . . .*

"What are all these copies doing, here in the window?" Terry demanded loudly. He wasn't smashed, he was only putting it on—he'd virtually stopped drinking since he'd gone to work for Kennedy. Maybe the book jacket had sobered him, too, and he didn't want to lose the mood of festivity. "How are people going to buy them if they're stuck in the window?" He pointed to each of the three F's on the jacket blow-up as if he were picking them off in a shooting gallery. "Fear—fancy—faith," he proclaimed, pointing, his thumb dropping like a pistol's hammer. "That's the whole human story. In a nut-shell."

"That isn't what *I* thought you were going to say!" Sheilah teased him, and Liz said dryly:

"You mean fashion—he left out fashion."

"Not to mention fecundity," Nancy said.

"God, what a one-track mind."

"You'd have one too, if you were me!"

We were all talking at once now, and laughing; all of us except Russ. He was gazing up at the blue towers of books with a kind of fearful absorption; his eyes glittered in the soft floodlights. He'd dreamed of it so long and so often—and it had, impossibly, happened: that was *his* book heaped high above him, he was scheduled to appear on "The Author Meets the Critics" the following week; all this and more had happened to him and he couldn't quite believe it. *Those are pearls that were his eyes . . .*

"Yes, it's real," I said with a grin.

His eye caught mine, but he didn't produce even the ghost of a smile.

"I wish Chris could see this." I hadn't meant to say it—or maybe I had; anyway, I did. He nodded rapidly, and swallowed, his hands jammed deep in his jacket pockets. I saw it, then. That air of awkward diffidence was not excessive modesty, but naked fear: he had leaped astride a tiger, and he didn't know where it was taking him—or whether he could ever dismount and return alive. *Nothing of him that doth fade but doth suffer a sea-change—*

"It's a wonderful book, Russ," Kay murmured.

He turned to her eagerly. "Did you like it? Really?"

"Really and truly." She nodded, smiling the old presumptuous smile. "It has sweep and poignance and grandeur—the love scenes are overpowering. And my God, what a picture it'll make! Who've you got in mind for the lead?"

"Why, Fonda, of course!" Terry guffawed. "With John Garfield and Dana Andrews as the devoted buddies."

But Kay only grinned. "Oh, but I'm serious. Russ is going to be the great writer of our generation."

"Do you really think so?" I said.

"Absolutely. Don't you? Don't tell me *you've* lost faith, of all people..."

"I remember a snowy night on the way to—"

"Oh, you're not going to rake up dead ashes at a time like this?"

"It just interests me, that's all," I said. "Remembering."

"George, you've become vindictive. You've changed."

"Not me, Kay. I'm not the one who's changed."

"All right—go to a neutral corner, both of you," Terry broke in.

"Yes, let's kiss and make up, George," Kay agreed quickly. "George is still cross with me because of one of those hectic wartime encounters, and I don't blame him. I *was* impossible— after two solid months of batting around in jeeps and tanks, eating on the run, spam and hash and more spam, and screaming into a pick-up mike at all hours, you turn into one quivering, exposed nerve..." Her lips broke into a dazzling, carefully tremulous smile. "I'll admit it—I was wrong."

"No! About what?"

"About Russ. I thought his talent was for film. I was dead wrong—it's both novelistic *and* cinematic."

We all laughed.

"Only the novel is more important," Sheilah said suddenly. "I mean, isn't it?—the way Chopin's more important than Hoagy Carmichael."

"Oh, don't knock old Hoagy," Russ protested. "He was our Pied Piper."

"On our way to the cave in the mountains?" Kay asked him.

"Yes, but who knows what was inside that cave?" Russ passed his hand once through his hair. "Maybe those kids were happier inside that mountain than they'd ever been before."

"They were," Kay said. "Believe me, they *were* . . . Write us a brilliant screenplay," she said softly. "You've written the great novel, now make a great picture. Why not?"

"Why not?" Russ's eyes were alive with that burning, eager glance I remembered. *Sea-nymphs hourly ring his knell.* Disquieted, shaken I looked at Sheilah, but she was laughing at something Baxter was saying, her fey Irish face filled with innocent delight.

7

THAT WAS HOW it all started up again—the old fascination, immolation, whatever it was—that instinctive sway toward Kay and everything she stood for, that Russ neither could nor wanted to prevent. He wasn't "over it," as I'd known perfectly well. It was simply a matter of time.

And who am I to talk, anyway. We are never "over it"—any of us. There is no immunity. It's like malaria without atabrine: the recurrences come, and leave, and come again—a month, a year, a lifetime later, and we shiver and sweat every bit as intensely as we did the first time...

Things went rocking along like that through the spring. The book's very publication date—4-7-47—was enough to arouse anybody's sense of destiny; and Russ was always incorrigibly superstitious. *Full Fathom Five* climbed quickly to Number 1 on the *Times* best seller list, and clung there 5, 9, 14 weeks. All but a handful of the reviews were ecstatic. The studios were eager now; Russ's agent, Tip Longevin, was running a protracted auction for the film rights. Sam Goldwyn, flush with the success of *The Best Years of Our Lives*, was said to be personally interested.

Russ particularly wanted to write the screenplay. He'd never talked that way before, and I knew where that idea had come from. The following month he pulled precipitately out of graduate school and took a studio apartment over on Brimmer Street overlooking the Charles River Basin; he was all over the place, mostly down in New York City. When you called you never knew who was going to answer the phone.

It was a strange crew he'd begun to surround himself with; I didn't care much for them. They were pale and thin, with high foreheads and heavy tortoise-shell glasses and wispy blond hair, or squat and dark, with thick lips and bugging eyes. There were self-styled avant-garde theater directors, and fifth-rate poets, and rich young men who brought out special "commemorative editions" of little magazines; their women were flat-chested, and wore overlong skirts and Menalkas Duncan sandals. They drank sherry and Kümmel and were always talking about Reich; they had just discovered Anaïs Nin. They laughed when you didn't—and then they were still and distantly disapproving when you did.

I dropped by one evening in May to return the Empress— Russ had asked me to check the plugs and points for him, he'd said it was very important; he'd loaned her to me several times during the winter, and so I'd greased and oiled her as well. One of the high-domed types—I remembered him, a former *Advocate* editor—let me in. Figures sat on the floor or leaned against the mantel in a low, steady hum of talk, punctuated by some girl's single high, harsh laugh. From the phonograph came the staccato drone of a tenor sax, gurgling like a wide-open drain: Charlie Parker—whom these devotees never called anything but "Yardbird."

"Grog, boy!" Russ came up to me, a drink in each hand; his shirttail was out and his face was flushed. "Come on in and hunker down by the fire."

"I can't stay," I said. "I've got work."

"Work? Work? What's that? Come on—" he shoved one of the glasses in my hand "—you can stick around for a farewell drink."

I looked at him. "What do you mean, *farewell?*"

He raised his free hand—benediction, imprecation, judgment, it was hard to tell—then swung it across his body in a long, sweeping gesture. "Hitting the road, pardner. Heading for Lotus Land. Tomorrow at dawn."

"Hollywood?"

"And after that we're going over the big falls, Groggy. Kay and I. Unholy wedlock!"

"Wow," I said. I could feel my face freezing. "Hey, congratulations..."

"Come on—you can do better than that!" He clapped me on the shoulder, spilling a little of his drink; it looked like a stinger. I sipped at mine: it was. "Come on out with me, Grog-o. Be my best man. One dastardly turn deserves another."

"California?"

"No, Atlantis. Xanadu. What the hell did you think? I'm going to need your staunch moral support. Come on now, climb aboard."

I stared at him. "Russ *I* can't go out to California..."

"What is it—dough? I'm rolling in it. I'll stake you."

"That's out," I said sharply. "You know me better than that."

He threw open his hands. "Why are you so everlastingly touchy about money?"

"Maybe because I'm so everlastingly without it," I retorted. "I'm sorry, Russ. It's out of the question, you must be able to see that."

"I'd do as much for you, Giorgio. I *did*."

"I've got classes—exams. Nancy's getting close—you can see how it is..."

Voices rose behind him, an argument, and someone called: "The trouble with you, Haislip, you've been analyzed within an inch of your id!"

"So that's how it runs." Russ's face seemed all at once rather hard and narrow, his eyes onyx-black. "The old solidarity, all these years, good times and bad times... all just in *my* mind, ah? That it?"

"Russ, it's not that—I've got *work* here, a family."

"It's her, isn't it?"

"No—"

"Fall of '41, that crazy weekend at Brewster, the run back to Bennington."

"Russ, listen—"

"The trouble with *you* is your God damn memory. Why can't you *forget* something, once in a while? wipe the slate? Who the hell are you to judge people, anyway? Have *you* been such a five-alarm saint?"

"No," I said after a moment, and drank half the stinger. "Not remotely."

The buzzer had rung, there was a small commotion at the door, Russ's face changed. I turned. It was Sheilah—she had thrust her way through a couple of the limpsy, high-domed people, she started toward us and then stopped, swaying on her feet. Her face was dead white, her eyes were wild; she was watching Russ with the terrible, concentrated intensity of an assassin. Then she noticed me.

"Well—George! Come to offer best wishes, bon voyage? or perhaps you're going *with* them?—chaperon, chief mechanic?"

"No," I said. "I'm not going."

"What a shame—think how *cozy* it could be! One for all and all for one, share the wealth, isn't that the code?" Her eyes kept flashing from me to Russ and back again, she was gripping her handbag in her two hands. She was drunk, very drunk; her mouth quivered when she stopped talking. "Just dropped by to wish him all the best, then? a perfect lifetime of happiness—? Like me. Sure. Why not? Why in fucking holy hell not? It's all in a spirit of good clean fun, may the best man—or woman—win. Right?"

Across the room there was a low snicker of laughter, loud in the gathering silence, and a voice murmured, "My God..."

Sheilah whirled on the speaker—it was the former *Advocate* editor, Stynchon, I suddenly remembered his name—took one quick, threatful step toward him. "You shut up, you fatuous son of a bitch!" she hissed at him. "What do *you* know about God? or anything else?"

"Sheilah, don't you think—" Russ was saying.

"No!" She whirled back, a bitter half-smile on her stark white face. "No—I never think, never! I *feel*...But you won't mind, everybody out there thinks, don't they? in Malibu-by-the-sea, you'll be right at home—they're all cut-outs too, you can put them here and there and everywhere, shuffle them around, make them do all kinds of charming things to each other—and when you get tired of them you can go out and buy a whole boxful of *new* ones. It's so simple, isn't it?"

"Sheilah—"

"And then maybe, just maybe, someone will pick you up and put you in his toybox—maybe *you'll* become one of the cut-outs and oh, Christ! won't that be wonderful to see, won't that be funny!" But the laughter never came, her eyes suddenly swam full with tears. "And oh, dear Mary Mother of God, how I'll laugh to see it, I'll laugh myself sick!"

"Sheilah, please—"

But she had spun around again, flung her way through the two men in the hallway, weeping, had wrenched open the door without once looking back, and was gone. Russ started after her; I pushed my hand against his shoulder and stopped him dead.

"Let her go," I said.

He gazed at me agitatedly. "But she's—"

"Let her go! You've done enough damage as it is. More than enough...She's right," I told him. "You don't care who you hurt, or when, or why. You never did."

"Now, hold on," he began hotly.

"Maybe she's right—maybe we *are* just cut-outs to you, maybe that's all we've ever been. All of us. Is that why it's always come so easy?"

"No—wait, Grog..." His eyes had that hurt, pleading look.

"Wait?" I said. "Wait for what?"

"I can't help it," he burst out in a low voice. "I can't *do* anything else. You can't understand it and that's all right, I don't hold it against you, but that's how it is—*I can't fight it off.* Kay...Can't you even try to imagine—?"

That stung me: I'd had it once too often—and at the wrong time.

"—Suppose I did," I said savagely, "just let's suppose I did feel this same thing, dull and unimaginative as I am. Only I decided *not* to tear everybody apart, I decided not to play with other people's lives as if it was some lousy fucking Monopoly game." And I hated him then, I wanted to belt him right on his aristocratic nose. "Let's just suppose I *care*—at least enough so I've decided not to go around playing God."

"—You've always hated her guts," he said in a flat, musing tone, and I had no trouble with the transition, I knew who he was talking about, all right.

"You bet," I said. "I can read her like a New England primer. You think she'd have shown up at *that* party if the book hadn't come in a gusher? Forget it."

"You're trying to—"

"I'll tell you something, pal. She's a Discontented Woman. Class 3A, American Style. She'll always be longing for something that doesn't exist—greener grass, you know—and *you'll* be Private Enemy Number One. She'll never be satisfied with a thing you do, you'll be forever trying to score in a game you can't possibly win."

"Oh," he said tightly, "and just how do you come by all this fancy expertise?"

"Because I married one, too," I came back at him, "that's how!"

We looked at each other in silence, then: a long moment. I was half-sick at my admission—even Russ was shocked. We were frozen on dead-center—we could neither go forward nor back from this one and we both knew it.

Then he said: "If that's the way you want it, Grog."

"Goodbye and good luck," I repeated. "Something tells me you're going to need it this time. If you get lost out there and shoot up a flare, I hope *somebody* sends out a patrol—because it sure as hell won't be me."

There were bells, alarm bells jangling, the signal for imminent attack, and I tried to get everybody on the line but the platoon, a roomful of raffiné men and women in formal attire, laughed at me; a low derisive simpering. The enemy was assaulting in force right up the Charles River Basin—there was no time, no time at all and I couldn't find my helmet or my weapon. I ran into the CP to find Dutch, and the alarm bell resolved itself into the telephone. Ringing away in the black night. In the Quonset hut. Here in Cambridge.

I swung myself out of bed, sweating.

Nancy was saying, "My God—what time is it?"

"Quarter of two. Probably some God damn drunk misdialing."

She struck the pillow with a groan. "If it's one of your self-dramatizing friends—"

I picked up the receiver and snarled: "Hello!"

"... George." A dreamy voice, fading. A voice falling away, down wells, along echoing passages into deepest night.

"Yes? Who's this?"

"Just ... want say ... goodbye. G'bye, George ..."

"Sheilah! What's the matter?"

"—only one of them ... only that cares ..."

"Sheilah, are you all right? Where are you? Wait. Look, I'll get a—"

"Bye, George ... bless ..."

"Sheilah—"

The line broke, a fumbling clatter, the dial tone sang in my ear. I started pulling my trousers on over my pajamas.

Nancy said: "What are you doing?"

"Going out."

She sat up in bed, heavily. "Didn't you say Sheilah? Sheilah Gilligan?"

"That's right. She's in trouble—some kind of trouble."

"What's the matter?"

"I don't know."

"You don't know—for God's sake, George! Calm down. What's the matter with you? What's she doing—crying her eyes out?"

"No," I said tightly. "She's not crying."

"Well, what *is* it, then? It's two o'clock in the morning— you've got an *exam* in the afternoon ..."

"I know that."

"But this is crazy—what did she say?"

"I don't like the way she sounds. She sounds—" I didn't complete the thought, jammed my feet into my loafers.

"Oh my God." She struck the sheet with her fist. "She's nothing but trouble—they're *all* nothing but trouble. What about *me?*"

I looked at her. She had both hands clasped against her swollen belly, as if to thrust it at me.

"Have you had pains?"

"What? No, of course I haven't—but what if I should?"

"I'll call you. Soon as I can." I snatched up my wallet and keys from the bureau top.

"You're really going all the way over there ... They throw one of their lovers' tantrums and away you go, not a thought for anyone else—"

"I told you, I'll call you!"

"—don't you see, you can't wet-nurse them all—George! I'm asking you to *stay!*"

I ran hard all the way up to Mt. Auburn Street. By luck I

caught a cab cruising back to the Square from a late fare. He eased over for me and I threw myself in, gave him the address and said:

"This is life and death, and I'm not drunk and I'm not bullshitting. There's ten bucks in it if you get me there in ten minutes."

He threw me one hard look, then snapped his meter down and took off without a word. We whipped down the Drive, over the Harvard Bridge and down Massachusetts Avenue, deserted now except for an occasional delivery van. All I could think of was that rainy night with Chris, driving to Mattapan. Woman trouble. Let old George do it. Same old Jazz. At least I couldn't smack up the Empress on this run. The night air poured cool against my throat. I'd been scared sick, then—and it was nothing to the way I felt now. She had a knife, a Japanese ceremonial hara-kiri dagger Russ had given her. It had a curved wooden sheath and lovely floral designs etched on the blade, it was sharp as a razor; we'd kidded about it one night.

Sheilah had an apartment of her own beyond Symphony Hall, one of those beat-up old buildings on Gainsborough where they let musicians practice at all hours—I remembered hearing a piano thumping away through the walls one evening, at a birthday party for Russ the year before.

God *damn* that selfish, no-good, one-way son of a bitch!

The cabby made it in ten minutes, or damned near, anyway. I handed him the ten-spot and took the front steps three at a time. The downstairs door was never locked. I went up the two flights in a long, gliding dream, the sweat crawling in my scalp. At her door I knocked, called her name sharply twice. No answer. I called again, stood there, thinking. Russ had taken off in the Empress two days before. I knew the building had no super, and there wasn't time for that kind of finesse anyway. If I kicked the door in I'd wake half of Back Bay and bring the cops in force. But it couldn't be helped. I'd have to kick it in. I rattled the door knob in exasperation—and the door opened.

A light burning in the bedroom. Raincoat flung on the floor, small black kid ballet slippers on top of the upright piano, a welter of music scores in the chairs. The little wooden sheath was on the coffee table. Empty. The window over the airshaft was wide open, no screen. Jesus. I ran toward it—saw her then, sprawled on the floor beside the bed in a brocade kimono,

another of Russ's war souvenirs, her hair loose, one arm flung over her head. No blood. There was no blood. I almost cried out with relief. I picked her up—she was so *light*—and eased her onto the bed—and that was when I saw the little chocolate bottle lying on its side by the gold travel clock and a copy of *Hollywood Reporter* and the photo of Russ that Gwen Carrington had taken for the jacket of *Full Fathom Five*. Pills. She looked white as milk, her hair damp against her forehead and throat; her mouth was open. I couldn't tell whether she was breathing or not. I felt for a pulse. Yes, there was a pulse: but so *faint*—I snatched up the bottle, but there was no writing on it.
   Pills.

Mel was over at Peter Bent Brigham studying the heart, something to do with plastic valves to help keep it beating one day; he and Marge were living in Brookline. Right here in Brookline. I remembered the number—funny, always the numbers of friends. I phoned. It rang once, and before it could ring again Mel's voice answered crisply:

"Doctor Strasser."

"Mel? This is George. Mel, I'm at Sheilah's place, Terry's sister Sheilah. Mel, we've got trouble—she's out, she's taken pills."

"What kind of pills? How many?"

"I don't know—there's no label on the bottle."

"You say you're there, at her place—"

"Yes—she called me and I took off over here. I was talking to her twenty—well, maybe thirty minutes ago. I got a pulse, barely—"

"All right. Get her up. Get her moving."

"But she's *out*, Mel . . ."

"I know—*get her up, anyway.* Walk her! Up and down, up and down. Get some black coffee into her."

"Hadn't I better call an ambulance?"

"No—no need for that yet. It'll hurt her if it gets out—it could ruin Terry. Hold on, now. Get her moving. I'll be right over."

He was there in fifteen minutes. By that time I'd half-dragged, half-carried Sheilah to Los Angeles and back, while she groaned and muttered and fought me, a dream struggle in the little room; she didn't seem any more conscious to me than when I'd started. I was getting panicky by the time Mel showed up carrying a small black bag. He was wearing a seersucker jacket and khaki pants over *his* pajamas, but except for a slick blued sheen of stubble he looked flawless. He checked Sheilah with unobtrusive deft purpose, pumped out her stomach—a prolonged and hideous business I'd never encountered before—gave her an injection and put her to bed. I phoned Nancy; and then for a while we sat there smoking and talking while Sheilah lay pale and spent, her breath coming with the dry-gravel rattle of the dying, and the dun light eased its way through the sooted windows. Over on Huntington Avenue the early traffic had begun.

"I think I'd better call Terry," I said.

"What about her parents?"

"I'd rather not. Terry will know how to handle that—it's better if he does."

"All right. Well, I guess I'll take off. There's nothing more I can do here. I've got surgery at eight sharp."

"Jesus—*surgery,*" I muttered.

"Why not? Somebody's got to do it. Well, it's routine. And I got to bed early. You learn to grab your sleep whenever you can in this racket, believe me." For a moment he watched Sheilah critically, his eyes narrowed. "She'll be all right."

"Christ, I hope so."

"Her calling you is a good sign. Encouraging." His lips curved in that mournful smile. "For an unadventurous type, Virdon, you certainly do get yourself involved."

"Don't I, though."

"Because of Russ, right?" he said, tossing his head toward Sheilah. I nodded. "I thought so . . ." His eyes were large and dark now, without depth. "Have you ever stopped to wonder *why* you have to go around picking up after him?"

"—But it's her *life,*" I protested.

"I know, I know. Don't tell *me.*" He sighed—a long, weary, shuddering sigh. He looked much older than the rest of us—and now he was cross. "Crazy little fool . . . Why do they do it? Why? The world is so eager to break you down anyway, cell, tissue, bone—turn you to muck and ash—why help it along? . . . Do *you* understand it at all? Do you?"

Watching him steadily I nodded. "Oh, yes," I said.

"Well, that's more than I can say." Then, in another tone: "Shit, you understand everybody too well for your own good. Always did." His lips drew down, not without affection. "What the hell are you doing in History and Lit? You should have gone to divinity school. Tell me honestly: do you get a kick out of it? giving aid and comfort to all us poor sinners?"

"God, no," I said without a second's hesitation.

"Oi, weh—a closet masochist."

We laughed together softly, but it was true, in a way. Always missing my own bus, but flagging down theirs. It hurt, it always saddened me more than I would have believed; but there was no avoiding it, it was the way I was built.

He left then, with quiet purpose, the way he'd come. I made more coffee and stayed on, until Sheilah opened rheumy, glazed eyes that suddenly focused sharply, fearfully on me.

"Oh, George. Oh, you didn't . . ."

"Oh yes, I did. How you feeling?"

"How do you think I feel. Oh, George." And she began to cry, a weak, helpless weeping. "Damn you, anyway . . . What did you have to do that for?"

"Thrift, Horatio. Who would we get to play piano at our soirées when I'm department head?"

She sipped feebly at the coffee I gave her, coughed most of it up, and set the cup down with a little clatter. Then she looked at me without any expression whatever. "Now what?" she said softly.

"That's up to you, kid. All up to you."

"You *saw* what I did when it was all up to me. Jesus, I'll never get up the nerve to do it again."

"That's good. By the by, where's that Nipponese toad-stabber?"

"I threw it away. Two days ago. I was afraid I might—get tempted."

"You wouldn't kid me."

"No, I wouldn't kid you!" She looked like a sullen child who had been thwarted, not a lovely young woman who'd just tried to commit suicide out of unrequited love.

We talked about nothing at all for a while, then, till the sunlight reached in the upper corner of one of the windows and flooded the room.

"You know what I like about you?" Sheilah said. Her eyes were clearer now. "You never lecture people, browbeat them. If it were Terry instead of you—my God . . . You going to tell on me, George?"

"I'm trying to make up my mind. I suppose I ought to call him—unless you want to."

"You're such a good person. You are. I wish I could have fallen in love with you, George."

"So do I." I stood up and stretched. My head ached brutally, and I felt as if I'd been beaten with a ball bat. "Well, take it easy, kid. I've got an exam this afternoon and I'd better do some last-minute review, unquote."

Her head twisted on the pillow. "George . . . It's no good, you know. Nice try. Sorry to foul you up. But it's no good. There's still no sense in it."

"Yes. There is. We don't always see it, but there is."

"You're wrong. I'll never get over it. Never."

"That's right," I said. "You won't."

She hadn't expected that—she pushed herself up in bed with a funny little convulsive effort.

"Every time you think of him the wound will open. The pain will dull down, but the wound will always be there."

"How do you know that?" she whispered.

"Because I've been there, kid. But you get a kind of emotional second-wind. You'll see."

"How can you say that?" She was watching me very closely now, her brown eyes deadly grave. "Did you ever try it?"

I nodded. "Different way from yours. But the object was the same. It didn't work, either." I came back to her then and put my hands on her thin little shoulders. "You go on. You go on. It's why we're better than the monkeys—maybe the only reason. All that about symphonies and serums and radar is so much eyewash. What makes us better is that we find out life itself is essentially a defeat, a steady, losing game—and yet somehow we summon up the—the good courage to take what comes, and make out with it."

I let go her shoulders and straightened up again. "You're tuned in to the Answer Man," I told her, and winked. "Check it out."

"Thanks, George," she said, and rubbed one hand with the other. "Not just for coming over. But for sitting here with me. All this while."

"My pleasure," I said, and bent down and kissed her on her sweaty white forehead, wondering where or when I'd said that before. "Be good."

* * *

I didn't go back to the Quonset—there wasn't time. I munched on a Three Musketeers bar, borrowed a fountain pen from an undergraduate named Hazeltine, walked into Memorial Hall without a single, solitary thought in my head—and wrote the best exam I ever had. It just kept rolling out, I couldn't even keep up with the surge of ideas; it seemed to me I'd never seen things so clearly. I almost burst out laughing halfway through.

The Quonset was still broiling when I got home. Nancy was slumped in the butterfly chair—a gift from the departed Dalrymples—looking swollen and sweaty and truculent.

"Hi, Blondie," I said. "How's my long-suffering girl?"

"Suffering long. How'd you do?"

"Do? I was brilliant, *brilllllliant*—I threw whole new vistas into historical perspective."

"You *look* as if you just finished the Bataan Death March."

"Ah, well, looks, the outward shows—"

"Oh, cut it out, George!" She was glaring up at me, her lovely little mouth working; her upper lip was beaded with sweat. I went over to her and pressed her head against my hip.

"Not very much fun is it, honey? Sitting here in the heat, brooding."

"I'm *not* brooding! You'd brood too, if you had a nine-pound *som*ething kicking like a colt in your stomach."

"I know. And this lousy heat." I ran some tepid water in the sink and started shaving. "Tell you what: I'm going to take you away from all this."

"Hah."

"I'm going to take you up to Cronin's for a cold plate and a beer. You can have tripe, a banana split, gherkins—"

"What an obscene word."

"Gherkins? I always think of medieval varlets bearing trenchers of boars' heads into the main hall, flagons of foaming burgundy. Come on. Anything your exotic tummy desires. Price no object."

"Stop bringing up *money*—" Her eyes flashed at me irritably, narrowed at the late afternoon light. I put down the razor and turned. "What is it, Nan? What's the matter?"

"Did you really do all right on the exam?"

"Yes, I did—it's funny, everything just flowed like a mountain stream. Maybe we've been going at it the wrong way all these years."

"I worried about you. No sleep, no last-minute chance to bone up,... Is she all right?"

"Sure—I told you. Mel brought her out of it beautifully. She was resting when I left."

"I mean, is she *going* to be all right?"

I stopped shaving again. "I think so."

"She needs psychiatric help."

"I suppose she does. I daresay we all do."

"I don't know what you mean by that. She's always been unstable. These artists and their *temperaments*..." She threw out the last word between her teeth, and watching her askance in the little mirror I thought, Why, she's jealous—she's jealous of Sheilah's good looks. Or was it the pregnant woman's resentment of the free (and therefore available) female? Several weeks ago Sheilah had burst in on us, very drunk and raging, broken a coffee cup and fallen into a crying fit—I remembered Nancy's face stony with exasperated disgust... Why had I, who forgave all things in all people, to a fault, married so unforgiving a woman? Did I unconsciously want to convert her? or do opposites really attract, after all?

"What did she expect, anyway?" Nancy was saying now.

"I'm sure I don't know," I answered. The euphoria from the exam had vanished. "Life, maybe. Love. Giving. The sun, the moon, and all the stars. How should I know."

"Yes, that's about the size of it—and they make *you* risk everything, a year's hard work, sitting up studying till all hours of the night while *they*—" She broke off, kneading her belly absently, glaring out at the heat. "You were risking your whole *career,* going over there!"

I dropped the razor in the water and turned around. "Nancy, the girl *tried to take her life.*" My voice had got away from me a little, but I couldn't help it. "She could be dead by now—she would have been. Have you got that? Has it penetrated?"

She stared back at me for a moment, hard and unrelenting—then her eyes filled and she began to wag her head back and forth, querulously. "Oh, life is such a mess, a mess!" she exclaimed. "Such a lousy cheat..."

"What is it, Nan?" I asked again, ashamed of myself. "Let me help. What's the matter?"

"I heard from Liz. Today." She bit at her lower lip. "She and Hugh have broken up—she's getting a divorce."

"I see."

"Well, don't you care? No, you don't, I can see you don't."

"Nan—"

"That's all you can say—I *see*. It's terrible, terrible! She gave up her *career* for him! Her whole life is over..."

I turned around again, plucked the razor out of the dirty water and went on shaving. Nancy was racing on now, about Liz's plans—to go to Reno, to find a Midtown apartment, something in the East 60s, and Hugh's departure for England, where he'd been offered a curatorship at the Victoria and Albert... It was one of those funny moments in your life: that stained little mirror seemed like a truly magic glass giving on the world, a lens through which to view with consummate clarity the whole contradictory muddle, friends and strangers alike: Russ and Kay Madden off for the golden west to marriage and film careers, Nancy and I stuck in torrid Cambridge about to have a baby, Hugh and Liz divorcing, Chris and Dal now in a fashionable suburb outside Chicago, Sheilah struggling back into life again—

"—and you don't care at all," Nancy was telling me, her voice shrill and high in the little tin-roofed room, "of course not, she's only *my* best friend, she's not your sacred Chris or one of your God damned Fusiliers. You'd find excuses for *them* if they blew up the world with an A-bomb, you'd tell me they were trying to excavate a tunnel to China, or they didn't know it was loaded. Don't deny it! So sympathetic—and when something like this happens to a really fine person, my closest friend, you couldn't care less. God, you're something, sometimes! Let me tell you something—I'm *glad* Russ Currier's gone to California, I'm *glad* Terry's down in Washington and Dal and his heavenly, perfect Christabel are out in Chicago! I wish to God they were marooned in Zanzibar, then they could found a club and tell each other all day and all night how wonderful they are. Only then *you'd* like to be there, too, wouldn't you? Then you could record all the lengendary things they say about each other..."

I stared at her through the mirror, keeping my lip buttoned, waiting for her to run down. In a while she would give out, would weep a while, become snuffling and remorseful; and later would come sleep: she would lie on her side, her little hands cupped under her chin like some fairy child asleep in the wild wood, would slumber sweetly right on through the tropic night if the baby didn't kick too much...She was my wife, she was going to be the mother of my child, heart of my heart, flesh of my flesh—and standing there pretending to shave my upper lip I didn't for the life of me see how we could go on living together a week longer within the same four walls.

But we did. For the most part that's what my generation did—stuck it out. Why? Why did we put up with so much, take so much from each other—cling to each other when by any rational criterion we should have burst apart like exploding atoms? I thought remembering might give me the answer to that one. Maybe it still will.

V

Serenade in Blue

1

1948 WAS THE YEAR of the Berlin Airlift, of course, the year of the
birth of the state of Israel against formidable odds, and
Truman's impossible, underdog victory in November. It was a
season of surprises. I was never very wild about Harry myself
(that is, I wasn't until some of his successors came along), but
there was something deeply satisfying about that election to a lot
of us: the small-town bantam rooster knocking off the smug,
big-city operator; it was worth sitting up all night for—if only to
hear toplofty old H. V. Kaltenborn stuttering and sputtering
away. How could we *do* this to him? Well, we could and we did.

1948 was also the year of the movie version of *Full Fathom
Five,* which starred a convincing William Holden and received
three Oscar nominations. As you might have imagined, Kay had
a good part in the picture—the hero's socialite fiancée
contemptuous of his involvement with the war—but her
performance was curiously disappointing: she was certainly
photogenic, as they say, and in the final quarrel in the San

Francisco hotel room she was vindictive enough; but there was still that feeling you had from her earlier pictures—she was never completely and believably the character. What you were seeing was Kay Madden playing a role, the way she might do an imitation at a party; you could feel it in the audience around you—everyone became restless, vaguely dissatisfied whenever she came on camera.

And as you might also have imagined, she and Russ were married right after the première: a dismayingly ostentatious affair featuring pin-stripes and cutaways and white tulle and platoons of bridesmaids, and held at one of those multi- (which is to say non-) denominational California houses of worship which looked, as Terry said, like an Aztec's idea of a Catholic mosque. It was followed by a lavish reception—I almost said production—at Kay's parents' home in Santa Barbara. I still have the pictures here, the clips—there were spreads in all the West Coast papers, and the affair was deemed important enough for *Life* to do a modest feature ("Life Goes to a Wedding").

Here is Russ standing on a vast terrace of blue-and-yellow glazed tile bordered with boxwood hedges under that faultless Pacific sky, talking with Kay's father, a florid man with heavy jowls and distinguished silver hair ("the happy union of art and cultchuh," Dal has scrawled underneath this one); here are Kay and Russ, their hands joined, cutting into—or perhaps tunneling into—a cake that looks like the Alhambra doused in white icing (Nancy was incensed at Kay's wearing a white wedding gown with veil and train—"the blushing bride, after all the places *she's* been! She's been divorced, for heaven's sake, *divorced!*"—and only Chris said nothing); here is Russ, glass in hand, in vehement discussion with Cort Beauchamp, the handsome, youthful director of *Full Fathom Five,* and his best man on this day of days; here are Kay and Russ again, against a background of dancing couples, their arms entwined, right feet swung out in unison, grinning madly at the camera, as though just ending a song-and-dance number; and finally here they are, dressed for travel now in silk shantung and cashmere, standing in front of the Empress, which has been polished until that glorious deep Berkshire Green shines like glass (the *Life* writer had himself a whirl with the Empress: "Currier's elegant, aging East Coast status symbol parked among the flamboyant Jags

and custom Mercedes like a falcon among birds of paradise"—
how Jean-Jean would have roared with laughter); anyhow, there
they are, rich and famous and blithe and debonair, waving
goodbye to an ecstatic cast of thousands—well hundreds . . . and
yet if you look closely, you can catch something in Russ's eyes,
the merest flicker of uncertainty, almost alarm . . . But maybe
I'm only reading that into them now. It's easy enough to be
discerning after the fact.

It was the year Dal got started on his Grand Design too, a big
job with a plastics firm—something to do with polymer resins
and compression molding, something with a terrific future
anyway, unlimited possibilities—it was one of Dal's freewheeling, cockeyed letters and I wasn't any too clear about it. I
wrote him a postcard saying, *What the hell do YOU know about
plastics? You never took a single chem or physics course—and
you'd have flunked it if you had,* and he shot back a straight
wire: CHEMISTRY SHMEMISTRY AS LONG AS YOU'VE GOT A FAST
RETORT GET IT? YOU JUST STICK TO THE ACROPOLIS AND I'LL TAKE
CARE OF THE ACRYLICS.

Terry was based permanently in Washington now, heading
what sounded like a kind of foreign affairs advisory team, as
Jack Kennedy began to gear up early for the Senate; Sheilah
turned to her music with a vengeance—her senior recital at the
Conservatory was praised by Warren Story Smith of the *Post* as
the outstanding performance of her class; and the following year
she was accepted for study in harmony and counterpoint with
the venerable Nadia Boulanger. *You were right, Georgie,* she
wrote me from the Cité Universitaire that fall, *I'm back on key
now, why don't you rent out as a guru? It seems terrible you
never got to see Paris, you've GOT to come over, it's such a vital,
sensuous city, so full of beauty, history, all the important
things . . .*

And 1948 was also the year George Virdon left the sheltered
ivy walls and got himself a job.

It was Teddy that did it. Dear Teddy. Peering through the
hospital glass at this tiny, squirming replica of myself I felt
something I never had before—a sense of power, of bursting
exhilaration—and an obligation as holy as the Grail. A son. I
had a son of my own, to teach how to throw a ball, drive a nail,
ride a bike; a son to regale with all the past great deeds of men—a
son who would surpass me in everything, who would avoid the

traps that had snared me (or in which I snared myself), who would succeed where I had failed. The surging, soaring promise of it!

Nancy looked gutsy and noble, lying in the hospital bed. Elemental Woman, mother of the race. It wasn't a role she ever liked very much; but that day she laughed wearily and lazily—her nostrils were flared, her blue eyes held a hard-won triumph, a long knowledge: she'd done something no man could ever do, and done it very well. She wanted to name him Walter after her father; I suggested Terry; we compromised on Theodore, her mother's brother and a man I liked a good deal. We talked with suppressed excitement, our heads close, so as not to wake the other two mothers. I held her hand, and wiped her forehead with a cool cloth; I felt closer to her than I had in a long time, bathed in that dense, abiding affection. Later I went to look at Teddy again, was gripped with the standard panic that they'd get him mixed up with all the other babies, laughed that thought away nervously, struck up an absolutely indissoluble friendship with two other elated young fathers I knew I'd probably never see again, and went home feeling profoundly blessed. And altered. I'd joined the human race in still another way—the most important one of all; I knew it by the deep singing in my veins. *Continuity.* Why has that word always had so much meaning for me?

A month later I decided to give up the Ph.D grind and go to work. Nancy was pleased, more pleased than even I'd thought she'd be somehow. Student housing among the married veterans was no picnic—it had been a grim year for her, I knew. So many of her old classmates were already settling into elegant stone homes in Bucks County or Westchester; and her mother had become increasingly unhappy about what she referred to as "this vagabond student life."

And you say, What about all those dreams? the ardent pursuit of truth, the whys and wherefores—the dispassionate delving in the wastes of past events, trying to reduce that avalanche to order...Well: I'd have made a good historian, I know I would have; and maybe more than good, too. That word *relevance* you kids love so—it doesn't do it all, you know; it doesn't go deep enough. History can tell you *why*—and maybe even what to do about it, now and then...

Don't worry—I'm not cooking up any cheap excuses,

begging off; or blaming anybody, either. It was my choice: I made it. I decided teaching and research were luxuries I would simply have to forgo; that I was a father now, and I'd better get off my duff and make some money to take proper care of my family. I couldn't ask Nancy to give up anything else. Money was, finally, unanswerably, just too important for me to go merrily along, pretending it wasn't. I would do research on the side, or in another karma, maybe; not this one. I remembered what Norris Lydecker had told me at Russ's publication party; I talked to the people at Bicknell & Stout, across the river; they seemed moderately pleased with my academic record, and when I completed work on my MA I started with them, in the text department.

I liked it—even more than I thought I would: the sober, careful evaluation of material, eventually getting first-rate scripts from professors I knew and valued. Standards were still high, then—the student was expected to adhere to *them*, measure up to *their* excellence; and even though you were underpaid and overworked and a certain stealthy pandering to grosser tastes had already begun, you could tell yourself it was a profession not without honor...

And we found the place out in Belmont—an old house in very bad shape. Nancy liked it the moment she saw it, and after a little while I realized why: it defied easy classification—it was on the edge of a very good neighborhood, and it was a dignified old structure, at least on the outside. I borrowed the money, kept up the bank payments rigorously, and began to set aside a little here and there to pay off the loan. The house needed work—a great lot of work—but I was handy with tools, and I loved the release from incessant reading I got weekends in sanding floors or repairing sashes. It was a house with possibilities, I guess you could say.

I bought a car, too. I wanted to get a convertible, but Nancy put her foot down firmly on that; I picked up a '39 Chevvie for $225, and worked on it in odd moments. It was black, with that scarlet pinstripe, and after I'd given it a paint job it looked presentable.

Anyway, my life was launched, for happier or sadder—like everybody else's. But the center was Teddy. Sleep-befuddled I'd get up in the humming small hours for the feedings, hold his warm little body against my own with that slow, deep beat of love, and put him back down in his crib—Ronny's once, now passed on to us—with reluctance and hang there for half an hour watching over him, like some foolish, drowsy bear standing guard over his unlicked cub; thinking often as not of Ronny, of Chris; of all of us, scattered to the four winds again, bound on our lonely night-journeys, curving away through the astral dark to fame, obscurity, constancy, betrayal...

"Honestly, George," Chris cried into the wind, "did you ever see such a heavenly, glorious day?" She was braced high on the edge of the boat's cockpit, her head thrown back, her hair whipping around her face; she was wearing an old shirt and shorts of faded blue denim, and all morning the memories had come flooding back, rapturous and bright.

"No," I answered. "Not in years. Not—since Nauset."

"Where's Nauset?" Ron and Teddy asked together.

"Ask Daddy, Ron," Chris said, and winked at me. "Daddy'll tell you."

"Where's Nauset, Dad?"

"Let's see..." Dal, sprawled at the helm, squinted up at the quivering taut belly of mainsail.

"Doesn't want to remember," Terry said, and laughed his short, dry laugh.

"*Where* is it?" the kids called.

Hooking one hairy, muscular leg over the tiller Dal poured himself a drink from a bright red plastic thermos bottle. "It's a little bit north of South Carolina."

"No—where, where!" They were shrieking with delight now.

"It's east of the sun and west of the moon."

"No, where *is* it? Uncle Terry, why doesn't Daddy want to remember?" Ron demanded.

"Because that was where we beat the boys at softball," Chris said. That devilish, impulsive mood was upon her, I could tell. "We skunked 'em."

"Did they, Dad?" Ron said. "Beat you?"

Dal sipped again at the cup, his eyes hidden under the stained, floppy crew hat brim. "They cheated. Women, y'know."

"I like that! Liz was a demon at pitching—she struck them all out. Uncle George, too."

"Did she, Daddy?" Teddy asked me, his eyes wide.

"Yes, she did."

"Wow!"

"Jean-Jean threw the ball into the surf," Dal said. "Remember?" His eyes flickered at mine, shot out to sea again. He'd remembered the day, all of it; the row with Jean-Jean, the Fall of France. "Me and my big mouth," he muttered, and shook his head. "Was I as obnoxious as I think I was?"

"Only intermittently," Terry answered. "Mittently, you were perfectly swell."

"What else did you do at Nauset, Mummy? besides softball?"

"Oh, we had a picnic, and Daddy and Uncle George burned the hamburgers because they were mad over the ballgame. And we went swimming, and looked for shells, and we flew a big blue kite we had, and—oh, lots of things..." She smiled at me, but her eyes were grave. "Have you been back there?" I shook my head. "Let's go over this week sometime," she said to Dal. "Maybe there'll be surf. Oh God, it's so *good* to be at the ocean again!"

It was. The sun lay on the water dazzling, the sky held high whirling wraiths of cloud, dead white against the blue; gulls wove back and forth above us, beating clumsily and then falling away downwind in one long sweeping glide, the waves came in easy, tumbling rollers against the hull and spanked it smartly, sent spray drifting back over us now and then in tiny rainbow showers.

"Ready about!" Dal roared, a hoarse old-salt caricature, and Ron and Teddy, crouched forward, holding the jib sheets, chanted seriously: "Ready..."

"Hard alee!" Dal shoved the tiller over. There came that tentative, disembodied pause, the restive rear and dip of the bow, and we all ducked and shifted sides as the boom passed low overhead like a dark angelic wing; then the sheet racketed away through its blocks and the little boat canted, heeled over and ran off again while we crowded high on the weather rail. Teddy deftly snubbed down the jib sheet and made it fast on the cleat and Ron called, "That's right, that's it!" and Teddy looked back at me then, his thin pale face wild and prideful and happy.

"Daddy—you're *soaked!*"

"Right! So are you!"

He giggled and ducked his head and slapped his bony knees with his hands. He was such a merry little boy, he'd always been from the moment I saw him, not roaring and squawling like the other babies, face pinched with rage, but looking around beaming, his blue eyes wide and perfectly clear; smiling at this great stage of fools . . . Sunny, a sunny baby, my mother had called him, looking at him in wonder. Where had it come from? He rarely cried; I would come upon him in his crib, clutching at his toes and talking to himself by the hour, chuckling, bubbling away. I would poke him gently in the tummy to make him laugh, and then swing him up on to my shoulders and jog with him around the porch, feeling a contentment deeper than anything I'd ever known.

The summer he was three he got sick. To my astonishment Nancy became almost hysterical, pestering the doctors, arguing with them incessantly. She was convinced it was rheumatic fever, persisted in thinking so even after it became clear it was not. Teddy recovered in a month or so, but he'd lost weight and he seemed to tire easily, and Nancy kept him in a good deal and was reluctant to let him play with the neighbors' children. To get him away from his mother's overprotectiveness I formed a habit of going out with him Saturday afternoons. I took him to a marionette show—his eyes were huge with apprehension when the forty thieves hid in the oil jars to wait for Ali Baba; I took him to a rodeo and the circus at Boston Garden, which he loved most of all. He gained weight, and developed a passion for molding fanciful animals out of play-putty; and when Nancy became pregnant again in the fall of '51 she seemed to have shaken off that excessive anxiety over the boy.

Then had come this summer, the summer of 1952.

It hadn't seemed like an epidemic at first: a few cases of polio here and there, mainly in the south and midwest, a few of the usual warning articles in the papers and magazines. But Nancy was convinced it was going to be an epidemic—a bad one, perhaps the worst of all. Do we create epidemics out of our own morbid concern? I don't know. All I do know is, it turned into a long summer. Peg came in June—a breech birth, long and arduous and scary; there were complications, as the doctors like to say, Nancy was slow in recovering, she was having a lot of trouble nursing the baby; everything rubbed her the wrong way. Even when she was better there was an overweening tendency to wrench everything all out of proportion. Or so at least it seemed to me.

In July there was a sudden increase in the polio cases

reported—it was moving north and east with the heat; and Nancy turned wildly overanxious and forbidding. We couldn't go to the beach or the movies, we must avoid crowds, any gatherings at all; Teddy was not to play with other children under any circumstances. I came home early one afternoon to find him sitting by the window watching the neighbors' kids playing ball in the vacant lot beyond the house; I suddenly realized how pale and apprehensive the boy looked, how jumpy he was. This led to a long and inconclusive argument with Nancy, who was absolutely implacable, and after a while I let it go. Memories of the summer of '49 were still pretty fresh—the Hollander girl several houses down the street had got polio then, and a boy over on Trapelo Road who still couldn't walk. Maybe it *was* wiser in the long run. And it was only a few months until the cooler weather. Anyway, I did what nearly everyone else in America did that still, parched summer: changed into my work clothes and went and got a beer out of the refrigerator—and drove the thought away.

But why did I answer the telephone that evening a week or so later? I, who detest phone calls, who usually let it ring on without a qualm, until Nancy answers it. Why did Nancy dally in the children's bedroom with Peggy, even though she was already asleep? Why did I hurry in from the bathroom, all over lather, and pick it up? There *is* a divinity that shapes our ends, whatever we think. Chance. If I hadn't answered, if Nancy had...

Well. I did. And that voice, with such rare music in it, so vibrant and filled with life and warmth and the promise of all green things—the voice I would have recognized instantly in Mombasa or Mindanao, said:

"Well, George—Q.—Virdon."

"Chris!" There was that humming in my ears, under my heart, like high tension wires. "Where are you?"

"The Cape. We're staying with Dad. Thalatta, thalatta! After the agony of the Great Plains. Two heavenly weeks, George!"

"Great. How's Dal and the kids?"

"Noisy, querulous, omnivorous. Remember that sailing picnic we talked about last winter?—we thought we'd do it Saturday in Dad's old tub—he *says* it still floats. Can you make it?"

"Absolutely—we wouldn't miss it for worlds. Not for worlds. If it isn't imposing on you, I mean."

"Imposing! You fool, George, you perfectly lovely fool...
Oh, we've just had two gin-and-tonics and the wind is blowing
and the waves are washing against the bulkhead and it's all just
glorious! Come on down early, nine o'clock or so, and we'll have
us a lovely, rollicking day..."

I set the phone softly back in its onyx cradle, basking in a
slow surge of affections and memories, the low melody of her
voice.

When I turned Nancy was standing in the doorway, watching
me.

"Chris Dalrymple?" she said.

I nodded. "They've just come east, on vacation."

"I see. I'd like to have talked to her."

"Well..." I shrugged. "We'll be seeing them in a few
days—they've asked us to go sailing with them."

"—Sailing!" Teddy came racing into the room in his
pajamas, his arms rotating like a windmill. "Sailing, Daddy?
With the Dalrymples?"

"Right," I answered. "A life on the bounding main."

"Oh, boy! Sail—"

"Be quiet, Teddy," Nancy said. She was still watching me.
"And you accepted."

"Why—sure I did. Why not?"

She folded her lower lip in. "They don't know, then."

"Don't know what?"

"How things are, here."

"Look, we'll be out in a boat, on the Sound—"

"You'll have to tell them."

I looked at her slowly. "Tell them what?"

"Why, that we *can't* go—that there's a dangerous epidemic
all around us."

"Oh Mummy, can't we go? Just this once, can't we?"

"Teddy, go to your room," Nancy said. The boy's eyes shot
from one to the other of us, wide and hot with disappointment.

"Go hop into bed, Froggy," I told him gently. "I'll be along in
a minute."

He dropped his head and went quickly away down the hall.
When his door closed I said, "He's been looking forward to this
sailing trip for two years. You know that."

"You're actually thinking of taking him down there—
exposing him—"

"Nancy, you can't keep the boy locked up in this house week after week, like some kind of criminal."

"He's not *locked up*."

"Yes, he *is*—to all intents and purposes. Look at him— mooning around in here, coloring books, bouncing that balsa glider off the walls—he's had no sun, no real exercise. You heard him the other night—"

"A bad dream—"

"—it wasn't just a bad dream, he's on edge and nervous, crying over nothing at all. It's unhealthy as hell, an unhealthy pattern, can't you see that?"

"And so the solution is to expose him to a lot of strange kids in a strange environment." She broke off in angry wonder. "Sometimes I just don't understand you, George. Sometimes I don't think we're even living on the same continent, talking the same language."

"Maybe so," I said. "Maybe you're right."

I went back into the bathroom and rinsed my face, and then went into Teddy's room and read him the next chapter from the *The Wind in the Willows,* which happened to be the one in which Ratty gets swept away by the Seafarer's tales of high adventure in far-away, exotic lands, and Mole has to restrain him from a fevered departure. Chance. Teddy was very quiet when I finished. I thought he was going to ask me about going sailing, but he said nothing.

"Don't you want to go?" I murmured.

He nodded—a tentative, uncertain dipping of his chin; his eyes darted restively. "I don't know..."

I stroked his forehead. "What is it, Teddy? Tell Dad."

"I don't know," he repeated. But I'd seen that look in his eyes before, this summer. He was afraid. Afraid of everything. Afraid even to want what he longed for with all his heart. God damn it, she was making our boy *afraid.* I felt all at once hugely, irrationally angry. It was wrong, willfully wrong, this whole wretched regime of withdrawal, severity, dread... What the hell was happening to us? How was the boy ever to gain any confidence?

"Don't you really *want* to go?" I asked him. "Really and truly?" He nodded rapidly now, his eyes somber. "All right," I said. "We'll see."

Nancy was in the kitchen, heating bottles for Peg.

"Do you know what I think?" I said in a very different tone. "It's time we broke out of this. This whole weird, garrison-under-siege routine."

Her eyes widened, her face flattened with resentment. I'd realized some time ago that immaculate, groomed perfection was something she felt she could always fall back on, her armor against the world. Now, stripped of that, weary and disheveled and overweight, she felt defenseless, vulnerable. Poor Nan. I felt tender toward her. But then she raised one hand, dropped it against her thigh.

"You knew I couldn't go, anyway," she said in a dull, spent voice.

"Sure, you can—of course you can."

"No, I can't, I can't! What about Peg?"

"Mrs. Ames can stay with her. She can feed her the formula as well as anyone else."

"I'm just not up to it."

I paused. "Well, even if you don't feel like going, is it fair to deprive Teddy?"

"It's not a case of *depriving* anyone."

"No? Isn't it?"

"I see. That's it. The unfeeling mother punishing her helpless child." And her chin set in anger now. "That's rotten, George, that's really low."

"I'm sorry," I said. "I am, Nan." Watching her face, puffy with lack of sleep, the hollows under her eyes, I felt contrite, washed with affection. "But can't you see the other side? A chance, the chance of years to get out in a sailboat for a day, *one day,* and you—"

"There *isn't* any other side!" She waved a spoon wildly toward the window. "It's right out there, right now! 129 fresh cases reported last week. Right here in Massachusetts. No!" she said in a low, threatful tone. "He's not going."

"And I say he is."

We looked at each other for a long, a very long moment. It had never come to this before—not quite this. Our eyes locked defiantly—a childish and unseemly business, and I looked away first, vexed with myself, and lighted a cigarette.

"It seems to me you could quit smoking for these few weeks when I've asked you to."

I tamped out the butt without inhaling any of it, sat perfectly still while she pounded on shrilly about the 67% increase in cases in the northeast, the high frequency of the bulbar strain, the official warnings against chill, overexertion, travel. I'd learned early and painfully that if you hold to a position you believe in, really hang on resolutely enough, you're likely to win because the other person lets go sooner or later—loses interest, or gets deflected. It's not a very commendable faculty. I listened quietly, and thrust the pack of cigarettes back into my pocket and clasped my hands together over my knees, and after a while I said very quietly:

"This is necessary for him, Nan. He's looked forward to it for months and months, but it's more important than that. It's something every boy should experience. It's a part of life."

"Life—you talk about life! When you—"

"Yes. It's part of what gives a boy confidence, self-assurance, a sense of his worth in the world. And I'm not going to let you rob him of it simply because you've become paralyzed with fear and want to wrap him up in it, too."

She turned away then, a violent, awkward twisting of her body. "All right," she cried hoarsely, "go on, then! You always do what you want, anyway. And I know what this is. I know, d'you understand?... Go down there, then. Go on!"

She began to cry, then—a low, exhausted sobbing. But when I came up to her and put my arms around her she shrugged me off roughly. "No, leave me alone. Just—leave me alone, that's all..."

Now the sun was dancing over the blue sea, a sparkling magic shawl, and the little waves rolled and sank. Dal let Ron take the tiller for a spell, and we sang snatches of sea chanteys and big band tunes from the Fusilier days—only Chris remembered the lyrics—and watched the black, sinister cormorants diving and made bets as to where they'd surface. We anchored in a little cove on Naushonoy Chris knew about, and rowed ashore like pirates to a deserted beach where the sand was white as sugar and the beachgrass rippled silver in the onshore breeze. We swam, and Terry and I made a fire and toasted the hotdogs and buns while Chris fed the baby, and Dal served us perfect martinis. We talked about the conventions; Chris and I were all steamed up over Adlai.

"That acceptance speech—wasn't it glorious?" Chris said. "He's *my* idea of what a President ought to be—intelligent and witty and kind. And he's going to win."

"No, he isn't, sweetheart," her husband said.

"Oh, Dal! Can't we just pretend? just today? I don't see why he won't."

"That's because you're not paying attention to what happens in little old Ashtabula," Terry murmured. "What *they* want is a military Pappadaddy Warbucks with a grin as big as all outdoors."

"You were wrong in '48," she told him. "You both were. Sat up all night," she winked at me, indicating Dal. "Got more and more stinko with each passing hour. Took it as a personal affront. Can you imagine?"

"How could I know that Dewey was such a dim bulb? Stuffed-shirt store-window dummy..."

"You said it, I didn't!"

"Well, it won't happen this time, I'll tell you that. Going to be a sweep this time. Big one." He emptied his cup again and looked at Terry. "Your boy is going to drop this one."

"You think so?"

"Hell, yes. Ike'll carry 'em all in on his coattails."

Terry pushed his thin white feet back and forth in the sand, watching them. "We're worried. But we're not panicking. It's funny... people respect Lodge, they even admire him—but they don't *like* him. They like Jack. That's what's going to do it."

"But he raises emotional temperatures. He makes people care *too* much—for or against, it doesn't matter. The public figure of the future is going to be the cool cat. Style, not passion."

"Oh, Jack's got the image, if that's what's worrying you!"

"But you're not talking about qualifications," Chris protested. "Competence or—or experience or principles. Honestly, you two sound like a couple of ad agency flaks."

"That's it," Dal nodded. "That's the new name of the game."

"Is that really the way it's going?" I asked Terry.

He smiled his slow, thin-lipped smile. "Afraid so."

"Come on, Grog—don't be downhearted," Dal said. "You remember what Confucius say about—er, ah, carnal ravishment. Have another chota peg of Wog's grog. Or Grog's wog."

"As the case may be."

"As the case may be... *Here's* the shape of the future," he proclaimed, holding the shiny red plastic thermos high over his head. "Prototype—first hundred of its kind. Look at it—won't break, won't melt, won't warp, won't age. It's indestructible."

"What do you mean, it's indestructible?" I demanded. "I could smash it to bits with that stone, there."

"Sure—but the *pieces* are indestructible, Grog-o." And his red, round face squinted into its Chinese grin. "It'll last forever. Ten thousand years from now, when all the wood and steel and copper and asbestos has worn away, this will still be here. We figure we'll sell ten million of these in the next five years."

"Ten million," I said.

"That's the ticket."

"Well, *I* think it's hideous," Chris declared. "Hey, kids!" she shouted to Ron and Teddy, who were playing at the far end of the cove, "don't go wandering off, now!"

"Oh, let 'em explore a bit," Dal murmured. "Maybe they'll stumble on Kidd's treasure. Did you know he buried it around here somewhere?" He'd put on weight since he'd left Cambridge, most of it around the middle, but he still gave that impression of quick, husky energy; he played a tough, aggressive game of golf, I knew. Terry on the other hand was even thinner—as though layers on layers of himself had been stripped away; his face was cavernous, handsomer than before the war. He'd been staying at the Kennedy compound at Hyannis Port abstracting foreign affairs material for campaign speeches, and Chris had prevailed on him to run over for the day.

"No, it's a brand new world a-coming," Dal was saying; he was pleasantly smashed, his eyes blinking happily behind his glasses. "For example: the landmark date for this year you want to remember is June 2nd."

"June 2nd?" we echoed blankly.

"Check. That was the day the FCC lifted the freeze on construction of new television stations. Authorized 2,000 of them." He ran his tongue quickly around his lips. "Convey anything to you? Mmmh? Local reception—from towns, minor cities. There are 18 million sets in operation, right now. And it's only the beginning. There will be 100 million in a few years. Every family in the old US and A is going to have one—then two."

"Two in the same *house?*" Chris said incredulously.

"Check."

I said slowly: "And so whoever buys into one of these local television stations is going to make a great deal of money."

Dal threw back his head and roared. "Now you're thinking, Groggy! *Now* you're using the old beaneroo."

"And you've bought into one."

"Better than that, GV. I bought *all* of it." He gave me the slow, coony wink; independent as a hog on ice. "Station FFTV—in honor of the Fornicating Fusiliers. Or conversely."

"You're catching up, then," I couldn't help laughing. "On your Grand Design."

"Getting there, dad." His eyes rested on mine then, perfectly steady and penetrating, for all the chota pegs he'd downed. "The race is not always to the swift, Grog. Sometimes, but not always."

"Will you be operational this fall?" Terry asked him quietly.

"You bet. Want to buy some time for your boy?"

"Sure, we do."

"I'm going to hunt for shells," Chris announced. "Come on, George, let's let these two pirates carve up the world to their satisfaction, while we do something really worthwhile."

"Sour grapes, lover," Terry said.

"Oh, no!" She was smiling, but her eyes glinted green. "Lots of grapes—but they're not sour."

She picked up a funny little clawlike tool I remembered from before the war, and a net bag with thong ties, and handed it to me; and we went wading in the achingly clear water, bending and searching, and talked about the kids, and Nancy and Liz and my father, who had died of a stroke, and her father, who had received a Nobel Prize the year before, and Mel and Marge Strasser, who were living in Cleveland; and finally, inevitably of *Shadow Dance,* a recent movie Russ had written the script for, and which had played to very mixed reviews.

"What did you think of it?"

She shook her head. "I didn't like it. I wanted to, but—I don't know... that scene where the girl lets the man drown, and laughs at him. I don't mean there couldn't be people like that, I know there are. It's just that they're like *ideas* of people, not the people themselves. Maybe it's the way he wants people to be, or is afraid they'll be, or something. Of course it could be the acting."

"No," I said, "it's not the acting."

"I thought he'd go on writing novels. Or if he did movies

they'd be different—not these phony, sadistic ones."

"He's been working on a novel, I read somewhere."

"He *has* changed, hasn't he? In some irreversible way. I feel it—no more blue kites for Rusty. Do you hear from him much?"

I shook my head. "Christmas cards. We parted on a rather uncongenial note. But you could say I'm biased."

"Everyone's biased." Abruptly she bent over and drew up a shell like a rough translucent yellow coin. "Anomia." She held it to the sun, and it turned still paler and more opaline. "They're so fragile—and yet they survive. You can find them by the dozens, sometimes. Russ and I used to pretend they were money when we were kids; I always thought they were more beautiful than money could ever be."

"What are those tufts there? like hanging threads?"

"That's the byssus—its anchor. It attaches itself to rocks as it swims along. Then when it's tired of staying there, it lets go and drifts along to somewhere else."

We stared hard at each other a moment, then. She looked as lovely as she ever had; her face had strengthened, somehow— her chin was firmer, her mouth a bit more determined. She had cut her hair a touch shorter, but that was all. There was still that steady, guileless gaze, still shadowed, still brave and warm and full of life.

"A collector I write to told me he once found these pearls in a tortuma, an Inca tomb. Dozens of them, so beautiful he couldn't believe his eyes. He said all kinds of things raced through his mind—the immense fortune they must be worth, how his life would be changed, the irony of this exquisite beauty hidden there all these centuries. He blew on them impulsively—and they vanished, in a little cloud of dust. Time had eaten them away—all that was left was that beautiful nacreous shell…

"Where are the kids?" she said then in a new, brisk tone. "We'd better round them up—it's getting late." She called, her voice sweetly piercing on the warm air. "Let's go find them."

We walked quickly along the sand at the water's edge, turned a little headland. We could hear shouts now, shrill, windborne. We walked on through dusty miller and cockle shells and seaweed, rounded another spit of sand and there they were, a whole gang of kids, racing in a melée of wiry, half-naked bodies, out of which a red-and-yellow beach ball flew, bumped crazily off outstretched hands and rolled into the water, while the crowd tore after it tumbling and shrieking, the water lashing them in curving quicksilver flails.

"Ron!" Chris called. "Teddy! Come on—we've got to go back."

They detached themselves from the yelping crowd, came running toward us. Teddy was panting, sweaty, his body caked with sand and salt water; his hair stuck up on his head like some eerie ceremonial headdress; his eyes were shining. His shoulders were starting to burn.

"Oh, Daddy," he cried, "oh, I don't want to go—ever! We're having such fun..."

"I can see that." I swung him up on to my shoulder; I could feel his heart thumping, the sun's heat in his legs and arms. "But we've got to go home, Froggy. All good things have to end."

"Why, Daddy?"

"Because that's the law, Froggy." I smiled. "The biggest one of all."

The wind had fallen with the day. We crept back to harbor indolently, half-stupefied by the martinis, the sun and salt air. The kids lay on the cockpit seats like dead Indians, the baby slept in a papoose-like sling over Chris's shoulder. Dal gave me the helm and catnapped, his head bobbing like a doll's. The sun, low now, bathed the water in a harsh gold light that dazzled us. We talked in monosyllables, watching indifferently the black cage of a bellbuoy, the birds' wings of other sailboats, the points of land as they shifted and slid like cut-outs under their mats of green. I could feel my forehead smarting from the sun, the taut pull of salt rime on my arms and legs. A drowsy, sprawling contentment, everyone thinking his own thoughts now, thinking of autumn. August is such a premonitory month—or so it's always seemed to me: it isn't really summer, it's already leaning toward fall, the new season. For me Labor Day weekend has always been more of a demarcation than New Year. For that *is* the year, to me—September around to June, with the summer months a kind of pleasant appendage. The legacy of the academic year, I suppose. Maybe we never stop being what we've intended in our hearts to be...

We eased the boat in to the little dock and made her fast.

"Come on!" Chris called to the children. "Up, up, stir your stumps! All ashore that's going ashore."

Ron got dazedly to his feet, rubbing his eyes. He spoke to Teddy, shaking his shoulder. I started passing gear up to Dal. Stuffing our suits and towels into a duffel I watched Ron scramble up on the dock. Behind him Teddy reached upward clumsily, faltered—then toppled back into the cockpit with a thump. I leaped over to him.

"Teddy! You all right?"

He looked up at me, an odd, frightened glance, got up and fell against me, clutching at my legs. His face was flushed a deep red; sweat was streaming down his face and neck, he was bathed in sweat. Then while I mopped at his face with mounting uneasiness, he muttered, "Daddy, I feel sick—" and threw up in a hot spattering rush on the planking. Holding him, murmuring vague consoling sounds I could feel the heat on my palms. He was on fire, he was burning up—

"What'll we do with the drunk-en sailor?" Dal chanted lugubriously, and Chris said:

"You stop that, Dal. Poor sweety. It was all that racing around in the hot sun."

I picked Teddy up in my arms and climbed up on the dock. He cried out then—a low cry that alarmed me.

"What is it, Froggy?" I said. "What hurts?"

"My neck," he moaned, "—my neck . . ."

"Kid's gassed from all those chota pegs," Dal said; he was hurling odds and ends of gear into the back of the station wagon.

"Bring him over to the house for a while," Chris said, "let him lie down."

"No," I said. "No—I better get on home."

She looked at me quickly then; I saw her face change. "You worried?" she said softly.

I nodded. "Feel him."

She placed her hand on his forehead, his neck, his arm, withdrew it quickly. "Yes. I see."

"What's the problem?" Dal said, coming over toward us. "You mean you think he might have—" He broke off, blinking in the early evening light, staring at Teddy. "Aw, hell no—look, he's just knocked himself out."

"I better get going," I said—and just then Teddy gripped my arm convulsively and cried out, sharply now—a shrill cry of surprise and pain that froze us all rigid.

"—Can't move—my neck. Daddy!—"

"For God's sake, let's go," I said.

"I'll drive you," Terry answered. "I'll drive you up."

"No," Chris broke in, "—take him over to Hyannis Hospital. It's only twenty minutes away..."

"Sure," Terry said, "they've got good people there, a good staff. I know Wetherell over there. Just in case."

Holding Teddy, soothing his forehead with a wet handkerchief, filled with leaping dread, I tried to think what to do. Thoughts kept racing through my mind, clashing and fading: all those kids, Ron, the hour's drive up to Boston, the baby in the boat with Chris. Yes, we must move quickly, get over there. Just in case.

I said: "I'm heading for Hyannis."

"You don't know the way," Terry told me. "Follow me over."

"I'll go with you," Chris said. She touched my shoulder.

"Hey, wait a minute," Dal protested, "—look Chrissie, what about the baby? You can't do any good—"

"Dal, you pull yourself together," she said to him sharply. "He's sick, really sick—George needs me. The kids have *been* exposed, we've *all* been exposed, if it *is* polio," she said flatly, uttering the dread word for the first time. "And babies under two have the best immunity of all. Now go on home with them—I'll be back when I can."

We took off then, with Teddy in her lap, driving too fast along the south shore, hurrying through the weatherbeaten, homely towns, past cranberry bogs a rich green under the hot summer-pale evening sky. Teddy vomited again—a helpless, empty retching. I pulled over and Chris said tersely, "No. Better keep on going," and I picked up again, hurrying after Terry's blue Ford, listening to Teddy moaning in fear and pain, and Chris's voice murmuring reassurance.

The hospital looked incongruous, unreal; a sprawling background for summer dresses, the bare arms and legs of teenagers. I started to pull in beside Terry and Chris said: "No, no—go on, the emergency entrance, over there," and the note of urgency in her voice deepened the fear that already held my heart in a vise.

I ran around and lifted him out. His face was purple, contracted, he was gasping now, shoulders hunched, his neck drawn harshly, rigidly in. Once he muttered something, but I couldn't make it out; he was delirious, fighting for air, bathed in thick sweat. I wasn't able any longer to beat down my terror. So *fast* . . . surely nothing serious could happen so fast. And all the while the terror told me it could, it had.

The next two hours were worse. The polio specialist was there in twenty minutes—a peppery Cape Cod Yankee named Wetherell with a scar on his upper lip. He took tests, then a spinal tap. I told him everything I could think of that might be relevant, and he listened intently without saying a word.

When I was through he said: "Well, the overexertion is bad. Especially if he's been kept as quiet as you say. The fever is high. But he probably contracted it, if he did, some days ago."

"Then—it wasn't that crowd of kids at the beach?"

"It's extremely unlikely. But we can't know for certain."

"Was it the water? the swimming?"

"Probably not. But we don't know." His lips turned down in a brief, sad smile. "There's so much we don't know, Mr. Virdon." His eyes fastened on me again. "But you did the right thing, coming right on over here. Rather than subjecting him to a long drive to Boston. I'll tell you this: he's a very sick little shaver. It does not look good."

The vise turned again. Tighter. I went down to the lounge then and made the worst phone call of my life, to Nancy.

"—Hyannis!" she cried. "*Hyannis*—what can they do down there?"

"They have a—a polio unit here, if it should be necessary, they're fully equipped with—"

"Oh, my God, why didn't you bring him *home?* Mass General, at least."

"Nan—"

"The spinal, what does the spinal say?"

"They haven't got the results yet—I just got him *over* here. But Wetherell says the prognosis isn't good. His reflexes are poor, he's very, very sick. And the fever—"

"Oh, I can't stand it, sitting here. I can't stand it!"

"*Nancy*," I said unsteadily, gripping the edge of the phone booth, watching Chris sitting a few feet away, bent forward, hands clasped at her knee, "Nancy—try, darling, you must try to get hold of yourself! Terry's coming for you just as soon as he can. Everything that can be done is being done. We've got to hold on to ourselves now . . ."

I don't know what happened to the following hours and days;

where they went, what I did. It was like Mortellange—there was the same ominous, disembodied, hellish progression of blanks mixed with other moments so vivid they blinded, blinded—only of course it was worse, infinitely worse than Mortellange. Chris sat with me, hour after hour, not talking, just holding my hand, until Terry drove down from Boston with Nancy. When she came in I held her a long time; even her back felt brittle against my hands. Then we all sat, and walked—and waited. And phoned other specialists—Hillyer in Boston, and Mel out in Cleveland. And talked about nothing. And waited some more.

It was polio: spino-bulbar polio, the most deadly strain of that deadly virus—the spinal test confirmed it. They put Teddy in a lung; little Ted in that big impersonal monster. Dr. Wetherell had to do a tracheotomy; they set up intravenous feeding, pumped into his small, wasted body fluids and solutions I knew nothing about. And the fever kept climbing—103.6°, 104.4°, 105.2°; nothing seemed to break it, bring it down. The hardest part was not being allowed to be with him. I knew the lung was supposed to save him, I knew that, but I felt I had somehow yielded him to that iron cage that looked so deathlike, like a—

I caught a glimpse of his face once—a strained, gaunt white mask of a face, not Teddy's at all. Not Teddy.

Somewhere along the way the weather broke, the first east wind of autumn... We were alone, Nancy and I, in the falsely bright lounge with its pastel colors and seascapes; it was early morning, very early, a dove-gray iridescent sheen above the scrub pines. I was standing by the window, and Nancy was sitting on the edge of one of the couches and saying miserably:

"What I can't understand is why you let him wander off like that. You *knew* exposure to strange children was dangerous..."

"I didn't realize there were other kids there," I answered, cold in my own dark cold. "It's a privately owned island. There wasn't any way of knowing another boat had anchored down the coast a way."

"Did you think nobody else owned a sailboat? Why couldn't you have kept him with you, right there with you on the beach—at least that?"

"Wetherell says he probably caught it several days before—it's a minimum of three to five days incubation, you know that. It could even be as long as—"

"I'll never believe that. Never."

"—All right, then," I said flatly, angry at feeling nothing—nothing at all now—in the great cold fear that had invaded me. "Believe anything you want to, I don't care. Maybe you're right—" and then my voice broke. "God knows, maybe you're right. My fault. All my fault, I know..."

Silence again. Outside in the parking lot a nurse and an intern got out of a beat-up powder-blue '41 Buick convertible. The nurse said something I couldn't hear, and they both laughed—then the intern snatched something out of her hand and held it high above his head.

"No, come on, Al—oh, you rotten rat!" the nurse cried; she leaped for his hand, and they engaged in a playful twisting scuffle beside the car—abruptly hurried off toward the emergency entrance.

"...It was because you wanted to be with her," Nancy was saying in a low voice. "Wasn't it? Wasn't it?"

I turned and stared full at her. Her face was blotched and puffy from strain and lack of sleep, but her blue eyes held perfectly level on mine.

"What?" I stammered. "No—of course not, Jesus God, of course not—what are you *saying*...?"

But there had been that instant's tick of hesitation, and she had caught it. She nodded twice, stonily, and looked away. I pressed my face against the glass, which was curiously warm for five o'clock in the morning. To be with her... was it true? I'd told myself it was for Teddy, to get him out in the sun, sailing on the briny deep, but was that all of it? Had I—

The sky was completely overcast now, a high, filmy cirrus gliding in from mid-Atlantic. At least 50% of all polio cases recover completely. Another 25% suffer only slight after-effects which do not interfere with normal living. Approximately 17% are permanently crippled. Only 8%, somewhere between 6% and 9% roughly, maybe as low as 6%—

And *attitude*. They seemed to feel that an optimistic attitude was actually helpful. Nothing good or bad, but thinking makes it so. Was that true? A destiny that shapes our ends—was there one? was there, ultimately and implacably, somewhere out there beyond all the prating about accident and free will, a grim celestial magistrate who meted out our fates with a perfectly logical causality? did a flicker of weakness, a fleeting shadow of dereliction—

Someone was coming, coming quickly. I turned. Wetherell,

in operating room garb, his face more wizened, harder under the boxlike cap; the mask was dangling from one side, swinging free. He had not made a sound on the gleaming tan floors, but I'd heard him. Nancy was gone, I didn't know where.

"Mr. Virdon." He walked all the way up to me. I couldn't take my eyes from his face. When he got to me he said: "Let's sit down for a moment."

"No," I said. "I want to stand."

He nodded. "I have very hard news for you, Mr. Virdon. Very hard." I tried to say something, could not. "We lost him. Your little boy."

"... *Dead.*"

"The fever kept right on climbing, there was no stopping it. All the nerve centers were paralyzed. Everything that could be done we did, I guarantee it. I'm terribly sorry."

"Yes." Wetherell's crabbed Yankee face grew blurred, then magically, microscopically clear. I found myself wondering how he'd got that scar across his upper lip.

"I thought for a while we were going to be all right," he said. "And then it started soaring again... There's so much we just don't understand." He put his hand on my arm for a moment, withdrew it lightly and glared out at the parking lot. "Some day they'll isolate this damned, vicious virus, find out how it's transmitted, develop a serum—they're working on it now, night and day. They're close. I know that's no con—"

He broke off. Nancy was coming down the hall toward us, hurrying. Then she saw my face—and stopped.

"What is it?" she asked. "Is he better, is he—?" But her eyes were stony with terror: she knew, she'd felt it in the room, maybe; I don't know.

"Honey," I said. "Honey... you'll have to hang on. Hang on tight. Honey, he's gone. Teddy. Our Teddy. He's dead."

She gazed at me, and then at Wetherell, and then at me again, her lips parted, her eyes perfectly hollow. She made a low, incoherent sound deep in her throat, and then her head began to rock back and forth, a slow, mesmeric rhythm, her eyes distended.

Before I could move Wetherell slapped her—a smart, light blow on the cheek; she fell against him, sobbing.

"All right," he said. "All right, now. Let it go, let it go, now."

I stepped forward, and he passed her into my arms. "I'll be in administration for an hour or so, come see me then."

Afterward we sat in the car with the rain sweeping in milky waves over the blacktop, and Nancy wept hopelessly, inconsolably while I held her and wept, too, thinking of Dutch at Montélimar, and Dee and Opp; and those terrible moments seemed now like nothing at all. My son. All hope, all joy. This was worse than the war, infinitely worse—the whole world had been one cauldron of misery then and you walked toward it grimly, setting your teeth, hardening your heart. But *this*—out of a balmy summer holiday, to a lively little boy who had clapped in delight when Morgiana poured the boiling oil into the jars where the forty thieves were hiding to kill Ali Baba, who came racing into the bedroom mornings and pounced on top of me for the daily tussle, who made ferocious, misshapen dragons out of colored clay, and once said—

Oh Teddy, Teddy.

It wasn't possible. It simply was not possible that this could have happened.

But it had.

And the rain kept beating savagely on the roof of the car, a harsh comfort, and we clung to each other as if we were the last man and the last woman, on the verge of being drowned in the flood. The final one, with no ark and no survivors.

"—I didn't mean it, what I said," she moaned at some point. "What I said about you, I didn't mean it, I'm half crazy, a terrible thing to say—I *know* you loved him, more than anything, you've always been right here with me. I don't know why I said it, I don't, truly I don't . . ."

"It's all right, honey. I shouldn't have taken him. Oh God, I shouldn't have taken him. I only wanted him to have—"

But I couldn't finish the words, I couldn't finish. We had changed courts somehow, in some crazy way: now she was saying she didn't blame me for the sailing trip; but from that day on I was never entirely free of blaming myself, of the sense that I *had*—that I'd risked my boy in my own lonely, anguished need . . .

I cannot talk about the funeral. Not even now. Dal and Chris were my mainstays then. Dal walked with me for hours, in rain, in sun, just quietly there, at my side—I wanted only silence and he gave it. And when Nancy shut herself up in the bedroom for hours at a time it was Chris who came in and did the cooking and helped Mrs. Ames with Peg; who held me in her arms one sultry, gray afternoon, held me so gently and said again and again, "Oh George, I wouldn't have had this happen to you and Nan for the whole wide world. Oh God, I wish I could help you, I wish I could help you..."

The poliomyelitis epidemic, the worst in our history—worse than '35, worse than '49—finally, mercifully subsided. Neither Ron nor the baby nor our Peg got it. None among all that crowd of yelping kids at the beach. Only Teddy. And of course in a year—*one year*—they had isolated the virus and developed the serum.

God's punishment. Nancy thought so, I knew: punishment for sin. She only alluded to it twice in all the years to follow; she never mentioned Teddy's name again—not once.

There was only that still, blazing Saturday morning when the Dalrymples said goodbye—Chris weeping in perfect silence, even Dal's eyes filled with tears—when Nancy embraced them curtly, not weeping at all. I remember that moment. I remember Nancy later, standing at the bedroom window saying: "They're gone. I'm glad they're gone. I hope I never see them again." Her voice toneless and even.

"Nan," I protested, "you don't mean that."

"Oh, yes I do."

"Nan—they're good friends..."

"—*Friends*," she said in a dead, threatful tone that was more frightening to me than any shrieks or hysteria, "—don't talk to *me* about friends, I've had all I want to hear about friends."

"Nan, please try—"

She moved past me then, with sudden violent purpose, snatched something from my bureau top and flung it from her with a hoarse, low cry; it bounced all the way into the bathroom, off the edge of the tub, and clattered hollowly back across the tile floor. Chris's little cowrie shell—still amazingly unbroken. But she was on it in a series of quick running steps and had crushed it with one savage stamp of her foot.

"This—!" she panted. "I'm not ever going to look at this again. Never!"

And there was nothing, absolutely nothing I could say—I could only watch her while she ground and ground it into the blue tiles, her eyes fastened on me all the while in cold defiance.

All right, then. But what about punishment for the sin you *don't* commit? There's the dirtiest, cruelest joke of all . . .

We held on. I worked till all hours; read grimly and voraciously, mastered printing techniques and sales patterns, hunted up old professors at work on new manuscripts; stunned and flooded my heart with work. Nancy did too, throwing herself into polio therapy, the library board, half a dozen community activities. We would meet around midnight, talk while we undressed, and fall exhausted into bed. We made a kind of love, now and then. We even laughed now and then—not often, not long, but we did. But she'd become a stranger, Nancy. Part of her had drawn into itself, like one of Chris's sea creatures backing into its shell and blocking up the entrance with its own operculum. There was no reaching her.

And there would always come those moments when a bright red top found under the lilacs, a snatch of tune, a small mitten at the back of a closet, a child's footprint in the soft earth of the back yard would cut into me, sweeping Teddy back with terrible force, and I would go down into the basement and sit on one of the carpentry horses and give way to long, shuddering sobs, until the seizure finally wore itself out and let me go again. For the time. (Some things *are* irreparable, you know.) And then I would wipe my face and climb back upstairs again, where the world—impossibly, capriciously—was going along exactly as it had before.

2

IT WAS THE HORN—I'd have known it anywhere, any time: that sonorous, windborne clarion call that could always make you think of heralds in royal tabards, of cuirassiers, and Roland deep in the rocky gorges of Roncesvalles...

"Who can *that* be?" Nancy said, frowning.

"I don't know," I answered. But I did. I got up from the table and hurried down the hall, caught in the old sharp surge of affection—and a certain uneasiness; I opened the front door and there was Russ, all right, just getting out of the Empress. He slammed the door behind him with a quick, contemptuous snap of his wrist, and dust rose in a thin, dry cloud. There was no one else in the car.

"Not Belmont, Grog. Not *Belmont*..." He gazed up at the house, affronted, shading his eyes although it was dusk and there was no sun. He was wearing a maroon blazer with gold buttons and a blue paisley cravat.

"Everybody's moving out here," I said, "didn't you know? Here and Concord. It's got cachet."

We looked back at the house together.

"Yes, I see it. I see it now." Squinting he held up his hands, palms flat, thumbs extended, as though framing it for a camera shot. "It does have a kind of indefinable—a kind of ineffable—"

"Up yours, Currier." We laughed together; but the old place did seem shabby, depressing in a way I'd never noticed before. Why was that? I turned around. Behind Russ the Empress looked battered and dirty, the body coated with dust and caked mud; the luggage rack was bent grotesquely sideways.

"What have you been doing—running her on some third-rate stock car track?" I demanded. "Reshooting *The Grapes of Wrath?*"

"Terrible trek, Grog. Terrible. Eighty days across a continent of shifting sand. Strong men cried when we had to eat the lead camel ... She's had it," he said, and thumped the long, angular hood with the heel of his hand. "The grand old Empress. She's done for. Like our youth."

"Nonsense—her best years are still ahead of her ..."

We looked at each other, then—really looked at each other. He was still as handsome as ever—the slim head, the close-fitting, dark hair, the fine straight nose; but I saw crow's feet now at the corners of his eyes, and a new tightness around his mouth. And I could tell from his expression that he'd noticed changes, too. A long, naked moment while we watched each other, wondering, remembering. . . . Then I caught that sudden droll twist at the corner of his mouth, the glint of hilarity in his eyes.

"I've come home, Grog: is all forgiven?"

I laughed; there was nothing to do but laugh, there never was. "Come on in, you dizzy son of a bitch," I said. "You're just in time for some fatted calf."

We started up the steps; the door was open, Nancy was standing there.

"Russ Currier!" I saw her face change, her eyes narrow. But she smiled—a slow, questioning, ambivalent smile. "What a surprise! What brings you back to us poor mortals?"

"Banished." He laughed hugely, and embraced her. "Hurled into Tartarus. For—for harboring illicit designs on Pallas Athene. But hell, you've got to get your kicks somewhere."

At dinner we talked about a dozen things, but mostly about the election, which was that very day.

"What timing!" I said.

"Pure accident, Grog. I left the Coast five days ago."

"But you *did* vote."

"My God, yes. Absentee ballot. What do you take me for? This time of all times." He raised his glass. "Here's to Adlai, the last gentleman of politics."

"That's just about it, isn't it?" I drank with him. "You think he can win?"

"Win—he's *got* to win." He caught a certain faint gleam in Nancy's eye then, and stared at her. "You're not—no, Nancy, no! You're for Stevenson, aren't you?"

She smiled now. "Not exactly."

"You're kidding..." And he turned to me in consternation.

"Oh yes, I'm for Adlai," I told him. "To the hilt."

"Blazes, Grog-o." He had himself in hand again. "You mean to tell me you can't control your own everloving spouse?"

"Not I," I said. "Can you?"

His eyes flickered at me and away. "You're right," he murmured. "It's a silly question."

"Now Russell," Nancy said. "You're not going to turn into one of those dreary people who says if a woman votes for the opposition she's canceling her husband's vote, are you?"

"Why, no."

"The Dalrymples vote differently. Lots of couples do. How about you and Kay—are you voting the same ticket?"

He gave a tight, lean smile. "Kay and I are not in agreement on anything. Anything at all... In fact, we've gone our separate ways."

"Oh—I'm sorry," Nancy said.

"I don't know whether I am or not," I said, and we laughed.

"Yes, well, all bad things must come to an end." Russ emptied his glass. "No, but seriously, Nancy: when you've got the chance to vote for a mind as superior as Adlai's—"

"Maybe more than intellect is involved," she said. "That never seems to occur to you Stevensonians."

"Oh, but Ike!—the corporation general with the Howdy-Doody grin. Going to Korea—isn't that big of him, though! What a cheap shot. And that creep Nixon. I could tell you tales about him that would curl your hair." And he proceeded to do just that—about the Helen Gahagan Douglas campaign on the coast, the anonymous phone calls, the foul avalanche of smears and slander. "Talk about McCarthy—Tricky Dicky's every bit as rabid. He's pathological."

"Have you ever noticed? Somebody is always pathological if his convictions run counter to yours," Nancy observed in what I had begun to think of as her Head Mistress voice.

"Nancy's been working with the League of Women Voters," I put in.

"Great." Russ nodded; he was still watching her warily. "But you *are* going to vote for Kennedy for the Senate."

"I may," she said with a smile. "I haven't made up my mind yet."

"Terry's been working on her," I added. "He's almost got her convinced."

"Terry?" he said. "He's here? in Boston?"

"Hell yes, everyone's been in the trenches all fall. It's make-or-break time for Jack, this one."

"If he were running in California he'd win in a walk. The women are downright tumescent about him out there. How about you, Nancy—do you want to leap into bed with him?"

She gazed back at him flatly, her eyes a very deep blue. "Not remotely," she answered.

"Sure, just kidding. Just waxing facetious."

It was curious, sitting here in our home, with Russ the visitor, the outsider. Nan and I were "together," a couple, to all intents and purposes—part and yet not part of that passionate group solidarity and craving which marked our generation: Fusiliers or fraternities in college, bound together in the Army, and then rushed into corporate business and marriage and parenthood—a man seemed actually diminished in most eyes if he didn't belong to a family or an institution . . . Russ even seemed to sense something of this—he was arch, and then diffident, and then overweening again; he watched Peg in her high chair with a kind of fearful fascination, this alien world of infant ritual.

"I was sorry to hear about Teddy," he murmured while Nancy was putting Peg to bed.

"That's all right." I felt suddenly angry with him for bringing it up, angry with myself for being angry. "It's over now—we're over it." To change the subject I brought up the most recent picture I knew he'd written, but he brushed it aside; he was through with films for a while, he was back on the novel, he'd just about wound it up. We talked briefly about *Invisible Man,* and William Styron and Malcolm Lowry, but his mind wasn't on any of that, either. He wanted to know about the old crowd, how they were doing; he wanted to roam around Cambridge.

"Tell me about J. Pierpont Dalrymple. How's he coming with that Monopoly game time-table of his?"

"Full blast. He's into plastics, television, the market—he's going in all directions. They've got a big place out in Lake Forest now, with stables and a tennis court and a swimming pool. And a lovely little girl named Julie. They were east this summer, we went sailing—" I broke off; I didn't want to go on with that.

"He's over thirty, isn't he? He must be behind schedule, no matter how you look at it. He still owes me a case of choice, the lousy welsher."

"He says the race is not always to the swift."

His eyes met mine, then, and I caught a flash of the old, hot rivalry—and something else, too, something I couldn't read; then he threw off the rest of his drink.

"Let's run down to the Square—check out some of the old haunts. You game?" The old infectious excitement was working in him again, his eyes were snapping. "Let's go over and see Shafty Kennedy—I don't suppose they call him Shafty any more, now he's the rising politico. He'll be there, won't he?"

"Terry'll be there, too," I said.

He looked at me. "He doesn't—hold things against me, does he?"

"I couldn't tell you, pal. I don't know how he feels about you."

"But it was five years ago..."

"That's true."

"Weren't you planning to run over there, whoop it up a little?"

"No—we were going over to some friends—they've got a TV set."

"We can do that later—let's cruise around a while first."

"All right. How about it, Nan?" I said.

"No—you boys go on over. Something tells me I wouldn't be too welcome at Democratic Headquarters tonight. I'll meet you at the Merwins' later on."

So Russ and I took off together. The Empress was in terrible shape. Terrible. She was missing, fading badly on the upgrades. The carburetor needed an overhaul—either that or the fuel pump was shot. It actually hurt me to listen to her.

"You're the world's worst auto mechanic, Currier," I told him. "You're wrecking this chariot through sheer neglect, you realize that?"

"That's why I came directly to you, Grog. For expert automotive R&R."

"Yeah, but you haven't even given her—"

"Groggo, you don't understand—there was never time to do anything like that out there. Let's not talk about it. I want to pub-crawl in Olde Cambridge—where everything begins and ends. And forget everything else."

We checked in at McBride's, and then Cronin's, and then the Oxford Grille. TV sets were flickering away, there were commentators and wavering columns of election figures, but the atmosphere was curiously dull; the undergraduate of the '50's seemed sober and subdued—we missed the rambunctious bedlam of the post-war days, with Chid and Blazer in worn chinos and white buckskins, thumping the table in time to the juke box and bellowing: "*Caldonia! Caldonia! What-makes-your-big-head-so-hard?*—ROCKS!" The self-assertion, the uncaring exuberance were gone. Russ felt it, too—he kept peering around irritably.

"Is this really the OG, the place that launched a thousand drunks? What's the matter with these kids?"

"Too much post-war money. Too many fins on their cars," I said. "And Korea."

"Yeah. *That* mess..."

Everything seemed bewitched that evening, laid under some malignant spell. That night of all nights Conger came by, as you could know he would; Conger, inevitably in gray flannel, with his bland, frozen-pudding face. He saw me and grinned slyly, tossed his head toward the TV set and said: "It's looking awfully good, Virdon. Awfully good!" He was actually rubbing his hands. He started to pause by our booth, then caught sight of Russ's face and moved away.

Russ said loudly: "What's he doing here—hasn't the son of a bitch graduated *yet?*"

"He's working over there in University Hall."

"*Conger—?*"

"Yeah. A career in higher education."

"That tears it. Let's move on."

The crowd at Kilby Street was thinner than I'd expected. At Lodge headquarters across the street people were pouring in and out, a band was playing lustily—there was a jubilant, expectant air.

"It doesn't look too good," I said.

"Now, don't panic, Grog. Wait till the urban vote starts to roll in. Don't forget '48."

"Check."

"Don't sell the average American short—he knows what the score is, he's not going to turn his back on the party that's fought for him all along, the party that nominated a Stevenson."

"I hope you're right," I said. I was already feeling doubts; maybe it was living with Nancy.

The crowd was light enough that you could make out different small groups, talking rather quietly. The PA system was growling out canned music, Jo Stafford singing *Jambalaya*. There were TV sets here, too, and two girls in bright green dresses were erasing and writing down figures on blackboards.

Terry was in the middle of the floor, talking to Ken O'Donnell and Eunice Kennedy and an older man I didn't know; he raised his chin and winked. When I reached him I said: "I brought you an old friend. An *old friend*," I repeated.

He saw Russ then, and his face changed before his eyes did—for a second or two my forebodings were very real. Then he grinned and put out his hand.

"Russ! What perfect timing." He introduced us to the others; the older man was Larry O'Brien. Their smiles were forced; the tension was almost palpable. They knew about Russ—both O'Donnell and Eunice had read *Full Fathom Five*—but right now he was too vivid a reminder of Beacon Hill and the Somerset Club and the Harvard Board of Overseers—that assured, entrenched, frosty Brahmin world whose adherents were right there across the street, whooping it up so ecstatically for Lodge.

"Are you a product of your class or have you risen above it?" Eunice teased him. For all the months of receptions and speeches, she looked marvelous, her deep oak hair swirling about her throat, her wide-set eyes sparkling.

"Neither, really—I dove under it and came up on the other side," Russ answered; he was instantly attracted to her, I could tell. "In fact I'm such a traitor I've even earned my own living."

"You're wicked!" she laughed, but her eyes glinted.

"Don't you know the only two classes are those who believe the incredible—and those who do the improbable?"

"I *like* that—will I remember it tomorrow?"

"I'll send you a copy of my new book. That's the epigraph for it."

Jack Kennedy came up then with Dave Powers and wanted to know what the unseemly hilarity was all about.

"Senator," Russ said, "can I have your autograph?"

Jack frowned—then his face broke into that irrepressible, mischievous grin. "Tolstoy! You've conceded, then?"

"Conceded—I *voted* for you! Still again. They've probably confiscated all the Democratic votes in California, but it's there."

"How considerate of you to fly east for our victory celebration. Now I call that dedication." Jack was the only person in that great barn of a room who looked poised and confident, perfectly at ease. "Can't you give Lodge a job in the studios, Currier? something to write? He used to be a reporter..." He looked very changed—he was still quite thin but his face was more resolute, less boyish and callow; the head—that wonderfully shaped head—with a new hair style now.

Bobby came up in that brusque, rather surly way he had and called his brother away to meet someone. New returns came in, and there was a slow, hesitant surge toward the big boards. The figures were dismaying; Eisenhower was winning nearly everywhere, winning big; the margin seemed to be growing by leaps and bounds. Jack was ahead, but not by much, and his lead was dwindling steadily. I heard the word "sweep" here and there around me. I looked at my watch: it wasn't even eleven.

There is nothing sadder than a campaign headquarters on a losing night: the forced joviality can make you actively sick.

"Well, it's early yet," Russ said hollowly. "Let's go some place and get a drink."

He wanted to revisit the Statler Bar, but the vindictive hilarity of the GOP stalwarts there drove us out again. We cruised round and round aimlessly, the fuel pump on the Empress clearly getting worse and worse, and finally wound up in an Italian joint behind Dock Square, where most of the inmates looked and acted as gloomy as we felt. Ike was leading

Stevenson by nearly 200,000 in Massachusetts, and by over four million nationwide. Russ was thunderstruck—he kept gazing at the returns in angry shock.

"It's impossible! They *can't* pick that back-slapping golf player over Adlai, they wouldn't be that stupid. Jesus, did you see Ike embracing that bastard McCarthy in Wisconsin? Ah, you've got no idea what it was like out there, Grog. These last couple of years. Yeah, I know, you read the papers, but that was only the tip of the iceberg. It was contemptible—all that money, all that power, and they broke and ran like weasels. I want to tell you, if Ike wins, McCarthy will run the country: there'll be thought control, press censorship, travel restrictions, ID cards—the works. You think I'm spinning, you wait. You won't even have to pay your electric bill—you'll be able to read by the light of the God damn witch burnings..."

I sat listening to him, my face in my fists, shifting back and forth between flat disbelief and a hollow alarm that he might be right. He wasn't even watching the TV screeen now; he ordered another round of drinks, and unreeled a disquieting tale of directors jibbering in panic, producers informing on their stars and stars informing on their writers, half the colony howling patriotism at every turn. But watching him I knew he didn't really want to talk about that; he was stalking something else—a starving animal circling a baited trap. He got around to it with the next drink.

"Well. You warned me, Grog. You warned me. And you were right." He rocked forward on his elbows. "You know, I hated you for saying what you did that night before I left for the coast. I made up my mind I was never going to see you again, you know that?" He frowned. "But you read her like that old New England primer, didn't you? right from the beginning."

"It wasn't hard," I said.

"No—I suppose not. The Mad Miss Madden. And I know you'd never ask. But in a way I owe you the story. How it was. You and nobody else."

"You don't owe me anything."

"Yes, I do—if only because you made that admission of your own that night. To try to jolt me out of it. It must have been painful for you."

I remembered what I'd said, then. "Look, Russ," I said uncomfortably, "I don't need to hear it. I'd rather—"

"But you don't understand—I've *got* to tell someone!" he cried with the old hot intensity; then threw himself back in his chair with a shrug. "And you're elected. On election night. Joke.

"It started out merrily enough," he murmured, as though he were pleading his case before an unsympathetic audience. "When you're on top out there the view is breathtaking, the attentions are disarming, the surroundings are all so damned sybaritic. It's like a kid's fairyland where everyone can play king—only not for long. Not for very long...

"The house was at the core of it. If you're a king you've got to have a palace. Perfectly simple, Grog, you can see the logic there, can't you? So we built this pleasure dome, out at Malibu. All glass and cypress and brushed aluminum, hanging there above the sea. Our glass house. It was Kay's doing—she went wild over it. It became an obsession with her, she'd spend whole afternoons with architects and landscapers and pool people; the blueprints changed from day to day. At first I indulged her—I thought it was compensatory, she'd had those bad notices on *Fathom* and then she'd walked off a picture right after that, and Fennerman had begun to have trouble getting work for her. But I can see now it was more than that—a lot more.

"Anyway, the house was fantastic. It had living rooms beyond living rooms, constructed on half a dozen levels, there were dens and billiard rooms and bars, there were circular iron staircases and graystone terraces and massive decks overlooking the ocean. And at the heart of it was the pool—but not what *you* think of as a pool, Grog. No, this one meandered through half the house—outdoors, indoors, it wound through the high glass rooms like a great green anaconda. Maybe it was beautiful, maybe it was hideous, I don't know—how in Christ's name can you *judge* something like that? I can't. It ran over rock outcroppings that had been brought in from the Sierras, it fanned out again in cunningly placed pools and grottos edged with ferns and dwarf palms and a dozen other exotic plants: a bloody jungle under glass. And everywhere were these underwater lights, cleverly concealed beneath rocks, or in that God damned rain forest, that kept turning the water from turquoise to emerald to amber...

"A pleasure dome." He finished his drink again, motioned for another. "And the cost—! Jesus. When I began to get the picture I was horrified. '*We* can't afford this,' I said, 'we can't *begin* to handle something like this! Who do you think I am, the Aga Khan?' 'I've got money of my own,' she told me. 'Relax.'

"I knew that was a lie—she never had any money, she ran through it like the sands of Sahara, she never could hang on to a nickel if there was any place to spend it. I knew she meant Daddy and those big shiny new jet planes of his and I got sore, and we had a row about that; and then I thought, What's the difference, he's always given her money anyway, all she wanted, once the place is completed we'll have a final understanding, and that'll be that.

"But that wasn't that. The house was only the beginning. Kay was ecstatic when it was finished. 'Oh, Rousseau'—she'd taken to calling me that for reasons unknown—'it's sensational, it's divine!' She loved to swim naked through the long, cool rooms, rolling over and over, those gorgeous breasts and ass fading and reappearing like slick golden globes. Once in a while I swam with her, but I never liked it—it made me nervous. With the great, gray Pacific out there in front of us, that magnificent sweep of sand and the breakers furling in like time itself, I could never understand why she wanted that coiling hot-house waterway. But she said it, finally, rolling over and over in the amber rock pool: 'Oh baby—what a set!'

"Which was what it was all about, of course. Because then the parties began. And nobody's as good as Kay at throwing parties. Nobody. She's got that instinctive sense of personal drama— what would draw people, tickle their curiosity. She loved themes. There were Jazz Age parties, there were Old Persia parties with all the woman running around in those filmy transparent pants, there were Chinese parties and Art-Deco parties, there was even a Doris Day party as American as Mom's humping apple pie—but her most inspired productions were restagings of scenes from old movies, in which she would play Garbo to some young male lead's Frederic March, Janet Gaynor to some stud's Ronald Colman, Lombard to somebody else's Gable. And of course she had an unerring instinct for which stars in the colony were rising, which were not; what directors might be enticed over, and impressed...

"It was all very exciting. And exhausting. I was writing less and less, and what work I did get around to was lousy, working off hangovers as I was, half-stunned. The brass at Columbia didn't like the two scripts I'd been assigned, and Cort didn't even try to defend the second one. The signs were ominous, but I wasn't reading them—I was still running around starry-eyed and dazzled by all my good fortune, still thinking of Hollywood as a place where people would use this glorious medium for something more than a bucket of tapioca. I didn't know how things worked, how power was wielded or where its source lay—I guess there was a part of me that didn't want to know. And I made a lot of mistakes. Big ones."

He sighed again, his chin on his chest, gazing at nothing. "We'd already started to skid, Grog. It's such a *quick* world out there! We'd already begun to skid, and we didn't know it—at least *I* didn't know it—and then we were sliding fast, almost falling. And still I didn't get it. I showed up at the studio and ground out the pages, and what I did was molded and stretched and twisted like dough and made into something else, some very different confection—there were times I couldn't recognize anything I'd done in what I saw later. Nothing. And maybe that was just as well ... *Kay* knew what was happening, though—she knew, and she was doing something about it. Oh yes."

He threw up his hand, glaring hard at me. "Don't get me wrong: I don't want to sound as if I didn't know what was going on—at least some of it. I did. I knew she was spending a lot of time with other men now—rising young directors, producers who were putting new packages together, even old friends of Uncle Lorenzo who might offer her a part. I'd run into her at Chasen's or Romanoff's or on location out in the valley—that was when she started seeing a lot of Matt Driessen. Of all the new phony-macho types I hated him most. Those crotch-bound pants and shirt unbuttoned down to his hairy navel, and the face of a Vegas pimp. I'd say to myself, Okay, okay, all right. Hell, I've never been a prude, Grog, you know that. I knew she played around—or I suspected she did. But discreetly; and I figured, All right, as long as it's casual and discreet, that's the way things go out here, I can handle it, roll with it. Maybe I even encouraged it some by ignoring half of what went on, ducking a few of those incessant parties, trying, trying, *trying* to get back to work ...

"But we were sliding fast now, that long, tumbling slide. People who'd pursued us wildly when we first got out there didn't have time for us now—or, the most dangerous sign of all, couldn't even bother with an excuse; and Kay grew more hostile and aggressive. She was obsessed about everything. Even her body. There she was with that incredible golden body God or somebody had given her—and she began to spend half her time worrying about it. She'd come up out of that enormous scallop-shell bath tub that always made me uneasy—it always made me think of Chris's shells; I mentioned it once and Kay laughed—you remember that laugh of hers, as though the whole world were an audience for one of her private jokes—and cried: 'How clever of you! To figure that out all by your lonesome. Doesn't it remind you of how much better you've done?'— anyway, she'd rise up from it like Botticelli's Venus and stand in front of this three-panel mirror, studying herself, examining that perfect, perfect body for half an hour at a time, running her hands down her flanks or lifting her lovely breasts, first one and then the other, as if to detect the slightest, most infinitesimal change. And when I'd move up to her and take her in my arms she'd wrench herself away from me crying, 'No no no—let me alone, don't touch me—!'

"That's the way she was—sex with her was either a mad, whiplash duel, or nothing at all. She never *enjoyed* sex, the way other women do. Only a wild, fantasy-ridden tease ever brought her off—and even then you never really knew. It was all wrong, I knew it was all wrong; and yet I couldn't help myself...

"And now this fierce preoccupation with aging—which was so ironic, because no woman ever mocked time with her face and body the way she has. She began wearing younger and younger clothes, displaying more and more of herself: backless, sideless, frontless—but *never* sexless. You know. That taunting banter of hers—and her dissatisfactions: everything I did displeased her now. Then Hedda Hopper ran an item in her column on Kay and Driessen, and I called her on it—which only provoked another row.

"'Oh for God's sake, Rousseau, let's be just a little sophisticated about things, can't we? You'd think we were five-year-olds. You never *experiment.'*

"'Experiment! You call—'

"'Oh, don't be such a fucking Boston snob! Non-fucking, that is. You never get with it at all... Why don't you shop around a little yourself, try something different—it might inject a little life into your scripts! Even yours.'

"That kind of thing. And worse. Sometimes much worse. Which led to more fights. We always fought, from the very beginning, but now it was different: now there was a really nasty edge to our quarrels that hadn't been there before."

He started to pick up his glass, pushed it away. "And then came the night that ripped it all apart. For good and forever. I'd been working on a lousy third-rate script with Chambers and I came home late. The house was dark. I figured she was out with someone. I came in the back way, I didn't bother to turn on the lights. As I started across the living room toward the bar I heard the laughter and stopped. The only light was from those colored underwater floods that kept flickering across the walls and ceiling like flames. And there they were—Driessen and another man and Kay. They were in the rock pool together, naked, their bodies sleek and shining as they moved through the still, amber water, locked together. All of them. I watched them. God help me, I just stood there and watched them—at their games. I couldn't seem to move. They were all over her, in and out of her, together, separately, in tandem, and she was laughing that wild, metallic laugh of hers, head thrown back, long hair trailing gold behind her; loving it all, exulting in it. And then in a ritual she had clearly performed before, it was so effortless, she threw herself backward, her body arched, and dove straight to the bottom of the pool and burst to the surface among them in a white rush of water, and now she was fondling and kissing and swallowing those two cocks, sliding over them, down the length of them, greedily swallowing those male bodies ten years younger than hers as though she wanted to take into herself all of them, all of their youthful elixir; now astride their shoulders, now slipping between their legs and holding there, all open mouth and searching tongue...

"And then from behind the rocks a girl swam into view, a baby-faced starlet named Belinda Briles who'd been trying to get bits at 20th; and she and Kay performed now, a rolling, sliding ritual, head to pelvis, all teasing fingers, tongues, their faces contorted, while the men watched, and laughed, and swam to join them.

"I started to move, then—and that was when I saw the man. Sitting on the rattan couch in the near darkness. Perfectly motionless, watching. Just the cropped head and a glint of silver-rimmed glasses, the blur of a pale silk shirt, but I knew. Vic Gabruda, the producer. Something in the way he sat there told me he'd already seen me, but he gave no sign. Gabruda, who'd stood the industry on its ear with his last three pictures, whose stock-in-trade was shock: girls' faces slashed with razors, bodies crushed in garbage trucks, guts spilled over laden dining tables. Gabruda, who'd told me not two weeks before that he was looking for 'irreverent' new scripts, who was casting now for *Den of Thieves*. I stared at him for three, four, five seconds. And still I didn't move.

"God, how I hate myself for that! You wouldn't think you could hesitate at a time like that, would you? But I did. It's the worst thing I've ever done in all the world. Then the disgust took over. And the rage. And I roared: 'Get out! Get out of here, every motherfucking one of you—*out!*"

"And they just floated there, looking up at me in surprise, while I called them every filthy name I could remember or invent—and then Kay began to laugh wildly, insanely and then they were all laughing, splashing about and howling like hyenas, and Kay was pelting water at me, soaking me. I thought, She knew: she *knew* I was coming home tonight—she knew all along... And still Gabruda went on sitting there, perfectly inert, as though this was all part of the exhibition too, a hugely comic climax to the whole dirty scene."

Russ rubbed his eyes, picked up his drink again and emptied it. I wanted to say something, but there was clearly nothing at all to say.

"Well, then I went crazy. I ran and got that Jap Nambu 7-mm I had and they stopped laughing then—everybody stopped laughing, and they got out of the pool and left. As they were. Gabruda was already gone. And then I went and hid the pistol because by then I was afraid I was going to use it. I very nearly did, Grog. Oh so nearly. As it was I damned near killed her. And I *wanted* to kill her, I wish I had..."

"All right," I said quietly.

"I know, I know. I never thought I could kill anybody—not that way. But I see you can, any time, any place given the—the proper conditions. Oh, yes." He gazed down at his hands in fearful wonder. The seal ring was still there, glowing pale gold. "I can feel her wet throat in my hands right now, I was going to choke her—I *would* have choked her to death if it hadn't been for her eyes. There was fear there, sure, but there was something else, too—a flash of secret delight, some crazy inverted ecstasy—yes, really! *ecstasy*—she was getting her rocks off in a way she never had before. And that sickened me utterly. I threw her to the floor and she lay there holding her throat, gasping, her body shuddering and writhing on the tiles as if she were rendering a passage with death itself.

"'This is all of it, Kay,' I told her when I got my voice again. 'The end of Ancient Rome.' And I got in the Empress and drove way deep into Mexico that night, down the coast, watching the sea and trying to calm down. And when I came back I was over it.

"Well, we fought our way through the divorce—and she won there, too, what with all of Daddy's lawyers: she got the house, and half of what I had left from *Shadow Dance,* and a big alimony judgment. I rented a small place out in Pacific Palisades, I still wanted to be near the sea. And she still had the last word, Grog. Trust Kay. One night I was running off a print of *Fathom,* I wanted to study the transitions again, and all of a sudden I wasn't watching *Fathom* at all. I was watching Kay, stark naked, in all kinds of provocative poses, playing with herself, then having sex with an actor I'd seen somewhere before, and another man I didn't know—and then there *I* was, in bed with her, *our* bed in the Great Glass House, and we were screwing—she was sitting astride me, she always liked that position best though I don't know what bloody difference it made, she was always ravenous for more right afterward—and now she was laughing, I could see her, laughing at the camera and winking...

"I began to shake like a fever victim. I thought, If she did *this,* if she allowed these to be made and took the trouble to splice them in the reel, where are the other prints? Who is sitting around laughing with her right now, watching them? What else has she done?

"I ran out on the little deck and gripped the railing and looked out to sea. I felt as if I were on fire, burning up from the inside, and all that would be left of me would be an ashy shell. Far, far out there was a destroyer, running down to Dago, I spotted the silhouette instantly. I wanted to cry, and couldn't. The sea—all my life it's been such a—such a source of everything clean and good. And now even the sea seemed to have gone treacherous and foul."

He puffed his lips and threw out his thumbs, palms up, an umpire's *out* gesture. "So there it is. How to sink a Currier—in celluloid. Kay scored with Gabruda, by the way—he's promised her a lead in his next slaughterhouse epic—which was precisely what she was after. And I was through, after that. Really through . . . That Faustian legend—it's all wrong, Grog—I'll tell you how it really goes. Faust makes the pact all right, signs away his immortal soul for unlimited wealth and power, the most beautiful woman in the world, etcetera-etcetera—only he never sees any of it. He's screwed—the Devil hasn't had the slightest intention of coming through, all along. That's your *real* switcherooney."

He broke off then, fiddled with his empty glass, gazing stupidly at the flow of meaningless numbers on the TV screen above our heads that were to mean so much, that were our political hieroglyphics for the next decade—maybe longer, much longer—

". . . I've messed up, Grog. Royally. I did it all wrong. I wanted to catch the old brass ring every time around—I was so *sure* I was going to. I've blown all these years, and I haven't got a God damn thing to show for it. Not one . . .

"How is she?" he asked me then, in a low voice; that look of naked pleading was in his eyes. "Chris? Is she all right?"

"Chris is fine," I answered. "As full of life as ever."

"Good," he said, and nodded. "Fine. I'm glad to hear that."

After a silence I said: "You haven't asked about Sheilah." His eyes shot up to mine, slipped away again. "She's living in Italy now. In Spoleto. She had a concert at Town Hall, last year. We went down for it."

He nodded again. "How is she?" he asked uncertainly. "I mean, how's she getting along? she herself?"

"She's living, Currier," I said flatly, "she's gone on living." I felt suddenly all out of patience: with the whole appalling Hollywood saga, with his asking about Sheilah like this, with myself for sitting here half-shot when I ought to be home and in bed, with the American public for choosing the blowsy pap of Ike and Nixon over Adlai; with all that high, burnished promise of 1945 sliding greasily on down the drain. "How in hell should *I* know how she feels?" I retorted. "Don't ask a God damn fool question like that. You're the frigging psychological novelist."

"I'm sorry. I know it's stupid to say—but I've never forgiven myself for that."

"Good. That makes two of us. Twenty-two."

He bit his lip. "You still hold it against me. Terry does, too."

"She's only his sister."

"God, ever since Chris and I broke up it's all been downhill. You know that?" He ran his hand back through his hair, the old gesture I remembered. "It all began when I lost Chris."

"You didn't lose Chris," I said very slowly and quietly. "You threw her away."

He looked at me fearfully again. "I know, I know . . . What's the *matter* with me, George? Why is it I never realize the value of a thing until I've lost it?"

"Is that a rhetorical question?" I said.

"No—!" He glared at me unhappily, and now I could see tears hanging in his eyes. "Christ almighty, I'm asking you!"

"Then . . . you ought to care more about people, and less about—other things."

"—But I *do,* George. I do. In my own way. I just can't seem to . . ." He shook his head again, ponderously, his jaw set, and I saw he was drunk. Very drunk. I looked away at the TV screen but that was no consolation—the score was worse than ever, Ike was leading by five million plus now, it was all over. Maybe Stevenson had already conceded, for all I knew.

"Let's get out of here," Russ was saying, "—let's run out to the Totem Pole."

"You're bombed."

"Not really. Just mellow. If I could just sit there a while—it was the high point. You know? Everything downhill—after Chris. If I could just sit around out there . . ."

We went weaving out into raw November night, trying to remember where we'd parked the Empress. A bunch of college kids went roaring by in one of the fat, new, chrome-laden convertibles with tail fins five feet in the air, sporting a fantastic pink paint job: 1952 Pepto-Bismol pink. Well, maybe they were having the time of their lives cruising the main drags, making the week-end runs to Wellesley and Northampton, and groping their way into sex in secluded lakeside roads—maybe they were having more fun than we did. I didn't think so, but maybe they were. In front of the paper vendor's hutch at the corner of Congress Street the bundled morning editions were thumping off the tailbed of a truck. *GOP SWEEP!!!* the headlines blared. *Ike, Herter Win.*

"Look at that." Russ aimed a kick at one of the bundles and

missed. I yanked him away. "Trouble with us was, we were miseducated," he went on doggedly, glaring at his shoes. "Realize that? The good man wins, Veritas will triumph, standards will conquer all—that's what they taught us. Like shit! When the actual, ball-breaking *fact* of the matter—"

Then I saw it and stopped dead. A long black tear running along the back of the canvas top of the Empress, from frame to frame.

"*Russ,*" I said.

"Jesus..." He'd seen it too, now. "It's cut," he exclaimed thickly, feeling it with his fingers as though it might burn. "It's cut!" He thrust a hand into the deep slash in the back then, plunged in head and shoulders.

"Russ," I called. "Unlock the door!"

He pulled himself out and straightened, staring at me. His face was white, perfectly expressionless. "It's gone," he said. "They took it."

"Took what?"

"They took it. The manuscript."

"The book?" I murmured. "The new book?"

"And my old Royal portable. One I bought with that second mustering-out check. You remember."

"But your *book...*"

"What would they want to take the manuscript for?"

"A carbon," I said, with growing alarm. "You've got a carbon, haven't you?"

He shook his head. "No. No carbon. The first part, yeah—nothing after that. I can't write if there's a carbon in the carriage." He kept crouching down and looking under the wheels, below the running board, as though it might still be right there somewhere. "Now, who would do a thing like that... It was in an attaché case, a pigskin case." The almost abstracted calm with which he said this, after the maudlin recital in the bar, amazed me. "I can understand the typewriter. But hell, a manuscript—"

"We'll get the police," I said.

"Think it'd do any good?"

"Let's find Terry. He knows the brass all over town."

"Terry? He won't want to see us—not after tonight, anyway. Hell, he's probably gone to bed. It's after two."

We drove over there anyway. To our astonishment both

headquarters were still open; the two bunting-draped façades confronted each other like rival saloons in a western gun duel, blazing light in the early morning darkness. The air was clear and cold.

"The old guard dies but never surrenders," Russ murmured. The long room was nearly deserted. They were still there—the campaign managers and lieutenants, the vulnerable young office workhorses: tight-lipped, tense, glassy-eyed. Only Jack was still as casually confident as ever, laughing, sipping coffee, telling jokes. He was holding—a slender margin, but he was holding it; almost alone among all the Democratic contenders he was standing against the landslide.

"Had to come back, didn't you?" Terry said to us, his lip curling. "Couldn't quite give up on him. You amateurs."

"Actually, Terry, we've got a problem," I said. "A big one." I told him about the theft. He asked a few questions, and then made a phone call.

"I got Riordan," he said. "He's going to see what he can do. There's a fairly good chance they might recover the typewriter. But the manuscript—Jim says they usually throw something like that away when they see they can't fence it." He looked at Russ a moment. "How is it you didn't have them in the trunk?"

"Trunk's full of junk, Terry. Besides, I thought it'd be safe enough in the back seat. After all—hell, Boston isn't Algiers..."

"You've been away, Currier. We've got vandals now. Like everywhere else." Terry went off to confer with someone about the Berkshire County returns. We hung around in stony resignation, watched Stevenson concede—an emotional moment; I'd never seen Adlai at a loss for words before. I knew I ought to go home, I had an editorial meeting at eleven, but I couldn't bear to. The hours crept along, somehow. I kept thinking of that maiden speech of Jack's at Central Square, and Russ sprawled on the running board of the Empress, choking with mirth, and Terry glaring down at him. It was only six years...

"Why the devil doesn't he concede?" Terry demanded hotly, staring at the headquarters across the street. "Doesn't he know he's beaten?"

"Would *you?*" Jack said with his easy smile, and moved away.

Around four-thirty people began to filter in—beaming,

preening faces that hadn't been here at eleven; among them were the balding heads and fleshy jowls of old pols.

"Look at them," Terry said with a cold, cynical smile. "You couldn't find one of them this fall, when we were screaming for help. Bad-mouthed us all the way—sniped at Larry, tried to take over our regional headquarters. Now they'll say they knew it all the time, Kennedy was a winner. Sunshine patriots." Someone put a new record on the PA system, *Wheel of Fortune,* and now there was general laughter. "Ah, it's a dirty, dirty business, George." The strain of an interminal succession of 16-hour days rang in Terry's voice. "You can't know how dirty. You have to tell yourself—it will be worth it. Once he's there. Then it'll all be worth it."

Around us the headquarters was filling up rapidly; there was much laughter, and that anticipatory hum that precedes victorious events. I saw a television crew setting up; several photographers were standing around. I was surprised—and horrified—to find it was six-thirty; outside it was getting light. Jack's margin was increasing now—62,000, 65,000. Tired as we were, depressed by the disastrous national results, it was impossible not to feel a slow, deep surge of elation—at least one of our own had made it. Russ had been spiking his coffee with a bottle somebody'd told him about hidden in one of the desks, and was waxing so exuberant you'd have thought the triumph was his. Every time fresh returns were chalked on the board we cheered and pounded each other on the back. Even Kenny O'Donnell was smiling.

Just after seven a rising murmur flowed over the crowd, and there was a rush toward the doors. I saw Lodge—it was clearly he, you couldn't mistake the white, coldly handsome face, the dark, perfectly tailored suit—get quickly into a car and drive away.

"There he goes!" Terry exulted, "—the sacred cod himself. He's through, he's done for!"

Ten minutes later Bobby Kennedy was standing on a desk trying to read Lodge's congratulatory wire and being drowned out by this stamping, roaring crowd that had materialized out of nowhere. Flashbulbs danced their festive lightning; in front of the curtains Jack was besieged by some of the recent arrivals, who jostled and shoved each other in an effort to squeeze into the pictures with him.

The idea for the triumphal parade was Russ's, of course. The victory party was postponed until that evening, I heard Bobby telling Terry—if they tried to hold it now everybody would collapse in a heap. We poured out into the street, and Russ was saying, "A Roman triumph, why not? Right now! Let's go out with a roar, God damnit—come on!" He was fumbling with the catches to the top of the old convertible. Together we unhooked the posts and flung the canvas back in a crazy heap, and Terry leaped in and sat on top of it; and everyone began piling in. One of the girls in Kelly green got up beside him, and a quiet, red-haired man named Shaughnessy I'd met earlier. People kept crowding into the Empress; a jolly, freckle-faced girl plunked herself on my lap and said: "Hi! I'm Maggie. I hope you don't mind—there's no more room."

"*Mind!* He loves it," Russ crowed. "Just like old times, Grog-o." Other cars were filling up behind us now, honking their horns. He threw the Empress in gear and we wound our errant way all over Boston: down through Chinatown into the South End, past the site of the Cocoanut Grove, closed after that terrible fire the autumn after our own New Year's Eve explosion; back up Washington Street past the rerun movie houses, where Chris had wept quietly beside me through the last scenes of *Anna Karenina*; along Boylston and then Charles Street between the immaculate Garden and the scruffy Common— patrician and plebeian, the two faces of Beantown-by-the-Bay; down Beacon and out Commonwealth Avenue, past Garland, where we used to pick up Ann Rowen, married now to an engineer in far-away Seattle—the only one of us who hadn't come home after the war; on past Fenway Park, past Jean-Jean's sybaritic apartment in the Fens, and the party that had ended—and started—everything; Russ riding the horn, the following cars echoing the Empress' deep bugle strains, the dawn wind tearing at our foreheads. A cop on Massachusetts Avenue grinned and raised his stick in salute and we waved back, Terry pumping his clasped hands high above his head, a boxer mitting the crowd. The girl in green was laughing hysterically, her teeth chattering.

"Too cold!" she was shrieking, clutching Terry's bony frame. "Oh! Too—cold! . . ." On to Soldiers Field Road past the leaden, still plate of the river, past the Stadium, singing the Harvard victory song now, the words coming back to us, clinging to one another frantically, half-frozen, light-headed with sleeplessness, our voices hoarse; on into Harvard Square with the early commuters glancing at us in disapproval or delight; to wind up, chilled to the bone, our eyes streaming tears, in the Hayes Bickford's, where we sprawled over three tables, wolfing down Danish pastries and gulping coffee in thick china mugs.

"*Now* where's that fatuous bastard Conger?" Russ demanded.

"Beats me." I was so cold I couldn't feel the cake between my fingers. Everyone was chattering at everyone else, saying nothing, just trying to get warm.

"You remember Conger," Russ said to Terry.

"Yeah, I remember him."

"Let's go over to University Hall and give him a bad time. Take away his bursar's card." For some reason this struck us all as immensely funny; Russ watched us like a terrier, his head cocked, pleased with the effect. "Let's strip him naked and tie him to the John Harvard statue, see how he carries that off. I know—let's take him to Scratchy Scarborough's class and make him take notes."

"Scratchy's dead."

"No!" Russ gazed at me slackly. "But—Scratchy was interminable—I mean he was illimitable."

"Lodge can take his class," Terry said suddenly. "Yeah! The Role of the Aristocrat in Western Civilization. The Brahmin as Horse's Ass. Phony son of a bitch—he won't be able to run for dog-catcher in this state when we get through with him."

"Oh, Ike'll give him a cabinet post," Shaughnessy said matter-of-factly. "Forget him."

"The hell I will—I've waited six long years for this day!" I was astonished at the vindictive heat in his voice. "And you know how long the Kennedys have waited?—since 1916."

"Oh—when old Lodge beat out Honey Fitz," Russ murmured.

"Well, now we're even," Terry hissed at us, his eyes blazing. "Snotty blue-blood bastard—we don't have to take shit from any of them! Ever! Don't tell *me* revenge isn't sweet."

"I'm a snotty blue-blood bastard, Gilligan," Russ said.

"What? No, you're not—not like *them*, you never were."

"Oh, yes. Same schools, same background." Russ looked surly and morose now, his hair in his eyes. "Aristocrats. Natural aristocrats. Like Scratchy Scarborough. Like Adlai Stevenson."

"Come off it, Currier. I'm talking about—"

"No no no, Gilligan—you're right. That's exactly it." He looked around the table wrathfully, his face drained of all color. "What the hell am I celebrating for?—the finest man, the noblest man of this century just got beat—by a five-star, glad-handing, Kansas moron . . . and *you're* happy about it," he said with low, sudden savagery to Terry, "aren't you?—you never gave a damn about Adlai, you hated his guts, you *wanted* him to crash . . ."

"Now listen, Currier—"

"Let me give you something, Gilligan. For your files. He's worth a hundred Kennedys any day—he's a better man right now, beaten, then your glamor boy will ever be, if he gets to be Emperor of the frigging Universe!"

"All right, that did it!" Terry snarled. He shoved back his chair, but I was quicker, I'd seen this coming from the moment Terry made that crack about blue-bloods; I had Russ on his feet and was moving him toward the door past staring, affronted faces, muttering, "Come on, now, you've had your say, now let's get out of here—"

"Yeah, get him out of here before I make him eat that," Terry shouted after us.

"He's tanked, Terr," Shaughnessy was saying to Terry, "he doesn't know what he's saying, let it go . . ."

"Oh yes—he knows what he's saying, all right," I answered, for no reason I could explain, "don't you worry about that!" I propelled Russ out into the Square and hurried him toward the Empress, still muttering to myself. Russ, curiously, put up no resistance: all the fire and fury had gone out of him. He mumbled, "Take her, will you, Grog?" and slumped deep in the rider's seat. I drove home in a jumble of contradictory emotions, re-enacting long dead-and-gone episodes. Beside me Russ was sound asleep, his head lolling on the worn leather.

About a quarter of a mile from the house the Empress began coughing and bucking, and right after that she quit entirely. The fuel pump was gone. I coasted down the slight grade and parked in front of the house, and woke up Russ. He climbed out of the car like an automaton.

Nancy was in the kitchen, feeding Peg, and looking perfectly fresh and immaculate, every hair in place.

"Well—you boys had yourselves a night, I see." Her tone was

light, but the look in her eyes was not encouraging. Russ failed to detect it, however.

"A brief, fond sojourn down memory lane," he said.

"Is that what it was."

"Kennedy won," I said. "Barely."

"Yes. I just heard."

"One ray of celestial light, in a sea of darkest night. Old poem." Hands on his knees Russ bent toward Peg. "Hi there, sweetie. How many hearts are *you* going to break today, mmmh?" She gazed back at him gravely, her eyes—Nancy's eyes—steady and accusatory and blue. He straightened with a sigh; running his hand through his hair he wandered away into the living room.

Nancy pressed her hands firmly down the front of her apron. "We missed you. At the Merwins'. I waited till after one."

"I'm sorry," I said. "To tell the truth, I didn't think you'd miss us very much."

Her mouth tightened. "That's not the point. Is it?"

"We had some trouble. Somebody broke into the Empress and stole Russ's manuscript. The new novel."

"Oh—that's a shame." But I could tell what she was thinking.

"It was locked," I said. "They slashed the canvas top. Took the novel and his old typewriter."

"That's a shame," she repeated; she was fussing over Peg, her hands moving in quick, jerky motions. "Well: what are you going to do now?"

"Do? I'm going to go to work. I guess I'd better shower and shave."

"It seems like a good idea." She straightened. "Have you had breakfast? or did you drink it?"

I stared at her now, said: "We ate at the Square."

"The Square—oh yes, *Harvard Square*," she said as Russ came wandering back into the kitchen, "of course, I might have known!" The quiver of suppressed rage in her voice was unmistakable now. "Drink to all the happy hours, drink to the carefree days..."

"Just a night on the town," Russ broke in, "you don't begrudge us that, do you, Nancy-girl? a few hours, for old time's sake?"

She looked at him from under her brows for a second or two; then her head came up.

"Nan," I said, "let's just—"

But I was too late; or perhaps nothing could have averted it anyway, what followed.

"—Maybe *you've* got used to living that way," she said in her District Attorney voice, low and very incisive, "maybe that's what they do out there—play all night and sleep it off all day. But we don't, Russell. We have work to do. You know? You drop in on us out of nowhere—no card, no phone call, no advance warning at all—just drive up with a flourish and expect us to drop everything and obey your every whim. Well, we don't work that way, Russell—a lot of people don't, they have their own lives to live, astounding as that may sound to you. Now you may not know it but we've been through a lot this year, it's been a hard year, a—an unhappy year for us, and you'll pardon us if we're not exactly enchanted with your charming sense of irresponsibility!"

"Nancy," I said.

"I'm sorry—I've had it with your school-boy melodramatics and your selfishness and your casual bad manners, Russ. I've had it up to here! You're not welcome in this house, any time you please—we've got our lives to live, we're not *in* your God damned stupid movies!—"

"Nancy," I said, and my voice was shaking now, I couldn't manage to steady it, though I *was* able to hold it low, "Nancy, Russ Currier is my friend. He is also our guest, and *he will enjoy the hospitality of this house.* Now let's not have any more about it. Is that clear?"

"No, George, look—" Russ was pulling urgently at my sleeve now, "—it's all right, I spoke out of turn. I had no business busting in on you like this—I'm truly sorry. I am . . ."

Nancy stood glaring at us—at me more than at Russ—her breasts heaving; then she snatched up Peg, who was still staring at us wide-eyed, as if we were some race of fascinating creatures out of her picture books, and stalked out of the room and on upstairs.

"*Now* look what I've done," Russ muttered so inanely it almost made me laugh.

"Relax," I said. "She'll get over it."

"No, I've got to be taking off, anyway—I'm heading for Paris. I've had enough of the old US and A to last me a while. Quite a while. Just give me a lift down to the Square, will you?"

"What about the Empress?"

He shrugged. "You want her?"

"Want her!"

"I know she's not much of a gift as she stands."

"Russ, I can't just accept her, just like that..."

"Sure you can, of course you can. *I* did, didn't I?" And he smiled, his face all at once shadowed with fond recollection and regret. "She should have been yours, anyway—I beat the hell out of her, I know. I didn't treat her right. I mean it: she's yours, if you want to patch her up."

"Well, thanks," I said lamely. "I *would* like to fix her up—she means a lot to me... to all of us. What about your stuff in the trunk?"

"Keep it, throw it away—whatever suits your fancy." He laughed harshly—he seemed half wild to get out of the house now. "I want to travel light."

I went to the foot of the stairs and called: "Nancy! I'm taking the Chevvie, I'm driving Russ over to Boston." There was no reply. "Let's go," I said.

Running back into town still again, I said: "Where do you want to go?"

"Statler."

"The Statler! Oh look, come on Russ—"

"No, it's better this way, it really is. I'm going to get a flight over as soon as I can. I'm ready."

I looked at him. "Aren't you going to Mt. Vernon Street?"

"No. No prodigal entrances. That's something I'm not up to... I think I'd kill the Old Gentleman if he started in on me right now."

I glanced at him, but he was staring out of the window, his mouth working. "The filthy little shit won after all, didn't he?" he said after a long pause, in a dull, musing tone.

"Who won?"

"Hitler. The fucking Krauts. They won, anyway. I can see that now. We broke them, but they took over our world anyway. Uprooted—the way they were after the first war. Psychologically split. We're getting to be just like them: scared of any dissent, wallowing in violence, the Extreme Solution to everything. Shouting, 'Kill him! Kill him!' at the movies. Screaming for more blood—even in sports. Slandering anybody who doesn't share our group hysteria... Can't you feel it in yourself—the terrific pull toward it? I can. God knows I can—I even fooled around with it in my last picture—not that they'll ever make it. We're all gone, George. We're done for. O brave new world, that has such jackals in it . . ." When I said nothing he turned to me in a kind of soft, raging entreaty. "Can't you see it, for Christ sake? You've read plenty, seen enough, you know how this world goes . . . Shit, we deserve everything we get, you know it yourself."

No, I thought, pulling in at the Statler entrance. Not everything. Aloud I said: "You may be right."

"You *know* I'm right!"

"But we're all there is to work with, Russ. For better or worse. If we throw up our hands, nothing can be saved. Nothing."

He stared at me very hard—then his lips broke into the old, fond smile. "Dear Grog: the Keeper of the Ark. I love you, you dumb bastard—in spite of everything." He got out, hauled out his two suitcases.

"Well . . ." He looked around restlessly; toward Beacon Hill, Cambridge, the South End. "I'm off, Grog-o. What the hell—a new life."

"Take care," I said.

3

"A *battlefield,* DADDY?" Peg said doubtfully. "It doesn't *look* like a battlefield."

"That's because it was years and years ago, dim-wit," Ron told her. "Gee, what a dim-wit."

"Ron," Chris said, "don't tease her, now. You're too old for that kind of thing."

"Well, it's true—she wasn't even *born* then."

"I know. Eat your lunch." Placidly she watched her son. He was sixteen now, slender and dark and restless, with Russ's flashing eyes: yet his mother's son, too. For a moment I watched him, feeling the strangeness of the day, the place. *Sixteen* . . .

"He's making it all up, sweetheart," Dal informed Peg confidentially; he was drawing the cork from a bottle of wine with a silver-plated tire-bouchon he'd bought in Dijon two days before. "He's just angling for your sympathy."

"Sympathy?" Peg echoed.

"Dal," Chris laughed, "you stop that nonsense—you're confusing the children."

456

"Confusing!—I'm setting 'em straight."

"Uncle Dal's making jokes again," Nancy said lightly to Peg, but there was the faintest edge in her voice. "Daddy was very very brave here, right here where you're sitting. In World War II."

"Daddy was very very scared, was what he *was*," I murmured, and Nancy said with irritation:

"Oh, George—honestly . . ."

"Well, they're long ago and far away, those days," I said. Children distend issues so—their need for simplification always throws things like this into high relief. "Let's hope they never come again."

"No, they'll come somewhere else next time," Dal said, pouring wine. "What do you think's been going on in Algeria for the past five years? or Indo-China?"

"Was it a big battle, Daddy?" Peg asked me.

"No—as battles go it was a small one. But even a small battle can seem very big when you're in it."

I smiled, but Peg studied me gravely, a piece of French bread clutched in her fist. She'd always been like that, observing the world's alarums and excursions with the same watchful, steady gaze, serenely appraising; Nancy's in miniature. Yet I'd always been conscious of a special affinity between us—the way she tried, even when she was very little, to mend her favorite toys, put away her treasures; the way she seized certain moments in memory. She would remember this afternoon in a wonderfully foreign country far from home, and the grown-ups' voices touched with cynicism, resentment, levity—I knew she would remember it. "She's got her mother's face but her father's fixations," Terry had said of her once, and we'd all laughed . . . yet there was an edge of doubt now in that level blue gaze.

"No, it was true, it happened," I said, pointing. "The Germans were up there. And we were down here, by the river."

She nodded then, looked up the long open field to where the clear line of woods began, all lush and drowsy in the midsummer heat; extended one of her small round arms. "I'd rather be up there than down here."

I laughed, and Dal said: "That's it, honey—you should have been running the show. You've got more sense at seven than your Daddy ever did. You ought to be a general."

"A general?" Julie, who was a year older then Peg, cried, her mouth full of food.

"No, you dope," Ron said, "Dad's just kidding around—haven't you learned that yet? You have to go to school and study, to be a general."

It was odd sitting there at the side of the field, watching the plane trees along the side of the stream; down the road two farmers in faded blue shirts moved languidly, as though bound in the rhythm of the hot season; the sun beat down richly. It was both difficult and fearfully easy to feel that other midsummer afternoon, with the always comforting smell of newly torn earth, the always repellent stink of cordite; to feel the quiet—the eerie, unreal quiet—screaming out of those woods—and then without any warning whatever the brittle, shuttling racket of the Spandaus and the ear-splitting pa-*krack!* of 88s; and then later, light-years later, the silence again, the hot dust sifting away northward, and Opp, his sweat-soaked face pressed hard against the grass, saying: "Remember those fucking steel company ads, Vird? in *Colliers?* the ones that said, *The World Moves Forward With Steel?* This must be what the sons of bitches had in mind . . ."

I hadn't sought it out—that's what was so curious. We'd been driving from Troyes to Reims, Chris wanted to see Reims Cathedral before we returned to Paris, and Dal was hunting rather aimlessly for a chateau near Romilly he'd stayed in during the drive across France; and all of a sudden, obediently trailing the Dalrymples' gorgeous Bentley convertible in our little blue Dauphine, I was flooded with a sheerly animal sense of recognition. I pulled off onto the shoulder and honked the funny horn, then stuck my arm out of the window, palm forward, and waggled my hand in tight circles—the old platoon leader's assemble-here-to-me-now. The Bentley had stopped with a jerk, the heads had all turned; it was backing slowly toward us.

"What's the matter?" Nancy asked.

"I was here," I said. "Right here."

"You were? How do you know?" Why could she never believe me? Even here.

"I just know, that's all. Let's stop."

I owed the trip to France to Chris—and to Liz. We'd begun seeing the Dalrymples again. They had come east to visit Chris's father three years before, and I'd made a point of inviting them to stay with us overnight. Chris had chosen not to see Nancy's intentional coolness, and Dal had gone out of his way to catch up some of the old affection—he brought Nancy a number of funny presents, made her laugh. While she still deplored his manners she'd come to admire the brilliant success *Newsweek* had called "meteoric." The Dalrymples moved in a world far beyond ours, it was obvious; but they were unassuming and warm, and we had a good time together again—even Nancy. On their last visit in the spring they'd been full of plans for another trip to Europe this summer; they had been going abroad for several years now.

Suddenly Chris had said: "Say, why don't you come with us?"

Nancy had laughed awkwardly. "Oh, we couldn't."

"Why not?"

"Well, there's Peg—"

"Julie's no older than Peg. Bring her along, too—it'll be great for the kids. Oh, say you'll come!" The old exuberant gaiety was in her eyes. "We're renting a car—you can, too. There's so much we'd love to show you. We'll just drive around, stop wherever the mood hits us. You've never even *seen* Paris, George—it's a crime! A distinguished editor, and you've never been to Paris. All those glorious things to see—I've felt guilty every time because you weren't there to share in it, too. Come *on,* Virdons—if you don't go now you'll just keep putting it off and putting it off, and finally you'll never go at all..."

We talked about it after they'd left for Chicago. Nancy was opposed—we'd just moved into the old Federal farmhouse out in Holliston, and she'd begun talking about having another child, a logic that amused and irritated me: new house, new baby. But for me, that clinched it.

"Once you're pregnant and have the baby, we'll be really pinned down. Let's do it now."

"But there's too much to do *here,* darling—the wainscoting in the dining room, the living room beams to restore..."

What saved the situation—and avoided a series of nasty arguments, because I was determined we should go, and she was equally determined we should not—was her discovery that Liz would be in Paris in August on her way to the Greek Islands, and that, with a little planning, we could all meet at the same time. Nancy was all for the trip, then—she began collecting guides and annotating maps with a vengeance.

"How fortunate for me Liz decided to stop off in Paris," I said.

I drew the Battalion Adjutant stare. "Yes, she's one of *my* friends... You told me you *liked* Liz."

"I do. You know I like her."

"Well then, why make an issue of it? We're going to be traveling with the Dalrymples."

"You've said you like *them*. Don't you?"

"Yes, of course."

"And you see Liz several times a year, as it is."

"You know, George, you sound actually resentful."

"Oh Nan, come on..."

"Yes, I value my friends—at least I'm able to avoid quarreling with them every time we get together."

Which closed out that exchange. The irony in all this was that I was really very impressed with Liz. She hadn't slipped into self-pity or vindictiveness or gone running home to Daddy after her marriage had broken up, the way so many of the girls of our generation had. Instead she'd refused both alimony and a large settlement—after all, she said, there were no children and Hugh had only his museum salary. She had picked herself up and gone to Paris and worked on the lowest level as an apprentice in the cutting and fitting rooms of Givenchy. She'd haunted the museums, too, steeping herself in the history of costume and design for two arduous years. Then she'd come back to Seventh Avenue and learned the garment trade inside out. It was only after that she'd joined forces with a plump, pretty young fabric and print designer named Margo Gunderson and struck out on her own.

It takes guts as well as talent to be an innovator in the world of fashion, and Liz had both. After a year or two she began to make a name for herself. She was the first really to specialize in co-ordinates—clothes of subtle colors and sensuous fabrics that could be worn one way for evening, in another combination for afternoon— easy, lithe clothes that fit the American body in a new, fluid way the great couturiers would soon imitate. She designed Oriental tunics and pants suits long before they became popular.

Yet she was always selective—and astonishingly honest. "Some women simply can't *wear* slacks, and shouldn't ever try—they look like ducks or someone standing in a manhole," I

remember her saying once. "Style is what *you* look well in, feel
attractive wearing." Simplicity, grace, flair—distinction of
line—never went out of style; it was the crudely sensational, the
calculatedly bizarre that withered on the vine. LIZ PAYNE, the
label read in small sans-serif capitals—and in time discerning
clients like Lauren Becall and Babe Paley and Pamela Harriman
sought that label.

She even began to design jewelry, to complement her clothes:
bold, arresting creations using semi-precious stones ("I'm bored
with diamonds," *Vogue* quoted her), exotic woods or bits of
shell, ivory and coral; the wide bracelet of ifil or snakewood
scored with tourmalines or mother-of-pearl became a Liz Payne
trademark. She was famous—all at once, it seemed, you turned
around and saw her designs in the big fashion ads in the *New
Yorker* and *Harper's Bazaar*. Her New York shows were already
legends.

Nancy saw more and more of her as time went on. Certain old
Wellesley classmates and a few more recent friends would meet
down in New York City several times a year, stay at the Plaza,
eat at Cherio or Giovanni's, and inevitably wind up at the
apartment Liz and Margo shared, a Sutton Place duplex with an
almost feudal view of the East River. It was, like everything Liz
put her hand to, flawless. The draperies were of ancient brocade,
of precisely the right shades of fawn; there was a delicate Queen
Anne writing desk, a Récamier divan upholstered in pale green
silk, a fine Louis XVI chair, there were very dark, polished floors
with antique rugs of perfectly faded hues; the walls held Chinese
scrolls as elusive as dreams, and fierce Daumier prints; and they
all harmonized superbly. Through its light, cool elegance a
Burmese cat paraded like some eastern divinity.

I don't know what they talked about at these gatherings—
they were, properly enough, gatherings of women: theater and
clothes and interiors, I suppose. I guess that sounds pretty
patronizing—I'm not altogether free of a certain resentment; for
all I know they discussed tensions in the Middle East or woman's
changing role in tomorrow's world. What I *do* know is that they
came to assume an increasingly absorbing role in Nancy's life.
As the time for one of these sessions approached she would grow
curiously preoccupied, anticipatory, almost rapt. I couldn't read
her at all. On her return she would be utterly changed—tense, on
edge, barely containing her dissatisfaction with everything

around her—Peg, me, the new house, the maid, life itself.

"Yes yes yes—*and* the laundry *and* the dishes *and* the shopping *and* the school runs *and* what else?" Her voice was shrill in a new way that set my teeth on edge. She would be wearing a suit or a piece of Liz's jewelry she'd picked up in New York—she was always coming back with some new booty now. "She's in bondage—do you realize that?—the American housewife. No, I don't suppose you do, but it's true anyway. In complete bondage to a lot of stupid, out-worn rituals. Yes!" And she would stalk off upstairs with a kind of exasperated willfulness while Peg and I looked at each other, and then away.

I came to dread these New York forays. I'm ashamed to say it, but I did. I *wanted* her to have a good time—and freedom on her own, too, freedom to grow and change. In fact I encouraged it. But why should that very freedom need to turn back, harsh and bitter, on those who offered it openly—and who were trying to pay for it? Burdened with work—old man Bicknell had moved me up to chief textbook editor the year before, which only meant more pressure, more crises and cost estimates— swamped with work as I was it was only after some time that I began to see Nancy's trips for what they were. They were benders. In their way. Dear, practical, circumspect Nancy, who never drank more than two cocktails, whose contempt for heavy drinkers was summary and huge—they were three-day spinners all the same, with the six-weeks' drying-out period bound in surly resentment precisely like the alcoholic's . . . And there was more than that, too, I began to perceive—an unspoken but dismaying series of contrasts: her freedom in New York versus her routines in Holliston, her romantic old life with Liz versus the daily treadmill with me now, her conversations with Liz versus her silences with me—and finally, astonishingly, Liz's nature versus mine, Liz versus me . . .

I don't know why I found the implications of that final comparison so shocking; but I did. My generation saw such things with rather distressing rigidity—it was another facet of our naiveté, our ruinous upbringing, I suppose; we were so woefully insensitive, even while feeling we were so marvelously sophisticated. Oh sure, there were Sappho and Leonardo da Vinci and André Gide, we'd read our Freud and Krafft-Ebing (had we read them a touch *too* avidly, perhaps?), there had been certain friends and acquaintances at college we viewed with equanimity (we told ourselves proudly) and genuine admiration for their often exceptional abilities—but it was a world apart from ours, somehow: perilous, unstable, the obsessive choice of a Bloomsbury poet, say, or a Provençal painter...

But to sit in your office on a given afternoon in your shirtsleeves, surrounded by the clamor of typewriters and phones, and consider the possibility that your wife, *your own wife* could actually prefer—

I tried to take hold of this thought; I struggled with it at odd moments, in the small hours. What dissatisfactions had thrust her on this course? Had I encouraged it, intensified it by my own preoccupations, by my failure to overcome the pattern of almost involuntary withdrawal that had enveloped us after Teddy's death? We cause so many things to happen in this world, without ever meaning to... Had her awareness of my old love for Chris brought on this insecurity in her? But *was* it insecurity—why in any case did I want to call it that? Wasn't that simply another kind of male ego-preening? And why for instance did I feel this attraction of hers had to be rooted in dissatisfaction—why shouldn't she be happy in female company if she was? Yet *was* she, really? Was I distorting this, making more of it than I should be, out of my own sense of guilt?

Round and round. I tried to spend more time with her, to draw her out, find out what she was thinking; but Nancy was never interested in moods, in nuances. Abstract ideas—I don't believe they really existed for her. Her concerns all had hard edges to them: what she could touch, hold, fashion, make her own... Mind you, I'm not disparaging that. God knows we need people with such proclivities. Only—it meant that we just could never really discuss them. And so the situation persisted, and deepened.

We approached this fearsome territory only once, during an argument after one of those post-Manhattan withdrawal periods. As usual, the argument was over money; and as usual, it took place just after midnight. Why do the most destructive domestic quarrels invariably occur just before bedtime? You could say, Because that's the only time husband and wife share together, with the day's work over and the children in bed. But that doesn't answer it, really.

Anyway, the row was over the hiring of a live-in maid. Nancy felt she must have one—the new house was an awful lot to keep up with; the daily woman was inadequate, she needed professional help for meals and entertaining. Nancy marshaled her arguments beautifully; she always did.

"That's a tremendous expense," I said. I'd got a raise—another one, a big one—but the new house she'd had her heart set on, the second car, the dishwasher and TV sets and hi-fi had eaten it up. I was farther behind than I'd been before the raise, and it angered and frightened me. Things. Things. "Do you realize what it would run us? We're not in that class."

"That's ridiculous—you're in the class you aspire to, make your own. You know that."

"No, I don't know that. We've got heavy payments on this house, school expenses coming up for Peg. It seems to me Ella is perfectly adequate."

"That's because you don't have to cope with her. I do. She's slipshod and unreliable, always going home early. A live-in maid would be here all the time. And I'd be freer for other things."

"What other things?" I asked.

She stopped brushing her hair and turned on the seat. "Well, for one thing I might like to get back into magazine work." My face must have shown something because her jaw set firmly. "Is there some special, divine reason why I can't have a life of my own, a job? like yours? Is there?"

I put down the shoe I'd been holding in my hand. "Nan, you know I wouldn't mind your working at something you like. When you can."

"Peg is school age."

"It's *you* who've been talking about having another child . . ."

"Well, now I don't know. I just don't know. I'd simply sink back into the deadly-dull old pattern. Kinder, Küche, Kirche—no!" she said with sudden low violence. "I have ambitions, too, you know—whether it's ever occurred to you or not. I could have done something with my life."

"You *have,*" I said, "you've got—"

"Oh, don't be ridiculous! I've done nothing, nothing! *Liz* didn't let herself be trapped, like a bug in a Mason jar—look at her! She did something with *her* life."

It was too late, I was too tired and on edge; it had been a bad week for me. The sullen resentment in her eyes was all at once too much. I said: "Well, you sure as hell pressed for marriage, Nancy. You wanted it *then* all right enough . . . Maybe you should have gone on being Liz's roommate."

She stared at me, then—a curious expression of hatred, fear, surprise, a kind of furtive awareness—of exactly what I couldn't really tell. A long, a very long moment. Then, "That's perfectly disgusting!" she snapped, and stomped into the bathroom and slammed the door.

... But for now there was Paris. Paris was glorious, Paris was venerable and muted and strident, burnished like banks on banks of precious jewels—it was everything I'd imagined and longed for. Paris swallowed me up—I hadn't felt such leaping excitement in years. Everything pleased me: the majestic sweep of the boulevards, the festive affiches, the painters working with still intensity beside bridges, the easy intimacy of the cafés terrasses, the gendarmes with their blue capes and white billy-clubs, shifting the flow of traffic with stately, archaic flourishes; and everywhere you turned the thunderous beat of history: the Invalides, the Little Corsican's last resting place, gloomy and sepulchral behind the green canopy of the plâtanes; the high-gabled grimness of the Hôtel de Ville, with its halberded iron railing where Robespierre's followers had impaled themselves when they'd leaped in panic from the windows; the great twin towers of Notre Dame soaring up and up in sublime majesty—Notre Dame, where everything had happened, where even Protestant Henry of Navarre had found it wise to go to mass; the Arc de Triomphe planted at the crest of the Champs-Elysées like the battle monument to end them all; and there were fresher memorials, too—already-dull bronze plaques on the somber walls of buildings: *André Bergeron, age 19, killed on the 18th of August, 1944 during the liberation of Paris...*

The children, sobered by our voices, squinted up in awe at the great men of France in their niches, these stone figures whose stern faces seemed to say: "Take care! You are no longer on casual ground. The stones beneath your feet have borne the weight of conquerors, philosophers and kings..." Paris lapped us round, enveloped us in braying horns, the flatulent bellow of Lambrettas, the stern tolling of great bells; street signs sent up a continual storm of images: Boulevard Murat, Quai Voltaire, Rue des Arquebusiers, Rue de l'Estrapade, Rue Vercingetorix; and at the very base of our nostrils lay the smell of Paris—an intense redolence compounded of coffee and wine and soap and urine and antiquity...

There was everything to see and we tried to see everything.

The kids went wild at the intimate little Cirque Médrano, with its fantastic jugglers and low-wire artists and lady lion tamers; the last of the Fratellinis—that great family of clowns—was performing, and the skits bore no resemblance to the formless routines of the American big-top. There is no true humor on this earth which is not brushed with sadness. Peg's eyes were round and solemn behind her giggling fits of laughter. She knew that already, somehow; her generation was going to be radically different from mine, then—and maybe that wasn't such a bad thing either.

We went to the Luxembourg Gardens, where other children were sailing sturdy little white-hulled boats or riding ponies, or watching a raucous puppet show that caught me with a throb of naked anguish I couldn't suppress. Teddy. Teddy. I turned away. Above the basin, beyond the balustrade stood the great ladies of France. I remembered Jean-Jean the afternoon of the Totem Pole evening, and watched Chris pointing out something to Julie: the proud carriage of her head, her eyes flashing with that fine high excitement, that passionate *giving* of herself to life that would never falter, never die away—

She looked up and saw me then and said, still smiling: "What are you thinking?"

"That Jean-Jean was right." She shook her head, she didn't remember. "That you ought to be up there. With all the other queens."

"Oh, George—you're making that up!"

"No, I'm not."

"Did he really say that? Bless him."

"Hell, that was one of Jean-Jean's opening gambits," Dal broke in on us. "Instead of telling a broad she ought to be in pictures, he'd tell her she ought to be enthroned in the Jardin de Lux."

"You remember that?" I said.

"Sure, I do."

"When was it, then? When did he say it?"

"Totem Pole weekend. At Currier's digs. The furniture was all covered in white." He watched me a moment, enjoying my surprise. "You're not the only joker with a golden memory."

Later that day he and I were sitting at a table in the private bar of the Elysée Park, that newest playground for the favorites

of the gods, resting our feet. We'd left the younger kids back at
the hotel, and were waiting for everyone to show up. The girls
were dressing, Ron had gone off sightseeing on his own; and it
was here we were to meet Liz, who had got in from New York
that morning and whom I secretly envied for staying at the
George V. I sat there happily, tired, bathed in foreignness. Every
language bears its own timbre beyond the meaning of the words
themselves: French has few cello tones, it runs in high, quick
rhythms, pizzicato. Even so, I was beginning to pick up a lot of
it, even after all these years. And it was quite a show. I saw Alain
Delon, looking sullen and spoiled and impossibly handsome;
Gina Lollobrigida was the center of a particularly lively party;
and sitting by himself in a corner the incomparable Pierre
Fresnay, now enjoying a big come-back, looking like a
greyhound among poodles. Everywhere were young starlets—
vedettes, they seemed to call them; why was that? The handsome
room was riotous with their ripe young bodies, their pouting
lips.

"Will you look at all this gorgeous, succulent stuff," Dal
marveled. "Takes you back, doesn't it, Grog?"

"Too far for me," I said. "I never cruised in these circles."

"You should have been here during the liberation, Groggy.
At the Grand Rigord we had one whole floor, and the chicks
were running naked as jay-birds up and down the halls—they'd
come running into your room and jump right into bed with
you—boom! and then go racing off somewhere else, and
another one would come barreling in. Talk about nonstop
saturnalias! Fifteen years ago, almost to the day. Jee-suss:
fif-teen years..." He sighed through his nose, and drank.

"Guy I knew had a week with an actress, down in Cannes. On
R&R. A really stunning babe. He said the only way she could get
off was if he tied her down to the bedposts, tight, so she couldn't
move a muscle, and then kissed her on the belly. Just kissed her.
Otherwise she couldn't make it. What do you think of that?"

"Fantastic."

"Just goes to show: one man's prong, another man's wrong."

"I'll bet you made that up."

"I did, Grog. I most certainly did. And variations. Want to
hear a few?"

"Not right away."

The girls came in then, a bit self-conscious in that citadel of alien glamour, pleased to see our American faces, hear our reassuring voices. They both recognized Lollobrigida as they sat down.

"She *is* beautiful," Chris said. "It isn't just the cameras."

"I think she's common," Nancy said.

"No—there's real vitality there, a sense of life." Chris smiled softly, admiring the star, basking in the little adventure of the moment, its unreality. I looked at the actress critically now, as if I were going to hire her. Yes, there was beauty of a sort, a kind of sensuous perfection of feature, sultry, provocative...but if beauty meant grace, a Matisse painting, the airy, sunlight dance of all green-gold things, alive, *in life*—

"That's Pierre Fresnay," I murmured, moving my eyes from her. "Over there."

"Oh—yes. The French officer. In that war picture—"

"Grand Illusion."

"He was killed trying to escape." And now that old shadow had flooded her gaze. "It seems so long ago, doesn't it?"

"Yes." I'd have given the very world to have taken her hand in mine at that moment—anything God or the devil might have required of me. I dropped my eyes, raised my drink to my lips, glanced at Nancy: her face was transformed, her eyes the clearest, brightest blue. Liz was coming toward us through the crowd, looking slender and assured and marvelously high-style. Heads turned, eyes followed her—and this was Paris, this was the lair of the haut monde.

"Darling!" She embraced Nancy, who had risen and moved toward her; greeted us all one by one. Dal, who hadn't seen her since our wedding, was bowled over.

"Liz baby," he cried, "you look super-sensational..."

She did—she was a very striking woman now. Too thin as a girl—at least for my taste—her hawklike features had deepened. She was wearing a long dress of heavy, cream-colored satin with a high halter and practically no back; it moved with her like a second skin—even I could tell it could only be a Liz Payne. She was wearing matching cream pumps, and one wide amber bracelet with a Renaissance clasp. People were staring at our table now—it pleased me obscurely.

"Jaded-but-still-ravishing is the phrase, isn't it?" We laughed, liking her, remembering old times. Her wry humor suited thirty-six far better than eighteen. "God, what I wouldn't give just to take two weeks off—just go off somewhere and swim. For two solid weeks. Instead of dreaming up an entire wardrobe for Tina Rinarchos."

"Come away with me, lover," Dal said. "We'll play beautiful golf together."

"You'll cheat, Dalrymple—I know you."

"They're stealing your designs," Nancy broke in. "We saw them all along St. Honoré."

"Darling, theft is always the sincerest form of flattery. Who said that, George?"

"You did."

"No, I mean who originated it?"

"You did," I repeated, and everyone laughed.

"George, you're a rogue. That's the heart and soul of American business—thievery with variations. Wouldn't you say, Dal?"

"You see? She understands me," Dal informed us. "Always did. I married the wrong woman."

"Had your chance, Wog." She laughed easily, watching him. There was something a little formidable about Liz; under her chic good looks and quiet competence there was a trace of that special steely self-assertion New York demands of its more flamboyant successes. "What's with your Grand Design, by the way?" she asked Dal. "That German General Staff time-table you had."

"Oh, I gave that up long ago."

"No, he hasn't," Chris said mischievously, "I made so much fun of it he burned it in the fireplace one evening—but he was putting me on. He'd committed it to memory all along."

"I've been hearing things about you," Liz pursued. "I hear you've put a small fortune into cancer research. Is that true?"

I glanced at Dal, but his expression was more inscrutable than ever. "Where'd you hear that?"

"Spies. And you're backing that reform candidate for Congress, what's-his-name—Pelletier. Anything to that?"

"Tax write-off," he said uncomfortably.

Liz laughed again. "You're going to destroy that ruthless-young-tycoon image if you don't watch out."

"Not a chance. I'm going to rack up a pile, and stick it all in a numbered Swiss account. And then I'm going to buy a villa on the Riviera and lie in bed all day long, with a baker's dozen of these delectable chicks crawling after me over the counterpane."

"Darling," Chris said to him, "you'd be bored to tears in two weeks."

"Sure I would. But what a way to go."

Ron came hurrying up to us then, eyes dark with excitement. "Dad! Know who I just met? at the door? Catherine Deneuve! The door was going to bump against her and I held it for her and she smiled at me and said, 'Merci, Monsieur.' Just like that! What a woman!"

"Ron," his mother reproved him gently, "this is Liz Payne—you haven't met her."

He broke off. "Oh—I'm sorry. How are you, Miss Payne."

"Hello, Ron. You're—" She stopped in a curious small confusion; I'd never seen Liz nonplussed before—there was a swift, flat tensing of her features; then it vanished. "What a—what a fine-looking boy," she exclaimed softly. I found myself staring at him hard. She had never met Ron before: had familiarity dulled the points of resemblance for me?

"Why shouldn't he be?" Dal was saying.

"—I'm glad he took after Chris and not you, Dalrymple," Liz went on easily, "that I *will* say."

"With her looks and my brains the boy can't lose."

"Where are you at school?" Liz asked Ron.

"Andover, Ma'am. I'm an upper middler."

"Don't you dare call me Ma'am, Ron! Call me Lizzie or Pog-Wog or anything you want to—but not Ma'am. What's the good of being in Paris if you feel 103?"

We talked idly about Jean-Jean then, and about France—the Revolt of the Generals the spring before, and the spanking new Fifth Republic, and de Gaulle; and that made us think of Jack Kennedy's surprise run for the Vice Presidential nomination in '56, and his Presidential chances for '60; and Terry, who was now heading up his foreign affairs advisory team . . . It was pleasant sitting here in this 'ultra-posh Parisian lounge, surrounded by the beautiful people; basking in this reunion of old friends. The setting, the moment made me think of the beach picnic at Nauset, and what Dal had said about the rich being trustees of their wealth, their obligation to use it for the common good. Now he was doing it—one of the very few who was—a touch ashamed that Liz had caught him out . . . How American we were! That eager, almost foolish willingness of heart, the need to extend the open hand. Of course more often than not we extended it at the wrong time, or to the wrong person. Or after our own initial greediness had been sated. But didn't the gesture matter at all, the naked act itself?

"But what about Russ Currier?" Liz was saying. "*He* was the Fox Entry ringleader—why isn't he here?"

There was a short silence while Dal and I glanced at each other.

"What's the matter? He's right here in France, isn't he?" Liz looked around at us. "Or have I said something I shouldn't have?"

"Now why spoil a perfectly happy, boozy holiday?" Dal asked.

"Russell," Nancy said, "has become a highly abrasive element."

"All he can do is put you down."

"I doubt if he'd be doing *that*." Dal looked up with a trace of belligerence. "What's he been doing? Bunch of creepy mixed-up art movies. Hell, he never finished that other novel, did he?"

"He lost it," I said.

"But Jesus—that was seven *years* ago...I haven't been sitting on my butt the past seven years, Grog. And neither have you."

"He married a Frenchwoman, didn't he?" Liz asked. "After Kay Madden?"

"She's a countess," Ron burst out.

"Well, there's countesses and countesses, you know. Barefoot, bare-ass—"

"Dal—"

"His old man made a settlement on him. In the continental manner. Hell, he's clipping Daddy's coupons—that's probably why the broad married him."

"Now how in hell do you know that?" I demanded.

"Financial grapevine, Grog. Tom Batchelder told me. He's with Bay State now. Yeah, always sneering at his old man, but I notice he's not averse to taking the dough when, as and if."

"Where's he living?" Liz pursued.

"Place on the Loire," I said. "Near Saumur. It's called Les Cèdres."

"The Cedars," Chris murmured. "That's a lovely name."

"Why doesn't he just call it Chequers and be done with it?"

"Simmer down, Dal," I told him. "It's a country house. An estate."

"Like Jean-Jean," Liz said, her thumb against her teeth. "As close as he could get. Of course." We all thought about that for a moment, and then Liz said: "Oh, come on, you two. Stop sparring and give him a ring. That's what you really want to do, isn't it?"

"I don't know that it is," I said.

"Sure you do." Dal was wearing his sleepy Chinese look. "You think he's so effing romantic and all. Call him up."

"Not me. To tell you the truth, we didn't part under the happiest of circs, last time out."

"—Now don't you blame me for that, George Virdon," Nancy cried. "My God, they never even showed up at a party we were invited to—drove around Boston all night in that sacred ibis of a convertible like a bunch of high-school kids."

"Oh, hell," I said. "Go ahead and give him a ring, Dal."

"Don't look at me, pal. I haven't seen him since your wedding, and that was twelve years ago."

"Come on. I'll toss you for it. Loser phones."

"All right."

He pulled a wad of French coins out of his pocket, selected one and flipped it high in the air, a silvery blur in the dim light; caught it deftly and slapped it on the back of his hand.

"Tails," I said. He raised his hand and covered it again instantly, but I'd seen it was tails.

"Move out, dad," I said.

"Best two out of three."

"Dal, you're impossible," Liz told him.

He sighed. "Okay. Give me the address."

"How can you make a long-distance phone call?" Chris said. "With your French?"

"I'll charm the operator. There's one language they all comprenez, sister. Know what I mean?" He shot me his coony wink and moved off, heavy and deliberate in his flashy Madras jacket. I didn't know whether I was elated or sorry I'd won.

In ten minutes or so he was back. "Got 'em," he said. "*Her,* anyway. One of those hoity-toity ancestral types. Only speaks French."

"I told you so," Chris said.

"Currier wasn't there, but he's going to be back tomorrow. From some eerie place I never heard of." He threw himself back in his chair. "Well: shall we sashay down there tomorrow? are you game?"

"Darling, did she *invite* us."

"What? Sure, she did. Of course she did." He grinned at us then—a devilish little boy's grin. "I told her we'd be there. With cap and bells."

There is no river in the world quite like the Loire; it seems broader and flatter than other rivers, it is somehow invested with a greater serenity and luminosity and grace. It reflects the sky's moods more subtly, its blues are deeper, its grays run a marvelous gamut from polished steel to the softest roseate dove. Today it was almost cerulean under a still, hazy sky. The road meandered beside it, then swung away through a beech wood, climbed gently—and at the end of a little grove of cedars the chateau confronted us, gloomy and gaunt with its twin turrets and dense slate roofs; there were gate towers, outbuildings, a greenhouse pressed close against the walls. Leading the way in the Dauphine I paused involuntarily.

"A castle, a castle!" Peg cried, and bounced up and down on the seat.

"Are you sure this is the right place?" Nancy demanded.

"Regarde donc ce signe illustre," I said grandly, and pointed to an exfoliate iron design in the gate with the letter P, and below it the legend *Les Cèdres*.

"So he actually did it," Liz murmured from the back seat.

The moat was wide and deep, and nearly empty of water. We drove across the drawbridge, our tires rumbling on the heavy planking, and stopped in the courtyard. The Bentley pulled in beside me and we all got out.

"Well," Dal said, staring up, "it isn't much, but we call it home."

"Keep your voice down," Chris said, but she threw me one of her best wild-surmise glances. Even the kids were subdued.

A man was standing on the front steps, observing us with that near-hostility the French adopt when they don't recognize someone and aren't sure they want to, either. An immense blue

Irish wolfhound was poised motionless beside him.

"The seneschal," Dal murmured. "Up visors. Mind that basilisk, now."

"Be quiet, Dal."

"Hot dog." He swung Julie up on to his hip. "Come on, baby, put on your best hauberk and Daddy'll take you down to see the torture chamber."

I laughed—I too felt hilarious, I didn't know why. "Good day," I said to the butler or porter or man-at-arms or whatever he was in my best French, which was stilted but still serviceable. "We are friends of Mr. Currier, old friends from university days, we called yesterday and spoke with—" I paused: what did you say? Madame Currier? Countess de Palantreuil? "—with Madame la Comtesse," I finished a touch lamely.

With a gesture he turned, the great wolfhound wheeling with him, and we followed them through a gloomy vestibule into what I suppose was the main hall. "If you would wait here, please." He went away up a long flight of stone stairs.

We stood in the great room like country cousins and stared at everything, as full of wonder as the children. There was a fireplace of heroic proportions, a refectory table at least 20 feet long, nicked and scarred and patinaed with time, with thronelike chairs at either end. The walls were decked with weapons, bristling trophies. I saw a shield with three gold oak leaves on a blue field, and another with a boar's head, jet black against a blood-red background.

"Is this real, or is it an old set for *The Man in the Iron Mask?*" Dal queried.

"It's real, all right," Chris answered him. "That's one of the handsomest armoires I've ever seen."

But Dal had hit on something, all the same—there was an air of neglect about the place: dust lay heavy on the great table, the tapestries were badly frayed, the little formal garden beyond the French doors was a tangle, choked with high grass. We all were looking at one another now, uneasily. The moment grew.

"Going to make a dramatic entrance," Dal offered. Still carrying Julie he was rocking up and down on the balls of his feet, something he did when he was irritated or impatient. "What do you suppose his title is? Count-Consort? or maybe *Discount?*"

"Be still, Dal," Chris hissed at him.

Someone was coming down the great staircase—light, unhurried steps. We turned. I thought, Now it will happen, at last and finally—they will look each other in the face, Russ and the boy, they will stand there face to face and all the mysteries and confusions of 16 years will—

A woman, our age—or possibly a bit older—with deep-set eyes, high cheekbones, long blond hair woven about her head in a tightly braided coronet. In spite of myself, prepared for almost anything, I started—the resemblance to Kay Madden was staggering. Not that she was a physical replica; there was none of the flawless symmetry of Kay's face, the sheer vapid good looks. It was her manner—that supremely assured, lazily arrogant amusement. Only this was the real thing. Her eyes gleamed like the axes and broadswords on the walls beyond her. I thought—I almost said aloud, No, oh no, he hasn't done it again—not after all that misery and—

"The friends of Russell's!" she exclaimed in excellent English with barely a trace of accent; her voice was lower than Kay's, and harsher. "What a charming surprise! I am Clothilde. You are touring, then? En famille, I see. You must forgive me, I had no idea you would be driving near us."

I looked inquiringly at Dal—we all did; frowning at her, he set the child down. "Why yes, we drove down today. You said—"

"Russell will be so sorry not to see you. He is in Sidi Bou Noura now. On location."

"But," Dal stammered, "—you said he was going to be back today."

"Why no, I did not!" She laughed once, shaking her head, facing him as one might an unruly small child. "I told you—it was you who telephoned?—I told you he will not be coming back for a month at least." She searched our faces then, her smoke-gray eyes wide. "Ah, what a malentendu, eh?"

"Yes, a misunderstanding," Chris said. "We're sorry to have broken in on you like this. My husband's French leaves something—"

"But you speak English!" Dal burst out accusingly, "you speak perfect English."

"But of course. What do you take me for?"

"But you were speaking French..."

"*You* were speaking French!" She laughed again, hugely amused. "How was I to know you would not understand what I was saying?"

"I did, I did understand," Dal repeated stubbornly, "you distinctly said he—"

"It's quite all right, Madame," Liz interrupted him firmly, in flawless French. "Our profuse apologies for breaking in upon you so barbarously."

Clothilde Currier turned quickly. "Ah—you should have made the call, perhaps!"

"Perhaps so."

We laughed, all of us except the children; there was really nothing else to do. A moment longer the women chatted, and then Clothilde Currier said: "You will excuse me? I have guests."

"Of course."

She accompanied us out to the courtyard. Overhead clouds were gathering sullenly in the heat, soot towers washed with silver; puffs of wind swept a few of last year's leaves in tiny fierce eddies over the worn stone.

"Russell would have enjoyed showing you about—he loves this old ruin so. Even its frightful history he finds enchanting. He is such a romantic. I like to tease him—I tell him he was born seven centuries too late."

"What frightful history, Ma'am?" Ron asked.

"Ron," his mother said.

"No—why shouldn't the boy ask?" She gazed at Ron a long moment, her eyes wide and piercing—then, even more sharply, at Chris. She seemed on the point of saying something, changed her mind and said instead: "You want to hear it, do you? Very well, you shall. My ancestor Gaspard de Palantreuil held a banquet for his wife's lover. Or perhaps he was not her lover, no one knew, but Gaspard was sure. Gaspard was always sure!" She laughed once, watching Ron intently. "It was long, long ago, during the Wars of Religion. At the great table in there, Gaspard stood up and proposed a toast: 'To the rewards of all adulterers!' and as he raised the goblet to his lips two of his men-at-arms struck Hubert des Barres dead where he was sitting."

"*Des Barres?*" I heard myself say in amazement. "Des Barres?"

"Yes, that was the lover's name—it is a very proud French family—Guillaume des Barres twice unhorsed Richard Coeur de Lion of England. And Gaspard turned to his wife Hélène and said, 'Why are you not drinking? You must always join in a toast.' And he went up to her and forced her to drain her goblet."

Her wide gray stare was still bent on Ron, who was watching her unsteadily now; Julie's eyes were squeezed tightly shut—I knew she was very close to tears.

"And the Lady Hélène gestured to one of the men-at-arms to fill her goblet again, and she smiled at Gaspard and said: 'Another toast—to the imperishable glory of your house, my gracious lord,' and she drained that goblet, too. And then she excused herself from the company and mounted to the blue tower, that one there, and gathered her two little boys in her arms and threw herself from that window—and they landed right where you are standing." Her extended arm fell, the finger pointing. "And that stone—see it? it is unlike all the other stones—turned black from the shame of it. At least that is the legend."

There was a short silence; the sky above the towers was darker now, churning heavily; the wind was cool. I glanced at Peg; she was gripping my hand tightly and scowling down at the great discolored flagstone. At that moment Julie began to cry—great, gasping bellows, her eyes still shut.

"There, there," Chris said, holding the child to her breast, "it's all right, darling. It's all right, now."

"What a fearful thing to do," Liz said.

"Isn't it?" Clothilde Currier laughed above the child's crying. "What a pity no one has the spirit for such deeds these days..."

"Perhaps we lack sufficient inspiration," Liz returned, and her eyes were cold.

"Perhaps." Briskly Clothilde Currier said goodbye, and went inside. The mighty oak door shut like a cannon booming.

"And thank—you—Lady Dracula," Dal said. "Jesus, what a bitch."

"Honest to God, Dal." Chris was still trying to comfort Julie. "Sometimes you beat everything on earth."

"She *said* he'd be back tomorrow, I heard her say it."

"She could have said he'd joined the Foreign Legion, for all you know." The rising wind whipped her hair around her forehead and cheeks. "Come on, let's get out of here before we all get turned into gnomes or something."

The Bentley took off with a roar; I watched it rumble over the drawbridge and race on down the road. A few drops of rain fell; a random, isolated tapping on the stones.

"Come on, Peg, hurry it up," Nancy was saying. "We're going now."

I looked down. Peg's hand still gripped mine tightly; she hadn't once moved.

"Honey," I said.

She looked up at me then. That steady, serene gaze was gone; her eyes were hollow and wide—a consternation too deep even for tears. "Daddy—" she murmured, so faintly I could only tell by the movement of her lips; her body was rigid.

"Come on, let's go," Nancy called, "it's raining." She swung open the door, and turned. "What's the matter now?"

"She's frightened," I said. "The story frightened her.— Honey-girl," I said. "She's a mean person. Yes. Cruel. She told you that story to hurt you. Frighten you."

"Goodness sake, George." Nancy banged the car door shut again. "Don't fill the child's head with such thoughts."

"Why not?"

"Because it's stupid, that's why! Darling, it's nothing," she said soothingly, "it's—it's just a fairy story, darling, a fairy tale, there weren't any such people—"

"*No*," I said. I was filled with a slow, heavy anger. "No, it's not a fairy tale. It's *real*—that woman is real. And she's cruel."

"Look, George, what possible good—"

"—*Here* is where I learned it," I said, my voice shaking all at once, and I pointed down at the stones, "right here I learned just how cruel men can be. I never believed it till then . . . She's not going to grow up the way we did, Nan—she's not going to! You hear me?"

"George, she's a baby—"

"She's seven," I said. "She's old enough to face this."

"George, you can't—"

"He's right, Nan," Liz said evenly. "He's right. Listen to him, now."

Nancy fell silent, glancing uncertainly from one of us to the other. I crouched down in the courtyard, still holding Peg's hand. Nothing had ever seemed so important as this moment—not in a long, long time.

"Honey-girl, you must learn what is true and what isn't. We all have to. Maybe Mother's right, and that story never really happened. But that doesn't matter—it is cruelty that matters. Cruelty exists. In the world." I held her eyes with mine. "And it's important to see it for what it is. And not pretend it isn't there, or be frightened by it, or be fooled by someone trying to act pleasant while she's being cruel."

"But why, Daddy?" Her eyes filled with tears at last, and I felt better. "Why did she do that?"

"I don't know, Peg. Maybe she gets pleasure out of being cruel, hurting others. Some people do. Maybe she didn't like us—maybe we reminded her of something she hates and fears. I don't know . . . Do you remember the clowns? In the circus, back in Paris? The one who kept building that funny little house of blocks in different ways, and the other one kept coming by and knocking it all down? Well, it's like that clown. There are men like that in her story, there were men like that just a few years ago, here in France, in Germany—there always are, everywhere. At home, too. It's in all of us, honey-girl—you, me, everybody." It was raining harder now, the storm clouds rushing by low overhead, boiling above the castle towers. In the distance the river lay like old iron.

"And sometimes we have to stop it, put an end to it if it gets bad enough. But the most important thing is to admit what someone says or does *is* cruel, and not lie to ourselves about it. Even if it hurts us, and scares us sometimes. We have to face up to it. Do you see, honey?"

She was weeping now, but the lost look was gone. I held her shoulders and thought: *No*—no-fairy tales, no fantasies that swirl their way into nightmares, and stalk the shadows . . .

"But Daddy." I could almost feel her worrying the thought. "If it's in all of us . . ."

"Yes, that's right. That's why we must all try to be as honest and as good as we know how." I hugged her to me—an embrace that was like drowning; released her. "Now hop in the car."

By the time we reached Paris it was late, the neon signs bleeding vermilion and emerald through the slick dark, the trees swaying proudly in the storm wind. I dropped Nancy and Peg at our hotel, and then drove Liz on up to the George V, through the streaming jewels of light around the Etoile. I felt depressed, disconsolate out of all proportion to the incident, the day's journey. I couldn't seem to get Russ out of my mind. Or the Countess Clothilde. Or Peg.

"I'm sorry it was such a bust," I said. "The whole excursion."

She gave me her easy grin. "Can't win 'em all. It was my fault, really."

"What? No, it wasn't."

"Sure, it was. I talked you and Dal into phoning. I ought to have kept my mouth shut."

"We wanted to, anyway. And yet even then I had the feeling it would end badly. I don't know why."

"Maybe we shouldn't ever go back."

"Oh, don't say that . . ." I grinned, to take the force out of my words.

"Ah, if youth only understood, if old age only could," she recited with her wry, hoyden smile. "We only become what we were meant to be all along, I think sometimes. If we're lucky, I mean."

Drawing up before the hotel I looked at her then, thinking of that afternoon at Nauset Beach, with Chris and Russ running with the great blue kite, and what Liz had said about destiny. Liz and I had always been able to talk simply and easily. We had a lot in common. She was like the sister I'd never had—a very talented, steady sister—there was that purposeful competence you had to like; and there was also the affinity between two people who recognize the value of each other's work, the measure of discipline and self-sacrifice needed to get it done . . . but now there was more than that—her old, restless vulnerability was gone, replaced by an acceptance of who and what she was. *There* was where her strength lay. I hadn't seen that so clearly before. I shut off the motor. The chasseur hurried toward us but I waved him away.

"You're happy, aren't you, Liz?" I said. "Really happy." She nodded. "Much happier than you ever were in college."

She nodded again soberly. "That wouldn't be hard—I was a very unhappy girl in college. And later, too."

"You've come to terms with yourself," I heard myself say. "Completely. Haven't you? You're one of the few people I know who's ever done that."

She paused, watching me steadily. "I mistook myself for someone else—for a long time," she said with slow deliberation, as though exploring the thought. "Now I can look at myself clearly. As I am." Her lips curved in the sad, sardonic smile. "I can even forgive myself—even rejoice in the kind of person I am. That's a lot, for me."

Her gaze held firmly on mine. Surrounded by the gleaming Paris dark we looked at each other for a long moment.

"It's not a road for the faint of heart, George," she said, and pressed one of her fine, expressive hands on the other. "The *real* road, I mean—not the freedom fantasy bit. Speaking of fantasies. For some people it's just an evasion of growing up... It's all a crush—a schoolgirl crush," she said softly. "You do know that, don't you?"

"I don't know," I said after a pause. "There are so many things in this world I don't know."

"She *wants* the life with you. Marriage—that's what she was always bound and determined to have. Wife and mother, the whole works. That's her bag, really. It is. She's one of those gals who always says what she could have been if she'd only 'had the time'—without any real intention of putting in the *work* involved. It's a kind of approval she wants, needs. Well, who doesn't? I know it hasn't been easy for you, any of it. Losing Teddy—"

"Yes," I said.

She leaned forward then and kissed me on the cheek. "Well, I wish *I'd* drawn you for a father, I'll say that. Does that horrify you?"

"No," I said. "I'm honored."

She swung away and out of the car. "Don't see me in, go on back." Leaning in the window she gave me the wry, roguish grin once more. "And just think how lucky you are not be to married to the Countess Clothilde!"

I watched her move off toward the soft orange lights of the hotel, tall and proud: a lady of high fashion—and oh, so much more than that.

4

TIME GOT AWAY. The gathering rush of years, as they say. I thought time had passed quickly enough before the war ("World War Two," the kids say now, with the accent on the *two*, which always irritates me until I think: Of course, it's history to them—God, it was 20—or 25—or 30 years ago)... But the very sun-and-honey vividness of those days had always held them in a luminous, crystalline stasis for me; beyond time.

Everything *is* relative, as Terry is fond of saying with his sardonic smile. The post-war years gathered speed with infinite subtlety, the most seductive of con games. I remember what Peaches Maitland, the Grand Prix champion, told me once at a party. "The interesting thing is, at a certain speed everything is reversed: you're driving the car, racing past trees and poles and houses—and then you're not, you're not driving *anything,* you're sitting in a goofy trance, absolutely motionless, a floating mindless projectile, and all those trees and houses are swooping at *you*, with a malicious intelligence all their own. That's when it's most dangerous..."

Cars. I keep coming back to them, I can't help it. We loved cars so, my generation. You start out fooling around with junk jalopies, stripping them down, souping them up, giving them weird paint jobs, and the first drive down Main Street to Lamprey's Drug Store in your own wheels is a moment you will never forget; you move on to Model A's with rumble seats, a gang of you following the football team to nearby towns, and it's really and truly an open road—you can feel it, woods and shocked cornfields and the smell of burning leaves, you *know* it's true; in the newsreels you watch FDR driving that specially designed Ford V-8 of his, tearing over the backroads of Dutchess County, his hat brim flaring up at the front like a roughrider's, and you take a measure of courage from this man who can't walk a single step unaided—and who has nonetheless managed to travel so very far; you revel in those brief pre-war months with the Empress, when nearly every car seems to have a touch of individual distinction, and automotive pride has a fierce, definable source—you're abruptly flung into the sepia world of jeeps and weapons carriers, mud and dust and olive drab; and then you come back, struggling to make things fit again, get your feet under you—and when finally you gaze around you the cars all look the same, and they don't look like cars at all, they look like bombs or blimps or killer whales... and it isn't an open road any more, not remotely, it's all a macadam track, an eight-lane freeway—which isn't a *freeway* at all, the very term is preposterous—bound up and tangled in a thousand cloverleafs and off-ramps, going nowhere that you can see...

We thought we could control those cars, that open road—we were so sure of it! If we drove well, you know; kept alert, a certain steadiness, watched for the signposts. And it wasn't true, we woke up to find ourselves in Maitland's mindless projectile, with everything flashing by so fast, so diabolically fast... Where *did* the time go, all those years? You pressed on with the demands of the job (there were always more of them), the mounting needs of your wife and children (there were even more of these)—and all at once, it seemed, you looked up with a slow, heavy sense of shock to discover that Amanda was hitting tennis balls against the garage and cool young men were driving up in candy-colored cars to take Peg to their dances; when you shaved mornings your stubble had gray in it—yes, unquestionably, more gray than brown; your thighs sometimes quivered after a few flights of stairs.

Only moments brought things up short, checked the rush of the infernal freeway. Amanda going off to school the first day, whirling around with that defiant grin: "If I don't like it I'm coming right on back home. I am!" Ron graduating from Harvard, looking even thinner and taller than he was in his cap and gown, standing between Dal and Chris. I took the snapshot myself, against the old Fox Entry doorway in the Yard. I have it right here. Chris is smiling up at him proudly, a touch uncertainly. Dal is squinting at me and saying something out of the corner of his mouth to Julie, who is giggling and pinching Billy, who is six years old here and cross about something. I can never look at that shot without a certain foolish flow of satisfaction—we'd had no caps-and-gowns ourselves, no commencement: the day we should have graduated found us on Omaha Beach or Saipan or half a thousand leagues from any land at all; when it finally came, after the war, no one cared. Ron's had to do for us. Here are several more pictures—Nancy's smiling there, and Peg, with her arm around Julie. Only Ron is somber, his slender, handsome face troubled and unsure.

All those moments... Jack Kennedy's Presidential victory (another cliff-hanger) and Terry's jubilant, almost incoherent phone call from Hyannis the following afternoon. The inauguration, the young man without an overcoat (young, we would always see him as young because he was of our generation—and because, God help us, we would have no other choice), speaking so vigorously and incisively in front of the soured, bundled-up old men who had commanded us in the war, made the guns we'd fired; watching, listening we'd felt a sudden, fierce pride such as we'd never known before—this was *our* administration, *our* generation come to power at last: the coxswains and platoon leaders and bombardiers we'd served with were in the driver's seat now. The Camelot years pleased us deeply, even when we didn't agree with everything Kennedy was doing: it was, we felt, just about the way we'd have tried to do things if we'd been President—hold witty, wide-open press conferences and lively parties, impromptu ball games on the green lawns after work; invest the office with grace and dignity again—maybe even some true substance, given time...

And then that deceptively springlike November afternoon

that for years afterward so many of us couldn't recall without a
dart of helpless, raging sorrow. Numb with shock we phoned
each other for days, back and forth—we had to talk about it,
around it, as if that might somehow reduce its stunning,
causeless brutality. I remember Chris's voice hoarse with
weeping, her bereft, angry dismay: "—But he was *our*
President!"... In an hour he was gone, and our generation's
hour in the sun was gone too, for good—power had passed back
to the shrewd, conniving old men of the 30s, before we'd even
had a chance to get started. We watched the funeral on
television, drinks in our hands, eyes brimming with tears,
thinking bitter, wrathful thoughts: we were back in the war—the
uncaring shell had struck our leader down, the crafty bully had
succeeded to command.

We were all shaken; it was a blow Terry never recovered
from. He never once alluded to it in all the time I've known him,
but Eddie Shaughnessy told me later that in the plane flying
back to Washington that evening Terry in his grief went raving,
ranting mad, cursing Lyndon Johnson to his face for a
self-serving, power-crazy swine, screaming why had it happened
in Dallas, why *in Texas*—! Two of them had only just prevented
him from physically attacking the new President of the
Republic. He was through in the Administration after that, of
course—he was through in Washington for that matter. He
came back to Boston and assumed that patent cover for doing
nothing at all: "management consultant." Then he had a
complete nervous collapse, and lay huddled in a blanket
sweating and moaning, while some of us stayed with him in
relays. Sheilah flew back from Spoleto to be with him. Slowly,
very slowly he got better, sat for hours on the deck of the
Scituate summer house bundled up in an old flier's jacket and
boots, drinking, staring implacably at the ice along the shore.

The Assassination (that's what it became for us, just as World
War II remained The War) had been a thunderbolt. Vietnam
was like a pestilence: the subtle increase of uniforms, an
occasional busload of kids going south to the army camps, a
rather disorganized demonstration in front of the town hall—
and all the while the muscular, optimistic announcements telling
us all was well, going very well indeed, it was only a matter of
three months, six months, a year or so.

So stealthy. Our war had been Pearl Harbor, ten million men

under arms, full conversion, Rosie the Riveter, *I Came Here to Talk for Joe,* Ernie Pyle and Major Glenn Miller, the Four Freedoms flung in the teeth of the Axis, and back there behind us in Washington, General George Marshall like a supremely competent, stern-but-sympathetic father... What the hell did we have to do with military adventures in the rain forests of Southeast Asia? What made it worse was that we persisted in believing Jack would have stopped it. We deplored it, and wrote angry letters and supported the first protesters; but still it remained remote, ephemeral, something far away.

And then one night it all came home. Ron was sitting across from me here in the study with his hands hanging in his lap and saying: "What do you think I ought to do? Dad wants me to go into pre-med, go for a medical deferment. But hell, I hate medicine. I'm not good at it, I never was."

"And your mother?"

He paused. "She wants me to bug out. Canada or whatever. She says she'll back me if I go. Send me bread. Until I get a job. Some of my friends are doing it." He looked away unhappily into the hot summer night.

"How about you, Ron? How do you feel?"

"I don't know. I just don't know. Maybe I should. *Nothing* seems right, nothing I can think of. That's why I ran out here—I thought you could rap with me about it. You were in World War Two."

"Your Dad was in the war," I said.

"Ah, it was all calvados and jeep rides, a happy rip-off—I've heard him. You were in the *real* war. Mother's told me."

I started to answer him and stopped. He wasn't hitting me for a $20 loan, or the use of the Empress on a hot date now. He was better than I was, finer-spun material, and there was something humbling and saddening in the realization. And he felt things so deeply—there was his mother's quickened sensibility and passion; Russ's, too. The world is a comedy to those who think, a tragedy to those who feel, somebody had said. Was that true? Probably. And what about those poor devils who both thought *and* felt?

Now—right now—he was frightened. That scooped-out, hollow, distending fear, the flutter of immense black wings: I remembered it. The old aboriginal dread of a pitiless universe—once a man has felt it he is never the same again.

"I don't know about the medical thing," I said slowly, "I don't know if there's time for that anyway, if you've drawn a low number. But Canada—I think it would be a big mistake for you. Protests are one thing, but leaving altogether—"

His head came up. "But then—that means the *Army*..."

"Yes." I took a deep breath. "We're slipping into one of our hysterical national binges, Ron: guilt-induced phony heroics. We know God damned well we're doing the wrong thing—and whenever we get defensive out of guilt we're dangerous. Everyone is. It's going to be worse than the McCarthy days. We're ashamed of this war—some of us anyway, and a lot more of us are going to be—and that will only turn the movers and shakers all the more vindictive and self-righteous. I don't know why they can't ever admit they're wrong, that a policy is stupid and suicidal, entirely against the very idea of America itself; but they can't."

"Well, but if that's the case—"

"Let me finish. What it means is, you'll never draw a pardon if you skip, Ron—not for years, anyhow. Maybe never. Can you handle that? Some men can, without hurting—write it off, drift around Scandinavia, vegetate or find work in Saskatchewan, make out as best they can in the sad company of exiles... It could be a life sentence, you know. There *are* men, who can and must live that way; but I don't think you're one of them. You'll turn bitter—"

"Bitter! I'm bitter right now."

"No, you're not. You think you are but you're not. Forgive me, kid, but you don't know what bitterness *is*. I hope to God you never do... Or you'll turn nasty, uncaring—I mean deeply uncaring; and for you that will be a kind of death." I leaned back in my chair, remembering, not wanting to remember. "Anyway, that's my opinion. For what it's worth."

Ron was staring hard at me, his eyes dark with distrust. "So you're telling me I ought to go into the Army, then. Become a part of this filthy war."

"Only as the least of several distinct evils, Ron."

"Wow... I never thought you'd say anything like this."

"I didn't, either. But there it is. You asked me."

"Would you do it? if you were my age?"

I paused. "Yes. I think so... That doesn't say it would be right."

After a little he thanked me, said he'd have to think about it some more, and left. It had seemed right to me, what I'd said, it seemed like sound advice, for the kind of boy Ron was. But later, much later that night, lying there in bed staring at the ceiling, the car lights sliding pale rectangles over the plaster, all I could see was the long, white jackstone parade of crosses at Salerno, and Debremont, all those neat white graves, and what had led to them. Would I have given him that advice if he'd been my own son? if he'd been Teddy? And then I thought of Dal, and Chris, and I was more afraid, and disgusted with myself. Hell, it was easy enough for me to say, 42 and getting fat in the ass. The point was not whether I would have served if I'd been his age: would I have served *again*, knowing what I knew of what war did to a man—pumping him full of inverted pride, making destruction easy for him, so easy, indoctrinating him with the sacred importance of the group—squad, platoon, battalion (yes, and then later the company, agency, corporation) over the individual? turning him vindictive and brutal far more cruelly than exile might ever do?

And I convinced him; I guess I did—more than anyone else, anyway. In any event he went in, which led to a phone call from Chris I won't ever forget.

"—after all you went through, the terrible *misery* of it—George, George, your hands were still shaking after you got home, sometimes! Do you remember that? *I* do..." The terror kept bleeding through her rage. "What did you tell him, what did you *tell* him? Don't you remember any of it at all—!"

"Chris, it's not just a—"

"Have you really become like the rest of them, sitting around at the club and gassing on about its not being so bad really, we had a hell of a lot of fun, didn't we, fella—"

"Chris, please listen—"

"—or have they got to you too, talked you into believing we're leading a crusade out there?"

"You know better than that."

"I don't, I don't know anything. All I know is I'm sick to my very guts! How could you urge him to go to war, George—you of all people? How *could you do it!*"

"I didn't urge him, Chris, I only gave what I thought was—"

But she had broken down then, and hung up on me. Chris had hung up on me. She felt I had betrayed her—I, who would cheerfully cut off my right hand if it would spare her one day's unhappiness.

They shoved him in the infantry—where else does a comp lit major wind up in his country's service?—and sent him to Vietnam in the first big troop build-up of '66. Nights I would find myself peering at the film clips in the seven o'clock news with a kind of sick fascination, afraid I might recognize him; fearing for those other Rons and Opps and Dees; hating LBJ for his John Wayne-Texas-macho talk about bringing back the old coonskin, hating all those civilian advisers whose participation in *our* war had been such a lark, such an intoxicating adventure, with their parties at Claridge's or Foyot's, and heady staff conferences and requisitioned castles and cameramen on guided tours; cursing them (as much as I ever had the Wehrmacht) for their thinly veiled racial contempt, their computer statistics and buoyant, tough-minded pragmatism, their murderous want of humanity...

And then Dal phoned me that Ron had been hit. I had to sit down by the phone stand and clamp my arms to my sides.

"How is it? How bad is it?"

"He didn't say—only that he was wounded in the back and arm. I'm trying to find out now." His voice was quiet, utterly factual. "I gather it's not too bad because he wrote the letter himself and it sounds loose. They helicoptered him right out of there to Tan Son Hut; he's in Tokyo now."

"How's Chris taking it?"

"Well, she's shook up. She'll be okay in a couple of days. She'd be speaking to you herself but she's still a little cut up about the letter."

"What letter?" I said.

"Nancy's letter—Nancy wrote her a while back, read her off... Didn't you know about that?"

"No," I said. "I didn't. I certainly didn't."

"Oh, Christ." He sighed. "Look, it's a woman squabble—Nancy apparently got sore at Chris for sounding off at you when Ron decided to go in. Don't let it get you. Hell, it'll blow over... Grog? You still there?"

"Yes," I said, "I'm here. Let me know when you hear anything more, will you?"

"Sure thing. Take care."

"Take care."

Nancy was sitting on her bed, brushing her hair and watching an old black-and-white movie on TV. "Who was that?" she said.

"Dal. Ron's been wounded."

"Oh, how awful. Will he be all right?"

"They don't know. They hope so." I walked up to the edge of her bed. "When did you write Chris?" I asked quietly.

Her eyes swung up to mine, very flat and blue. "I don't remember, really—some months ago. Why?"

"Why don't you try," I said. "Try to remember."

She lowered the brush. "Now, just a minute—"

"What did you say to her?"

"I didn't realize we were required to report our correspondence to each other."

"On this one we are. *What did you say to her?*"

Her jaw set. "All right. I told her I was sick and tired of your having to bear the blame for Ron's being in the Army, as though for heaven's sake it were some kind of badge of disgrace, wearing your country's uniform. And that if she had any *further* ideas about berating you for simply trying to give that confused boy some sound advice—"

"You laid into her like that, knowing she had a boy in Vietnam—no!" I almost shouted. As I've said, I'll go along for a long time, a very long time—and then all of a sudden I've had it and I don't care where it leads, who gets hurt or how much. And now the old fear and rage had hold of me. "No!" I said again. I leaned down and gripped her by the arm, very firmly. "You had no right to write a letter like that! You have no right to talk about this war—you don't know anything *about* this war, or about *any* war! You got that?"

"George, let go of my arm."

"I want this to penetrate. All the way . . . So solicitous and noble, defending me from the barbarians—no! Now, you're going to write her another letter, apologizing for the things you said. Have you got that?"

"Don't you talk to me like some grubby top sergeant!"

"Then don't act like a general fuck-off! And a trouble-maker." I brought my eyes very close to hers. "You are going," I said slowly and distinctly, "to write a letter of condolence and apology. And you are going to write it tomorrow. And that's it." And I released her arm.

She hugged it with her other hand, but aside from that she

didn't move. She'd got over her fright now; her eyes were hard as sapphires.

"...Just can't bear to see her criticized, can you?" she whispered, but it sounded like a shout. "Just can't *live* without her. Can you?"

I leaned down again. "We won't talk about who we can or can't live without," I said. "Either of us.—You wanted to tear it apart for good, didn't you, Nan? Didn't you?"

"No—that's not true..."

"Then what you said about me isn't true, either." And I went down to my study and read until two-thirty.

How do you go on, after moments like that one? Well, you do. Or you don't. To tell the truth, we were not a divorcing generation. Some of us did, but they were in the minority. That came later. And of course there were the kids, the obligations—the habit of monogamy. Was that what it was? Anyway, that was how it worked. This time it was Nancy who gave way, for a change—that is to say she did write Chris, and I presume it was a good letter for Chris replied with warmth. Ron recovered. But he didn't look me up when he came back through Boston.

What else happened, those years of the demonic freeway? Dal got richer and richer—he had moved into electronics, some tie-in with Japanese firms I never could understand; he owned or controlled three more television stations, he was in real estate and stock options, and of course oil. He had built a summer place for Chris on Cape Cod, at Chatham, a great rambling structure abounding in decks and boat houses; he had a big, fast sloop and an even faster power cruiser which slept eight. He'd gone far, far beyond his Monopoly game plan now—he collected board memberships like crackerjack prizes, there was even talk of his running for the Senate in Illinois, but he openly ridiculed the notion. And there was the other side, too—that early conviction of his about the power of money: he poured hundreds of thousands into medical research and hospitals and political reform candidates, but he would never talk about that side, he even disparaged it—it was as if such ventures were a secret vice, or a religious tithe.

And they traveled. I don't know whether it was the dislocations of the war, or the remembered poverty of the Great Depression, or a genuine desire to see, to know, but we were a generation that loved to travel. The Dalrymples journeyed to

Greece, to Antigua, to Africa, to Japan. Dal's postcards were still the same whacky, freewheeling communiqués. I have several here—one is postmarked Nairobi and reads: *The exotic animals are right out there in the bush but are of course invisible because of their natural markings. At night they come to the waterhole just below our window & yowl & trumpet & screech & mew & hiss. But you can't see them then because of course it's dark. The natives are blue, the dust is red, the flies are black. Fortunately the Haig & Haig & Haig & Haig is golden brown. Cheers.*

Chris's letters, less frequent, are lively and rich and warm—glimpses of a landscape nobody else would have caught. She kept up her collecting and published a quiet, beautiful book on shells of the Caribbean. Julie, happy-go-lucky and outgoing, went off to the University of Wisconsin; Billy, stubborn and practical like his father, came east to Choate.

Russ we heard of distantly, indistinctly, like the off-stage alarums in Shakespearean battles. He had a fair success with *Jeux des Imbéciles,* a film he wrote and directed; he published a novel, *Chance of Anger,* about a dying French aristocrat, which garnered enthusiastic reviews but had a disappointing sale; he wrote articles for—astonishingly—a monarchist magazine in Paris; he had parted with Clothilde, he was back with her again; they were divorced; he was often seen with the rising young film star Thérèse Renaudin; I have a picture cut from *Paris-Match* a French publisher sent me, of Russ skin-diving off Corsica with the jet-set film-maker Roger Vaugirard; he looks as slender and youthful as ever—yet he is staring at the camera with the most curious expression, as if what he'd seen 20 fathoms down had changed his very chemistry...

5

"AH—HERE'S A coruscating little item," I said. I flipped the *Herald* open at a new page.

"What's carskating?" Amanda asked, as I knew she would.

"Sparkling, dazzling, radiant. Like your rejuvenated old Dad this fine June morning." Holding the paper aloft I read: *"Among the early arrivals for the Harvard Class of 1944's 25th Reunion were Knowles Fletcher and his exotic Oriental bride Mai Soong, who emerged from the cargo hatch of a Navy PBY at Logan International Airport riding a snow-white unicorn."*

"Snow-white unicorn," Peg said. She was a sophomore at Radcliffe now, and far beyond this kind of horsing around. "Honestly, Pa."

"Is she really Chinese?" Amanda wanted to know.

"She really is." I read on: *"'Fluff and I wouldn't have missed our 25th for all the oil in China,' Mai Soong informed this reporter. 'After all, where would the Mysterious East be without Harvard? Or conversely.'"*

"Why did you call him Fluff?" Peg asked.

"That's a good question and I can't answer it."

"Because his head is full of feathers," Amanda decided, twisting around on her chair. "Because he's got a—"

"Hush!" I raised a peremptory hand and my family stared at me. The phonograph in the living room was playing Tommy Dorsey's *Song of India,* and Bunny Berigan had just burst into the darting, soaring trumpet solo that never failed to shoot me back on a laserbeam to the Riverside Ballroom, and Dal dancing with Liz in that funny, hunch-shouldered way he had, pointing toward the bandstand. I glared fiendishly at Amanda until the ride was over, then lowered my hand. "All right," I proclaimed. "Life can go on."

"Your father," Nancy informed her daughters, "is going to be impossible all day. For *four* straight days. And there's nothing any of us can do about it." But she smiled at me indulgently.

"Now, I want everybody saddled up at 1100 hours," I told them. "You may bring anything and everything you want to—but anything you forget will be forgotten forever. We are not—repeat, *not*—coming back for it."

"Check!" Amanda shouted; then her face fell. "What if it rains?"

"It can't rain. I absolutely forbid it."

"It rained last year with the class of '43," Peg said.

"*That* bunch of bums. They're not the Double Four."

I went outside and walked slowly around the Empress, feeling like Wiley Post about to take off for the round-the-world record. I'd got Barney Dietz to replate the chrome on those magnificent radiator louvers. A sailmaker over in Plymouth named Jot Snow had long since mended the tear in the top, which was impeccably folded back now, and snapped down. Over the years I'd filled her dents and creases with lead and filed them down, and I'd built up nine—yes, nine—coats of lacquer on her body; as I said, I hadn't been able to get precisely that original green, but it was close, very close. And I'd just polished and repolished her within an inch of her charmed life. There she stood, proud as a peacock—as though it were the fall of 1940 again, and Dal were yelling at us to come on, let's move it or we'd never pick up the girls and make it back to the Stadium in time for the kick-off—

I whirled around and ran into the house. "Come on," I called, "let's go! Let's move out..."

Nancy said: "But George—it's only ten!"

"Never mind. This is it."

The weather was perfect—clear and cool, with northwest breezes, as I was sure it would be; we cruised along with our crimson-and-white reunion sticker blazing on the windshield, and the sun racing through the green latticework of leaves overhead.

"Perverse," Nancy declared, though she was smiling, holding the brim of her straw hat lightly. Nancy had really got herself up for this clambake. She was nicely tanned—she'd taken up tennis at the club for the past three years, along with consciousness-raising sessions—even a bout of yoga—and she'd dieted rigorously; her hair had been cut and styled by a very expensive, waspish young man in Boston, and it was still that fine, silvery blond; her face looked young and serene under the wide brim. "Harries us like a drill sergeant, and then wanders all over every back road he can find."

"I want to let it build," I said—and grinned at myself in surprise. It was what I used to say to myself a quarter of a century before. I made a leisurely pass through the Wellesley College campus, and drove around the Longwood Cricket Club. On one court the white-clad figures stopped their play and stared and waved their rackets, and I waved back, slowing a bit more to let them have a good look at the Empress.

"Daddy, we've *done* all this a thousand times," Peg said.

"Got to touch all the bases," I told her. "Can't miss a thing today."

Running through Brookline the Shattucks passed us in their Chrysler station wagon, the kids waving frenziedly from the tailgate, and we tooted horns at each other. The Stadium looked venerable and sleepy in the June sunlight, and the river was a soft, deep blue. At the University Theater—now unfortunately renamed the Harvard Square Theater—*Casablanca* was playing, as a tribute to the class of '44.

"Bogey!" I exclaimed. "A Bogey film at the UT."

"Pa," Peg said, "you've gone bonkers, no kidding."

"Here's looking at *you*, kid . . ."

On Quincy Street in front of the Union they kept rolling up in taxis from Logan Airport, in rented limos, in Buick wagons and Mercedes and Corvettes and Thunderbirds; and Harry Bradner, a senior executive at CBS, looking congenial and distinguished even in the floppy-brimmed white-and-crimson Reunion hat, greeted us all. But there was only one Empress, and they crowded around it as I knew they would, classmates and wives and children, their cries edged with awe and remembered delight:

"—a Packard convertible!"

"The Empress—you remember the Empress, Jeanie..."

"Dig that chariot! What a restoration job, Virdon."

"That car isn't restored, it's transubstantiated!"

We milled around inside the gates, greeting one another with a bonhomie that was a touch high-key, struggling to recall names, making introductions. Our wives watched one another warily, assaying styles, skirt lengths, faces and figures after twenty-five hasty years; if we were nostalgic they were analytical—some of them looked downright worried; but perhaps it was only the drive to Cambridge with the kids. Laughing, talking too loudly we poured into the Union to check in.

Half an hour later, the back seat piled with a crazy collection of Reunion hats and ties, *Veritas*-inscribed wastebaskets, rain jackets and tote bags and ashtrays, we eased our way down Holyoke Street and pulled up in front of the House, where a clear, vibrant voice called: "*Who* is driving that glorious convertible dreamboat!" and three heads were hanging out of a window above us, over a sheet adorned with crimson block letters that read: *FOX FUSILIERS FOREVER—44*. The head in the middle was Chris's; I blew her a kiss.

We'd drawn adjoining suites on the same floor, though in different entries. Dal had wangled it. We got ourselves settled in sketchily, and then came in through the connecting fire door—it was still open, I was pleased to see, its glass disc cunningly removed—and greeted the Dalrymples.

"Grog, boy! Welcome home. How about a swifty? just to prime the pump, don't you know." Dal had brought along a handsome portable bar with its own ice-maker and glasses with the Harvard seal, and a phonograph covered in Russian calf which was already playing Gene Krupa's *Drum Boogie*. Winking he handed me a drink. He'd lost more hair; there was only a thin, sandy fringe high on the top of his head which made his jaw look harder and more aggressive. Julie and Billy were already rigged out in Harvard T-shirts. Ron, who had been sitting by himself in a corner of the room, came over and said:

"How are you, Mr. Virdon."

"Fine, Ron," I said. "It's good to see you again."

"Hey, what's this *Mr. Virdon* routine?" his mother inquired. "That's Uncle George, your indulgent old godfather."

"He can call me anything he wants," I said easily, though I felt sad, watching his cool, distant gaze. He still looked painfully thin. After he got out of the Army he'd surprised everyone—and delighted me—by deciding he wanted to be a marine biologist, like his grandfather, and had gone back for the extra degree; but he hadn't come by the house to spend a weekend or borrow the Empress as he always had before. He greeted Nancy and Peg and Amanda rather perfunctorily and went back to the far corner and sat down again, looking ill at ease. He seemed mildly contemptuous of our eager camaraderie. And why not? I thought. Yet we, too, had put in *our* time; and we didn't intend to let him spoil our mood—not on this day of days.

Mel and Marge Strasser came in then, with their two kids; and half an hour later Terry brought his new wife, Ingrid, whom the Dalrymples hadn't met.

"Yeah, I married a Swede!" he exclaimed. "Can you imagine?—*me? Now* let's see them call me a henchman in the Irish mafia . . ." He looked stooped; his eyes flashed restlessly around the old room. Eddie Shaughnessy had talked him into working for Bobby, and the second assassination had been cataclysmic. He'd drawn into himself again, refused contact with any of us, even Sheilah, and would probably have gone completely to pieces if it hadn't been for Ingrid. He'd run into her one weekend at Shaughnessy's place on the Vineyard. She'd been just what he needed, her calm resilience absorbing his paranoid savagery—he was obsessed with the idea of an anti-Kennedy conspiracy launched by some amorphous oil-cum-munitions clique. She kidded him out of his darker moods and got him moving again. But his face was drawn and deeply lined—the face of a man on the thin edge of ungovernable rage; he looked much older than any of the rest of us.

"Where's Currier?" he asked at one point. "He's coming, isn't he?"

"Beats me," I said. "I wrote to him, the last address I had, I offered to meet him in the Empress. He never answered."

"He wouldn't miss *this* . . ."

"Don't be too sure."

"He broke up with that countess, didn't he?"

"Yeah. She dropped him," Dal said.

"Now darling," Chris chided, "you don't know if that's true or not."

"Sure, it's true—she left him and married that racing driver, the Italian, what's-his-name."

"Oh, let's not talk about Russ Currier," Nancy protested.

"Why's that?"

"He's such a *discordant* element."

But our thoughts had to be on him, all the same. He'd always been—well, spokesman, catalyst, leader of our particular revels; the unpredictable element. We wanted to talk about him; and there was a good deal to talk about. He'd had a huge success recently with *Weep For Memory:* the novel had been a surprise best seller, despite indifferent reviews—and then Russ had astonished everyone by turning down lucrative offers from the big studios and making the picture on his own. It had just won first prize at the Cannes Film Festival: there had been heavy attendant publicity, and a laudatory article in *Newsweek*. He'd recouped his losses, it seemed—and then some...

After several drinks we went up to Harkness Commons and stood in an interminably long reception line to shake hands with the president, who did not seem as delighted to see us as he might have been. Then we milled around on the lawn under a vast tent and watched the dimly remembered faces swim into view out of the humid twilight. There was Bill Rendle, who'd been caught in the Haynes-Bjornson granaries scandal in '63, and had bounced right back with Prentiss, Starkie. There was Bur Procter, whose former wife had shot him in the neck with a .22-caliber pistol in an argument, it was said, over Bur's use of lighter fluid in the barbecue. There was Blazer Blassingham, who had blown up to 195 pounds and operated a truck rental agency in Duluth, and Chid Bierce, who was with IBM in Poughkeepsie. There was Coker Blenham, now predictably a big wheel in New York advertising, and married to a former stage actress; and Fletcher, equally predictably, perched in some unclassifiable niche in the upper echelons of *Time*. And of course there was my old nemesis Conger, still with University administration, and now choleric about the student occupation of University Hall that spring, and vengefully gleeful over what he referred to as "The Big Showdown."

And so we stood and drank and chatted, measuring one another—which is to say ourselves. Nothing—not marriage or the birth of a child or the death of a parent—forces so harsh a self-appraisal as one's 25th Reunion: here, for all the crowd of overalert women and overcasual men, there are really only two individuals—the *you* of 25 years ago, with your ignorance and innocence and dreams of glory; and the *you* of now, lined, the fat setting in your muscles, desire succumbing grimly to resignation...no wonder nearly everyone behaves badly.

"Spider, boy! You made it back..."

"They went forth to battle, but they always fell."

"And conversely, dad!"

"And conversely."

Maybe Harvard reunions exert more pressure than most. Every university puts its mark on its sons to a greater or lesser degree, stamps them indelibly with one salient characteristic. With Yale it is financial ambition; with Princeton, social arrogance; with Columbia, practicality; with Dartmouth, macho dominance. For us, gentlemen of Cantabrigia, it is pride of intellect—we have to "shine" somehow, some way; part of us had never doubted that we would—somehow. Nothing had quite been able to knock that out of us.

And yet it wasn't true—we knew it: we were corporation men, most of us, built into the huge monolithic structures that, sadly enough, had become the hallmark of our time. Only a few—a very few—had taken the lonely, perilous high road we'd been taught was "the Harvard way": there was Clay Newell, who had gone to live with the Brazilian aborigines, and Sumner Fein, who was an expert on ancient woodwind instruments; there was Harrison Gaunt, who'd been battling the fire ant deep in Alabama for two decades. But for most of us...

Monday started off fittingly enough with the memorial service for the class dead. Bill Coddington, who'd played in the line beside Rhino Tanahill, wearing bifocals now, his hair snow white, delivered a moving sermon; and standing there in Memorial Church with your head bowed, while the great bell tolled and tolled, thinking of Jean-Jean and Rhino and all the others, it was hard suddenly to keep the tears from starting, to restrain angry sorrow at all the cruel waste—by iron, by fire, by water—that the world had not, somehow, been more altered by the sacrifice.

And then came those damned symposia. It's a peculiar Harvard affliction—we feel if we sit around a table and hold forth on a subject (almost any subject will do), analyze it, worry it, examine it from every conceivable angle we are upholding fair play, the right of dissent, that proud tercentenary banner of Intellect, untrammeled and supreme...

So there were symposia everywhere you turned—on city planning, on the New Woman and the mass media and the peaceful uses of the sea floor; above all, on the student strike of that spring. This was a sore point—it had hit us at the very core of our pride. We'd known it couldn't happen at Harvard. Riots and violent confrontations were one thing at Berkeley or even Columbia—but not Cambridge: this was the citadel of reason and good will, where men of intellect listened, and weighed, differed if need be, and gave measured—nay, profound— reply... but then it *had* happened—the whole squalid scenario of seizure and demands and then the police, and broken heads and blood. *In the Yard.* Harvard was like everywhere else, then; we were not unique.

Now, here were undergraduates who had taken part in these demonstrations; and instead of reason and good will there were loud and angry exchanges. Pat Leveridge, who'd been wounded twice in the Rhine Crossing, got up and said, "I'm *proud* of this country with all its faults, I'm *proud* of what it stood for 25 years ago, what it still stands for... Don't you boys recognize a debt to be paid here?"

And a senior, a boy with a square, serious face answered: "Yes, I acknowledge a debt—but only up to a point. Should I be forced to commit crimes for my government? and if so, what crimes?"

Blazer cried: "But you can't think that way—love of country is unconditional!"

And the boy replied levelly, "Why should it be? What if it destroys the very decency of its own citizens? *You* may have struck that bargain, but I don't see why we should..."

We wanted to understand the kids—hell, they were *our* kids, a lot of them—we'd given them their standards, pleaded and remonstrated with them. But that memorial service—we'd lost more, many more of our class than we'd realized, somehow— got in our way. The old memories had come flooding back—the beaches, the foxholes, the aid stations... There we sat, nine in

every ten of us veterans of that war, over half of us feeling we
were more successful than our fathers had been, three-quarters
among us believing a Harvard degree had helped us substan-
tially in our careers. Now in our forties, moderately pleased at
seeing one another again, we wanted to remember our better
moments; but the kids were there, articulately there, and they
wouldn't let us. *Had* we become part of a murderous industrial
juggernaut, a new imperial Rome? It certainly looked that way
to these somber-faced young men. And if we had, how had we
got that way? We'd always seen ourselves—mostly without
self-pity or a thirst for vengeance—as victims; how had we all at
once been twisted into hawk-faced executioners?

Even our own night at Pops that evening, with the Boston
Symphony playing our old fight songs and Miller and Dorsey
tunes, couldn't clear the air—we were still snatching at rhythms
that kept eluding us. When even Mel Strasser—whose son Jeff
was a junior now majoring (to Mel's horror) in classics—turned
to me at the very moment Arthur Fiedler, our reunion hat on his
head, was leading the BSO's rendition of *In the Mood,* and said:
"I can't fit it together, George—it's as though it's happening to
three other guys," I knew how deeply we were all shaken.

The outing next day at the Tashawena Country Club didn't
pull it together either; not even a dizzying round of golf and
tennis and a disorderly fathers-and-children softball game could
keep us from dwelling on it. We sat around the umbrellaed
tables later, sipping gin-and-tonics, and talked about Apollo 10
and the collapse of the Go-Go funds and the *Pueblo*
case—about everything, in short, except what we were thinking;
and after a while our wives joined us, looking impossibly fresh
and appealing in their rippling summer dresses, and our spirits
revived. We ordered drinks and canapés, and made cracks about
Oh! Calcutta! while the sun sank behind the trees like a vast
orange wafer, and the air cooled. The older kids came from
whatever they'd been doing and joined us, and we felt all of a
sudden paternal and proud: maybe we hadn't done so badly,
after all. We dined on lobster tails and Caesar salad; flash-bulbs
went off in festive sapphire blossoms, white-jacketed waiters
flitted here and there like ghosts; the twilight deepened; there
was a brief, premonitory pause—and at the far end of the terrace
under the high blue-and-amber pavilion the orchestra struck its
first chords, dominated by the brassy, biting horn that, along

with Benny Goodman's clarinet and Tommy Dorsey's trombone, sang for our naive and fragile youth more than any other single thing.

"Harry James!" Chris cried. "Is that really Harry James?"

"The one and only," Dal said. "Price no object."

"Oh, don't be mercenary—feel that beat!" Her eyes sparkled and danced in the swaying pastel light from the paper lanterns. "Are you ready, George?" she demanded with the old mischievous grin. "Ready to swing out?"

"Daddy?—*dance?*" Peg was looking at me as if I were an aardvark.

"You bet. He's a five-alarm rug-cutter."

"Rug-cutter!" Julie laughed wildly. "Oh Mom, you're priceless."

"You just watch our smoke... Oh, you didn't *tell* me you'd got Harry James! Remember Lake Compounce, when those sailors came in and—"

She broke off. I looked up, saw her staring hard into the deepening dusk, her face arrested in its high excitement, shadowed with amazement, wonder, a kind of fright. I knew who it was even before the voice said:

"Damn it all, do I have to get you people out on the floor *every* time?"

It was Russ all right. He was wearing a blue blazer with white flannels—the first real white flannels I'd seen in years. He looked slender and tanned and handsome; his hair, dark as ever, swung back low along his brow, and he still had all of it. We got to our feet in a quick, bumping commotion.

"I knew it!" I said. "I had faith..."

"Did you, Grog?" He smiled at me slowly, shaking hands. He was alone, I knew.

"Well, Russell—Q.—Currier," Chris said lightly. "*Where* have you been?"

"Yeah, where've you been hiding out?" Dal wanted to know. "You've missed the first half."

Talking all at once, we greeted him in a crazy mixture of attitudes. Terry was ebullient, Dal reserved, Nancy very awkward; Chris was the only one of us who looked perfectly at ease.

"You haven't met some of the kids," she was saying. "This is Julie—and Peg Virdon. And you remember Ron."

"Of course—the baby! From Busy School days. All grown up."

Ron rose and he and Russ shook hands, rather formally. I don't know what I expected after all these years—an electric shock of recognition, a violent embrace, some kind of emotional response. But life doesn't move like that, it seems. Their dark eyes met once, held and dropped away indifferently. I was conscious of a taut, nameless anger—involuntarily I glanced at Chris. Something anguished and raging flickered for only an instant over those fine-boned features—then her eyes met mine, and the corners of her lips twitched in a curious, rueful smile.

"I'm so happy to meet you at last," Ingrid was telling Russ. "They said you weren't coming, and we were all so disappointed—"

Now classmates from nearby tables had recognized him; they pressed close around him, and the cries of welcome and congratulation fell on him like warm rain. Standing at our table we all looked at one another for a moment.

"Well, *I* want to dance," Chris announced. "Come on, you crazy hep cats—don't let this glorious music go to waste! One last fling—we deserve one. Don't we deserve one, Georgie?"

"Solid-old-man."

We got out there quickly then. Yes, there was Harry James, out front just the way he used to be, giving the downbeat with two fingers, that gleaming horn dangling with easy professional disdain from his left hand. We'd caught him a thousand years ago at the Riverside, when his vocalist had been a skinny, big-eared, not too confident kid named Frank Sinatra. Like Basie and Herman he had persevered, hung on through the mesmeric bleating of bop, the ear-splitting cacophonies of rock-and-roll, rock-a-billy, acid rock, new sound and God alone knew what else; playing the kind of music we loved. He was still there, and we loved him for that alone. The faces behind him were young, but there were a few we thought we recognized— was that Corky Corcoran on tenor, was that really Louis Bellson on drums?—and we nodded and grinned and even waved up at the bandstand, spinning and gliding as the mood took us, singing fragments of the half-forgotten honey-gold melodies:

I cried for you...
What a fool I used to be...
Now I found two eyes—just a little bit bluer—
I found a heart—just a little bit truer—
I cried for you...
Now it's your turn to cry over me...

Bathed in the past we danced on in the cool, murmuring evening, cutting in on one another the way we used to, recalling the variations, stepping them out, while the kids watched in amazement from the sidelines. We embarrassed them, no question about it—our recaptured fervor, the simple force of our emotion. At one point I went up to Peg and inveigled her out on the floor. She came willingly enough, but it was duty—dull, dead duty: she didn't *believe*, and that was all there was to it. So I let her go and cut in on Dal—the number was *Blues in the Night*—just to shake him up.

"All right, Georgie," Chris said. "Let's show 'em!" Her sage-green dress was of the thinnest cotton, and short enough to show off those fine legs and exciting knees I admired so. It had a deep, square neckline and soft Camelot sleeves—the simplicity that was always Chris. Beyond her slim head I could see the eyes of the other wives slide over her with that ever-so-faint tightening of the lids which means only one thing; I laughed out loud.

"Are you making fun of me, Georgie?"

"*Me*—no! Heaven forbid..."

Around us were women I'd known as rather dowdy girls, made up now to the teeth, there were even (Nancy had informed me crisply) a few discreet face-lifts; there were the old sought-after beauties of Smith and Wellesley and Bryn Mawr...and they all paled beside Chris. It was true, what I'd known back in 1940—hers was the beauty that never changed: the high promise of life itself sustained it.

"I was just thinking how happy I am right now," I said.

"Good...Don't make *too* much of it now, will you?" She paused. "I mean, it isn't absolutely everything—"

"It's only *almost* absolutely everything."

We laughed together as if at an old joke only we understood. Up on the stand Harry James lowered the trumpet from his lips and smiled down at us, his eyes ice-blue in the soft light, and

Chris gave him back her exuberant, vulnerable smile. Near us Ron was dancing with Peg, a curious half-twist, half-fox trot, touching and not touching, a style that irritated me. Chris saw me watching them.

"That's the first time I've seen him dancing since—since he graduated."

"He's all right," I said.

"No, he's not. But maybe he will be. I pray he will be."

"So do I . . . with all my heart," I told her in a low, even tone, though there was no need to drop my voice, the brass team was blaring high and shrill: *A woman's a two-faced, a worrisome thing, who'll leave you to sing—the bluuuues—in the niiiight . . .*

"—He's never forgiven me," I heard myself say.

"He's never forgiven any of us." She smiled at me sadly, shook her hair back. The number ended and we paused, clapping. The band broke into *Prince Charming*.

"Dear George. It's funny. He's always in the middle of *our* lives, isn't he? Ron. As though he were our son—yours and mine . . . It's funny, isn't it?"

"No," I said, "no, it's not. If—"

A hand clapped me on the shoulder then, once—a single tap that brought back every prom of our youth as nothing else could. Russ, looking romantic and eager—and so young. He's beaten the rap, I thought with a resentful twinge; somehow he's found out how to cheat the clock. Prince Charming.

"Just a brief turn on the floor," he was saying, "for old time's sake?"

"But of course," I answered in my broadest French accent.

"Actually I'm not sure you can still keep up with me, Chrissie."

"Try me!" she said, and her green eyes flashed at him. "Just try me."

They moved off without effort, and I watched them go. His limp had vanished, the years had erased that; and Chris was Chris. They swung into their Lindy, breaking, closing, perfectly controlled; the floor began to clear away a bit around them. Someone called, "Just like Norumbega!" and the other faces watched them—flushed, indulgent, bound in memory. I saw Terry on the stand talking to James, who nodded and bent over his rhythm section: the beat broke, altered to rhumba, then conga, then the Charleston—and Chris and Russ, after a sudden hitch, laughing, were shifting styles flawlessly, too; and then James took them back to a wickedly fast *Sweet Georgia Brown,* the brass sections on their feet, horns swinging like cannon out over the ballroom. Ron and Julie were gazing at their mother in stupefaction, their mouths open. Nearly everyone had stopped dancing now; there were cries and bursts of cheering:

"Hubba hubba!"

"Let's go—*Totem Pole . . .*"

"Our-team-is-re-e-e-ed *hot!*"

The number closed in a tumultuous crash of drums and horns, with Chris still spinning and swirling, her skirt snapping green around her thighs. The roar surpassed even the response to *In the Mood* the night before; we swept toward them instinctively. Chris was flushed and distracted, laughing.

"You!" she called to a grinning Terry. "You perfect sneak!—I saw you up there."

"I had to see if you could still swing out."

"Least they can give us is a statuette of John Q. Harvard," Russ said. "After that. Or a miniature goldfish." He was pale under his tan, pressing a handkerchief to his cheeks.

"I thought for a while there it might be coronary time," Dal told him.

Russ laughed boisterously. "Mel's here, isn't he? and anyway, what a way to go. That's still your line, isn't it?"

"That's still my line."

That got us rolling; we called for all the old tunes we remembered, or thought we remembered. Chris was as besieged as a USO hostess—everyone wanted to dance with her; her face was flushed to that deep apricot glow, her head was flung back happily. She danced with Russ again, and then again, a rhumba, her lithe body turning indolently under his upraised arm in the glow of the paper lanterns. Dal's eyes narrowed, watching them.

"Old Chris is really having herself a ball, isn't she?"

"Well," Terry said, "you've got to admit you could never keep up with her out there."

Dal turned and looked at Gilligan for a moment. "That's right, Trog-o. I never could." And he moved off toward the bar, slow and purposeful as a badger.

By now the floor was really crowded. I danced with Marge and Mai Soong and again with Nancy. At one point I saw Ron and Peg, their eyes closed, holding each other very close, barely moving, and my throat all at once ached with a sadness I couldn't fathom and didn't want to.

> *Each old refrain*
> *Keeps returning as I remain*
> *With my memories of blue champagne—*
> *To toast the dream that was you...*

And finally, flushed and noisy, we piled into the Empress— nine of us: a new record, Terry joyfully proclaimed—and drove back to Cambridge through the balmy North Shore night, singing *Stairway to the Stars* and *Skylark* and *Sentimental Journey* and finally, inevitably *Stardust,* with Chris's sweet pure contralto soaring up out of our wobbly chorus; and it hadn't been 29 years at all, there hadn't been any World War II or Joe McCarthy or Bay of Pigs or Assassination or Vietnam, no shocks or gulfs or losses; what the hell—it was, as Dal said wonderingly, only yesterday...

One pays for all one's pleasures, however; and the bill was rendered back at the Hasty Pudding Club, improbably—nay, impossibly—our Reunion headquarters, where the festivities went racketing giddily along.

"You realize this is the first time I've ever seen the inside of this snotty place?" Dal muttered, watching Conger who looked (and indeed was) perfectly at home here.

"Inside!" Mel retorted, his eyes dark as onyx, "—I never even knew where the hell it was..."

It was then that Coker Blenham asked if we'd meet with him on a matter of some urgency; we nodded, and watched him move on to Blazer, and then Spider Hoadley, a senior stockbroker with Dale, Hallowell, and then Walt Fenstermacher, who was head of Phoenix Electronics. Upstairs, in some kind of committee room, Coker moved to the head of a long table and stood there while we took seats, hands jammed in his pockets, his belly straining against his alligator belt. The bland, genial smile was gone now, and there was a hint of strain around those deceptively pale blue eyes.

"I hope you're nicely smashed," he began. "Full of nostalgia and gratitude for all the things Harvard did for you—or *would* have if you'd been here to enjoy them, instead of wandering around on Okinawa or Anzio Beach. Because we are in trouble.

Serious trouble. We're $200,000 short on the Gift." He paused, looking around the table. "I know you've all given generously— some of you more than generously— and you know how grateful we are to each of you. But the grim facts are that we now have"—he glanced at his watch—exactly 42 hours until our Gift Chairman has to deliver that check on the podium. And frankly, I can't hear him saying—he's worked his tail off on this—I can't hear him saying, 'I'm awfully sorry, Mr. President, the class couldn't meet our pledge, we crapped out in the clutch. The Double Four is a fourflusher'— somehow I just can't hear him saying those words. That's why I've called you up here—you're the only men who can bail us out. If you don't cut it, we go down."

There was another silence, a longer one. Downstairs the band had just finished *Chattanooga Choo-Choo* and there were cries of "Yayyy! Go, go, go!"

"Hold on, Coke," I said. "I'm just a poor textbook editor—I don't even know what I'm doing in this august company. I've already given just about everything I own except my soul and the mortgage on the house."

"We don't want your money, Virdon. We wouldn't take it if you gave it to us." Coker Blenham was grinning at me broadly now, and I began to see why all the big-time accounts at Vance, Siergerson were so frantic to get him. "I brought you up here as conscience and inspiration." He turned to the others, and now he wasn't smiling. "I have some interesting information for you heavy hitters to ponder. George, here, has given more than any of you." He stared stolidly into their surprise. "That's right. In proportion to his income. I know almost exactly what each one of you makes—I've made it my business to know, and you can forgive me or condemn me as the spirit moves you." He leaned forward over the table, his round, affable face suddenly quite hard. "Some of you guys make more in one year than George will in a lifetime—there he sits, over there in that musty office on Marlborough Street, working half the night putting together text books for your wayward kids to read...and *he* comes in with it! He knows what Harvard's meant to him. And so do you guys—and you're sitting there on your butts with '44's reputation on the line..."

Now he deftly shifted gears, switched from threat to flattery. "Look, it's bad enough we can't match '43's gift—half those bastards are fourth-generation millionaires, I know, I know. At least you've made it on your own. I know, you're all hassled up over the Trouble, I've been listening to you since we got here. Some of you think the place is crawling with bomb-heaving Bolsheviks. Book-burnings in the Yard, group sex on the steps of Widener. Well, that's pure bullshit, and you know it just as well as I do. All this activist crap is going to dry up and blow away, and what's going to remain is—Harvard. In a word. And it will."

As if on cue the orchestra burst into a swing version of *Wintergreen,* our old half-time band favorite at the Stadium. Coker led the laughter, said: "*Somebody* down there loves us." He opened his hands. "Look—it's the one, single, solitary time in your misspent lives Harvard is asking you to stand up and be counted: our 25th. Come on now boys. Walt, Spider, Dal—I'm pleading with you. Don't let us down. Not now."

There was another short pause—then Dal threw himself back in his chair and said: "All right. I'm game." He looked directly across the table. "Currier?—what do you say? I'll match anything you do." He grinned easily. "You always said I owe you a case of choice—I've always felt you owe me one."

Russ glanced at him sharply. "Some case," he laughed awkwardly.

"That's right. Vintage 1940. A really good year..." Dal nodded slowly, his eyes still on Russ. "I'll put up fifty—in memory of Jean-Jean and Rhino. Will you match it?"

"... Fifty thousand," Russ muttered. "Jesus Christ, Dalrymple, you've got to be kidding—"

"Unless of course you don't feel they deserve it."

Their eyes locked; it was utterly quiet in the room. Watching them I realized the dance wasn't over. I glanced at Blenham; he was standing perfectly motionless, letting the silence grow in order to increase the pressure.

Then Russ said in a tight, dry voice: "All right. I'll match you."

"Wonderful!" Coker exclaimed. "That's the old college try."

"But I can't raise it immediately, just like that—it'll have to be a pledge..."

"That's good enough for me." Blenham's voice was genial and booming again. "All right, now who else will come in on this?"

"Blazer?" Dal said idly; he seemed strangely depressed by the duel. "You knew Rhino as well as any of us. Except Mel."

Blassingham rolled his eyes at the ceiling. "Okay, hit me for ten. Jesus, I can't let old Virdon show me up for a piker."

The palaver went on. After some hassling Dal stretched and said: "Hell, it's getting late—we're missing all the fun. Come on, Walt," he said to Fenstermacher, "stop your pussyfooting—let's see you part with some of those big-assed electronic profits of yours." He looked down the table coolly. "We'll pick it up, Coker—Walt and I. Whatever you need to make up the difference."

As we left the room I saw Russ's gaze, black with anger, burning into the back of Dal's stolid, sunburned neck.

6

"OH, THESE KIDS don't want to hear about all that stuff," Russ was saying lightly to Ingrid. "Sacrifice and pro patria mori. And they're right, you know? They're absolutely right. That's all dead ashes."

We were slumped in various states and stages of exhaustion in the Dalrymples' suite—near the very window, in fact, from which Dal had lowered a girl named Sue Trumbull on a rope of tied-together bedsheets one dark night into a foot of freshly fallen snow. We'd closed the Pudding, and Dal had invited several of us in for a nightcap. Some of the kids had come in from their dance at Dunster House after that, and we'd turned to them rather awkwardly: the generation gap had never seemed wider than it did at that late hour—their apparently inexhaustible energy had begun to irritate us a bit. Sometimes I think half the world's troubles come about because people won't go to bed when they should.

"What a shame you weren't here for the symposia yesterday,"

Dal informed Russ suddenly. "You'd have been a bleeding hero."

"Well, I'll tell you this, Dalrymple. If I were this kid's age"—he indicated Mel Strasser's boy Jeff—"I'd have been out there—I'd have hit University Hall with the first wave."

Dal studied him a moment. "Yeah. You probably would have, at that."

"Please," Chris cried, "no more politics, okay?"

"Why not?"

"Because this is neither the time nor the place."

"If this isn't, when is?" Leaning back in his chair, one arm dangling, Russ studied Dal a moment, a thin half-smile on his lips. "You know why you're hot about it, Wog? *Really* why? Because the kids dug up all that dirty laundry and hung it out to dry. That's what you never wanted out in the open. Right?"

"Oh, come off it, Currier! Those kids broke in like any second-story man, they stole private documents, burned them like a bunch of delinquents—and you want to build them up into a lot of Emile Zolas."

"And so they're supposed to keep waltzing meekly off to your big business war, without a murmur of dissent. Is that it?"

"Oh for Christ sake, Currier!"

"Dal—" Chris said sharply, but now he was sore, he wasn't about to drop it. The dance still wasn't over.

"Look," his voice was hoarse and blurred from too much liquor, too little sleep, "it wasn't a very pleasant business, our war—we all did things we didn't want to do. But we had the maturity to see it in the bigger context. We knew who the enemy was…"

"Well, that's more than we can say, Mr. Dalrymple," Jeff Strasser said quietly. "We're not so sure of that, you see." He looked around the room, a bit intimidated by the gathering silence, but constrained to go on. "That's what I've tried to tell Dad—your generation never *wanted* to rattle the cage, you never wanted to question things. We do."

"That's tommyrot—we questioned plenty, from the Depression right on through NRA, Lend-Lease… We didn't rush happily off to war—ask George, or Terry, or anybody here if we did." Dal jabbed at the nose-piece of his glasses. "Why do you have to make us out such unfeeling monsters? It's probably hard for you to believe, but we were once every bit as troubled as you are now. We thought we—"

"No!" I turned, we all did. Ron was on his feet, his face taut and strained. "How *can* we relate to it—your show-window world? No—you taught us about America the Generous, you covered up that other world, the *real* world—you wouldn't look at it! But you knew it was there, all along—a stinking black sewer—"

"All right, Ron, that's enough!" Dal snapped. "Let's drop it, all right?"

"Let him speak," Russ broke in. "This isn't one of your dummy corporations now, Dalrymple. What's the matter—you afraid of what you might hear?"

"Power demands responsibility," Dal hammered thickly on, trying to ignore Russ, his hand chopping at the air, "the business world—it means obligations, a lot of very hard choices, you'll see, it's not a—"

"How about the ego-trips and joy rides," Ron came back, "what about them? You wouldn't give them up for anything, don't tell me you would! All those fat profits turned into napalm."

"Ron," Chris said in visible distress, "you know better than that, your father's never been into anything remotely like that—he's given a great deal to all kinds of—"

"Sop." His lip curled in savage contempt. "To sugar the pill. You never cared—you wanted the money and the power, and everything else could go to hell on a sled! Sure, what's wrong with starching a few hundred thousand radical kids, as long as the old plant keeps humming along!"

I didn't know where to look, or what to do. I stole a glance at Peg: her eyes met mine, flat and steady and coolly condemning. I was shocked in spite of myself, in spite of what I knew; I tried to ride it down, and I couldn't. We'd loved them so, these kids of ours, and we'd failed them—that was clear enough: we'd bought them hula hoops and TV sets and sent them to expensive schools and taken them with us to Copenhagen or Taormina; but we hadn't done it right, somehow. Of all the things we might have been we wanted to be good parents—and it was here, precisely here, we'd failed. We'd sought their love so desperately, and they'd withheld it because—because we didn't command their respect any more. Was that it? We stared at them hollowly— caught out in our fear.

"Ron, that's not fair," Dal was stammering, "—good Christ, kid, *I* didn't send you to Vietnam..."

"No? No? If you didn't, who did? Money, you're always saying money is the real power, capital calls the tune—all right, then! Why did you let it happen, tear half the world apart, brush-fire wars everywhere, Jesus, *brush-fire wars*—! You had the power—why did you give in on everything?" he cried, and now the naked anguish in his face was terrible to see. "No, you sold us out, you sent us out there because you couldn't stop lying, you couldn't face the truth about yourselves—!"

Again a silence. I glanced at Dal—I couldn't for the life of me tell whose expression was more agonized, his or Ron's.

"*Ron*," Chris said in a low, even voice, "Ron, you have no right to speak to your father like this. You will apologize, do you hear?"

"... No, Mother." And now his eyes were full of tears. "Not about this. About anything else. But not about this."

He turned quickly and walked out of the room. Peg rose and followed him, and then Jeff and Julie and the Blassingham girl.

Nancy said: "Peg—!"

"Let her go," I told her.

"But it's late..."

"Yes. Isn't it."

There was a little stir of movement in the room. Dal looked stunned, as if he'd been hit on the side of the head; those white spots had appeared at the corners of his nostrils, but there was no fight in him. None whatever. Across the room, still slouched in the big chair, Russ was twisting and twisting the seal ring on his finger—an almost eager expression on his face. Chris was watching them both; the tears were glittering in her eyes. On the phonograph Frank Sinatra was calmly singing *All Or Nothing At All.*

Nancy routed me out before five the next—the same—morning. I'd only just crawled into bed around three, my mouth woolly and my head hammering. I asked her crossly if she had gone crazy or had merely decided to be impossible.

"George, she hasn't come in. Peg. She hasn't come in at all. It's daylight!"

"Damn good chance."

"She's never done anything like this before—George! Did you hear me? Are you awake?"

"Come on, Nan. She can take care of herself."

. "George, I'm worried! God knows what they might have got into, these kids."

I dragged myself out of bed, pulled on some clothes and went downstairs. The Empress wasn't there, but I wasn't worried especially—Ron had asked me if he could borrow her after we'd got back from the North Shore and I'd been happy to give him the key again.

I crossed Memorial Drive and walked along the river bank, watching the morning mist curling up from the pewter sheen of the water. It was going to be clear again, and a scorcher. Off toward Watertown there was a sound of heavy equipment grinding: tractors. After a while I strolled back to the house and sat down on the entry steps, my hands on my knees. In about ten minutes the Empress rolled up, loaded with kids. They were chattering and laughing and shushing one another; then they began climbing out, untangling like a lot of happy young reptiles, stretching and groaning. Except for the jeans and guitars and the profusion of long hair they looked pretty much the way we had. Sandra Strasser was wearing a purple tank top that had lettered on it: *Follow me to an uncomplicated love.* Softly they called farewells, insults and other nonsense—there was the same old hilarity over having done something wickedly daring I remembered. Then a boy I didn't know turned and I saw he was wearing a T-shirt stamped with the clenched red fist of the Revolt, and around it was stenciled, WAR IS GOOD BUSINESS—INVEST YOUR SON, and I could feel myself stop smiling.

Ron was lifting a ditty bag out of the floor of the back seat. Peg swung herself toward him under the wheel, and he took her hand—an easy, warm gesture. She said something, then held up her face to his as though it were a mirror, and they kissed. He murmured something in reply and she nodded, and ran her hand softly up and down his chest. She saw me then; but instead of pulling away nervously she smiled at me—her steady, quiet smile. I got to my feet feeling middle-aged and inept.

"Well," I said, rather creakily, "big night on the town."

"Hello, Mr. Virdon," Ron said. "Thanks for the Empress." And to Peg: "See you for lunch?"

"Groove."

He bounded off up the stairwell.

"Oh, Pa," Peg said, "it was lovely! We went to the shore, this place Jeff knew about, there's a cliff and a beach. And we sang songs, and watched the sun come up, all big and orange—I never knew it was so huge. Right at the horizon, I mean."

"It is, isn't it?" I said. "Your mother's a bit upset."

She looked at me then. "I'm grown up now, Pa."

"I know that," I said. "But she doesn't."

"She'll have to learn it then. Remember what you said that time in France? by the castle? About what's true and what isn't, and lying to yourself about it?"

"Yes," I said. "I remember."

"Well," she grinned, "maybe you'd better say it to Mother. Again." Walking up the stairs with me she suddenly put her arm around my waist. "Hey, I'm—I just fell in love, Pa."

"Have you, now," I said, and winked at her. "And how do you know that?"

"I don't know. I just am."

"That's the only way," I said.

She nodded rapidly, "With—you'll never guess. With Ron! Isn't that weird? I mean, after all these years?"

I hugged her; I felt obscurely pleased, and also saddened—a sharp sinking and lifting of my heart. She was so young!—And yet she was so steady, too.

"Well, honey," I said. "Well, honey-girl."

The final formal dinner dance was at the Copley—now brashly renovated and renamed the Sheraton-Plaza, though we stubbornly persisted in calling it the Copley—where we'd held our last prom, that Yale Game weekend before Pearl Harbor; the dance Russ and Kay Madden had tried to pretend they weren't seeing each other. Maybe the setting was just unlucky. Ron and Peg and the rest of the kids were off on some excursion of their own, but the fall-out from the explosion of the night before still lay over us. We were all off-balance.

No one ever looked better in a white dinner jacket than Russ; and tonight he was decked out in his maroon cummerbund, too. The old headlong excitement was working in him—it was as if yesterday's confrontations with Dal had tripped a hidden spring. During dinner he regaled us with a succession of stories, the last about eating goat with the hair still on it, under the fierce eye of a Bedouin chief while on location in the Sahara.

"Weren't you afraid you'd get deathly sick?" Chris asked him.

She looked spectacular in a Liz Payne original of white matte silk jersey which crossed ingeniously over her breasts and then fell away in soft, sinuous folds—in that classic Grecian line; her arms were bare. Her only jewelry was tiny gold scallop-shell earrings Dal had had designed for her.

"Couldn't afford to," Russ answered. "To have upchucked would have been a mortal insult—they'd probably have massacred us all on the spot and thrown us in the pot, too."

"You're supposed to belch lustily, I believe," Dal offered. Tonight he was taciturn, almost surly; he kept wrenching his neck around in the collar of his dress shirt.

"Dal!" Nancy protested.

"Fact of desert life. Louder you belch the greater the compliment to the cuisine."

"Did you belch lustily, Russ?" Chris asked him; she seemed unnaturally vivacious, on edge; one hand kept going to her throat.

He shook his head. "I was too busy averting my eyes."

We laughed half-heartedly. The trouble with reunions is that every moment is programmed, the dials have all been set too high; there's no chance to sit and think anything through, or simply let your nerves disentangle. Everyone is running on pure emotion—nostalgia, ambition, resentment, regret—and pure emotion has no gyroscope, it soars and plunges like an unbalanced kite; it is sure to impale itself on a tree branch sooner or later. In our exhaustion we drank far too much, danced listlessly with one another's wives, or wandered around affecting a hearty camaraderie with men we'd never particularly cared for. Even Harry James looked weary, watching us from the stand, thinking perhaps of all those errant college generations he'd made music for, vanished bands and nights of glory, and young men who'd died in wars that seemed important at the time...

The evening rocked along, but not convivially. At some point I found myself standing at the bar with Dal, half-listening to Chid Bierce recounting his efforts to start master point tournaments at his club; I looked away, and met Conger's bland, frozen-pudding face. I was silent, but Conger nodded to us, falsely congenial.

"Well, there's no flame like an old flame," he observed, gazing airily about him. "How permissive of you, Dalrymple. Though I gather anything goes these days. Anything." His codfish mouth drew down primly, but there was no disguising the gleam of smug delight in his eyes. "Do you suppose they'll come back?"

"What the hell are you talking about, Conger?" I demanded.

"Why, Currier and the irrepressible Chris Dalrymple. They took off some time ago in your museum piece. Didn't you know?" He started to say more, saw something in my face that changed his mind, and moved away into the crowd with a shrug.

"The Empress?" Dal was saying. "Gone off in the Empress?" He stared at me blankly, then his face hardened. "All right, Grog. What goes on?"

"I don't know," I said. "He asked me for the key—he said he wanted to take the Empress for a spin. One last time, he said. I didn't know anything about—this..."

He gave me another long, very hard look, then swung away to the bar and turned his back on me.

That finished whatever festivity was left in the evening. We hung around for a while longer, but they didn't come back and it certainly didn't look as though they were going to. Dal was practically glued to the bar by then; I pried him away as casually as I could, and we took one of the chartered buses back to Cambridge. Of course I had to explain to the others that Russ had borrowed the Empress, and Chris's absence let the cat out of the bag. Nancy turned elated and garrulous then, in a way that set my teeth on edge. Dal was completely silent.

Back at the house we went through the fire door into the Dalrymples' suite. I'd hoped against hope they might be here, but they weren't. Dal stared absently into the fireplace for a moment, then walked off down the hall, and I heard the front door slam. I started after him.

"Where are you going?" Nancy said.

"I'm going to keep him company for a while."

"Oh honestly, George..." Her expression was a nice balance of gratification and annoyance. "*You* can't do any good—can't you see that? It's gone beyond that, now."

I moved up to her. "Nan," I said, "Dal stood by me on the worst day of my whole life. If he wants me to stick around, I'm going to."

I caught up with him outside, by the high wrought-iron gates. He turned and saw who it was, waited indifferently, and then moved on. In silence we walked along the embankment; the river gleamed like ink under the lights. In the center of the bridge Dal stopped and leaned on the parapet, gazing downstream. A group of kids was sprawled there on the grass, drinking beer, and a transistor radio was playing that fine Beatles tune, *Strawberry Fields Forever*.

"Can a bald, tired old grad find happiness at his 25th?" he said with a radio announcer's falsely genial inflection. "Come back to ivy-draped Cambridge and find out. If you've got the guts for it ... Look at me," he said suddenly. His voice was thick, but he wasn't drunk. "No—go ahead. Take a look. You think you're looking at your old hot-shot roommate, you think you're facing a media-and-plastics entre*p*reneur—well, that's where you're wrong. Dead wrong. What you're really looking at is a villain. Yep. *The* villain, Grog-o. Ain't that delicious? Eating the Poor, Defenseless Younger Generation on a platter of rolled steel. With napalm sauce."

"He's all right," I answered. I was relieved that he wanted to talk, and that he was launched on Ron. "It's not you, it's the whole system. He knows you're the best of it. They've got to blow off—and he does especially. Don't you remember how we ranted and roared at everything when we got home, back in '46? Now *we're* a symbol, that's all."

"Sure, sure. Everything's a symbol." He was silent a moment, listening to the kids' laughter, the tinny racket of the radio. "But to tell me off like that, to accuse me ... the hate in his eyes! Did you see it, Grog? Did you? The *hate* ..." He gripped me by the arm, hard. "*Am* I to blame, George? the way he said? Am I?"

"No ... Well, hell, we all are, in a way." I wanted to say exactly the right thing, and I knew I couldn't. "We didn't start the lousy, frigging war—but sure, we should have done more to stop it."

"Yeah, sure. I know." He started walking again. "But to blast me like that, in front of everybody—"

"It just came out," I answered, wishing I were home now and in bed, wishing there had never been a 25th Reunion or a Harvard University or a Boston. "It's been boiling around there inside him—and then it all came rushing out."

"He's so violent, Grog!"

"Yeah—he speaks before he thinks, he always did. That quick Italian thing—"

I froze there, blinking, shocked at what I'd said, not really believing I could have said those words. But I had. I certainly had. Jesus. I glanced at Dal with real horror. His gaze was perfectly impassive. Those tell-tale white blotches at his nostrils hadn't appeared; there was only the flexing of a muscle in his cheek.

"I know," he answered quietly.

"—I don't know what I'm talking about." I said, "I'm stewed to the eyeballs. Too much booze."

"I tried to be a father to him," he went on, as though I hadn't spoken. "A real father. I did. Tried to—you know, teach him things here and there, listen to him, talk his hang-ups out with him. You know. As much of a father as I knew how to be, anyway."

"... You knew, then," was all I could manage to say.

"Long ago. Chris told me. But I knew, long before that, even. Hell, you'd have to be blind." He wrenched his neck around in the dress collar. "I didn't care. I wanted Chris—she was all I wanted, all I've ever wanted. In this world. That's God's truth, Grog. Nothing else ever mattered, beside her..." And his eyes glittered in the car lights. "The one, single, solitary thing—"

Abruptly he turned off the drive and started along the bridle path past the Newell Boat House. I moved beside him, saying nothing, furious with myself for the slip—and yet also curiously glad: it had struck down a barrier that should never have been there between us. Wasn't that true?

"All these years," he was saying, his voice low and even. "I wanted to give her everything, Grog. And the boy. Everything I could. Christ, I even went skin-diving with her in Jamaica, hunting for some goofy sea shell she needed for her collection. Can you imagine *me—skin-diving?* I was scared shitless the whole time." He tried to chuckle, but it didn't come off. "But it never reached her. Never touched her heart, you see. And I always loved her, even though I knew I didn't deserve her—not really."

He scuffed his shoes in the soft earth of the path. "Son of a bitch used to run cross-country down here, didn't he? The short-distance runner... Now she's left me. I guess I always knew she would. Sooner or later. What could I expect?"

"She hasn't," I said, but my voice lacked conviction. "She wouldn't do that."

"I knew it," he went on doggedly. "I always knew he was what she wanted. That I couldn't ever make it right for her, no matter what I did. I knew. But I tried, anyway. Oh Christ, how I tried! ... Well, what the hell. What the hell."

"She thinks the world of you," I murmured. "I know she does."

"Yeah, sure ... First the boy, and now Chris. All these years, and he's still beaten me ... Jesus God," he cried all at once, "can't he leave a man *anything*—? Anything at all?"

He began to weep, a tight, rhythmic shaking of his big shoulders. "I was all wrong, George. All stupid wrong—I thought if I loved, kept on loving, gave with all my heart, it would be enough, it would make up for all the rest. But you see?—it never does. It never does."

I stood there watching him, the naked suffering in his face. He'd lived with that bleak knowledge all those years. All those years on years. He'd gone on, father to another man's son, a good father, a loving husband. A solid man. That was worth something, wasn't it? Jesus God, wasn't it?

He walked on again, aimlessly. The river was dark and still; the reflected lights along shore drifted in its depthless expanse like small, elusive moons. I reached out and put my hand on his shoulder.

"Look, Dal, don't jump to a lot of hopeless conclusions now. It may not be—"

I broke off. We'd come upon the car so suddenly, parked there where a car wasn't supposed to be, on the edge of the path under the trees, that for a second or two I simply didn't believe what I was seeing. It was unmistakably, impossibly, the Empress; and Russ and Chris were sitting in it—I could make out her white gown, his white jacket. I didn't know what to do. I began to draw Dal away, toward the water—then he, too, recognized the car and stopped. He made a soft, inarticulate sound deep in his throat. Then he swung completely around and started walking back toward the bridge.

But Chris had seen us—her door opened, she came toward us quickly.

"Dal?" she called softly. Behind her I could see Russ getting out on the driver's side. "Dal? George?" she called again. "Is that you?"

Dal stopped then. He shook off my hand but he stood there, his head down, waiting; he looked like an old bear, cornered and beaten, waiting for the final rush.

"What a crazy coincidence!" Her laughter sounded high in pitch, a bit forced in the night air. "What are you two doing down here? We've been out to Norumbega, we were just—"

"—I don't want to hear it," Dal said hoarsely; his face was drained of all color. "Let's drop it, all right?"

She paused, her eyes going from one of us to the other and back again, her body caught in a sudden fierce agitation. Russ had come up silently behind her.

"Yes—Russ asked me to go for a drive with him, a quick spin for old time's sake, and then we got to—"

"I don't want to hear about it," Dal repeated, "I can see how it is—Jesus, don't you think I *know*...?"

"Dal," she cried then. "What are you thinking? Are you actually—Dal! You fool! You total fool...Look at me!"

He did; we both did. Her head was back, her breasts heaving under the soft, pale silk, her eyes flashing; she looked passionate and angry and utterly beautiful. "All these years, and you don't even believe—"

"Chris—"

"No!—You *will* listen to me!...All right," and she whirled around to Russ, her hair whipping about her head. "Go on! Tell him. Tell him what happened between us tonight—everything!"

"Chris, let's—"

"Oh, no! You don't know what to believe—is that it? All right, believe it now! Go on, Russ. Tell him!"

The two men stood there staring at each other hard. Then Russ's glance wavered away, he looked down at his feet.

"She—I want her to come away with me. To Paris," he said with sudden urgency. "A new life. I told her I love her—from the beginning I've loved her, I know it now, I need her." He stopped, ran his hand through the fine black hair. "She turned me down. Flat. Just now. I can't believe it, somehow—I mean when you think of all we had together, all we *were* together—"

"Go on," Chris broke in on him grimly.

"She said—she loves you."

"All right," Chris said. "You see? You wanted it all—there it is...What's the *matter* with you?" she cried hotly, and now she included me in her angry gaze. "Haven't you learned anything? all these years? Chrissie, our Chrissie, the party simply can't begin without our Chris. You made a mascot out of me, all of

you—locked me up in the past. Time Capsule 1940. Now cut it
out! I'm not a mascot, or some keeper of the eternal flame—or a
statue in the Luxembourg Gardens, either... why can't you see
me, *me!*—not your stupid romantic idea of me. I'm flesh and
blood, a woman who made some big mistakes and lived with
them—I climbed out of that quaint time capsule... I haven't just
been cataloging shells all these years, bringing up our kids. I'm a
person who changes, I've *grown up*—and by God, it's time all of
you did, too!

"Of course I love Russ," she turned to Dal, "I'll always love
that Russ—a part of me will, anyway. I loved the girl I was then
too, running on the beach, sailing kites. Only it just so happens I
stopped being that girl a long, long time ago..."

She shook her head. There was the same tightening at the
corners of her eyes I remembered from that far-away night when
Mel had examined the cut on her forehead. And she had laughed
that ringing, valiant laugh of hers and cried: "You're both
loony—sometimes you Fox Entry types carry loyalty too far!"

"We've come a long way since the Quonset-hut days, Dal,"
she was saying now in a very different tone. "We've spent a lot of
years growing up, you and I—hard years, some of them. We've
learned to face the present together. Yes, the present! Don't
forget it. I've watched you, and helped you, I've seen you damn
near kill yourself to make a life for us, a good, full life—and here
you still don't believe I love you. You idiot! You've been a father,
a *real* father to my son—"

She turned passionately toward Russ again and I thought in
deep alarm, Oh no—she's not going to tell him here, now, it'll
kill Dal if she does...

"Yes, Ron," she was saying hotly, "the *baby,* you call him,
from Busy School days, it might just interest you to know—"

But she checked herself then with a visible effort, and said:
"—to know Dal's been a wonderful father to him, loving and
understanding and helpful. Don't be misled by last night. Don't
be!—Ron's a man, Dal," she said, quite softly now, "he's even
man enough to talk back to you, speak his mind. But *you* did it,
you helped make this son of ours into a man. You made it
possible. *He's* grown up, too—that's part of it." Her eyes flashed
up at Russ. "You grow up out of loving, out of hurting—not out
of games or movies, or living in some romantic past that never
was."

"—You're punishing me," Russ burst out, "you're trying to get back at me for what's over and gone! What we had was so rare, Chrissie—such a rare thing..."

"Yes," she answered slowly. "It was." Her eyes were dark now, deadly grave. "I loved you so completely I couldn't believe you didn't love me in the same way, I couldn't even *imagine*—" She broke off. "Love is a funny thing, Rusty. It's like that sea god that kept changing his identity every time someone grabbed hold of him—"

"No," he cried in great agitation, "that's not so, there's only one kind of love and it's forever—that's what I didn't see! But I see it now, I..."

"Oh, Russ. Russ. You troubled, troublesome boy." Her lovely head cocked, she studied him a moment in frank wonder. "You haven't aged a day, do you know that? That's just what's wrong. Handsome, witty, talented, wealthy, well-born... they gave you all the graces, didn't they? All but one. All but the capacity to *care*—to the point of suffering. You've never really cared. Have you, Rusty?"

"That's not true—"

"Yes. Yes, it *is* true... You've forced your passions," she said without rancor. "You're forcing them now."

"I'm not, I tell you I'm not! Don't you think I even know my own feelings? You're punishing me again, it's—"

"No." And she smiled at him sadly. "Oh, no. I've wanted to, sometimes—but I never could. I can't now. It's simply a law of nature, Rusty. And you've violated it. A betrayal of life itself... Style," she said, evenly, holding his gaze with hers, "you always used to talk about style, Russ. Well, let's go out with a little honesty—and a lot of style." She paused. "We owe it to each other. At least that."

Russ started to protest, broke off with a wordless exclamation. Then he laughed once. "Yeah, you're right—this scene's played long enough. Wouldn't you say?" He set his hands, thumbs extended, as though to frame it all. "End four shot, dolly out to medium long shot of Empress, backed by Stadium; slow dissolve... Only what if there was no film in the effing camera all the while?"

But this time none of us laughed. He looked at us one last moment, shrugged and walked swiftly off toward Larz Anderson Bridge, his jacket white against the night. We stood there together, watching him go. Then Dal reached out and took Chris's hand.

"I'm sorry, honey," he murmured. "I sold you short. I didn't mean to."

"Don't belittle what we are, Dal." She looked up into his face, searchingly. "What we did. We learned to face the present together, you and I. It took some doing. Don't forget it."

He nodded. "I was afraid—that's the trouble. I've always been."

"Everyone's afraid," she said lightly; her mood had changed with Russ's departure. "Isn't that right, Georgie?"

"Amen to that," I said.

"George has been scared by experts. And he was as bad a romantic as Russ or you. Well—almost. In his own way. But he got over it." She winked at me, and I saw the old lively mood had taken her. "He grew up more than any of you," she said to Dal. "You know that? You put *him* in a capsule, too—the loyal retainer. But he wouldn't stay there." She put her free arm through mine and hugged it once. "Well," she said, "shall we drive on back in style?"

So it was over. Where it had all started. The next day we said our uneasy farewells. We really had nothing more to say to each other, and we knew it. Russ flew east to Paris, alone; the Dalrymples flew west to Chicago; we Virdons climbed into the Empress, and I looped around past Mem Hall and the Square before starting for home, driving slowly, because I knew this was for the last time. Amanda was fretful and tired; Peg was holding her new-found emotion deep inside her, a little frightened, and very proud. Only Nancy was light-hearted.

"What a fun time!" She threw herself back in the seat and placed her hands behind her head, something she always did when she was pleased with things. "What a delightful change. For all four of us."

"And you were so reluctant to go," I reminded her.

"I know—isn't that silly?"

And she smiled at me, wrinkling her nose, and gazed serenely at the feathered canopy of Chestnut Hill. She was content—it had all worked out so satisfactorily: Russ returning to Europe without Chris, who was going on through life with a man she didn't love; Dal forced to go on, too, enduring that knowledge.

They had all lost, they were all torn up in their different ways.

The only trouble was she didn't know the score, the real score; and I was not going to tell her how pitifully wrong she was...

Yet it wasn't quite over—not quite. Later that evening—when we were getting ready for bed and Nancy said casually, "This thing between Peg and Ron—I think it would be just as well if they didn't see too much of each other for a while, don't you?"—I was ready.

"No," I said very quietly. "No, Nan."

"Why—what are you trying to say?"

"I'm not *trying* to say anything: I'm saying it. Leave them alone. I mean it. Let them find their own way."

She turned to face me directly. "George, it's *not good,*" she said in her Supreme Court voice. "He's a *very* disturbed boy."

"We're all disturbed."

"You know perfectly well what I mean. Ever since Vietnam—"

"No, I don't," I said. "Personally I think she's good for him, he's good for her. Though it's no business of mine—and that's the way it's going to be around here: no business of ours."

"George, you've said yourself—"

"No meddling," I interrupted. "You hear me? Don't go *too* far, Nan. Don't push your luck too far..."

She blinked at me—in surprise, in anger, her neat little pink mouth open.

"I mean it, Nan. Lay off. If I find out you've tried to mess in this I'm going to be very, very angry."

"Well," she said, after a pause, with a quick, high laugh, "*you're* in a jovial mood!"

"Actually I am," I said. "It just takes me this way."

She turned back to her three-panel mirror, her set face smooth in the glass. "I'm certainly glad we don't have a reunion every year."

"I'll sign that," I said.

7

THE RAIN HAD STOPPED, the weather was clearing to the northwest. There was a flare of orange on the bookcases, a last ray of sunlight low in the trees; then it faded, and the day sank quickly into dusk. Water was still dripping from the eave outside the study window. Time present, time past. Ron was sitting quite still, his long legs stretched out straight, fingers laced in front of his chin.

"That's it," I said. "All I remember, anyway. From here on in it's up to you."

"I never saw Dad cry," he murmured to himself. "Not once." Abruptly he leaned forward, picked up a copy of *Weep For Memory* and peered hard at the back ad photo of Russ: the slender, handsome head, the intense dark eyes. A studio portrait.

"My father," he said flatly. "What do they say? My *natural* father. Natural..." He put the book down again and gripped his hands; I could feel him going round and round on it all, trying to think it through. "I see," he said after a moment. "*He's* the one who's always been afraid, isn't he?"

"A lot of people are," I said.

"Sure—but he was afraid the wrong way. You know? He—ducked it. In spite of all the big-deal, high-adventure bullshit. He dramatized things, he didn't *live* them."

"Don't forget, kid, one turn of the dial and any of us could have gone in an altogether different direction. Even Russ. Maybe Russ most of all. He wasn't bad, you know—he went bad; Kay Madden was just too much for him."

But he was full of his own discoveries. "That's why Mother didn't tell him about me that night . . . It was such a rough deal; she'd carried it so long: he didn't deserve to know what she'd gone through. What Dad had gone through. Just waltz into it, like that—that I was his son. It would have given him a—I don't know, some kind of importance. And he didn't rate it."

"Something like that."

"You have to pay your own way, don't you?" he said, as if he'd been the first member of the race to come upon that hard, indispensable truth. "Mother learned that—early. Dad did, too. But he still hasn't learned it, has he? Currier. You've got to earn your way: it's as simple as that."

"And as complicated."

"Yeah." He grinned briefly. "Name of the game. I'm sorry I blew off that night. At Dad. Pretty childish, really."

"I'd say it was natural enough. True enough, too, in a way."

"Oh, I meant it—I'm not going back on that. And yet it isn't that simple. You know, it was Dad who encouraged me most, about going back to school, going into oceanography. 'Save it, Ron,' he told me, you know, in that go-get-'em way he has, 'save that sea out there—it's the most important thing you could ever hope to do.' I said, 'For Christ sake—those are *your* plastic containers cluttering up the sea floor, that's *your* crude oil sliming up the beaches!' and he said, 'All right, I was wrong, I was *wrong*—now come on and help bail me out! Will you?' Can you imagine—R. G. Dalrymple saying he was wrong? Talk about cataclysms! I said: 'Who do you think I am, Jacques Cousteau?' 'Well,' he yelled, 'you can try, can't you?' Jesus, I had to laugh, even then, and after a minute he did, too. One thing about Dad: he can drive you up the wall, but he's always had a sense of humor. That was when he got that Management of

Oceans thing started, the big umbrella organization—God knows how much bread he's thrown into that caper."

"Bread upon the waters," I couldn't resist saying, and he laughed, then sobered again, his eyes roaming over the letters and pictures on the floor around us.

"Only—why didn't you gamble more, take some chances? Why did you all play it so cozy?"

I smiled—a sad, slow smile. "Well—the world bent us that way, for one thing. We feared poverty from the Depression, we hated it like death. We'd watched our parents turn desperate and bitter. And then we drew the war—our war—and we feared that enough, God knows; and so we hated death like poverty."

"And conversely," Ron murmured with a wry half-smile.

"Yes—and conversely. If there was anything we learned it was that there wasn't one hell of a lot in this world that one man could accomplish on his own. Working in a mill, crouching in a foxhole—maybe it wasn't the sort of education that encouraged taking bold risks... So we tried to make up for it, too fast, too foolishly; and we settled for security—and family." I sighed; the room was almost dark now. "That's why we were so shaken when you turned on us. You kids. We felt doubly betrayed— we'd put all our money on you."

"But that was your mistake," he said with a flash of the old defiance. "You made claims on us you had no right to make. As if we were some kind of investment."

"Yes."

"Risks are—they're everything..."

"That's true. When you can figure out the right ones to take. But maybe we'd already taken too many of a different kind." I stirred uncomfortably; I felt stiff in the joints, I'd been sitting too long. "Sure, we fouled up, we Fusiliers—you don't have to tell me that. But don't write us off *too* quickly, kid. We were naive, and misguided, sure—but we cared. We *cared,* Ron. We had passion and enthusiasm—we believed with all our hearts in heroes, and hopeless causes, and excellence—in all the valiant, transient, menaced things. And sometimes we died for them. And for other things, too, that we didn't always have a name for..."

I leaned forward and snapped on the desk lamp. I wanted to watch his eyes—all at once it seemed terribly important to make him see this. "We didn't do so badly, when you add it all up:

millions of us fought Joseph McCarthy—and some of us paid
for it, too; we marched at Selma, a lot of us were down there at
the Washington Monument with you kids, in '69 . . . We did help
to put the world back together again after the war. Our war.
Remember that. We just did it in too big a hurry, that's where we
blew it—we kept trying to make up for all that lost time. And the
old men went right on running things, hanging around our necks
like stones. That's half our trouble, Ron, that's why we're often
so difficult to get along with: we've had to take the blame for
your world—and we never quite held the real power. Only those
thousand days of Camelot. Some of us tried now and then, you
know. It wasn't all dance bands and convertibles . . ."

I stopped. The boy's eyes held that distant, wary look; if he
didn't feel these things, how in hell could I convey them? I picked
up the piece of ancient marble molding from my desk and said:

"Can you face up to it, Ron?"

His head came up then, his eyes widened. "Face up to what?"

"Losing your innocence. Every generation has to, sooner or
later. Every generation sells out; one way or another. It's always
been hard to face up to the moment—you're going to find out
how hard it is, too. It's a lot easier to drop out than face up,
however badly. Day by day. Yes, it is. Maybe *your* innocence is
dropping out."

"Well, if it is," he came back at me, "I've faced up to that now,
by God. And anyway, it's still better than conforming. Isn't it?"

"Maybe. As long as you get over it . . . The point is, you'll
have to forgive us, Ron. For all our faults. Sooner or later you'll
find you're us, we're you. You're still *our* kids. We taught you
how to think, how to weigh and measure—we gave you values
even if you did decide to fight some of them. That's your
privilege: but you're our kids. We may even have taught you to
care; at least we tried, some of us . . .

"The thing I guess we didn't want you to discover—but the
thing you've got to find out for yourselves—is that everybody
loses: that's what it means to join the human race." I grinned at
him. "Tell you what: you forgive us our conformity and we'll
forgive you your withdrawal. Okay?"

"Fair enough." He shook his head as though to clear it,
expelled a lungful of air. "What a relief it's been—listening to
you, hearing about it all. Hey, I want to apologize for what I said
to you out in the garage."

"Forget it."

"It's weird, not knowing who your father is—it's as though you're floating around, not anchored to solid ground ... Though why should it matter so much?—I mean, if you break it down. The real thing isn't genes at all, you know? It's who really put you together, right down the line." For a few seconds he gazed out at the dark, his lower lip thrust forward. "You know, I'm sorry for him. Currier. But I really don't want to have anything to do with him. *You're* my father, really," he said with sudden shy force. "You know that? After Dad, of course. That's not such a flaky thought, is it?"

"No," I said.

"It can't have been a breeze for you, either. These past few years." Stretching again he eyed me uncertainly. "I guess you feel I've been—well, evasive about Peg."

"No," I said. "We married too fast—all of us did. Maybe it was our besetting sin. If it was, we've paid for it. St. Paul says it's better to marry than to burn, but he never went into the problem of marrying and *still* burning." I set down the piece of Italian stone. "I hope you two have had a resounding sex life."

His eyes flashed out at me, he colored faintly—he'd never in his life expected me to say anything like that; then his face broke into his mother's smile. "As a matter of fact, we do!"

"Nothing could make me happier," I said.

"Actually we've been talking about getting married," he went on. "In April. We thought we might go down the Cape, stay in Grandpa's old place. I can work over in the lab at Woods Hole, I like it there."

"Then you'll need wheels," I said. I opened the top right-hand drawer of the desk and took out the key to the Empress and tossed it to him. He caught it deftly, peered at it in surprise.

"Well no, I didn't mean—"

"I'd like you to have her, Ron. For keeps. I've had the fun of her—those days are over, anyway. She's all yours."

Smiling at me he shook his head, a bit embarrassed. "Well, thanks—she's a great car. A grand car. But I don't—I hope you won't be offended. But she was your chariot. She was for another time, another set of dreams. Not ours. We've got to have our own wheels."

"I see." I felt deeply disappointed—so disappointed it amused me in spite of myself. "Well, I hope you borrow her once in a while."

"Sure—I'd like to."

We heard the Pontiac then, pulling into the drive.

"Here they are," Ron said, and his face took on a trace of that high excitement I remembered. Peg was in that car. And now he was free. As we got up he seized my hand—a quick, sure gesture. "Thanks," he said. "Thanks for—unreeling it all."

"It was my pleasure," I said. "Now run along and say hello to Peg... You two turn toward the summer, now."

I could hear their voices in the kitchen—Amanda shrieking with laughter, Nancy giving directions. I slipped out the sunporch door and walked over to the garage. The air was clear and cold, the stars were coming out through the rifts in the clouds. I threw on the workshop lights. The Empress gleamed and glinted like a sleeping queen.

"Well, old girl," I said to her, "I guess you stay with me. They don't want you, sweetheart. Fancy that. Good, then; good. I'm the only one who went on caring about you anyhow." I ran my hand over the clean chrome edge of her radiator, the deep swell of a fender. "Chris was right—it's the present that matters. The kids, doing right by them, making the best of what you've drawn. But when they're gone—and it won't be long now—why, every now and then we'll take us a spin, you and I, we'll run down to Nauset for old time's sake... And remember: there's something to be said for a band of brothers. Maybe even our quarrels will add up to something in the end. Who knows?

"No, it wasn't all dance bands and convertibles. But you mattered, old girl. You mattered a lot—don't ever think you didn't... As Chris says: with a little honesty—and a lot of style."

I covered her up again and went outside. It had blown clear; all the stars were out now, bobbing and gleaming in jeweled triads, in lazy clusters, in endless drifting dusty incandescence. The stars are dying all the time—I read that somewhere— blazing into life and then burning away; though I guess I'll never believe it, really.

Well. Stars. Stardust...